"The book has beautiful descriptions of the land and animals of Rhodesia, good dialogue, a little sex, some use of Matabele language and enough historical fact to show that Smith has done his research . . . well done."

Houston Chronicle

◆ ◆

"A memorable tale . . . leaves you with the hope that Smith will continue to recount the saga of the Ballantynes."

Associated Press

◆ ◆

"Smith is an excellent writer who makes his audience know the characters and their vividly described land. *The Angels Weep* will send those who have not read the previous two novels rushing to the shelves for more."

Library Journal

Other Novels by Wilbur Smith

THE DELTA DECISION
FLIGHT OF THE FALCON
MEN OF MEN

THE
ANGELS
WEEP

WILBUR SMITH

FAWCETT CREST • NEW YORK

A Fawcett Crest Book
Published by Ballantine Books
Copyright © 1982 by Wilbur Smith

Library of Congress Catalog Card Number: 82-45885

ISBN 0-449-20497-9

This edition published by arrangement with Doubleday & Company, Inc.

Manufactured in the United States of America

First Ballantine Books Edition: October 1984

This book is for my beloved wife
DANIELLE ANTOINETTE

But man, proud man,
Dress'd in a little brief authority,
Most ignorant of what he's most assur'd,
His glassy essence, like an angry ape,
Plays such fantastic tricks before high heaven
As make the angels weep.

Measure for Measure
William Shakespeare

PART I
- 1895 -

THREE HORSEMEN RODE OUT FROM THE EDGE OF THE FOREST with a restrained eagerness that not even weary weeks of constant searching could dull.

They reined in, stirrup to stirrup, and looked down into another shallow valley. Each stalk of the dry winter grass bore a fluffy seed head of a lovely rose color, and the light breeze stirred them and made them dance, so that the herd of sable antelope in the gut of the valley seemed to float belly-deep in a bank of swirling pink mist.

There was a single herd bull. He stood almost fourteen hands tall at the withers. His satiny back and shoulders were black as a panther's, but his belly and the intricate designs of his face mask were the startling iridescent white of mother-of-pearl. His great ridged horns, curved like Saladin's scimitar, swept back to touch his croup, and his neck was as proudly arched as that of a blood Arabian stallion. Long ago hunted to extinction in his former southern ranges, this noblest of all the antelopes of Africa had come to symbolize for Ralph Ballantyne this wild and beautiful new land between the Limpopo and the wide, green Zambezi rivers.

The great black bull stared arrogantly at the horsemen on the ridge above him, then snorted and tossed his warlike head. Thick mane flying, sharp hooves clattering over the stony ground, he led his chocolate-colored brood mares at a gallop up and over the far ridge, leaving the watching men mute at their grandeur and their beauty.

Ralph Ballantyne was first to rouse himself, and he turned in the saddle toward his father.

"Well, Papa," he asked, "do you recognize any landmarks?"

"It was more than thirty years ago," Zouga Ballantyne

murmured, a little frown of concentration puckering an arrowhead in the center of his forehead, "thirty years, and I was riddled with malaria." Then he turned to the third rider, the little wizened Hottentot, his companion and servant since those far-off days. "What do you think, Jan Cheroot?"

The Hottentot lifted the battered regimental cap from his head and smoothed the little peppercorns of pure white wool that covered his scalp. "Perhaps—"

Ralph cut in brusquely. "Perhaps it was all merely a fever dream."

The frown on his father's handsome, bearded features sharpened, and the scar upon his cheek flushed from bone porcelain to rose, while Jan Cheroot grinned with anticipation; when these two were together it was better entertainment than a cockfight any day.

"Damn it, boy," Zouga snapped. "Why don't you go back to the wagons and keep the women company." Zouga drew the thin chain from his fob pocket and dangled it before his son's face. "There it is," he snapped, "that's the proof."

On the ring of the chain hung a small bunch of keys, and other oddments, a gold seal, a St. Christopher, a cigar cutter and an irregular lump of quartz the size of a ripe grape. This last was mottled like fine blue marble and starred through its center with a thick wedge of gleaming native metal.

"Raw red gold," said Zouga. "Ripe for the picking!"

Ralph grinned at his father, but it was an insolent and provocative grin, for he was bored. Weeks of wandering and fruitless searching were not Ralph's style at all.

"I always suspected that you picked that up from a peddler's stall on the Grand Parade at Cape Town, and that it's only fool's gold anyway."

The scar on his father's cheek turned a furious red, and Ralph laughed delightedly and clasped Zouga's shoulder.

"Oh, Papa, if I truly believed that, do you think I would waste weeks of my time? What with the railroad building and the dozen other balls I am juggling, would I be here instead of in Johannesburg or Kimberley?"

He shook Zouga's shoulder gently, the smile no longer mocking. "It's here—we both know it. We could be stand-

4

ing on the reef at this very moment, or it could be just over the next ridge.''

Slowly the heat went out of Zouga's scar, and Ralph went on evenly, "The trick, of course, is to find it again. We could stumble over it in the next hour, or search another ten years.''

Watching father and son, Jan Cheroot felt a small prick of disappointment. He had seen them fight once before, but that was long ago. Ralph was now in the full prime of his manhood, almost thirty years of age, accustomed to handling the hundreds of rough men that he employed in his transport company and his construction teams, handling them with tongue and boot and fist. He was big and hard and strutty as a gamecock, but Jan Cheroot suspected that the old dog would still be able to roll the puppy in the dust. The praise name that the Matabele had given Zouga Ballantyne was Bakela, the Fist, and he was still fast and lean. Yes, Jan Cheroot decided regretfully, it would still be worth watching, but perhaps another day, for already the flare of tempers had faded and the two men were again talking quietly and eagerly, leaning from their saddles toward each other. Now they seemed more like brothers, for although the family resemblance was unmistakable, yet Zouga did not seem old enough to be Ralph's father. His skin was too clear and unlined, his eye too quick and vital, and the faint lacing of silver in his golden beard might have been merely the bleaching of the fierce African sun.

"If only you had been able to get a sun sight; the other observations you made were all so accurate," Ralph lamented. "I was able to go directly to every cache of ivory that you left that year.''

"By that time the rains had started," Zouga shook his head, "and, by God, how it rained! We hadn't seen the sun for a week, every river was in full spate, so we were marching in circles, trying to find a ford—" He broke off, and lifted the reins in his left hand. "But I've told the tale a hundred times. Let's get on with the search," he suggested quietly, and they trotted down off the ridge into the valley, Zouga stooping from the saddle to examine the ground for chips of broken reef, or swiveling slowly to survey the skyline to try and recognize the shape of the crests or the blue loom of a distant kopje against the towering African sky, where the fair-weather cumulus sailed high and serene.

"The only definite landmark we have to work on is the site of the ruins of Great Zimbabwe," Zouga muttered. "We marched eight days due westward from the ruins."

"Nine days," Jan Cheroot corrected him. "You lost one day when Matthew died. You were in fever. I had to nurse you like a baby, and we were carrying that damned stone bird."

"We couldn't have made good more than ten miles a day." Zouga ignored him. "Eight days' march, not more than eighty miles."

"And Great Zimbabwe is there. Due east of us now." Ralph reined in his horse as they came out on the next ridge. "That is the Sentinel." He pointed at a rocky kopje, the distant blue summit shaped like a crouching lion. "The ruins are just beyond, I would never mistake that view."

For both father and son, the ruined city had a special significance. There within the massive stone-built walls, Zouga and Jan Cheroot had found the ancient graven bird images that had been abandoned by the long-vanished inhabitants. Despite the desperate straits to which they had been reduced by fever and the other hardships of the long expedition from the Zambezi River in the north, Zouga insisted on carrying away with him one of the statues.

Then many years later it had been Ralph's turn. Guided by his father's diary and the meticulous sextant observations that it contained, Ralph had once again won through to the deserted citadel. Though he had been pursued by the border impis of Lobengula, the Matabele king, he had defied the king's taboo on the holy place and had spirited away the remaining statues. Thus all three men had intimate knowledge of those haunting and haunted ruins, and as they stared at the far hills that marked the site, they were silent with their memories.

"I still wonder, who were the men who built Zimbabwe?" Ralph asked at last. "And what happened to them?" There was an uncharacteristic dreamy tone to his voice, and he expected no answer. "Were they the Queen of Sheba's miners? Was this the Ophir of the Bible? Did they carry the gold they mined to Solomon?"

"Perhaps we will never know." Zouga roused himself. "But we do know they valued gold as we do. I found gold foil and beads and bars of bullion in the courtyard of Great Zimbabwe, and it must be within a few miles of where we stand that Jan Cheroot and I explored the shafts that they drove into the earth, and found the broken reef piled in dumps ready for crushing.'' Zouga glanced across at the little Hottentot. ''Do you recognize any of this?''

The dark pixie face wrinkled up like a sun-dried prune as Jan Cheroot considered. ''Perhaps from the next ridge,'' he muttered lugubriously, and the trio rode down into the valley that looked like a hundred others they had crossed in the preceding weeks.

Ralph was a dozen strides ahead of the others, cantering easily, swinging his mount to skirt a thicket of the dense wild ebony, when abruptly he stood in the stirrups, snatched his hat from his head and waved it high.

''Tally ho!'' he yelled. ''Gone away!''

And Zouga saw the burnt gold flash of fluid movement across the far slope of open ground.

''Three of the devils!'' Ralph's excitement and his loathing was clear in the pitch and timbre of his voice. ''Jan Cheroot, you turn 'em on the left! Papa, stop them crossing the ravine!''

The easy manner of command came naturally to Ralph Ballantyne, and the two older men accepted it as naturally, while none of them questioned for an instant why they should destroy the magnificent animals that Ralph had flushed from the ebony thicket. Ralph owned two hundred wagons, each drawn by sixteen draft-oxen. King's Lynn, Zouga's estates, taken up with the land grants that the British South Africa Company had issued to the volunteers who had destroyed the Matabele king's impis, covered many tens of thousands of acres that were stocked with the pick of the captured Matabele breeding herds running with blood bulls imported from Good Hope and old England.

Father and son were both cattlemen, and they had suffered the terrible depredations of the lion prides which infested this lovely land north of the Limpopo and Shashi rivers. Too often they had heard their valuable and beloved beasts bellowing in agony in the night, and in the dawn found their ravaged carcasses. To both of them, lions were the worst kind of vermin, and they were elated with this rare chance of taking a pride in broad daylight.

Ralph yanked the repeating Winchester rifle from the leather scabbard under his left knee as he urged the chestnut gelding into full gallop after the big cats. The lion had been the first away, and Ralph had only a glimpse of him, swaybacked and swing-bellied, the dense ruff of his mane fluffed out with alarm, padding majestically on heavy paws into the scrub. The older lioness followed him swiftly. She was lean and scarred from a thousand hunts, blue with age across the shoulders and back. She went away at a bounding gallop. However, the younger lioness, unaccustomed to men, was bold and curious as a cat. She was still faintly cub-spotted across her creamy gold belly, and she turned on the edge of the thicket to snarl at the pursuing horseman. Her ears lay flat against her skull, her furry pink tongue curled out over her fangs, and her whiskers were white and stiff as porcupine quills.

Ralph dropped his reins onto the gelding's neck, and the horse responded instantly by plunging to a dead stop and freezing for the shot, only the scissoring of his ears betraying his agitation.

Ralph tossed up the Winchester and fired as the butt plate slapped into his shoulder. The lioness grunted explosively as the bullet thumped into her shoulder, angled for the heart. She went up in a high sunfishing somersault, roaring in her death frenzy. She fell and rolled on her back, tearing at the scrub with fully extended claws and then stretching out in a last shuddering convulsion before slumping into the softness of death.

Ralph pumped a fresh round into the chamber of the Winchester and gathered up the reins. The gelding leaped forward.

Out on the right Zouga was pounding up the lip of the ravine, leaning forward in the saddle, and at that moment the second lioness broke into the open ahead of him, going for the deep brush-choked ravine at a driving run, and Zouga fired still at full gallop. Ralph saw dust spurt under the animal's belly.

"Low and left. Papa is getting old," Ralph thought derisively and brought the gelding crashing down to a stiff-legged halt. Before he could fire, Zouga had shot again, and the lioness collapsed and rolled like a yellow ball on the stony earth, shot through the neck a hand's span behind the ear.

"Bully for you!" Ralph laughed with excitement, and kicked his heels into the gelding's flank as they charged up the slope, shoulder to shoulder.

8

"Where is Jan Cheroot?" Zouga shouted, and as if in reply they heard the clap of rifle fire in the forest on the left, and they swung the horses in that direction.

"Can you see him?" Ralph called.

The bush was thicker ahead of them, and the thorn branches whipped at their thighs as they passed. There was a second shot, and immediately afterward the furious ear-numbing roars of the lion mingled with Jan Cheroot's shrill squeals of terror.

"He is in trouble!" Zouga called anxiously, as they burst out of the thick scrub.

Before them there lay parkland, fine open grass beneath the flat-topped acacia trees along the crest of the ridge. A hundred yards ahead Jan Cheroot was tearing along the crest, twisted in the saddle to look over his shoulder, his face a mask of terror, his eyes huge and glistening white. He had lost his hat and rifle, but he was lashing his mount across the neck and shoulders, although the animal was already at a wild uncontrolled gallop.

The lion was a dozen strides behind them, but gaining with each elastic bound as though they were standing still. Its heaving flank was painted slick and shiny with bright new blood, shot through the guts, but the wound had not crippled nor even slowed the beast. Rather it had maddened him, so that the blasts of sound from his throat sounded like the thunder of the skies.

Ralph swerved his gelding to try and intercept the little Hottentot and alter the angle to give himself an open shot at the lion, but at that moment the cat came up out of its flat, snaking charge, reared up over the bunched and straining quarters of the horse, and raked them with long curved talons so that the sweat-darkened hide opened in deep parallel wounds and the blood smoked from them in a crimson cloud.

The horse shrieked and lashed out with its hind hooves, catching the lion in his chest, so that he reeled and lost a stride. Immediately he gathered himself and came again, quartering in beside the running horse, his eyes inscrutably yellow as he prepared to leap astride the panic-driven animal.

"Jump, Jan Cheroot!" Ralph yelled. The lion was too close to risk a shot. "Jump, damn you!" But Jan Cheroot did not appear to have heard him; he was clinging helplessly to the tangled flying mane, paralyzed with fear.

The lion rose lightly into the air and settled like a huge bird on the horse's back, crushing Jan Cheroot beneath his massive, blood-streaked body. At that instant, horse and rider and lion seemed to disappear into the very earth, and there was only a swirling column of dust to mark where they had been. Yet the shattering roars of the enraged animal and Jan Cheroot's howls of terror grew even louder as Ralph galloped up to the point on the ridge where they had disappeared.

With the Winchester in one hand he kicked his feet from the stirrup irons and jumped from the saddle, letting his own momentum throw him forward until he stood on the edge of a sheer-sided pitfall at the bottom of which lay a tangle of heaving bodies.

"The devil is killing me!" screamed Jan Cheroot, and Ralph could see him pinned beneath the body of the horse. The horse must have broken its neck in the fall; it was a lifeless heap with head twisted up under its shoulder, and the lion was ripping the carcass and saddle, trying to reach Jan Cheroot.

"Lie still," Ralph shouted down at him. "Give me a clear shot!"

But it was the lion that heard him. He left the horse and came up the vertical side of the pit with the ease of a cat climbing a tree, his glossy muscular hindquarters driving him lightly upward and his pale eyes fastened upon Ralph as he stood on the lip of the deep hole.

Ralph dropped on one knee to steady himself for the shot and aimed down into the broad golden chest. The jaws were wide open, the fangs long as a man's forefinger and white as polished ivory; the deafening clamor from the open throat dinned into Ralph's face. He could smell the rotten-flesh taint of the lion's breath, and flecks of saliva splattered against his cheeks and forehead.

He fired, and pumped the loading handle and fired again, so swiftly that the shots were a continuous sound. The lion arched backward, hung for a long moment from the wall of the pit, and then toppled and fell back upon the dead horse.

Now there was no movement from the bottom of the pit, and the silence was more intense than the shattering uproar that had preceded it.

"Jan Cheroot, are you all right?" Ralph called anxiously.

There was no sign of the little Hottentot; he was completely smothered by the carcasses of horse and lion.

"Jan Cheroot, can you hear me?"

The reply was in a hollow, sepulchral whisper. "Dead men cannot hear—it's all over, they have got old Jan Cheroot at last."

"Come out from under there," Zouga Ballantyne ordered as he stepped up to Ralph's shoulder. "This is no time to play the clown, Jan Cheroot."

◆ ◆ ◆

Ralph dropped a coil of manila rope down to Jan Cheroot, and between them they hauled him and the saddle from the dead horse to the surface.

The excavation into which Jan Cheroot had fallen was a narrow trench along the crest of the ridge. In places it was twenty feet deep, but never more than six feet wide. Mostly it was choked with creepers and rank vegetation, but this could not disguise the certainty that it had been dug by men.

"The reef was exposed along this line," Zouga guessed as they followed the edge of the old trench. "The ancient miners simply dug it out and did not bother to refill."

"How did they blast the reef?" Ralph demanded. "That's solid rock down there."

"They probably built fires upon it and then quenched it with water. The contraction cracked the rock."

"Well, they seem to have taken out every grain of the ore body and left nary a speck for us."

Zouga nodded. "They would have worked out this section first, and then when the reef pinched out they would have started sinking potholes along the strike to try and intercept it again." Zouga turned to Jan Cheroot and demanded, "Now do you recognize this place, Jan Cheroot?" And when the Hottentot hesitated, he pointed down the slope. "The swamp in the valley down there, and the teak trees—"

"Yes, yes." Jan Cheroot clapped his hands, and his eyes twinkled with delight. "This is the same place where you killed the bull elephant—the tusks are on the stoep at King's Lynn."

"The ancient dump will be just ahead." Zouga hurried forward.

He found the low mound covered by grass, and Zouga went down on his knees to scrabble among the grass roots, picking out the chips of white sugar quartz, examining each one swiftly and discarding it. Occasionally he wet one with his tongue, held it to the sunlight to try and highlight the sparkle of metal, then frowned and shook his head with disappointment.

At last he stood and wiped his hands on his breeches.

"It's quartz all right, but the ancient miners must have hand-sorted this dump. We will have to find the old shafts if we want to see visible gold in the ore."

From the top of the dump Zouga orientated himself rapidly.

"The carcass of the bull elephant fell about there," he pointed, and to confirm it Jan Cheroot searched in the grass and lifted a huge thighbone, dry and white as chalk, and at last after thirty years beginning to crumble.

"He was the father of all elephants," Jan Cheroot said reverently. "There will never be another like him, and it was he that led us to this place. When you shot him he fell here to mark it for us."

Zouga turned a quarter circle and pointed again. "The ancient shaft where we buried old Matthew will be there."

Ralph recalled the elephant hunt as his father had described it in his celebrated book *A Hunter's Odyssey*. The black gunbearer had not flinched from the great bull elephant's charge, but had stood it down and handed Zouga the second gun, sacrificing his own life for that of his master. So Ralph understood and remained silent as Zouga went down on one knee beside the rock pile that marked the gunbearer's grave.

After a minute Zouga rose and dusted off his knee and said simply, "He was a good man."

"Good, but stupid," Jan Cheroot agreed. "A wise man would have run."

"And a wise man would have chosen a better grave," Ralph murmured. "He is plumb in the center of a gold reef. We will have to dig him out."

But Zouga frowned. "Let him lie. There are other shafts along the strike." He turned away, and the others followed him. A hundred yards farther on Zouga stopped again. "Here!" he called with satisfaction. "The second shaft—there were four of them altogether."

This opening had also been refilled with chunks of native

rock. Ralph shrugged off his jacket, propped his rifle against the bole of the nearest tree, and climbed down into the shallow depression until he stooped over the narrow blocked entrance.

"I'm going to open it up."

They worked for half an hour, prizing loose the boulders with a branch of a leadwood and manhandling them aside until they had exposed the square opening to the shaft. It was narrow, so narrow that only a child could have passed through it. They knelt and peered down into it. There was no telling how deep it was, for it was impenetrably black in the depths, and it stank of damp, of fungus and bats, and of rotting things.

Ralph and Zouga stared into the opening with a horrid fascination.

"They say the ancients used child slaves or captured Bushmen in the workings," Zouga murmured.

"We have to know if the reef is down there," Ralph whispered. "But no grown man—" He broke off and there was another moment of thoughtful silence before Zouga and Ralph glanced at each other and smiled, and then both their heads turned in unison toward Jan Cheroot.

"Never!" said the little Hottentot fiercely. "I am a sick old man. Never! You will have to kill me first!"

♦ ♦ ♦

Ralph found a stump of candle in his saddlebag, while Zouga swiftly spliced together the three coils of rope used for tethering the horses, and Jan Cheroot watched their preparation like a condemned man watching the construction of the gallows.

"For twenty-nine years, since the day I was born, you have been telling me of your courage and daring," Ralph reminded him as he placed an arm around Jan Cheroot's shoulder and led him gently back to the mouth of the shaft.

"Perhaps I exaggerated a little," Jan Cheroot admitted as Zouga knotted the rope under his armpits and strapped a saddlebag around his tiny waist.

"You, who have fought wild men and hunted elephant and lion—what can you fear in this little hole? A few snakes, a little darkness, the ghosts of dead men, that's all."

"Perhaps I exaggerated more than a little," Jan Cheroot whispered huskily.

"You are not a coward, are you, Jan Cheroot?"

"Yes," Jan Cheroot nodded fervently. "That is exactly what I am, and this is no place for a coward."

Ralph drew him back, struggling like a hooked catfish on the end of the rope, lifted him easily and lowered him into the shaft, His protests faded gradually as Ralph paid out the rope.

Ralph was measuring the rope across the reach of his outstretched arms. Reckoning each span at six feet, he had lowered the little Hottentot a little under sixty feet before the rope went slack.

"Jan Cheroot!" Zouga bellowed down the shaft.

"A little cave." Jan Cheroot's voice was muffled and distorted by echoes. "I can just stand. The reef is black with soot."

"Cooking fires. The slaves would have been kept down there," Zouga guessed, "never seeing the light of day again until they died." Then he raised his voice. "What else?"

"Ropes, plaited grass ropes, and buckets, leather buckets like we used on the diamond diggings at New Rush—" Jan Cheroot broke off with an exclamation. "They fall to pieces when I touch them, just dust now." Faintly they could hear Jan Cheroot sneezing and coughing in the dust he had raised, and his voice was thickened and nasal as he went on, "Iron tools, something like an adze," and when he called again they could hear the tremor in his voice. "Name of the great snake, there are dead men here, dead men's bones. I am coming up—pull me up!"

Staring down the narrow shaft, Ralph could see the light of the candle flame wavering and trembling at the bottom.

"Jan Cheroot, is there a tunnel leading off from the cave?"

"Pull me up."

"Can you see a tunnel?"

"Yes, now will you pull me up?"

"Not until you follow the tunnel to the end."

"Are you mad! I would have to crawl on hands and knees."

"Take one of the iron tools with you, to break a piece off the reef."

"No. That is enough. I go no farther, not with dead men guarding this place."

"Very well," Ralph bellowed into the hole, "then I will throw the end of the rope down on top of you."

"You would not do that!"

"After that I will put the rocks back over the entrance."

"I am going." Jan Cheroot's voice had a desperate edge, and once again the rope began slithering down into the shaft like a serpent into its nest.

Ralph and Zouga squatted beside the shaft, passing their last cheroot back and forth and waiting with ill grace and impatience.

"When they deserted these workings, they must have sealed the slaves in the shaft. A slave was a valuable chattel, so that proves they were still working the reef and that they left in great haste." Zouga paused, cocked his head to listen, and then said, "Ah!" with satisfaction. From the depths of the earth at their feet came the distant clank of metal tool on living rock. "Jan Cheroot has reached the working face."

However, it was many minutes more before they saw the wavering candlelight in the bottom of the pit again and Jan Cheroot's pleas, quavering and pitiful, came up to them.

"Please, Master Ralph, I have done it. Now will you pull me up, please?"

Ralph stood with one booted foot on each side of the shaft and hauled in the rope hand over hand. The muscles of his arms bulged and subsided under the sleeves of his thin cotton shirt as he lifted the Hottentot and his burden to the surface without a pause; and when he had finished, Ralph's breathing was still even and quiet, and there was not a single bead of perspiration on his face.

"So, Jan Cheroot, what did you find?"

Jan Cheroot was coated all over with fine pale dust through which his sweat had cut muddy runnels, and he stank of bat guano and the mushroom odor of long-deserted caves. With hands that still shook with fear and exhaustion, he opened the flap of the saddlebag at his waist.

"This is what I found," he croaked, and Zouga took a lump of the raw, rough rock from him.

It had a crystalline texture that glittered like ice and was marbled with blue and riven by minute flaws and fissures, some of which had cracked through under the pounding of the iron adze with which Jan Cheroot had hacked it from the rock face. However, the shattered fragments of shining quartz were held together by the substance that had filled every crack and fault line in the ore. This cement was a thin malleable layer of bright metal that twinkled in the sunlight when Zouga wet it with the tip of his tongue.

"By God, Ralph, will you look at that!" And Ralph took it from his father's hand with the reverence of a worshiper receiving the sacrament.

"Gold!" he whispered, and it sparkled at him, that lovely yellow smile that had captivated men almost from the time they had first stood upon their hind legs.

"Gold!" Ralph repeated.

To find this glimmer of precious metal they had labored most of their lives, father and son, they had ridden far and, in the company of other freebooters, had fought bloody battles, had helped destroy a proud nation and hunt a king to a lonely death.

Led by a sick man with a swollen, crippled heart and grandiose dreams, they had seized a vast land that now bore that giant's name, Rhodesia, and they had forced the land to yield up, one by one, its riches. They had taken its wide, sweet pastures and lovely mountain ranges, its forests of fine native timber, its herds of sleek cattle, its legions of sturdy black men who for a pittance would provide the thews to gather in the vast harvest. And now at last they held the ultimate treasure in their hands.

"Gold!" Ralph said for the third time.

◆　◆　◆

They struck their pegs along the ridge, cutting them from the acacia trees that oozed clear sap from the ax cuts, and they hammered them into the hard earth with the flat of the blade. Then they built cairns of stone to mark the corner of each claim.

Under the Fort Victoria Agreement, which both of them had signed when they volunteered to ride against Lobengula's impis, they were each entitled to ten gold claims. This naturally did not apply to Jan Cheroot. Despite the fact that he had ridden into Matabeleland with Jameson's flying column and shot down the Matabele *amadoda* at the Shangani River and the Bembesi Crossing with as much gusto as had his masters, yet he was a man of color, and as such he could not share the spoils.

In addition to the booty to which Zouga and Ralph were

entitled under the Victoria Agreement, both of them had bought up many blocks of claims from the dissolute and spendthrift troopers of Jameson's conquering force, some of whom had sold for the price of a bottle of whisky. So between them they could peg off the entire ridge and most of the valley bottoms on each side of it.

It was hard work but urgent, for there were other prospectors abroad, one of whom could have followed their tracks. They worked through the heat of noon and by the light of the moon until sheer exhaustion forced them to drop their axes and sleep where they fell. On the fourth evening, they could stop at last, content that they had secured the entire reef for themselves. There was no gap between their pegs into which another prospector could jump.

"Jan Cheroot, there is only one bottle of whisky left," Zouga groaned, and stretched his aching shoulders, "but tonight I am going to let you pour your own dop."

They watched with amusement the elaborate precautions which Jan Cheroot took to get the last drop into his brimming mug. In the process the line around the bottom that marked his daily grog ration was entirely ignored, and when the mug was full, he did not trust the steadiness of his own hand but slurped up the first mouthful on all fours like a dog.

Ralph retrieved the bottle and ruefully considered the remnants of the liquor before pouring a dram for his father and himself.

"The Harkness Mine," Zouga gave them the toast.

"Why do you call it that?" Ralph demanded, when he lowered his mug and wiped his mustache with the back of his hand.

"Old Tom Harkness gave me the map that led me to it," Zouga replied.

"We could find a better name."

"Perhaps, but that's the one I want."

"The gold will be just as bright, I expect," Ralph capitulated, and carefully moved the whisky bottle out of the little Hottentot's reach, for Jan Cheroot had drained his mug already. "I am glad we are doing something together again, Papa." Ralph settled down luxuriously against his saddle.

17

"Yes," Zouga agreed softly. "It's been too long since we worked side by side in the diamond pit at New Rush."

"I know just the right fellow to open up the workings for us. He is a top man, the best on the Witwatersrand goldfields, and I'll have my wagons bringing up the machinery before the rains break."

It was part of their agreement that Ralph would provide the men and machinery and money to run the Harkness Mine when Zouga led him to it. For Ralph was a rich man. Some said he was already a millionaire, though Zouga knew that was unlikely. Nevertheless, Zouga remembered that Ralph had provided the transport and commissariat for both the Mashonaland column and the Matabeleland expedition against Lobengula, and for each he had been paid huge sums by Mr. Rhodes's British South Africa Company, not in cash but in company shares. Like Zouga himself, he had speculated by buying up original land grants from the thriftless drifters that made up the bulk of the original column and had paid them in whisky carried up from the railhead in his own wagons. Ralph's Rhodesian Lands Company owned more land than did even Zouga himself.

Ralph had also speculated in the shares of the British South Africa Company. In those heady days when the column first reached Fort Salisbury, he had sold shares that Mr. Rhodes had issued to him at £1 for the sum of £3-15s-od on the London stock market. Then, when the pioneers' vaunting hopes and optimism had withered on the sour veld and barren ore bodies of Mashonaland, and Rhodes and Jameson were secretly planning their war against the Matabele king, Ralph had repurchased British South Africans at eight shillings. He had then seen them quoted at £8 when the column rode into the burning ruins of Lobengula's kraal at GuBulawayo and the company had added the entire realm of the Matabele monarch to its possessions.

Now, listening to his son talk with that infectious energy which even those hard days and nights of physical labor on the claims could not dull, Zouga reflected that Ralph had laid the telegraph lines from Kimberley to Fort Salisbury, that his construction gangs were at this moment laying the railway lines across the same wilderness toward Bulawayo, that his two hundred wagons carried trade goods to more than a hundred of Ralph's own trading posts scattered across Bechuanaland and Matabeleland and Mashonaland, that as of today Ralph was a half owner of a gold mine that promised to be as rich as any on the fabulous Witwatersrand.

Zouga smiled to himself as he listened to Ralph talk in the flickering firelight, and he thought suddenly, "Damn it, but they might be right after all—the puppy might just possibly be a millionaire already." And his pride was tinged with envy. Zouga himself had worked and dreamed from long before Ralph was born, had made sacrifices and had suffered hardships that still made him shudder when he thought about them, all for much lesser reward. Apart from this new reef, all he had to show for a lifetime of striving was King's Lynn and Louise—and then he smiled. With those two possessions, he was richer than Mr. Rhodes would ever be.

Zouga sighed and tilted his hat forward over his eyes, and with Louise's beloved face held firmly in the eye of his mind, he drifted into sleep, while across the fire Ralph still talked quietly, for himself more than for his father, and conjured up new visions of wealth and power.

◆ ◆ ◆

It was two full days' ride back to the wagons, but they were still half a mile from the camp when they were spotted, and a joyous tide of servants and children and dogs and wives came clamoring out to greet them.

Ralph spurred forward and leaned low from the saddle to sweep Cathy up onto the pommel so violently that her hair tumbled into her face and she shrieked breathlessly until he silenced her with a kiss full on the mouth, and he held the kiss unashamedly while little Jonathan danced impatiently around the horse shouting, "Me, too! Lift me up, too, Papa!"

When at last he broke the kiss, Ralph held her close still, and his stiff dark mustaches tickled her ear as he whispered, "The minute I get you into the tent, Katie my love, we will give that new mattress of yours a stiff test."

She flushed a richer tone of pink and tried to slap his cheek, but the blow was light and loving. Ralph chuckled, then reached down and picked Jonathan up by one arm and dropped him into the gelding's croup behind the saddle.

The boy wrapped his arms around Ralph's waist and demanded in a high, piping voice: "Did you find gold, Papa?"

"A ton."

"Did you shoot any lions?"

"A hundred."

"Did you kill any Matabele?"

"The season's closed," Ralph laughed, and ruffled his son's dark, thick curls, but Cathy scolded quickly.

"That's a wicked thing to ask your father, you bloodthirsty little pagan."

Louise followed the younger woman and the child at a more sedate pace, stepping lightly and lithely in the thick dust of the wagon road. Her hair was drawn back from her broad forehead and hung down her back to the level of her waist in a thick braid. It emphasized the high arches of her cheekbones.

Her eyes had changed color again. It always fascinated Zouga to see the shifts of her mood reflected in those huge slanted eyes. Now they were a softer blue, the color of happiness. She stopped at the horse's head, and Zouga stepped down from the stirrup and lifted the hat from his head, studying her gravely for a moment before he spoke.

"Even in such a short time I had forgotten how truly beautiful you are," he said.

"It was not a short time," she contradicted him. "Every hour I am away from you is an eternity."

It was an elaborate camp, for this was Cathy and Ralph's home. They owned no other, but like gypsies moved to where the pickings were richest. There were four wagons outspanned under the tall, arched wild fig trees on the bank of the river above the ford. The tents were of new snowy canvas, one of which, set a little apart, served for ablution. This contained a galvanized iron bath in which one could stretch out full length. There was a servant whose sole duty was to tend the forty-gallon drum on the fire behind the tent and to deliver unlimited quantities of hot water, day and night. Another smaller tent beyond held a commode whose seat Cathy had hand-painted with cupids and bouquets of roses, and beside the commode she had placed the ultimate luxury, scented sheets of soft colored paper in a sandalwood box.

There were horsehair mattresses on each cot, comfortable canvas chairs to sit on, and a long trestle table to eat off under the fly of the open-sided dining tent. There were canvas coolers for the champagne and lemonade bottles, food safes screened with insect-proof gauze, and thirty servants. Servants to cut wood and tend fires, servants to wash and iron so that the women could change their clothing daily, others to make the beds and sweep up every fallen leaf from the bare ground between the tents and then sprinkle it with water to lay the dust, one to wait exclusively upon Master Jonathan, to feed him and bathe him and ride him on-a shoulder or sing to him when he grew petulant. Servants to cook the food and to wait upon the table, servants to light the lanterns and lace up the flies of the tents at nightfall, and even one to empty the bucket of the hand-held commode whenever the little bell tinkled.

Ralph rode in through the gate of the high thornbush stockade that surrounded the entire camp to protect it from the nocturnal visits of the lion prides. Cathy was still on the saddle in front of him and his son up behind.

He looked about the camp with satisfaction and squeezed Cathy's waist. "By God, it's good to be home, a hot bath, and you can scrub my back, Katie." He broke off and exclaimed with surprise, "Damn it, woman! You might have warned me!"

"You never gave me a chance," she protested.

Parked at the end of the row of wagons was a closed coach, a vehicle with sprung wheels, the windows fitted with teak shutters that could be raised against the heat. The body of the coach was painted a cool and delightful green under the dust and dried mud of hard travel, the doors were picked out in gold leaf, and the high wheels piped with the same gold. The interior was finished in glossy green leather with gold tassels on the curtains. There were fitted leather and brass steamer trunks strapped to the roof rack, and beyond the coach in Ralph's kraal of thornbush, the big white mules, all carefully matched for color and size, were feeding on bundles of fresh grass that Ralph's servants had cut along the river bank.

"How did Himself find us?" Ralph demanded as he let Cathy down to the ground. He did not have to ask who the visitor was, this magnificent equipage was famous across the continent.

"We are camped only a mile from the main road up from the south," Cathy pointed out tartly. "He could hardly miss us."

"And he has his whole gang with him, by the looks of

it," Ralph muttered. There were two dozen horses in the kraal with the white mules.

"All the king's horses and all the king's men," Cathy agreed, and at that moment Zouga hurried in through the gate with Louise on his arm. He was as excited by their visitor as Ralph was irritated.

"Louise tells me that he has broken his journey especially to talk to me."

"You had better not keep him waiting then, Papa," Ralph grinned sardonically. It was strange how all men, even the aloof and coolheaded Major Zouga Ballantyne, came under the spell that their visitor wove. Ralph prided himself that he alone was able to resist it, although at times it required a conscious effort.

Zouga was striding eagerly down the row of wagons toward the inner stockade with Louise skipping to keep up with him. Ralph dawdled deliberately, admiring the remarkable animals that Jonathan had molded from river clay and now paraded for his approbation.

"Beautiful hippos, Jon-Jon! Not hippo? Oh, I see, the horns fell off, did they? Well then, they are the most beautiful, fattest hornless kudus that I have ever seen."

Cathy tugged at his arm at last. "You know he wants to speak to you also, Ralph," she urged, and Ralph swung Jonathan up onto his shoulder, took Cathy on his other arm, for he knew that such a display of domesticity would irritate the man they were going to meet, and sauntered into the inner stockade of the camp.

The canvas sides of the dining marquee had been rolled up to allow the cool afternoon breeze to blow through it, and there were half a dozen men seated at the long trestle table. In the center of the group was a hulking figure dressed in an ill-fitting jacket of expensive English cloth that was closed to the top button. The knot of his necktie had slipped and the colors of Oriel College were dulled with the dust of the long road up from the diamond city of Kimberley.

Even Ralph, whose feelings for this ungainly giant of a man were ambivalent—hostility mixed with a grudging admiration—was shocked by the changes that a few short years had wrought on him. The meaty features seemed to have sagged from the bones of his face, his color was high and unhealthy. He was barely forty years of age, yet his mustache and sideburns had faded from blond to dull silver, and he looked fifteen years older. Only the blue eyes retained their force and mystic visionary glitter.

"Well, how are you, Ralph?" His voice was high and clear, incongruous in such a big body.

"Good afternoon, Mr. Rhodes," Ralph replied, and despite himself let his son slip from his shoulder and lowered him gently to the ground. Instantly the child darted away.

"How is my railway progressing while you are out here enjoying yourself?"

"Ahead of schedule and below budget," Ralph countered the barely veiled rebuke, and with a small effort broke the hypnotic gaze of those blue eyes and glanced at the men who flanked Mr. Rhodes.

On his right was the great man's shadow, small, narrow-shouldered and as neatly dressed as his master was untidy. He had the prim but nondescript features of a schoolmaster, and receding wispy hair, but keen and acquisitive eyes that gave the lie to the rest of it.

"Jameson," Ralph nodded coolly at him, using neither Dr. Leander Starr Jameson's title nor the more familiar and affectionate "Dr. Jim."

"Young Ballantyne." Jameson slightly emphasized the diminutive and gave it a faintly derogatory twist. From the very first, their hostility had been mutual and instinctive.

From Rhodes's left rose a younger man with straight back and broad shoulders, an open, handsome face, and a friendly smile which showed big, even white teeth.

"Hello, Ralph." His handshake was firm and dry, his Kentucky accent easy and pleasant.

"Harry, I was speaking of you this very morning." Ralph's pleasure was obvious, and he glanced at Zouga. "Papa, this is Harry Mellow, the best mining engineer in Africa."

Zouga nodded. "We have been introduced." And father and son exchanged a glance of understanding.

This young American was the one that Ralph had chosen to develop and operate the Harkness Mine. It meant little to Ralph that Harry Mellow, like most of the bright young bachelors of special promise in southern Africa, already worked for Cecil John Rhodes. Ralph intended to find the bait that would tempt him away.

"We must talk later, Harry," he murmured, and turned to another young man seated at the end of the table.

"Jordan," he exclaimed. "By God, it's good to see you."

The two brothers met and embraced, and Ralph made no effort to hide his affection, but then everybody loved Jordan. They loved him not only for his golden beauty and gentle manner, but also for his many talents and for the warmth and real concern that he extended to all about him.

"Oh, Ralph, I have so much to ask, and so much to tell you." Jordan's delight was as intense as Ralph's.

"Later, Jordan," Mr. Rhodes broke in querulously. He did not like to be interrupted, and he waved Jordan back to his seat. Jordan went instantly. He had been Mr. Rhodes's private secretary since he was nineteen years of age, and obedience to his master's least whim was part of his nature by now.

Rhodes glanced at Cathy and Louise. "Ladies, I am sure you will find our discourse tedious, and you have urgent chores to attend to, I am certain."

Cathy glanced up at her husband and saw Ralph's quick annoyance at the artless presumption with which Mr. Rhodes had taken over his camp and all within it. Surreptitiously Cathy squeezed his hand to calm him and felt Ralph relax slightly. There was a limit to even Ralph's defiance. He might not be in Rhodes's employ, but the railway contract and a hundred cartage routes depended upon this man.

Then Cathy looked across at Louise and saw that she was as piqued by the dismissal. There was a blue spark in her eyes and a faint heat under the fine freckles on her cheeks, but her voice was level and cool as she replied for both Cathy and herself, "Of course you are correct, Mr. Rhodes. Will you please excuse us."

It was well known that Mr. Rhodes was uncomfortable in the presence of females. He employed no female servants, would not allow a painting or statue of a woman to decorate his ornate mansion at Groote Schuur in the Cape of Good Hope; he would not even employ a married man in a position close to his person, and immediately discharged even the most trusted employee who took the unforgivable plunge into matrimony. "You cannot dance to a woman's whims and serve me at the same time," he would explain as he fired an offender.

Now Rhodes beckoned Ralph. "Sit here, where I can see you," he commanded, and immediately turned back to Zouga and began rapping out questions. His questions cut like the lash of a stock whip, but the attention with which he listened to the replies was evidence of the high regard he had for Zouga Ballantyne. Their relationship went back many years, to the early days of the diamond diggings at Colesberg kopje, which had since been renamed Kimberley after the colonial secretary who accepted it into Her Majesty's dominions.

On those diggings, Zouga had once worked claims which had yielded up the fabulous "Ballantyne Diamond," but now Rhodes owned those claims, as he owned every single claim on the fields. Since then, Rhodes had employed Zouga as his personal agent at the kraal of Lobengula, King of the Matabele, for he spoke the language with colloquial fluency. When Dr. Jameson had led his flying column in that swift and victorious strike against the king, Zouga had ridden with him as one of his field officers and had been the first man into the burning kraal of GuBulawayo after the king had fled.

After Lobengula's death Rhodes had appointed Zouga Custodian of Enemy Property, and Zouga had been responsible for rounding up the captured herds of Matabele cattle and redistributing them as booty to the company and to Jameson's volunteers.

Once Zouga had completed that task, Rhodes would have appointed him Chief Native Commissioner, to deal with the indunas of the Matabele, but Zouga had preferred to retire to his estates at King's Lynn with his new bride and had let the job go to General Mungo St. John. However, Zouga was still on the Board of the British South Africa Company, and Rhodes trusted him as he did few other men.

"Matabeleland is booming, Mr. Rhodes," Zouga reported. "You will find Bulawayo is almost a city already, with its own school and hospital. There are already more than six hundred white women and children in Matabeleland, a sure sign that your settlers are here to stay at last. All the land grants have been taken up, and many of the farms are already being worked. The blood stock from the Cape is taking to the local conditions and breeding well with the captured Matabele cattle."

"What about the minerals, Ballantyne?"

"Over ten thousand claims have been registered, and I have seen some very rich crushings." Zouga hesitated, glanced at Ralph, and when he nodded, turned back to Rhodes. "Within the last few days, my son and I have rediscovered and pegged the ancient workings I first stumbled on in the sixties."

"The Harkness Mine," Rhodes nodded heavily, and even Ralph was impressed by the range and grasp of his mind. "I remember your original description in *Hunter's Odyssey*. Did you sample the reef?"

In reply, Zouga placed a dozen lumps of quartz upon the table in front of him, and the raw gold glistened so that the men around the table craned forward in rapt fascination. Mr. Rhodes turned one of the samples in his big mottled hands before passing it to the American engineer.

"What do you make of these, Harry?"

"It will go fifty ounces a ton," Harry whistled softly, and looked up at Ralph. "How thick is the reef? How broad is the strike?"

Ralph shook his head. "I don't know; the workings are too narrow to get into the face."

"This is quartz, of course, not the banket reef like we have on the Witwatersrand," Harry Mellow murmured.

The banket reef was named after the sweetmeat of toffee and nuts and almonds and cloves which the conglomerated reef so much resembled. It was made up of the sedimentary beds of ancient buried lakes, not as rich in gold as this chip of quartz, but many feet thick and extending as wide as the broad lakes had once stretched, a mother lode which could be mined for a hundred years without exhausting its reserves.

"It's too rich," Harry Mellow repeated, fondling the sample of quartz. "I can't believe that it will be more than a stringer a few inches thick."

"But if it isn't?" Rhodes demanded harshly.

The American smiled quietly. "Then you will not only control nearly all the diamonds in the world, Mr. Rhodes, but most of the gold as well."

His words were a sharp reminder to Ralph that the British South Africa Company owned fifty per cent royalty in every ounce of gold mined in Matabeleland, and Ralph felt his resentment return in full force. Rhodes and his ubiquitous BSA Company were like a vast octopus that smothered the efforts and the fortunes of all lesser men.

"Will you allow Harry to ride with me for a few days, Mr. Rhodes, so that he can examine the strike?" Ralph's irritation sharpened the tone of his request, so that Rhodes's big shaggy head lifted quickly and his blue eyes seemed to search out his soul for a moment before he nodded, and then with a mercurial change of direction abandoned the subject of gold and shot his next question at Zouga.

"The Matabele indunas—how are they behaving themselves?"

This time Zouga hesitated. "They have grievances, Mr. Rhodes."

"Yes?" The swollen features coagulated into a scowl.

"The cattle, naturally enough, are the main source of trouble," Zouga said quietly, and Rhodes cut him off brusquely.

"We captured less than a hundred and twenty-five thousand head of cattle, and we returned forty thousand of those to the tribe."

Zouga did not remind him that the return was made only after the strongest representation by Robyn St. John, Zouga's own sister. Robyn was the missionary doctor at Khami Mission Station, and she had once been Lobengula's closest friend and adviser.

"Forty thousand head of cattle, Ballantyne! A most generous gesture by the company!" Rhodes repeated portentously, and again he did not add that he had made this return in order to avert the famine which Robyn St. John had warned him would decimate the defeated Matabele nation, and which would have surely brought the intervention of the Imperial Government in Whitehall and possibly the revocation of the Royal Charter under which Rhodes's company ruled both Mashonaland and Matabeleland. Not such an outstanding act of charity, after all, Ralph thought wryly.

"After giving back those cattle to the indunas, we were left with less than eighty-five thousand head; the company barely recouped the cost of the war."

"Still the indunas claim they were given back only inferior beasts, the old and barren cows and scrub bulls."

"Damn it, Ballantyne, the volunteers earned the right to first pick from the herds. Quite naturally they chose the prime stock." He shot out his right fist with the forefinger aimed like a pistol at Zouga's heart. "They do say that our own herds, chosen from the captured cattle, are the finest in Matabeleland."

"The indunas don't understand that," Zouga answered.

"Well then, the least they should understand is that they are a conquered nation. Their welfare depends on the good-will of the victors. They extended no such consideration to the tribes that they conquered when they lorded it across the continent. Mzilikazi slew a million defenseless souls when he devastated the land south of the Limpopo, and Lobengula, his son, called the lesser tribes his dogs, to kill or cast into slavery as the whim took him. They must not whine now at the bitter taste of defeat."

Even gentle Jordan, at the end of the table, nodded at this. "To protect the Mashona tribes from Lobengula's depredations was one of the reasons why we marched on GuBulawayo," he murmured.

"I said that they had grievances," Zouga pointed out. "I did not say that they were justified."

"Then what else do they have to complain of?" Rhodes demanded.

"The company police. The young Matabele bucks whom General St. John has recruited and armed are strutting through the kraals, usurping the power of the indunas, taking their pick of the young girls—"

Again Rhodes interrupted. "Better that than a resurrection of the fighting impis under the indunas. Can you imagine twenty thousand warriors in impis under Babiaan and Gandang and Bazo? No, St. John was right to break the power of the indunas. As Native Commissioner, it is his duty to guard against resurgence of the Matabele fighting tradition."

"Especially in view of the events that are in train south of where we now sit." Dr. Leander Starr Jameson spoke for the first time since he had greeted Ralph, and Rhodes turned to him swiftly.

"I wonder if this is the time to speak of that, Dr. Jim."

"Why not? Every man here is trustworthy and discreet. We are all committed to the same bright vision of Empire, and the Lord knows, we are in no danger of being overheard. Not in this wilderness. What better time than now to explain why the company police must be made even stronger, must be better armed and trained to the highest degree of readiness?" Jameson demanded.

Instinctively Rhodes glanced at Ralph Ballantyne, and

Ralph raised one eyebrow, a cynical and mildly challenging gesture that seemed to decide Rhodes.

"No, Dr. Jim," he spoke decisively. "There will be another time for that." And when Jameson shrugged and capitulated, Rhodes turned to Jordan. "The sun is setting," he said, and Jordan rose obediently to charge the glasses. The sundowner whisky was already a traditional ending to the day in this land north of the Limpopo.

◆ ◆ ◆

The brilliant white gems of the Southern Cross hung over Ralph's camp, dimming the lesser stars, and sprinkling the bald domes of the granite kopjes with a pearly light as Ralph picked his way toward his tent. He had inherited his father's head for liquor, so that his step was even and steady. It was ideas, not whisky, which had inebriated him.

He stooped through the fly of the darkened tent and sat down on the edge of the cot. He touched Cathy's cheek.

"I am awake," she said softly. "What time is it?"

"After midnight."

"What kept you so long?" she whispered, for Jonathan slept just beyond the canvas screen.

"The dreams and boasts of men drunk with power and success." He grinned in the dark and dragged off his boots. "And by God, I did my fair share of dreaming and boasting." He stood to strip off his breeches. "What do you think of Harry Mellow?" he asked with an abrupt change of pace.

"The American? He is very—" Cathy hesitated. "I mean, he seems to be manly and rather nice."

"Attractive?" Ralph demanded. "Irresistible to a young woman?"

"You know I don't think like that," Cathy protested primly.

"The hell you don't," Ralph chuckled, and as he kissed her, he covered one of her round breasts with his cupped hand. Through the thin cotton nightdress it felt taut as a ripening melon. She struggled genteelly to free her lips from his and to prize his fingers loose, but he held her fast, and after a few seconds, she struggled no more, and instead she slipped her arms around the back of his neck.

"You smell of sweat and cigars and whisky."

"I'm sorry."

"Don't be, it's lovely," she purred.

"Let me take off my shirt."

"No, I'll do it for you."

Much later Ralph lay upon his back with Cathy snuggled down against his bare chest.

"How would you like to have your sisters come down from Khami?" he asked suddenly. "They enjoy camp life, but even more, they like to escape from your mother."

"It was I who wanted to invite the twins," she reminded him sleepily. "You were the one who said they were too—unsettling."

"Actually, I said they were too rowdy and boisterous," he corrected her, and she raised her head and looked at him in the faint moonlight that filtered through the canvas.

"A change of heart—" She thought about it for a moment, aware that her husband always had good reason for even his most unreasonable suggestions.

"The American," she exclaimed, with such force that behind the canvas screen Jonathan stirred and whimpered. Instantly Cathy dropped her voice to a fierce whisper. "Not even you would use my own sisters—you wouldn't, would you?"

He pulled her head down onto his chest again. "They are big girls now. How old are they?"

"Eighteen." She wrinkled her nose as his damp, curly chest hairs tickled it. "But, Ralph—"

"Old maids already."

"My own sisters—you wouldn't use them?"

"They never get to meet decent young men at Khami. Your mother frightens them all off."

"You are awful, Ralph Ballantyne."

"Would you like a demonstration of just how awful I can be?"

She considered that for a moment, and then, "Yes, please," she giggled softly.

◆ ◆ ◆

"One day I will be riding with you," Jonathan said. "Won't I, Papa?"

"One day, soon," Ralph agreed, and ruffled the child's dark curling hair. "Now I want you to take care of your mother while I am away, Jon-Jon."

Jonathan nodded, his face set, the tears grimly restrained.

"Promise?" Ralph squeezed the small body that he held

on his lap, and then he stooped from the saddle and stood the child beside Cathy, and Jonathan took her hand protectively, though he did not reach to her hip.

"I promise, Papa," he said, and gulped, staring up at his father on the tall horse.

Ralph touched Cathy's cheek lightly with his fingertips.

"I love you," she said softly.

"My beautiful Katie." And it was true. The first rays of sunlight in her hair turned it into a bright halo, and she was serene as a madonna in the deep fastness of their love.

Ralph spurred away, and Harry Mellow swung his horse in beside him. It was a fine red thoroughbred from Mr. Rhodes's private stable, and he rode like a plainsman. At the edge of the forest, both men turned to look back. The woman and child still stood at the gate of the stockade.

"You are a lucky man," Harry said softly.

"Without a good woman, there is no today, and without a son, there is no tomorrow," Ralph agreed.

◆ ◆ ◆

The vultures were still hunched in the treetops, although the bones of the lions had been picked clean and scattered across the stony ground of the ridge. They had to digest the contents of their bloated bellies before they could soar away, and their dark misshapen bodies against the clear winter sky guided Ralph and Harry the last few miles to the ridge of the Harkness claims.

"It looks promising." Harry gave his guarded judgment that first night as they squatted beside the campfire. "The country rock is in contact with the reef. You could have a reef that continues to real depth, and we have traced the strike for over two miles. Tomorrow I will mark out the spots where you must sink your prospect holes."

"There are mineralized ore bodies right across this country," Ralph told him. "The continuation of the great gold crescent of the Witwatersrand and Pilgrims Rest and Tati goldfields curves right across here—" Ralph broke off. "But you have the special gift; I have heard them say you can smell gold at fifty miles."

Harry dismissed the suggestion with a deprecating wave of his coffee mug, but Ralph went on, "And I have the wagons and capital to grubstake a prospecting venture and to develop the finds that are made. I like you, Harry. I think we would work well together, the Harkness Mine first, and after that, who knows, the whole bloody country, perhaps.''

Harry started to speak, but Ralph put a hand on his forearm to stop him.

"This continent is a treasure chest. The Kimberley diamond fields and the Witwatersrand banket, side by side, all the diamond and gold in the one bucket—who would ever have believed it?"

"Ralph." Harry shook his head. "I have already thrown in my lot with Mr. Rhodes."

Ralph sighed and stared into the flames of the fire for a full minute. Then he relit the stump of his dead cheroot and began to argue and cajole in his plausible and convincing way. An hour later as he rolled into his blanket, he repeated his offer.

"Under Rhodes you will never be your own man. You will always be a servant."

"You work for Mr. Rhodes, Ralph."

"I contract to him, Harry, but the profit or loss is mine. I still own my soul."

"And I don't," Harry chuckled.

"Come in with me, Harry. Find out what it feels like to bet your own cards, to calculate your own risks, to give the orders instead of taking them. Life is all a game, Harry, and there is only one way to play it—flat out."

"I'm Rhodes's man."

"When the time comes, then we will talk again," Ralph said, and pulled the blanket over his head. Within minutes his breathing was slow and regular.

◆ ◆ ◆

In the morning Harry marked the sites for the prospect bores with cairns of stone, and Ralph realized how cunningly he was quartering the extended line of the reef to pick it up again at depth. By noon Harry had finished, and as they saddled up, Ralph made a swift calculation and realized it would be another two days before Cathy's twin sisters could arrive at the base camp from Khami Mission.

"Seeing that we have come so far, we should make a sweep out toward the east before turning back. God knows what we could find—more gold, diamonds." And when Harry hesitated, "Mr. Rhodes will have gone on to Bulawayo already. He'll be holding court there for the next month at least; he won't even miss you."

Harry thought for a moment, then grinned like a schoolboy about to cut his classes to raid the orchard. "Let's go!" he said.

They rode slowly, and at each river course, they dismounted to pan the gravel from the bottom of the stagnant green pools. Wherever the bedrock outcropped above the overburden of earth, they broke off samples. They searched out the burrows of ant bear and porcupine and the nests of the swarming white termites to find what grains and chippings they had brought up from depth.

On the third day, Harry said, "We've picked up a dozen likely shows of color. I particularly liked those crystals of beryllium; they are a good pointer to emerald deposits."

Harry's enthusiasm had increased with each mile ridden, but now they had reached the end of the outward leg of their eastward sweep, and even Ralph realized that it was time to turn back. They had been out five days from the base camp, they had exhausted their coffee and sugar and meal, and Cathy would be anxious by now.

They took one last look at the country that they must leave unexplored for the time being.

"It's beautiful," Harry murmured, "I have never seen a more magnificent land. What is the name of that range of hills?"

"That's the southern end of the Matopos."

"I have heard Mr. Rhodes speak of them. Aren't they the sacred hills of the Matabele?"

Ralph nodded. "If I believed in witchcraft—" He broke off and chuckled with embarrassment. "There is something about those hills."

There was the first rosy flush of the sunset in the western sky, and it turned the polished rock of those distant, brooding hills to pink marble, while their crests were garlanded with fragile twists of cloud colored by the slanting rays to ivory and ashes.

"There is a secret cave hidden in there where a witch who presided over the tribes used to live. My father took in a commando and destroyed her at the beginning of the war against Lobengula."

"I have heard the story; it is one of the legends, already."

"Well, it's true. They say—" Ralph broke off and studied the turreted range of rock with a thoughtful expression. "Those are not clouds, Harry," he said at last. "That's smoke. Yet there are no kraals in the Matopos. It could be a bushfire, but I don't think so; it's not on a broad front."

"Then where is the smoke coming from?"

"That is what we are going to find out," Ralph replied, and before Harry could protest, he had started his horse and was cantering across the plains of winter grass toward the rampart of bare granite that blocked off the horizon.

♦ ♦ ♦

A Matabele warrior sat aloof from the men who swarmed about the earthen kilns. He sat in the meager shade of a twisted cripplewood tree. He was lean, so that the rack of his ribs showed through the covering of muscle under his cloak. His skin was burned by the sun to the deep black of carved ebony, and it was glossed with health, like the coat of a trained thoroughbred, blemished only by the old, healed gunshot wounds on his chest and back.

He wore a simple kilt and cloak of tanned leather, no feathers or war rattles, no regimentals of fur or plumes of marabou stork upon his bared head. He was unarmed, for the white men had made roaring bonfires of the long rawhide shields and carried away the broad silver assegais by the wagonload; they had confiscated also the Martini-Henry rifles with which the company had paid King Lobengula for the concession to all the mineral wealth beneath this land.

On his head the warrior wore the headring of the induna; it was of gum and clay, woven permanently into his own hair and black and hard as iron. This badge of rank announced to the world that he had once been a councillor of Lobengula, the last king of the Matabele. The simple ring declared his royal bloodline, the Zanzi blood of the Kumalo tribe, running back pure and unbroken to old Zululand, a thousand miles and more away in the south.

Mzilikazi had been this man's grandfather; Mzilikazi who had defied the tyrant Chaka and led his people away toward the north. Mzilikazi, the little chief who had slaughtered a million souls on that terrible northward march, and in the process had become a mighty emperor, as powerful and cruel as Chaka had ever been. Mzilikazi, his grandfather, who had finally brought his nation to this rich and beautiful land, who had been the first to enter these magical hills and

34

to listen to the myriad weird voices of the Umlimo, the Chosen One, the witch and oracle of the Matopos.

Lobengula, son of Mzilikazi, who ruled the Matabele after the old king's death, had been the young man's blood uncle. It was Lobengula who had granted him the honors of the induna's headring and appointed him commander of one of the elite fighting impis. But now Lobengula was dead, and the young induna's impi had been blown to nothing by the Maxim guns on the bank of the Shangani River, and the same Maxim guns had branded him with those deeply dimpled cicatrices upon his trunk.

His name was Bazo, which means "the Ax," but more often now men spoke of him as "the Wanderer." He had sat beneath the cripplewood tree all that day, watching the ironsmiths perform their rites, for the birth of iron was a mystery to all but these adepts. The smiths were not Matabele but were members of an older tribe, an ancient people whose origins were somehow interwoven with those haunted and ruined stone walls of Great Zimbabwe.

Although the new white masters and their queen beyond the seas had decreed that the Matabele no longer own *amaholi*, slaves, yet these Rozwi ironsmiths were still the dogs of the Matabele, still performed their art at the behest of their warlike masters.

The ten oldest and wisest of the Rozwi smiths had selected the ore from the quarry, deliberating over each fragment like vain women choosing ceramic beads from the trader's stock. They had judged the iron ore for color and weight, for the perfection of the metal it contained, and for its purity from foreign matter, and then they had broken up the ore upon the rock anvils until each lump was the perfect size. While they worked with care and total preoccupation, some of their apprentices were cutting and burning the tree trunks in the charcoal pits, controlling the combustion with layers of earth and finally quenching it with clay pots of water. Meanwhile, yet another party of apprentices made the long journey to the limestone quarries and returned with the crushed catalyst in leather bags slung upon the backs of the baggage bullocks. When the master smiths had grudgingly approved the quality of charcoal and limestone, then the building of the rows of clay kilns could begin.

Each kiln was shaped like the torso of a heavily pregnant

woman, like a fat, domed belly, in which the layers of iron ore and charcoal and limestone would be packed. At the lower end of the kiln was the crotch, guarded by symbolically truncated clay thighs between which was the narrow opening into which would be introduced the buckhorn nozzle of the leather bellows.

When all was ready, the head smith chopped the head off the sacrificial rooster and passed down the line of kilns, sprinkling them with hot blood while he chanted the first of the ancient incantations to the spirit of iron.

Bazo watched with fascination and a prickle of superstitious awe on his skin as fire was introduced through the vaginal openings of the kilns, the magical moment of impregnation which was greeted with a joyous cry by the assembled smiths. Then the young apprentices pumped the leather bellows in a kind of religious ecstasy, singing the hymns which insured the success of the smelting and set the rhythm for the work on the bellows. When each fell back exhausted, there was another to take his place and keep the steady blast of air driving deeply into the kiln.

A faint haze of smoke hung over the workings; like sea fret on a still summer's day, it rose to eddy slowly around the bald peaks of the hills. Now at last it was time to draw the smelting, and as the head smith freed the clay plug from the first kiln, a joyous shout of thanksgiving went up from the assembly at the bright glowing rush of the molten metal from the womb of the furnace.

Bazo found himself trembling with excitement and wonder, as he had when his first son had been born in one of the caves in these selfsame hills.

"The birth of the blades," he whispered aloud, and in his imagination he could already hear the dinning of the hammers as they beat out the metal, and the sizzling hiss of the quenching that would set the temper of the edge and point of the broad stabbing spears.

A touch on his shoulder startled him from his reverie, and he glanced up at the woman who stood over him, and then he smiled. She wore the leather skirt, decorated with beads, of the married woman, but there were no bangles or bracelets on her smooth young limbs.

Her body was straight and hard, her naked breasts symmetrical and perfectly proportioned. Although she had already suckled a fine son, they were not marred by stretch marks. Her belly was concave as a greyhound's, while the skin was smooth and drum tight. Her neck was long and graceful, her nose straight and narrow, her eyes slanted above the Egyptian arches of her cheekbones. Her features were those of a statuette from the tomb of some long-dead pharaoh.

"Tanase," said Bazo, "another thousand blades." Then he saw her expression and broke off. "What is it?" he asked with quick concern.

"Riders," she said. "Two of them. White men coming from the southern forests, and coming swiftly."

Bazo rose in a single movement, quick as a leopard alarmed by the approach of the hunters. Only now his full height and the breadth of his shoulders was evident, for he towered a full head over the ironsmiths about him. He lifted the buckhorn whistle that hung on a thong about his neck and blew a single sharp blast. Immediately all the scurry and bustle among the kilns ceased and the master smith hurried to him.

"How long to draw the rest of the smelting and break down the kilns?" Bazo demanded.

"Two days, oh Lord," answered the ironworker, bobbing respectfully. His eyes were bloodshot from the smoke of the furnace, and the smoke seemed to have stained his cap of white hair to dingy yellow.

"You have until dawn—"

"Lord!"

"Work all night, but screen the fires from the plain." Bazo turned from him and strode up the steep incline to where twenty other men waited below the granite cap of the hill.

Like Bazo they wore only simple leather kilts and were unarmed, but their bodies were tempered and fined down by war and the training for war, and there was the warrior's arrogance in their stance as they rose to acknowledge their induna, and their eyes were bright and fierce. There was no doubt that these were Matabele, not *amaholi* dogs.

"Follow!" ordered Bazo, and led them at a trot along the lower contour of the hill. There was a narrow cave in the base of the cliff, and Bazo drew aside the hanging creepers that screened the mouth and stooped into the gloomy interior. The cave was only ten paces deep, and it ended abruptly in a scree of loose boulders.

Bazo gestured, and two of his men went up to the end wall of the cave and rolled aside the boulders. In the recess beyond, there was the glint of polished metal like the scales of a slumbering reptile. As Bazo moved out of the entrance, the slanting rays of the setting sun struck deeply into the cave, lighting the secret arsenal. The assegais were stacked in bundles of ten and bound together with rawhide thongs.

The two warriors lifted out a bundle, broke the thongs and swiftly passed the weapons down the line of men until each was armed. Bazo hefted the stabbing spear. The shaft was of polished red heartwood of mkusi, the bloodwood tree. The blade was hand-forged, wide as Bazo's palm, and long as his forearm. He could have shaved the hair from the back of his hand with the honed edge.

He had felt naked until that moment, but now, with the familiar weight and balance in his hand, he was a man again. He gestured to his men to roll the boulders back into place, covering the cache of bright new blades, and then he led them back along the path. On the shoulder of the hill, Tanase waited for him on the ledge of rock which commanded a wide view across the grassy plains, and beyond them the blue forests dreamed softly in the evening light.

"There," she pointed, and Bazo saw them instantly.

Two horses, moving at an easy canter. They had reached the foot of the hills and were riding along them, scouting for an easy route. The riders peered up at the tangle of boulders and at the smooth, pearly sheets of granite which offered no foothold.

There were only two access trails to the valley of the ironsmiths, each of them narrow and steep, with necks which could be easily defended. Bazo turned and looked back. The smoke from the kilns was dissipating; there were only a few pale ribbons twisting along the granite cliffs. By morning there would be nothing to lead a curious traveler to the secret place, but there was still an hour of daylight, less perhaps, for the night comes with startling rapidity in Africa above the Limpopo River.

"I must delay them until dark," Bazo said. "I must turn them before they find the path."

"If they will not be turned?" Tanase asked softly, and in reply Bazo merely altered his grip on the broad assegai in his right hand and then quickly drew Tanase back off the rocky ledge, for the horsemen had halted and one of them, the taller and broader man, was carefully sweeping the hillside with a pair of binoculars.

"Where is my son?" Bazo asked.

"At the cave," Tanase replied.

"You know what to do if—" He did not have to go on, and Tanase nodded.

"I know," she said softly, and Bazo turned from her and went bounding down the steep pathway with twenty armed *amadoda* at his back.

At the narrow place which Bazo had marked, he stopped. He did not have to speak, but at a single gesture of his free hand his men slipped off the narrow trail and disappeared into the crevices and cracks of the gigantic boulders that stood tall on either hand. In seconds there was no sign of them, and Bazo broke off a branch from one of the dwarfed trees that grew in a rocky pocket, and he ran back, sweeping the trail of all signs that might alert a wary man to the ambush. Then he placed his assegai on a shoulder-high ledge beside the path and covered it with the green branch. It was within easy reach if he was forced to guide the white riders up the trail.

"I will try to turn them, but if I cannot, wait until they reach this place," he called to the hidden warriors. "Then do it swiftly."

His men were spread out for two hundred paces along both sides of the trail, but they were concentrated here at the bend. A good ambush must have depth to it, so if a victim breaks through the first rank of attackers, there will be others waiting for him beyond. This was a good ambush: in bad ground on a steep, narrow trail where a horse could not turn readily nor go ahead at full gallop. Bazo nodded to himself with satisfaction, then unarmed and shieldless, he went springing down the trail toward the plain, agile as a klipspringer over the rough track.

◆ ◆ ◆

"It will be dark in half an hour," Harry Mellow called after Ralph. "We should find a place to camp."

"There must be a path." Ralph rode with one fist on his hip and the felt hat pushed back on his head, looking up the wild cliff.

"What do you expect to find up there?"

"I don't know, and that's the devil of it." Ralph grinned

over his shoulder. He was unprepared and twisted off balance, so when his horse shied violently under him, he almost lost a stirrup and had to grab at the pommel of the saddle to prevent himself going over, but at the same time he yelled to Harry.

"Cover me!" And with his free hand Ralph tugged the Winchester rifle from its leather boot under his knee. His horse was rearing and skittering in a tight circle, so he could not get the rifle up. He knew that he was blocking Harry's line of fire, and that for those long seconds he was completely defenseless, and he swore helplessly, anticipating a rush of dark spearmen out of the broken rock and scrub at the foot of the cliff.

Then he realized there was only one man, and that he was unarmed, and again he yelled at Harry with even more urgency, for he had heard the clash of the breechblock behind him as the American loaded and cocked.

"Hold it! Don't shoot!"

The gelding reared again, but this time Ralph jerked it down and then stared at the tall black man who had stepped so silently and unexpectedly out of the crevice of a fractured granite block.

"Who are you?" he demanded, his voice rasping with the shock, which still screwed his guts into a ball and charged his veins with a rush of quick blood. "Damn you, I nearly shot you." Ralph caught himself, and this time repeated in fluent Sindebele, the Matabele language, "Who are you?"

The tall man in the plain leather cloak inclined his head slightly, but his body remained absolutely still, the empty hands hanging at his sides.

"What manner of question is that," he asked gravely, "for one brother to ask another?"

Ralph stared at him, taking in the induna's headring on his brow and the gaunt features, scored and riven by the crags and deep lines of some terrible suffering, a sorrow or an illness that must have transported this man to the frontiers of hell itself. It moved Ralph deeply to look upon that face, for there was something, the fierce eyes and the tone of the deep, measured voice that was so familiar, and yet so altered as to be unrecognizable.

"Henshaw," the man spoke again, using Ralph Ballantyne's Matabele praise name. "Henshaw, the Hawk, do you not know me? Have these few short years changed us so?"

Ralph shook his head in disbelief, and his voice was full of wonder. "Bazo, it is not you—surely it is not you? Did you not after all die with your impi at Shangani?" Ralph kicked both feet out of the stirrups and jumped to the ground. "Bazo. It is you!" He ran to embrace the Matabele. "My brother, my black brother," he said, and there was the lift and lilt of pure joy in his voice.

Bazo accepted the embrace quietly, his hands still hanging at his sides, and at last Ralph stood back and held him at arm's length.

"At Shangani, after the guns were still, I left the wagons and walked out across the open pan. Your men were there, the Moles That Burrow Under a Mountain." That was the name that King Lobengula himself had given to Bazo's impi, *Izimvukuzane Ezembintaba.* "I knew them by their red shields, by the plumes of the marabou stork and the headbands of fur from the burrowing mole." These were the regimentals bestowed upon the impi by the old king, and Bazo's eyes turned luminous with the agony of memory as Ralph went on. "Your men were there, Bazo, lying upon each other like the fallen leaves of the forest. I searched for you, rolling the dead men onto their backs to see their faces, but there were so many of them."

"So many," Bazo agreed, and only his eyes betrayed his emotion.

"And there was so little time to look for you," Ralph explained quietly. "I could only search slowly, with care, for some of your men were *fanisa file.*" It was an old Zulu trick to sham dead on the battlefield and wait for the enemy to come out to loot and count the kill. "I did not want an assegai between my shoulder blades. Then the laager broke up and the wagons rolled on toward the king's kraal. I had to leave."

"I was there," Bazo told him, and drew aside the leather cloak. Ralph stared at the dreadful scars and then dropped his gaze while Bazo covered his torso again. "I was lying among the dead men."

"And now?" Ralph asked. "Now that it is all over, what are you doing here?"

"What does a warrior do when the war is over, when the impis are broken and disarmed, and the king is dead?"

Bazo shrugged. "I am a hunter of wild honey now." He glanced up the cliff at where the last smoke wisps were blending into the darkening sky as the sun touched the tops of the western forest. "I was smoking a hive when I saw you coming."

"Ah!" Ralph nodded. "It was that smoke that led us to you."

"Then it was fortunate smoke, my brother Henshaw."

"You still call me brother?" Ralph marveled gently. "When it might have been I who fired the bullets—" He did not complete the sentence but glanced down at Bazo's chest.

"No man can be held to account for what he does in the madness of battle," Bazo answered. "If I had reached the wagons that day," he shrugged, "you might be the one who carried the scars."

"Bazo," Ralph gestured to Harry to ride forward, "this is Harry Mellow; he is a man who understands the mystery of the earth, who can find the gold and the iron which we seek."

"Nkosi, I see you." Bazo greeted Harry gravely, calling him "Lord" and not allowing his deep resentment to show for an instant. His king had died and his nation been destroyed by the weird passion of the white men for that accursed yellow metal.

"Bazo and I grew up together on the Kimberley diamond fields. I have never had a dearer friend," Ralph explained quickly, and then turned impetuously back to Bazo. "We have a little food; you will share it with us, Bazo." This time Ralph caught the shift in Bazo's gaze, and he insisted. "Camp with us here. There is much to talk about."

"I have my woman and my son with me," Bazo answered. "They are in the hills."

"Bring them," Ralph told him. "Go quickly, before darkness falls, and bring them down into camp."

♦ ♦ ♦

Bazo alerted his men with the dusk call of the francolin, and one of them stepped out of the ambush onto the path.

"I will hold the white men at the foot of the hills for tonight," Bazo told him quietly. "Perhaps I can send them away satisfied without trying to find the valley. However, warn the ironsmiths that the kilns must be quenched by dawn tomorrow, there must be no shred of smoke.''

Bazo went on giving his orders, the finished weapons and freshly smelted metal to be hidden and the paths swept clear of spoor, the ironsmiths to retreat along the secret path deeper into the hills, the Matabele guards to cover their retreat. ''I will follow you when the white men have gone. Wait for me at the Peak of the Blind Ape.''

''Nkosi.'' They saluted him and slipped away, silent as the night-prowling leopard, into the failing light. Bazo took the fork in the path, and when he reached the rocky spur on the prow of the hill, there was no need for him to call. Tanase was waiting for him with the boy carried on her hip, the roll of sleeping mats upon her head and the leather grain bag slung on her back.

''It is Henshaw,'' he told her, and heard the serpentine hiss of her breath. Though he could not see her expression, he knew what it must be.

''He is the spawn of the white dog who violated the sacred places—''

''He is my friend,'' Bazo said.

''You have taken the oath,'' she reminded him fiercely. ''How can any white man still be your friend?''

''He was my friend, then.''

''Do you remember the vision that came to me, before the powers of divination were torn from me by this man's father?''

''Tanase''—Bazo ignored the question—''we must go down to him. If he sees my wife and my son are with me, then there will be no suspicions. He will believe that we are indeed hunting the honey of wild bees. Follow me.'' He turned back down the trail, and she followed him closely, and her voice sank to a whisper, of which he could clearly hear every word. He did not look back at her, but he listened.

''Do you remember my vision, Bazo? On the first day that I met this man whom you call the Hawk, I warned you. Before the birth of your son, when the veil of my virginity was still unpierced, before the white horsemen came with their three-legged guns that laugh like the river demons that live in the rocks where the Zambezi River falls. When you still called him 'brother' and 'friend,' I warned you against him.''

"I remember." Bazo's own voice had sunk as low as hers.

"In my vision I saw you high upon a tree, Bazo."

"Yes," he whispered, going on down the trail without looking back at her. There was a superstitious tremor in Bazo's voice now, for his beautiful young wife had once been the apprentice of the mad sorcerer, Pemba. When Bazo at the head of his impi had stormed the sorcerer's mountain stronghold, he had hacked off Pemba's head and taken Tanase as a prize of war, but the spirits had claimed her back.

On the eve of the wedding feast when Bazo would have taken the virgin Tanase as his first bride, as his senior wife, an ancient wizard had come down out of the Matopo Hills and led her away, and Bazo had been powerless to intervene, for she had been the daughter of the dark spirits and she had come to her destiny in these hills.

"The vision was so clear that I wept," Tanase reminded him, and Bazo shivered.

In that secret cave in the Matopos, the full power of the spirits had descended upon Tanase, and she had become the Umlimo, the Chosen One, the oracle. It was Tanase, speaking in the weird voices of the spirits, who had warned Lobengula of his fate. It was Tanase who had foreseen the coming of the white men, with their wonderful machines that turned the night to noonday and their little mirrors that sparkled like stars upon the hills, speeding messages vast distances across the plains. No man could doubt that she had once had the power of the oracle and that in her mystic trances she had been able to see through the dark veils of the future for the Matabele nation.

However, these strange powers had depended upon her maidenhead remaining unpierced. She had warned Bazo of this, pleading with him to strip her of her virginity and rid her of these terrible powers, but he had demurred, bound by law and custom, until it had been too late and the wizards had come down from the hills to claim her.

At the beginning of the war which the white men had carried so swiftly to Lobengula's kraal at GuBulawayo, a small band had detached from the main army; they were the hardest and cruelest, led by Bakela, the Fist, himself a hard, fierce man. They had ridden swiftly into these hills. They had followed the secret path that Bakela had discovered twenty-five years or so before and galloped to the secret cavern of the Umlimo. For Bakela knew the value of the oracle, knew how sacred she was, and how her destruction would throw the Matabele nation into despair. Bakela's riders had shot down the guardians of the caverns and forced their way within. Two of Bakela's troopers had found Tanase, young and lovely and naked in the deepest recesses of the cave, and they had violated her, savagely tearing the maidenhead that she had once offered so lovingly to Bazo. They had rutted upon her until her virgin blood splattered the floor of the cavern and her screams had guided Bakela to them.

He had driven his men off her with fist and boot, and when they were alone, he had looked down upon Tanase where she lay bloodied and broken at his feet. Then strangely, this hard, fierce man had been overcome with compassion. Though he had ridden this dangerous road for the sole purpose of destroying the Umlimo, yet the bestial behavior of his troopers had weakened his resolve, had placed some burden of recompense upon him.

Bakela must have known that with her virginity torn from her she had lost her powers, for he told her, "You, who were Umlimo, are Umlimo no longer." He had accomplished her destruction without using rifle or sword, and he turned and strode from the cavern, leaving her life in exchange for her virginity and the loss of her dark powers.

She had told the story to Bazo many times, and he knew that the mists of time had closed before her eyes and that now they shrouded the future from her, but no man could doubt that she had once possessed the power of the Sight.

Thus Bazo shivered briefly, and he felt the ghost fingers touching the nape of his neck as Tanase went on in her husky whisper.

"I wept, Bazo, my Lord, when I saw you upon the high tree, and while I wept, the man you call Henshaw, the Hawk, was looking up at you—and smiling!"

♦ ♦ ♦

They ate cold bully beef straight from the cans, using the blade of a hunting knife to spoon it out and passing the cans from hand to hand. There was no coffee, so they washed down the glutinous mess with sun-warmed drafts from the felt-covered water bottles, and then Ralph shared out his remaining cheroots with Harry Mellow and Bazo. They lit them with burning twigs from the fire and smoked in silence for a long time.

Close at hand a hyena warbled and sobbed in the darkness, drawn by the firelight and the smell of food, while further out across the plain, the lions were hunting, sweeping toward the moonrise, not roaring before the kill but coughing throatily to keep in contact with the other animals in the pride.

Tanase, with the child on her lap, sat at the edge of the firelight, aloof from the men, and they ignored her. It would have offended Bazo if they had paid undue attention to her, but now Ralph took the cheroot from his mouth and glanced in her direction.

"What is your son's name?" he asked Bazo, and there was a heartbeat of hesitation before Bazo replied.

"He is called Tungata Zebiwe."

Ralph frowned quickly, but checked the harsh words that rose to his lips. Instead he said, "He is a fine boy."

Bazo held out his hand toward the child, but Tanase restrained him for a moment with a quiet ferocity.

"Let him come to me," Bazo ordered sharply, and reluctantly Tanase let the sleepy child stagger to his father and climb into his arms.

He was a pretty toffee color, with a pot belly and chubby limbs. Except for the bracelets of copper wire at his wrists and a single string of beads around his waist, he was stark naked. His hair was a dark fluffy cap, and his eyes were owlish with sleep as he stared at Ralph.

"Tungata Zebiwe," Ralph repeated his name, and then leaned across to stroke his head. The child made no attempt to pull away, nor did he show any trace of alarm, but in the shadows Tanase hissed softly and reached out as if to take the child back, then dropped her hand again.

"The Seeker After What Has Been Stolen," Ralph translated the child's name, and caught the mother's dark eyes. "The Seeker After Justice—that is a heavy duty to place upon one so young," he said quietly. "You would make him an avenger of injustice inflicted before his birth?"

Then smoothly Ralph seemed to change to a different subject.

"Do you remember, Bazo, the day we first met? You were a green youth sent by your father and his brother the king to work on the diamond fields. I was even younger and greener when my father and I found you in the veld and he signed you to a three-year labor contract, before any other digger could put his brand on you."

The lines of suffering and sorrow that marred Bazo's features seemed to smooth away as he smiled, and for a few moments he was that young guileless and carefree youth again.

"It was only later I found out that the reason Lobengula sent you and thousands of other young bucks like you to the fields was to bring home as many fat diamonds as you could steal." They both laughed, Ralph ruefully and Bazo with a vestige of his youthful glee.

"Lobengula must have hidden a great treasure somewhere. Jameson never did find those diamonds when he captured GuBulawayo."

"Do you remember the hunting falcon, Scipio?" Bazo asked.

"And the giant spider that won us our first gold sovereigns at the Kimberley spider fights," Ralph continued, and they chatted animatedly, recalling how they had worked shoulder to shoulder in the great diamond pit, and the mad diversions with which they had broken the dreadful monotony of that brutal labor.

Not understanding the language, Harry Mellow rolled in his blanket and pulled the corner of it over his head. In the shadows Tanase sat, still as a beautiful ebony carving, not smiling when the men laughed but with her eyes fastened on their lips as they spoke.

Abruptly Ralph changed the subject again. "I have a son also," he said. "He was born before the war, so he is a year or two older than yours."

The laughter died immediately, and although Bazo's expression was neutral, his eyes were wary.

"They could be friends, as we are friends," Ralph suggested, and Tanase looked protectively toward her son, but Bazo did not reply.

"You and I could work side by side once more," Ralph went on. "Soon I will have a rich gold mine in the forests yonder, and I will need a senior induna in charge of the hundreds of men who will come to work."

"I am a warrior," said Bazo, "no longer a mine laborer."

"The world changes, Bazo," Ralph answered softly.

"There are no longer any warriors in Matabeleland. The shields are burned. The assegai blades are broken. The eyes are no longer red, Bazo, for the wars are finished. The eyes are white now, and there will be peace in this land for a thousand years."

Bazo was silent.

"Come with me, Bazo. Bring your son to learn the white man's skills. One day he will read and write and be a man of consequence, not merely a hunter of wild honey. Forget this sad name you have given him, and find another. Call him a joyous name and bring him to meet my own son. Together they will enjoy this beautiful land and be brothers as we once were brothers."

Bazo sighed then. "Perhaps you are right, Henshaw. As you say, the impis are disbanded. Those who were once warriors now work on the roads that Lodzi is building." The Matabele always had difficulty in pronouncing the sound of *r*, thus Rhodes was "Lodzi," and Bazo was referring to the system of conscripted labor which the Chief Native Commissioner, General Mungo St. John, had introduced in Matabeleland. Bazo sighed again. "If a man must work, it is better that he work in dignity at a task of importance with somebody whom he respects. When will you begin to dig for your gold, Henshaw?"

"After the rains, Bazo. But come with me now. Bring your woman and your son—"

Bazo held up one hand to silence him. "After the rains, after the great storms, we will talk again, Henshaw," Bazo said quietly, and Tanase nodded her head and for the first time she smiled, an odd little smile of approval. Bazo was right to dissemble and to lull Henshaw with vague promises. With her specially trained sense of awareness, Tanase recognized that despite the direct gaze of his green eyes and his open, almost childlike smile, this young white man was harder and more dangerous than even Bakela, his father.

"After the great storms," Bazo had promised him, and that had a hidden meaning. The great storm was the secret thing that they were planning.

"First there are things that I must do, but once they are done, I will seek you out," Bazo promised.

♦ ♦ ♦

Bazo led up the steep gradient of the narrow pathway through the deep gut of the granite hills. Tanase followed a dozen paces behind him. The roll of sleeping mat and the iron cooking pot were carried easily on her head, and her spine was straight and her step fluid and smooth to balance the load. The boy skipped at her side, singing a childish nonsense in a high, piping chant. He was the only one unaffected by the brooding menace of this dark valley. The scrub on each side of the path was dense and armed with vicious thorn. The silence was oppressive, for no bird sang and no small animal rustled the leaves.

Bazo stepped lightly across the boulders in the bed of the narrow stream that crossed the trail and paused to look back as Tanase scooped a handful of the cool water and held it to the boy's lips. Then they went on.

The path ended abruptly against a sheer cliff of pearly granite, and Bazo stopped and leaned on the light throwing spear, the only weapon that the white administrator in Bulawayo allowed a black man to carry to protect himself and his family against the predators which infested the wilderness. It was a frail thing, not an instrument of war like the broad, stabbing assegai.

Leaning his weight on the spear, Bazo looked up the tall cliff. There was a thatched watchman's hut on a ledge just below the summit, and now a quavering old man's voice challenged him.

"Who dares the secret pass?" Bazo lifted his chin and answered in a bull bellow which sent the echoes bouncing from the cliffs.

"Bazo, son of Gandang. Bazo, Induna of the Kumalo blood royal."

Then, not deigning to await the reply, Bazo stepped through the convoluted portals of granite, into the passageway that split the cliff.

The passage was narrow, barely wide enough for two grown men to walk shoulder to shoulder, and the floor was clean white sand with chips of bright mica that sparkled and crunched like sugar under his bare feet. The passage twisted like a maimed serpent and then abruptly debouched into a sweeping valley of lush green, bisected by a tinkling stream that spilled from the rock face near where Bazo stood.

The valley was a circular basin a mile or so across,

completely walled in by the high cliffs. In its center was a tiny village of thatched huts, but as Tanase came out of the mouth of the secret passage and stopped beside Bazo, both of them looked beyond the village to the opposite wall of the valley.

In the base of the cliff, the low, wide opening of a cavern snarled at them like a toothless mouth. Neither of them spoke for many minutes as they stared across at the sacred cave, but the memories came crowding back upon both of them. In that cavern Tanase had undergone the frightful indoctrination and initiation which had transformed her into the Umlimo, and on the rocky floor she had suffered the cruel abuse that had stripped her of her powers and made her an ordinary woman once more.

Now in that cavern another being presided in Tanase's place as spiritual head of the nation, for the powers of the Umlimo never die but are passed on from one initiate to another, as they had been from forgotten times when the ancients had built the great stone ruins of the Zimbabwe.

"Are you ready?" Bazo asked at last.

"I am ready, Lord," she replied, and they started down toward the village. But before they reached it, they were met by a weird procession of creatures, some of them barely recognizable as human, for they crawled on all fours and whined and yapped like animals. There were ancient withered crones with empty dugs flapping against their bellies, pretty little girls with pubescent breast buds and blank, unsmiling faces, old men with deformed limbs who dragged themselves in the dust, and slim youths with well-formed muscular bodies and mad eyes that rolled back into their skulls, all of them decked with the gruesome paraphernalia of the necromancer and wizard—bladders of lion and crocodile, skin of python and bird, skulls and teeth of ape, of man, and of beast. They ringed Bazo and Tanase, prancing and mewling and leering, until Bazo felt his skin itching with the insects of loathing, and he lifted his son high on his shoulder away from their touching, prying hands.

Tanase was unperturbed, for this fantastic throng had once been her own retinue, and she stood expressionless as one of the horrible witches crawled to her and slobbered and frothed over her bare feet. Dancing and chanting, the guardians of the Umlimo led the two wanderers into the village and then disappeared, slipping away into the thatched huts.

However, they were not alone. In the center of the village stood a *setenghi,* an airy, open-sided hut of white mopani poles, and a roof of neat thatch. In the shade of the *setenghi,* there were men waiting, but these were entirely different from the strange throng which had met them at the entrance of the village.

Each of these men sat upon a low carved stool. Though some of them were grossly fat and others skinny and stooped, they were all of them surrounded by an almost palpable air of dignity and authority. Though some were white-headed, with snowy woolen beards and deeply wrinkled faces, and others were in the prime of their life and powers, they all of them wore upon their heads the simple black headring of gum and clay.

Here assembled in the secret valley of the Umlimo were what was left of the leaders of the Matabele nation, men who had once stood at the head of the fighting impis as they formed the bull formation of encircling horns and crushing chest. Some of them, the eldest, remembered the exodus from the south driven by the mounted Boer horsemen; they had fought as young men under great Mzilikazi himself and still wore with pride the tassels of honor which he had awarded to them.

All of them had sat upon the councils of King Lobengula, son of great Mzilikazi, and had been on the Hills of the Indunas that fateful day when the king had stood before the assembled regiments and had faced eastward, the direction from which the column of wagons and white soldiers was entering Matabeleland. They had shouted the royal salute "Bayete!" as Lobengula poised his great swollen body on gout-distorted legs and then defiantly hurled the toy spear of kingship at the invaders who were still out of sight beyond the blue horizon. These were the indunas who had led their fighting men past the king in review singing his praises and the battle hymns of the regiments, saluting Lobengula for the last time, and then going out to where the Maxim guns waited for them behind the wagon sides and plaited thornbush walls of the white men's laager.

In the midst of this distinguished assembly sat three men—the three surviving sons of Mzilikazi, the noblest and most revered of all the indunas. Somabula, on the left, was the eldest, victor of a hundred fierce battles, the warrior for whom the lovely Somabula Forests had been named. On the right was Babiaan, wise and brave. The honorable scars laced his torso and limbs. However, it was the man in the center who rose from his ornately carved stool of wild ebony and came out into the sunlight.

"Gandang, my father, I see you and my heart sings," cried Bazo.

"I see you, my son," said Gandang, his handsome face made almost beautiful by the joy that lit it, and when Bazo knelt before him, he touched his head in blessing and then raised him up with his own hand.

"Baba!" Tanase clapped her hands respectfully before her face, and when Gandang nodded his acknowledgment, she withdrew quietly to the nearest hut, where she could listen from behind the thin reed wall.

It was not for a woman to attend the high councils of the nation. In the time of the kings, a lesser woman would have been speared to death for daring to approach an *indaba* such as this. Tanase, however, was the one that had once been the Umlimo, and she was still the mouthpiece of the Chosen One. Besides which, the world was changing, the kings had passed, the old customs were dying with them, and this woman wielded more power than any but the highest of the assembled indunas. Nevertheless, she made the gesture of retiring to the closed hut, so as not to offend the memory of the old ways.

Gandang clapped his hands, and the slaves brought a stool and a baked clay beerpot to Bazo. Bazo refreshed himself with a long draft of the thick, tart, bubbling gruel, and then he greeted his fellow indunas in strict order of their seniority, beginning with Somabula and going slowly down the ranks; and while he did so, he found himself mourning their pitiful shrunken numbers—only twenty-six of them were left.

"Kamuza, my cousin." He looked across at the twenty-sixth and most junior of the indunas. "My sweetest friend, I see you."

Then Bazo did something that was without precedent; he came to his feet and looked over their heads, and went on with the formal greetings.

"I greet you, Manonda, the Brave!" he cried. "I see you hanging on the branch of the mkusi tree. Dead by your own hand, choosing death rather than to live as a slave of white men.''

The assembled indunas glanced over their own shoulders, following the direction of Bazo's gaze with expressions of superstitious awe.

"Is that you, Ntabene? In life they called you the Mountain, and like a mountain you fell on the banks of the Shangani. I greet you, brave spirit.''

The assembled indunas understood then. Bazo was calling the roll of honor, and they took up the greeting in a deep growl.

"*Sakubona*, Ntabene.''

"I see you, Tambo. The waters of the Bembesi Crossing ran red with your blood.''

"*Sakubona*, Tambo,'' growled the indunas of Kumalo.

Bazo threw aside his cloak and began to dance. It was a swaying, sensuous dance, and the sweat sprang to gloss his skin and the gunshot wounds glowed upon his chest like dark jewels. Each time he called the name of one of the missing indunas, he lifted his right knee until it touched his chest and then brought his bare foot down with a crash upon the hard earth, and the assembly echoed the hero's name.

At last Bazo sank down upon his stool, and the silence was fraught with a kind of warlike ecstasy. Slowly all their heads turned until they were looking at Somabula, the eldest, the most senior. The old induna rose and faced them, and then, because this was an *indaba* of the most weighty consequences, he began to recite the history of the Matabele nation. Though they had all heard it a thousand times since their infancy, the indunas leaned forward avidly. There was no written word, no archives to store this history; it must be remembered verbatim to be passed on to their children and their children's children.

The story began in Zululand a thousand miles to the south, with the young warrior Mzilikazi defying the mad tyrant Chaka and fleeing northward with his single impi from the Zulu might. It followed his wanderings, his battles with the forces that Chaka sent to pursue him, his victories over the little tribes which stood in Mzilikazi's path. It related how he took the young men of the conquered tribes into his impis and gave the young women as wives to his warriors. It recorded the growth of Mzilikazi from a fugitive and rebel to, first, a little chieftain, then to a great war chief, and at last to a mighty king.

Somabula related faithfully the terrible *M'fecane*, the destruction of a million souls as Mzilikazi laid waste to the land between the Orange River and the Limpopo. Then he went on to tell of the coming of the white men and the new method of waging war. He conjured up the squadrons of sturdy little ponies with bearded men upon their backs, galloping into gunshot range, then wheeling away to reload before the *amadoda* could carry the blade to them. He retold how the impis had first met the rolling fortresses, the squares of wagons lashed together with trek chains, the thorn branches woven into the spokes of the wheels and into every gap in the wooden barricade, and how the ranks of Matabele had broken and perished upon those walls of wood and thorn.

His voice sank mournfully as he told of the exodus northward, driven by the grim bearded men on horseback. He recalled how the weaklings and the infants had died on that tragic trek, and then Somabula's voice rose joyfully as he described the crossing of the Limpopo and the Shashi rivers and the discovery of this beautiful, bountiful land beyond.

By then Somabula's voice was strained and hoarse, and he sank down onto his stool and drank from the beerpot while Babiaan, his half brother, rose to describe the great days—the subjugation of the surrounding tribes, the multiplication of the Matabele cattle herds until they darkened the sweet golden grasslands, the ascension of Lobengula, "the one who drives like the wind," to the kingship, the fierce raids when the impis swept hundreds of miles beyond the borders, bringing home the plunder and the slaves that made the Matabele great. He reminded them how the regiments, plumed and befurred, carrying their great color-matched war shields, had paraded before the king like the endless flow of the Zambezi River; how the maidens danced at the Festival of the First Fruits, bare-breasted and anointed with shiny red clay, bedecked with wild flowers and beads. He described the secret showing of the treasure, when Lobengula's wives smeared his vast body with thick fat and then stuck the diamonds to it, diamonds stolen by the young bucks from the great pit that the white men had dug far to the south.

Listening to the telling of it, the indunas remembered vividly how the uncut stones had glowed on the king's gross body like a coat of precious mail, or like the armored scales of some wondrous mythical reptilian monster. In those days how great had been the king, how uncountable his herds, how fierce and warlike the young men and how beautiful the girls—and they nodded and exclaimed in approbation.

Then Somabula sank down and Gandang rose from his stool. He was tall and powerful, a warrior in the late noon of his powers, his nobility unquestioned, his courage tested and proven a hundred times, and as he took up the tale, his voice was deep and resonant.

He told how the white men had come up from the south. To begin with there were only one or two of them begging small favors, to shoot a few elephants, to trade their beads and bottles for native copper and ivory. Then there were more of them, and their demands were more insistent, more worrisome. They wanted to preach a strange three-headed god, they wanted to dig holes and search for the yellow metal and the bright stones. Deeply troubled, Lobengula had come to this place in the Matopos, and the Umlimo had warned him that when the sacred bird images flew from the ruins of Great Zimbabwe, then there would be no more peace in the land.

"The stone falcons were stolen from the sacred places," Gandang reminded them, "and Lobengula knew then that he could no more resist the white men than his father, Mzilikazi, had been able to."

Thus the king had chosen the most powerful of all the white petitioners, Lodzi, the big blue-eyed man who had eaten up the diamond mines and who was the induna of the white queen across the sea. Hoping to make him an ally, Lobengula had entered into a treaty with Lodzi; in exchange for gold coins and guns, he had granted to him a charter to dig for the buried treasures of the earth exclusively in Lobengula's eastern dominions.

However, Lodzi had sent a great train of wagons with hard fighting men like Selous and Bakela leading hundreds of young white men armed like soldiers to take possession of the Charter lands. Sorrowfully Gandang recited the long list of grievances and the breaking of faith which had culminated in the clatter of Maxim guns, in the destruction of the king's kraal at Bulawayo, and the flight of Lobengula toward the north.

Finally he described Lobengula's death. Brokenhearted and sick, the king had taken poison, and Gandang himself had laid the body in a secret cave overlooking the valley of the Zambezi, and he had placed all the king's possessions around him, his stool, his head pillow of ivory, his sleeping mat and fur kaross, his beerpots and beef bowls, his guns and his war shield, his battleaxe and stabbing spear, and at the last the little clay pots of glittering diamonds he had laid at Lobengula's gout-distorted feet. When all was done, Gandang had walled up the entrance to the cave and slaughtered the slaves who had done the work. Then he had led the shattered nation back southward into captivity.

At the last words, Gandang's hands fell to his sides, his chin sank onto the broad scarred and muscled chest, and a desolate silence descended upon them. At last one of the indunas in the second rank spoke. He was a frail old man with all the teeth missing from his upper jaw. His lower lids drooped away from his watery eyeballs so that the inner flesh showed like pink velvet and his voice was scratchy and breathless.

"Let us choose another king," he began, but Bazo interrupted him.

"A king of slaves, a king of captives?" He laughed abruptly, scornfully. "There can be no king until there is a nation once again."

The ancient induna sank back and gummed his toothless mouth, blinking about him miserably, his mind altering direction in the way of old men. "The cattle," he murmured, "they have taken our cattle."

The others hummed in angry assent. Cattle were the only true wealth; gold and diamonds were white men's baubles, but cattle were the foundation of the nation's welfare.

"One-Bright-Eye sends unblooded young bucks of our own people to lord it in the kraals," complained another. "One-Bright-Eye" was the Matabele name for General Mungo St. John, the Chief Native Commissioner of Matabeleland.

"These company police are armed with guns, and they show no respect for the custom and the law. They laugh at the indunas and the tribal elders, and they take the young girls into the bushes—"

56

"One-Bright-Eye orders all our *amadoda,* even those of Zanzi blood, respected warriors and the fathers of warriors, to labor like lowly *amaholi,* like dirt-eating slaves, digging his roads."

The litany of their wrongs, real and fancied, was recited yet again by a succession of angry indunas, while only Somabula and Babiaan and Gandang and Bazo sat aloof.

"Lodzi has burned our shields and snapped the blades of the stabbing spears. He has refused our young men the ancient right to raid the Mashona, when all the world knows that the Mashona are our dogs to kill or let live as we choose."

"One-Bright-Eye has disbanded the impis, and now no man knows who has the right to take a wife, nobody knows which maize field belongs to which village, and the people squabble like sickly children over the few scrawny beasts that Lodzi has returned to us."

"What must we do?" cried one, and then another strange and unprecedented thing happened. All of them, even Somabula, looked toward the tall, scarred young man they called the Wanderer, and they waited expectantly for no one knew what.

Bazo made a sign with one hand, and Tanase stooped out through the entrance of the reed hut. Clad only in the brief leather apron, slim and straight and supple, she carried the roll of sleeping mat in her arms, and she knelt before Bazo and unrolled the mat on the earth at his feet.

The nearest indunas, who could see what was concealed in the roll, grunted with excitement. Bazo took it up in both hands and held it high. It caught the light, and now they all gasped. The design of the blade was by King Chaka himself; the metal had been beaten out and polished to burning silver by the skilled smiths of the Rozwi, and the bloodwood shaft had been bound with copper wire and the coarse black hairs from the tail tuft of a bull elephant.

"Jee!" hissed one of the indunas, the deep, drawn-out war chant of the fighting impis, and the others took up the cry, swaying slightly to the force of it, their faces lighting with the first ecstasy of the fighting madness.

Gandang put a halt to it. He sprang to his feet, and the chant broke off as he made an abrupt gesture.

"One blade will not arm the nation, one blade will not prevail against the little three-legged guns of Lodzi."

Bazo rose and stood facing his father.

"Take it in your hands, Baba," he invited, and Gandang shook his head angrily, but he could not take his eyes off the weapon.

"Feel how the heft of it can make a man of even a slave," Bazo insisted quietly, and this time Gandang stretched out his right hand. His palm was bloodless white with tension, and his fingers trembled as they closed around the grip.

"Still it is only one blade," he insisted, but he could not resist the feel of the beautiful weapon, and he stabbed into the air with it.

"There are a thousand like this," Bazo whispered.

"Where?" Somabula barked.

"Tell us where," clamored the other indunas, but Bazo goaded them.

"By the time that the first rains fall, there will be five thousand more. At fifty places in the hills, the smiths are at work."

"Where?" Somabula repeated. "Where are they?"

"Hidden in the caves of these hills."

"Why were we not told?" Babiaan demanded.

Bazo answered, "There would have been those who doubted it could be done, those who counseled caution and delay, and there was no time for talk."

Gandang nodded. "We all know he is right; defeat has turned us into chattering old women. But now," he handed the assegai to the man beside him, "feel it!" he ordered.

"How will we assemble the impis?" the man asked, turning the weapon in his hands. "They are scattered and broken."

"That is the task of each of you. To rebuild the impis and to make certain that they are ready when the spears are sent but."

"How will the spears reach us?"

"The women will bring them, in bundles of thatching grass, in rolls of sleeping mats."

"Where will we attack? Will we strike at the heart, at the great kraal the white men have built at GuBulawayo?"

"No." Bazo's voice rose fiercely. "That was the madness which destroyed us before. In our rage we forgot the way of Chaka and Mzilikazi, we attacked into the strength of the enemy, we went in across good shooting ground onto the wagons where the guns waited." Bazo broke off and bowed his head toward the senior indunas. "Forgive me, Baba, the puppy should not yap before the old dog barks. I speak out of my turn."

"You are no puppy, Bazo," Somabula growled. "Speak on!"

"We must be the fleas," Bazo said quietly. "We must hide in the white man's clothing and sting him in the soft places until we drive him to madness. But when he scratches, we will move on to another soft place.

"We must lurk in darkness and attack in the dawn, we must wait for him in the bad ground and probe his flanks and his rear." Bazo never raised his voice, but all of them listened avidly. "Never must we run in against the walls of the laager, and when the three-legged guns begin to laugh like old women, we must drift away like the morning mist at the first rays of the sun."

"This is not war," protested Babiaan.

"It is war, Baba," Bazo contradicted, "the new kind of war, the only kind of war which we can win."

"He is right," a voice called from the ranks of indunas. "That is the way it must be."

They spoke up, one after the other, and no man argued against Bazo's vision until the turn came back to Babiaan.

"My brother Somabula has spoken the truth—you are no puppy, Bazo. Tell us only one thing more, when will it be?"

"That I cannot tell you."

"Who can?"

Bazo looked down at Tanase, who still knelt at his feet.

"We have assembled in this valley for good reason," Bazo told them. "If all agree, then my woman, who is an intimate of the Umlimo and an initiate of the mysteries, will go up to the sacred cavern to take the oracle."

"She must go immediately."

"No, Baba." Tanase's lovely head was still bowed in deep respect. "We must wait until the Umlimo sends for us."

❖   ❖   ❖

There were places where the scars had knotted into hard lumps in Bazo's flesh. The machine gun bullets had done deep damage. One arm, fortunately not the spear arm, was twisted and shortened, permanently deformed. After hard marching or exercise with the weapons of war, or after the nervous tension of planning and arguing and persuading others to his views, the torn and lumpy flesh often seized up in agonizing spasms.

Kneeling beside him in the little reed hut, Tanase could see the cramped muscles and rigid contraction of sinews. She worked the ointment of fat and herbs with strong tapered fingers, into the crested muscle down his spine and the shoulder blades, following the rubbery contractions up his neck to the base of his skull. Bazo groaned at the sweet agony of her bone-hard fingers, but slowly he relaxed and the knotted muscles subsided.

"You are good for me in so many ways," he murmured.

"I was born for no other reason," she answered, but Bazo sighed and shook his head slowly.

"You and I were both born for some purpose which is still hidden from us. We know that—we are different, you and I."

She touched his lips with her finger to still him. "We will come back to that on the morrow."

She placed both hands on his shoulders and drew him backward until he lay flat on the reed mat, and she began to work on his chest and the rigid muscles of his flat, hard belly.

"Tonight there is only us," she repeated in the throaty purr of a lioness at the kill, delighting in the power she could wield over him with the mere pressure of her finger-tips and yet at the same time consumed by a tenderness so deep that she felt her chest crushing beneath the weight of it. "Tonight we are all the world." She leaned forward and touched the bullet wounds with the tip of her tongue, and his arousal was so massive that she could not encompass it within the span of her thumb and long fingers.

He tried to sit up, but she held him down with a light pressure against his chest; then she slipped the drawstring of her apron and with a single movement straddled him, both of them crying out involuntarily at the terrible yearning for each other's bodies. Then they were swept away together in a sudden exquisite fury.

When it had passed, she cradled his head against her bosom and crooned to him like an infant until his breathing was deep and regular in the dark hut. Even then, though she was silent, she did not sleep with him but lay and marveled that such rage and compassion could possess her at the same moment in time.

"I will never know peace again," she realized suddenly. "Nor will he." And she mourned for the man she loved and for the need to goad and drive him on toward the destiny that she knew awaited both of them.

♦ ♦ ♦

On the third day, the messenger of the Umlimo came down from the cavern to where the indunas waited in the village.

The messenger was a pretty girl-child with a solemn expression and old, wise eyes. She was on the very edge of puberty, with the hard little stones already forming in her mulberry-dark nipples and the first light fuzz shading the deep cleft in the angle of her thighs. Around her neck she wore a talisman that only Tanase recognized. It was a sign that one day this child in her turn would take on the sacred mantle of the Umlimo and preside in the gruesome cavern in the cliff above the village.

Instinctively the child looked to Tanase where she squatted to one side of the ranks of men, and with her eyes and a secret hand sign of the initiates, Tanase indicated Somabula, the senior induna. The child's indecision was merely a symptom of the swift degeneration of Matabele society. In the time of the kings, no one, child or adult, would have been in any doubt as to the order of precedence.

When Somabula rose to follow the messenger, his half brothers rose with him, Babiaan on one hand and Gandang on the other.

"You also, Bazo," Somabula said, and though Bazo was younger and more junior than some of them, none of the other indunas protested at his inclusion in the mission.

The child-witch took Tanase's hand, for they were sisters of the dark spirits, and the two of them led the way up the steep path. The mouth of the cavern was a hundred paces wide, but the roof was barely high enough to clear a man's head. Once long ago the opening had been fortified with blocks of dressed stone worked in the same fashion as the walls of Great Zimbabwe, but these had been tumbled into rough piles, leaving gaps like those in an old man's teeth.

The little party halted involuntarily. The four indunas hung back and drew closer together, as though to take comfort from each other. Men who had wielded the assegai in a hundred bloody battles and run in onto the guns of the white men's laager were fearful now as they faced the entrance.

In the silence a voice spoke suddenly from above them, emanating from the bare cliff face of smooth lichen-streaked granite. "Let the indunas of royal Kumalo enter the sacred place!" They were the quavering, discordant tones of an ancient beldam, and the four warriors looked up fearfully, but there was no living thing to be seen, and none of them could summon the courage to reply.

Tanase had felt the child's hand quiver slightly in her grip at the ventriloquistic effort of projection, and only Tanase was so attuned to the ways of the witches that she knew how the art of the voices was taught to the apprentices of the Umlimo. The child was already highly skilled, and Tanase shuddered involuntarily as she realized what other fearful skills she must have mastered, what other gruesome ordeals and terrible agonies she must already have endured. In a moment of empathy, she squeezed the child's narrow, cool hand, and together they stepped through the ruined portals.

Behind them the four noble warriors crowded with the timidity of children, peering around them anxiously and stumbling on the uneven footing. The throat of the cavern narrowed, and Tanase thought with a flash of grim humor that it was as well that the light was too bad for the indunas to make out clearly the walls on either hand, for even their warlike courage might have been unequal to the horror of the catacombs.

In a bygone age that the verbal history of the Rozwi and the Karanga tribes could no longer recount, generations before bold Mzilikazi led his tribe into these hills, another plundering marauder had passed this way. It might have been Manatassi, the legendary conquering queen, at the head of her merciless hordes, laying waste to the land and slaughtering everything in her path, sparing neither woman nor child nor even the domestic animals.

The threatened tribes had taken refuge in this valley, but the marauder had burst through the narrow pass, and the miserable host had fled into their final sanctuary in this cavern. The roof overhead was still coated with soot, for the marauder had not deemed it worthwhile to lay siege to the cavern. They had pulled down the protecting wall and blocked the entrance with piles of green brush and wood. Then they had started the fire. The entire tribe had perished, and smoke had mummified their remains. So they had lain down the years in banks and heaps, piled as high as the low roof.

As Tanase's party went forward, from somewhere ahead of them a faint bluish light grew in intensity, until Bazo exclaimed suddenly and pointed to the wall of human debris beside him. In places the parchmentlike flesh had peeled away so that the ivory skulls grinned at them, and the contorted skeletal arms seemed to wave a macabre salutation as they passed. The indunas were bathed in sweat despite the cool gloom, and their expressions were awed and sickly.

Tanase and the child followed the twisting pathway with unerring familiarity and came out at last above a deep natural amphitheater. A single ray of sunlight burned down from a narrow crack in the domed cavern roof. On the floor of the amphitheater was an open fireplace, and a tendril of pale blue smoke twisted slowly upward toward the opening high above. Tanase and the child led them down the rock steps to the smooth sandy floor of the amphitheater, and at her gesture the four indunas sank down gratefully and squatted facing the smoldering fire.

Tanase released the child's hand and sat a little to one side and behind the men. The child crossed to the far wall and took a handful of herbs from one of the big round clay pots that stood there. She threw the handful upon the fire, and immediately a great yellow cloud of acrid smoke billowed upward, and as it slowly cleared, the indunas started and exclaimed with superstitious dread.

A grotesque figure faced them from across the flames. It was an albino, with silver-white leprous skin. It was a woman, for the great pale breasts were massively pendulous, the nipples a painful boiled-pink color. She was stark naked, and her dense pubic bush was white as frost-struck winter grass, and above it her belly hung in loose balconies of fat. Her forehead was low and sloped backward; her mouth was wide and thin so that she appeared toadlike. Across her broad and flattened nose and her pale cheeks, the unpigmented skin had erupted in a tender, raw rash. Her thickened forearms were folded across her belly, and her thighs, splotched with large ginger-colored freckles, were widespread as she knelt on a mat of zebra skin and regarded the men before her fixedly.

"I see you, oh Chosen One," Somabula greeted her. Despite an enormous effort of will, his voice trembled.

The Umlimo made no response, and Somabula rocked back on his heels and was silent. The girl-child was busy among the pots, and now she came forward and knelt beside the gross albino, proffering the clay pipe she had prepared.

The Umlimo took the long reed stem between her thin, silvery lips, and the girl lifted a live coal from the fire with her bare hands and placed it on the vegetable ball in the bowl of the pipe. It began to glow and splutter, and the Umlimo drew a slow lungful and then let the aromatic smoke trickle out of her simian nostrils. Immediately the heavy sweetish odor of *insanghu* carried to the waiting men.

The oracle was induced in different ways. Before Tanase had lost the power, it had descended spontaneously upon her, throwing her into convulsive fits while the spirit voices struggled to escape from her throat. However, this grotesque successor had to resort to the wild hemp pipe. The seeds and flowers of the *Cannabis sativa* plant, crushed in the green and molded into sun-dried balls, were her key to the spirit world.

She smoked quietly, a dozen short inhalations without allowing the smoke to escape, holding it in until her pale face seemed to swell and the pink pupils of her eyes glazed over. Then she expelled the smoke with an explosive exhalation and started again. The indunas watched her with such fascination that they did not at first notice the soft scratching sound on the cavern floor. It was Bazo who at last started and grunted with shock and involuntarily grasped his father's forearm. Gandang exclaimed and began to rise in horror and alarm, but Tanase's voice arrested him.

"Do not move. It is dangerous," she whispered urgently, and Gandang sank back and froze into stillness.

From the dark recesses in the back of the cavern, a lobsterlike creature scuttled across the pale sandy floor toward where the Umlimo squatted. The firelight glinted on the glossy armored carapace of the creature as it reached the Umlimo and then began to climb up her bloated silver-white body. It paused in her lap, with the long segmented tail lifting and pulsing, its spiderlike legs hooked into the Umlimo's coarse white pubic curls, before it began climbing again, up over her bulging belly, hanging from one drooping pale breast like some evil fruit on the bough, upward it climbed, onto her shoulder, and then it reached the angle of her jaw below the ear.

The Umlimo remained unperturbed, sipping little puffs of the narcotic smoke from the mouthpiece of her pipe, her pink eyes staring blindly at the indunas. The huge, glittering insect crawled up her temple and then sideways until it stopped in the center of her crusted and scabbed forehead, where it hung upside down, and the long scorpion tail, longer than a man's forefinger, arched up over its horny back.

The Umlimo began to mutter and mumble and a rime of white froth bubbled onto her raw lips. She said something in a strange language, and the scorpion on her forehead pulsed its long segmented tail, and from the point of the red fang at the tip, a clear drop of venom welled and sparkled like a jewel in the dim light.

The Umlimo spoke again, in a hoarse, strained voice and an unintelligible language.

"What does she say?" Bazo whispered, turning his head toward Tanase. "What language does she use?"

"She speaks in the secret tongue of the initiates," Tanase murmured. "She is inviting the spirits to enter and take control of her body."

The albino reached up slowly and took the scorpion off her forehead. She held the head and body within her closed fist, only the long tail whipped furiously from side to side, and she brought it down slowly and held it to her own breast. The scorpion struck, and the rigid thorn fang buried itself deeply in her obscene pink flesh. The Umlimo's face did not alter, and the scorpion struck again and again, leaving little red punctures in the soft breast.

"She will die!" gasped Bazo.

"Let her be," hissed Tanase. "She is not like other women. The poison will not harm her—it serves only to open her soul to the spirits."

The albino lifted the scorpion from her bosom and dropped

it into the flames of the fire, where it writhed and withered into a little charred speck, and suddenly the Umlimo uttered an unearthly shriek.

"The spirits enter," Tanase whispered.

The Umlimo's mouth gaped open, and little glassy strings of saliva drooled from her chin, while three or four wild voices seemed to issue from her throat simultaneously, each trying to drown out the others, voices of men and women and animals, until at last one rose above them, and silenced the others. It was a man's voice, and it spoke in the mystical tongue; even its modulation and cadence were totally alien, but Tanase quietly translated for them.

"When the noon sun goes dark with wings, and the trees are bare of leaves in the springtime, then, warriors of Matabele, put an edge to your steel."

The four indunas nodded. They had heard this prophecy before, for the Umlimo was often repetitious and she was always obscure. They had puzzled over the same words before. It was this message that Bazo and Tanase had carried to the scattered peoples of the Matabele during their wandering from kraal to kraal.

The gross albino seer grunted and threshed her arms as though struggling with an invisible adversary. The pale pink eyes jerked in her skull, out of kilter with each other, so that she squinted and leered, and she ground her teeth together with a sound like a hound worrying a bone.

The girl-child rose quietly from where she squatted among the pots, and she leaned over the Umlimo and dashed a pinch of pungent red powder into her face. The Umlimo's paroxysm eased, the clenched jaw fell open, and another voice spoke, a guttural, blurred sound, barely human, using the same weird dialect, and Tanase strained forward to catch each syllable and then repeated calmly:

"When the cattle lie with their heads twisted to touch their flank, and cannot rise, then warriors of Matabele take heart, for the time will be nigh."

This time there was a slight difference in the wording of the prophecy from the one that they had heard before, and all of them pondered it silently as the Umlimo fell forward onto her face and flopped, limp as a boneless jellyfish. Slowly all movement of the albino's body ceased, and she lay like death.

Gandang made as if to rise, but Tanase hissed a warning,

and he arrested the movement and they waited; the only sound in the cavern was the click and rustle of the fire and the flirt of bats' wings high against the domed roof.

Then another convulsion ran down the Umlimo's back, and her spine arched, her hideous face lifted, but this time her voice was childlike and sweet, and she spoke in the Matabele language for all of them to understand.

"When the hornless cattle are eaten up by the great cross, let the storm begin."

Her head sagged forward, and the child covered her with a kaross of fluffy jackal furs.

"It is over," said Tanase. "There will be no more."

Thankfully the four indunas rose and crept back along the gloomy pathway through the catacombs, but as they saw the glimmer of sunlight through the entrance ahead, so their steps quickened, until they burst out in the valley with such indecent and undignified haste that they avoided each other's eyes.

That night, sitting in the open-sided *setenghi* on the floor of the valley, Somabula repeated the prophecies of the Umlimo to the assembled indunas. They nodded over the first two familiar riddles, and as they had a hundred times before, they delved inconclusively for the meaning, and then agreed: "We will find the meaning when the time is appointed—it is always the way."

Then Somabula went on to relate the third prophecy of the Umlimo, the new and unfamiliar riddle: "When the hornless cattle are eaten up by the great cross."

The indunas took snuff and passed the beerpots from hand to hand as they talked and argued the hidden meaning, and only when they had all spoken did Somabula look beyond them to where Tanase sat holding the child under her leather cloak to protect him from the night chill.

"What is the true meaning, woman?" he asked.

"Not even the Umlimo herself knows that," Tanase replied, "but when our ancestors first saw the white man riding up from the south, they believed that their mounts were hornless cattle."

"Horses?" Gandang asked thoughtfully.

"It may be so," Tanase agreed. "Yet a single word of the Umlimo may have as many meanings as there are crocodiles in the Limpopo River."

"What is the cross, the great cross, of the prophecy?" Bazo asked.

"The cross is the sign of the white men's three-headed god," Gandang answered. "My senior wife, Juba, the little Dove, wears that sign about her neck, given to her by the missionary at Khami when she poured water on her head."

"Is it possible that the white men's god will eat up the white men's horses?" doubted Babiaan. "Surely he is their protector, not their destroyer."

And the discussion passed from elder to elder, while the watch fire burned low and over the valley the vast shining firmament of the heavens turned with weighty dignity.

To the south of the valley, among the other heavenly bodies, burned a group of four great white stars that the Matabele called the Sons of Manatassi. They told how Manatassi, that terrible queen, had birth-strangled her offspring with her own hands, so that none of them might ever challenge her monarchy. According to the legend, the souls of the little ones had ascended to shine on high, eternal witness to the cruelty of their dam.

Not one of the indunas knew that the name by which the white men knew these same stars was the Southern Cross.

◆ ◆ ◆

Ralph Ballantyne was wrong when he predicted to Harry Mellow that by the time they returned to the base camp Mr. Rhodes and his entourage would have moved on to Bulawayo. For as they rode in through the gates of the stockade, he saw the magnificent mule coach still parked where he had last seen it, and beside it were a dozen other decrepit and travel-worn vehicles: Cape carts and surreys, even a bicycle with worn tires replaced by strips of buffalo hide.

"Mr. Rhodes has set up court here," Cathy explained furiously as soon as she and Ralph were alone in the bath tent. "I have made the camp too comfortable by half, and he has taken it over from me."

"As he does everything else," Ralph remarked philosophically as he stripped off his stinking shirt and flung it into the far corner. "I've slept in that for five nights, by God; the laundry boy will have to beat it to death with a club before he gets it into the tub."

"Ralph, you aren't taking it seriously." Cathy stamped

her foot in frustration. "This is my home. The only home I have, and now do you know what that—what Mr. Rhodes told me?"

"Have we got any more soap?" Ralph demanded as he hopped on one leg to free his breeches. "One bar will not be enough."

"He said, 'Jordan will be in charge of the kitchens while we are here, Mrs. Ballantyne; he knows my tastes.' What do you think of that?"

"Jordan is a damned fine cook." Ralph lowered himself gingerly into the bath and grunted as his naked buttocks touched the nearly boiling surface.

"I have been forbidden my own kitchen."

"Get in!" Ralph ordered, and she broke off and stared at him incredulously.

"What did you say?" she demanded, but in reply he seized her ankle and toppled Cathy, shrieking her protests, on top of himself. Steaming water and suds splattered the canvas walls of the tent, and when he released her at last, she was sodden to the waist.

"Your dress is soaked," he pointed out complacently. "Now you have no choice—take it off!"

Naked, she sat with her back to him in the galvanized bath, with her knees drawn up under her chin and her damp hair piled on top of her head, but still she continued her protest.

"Even Louise could bear the man's arrogance and misogyny no longer. She made your father take her back to King's Lynn, so now I have to bear him on my own!"

"You always were a brave girl," Ralph told her and ran the soapy flannel caressingly down her smooth back.

"And now the word has gone out to every deadbeat and drifter in Matabeleland that he is here, and they are riding in from every direction for the free whisky."

"Mr. Rhodes is a generous man," Ralph agreed, and tenderly slid the soapy flannel over her shoulder and down the front.

"It is your whisky," said Cathy, and caught his wrist before the flannel could reach its obvious destination.

"The man has an infernal nerve." For the first time, Ralph showed some emotion. "We will have to get rid of him. That whisky is worth ten pounds a bottle in Bulawayo." Ralph managed to slip the flannel a little further south.

"Ralph, that tickles." Cathy wriggled.

"When are your twin sisters arriving?" He ignored her protest.

"They sent a runner ahead; they should be here before nightfall. Ralph, give me that flannel immediately!"

"We will see how steely Mr. Rhodes's nerves really are—"

"Ralph, I can do that myself, thank you kindly; give me the flannel!"

"And we will also see how sharp Harry Mellow's reflexes are—"

"Ralph, are you crazy? We are in the bath!"

"We will take care of both of them with one stroke."

"Ralph, you can't! You can't—not in the bath!"

"We will have Jordan out of your kitchen, Harry Mellow overseer of the Harkness Mine, and Mr. Rhodes on his way to Bulawayo an hour after those two arrive—"

"Ralph, darling, do stop talking. I can't concentrate on two things at once," Cathy murmured.

◆ ◆ ◆

The tableau at the trestle table in the dining tent seemed unaltered since Ralph had last seen it, rather like one of the productions at Madame Tussaud's Waxworks. Mr. Rhodes even wore the same clothing as he dominated the tent with his expansive charisma.

Only the bit players seated in the position of petitioners facing the long table had changed. These were a motley bunch of out-of-luck prospectors, concession seekers and impecunious promoters of ambitious ventures, who had been attracted by Mr. Rhodes's reputation and millions like jackal and hyena to the lion's kill.

It was the mode in Matabeleland to display one's individuality by adopting eccentric headgear, and the selection which faced Mr. Rhodes across the table included a Scottish bonnet with an eagle feather pinned to the brim by a yellow cairngorm, a tall, brushed beaver girded with a green St. Patrick's ribbon, and a magnificent embroidered Mexican sombrero, the owner of which was relating a meandering tale of woe which Mr. Rhodes cut short. He did not enjoy listening as much as he did talking.

"So then, you've had enough of Africa, have you? But you haven't the passage money?" he asked brusquely.

"That's it exactly, Mr. Rhodes, you see my old mother—"

"Jordan, give the fellow a chitty to see him home, and charge it to me personally." He waved away the man's thanks and looked up as Ralph came into the tent.

"Harry tells me your trip was a great success. He panned your crushings from the Harkness reef at thirty ounces a ton; that's thirty times richer than the best banket reef of the Witwatersrand. I think we should open a bottle of champagne. Jordan, don't we have a few bottles of the Pommery '87 left?"

"At least I'm not providing the champagne as well as the whisky," Ralph thought cynically as he lifted his glass to the toast. "The Harkness Mine." He joined the dutiful chorus, and the moment he had drunk he turned on Dr. Leander Starr Jameson.

"What is this about the mining laws?" he demanded. "Harry tells me you are adopting the American mining code."

"Do you have any objection?" Jameson flushed, and his sandy mustache bristled.

"That code was drawn up by lawyers to keep themselves in fat fees in perpetuity. The new Witwatersrand laws are simpler and a million times more workable. By God, isn't it enough that your company royalty will rob us of fifty per cent of our profits?" As Ralph said it, it dawned upon him that the American mining code would be a smoke screen behind which the artful Rhodes could maneuver at will.

"Remember, young Ballantyne." Jameson stroked his mustache, and blinked piously. "Remember who the country belongs to. Remember who paid the costs of the occupation of Mashonaland and who financed the Matabele war."

"Government by a commercial company." Despite himself Ralph felt his anger rising again, and he clenched his hands on the table in front of him. "A company that owns the police force and the courts. And if I have a dispute with your company, who will decide it—surely not the BSA Company's own magistrate?"

"There are precedents." Mr. Rhodes's tone was reasonable and placatory, but his eyes were not. "The British East India Company—"

And Ralph's reply crackled: "The British Government eventually had to take India away from those pirates Clive, Hastings and that ilk, for corruption and oppression of the natives. The sepoy uprising was the logical outcome of their administration.''

"Mr. Ballantyne." Mr. Rhodes's voice always went shrill when he was excited or angry. "I am going to ask you to withdraw those remarks; they are historically inaccurate and by implication insulting.''

"I withdraw, unreservedly." Ralph was angry with himself now, he was usually much too coolheaded to allow himself to be provoked. There was no possible profit to be gained from a head-on collision with Cecil John Rhodes. His smile was easy and friendly as he went on. "I am sure we will have no need of the services of a company magistrate.''

Mr. Rhodes answered his smile with the same ease, but there was a steely blue flicker in his eyes as he raised his glass. "To a deep mine and a deeper relationship," he said, and only one other person in the tent recognized it as a challenge.

Jordan moved restlessly in his camp chair at the back of the tent. He knew these two men so well, loved both so dearly. Ralph his brother had been with him through all that lonely and tempestuous childhood, his protector and his comfort in the bad times and his joyous friend through the good.

Looking at his brother now and comparing Ralph to himself, it seemed impossible that two brothers could be so different. Where Jordan was blond and slim and graceful, Ralph was dark and muscled and powerful; where Jordan was gentle and self-effacing, Ralph was hard and bold and as hawk-fierce as his Matabele praise name implied. Instinctively Jordan looked from him to the big burly figure facing him across the camp table.

Here Jordan's feelings went beyond love itself to a kind of religious fervor. He did not really see the physical changes that a few short years had wrought in this godhead of his existence: the thickening of Mr. Rhodes's already bulky body, the bloating and coarsening of features already mottled with cyanosis caused by the laboring of the damaged heart, the reddish-blond curls receding swiftly now and slashed with gray at the temples. The way a loving woman places little store on the appearance of the man she has chosen as her own, so Jordan saw far beyond the marks of suffering and sickness and the racing years. He saw to the steely core of the man, the ultimate source of his immense power and brooding presence.

Jordan wanted to cry out to his beloved brother, to run to him and physically restrain him from the folly of turning this giant of a soul into an enemy. He had seen other men do just that and be ruthlessly crushed.

Then with a sickening slide in the pit of his stomach, he knew which side he would cast his lot if that dreaded confrontation ever forced a choice upon him. He was Mr. Rhodes's man, beyond brotherly ties and family loyalties, to the very end of life itself, he was Mr. Rhodes's man.

He sought desperately for some plausible excuse to break the tension between the two most important persons in his life, but relief came from beyond the stockade, in the delighted cries of the servants, the hysterical barking of the camp dogs, the crunch of cartwheels, and the excited shrieks of more than one woman. Jordan was the only one watching Ralph's face, so he caught the sly and smug expression as his brother rose.

"It seems we have more visitors," Ralph said, and the twins came into the inner stockade.

Victoria came first, as Ralph had expected that she would. She came on long shapely legs, outlined beneath the whirl and boil of her thin cotton skirts, barefoot in defiance of all ladylike pretensions, carrying her shoes in one hand, and Jonathan riding on her hip. The child was squeaking like a warthog piglet that has lost the teat.

"Vicky! Vicky, did you bring me anything?"

"A kiss on the cheek and a slap on the behind." Vicky laughed and hugged him. Her laughter was loud and gay and unaffected, her mouth was a little too large, but her lips were velvety as rose petals and sweetly shaped, her teeth were large and square and white as bone china porcelain, and as she laughed, her tongue, furry pink as that of a cat, curled between them. Her eyes were green and widespaced, her skin was that lustrous silky English perfection that neither sun nor massive doses of antimalarial quinine could mar. She would have been striking even without the dense tresses of copper-blond hair, ruffled by the wind and wild as the sea, that tumbled about her face and shoulders.

She riveted the attention of every man there, even Mr. Rhodes, but it was to Ralph she ran, holding his son on her hip still, and she threw her free arm around his neck. She was so tall that she had only to stand on her toes to reach his lips. The kiss was not long held, but her lips were soft and wet, the pressure of her breasts through her cotton blouse were springy and elastic and warm against his chest, and her thighs against his sent a shock up his spine, so that Ralph broke the embrace, and for an instant her green eyes mocked him, dared him to something that she did not fully understand, reveling in this heady sense of power over all mankind that she had not yet tested to its limits.

Then she tossed Jonathan to Ralph and whirled away to run barefoot down the tent and launched herself into Jordan's arms.

"Darling Jordan, oh, how we have missed you!" She forced him into a prancing jig around the stockade, shaking out her shining hair and caroling joyously.

Ralph glanced at Mr. Rhodes, and when he saw his expression of shock and unease, he grinned and released Jonathan, letting him race across to cling to Vicky's skirt and add his shrill voice to the uproar; then he turned to greet the second twin.

Elizabeth was as tall as Vicky, but darker. Her hair was polished mahogany, shot through with sparks of Burgundy, and her skin was gilded to the color of a tiger's eyes. She was slim as a dancer, with a narrow waist and shoulders supporting a long heron neck, and her breasts were smaller than Vicky's yet elegantly pointed, and though her voice was soft and her laughter a throaty purr, yet there was a mischievous quirk to her lips, a jaunty tilt to her head, and a measured sexual candor and awareness to the gaze of her wild honey eyes.

She and Cathy were arm in arm, but now she slipped out of her elder sister's embrace and presented herself to Ralph.

"My favorite brother-in-law," she murmured, and looking into her eyes, Ralph was reminded that though her voice was softer and her manner seemingly more restrained than that of her twin, yet Elizabeth was always the instigator and prime mover in any mischief that the pair conjured up. Thus close, her true beauty was apparent, less flamboyant than Vicky's perhaps, but the balance of her features and the depths beyond those golden-brown eyes were more disturbing.

She kissed Ralph, and the contact was as brief but even

less sisterly than had been the elder twin's embrace, and as she drew back from it, she slanted her eyes with a pretense of innocence that was more deadly than any brazening. Ralph broke the electric contact and looked to Cathy, making a comical moue of resignation and hoping that she still believed his studied avoidance of the twins was because he found them boisterous and childish.

Flushed and panting, Vicky released Jordan, placed her hands on her hips and asked Ralph, "Ralph, are you not going to present us to the company?"

"Mr. Rhodes, may I present my sisters-in-law," said Ralph with relish.

"Oh, the famous Mr. Rhodes," Vicky gushed theatrically, but there were little green sparks in her eyes. "It is such an honor to meet the conqueror of the Matabele nation, because, you see, King Lobengula was a personal friend of our family."

"Please excuse my sister, Mr. Rhodes." Elizabeth curtsied, and her expression was demure. "She intends no discourtesy, but our parents were the first missionaries to the Matabele, and our father sacrificed his life trying to help Lobengula while your troops were pursuing him to his death. My mother—"

"Young lady, I am fully aware who your mother is," Mr. Rhodes forestalled her sharply.

"Oh, good," Vicky chimed sweetly. "Then you will appreciate the gift that she asked me to present to you."

Vicky reached into the deep pocket of her long skirt and brought out a thin volume. It was bound in cardboard, not morocco leather, and the quality of the yellow paper was coarse and matt. She laid it on the trestle table in front of Mr. Rhodes, and when he saw the title, his heavy jaw clamped closed. Even Ralph quailed slightly. He had counted on the twins providing an unsettling influence, but he had not expected them to be so instantly explosive.

The book was entitled *Trooper Hackett of Matabeleland*, by Robyn Ballantyne, for the twins' mother wrote and published under her maiden name. There was probably not a man in the stockade who had not already read the slim volume, or at least heard of its contents, and if Vicky had thrown a live mamba on the table, their consternation could not have been more intense.

The contents of the book were so dangerous that three

reputable London publishers had rejected it, and finally Robyn St. John had published it privately and created an immediate sensation. In six months it had sold almost two hundred thousand copies and had been treated to extensive reviews in almost every influential newspaper both at home in England and abroad in the colonies.

The frontispiece of the book set the tone for the text that followed. It was a murky photograph that depicted a dozen white men in BSA Company uniform standing under the spreading branches of a tall wild teak tree and looking up at the corpses of four seminaked Matabele hanging by their necks from the topmost branches. There was no caption to the photograph, and the faces of the white men were too indistinct to be recognizable.

Now Mr. Rhodes reached out and opened the book at the gruesome illustration. "Those are four Matabele indunas who were wounded at the battle of Bembesi and who committed suicide by hanging rather than surrender to our forces," he growled. "They are not the victims of some atrocity, as this scurrilous piece of offal implies."

Mr. Rhodes closed the book with a snap, and Elizabeth exclaimed sweetly, "Oh, Mr. Rhodes, Mama will be so disappointed that you did not enjoy her little story."

The book described the fictional adventures of Trooper Hackett of the BSA Company expeditionary force, and his wholehearted participation in the slaughter of the Matabele with machine gun fire, the pursuit and shooting down of the fleeing survivors, the burning of the kraals, the looting of Lobengula's cattle and the rape of the young Matabele girls. Then Trooper Hackett is separated from his squadron and spends the night alone on a wild kopje, and while huddled over his campfire, a mysterious white stranger comes out of the night and joins him at the fire. Hackett remarks, "Ah, you have been in the wars, too, I see," leaning forward and inspecting the stranger's feet. "By God! Both of them! And right through—you must have had a bad time of it!"

And the stranger replies, "It all happened a very long time ago." Then the reader is left in no doubt as to whom he is dealing with, especially when the author describes his beautiful, gentle countenance and his all-seeing blue eyes. Abruptly the stranger breaks into a florid injunction to young Hackett.

"Take a message to England. Go to that great people and demand of them: Where is the sword that was given into your hand, that with it you might enforce justice and deal out mercy? How came you to give it up into the hands of men whose search is gold, whose thirst is wealth, to whom the souls and bodies of their fellow men are counters in a game, men who have transformed the sword of a great people into a tool to burrow for gold, as the snouts of swine for earth nuts?"

It was little wonder, Ralph smiled to himself, that Mr. Rhodes pushed the book away and wiped the hand that had touched it on the lapel of his rumpled Norfolk jacket.

"Oh, Mr. Rhodes," murmured Vicky, angel-faced and wide-eyed. "At the least you must read the inscription that Mama dedicated to you." She retrieved the discarded volume, opened the flyleaf and read aloud, " 'For Cecil John Rhodes, without whose endeavours this book would never have been written.' "

Mr. Rhodes rose from his seat with ponderous dignity.

"Ralph," he said quietly. "Thank you for your hospitality. Dr. Jim and I will be getting on to Bulawayo, I think. We have spent too long here as it is." Then he looked across at Jordan. "The mules are well rested. Jordan, is there a moon tonight?"

"There will be a good moon tonight," Jordan replied promptly, "and there are no clouds, so we will have good light for the road."

"Can we be ready to leave by this evening, then?"

It was a command, and Mr. Rhodes did not wait for a reply but stalked out of the stockade toward his own tent, and the little doctor followed him stiffly. The moment they were gone, the twins burst into merry, tinkling laughter and hugged each other ecstatically.

"Mama would have been proud of you, Victoria Isabel—"

"Well, I am not." Jordan's voice cut through their hilarity. He was white-faced and shaking with anger. "You are ill-mannered and silly little girls."

"Oh, Jordan," Vicky wailed and seized his hands. "Don't be cross. We love you so."

"Oh yes, we do. Both of us." Elizabeth took his other hand, but he pulled away from them.

"You do not have any idea in those giddy little heads how dangerous a game you are playing, not only for yourself." He strode away from them but paused for a moment in front of Ralph. "Nor do you, Ralph." His expression softened, and he placed his hand on Ralph's shoulder. "Please be more careful—for my sake, if not for your own." Then he followed his master from the stockade.

Ralph pulled the gold hunter from the inner pocket of his waistcoat and made a show of inspecting it.

"Well," he announced to the twins, "sixteen minutes to clear the camp. That must be a new record even for you two." He returned the watch to his pocket and put one arm around Cathy's shoulders. "There you are, Katie my love, there is your home again without a single stranger."

"That is not quite the case," murmured a soft Kentucky accent, and Harry Mellow rose from the log he had been using as a seat and removed the slouch hat from his curly head. The twins stared at him for a startled instant, then flashed each other a look of complete accord, and a remarkable transformation came over them. Lizzie smoothed her skirts, and Vicky pushed back the dense dangling tresses from her face, and their expressions became grave and their comportment ladylike.

"You may present the young gentleman, cousin Ralph," said Vicky in accents so refined as to make Ralph glance at her to confirm it was the same girl speaking.

When the mule coach drove through the outer gates of the stockade, there was one member of Mr. Rhodes's party who was not aboard.

"What did you tell Mr. Rhodes?" Cathy asked, hanging onto Ralph's arm as they watched the coach rolling away, a dark shadow on the moon-silver road.

"I told him that I needed Harry for a day or two more to help me lay out the development for the Harkness." Ralph lit his last cheroot of the day, and they began the leisurely stroll around the camp that was a little ritual of their life together. It was their time of contentment and delicious anticipation, the time when they talked over the events of the day just past and planned for the one ahead, at the same time touching each other as they walked, her hand in the crook of his arm, their hips sliding against each other, a closeness which would soon lead naturally and sweetly to the wide soft cot in the bell tent.

"Was that true?" Cathy asked.

"Semitrue," he admitted. "I need him for longer than a day or two, more like ten or twenty years."

"If you succeed, you will be one of the few men to get the better of Mr. Rhodes, and he will not like it."

Ralph stopped her and commanded, "Listen!"

From the inner stockade, there was the orange glow of the fire and the sound of a banjo being played with such rare skill that the limpid notes shimmered and ran into each other; like some exotic bird song, it rose to an impossible crescendo and then ceased so abruptly that the utter stillness trembled in the air for many seconds before the night chorus of the cicadas in the trees, which had been shamed to silence by the vaunting instrument, hesitantly recommenced. With it mingled the patter of soft palms and the twins' unfeigned exclamations of delight.

"He is a man of many talents, your Harry Mellow."

"The chief of them is that he can spot gold in a filled tooth across a polo field. However, I have no doubt your little sisters will come to cherish other accomplishments of his."

"I should send them to bed," Cathy murmured.

"Don't be the wicked elder sister," Ralph admonished, and the music started again, but this time Harry Mellow's soaring baritone led and the twins picked up the refrain in their true, clear voices.

"Leave the poor creatures alone; they have enough of that at home." Ralph led her away.

"It's my duty," Cathy protested halfheartedly.

"If it's duty you are after," Ralph chuckled, "then, by God, woman, I have another more pressing duty for you to perform!"

He lay stretched out on his back on the cot and watched her prepare for bed in the lamplight. It had taken her a long time to forget her upbringing as the child of Christian missionaries and to allow him to watch her, but now she had come to enjoy it, and she flaunted a little before him, until he grinned and leaned out of the cot to crush out the cheroot, then lifted both hands toward her.

"Come here, Katie!" he ordered, but she hung back provocatively.

"Do you know what I want?"

"No, but I know what I want."

"I want a home—"

"You have a home."

"With thatch and brick walls and a real garden."

"You have a garden, the most beautiful garden in the world, and it stretches from the Limpopo to the Zambezi."

"A garden with roses and geraniums." She came to him, and he lifted the sheet. "Will you build me a home, Ralph?"

"Yes."

"When?"

"When the railroad is finished."

She sighed softly. He had made the same promise while he was laying the telegraph line, and that was before Jonathan was born, but she knew better than to remind him. Instead she slipped under the sheet, and strangely his arms, as they closed around her, became home for that moment.

◆ ◆ ◆

In the southern springtime on the shores of one of the great lakes that lie in the hot depths of the Rift Valley, that mighty geological fault that splits the shield of the African continent like the stroke of an ax, there occurred at that time a bizarre hatching.

The egg masses of *Schistocerca gregaria,* the desert locust, that were buried in the loose earth along the edge of the lake released their flightless nymphs. The eggs had been laid in unusually propitious conditions of weather and environment. The swarms of breeding insects had been concentrated by unseasonable winds upon the papyrus banks of the lake, a vast food supply that heightened their fecundity. When the time came for them to spawn, another chance wind pushed them en masse onto a dry, friable terrain of the correct acidity to protect the egg masses from fungus infection while the mild humidity drifting up from the lake insured perfectly elastic egg casings from which the hatching nymphs were able to escape readily.

In other, less fortuitous seasons, the loss and wastage might be as high as ninety-nine per cent, but this year the kindly earth rendered up such a multitude of nymphs that it could not contain them. Though the hatching ground was almost fifty square miles, the insects were forced to crawl upon each other's backs in layers and drifts and banks ten and twenty deep, so that the surface of the desert seemed to become a single seething organism, monstrous and terrifying.

The constant agitation and stimulation of contact with their siblings wrought a miraculous change in this teeming tide of nymphs. Their color turned from the drab desert brown of their kind to a vivid orange and metallic midnight black. Their metabolic rate surged and they became hyperactive and nervous. Their hind legs grew longer and more powerful, their wings developed with startling rapidity, and they entered the gregarious phase. When they had molted for the last time and their newly fledged wings had dried, the last chance fluke of weather occurred. The tropical clouds along the valley escarpment blew away, and a terrible sun beat down upon the crawling mass of insects, the valley became an oven, and the entire swarm of mature locusts took spontaneously to the air.

In that baptism to flight, the heat that their bodies had sucked up from the baking earth of the valley was increased even further by their muscular activity. They could not stop, and they winged southward in a cloud that eclipsed the sun and stretched from horizon to horizon.

In the cool of the evening, this mighty cloud sank to earth, and the trees of the forest could not bear their weight. Branches as thick as a man's waist snapped off under the clinging masses of insects. In the morning the rising heat spurred them into flight once more, and they rose to darken the heavens and left the forest stripped bare of its tender spring foliage, so that the empty, twisted branches looked like the limbs of cripples in a strange, dead landscape.

Southward the endless flights poured across the sky, until far below them the silver ribbon of water that was the Zambezi River glinted dully in the shadow of their passing.

◆ ◆ ◆

The whitewashed walls of Khami Mission Station burned in the noon sunlight with the eye-aching brilliance of bleached bone. The family dwelling, surrounded by wide, shaded verandas and roofed with thick thatch, stood a little apart from the church and its attendant buildings, but all of them seemed to crouch below the line of wooded hills, the way that chickens huddle below the hen when there is a hawk in the sky.

From the front steps of the house, the gardens stretched down past the well to the little stream. At first, nearer the house, there were roses and bougainvillea, poinsettia and banks of phlox that formed bright bold slashes of color against a veld still brown from the long, dry winter just passed; but nearer the stream the fields of maize were tended by convalescents from the mission clinic, and soon on the tall green plants the immature cobs would begin to set. Between the rows of corn, the earth was hidden beneath the dark green umbrella leaves of new pumpkin plants. These fields fed the hundreds of hungry mouths, the family and servants and sick and converts who came from all over Matabeleland to this tiny oasis of hope and succor.

On the veranda of the main house, at a bare, hand-planed table of heavy mukwa wood, the family was seated at the midday meal. It was a meal of steaming salted maize bread baked in the leaves and washed down with *maas,* the cool, thick, soured milk from a stone jug, and in the opinion of the twins, the grace that preceded it was disproportionately long for such frugal fare. Vicky fidgeted and Elizabeth sighed at a volume that was carefully calculated not to exceed the knife edge beyond which it would attract her mother's wrath.

Dr. Robyn St. John, the doyenne of Khami Mission, had dutifully thanked the Almighty for His bounty but was going on, in conversational tones, to point out to Him that a little rain soon would help pollination of the immature cobs in the field and insure a continuation of that bounty. Robyn's eyes were closed, and her features were relaxed and serene; her skin was almost as unlined as that of Victoria's. Her dark hair had the same russet highlights as Elizabeth's, but there was just a fine silver mist at her temples to betray her age.

"Dear Lord," she said, "in Your wisdom You have allowed our best cow, Buttercup, to lose her milk. We submit to Your will, which surpasses all understanding, but we do need milk if this little mission is going to continue to work to Your glory—" Robyn paused to let that sink in. "Amen!" said Juba from the far end of the table.

Since her conversion to Christianity, Juba had taken to covering her huge black melon-sized breasts with a high-buttoned man's undervest, and among the necklaces of ostrich shell and bright ceramic trade beads around her neck hung a simple crucifix of rolled gold on a fine chain.

Apart from that she was still dressed in the traditional costume of a high-ranking Matabele matron.

Robyn opened her eyes and smiled at her. They were companions of many years, since Robyn had rescued her from the hold of the Arab slaving dhow in the Mozambique Channel, long before the birth of any of the children, when both of them had been young and unmarried; but it had only been shortly before his destruction by the company forces that King Lobengula had at last given his permission for Juba's conversion to the Christian faith.

Juba, the little Dove—how she had changed since those far-off days. Now she was the senior wife of Gandang, one of the great indunas of the Matabele nation, brother of King Lobengula himself, and she had borne him twelve sons, the eldest of whom was Bazo, the Ax, himself an induna. Four of her younger sons had died in front of the Maxim machine guns at the Shangani River and the Bembesi Crossing. Nevertheless, as soon as that brief, cruel little war had ended, Juba had returned to Khami Mission and to Robyn.

Now she smiled back at Robyn. Her face was a glossy full moon, the silky black skin stretched tightly over the layers of fat. Her dark eyes sparkled with a lively intelligence, and her teeth were a perfect and unblemished white. On her vast lap, within the circle of her arms, each as thick as a man's thigh, she held Robyn St. John's only son.

Robert was not quite two years old, a thin child, without his father's rugged bone structure but with the same strange yellow-flecked eyes. His skin was sallow from regular doses of antimalarial quinine. Like many infants born of a mother on the verge of menopause, there was a quaint, old-fashioned solemnity about him, like a little old gnome who had already lived a hundred years. He watched his mother's face as though he had understood each word she uttered.

Robyn closed her eyes again, and the twins, who had perked up at the prospect of a final amen, glanced at each other and slumped with resignation.

"Dear Lord, Thou knowest of the great experiment upon which Thy humble servant will embark before this day ends, and we are certain of Your understanding and protection during the dangerous days ahead."

Juba's understanding of the English language was just sufficient to follow this injunction, and the smile faded from her face. Even the twins looked up again, both of them so troubled and unhappy that when Robyn sounded the long-awaited "Amen," neither of them reached for the platters or jugs.

"Victoria, Elizabeth, you may begin," Robyn had to prompt them, and they chewed dismally for a while.

"You never told us it was to be today," Vicky spoke up at last.

"The young girl from Zama's kraal is a perfect subject. She started her chills an hour ago; I expect her fever to peak before sundown."

"Please, Mama," Elizabeth jumped up from her seat and knelt beside Robyn with both arms around her waist, her expression stricken. "Please don't do it."

"Now don't be a silly girl, Elizabeth," Robyn told her firmly. "Return to your seat and eat your food."

"Lizzie is right." Vicky had tears in her green eyes. "We don't want you to do this. It's so dangerous, so horrible."

Robyn's expression softened a little, and she placed one narrow but strong brown hand on Elizabeth's head. "Sometimes we have to do things that frighten us. It's God's test of our strength and faith." Robyn stroked the lustrous dark hair back from Elizabeth's forehead. "Your grandfather, Fuller Ballantyne—"

"Grandfather was touched," Vicky cut in quickly. "He was crazy mad."

Robyn shook her head. "Fuller Ballantyne was a great man of God; there were no limits to his vision and courage. It is only the mean little people who call such men mad. They doubted him as they now doubt me, but as he did, I shall prove the truth," she said firmly.

The previous year Robyn had, in her professional capacity as Medical Superintendent of Khami Mission, submitted a paper to the British Medical Association in which she set out the conclusions of twenty years' study of tropical malarial fever.

At the beginning of the paper, she had scrupulously acknowledged the work of Charles Louis Alphonse Laveran, who was the first to isolate the malarial parasite under microscopic examination, but then Robyn had gone on to postulate that the periodic paroxysms of chill and fever that characterized the disease were coincident with the segmentation of these parasites in the patient's bloodstream.

The august members of the British Medical Association were well aware of Robyn's reputation as a political trouble stirrer, a radical who flew in the face of their conservative convictions. They had never forgiven nor forgotten that she had impersonated a man to attend medical school and had desecrated their exclusive masculine preserve by obtaining her medical qualification under false colors. They recalled with pain the furor and scandal that she had conjured up when the governors of St. Matthew's Hospital, London, where she had received her training, had attempted, quite reasonably, to revoke her doctorate. Sourly they had looked on as she published a series of highly successful books, culminating in the infamous *Trooper Hackett of Matabeleland*, a vicious attack on the company in which a great deal of the association's funds were invested.

Naturally the honorable members of such an august body were above such mundane emotions as envy and malice, so none of them had grudged her the princely royalties from her publications, and when some of Robyn's outrageous theories on tropical diseases had finally been proven accurate and after they had been brought under pressure by Oliver Wicks, who was Robyn's champion and editor of the *Standard*, they had magnanimously retracted their previous refutations. Nevertheless, when Dr. Robyn St. John, previously Codrington, née Ballantyne, finally succeeded in hoisting and hanging herself on her own audacity and presumption, the members of the British Medical Association would not be numbered among the company of her mourners.

Thus they read the first part of Robyn's latest paper on malarial fever with mild alarm. Her theory on the coincidence of parasite segmentation and patient temperature change could only add luster to her reputation. Then with mounting joy they came to the second part and realized that once more she had placed herself and her reputation in jeopardy. Since Hippocrates had first described the disease in the fifth century B.C., it had been an uncontested fact that malaria, as its name implied, was transmitted by the foul airs of swampy ground and poisonous nights. Robyn St. John postulated that this was a fallacy, and that it was transmitted from a sufferer to a healthy victim by the physical transfer of blood. Then incredibly her paper went on to suggest that the carrier agents were the flying mosquitoes that were usually associated with the swamps and marshy ground where the disease proliferated. As proof Robyn cited her discovery, by microscopic examination, of the malarial parasite in the stomach contents of the insects.

Offered such an opportunity, her peers in the British Medical Association had been unable to resist the temptation to embark on an orgy of derision. "Dr. St. John should not allow her penchant for lurid fiction to intrude upon the sacred grounds of medical research," wrote one of her more charitable critics. "There is not the remotest shred of evidence that any disease can be transferred in the blood, and to look to the agency of flying insects to effect this mischief, is not far removed from belief in vampires and werewolves."

"They scoffed at your grandfather also." Robyn's chin was up now as she addressed her family, and in this mood the strength and determination of her features were daunting. "When he refuted their belief that yellow jack was an infectious or a contagious disease, they challenged him to provide proof."

The twins had heard this piece of family history a dozen times before, so they both paled in anticipatory nausea.

"He went into that fever hospital where all those eminent surgeons were gathered, and he collected a crystal glass of the yellow vomit from one of the patients who was dying of the disease, and he toasted his fellow surgeons with the glass and then he quaffed it down in front of them all."

Vicky covered her own mouth, and Elizabeth gagged softly and turned icily pale.

"Your grandfather was a courageous man, and I am his daughter," Robyn said simply. "Now eat up your lunch. I expect you both to assist me this afternoon."

◆ ◆ ◆

Behind the church stood the new ward that Robyn had built since the death of her first husband in the Matabele war. It was an opensided godown with waist-high walls. The thatched roof was supported on upright poles of mopani. In hot weather the breeze could blow through the structure unhindered, but in the rains or when it turned cold, then woven grass mats could be unrolled to close in the walls.

The sleeping mats were laid out in rows upon the clay floor, no attempt being made to separate families, so that healthy spouses and offspring were camped with the sick and the suffering. Robyn had found it better to turn the ward into a bustling community rather than have her patients pine to death. However, the arrangement was so congenial and the food so good that it had been difficult to persuade patients to leave after their cure had been effected, until Robyn had hit upon the ruse of sending all convalescents and their families to work in the fields or at building the new wards. This had dramatically reduced the clinic's population to manageable proportions.

Robyn's laboratory stood between the church and the ward. It was a small rondavel with adobe walls and a single window. Shelves and a workbench ran around the entire curved inside wall. In pride of place stood Robyn's new microscope, purchased with the royalties of *Trooper Hackett,* and beside it her working journal, a thick leatherbound volume in which she was now noting her preliminary observations.

"Subject: Caucasian female at present in good health—" she wrote in her firm neat hand, but she looked up irritably with pen poised at Juba's tragic tone and mournful expression.

"You swore on oath to the great King Lobengula that you would care for his people after he was gone. How can you honor that promise if you are dead, Nomusa?" Juba asked in Sindebele, using Robyn's Matabele praise name, Nomusa, Girl-Child of Mercy.

"I am not going to die, Juba," Robyn snapped irritably. "And for the love of all things holy, take that look off your face."

"It is never wise to provoke the dark spirits, Nomusa."

"Juba is right, Mama," Vicky supported her. "You have deliberately stopped taking quinine, not a single tablet in six weeks, and your own observations have shown the danger of blackwater fever is increased—"

"Enough!" Robyn slapped the table with the flat of her hand. "I will listen to no more."

"All right," Elizabeth agreed. "We won't try and stop you again, but if you become dangerously ill, should we ride into Bulawayo to fetch General St. John?"

Robyn threw her pen onto the open page so the ink splattered, and she leaped to her feet.

"You will do no such thing, do you hear me, girl? You will not go near that man."

"Mama, he is your husband," Vicky pointed out reasonably.

"And he is Bobby's father," Elizabeth said quickly.

"And he loves you." Vicky gabbled it out before Robyn could stop her.

Robyn was white-faced and shaking with anger, and some other emotion that prevented her speaking for a moment, and Elizabeth took advantage of her uncharacteristic silence.

"He is such a strong—"

"Elizabeth!" Robyn found her voice, and it rang like steel from the scabbard. "You know I have forbidden discussion of that man." She sat back at the desk, picked up the pen, and for a long minute the scratching of her nib was the only sound in the room, but when she spoke again, Robyn's voice was level and businesslike. "While I am incapacitated, Elizabeth will write up the journal—she has the better handwriting. I want hourly entries, no matter how grave the situation."

"Very well, Mama."

"Vicky, you will administer treatment, but not before the cycle has been established beyond any chance of refutation. I have prepared a written list of instructions for you to follow should I become insensible."

"Very well, Mama."

"And me, Nomusa?" Juba asked softly. "What must I do?"

Robyn's expression softened then, and she laid her hand on the other woman's forearm.

"Juba, you must understand that I am not reneging on my promise to take care of your people. What I will accomplish with this work is a final understanding of a disease that has ravaged the Matabele and all people of Africa since the beginning of time. Trust me, dear friend, this is a long step toward freeing your people and mine of this terrible scourge."

"I wish there was another way, Nomusa."

"There is not." Robyn shook her head. "You asked what you should do to help; will you stay with me, Juba, to give me comfort?"

"You know I will," Juba whispered, and hugged Robyn to her. Robyn seemed slim and girlish in that vast embrace, and Juba's sobs shook them both.

♦ ♦ ♦

The black girl lay on her sleeping mat against the low wall of the ward. She was of marriageable age, for when she cried out in delirium and threw aside the fur kaross, her naked body was fully matured, with a wide fertile spread of hips and hard-thrusting nipples to her breasts, but the heat of fever was burning her up. Her skin looked as brittle as parchment, her lips were gray and cracked, and her eyes glittered with the unnatural brilliance of the fever that was rushing down upon her.

Robyn pressed her hand into the girl's armpit, and exclaimed, "She is like a furnace, the poor child is at the climax," and she pulled her hand away and covered her with the thick, soft kaross. "I think this is the moment. Juba, take her shoulders. Vicky, hold her arm, and you, Elizabeth, bring the bowl."

The girl's bare arm protruded from under the kaross, and Vicky held her at the elbow while Robyn slipped a tourniquet of whiplash leather over her forearm and twisted it up until the blood vessels in the Matabele girl's wrist swelled up, purple black and hard as unripe grapes.

"Come on, child," Robyn snapped at Elizabeth, and she proffered the white enamel basin and drew back the cloth that covered it. Her hand was trembling.

Robyn picked up the syringe. The barrel of brass had a narrow glass inset running down its length. Robyn detached the hollow needle from the nipple at the end, and at the same time, with the thumb of her free hand she pumped up the veins in the girl's wrist with a stroking motion and then pierced the skin with an angled stab of the thick needle. She found the vein almost immediately, and a thin jet of dark red venous blood shot from the open end of the needle and pattered onto the clay floor. Robyn fitted the syringe nipple into the needle and slowly withdrew the plunger, watching intently as the fever-hot blood flowed into the brass barrel and showed through the glass inset.

"I am taking two cubic centimeters," she murmured as the line of moving red reached the graduation stamped in the brass, and she jerked the needle from the girl's skin and stanched the blood that followed it with the pressure of her thumb, dropped the syringe back into the bowl, and released the loop of the tourniquet.

"Juba," she said, "give her the quinine now and stay with her until she starts to sweat." Robyn rose with a swirl of skirts, and the twins had to run to keep up with her as she crossed to her laboratory.

As soon as they were in the circular room, Robyn slammed the door.

"We must be quick," she said, unbuttoning the cuff of her leg-of-mutton sleeve and rolling it high. "We must not allow any organisms in the blood to deteriorate." And she offered her arm to Vicky, who looped the tourniquet around it and began twisting it up tightly.

"Make a note of the time," Robyn ordered.

"Seventeen minutes past six," said Elizabeth, standing beside her and holding the enamel basin while she stared with a controlled horror at the blue veins under the pale skin of her mother's arm.

"We will use the basilic vein," Robyn said in a matter-of-fact tone, and took a fresh needle from the case on the desk.

Robyn bit her lip at the prick, but went on probing gently down toward her own swollen vein until suddenly there was an eruption of blood from the open end of the needle, and Robyn grunted with satisfaction and reached for the charged syringe.

"Oh, Mama!" cried Vicky, unable to restrain herself longer.

"Do be quiet, Victoria."

Robyn fitted the syringe into the needle, and without any dramatic pause or portentous words, expelled the still-hot blood from the fever-stricken Matabele girl into her own vein.

She withdrew the needle and rolled down her sleeve in businesslike fashion.

"All right," she said. "If I am right—and I am—we can expect the first paroxysm in forty-eight hours."

◆ ◆ ◆

The full-sized billiard table was the only one in Africa north of the Kimberley Club, and south of Shepheard's Hotel in Cairo. It had been transported in sections three hundred miles from the railhead, and Ralph Ballantyne's bill for cartage had been £112. However, the proprietor of the Grand Hotel had recouped his costs a dozen times over since he had set up the massive slate top on its squat teak legs in the center of his saloon bar.

The table was a source of pride to every citizen of Bulawayo. Somehow it seemed to symbolize the transition from barbarism to civilization that subjects of Queen Victoria should be striking the ivory balls across the green baize on the same spot where a few short years previously a pagan black king had conducted his grisly "smelling-out" ceremonies and gruesome executions.

The crowd of spectators in the barroom that lined all the walls and even stood on the long bar counter for a better view of the game were nearly all men of substance, for they had won their grants and gold claims by riding into this land in Dr. Jim's conquering column. They each owned three thousand acres of the sweet-pastured veld, and their share of the herds of Lobengula's captured cattle grazed upon them. Many of them had already driven their claim pegs into the rich surface reefs in which visible gold gleamed in the white Matabeleland sunlight.

Of course some of the reefs were unpayable stringers, yet already Ed Pearson had pegged an ancient working between the Hwe Hwe and Tshibgiwe rivers that had panned samples at five ounces to the ton. He called it the Globe and Phoenix, and Harry Mellow, acting on Mr. Rhodes's instructions, had surveyed the reef and estimated that there were two million tons of reserves, making it the richest gold mine in existence, except possibly for Ralph Ballantyne's Harkness Mine further south with its estimated five million tons of reserves at an incredible twenty ounces to the ton.

There was rich red gold and the good Lord alone knew what other treasure buried in this earth, and the mood was optimistic and boisterous. Bulawayo was a boomtown, and the spectators encouraged the two billiard players with raucous banter and extravagant wagers.

General Mungo St. John chalked his cue carefully and then wiped the blue dust from his fingers with a silk handkerchief. He was a tall man with wide shoulders and narrow hips, but as he moved around the green table he favored one long, powerful leg, an old gunshot injury, an affliction that no man dared mention in his presence.

He was coatless, with gold expanders holding his white linen shirt sleeves above the elbows, and his waistcoat was embroidered with silver and gold metallic thread. On a lesser man, such theatrical dress would have looked ostentatious, but on Mungo St. John it was correct as an emperor's ermine and purple.

He paused at the corner of the table and surveyed the lie of the ivory balls. His single eye had a predatory gleam to it, tawny yellow and strangely flecked, like the eye of an eagle. The empty socket of the other eye was covered with a black cloth patch and it gave him the air of a genteel pirate as he smiled across the table at his opponent.

"Cannon and losing hazard off red," Mungo St. John announced calmly, and there was a roar of comment in which a dozen voices were offering odds of five to one and better against the play, and Harry Mellow grinned boyishly and tipped his head in reluctant admiration of the big man's audacity.

The game they were playing was "Zambezi nominated three cushion," which is as far from ordinary billiards as the little gecko lizards on the barroom rafters were from the big, gnarled twenty-foot mugger crocodiles of the Zambezi pools. It was a local variation of the game, combining the most difficult elements of English and French billiards. The player's cue ball had to strike three cushions of the table before completing a scoring coup, but in addition to this monstrous condition, the player had to announce beforehand exactly how he intended scoring. This prevented him executing a fluke score, and if he did make an unannounced and therefore unintended winning stroke, he was penalized the points he should have won. It was a tough game. The stakes between the players were five pounds a point, but naturally the players and the spectators were free to offer side bets for or against the players making their nominated coup. With players of the caliber of Harry Mellow and Mungo St. John on the table, there was a thousand pounds or more riding on each stroke, and the voices that shouted the odds and those that accepted them were hoarse with tension.

Mungo St. John replaced the long black cheroot between his teeth, and he made a little tripod with the fingers of his left hand, then he laid the polished maplewood cue into the notch of his thumb and forefinger. There was a final flurry of bets, and then a silence fell over the crowded room. The air was blue with tobacco smoke, and the faces that strained forward were flushed and sweating. Mungo St. John lined up his white cue ball with his single bright eye, and across the table Harry Mellow took a slow breath and held it. If Mungo succeeded with the cannon, it scored two points, and another three points for the hazard off red, but that was not all that was at stake, for Harry had placed a side bet of fifty pounds against the score. He stood to lose or win over one hundred guineas.

Mungo St. John's face was grave as a professor of philosophy considering the riddle of the universe as he made a gentle practice stroke that he arrested with the leather button at the tip of the long cue almost touching the white ivory ball. Then he drew back the cue deliberately to its full travel. At the instant that he launched the stroke, the voice of a young woman cut through the bated silence of watching men.

"General St. John, you must come quickly."

There were only one hundred white women in the entire vast land north of the Shashi and south of the Zambezi rivers, of which probably ninety were already married and most of the others spoken for. A voice with such lovely ringing tones could have turned every male head down both sides of the Champs-Elysées, but in the billiard saloon of the Grand Hotel of woman-starved Bulawayo, it had the effect of a close-range broadside of grapeshot. A waiter dropped a tray laden with schooners of beer, a heavy wooden bench toppled over backward with a shattering crash as the six men seated upon it sprang to attention like guardsmen, an inebriated transport rider toppled backward off the counter on top of the barman who instinctively swung a round-arm punch at him, missed and swept a row of whisky bottles off the shelf.

The sudden uproar in the deep silence would have unnerved a marble statue of Zeus, but Mungo St. John completed his stroke with an almost creamy smoothness, his single yellow eye unblinking in the calm, handsome face as it followed the flight of the ball from the tip of his cue. The white ball thumped crisply against the far cushion, doubled the table, and the spin hooked it through the corner, striking the cushion at an angle that bled the speed off the ivory. It came trundling back and Mungo St. John lifted his left hand to let it pass under his nose; it touched the other white ball with just sufficient force to deflect it a hair's breadth and send it on to kiss the red ball like a lover. The contact robbed the cue ball of the last of its impetus, and it hovered on the edge of the corner pocket for a weary moment and then dropped soundlessly into the net.

It was a perfect cannon and losing hazard, nominated and executed, and a thousand pounds had been won and lost in those few seconds, but every man in the room except Mungo St. John was staring at the doorway in a kind of mesmeric trance. Mungo St. John lifted his cue ball from the net and respotted it, then as he chalked his cue again, he murmured, "Victoria, my dear, there are times when even the prettiest young lady should remain silent." Once again he stooped over the table. "Pot red," he announced, and the company was so entranced by the tall coppery-haired girl in their midst that no bet was offered or accepted, but as Mungo St. John took his cue back for the next stroke, Victoria spoke again.

"General St. John, my mother is dying."

This time Mungo St. John's head flew up, his single eye wide with shock, and the white ball screwed off down the table in a violent miscue as he stared at Vicky. Mungo let the wooden cue drop with a clatter onto the floor, and he ran from the barroom.

Vicky went on standing in the doorway of the barroom for a few seconds. Her hair was tangled into thick ropes on her shoulders by the wind, and her breathing was still so rough that her breasts heaved tantalizingly under her thin cotton blouse. Her eyes swept the sea of grinning, ingratiating faces, and then stopped when they reached the tall figure of Harry Mellow in his riding boots and breeches and the shirt open at his throat to show a nest of crisp curls in the vee. Vicky flushed and turned to hurry back through the doorway.

Harry Mellow tossed his cue to the barman and shoved his way through the disappointed crowd. By the time he reached the street, Mungo St. John, still bareheaded and in shirt sleeves, was mounted on a big bay mare, but leaning from the saddle to talk urgently to Vicky, who stood at his stirrup.

Mungo looked up and saw Harry. "Mr. Mellow," he called, "I would be obliged if you could see my stepdaughter safely out of town. I am needed at Khami." Then he put his heels into the mare's flanks, and she jumped away at a dead run down the dusty street.

Vicky was climbing up onto the driving seat of a rickety little cart drawn by two diminutive donkeys with drooping melancholy ears, and on the seat beside her sat the mountainous black figure of a Matabele woman.

"Miss Codrington," Harry called urgently. "Please wait."

He reached the wheel of the cart with a few long strides and looked up at Vicky.

"I have wanted to see you again—so very much."

"Mr. Mellow"—Vicky lifted her chin haughtily—"the road to Khami Mission is clearly signposted; you could not possibly have lost your way."

"Your mother ordered me off the Mission Station—you know that damned well."

"Please do not use strong language in my presence, sir," said Vicky primly.

"I apologize, but your mother does have a reputation. They say she fired both barrels at one unwanted visitor."

"Well," Vicky admitted, "that is true, but he *was* one of Mr. Rhodes's hirelings, and it *was* bird shot, and she *did* miss with one barrel."

"Well, I am one of Mr. Rhodes's hirelings, and she might have upped to buckshot, and the practice might have improved her shooting."

"I like a man of determination. A man who takes what he wants—and damn the consequences."

"That is strong language, Miss Codrington."

"Good day to you, Mr. Mellow." Vicky shook up the donkeys, and they stumbled into a dejected trot.

The little cart reached the outskirts of the new town, where the dozen or so brick buildings gave way to grass huts and tattered dusty canvas shelters and where the wagons of the transport riders were parked wheel to wheel on both sides of the track, still laden with the bags, bolts and bales that they had carried up from the railhead. Vicky was sitting upright on the cart, looking straight ahead, but anxiously she told Juba out of the side of her mouth, "Tell me if you see him coming, but don't let him see you looking."

"He comes," Juba announced comfortably. "He comes like a cheetah after a gazelle."

Vicky heard the beat of galloping hooves from behind, but she merely sat a little straighter.

"Hau!" Juba smiled with nostalgic sadness. "The passion of a man. My husband ran fifty miles without stopping to rest or drink, for in those days my beauty drove men mad."

"Don't stare at him, Juba."

"He is so strong and impetuous, and he will make such fine sons in your belly."

"Juba!" Vicky flushed scarlet. "That is a wicked thing for a Christian lady even to think. I shall probably send him back anyway."

Juba shrugged and chuckled. "Ah! Then he will make those fine sons elsewhere. I saw him looking at Elizabeth when he came to Khami."

Vicky's blushes turned a deeper, angrier shade. "You are an evil woman, Juba—" But before she could go on, Harry Mellow reined in his rangy gelding beside the cart.

"Your stepfather placed you in my care, Miss Codrington, and it is therefore my duty to see you home as swiftly as possible."

He reached into the cart, and before she realized his intentions, he had whipped a long, sinewy arm around her waist, and as she kicked and shrieked with surprise, he swung her up onto the horse's rump behind his saddle.

"Hold on!" he ordered. "Tightly!" And instinctively she threw both arms around his lean, hard body. The way it felt shocked her so that she relaxed her grip and leaned back just as Harry urged the gelding forward, and Vicky came so perilously close to flying backward over his haunches into the dusty track that she snatched at Harry with renewed fervor and tried to close her mind and shut off her body from these unfamiliar sensations. Her training warned her that anything that raised such a warmth in the base of her stomach, made the skin of her forearms prickle so, and rendered her breathless and deliriously light-headed must be unholy and wicked.

To distract herself she examined the fine hairs that grew down the back of his neck and the soft silky skin behind his ears, and found yet another sensation rising in her throat, a kind of choking, suffocating tenderness. She had an almost unbearable compulsion to press her face against the faded blue shirt and breathe in the virile smell of his body. It had the sharp odor of steel struck against flint, underlaid with a warmer scent like the first raindrops on sun-baked earth.

Her confusion was dispelled abruptly by the realization that the gelding was still in a flying gallop, and at this pace the journey back to Khami would be brief indeed.

"You are punishing your mount, sir." Her voice quavered and played her false, so Harry turned his head.

"I cannot hear you."

She leaned unnecessarily close so that her loose hair touched his cheek and her lips brushed his ear.

"Not so fast," she repeated.

"Your mother—"

"—is not that ill."

"But you told General St. John—"

"Do you think Juba and I would have left Khami if there was the least danger?"

"St. John?"

"It was a fine excuse to get them together again. So romantic, we should allow them a little time alone."

Harry reined the gelding down to a more sedate pace, but instead of relaxing her grip Vicky wriggled a little closer.

"My mother does not recognize her own feelings," she explained. "Sometimes Lizzie and I have to take things into our own hands."

Even as she said it, Vicky regretted having mentioned her twin's name. She had also noticed Harry Mellow look at Elizabeth on his only visit to Khami Mission, and she had seen Elizabeth look straight back. After Harry had left Khami in some haste with her mother's ultimate farewells ringing in his ears, Vicky had attempted to negotiate with her sister an agreement that Elizabeth would not encourage further smoldering glances from Mr. Mellow. In reply Elizabeth had smiled in that infuriating way she had. "Don't you think we should let Mr. Mellow decide on that?"

If Harry Mellow had been attractive before, Elizabeth's unreasonable tenacity had made him irresistible now, and instinctively Vicky tightened her grip around his waist. At the same time, she saw the wooded kopjes that marked Khami Mission Station looming ahead above the low scrubby bush, and she felt a sinking dread. Soon Harry would be confronted with Elizabeth's honey-brown eyes and that soft, dark flood of hair pierced with russet stars of light.

This was the only time in her entire life that Vicky could remember being free from surveillance, without her mother or Juba or, particularly, her twin being within earshot or touching distance. It was an exhilarating sensation added to all the other unfamiliar and clamorous sensations which assailed her, and the last restraints of her strict religious upbringing were swept away in this sudden reckless, rebellious mood. She realized with an unerring woman's instinct that she could have what she so dearly wanted, but only if she took direct bold action and took it immediately.

"It is a sad and bitter thing that a woman should be alone when she loves somebody so."

Her voice had sunk to a low purr, and it affected Harry so that he brought the horse down to a walk.

"God did not mean a woman to be alone," she murmured, and saw the blood come up under the soft skin behind his ears, "nor a man either," she went on, and slowly he turned his head and looked into her green eyes.

"It is so hot in the sun," Vicky whispered, holding his gaze. "I should like to rest for a few minutes in the shade."

He lifted her down from the saddle, and she stood close to him still, without averting her eyes from his face.

"The wagon dust has covered everything and left us no clean place to sit," she said. "Perhaps we should try further from the road?"

And she took his hand and quite naturally led him through the soft knee-high grass toward one of the mimosa trees. Beneath its spreading feathery branches, they would be out of sight of any chance traveler upon the road.

◆ ◆ ◆

Mungo St. John's mare was lathered in streaks down her shoulders and his riding boots were splattered with blown froth from her gaping jaws as he drove her over the top of the neck between the kopjes, and without pause pushed her down toward the white mission buildings. The mare's hoofbeats rang against the hills and echoed from the mission walls, and Elizabeth's slim skirted figure appeared on the wide veranda of the homestead. She shaded her eyes to peer up the slope at Mungo, and when she recognized him, hurried down the steps into the sunlight.

"General St. John, oh, thank God you have come." She ran to take the mare's head.

"How is she?" There was a wild, driven look upon Mungo's bony features. He kicked his feet from the stirrups and jumped down to seize Elizabeth by the shoulders and shake her in his anxiety.

"It started as a game—Vicky and I wanted you to come to Mama because she needs you—she wasn't bad, just a little go of fever."

"Damn you, girl," Mungo shouted at her, "what has happened?"

At his tone the tears that Elizabeth had been holding back broke with a sob and streamed down her cheeks. "She has changed—it must be the girl's blood—she is burning up with the girl's blood."

"Pull yourself together." Mungo shook her again. "Come on, Lizzie, this isn't like you."

Elizabeth gulped once, and then her voice steadied. "She injected blood from a fever patient into herself."

"From a black girl? In God's name, why?" Mungo demanded, but did not wait for her reply. He left Elizabeth and ran up onto the veranda and burst in through the door to Robyn's bedroom, but he stopped before he reached the bed.

In the small, closed room, the stink of fever was as rank as that of a sty, and the heat from the body in the narrow cot had condensed on the glass of the single window like steam from a kettle of boiling water. Crouched beside the cot like a puppy at its master's feet was Mungo's son. Robert looked up at his father with huge, solemn eyes, and his mouth twisted in the thin, pale face.

"Son!" Mungo took another step toward the cot, but the child leaped to his feet and silently he darted for the door, ducking nimbly under Mungo's outstretched hand, and his bare feet slapped on the veranda as he raced away. For a moment Mungo yearned after him, and then he shook his head and instead he went to the cot. He stood over it and looked down at the still figure upon it.

Robyn had wasted until the bones of her skull seemed to rise through the pale flesh of her cheeks and forehead. Her eyes were closed and sunk into deep leaden-purple sockets. Her hair, laced with silver at the temples, seemed dry and brittle as the winter grasses of the parched veld, and as he leaned to touch her forehead, a paroxysm of shivering overtook her that rattled the iron bedstead, and her teeth chattered so violently that it seemed they must shatter like porcelain. Under Mungo's fingers her skin was almost painfully hot to the touch, and he looked up sharply at Elizabeth, who stood beside him with a stricken expression.

"Quinine?" he demanded.

"I have given her more than I should—a hundred grains since this morning—but there is no response." Elizabeth broke off, reluctant to tell him the worst.

"Yes, what is it?"

"Before this, Mama had not taken quinine for six weeks. She wanted to give the fever a chance to strike, and to prove her theory."

Mungo stared at her aghast. "But her own studies—" He shook his head in disbelief. "She has shown herself that abstinence followed by massive doses—" He could not go on, as though the words might conjure up the specter he feared most.

Elizabeth had anticipated his fears. "Her pallor," she whispered, "the total lack of response to the quinine—I am so afraid."

Instinctively Mungo put his arm around Elizabeth's shoulders, and for a few seconds she shrank against him. Mungo had always enjoyed a special relationship with the twins; they had always been his willing accomplices and secret allies at Khami Mission, from the first day that he had arrived, dying of the suppurating gunshot wound in his leg. Though they had been barely pubescent at that time, the twins had not been proof against the strange mesmeric effect he had on women of all ages.

"Vicky and I tempted fate by telling you that Mama was dying."

"That's enough." He shook her gently. "Has she passed water?" And then, roughly, to cover the embarrassment between them, "Has she urinated?"

"Not since last night." Elizabeth shook her head miserably, and he pushed her toward the door.

"We must force her to take liquid. There is a bottle of Cognac in my saddlebag. Get lemons from the garden, a bowl of sugar, and a big jug of boiling water."

Mungo held Robyn's head while Elizabeth forced small sips of the steaming liquid between her white lips, and Robyn fought them in her delirium, hounded and driven by the terrible phantoms of malarial fever.

Then, as they worked, the icy chills that had racked Robyn's body gave way abruptly to a baking heat that desiccated her, and though she did not recognize either Mungo or Elizabeth, she drank thirstily from their hands, gulping and choking in her eagerness, even though she was so weak that when she tried to lift her head, it lolled and rolled to one side so that Mungo had to steady her. His hands, powerful and brutal-looking, were strangely tender and gentle as he cupped her chin and wiped away the drops that dribbled from her lips.

"How much has she taken?" he asked.

"Over four pints," Elizabeth answered, checking the level in the jug.

The light in the room altered as evening began to fall, and Elizabeth stood up and held her back as she went to the door and looked across the veranda at the road that led down from the neck.

"Vicky and Juba should have been home before now," she said, but her mother cried out again, and she closed the door and hurried back to the cot.

Suddenly, as she knelt beside Mungo, she became aware of the sharp ammoniacal odor that pervaded the room. She averted her eyes and said softly, "I must change her."

But Mungo did not rise. "She is my wife," he said. "Neither Vicky nor Juba are here, and you will need help."

Elizabeth nodded and drew down the bedclothes, and then whispered huskily, "Oh, sweet God."

"It is what we feared," Mungo said quietly, hopelessly.

The skirts of Robyn's nightdress were rucked up high around her pale, girlish thighs. They were sodden, as was the thin mattress beneath her, but it was not the sulphur yellow urine stain that they had hoped to see. Staring bleakly at the soiled bedclothes, Mungo recalled the piece of callous doggerel that he had heard the troopers of Jameson's column sing:

> Black as the angel
> Black as the ace,
> When the fever waters flow
> They are as black as disgrace.
> Soon we'll lay him down below,
> And chuck dirt in his face.

The reeking stain was black, black as old, congealing blood, the drainage from kidneys that were trying to purge the bloodstream of the wildfire anemia that was coursing through Robyn's body, the destruction of the red corpuscles that was the cause of the dreadful pallor. For the malaria had been transmuted to something infinitely more evil and deadly.

As they both stared helplessly at it, there was a commotion on the veranda and the door burst open. Victoria stood at the threshold. She was transformed, glowing from within, charged with that strange, fragile beauty of a young woman awakened for the first time to the wonder and mystery of love.

"Where have you been, Vicky?" Elizabeth asked. Then she saw the tall young man in the doorway behind her twin. She realized what Harry Mellow's bemused yet proud expression meant. She felt no resentment, no envy, only a small quick pleasure for Vicky. Elizabeth had never wanted Harry Mellow; she had teased her sister by pretending interest, but her own love was for a man she could never have, she had long ago resigned herself to that. She was happy for Vicky, but sad for herself, and Vicky misinterpreted her expression.

"What is it?" The glow faded from Vicky's lovely face, and she lifted a hand to her bosom as though to stem the panic that rose within her. "What has happened, Lizzie? What is it?"

"Blackwater," Elizabeth answered flatly. "Mother has blackwater fever."

She did not have to elaborate. The twins had lived their lives on a hospital station. They knew that the disease was peculiarly selective. It attacked only white persons, and Robyn's researches had linked that peculiarity to the use of quinine, which was restricted almost entirely to the whites. Robyn had treated fifty or more cases at the mission over the years. At first it had been the old ivory hunters and itinerant traders, then more recently the troopers of Jameson's column and the new settlers and prospectors that were swarming across the Limpopo River.

The twins knew that of those fifty cases of blackwater, only three had survived. The rest of them lay in the little cemetery beyond the river. Their mother was under virtual sentence of death, and Vicky flew to the bedside and knelt beside her.

"Oh, Mama," she whispered, stricken with guilt. "I should have been here."

◆ ◆ ◆

Juba heated rounded river stones in the open fire and wrapped them in blankets. They packed them around Robyn's body, and then covered her with four karosses of wild fur. She fought weakly to throw off the covers, but Mungo held her down. Despite the internal heat of the fever and the external temperature of the hot stones trapped under the furs, her skin was burning dry and her eyes had the flat, blind glitter of water-worn rock crystal.

Then as the sun touched the treetops and the light in the room turned to somber orange, the fever broke and oozed from the pores of her marble-pale skin like the juice of crushed sugarcane from the press. The sweat came up in fat, shining beads across her forehead and chin, each drop joining with the others until they ran in thick, oily snakes back into her hair, soaking it as though she had been held under water. It ran into her eyes faster than Mungo could wipe it away. It poured down her neck and wetted and matted the fur of the kaross. It soaked through the thin mattress and pattered like rain on the hard, dry floor below.

The temperature of her body plunged dramatically, and when the sweat had passed, Juba and the twins sponged her naked body. She had dehydrated and wasted, so that the rack of her ribs stood out starkly, and her pelvis formed a bony, hollowed basin. They handled her with exaggerated care, for any rough movement might rupture the delicate, damaged walls of the renal blood vessels and bring on the torrential hemorrhage which so often ended this disease.

When they finished, they called Mungo back from where he was sitting with Harry Mellow on the stoep of the mission. Robyn was comatose. Mungo set the lantern on the floor so that the feeble light would not trouble her.

"I will call you if there is any change." He sent the women away and sat on the stool beside the cot.

Robyn sank slowly during the night as the disease destroyed her blood, and in the dawn light she looked as though she had been sucked by some monstrous vampire.

He knew she was dying, and he took her hand, and she did not stir.

A soft rustle at the door made Mungo turn his head. Robert, his son, stood in the door. His nightshirt was threadbare and patched, too tight under the armpits, and the skirts were up above his knees. His thick, tangled curls flopped onto the broad, pale forehead, and he stared at Mungo unblinkingly, owl-eyed from sleep.

Mungo sat very still, for he sensed that any movement would put the child to flight like a frightened wild animal. He waited a hundred beats of his own heart, and at last the child shifted his gaze to his mother's face, and for the first time there was expression in his eyes. Slowly, a pace at a time, he crossed to the bed and hesitantly reached out to touch his mother's cheek. Robyn opened her eyes. Already they were glazed and sightless, looking beyond the dark frontiers which she had reached.

"Mummy," said Robert. "Please don't die, Mummy."

Robyn's eyes flickered from side to side, and then miraculously they focused on Robert's face. She tried to lift her hand, but it merely twitched and then relaxed again.

"Listen to me. If you die—" Mungo said harshly, and her eyes swiveled to him. "If you die," he repeated deliberately, "the child will be mine."

For the first time, she recognized him. He could see it, and his words had reached her. He saw the anger come alive in her eyes, saw the enormous effort that she made to speak, but she could make no sound, only her lips formed a single word.

"Never!"

"Then live," he challenged her. "Live, damn you!" And he saw her begin to fight again.

♦ ♦ ♦

Robyn's life forces rose and sank to the dreadful tides of the disease, baking fever followed icy chills, and the long, exhausted coma followed the bursting sweats. At times she raved in delirium, assailed by fantasies and demons from the past. Sometimes she looked at Mungo St. John and saw him as he had been so long ago, on the quarterdeck of his beautiful Baltimore clipper *Huron*, when Robyn had been in her early twenties.

"So handsome," she whispered. "So devilishly, impossibly handsome."

Then she was lucid for brief periods, and the fever added strength to her anger.

"You killed him—you killed him, and he was a saint," she whispered, her voice light but shaking with fury, and Mungo could not quieten her. "He was my husband, and you sent him across the river to where you knew the Matabele assegais waited. You killed my husband as surely as if you had driven the blade through his heart with your own hand."

Then her mood changed again. "Please, will you never let me be at peace?" she pleaded, her voice so weak that he had to lean over her to catch her words. "You know I cannot resist you, yet everything you stand for is an offense against me and my God, against me and the lost and leaderless people that have been given into my care."

"Drink," he ordered. "You must drink." And she struggled weakly as he held the jug to her lips.

Then the disease would tighten its grip upon her and sweep her away into the burning fever mists where there was no sense and no reality. The days and nights swung past in a blur. Sometimes Mungo would start awake—to find it was past midnight, and one of the twins was sleeping in the chair on the other side of the bed. He would rise, numbed with fatigue, to force Robyn to drink again.

"Drink," he whispered to her. "Drink, or die."

Then he sank back into his own chair, and when he awoke again, it was dawn, and his son stood beside the chair, staring into his face. As he opened his eyes, the boy darted away again, and when he called after him, Robyn whispered fiercely from the cot:

"You will never have him—never!"

Sometimes in the noonday, when Robyn was lying pale and silent, resting between the periodic onslaughts of the fever, Mungo could sleep for a few hours on the pallet set at the far end of the veranda, until Juba or one of the twins called him. "It has begun again." And he hurried to the cot and goaded and coaxed her from her lethargy and forced her to go on fighting.

Sometimes, sitting beside the cot, his own bony features now gaunt and haggard, he wondered at himself. He had possessed a hundred women more beautiful than this in his lifetime. He was well aware of the strange attraction he could still wield over any woman, and yet he had chosen this one, this one whom he could never possess. The one who hated him as fiercely as she loved him, who had conceived his son in a soul-consuming passion and yet kept him from the child with all her determination. She was the one who had demanded that Mungo marry her, yet vehemently denied him the duty of a wife, who would not allow him in her presence except now when she was too weak to resist, or on those rare occasions when her lust for him overcame her conscience and her revulsion.

He remembered one of those occasions only a month or so previously, when he had wakened in the backroom of his mud-brick hut on the outskirts of Bulawayo. There was a candle burning, and Robyn stood beside the camp bed that was the only item of furniture in his room. She must have ridden through the darkness and the wilderness to reach him.

"God forgive me!" she had whispered, and fallen upon him in a frenzy of desire.

In the first light, she had left him exhausted and stunned, and when he had followed her out to Khami Mission the next day, she had met him on the veranda armed with a shotgun, and he had known instinctively that if he tried to mount the steps to touch her, she would have killed him. He had never seen such loathing as there was in her eyes, for herself as much as for him.

Endlessly she had written to the newspapers, at home and in the Cape, denouncing almost every proclamation he made as Chief Native Commissioner of Matabeleland. She had attacked his conscripted labor policy which provided the ranchers and the miners with the black men they desperately needed to insure the continuance and the prosperity of this new land. She had condemned the levy of his native police force he used to keep order over the tribe. Once she had even stormed into an *indaba* he was holding with the tribal indunas and harangued them in fluent Sindebele in his presence, calling the indunas "old women" and "cowards" for submitting to the authority of Mungo and the British South Africa Company. Then not an hour later she had waited beside the path, in thick bush near the ford of the river, and had waylaid him as he rode back from the *indaba*. Naked as wild animals, they had made love upon her saddle blanket in the veld, and the fury of it came so close to mutual destruction that it left him shaken and appalled.

"I hate you, oh God, how I hate you," she had whispered, her eyes full of tears, as she mounted her horse again and galloped away, heedless of the thorns that ripped at her skirts.

Her exhortations to the indunas were blatant incitement to rebellion and bloody revolution, while in her book *Trooper Hackett of Matabeleland,* in which she mentioned Mungo by name, the words she put into his mouth and the actions she ascribed to him were a most virulent slander. Mr. Rhodes and other directors of the BSA Company had urged Mungo to take legal action against her.

"Against my own wife, sir?" He had slanted his single eye and smiled ruefully. "What a fool I would appear."

She was the most implacable and remorseless adversary he had ever known, and yet the thought of her dead desolated him, so that each time she sank back toward the abyss, so he sank with her, and when she rallied, so his spirits soared to match her.

Yet the play of emotion and the way in which he drained his own reserves to sustain her wearied him to the very core of his soul, and it went on and on, without respite, day after day—until finally Elizabeth broke in on the few hours of deathlike sleep which he allowed himself. He heard the emotion that shook her voice and saw the tears in her eyes.

"It's over, General St. John," she said, and he flinched as though she had struck him across the face and staggered groggily to his feet. He felt his own tears sting the rims of his eyes.

"I cannot believe it." Then he realized that Elizabeth was smiling through her tears, and she was proffering the enameled pot she held in both hands.

It stank of ammonia and the peculiar rotting odor of the disease, but the color of the fluid had changed from deadly black to light golden.

"It's over," Elizabeth repeated. "Her water has cleared. She's safe. Thank God, she's safe."

By that afternoon Robyn was well enough once more to order Mungo St. John to leave Khami Mission, and the following morning she tried to rise from the cot to enforce that order.

"I cannot allow my son to come under your evil influences for another day."

"Madam—" he started, but she swept his protest aside.

"So far I have resolved not to tell the child about you. He does not know that his father once commanded the most notorious slaving fleet that ever made the middle passage. He does not know of the thousands of damned souls, innocent children of Africa, whom you carried away to a far continent. He does not yet understand that it was you and your ilk that waged bloody and unprovoked war upon Lobengula and the Matabele nation, nor that you are the instrument of cruel oppression over them—but unless you leave, I shall change that resolve." Her voice crackled with some of its old force, and Juba had to hold her by the shoulders. "I order you to leave Khami immediately."

The effort left Robyn white and panting, and under Juba's gentle, chubby hands, she sank back against the bolster, and Elizabeth whispered to Mungo:

"She might have a relapse. Perhaps it would be best."

The corner of Mungo's mouth twisted up in that mocking grin that Robyn remembered so well, but in the golden depths of his single eye there was a shadow, a regret or a terrible loneliness, Robyn could not be sure.

"Your servant, ma'am." He gave her an exaggerated bow and strode from the sickroom. Robyn listened to his footsteps crossing the veranda and going down the steps. Only then did she push Juba's hands away and roll on her side to face the blank whitewashed wall.

At the crest, where the path ran through a saddle between the thickly forested hills, Mungo St. John reined in his mare and looked back. The veranda of the homestead was deserted, and he sighed and picked up the reins again and faced ahead down the road into the north, but he did not shake up the mare. Instead he frowned and lifted his chin to look into the heavens.

The northern sky was dark. It was as though a heavy curtain fell from the high heaven to the earth. It was not a cloud, for it had a peculiar density and body to it, like the poisonous plankton of the mysterious red tide which he had seen sweeping across the surface of the southern Atlantic, spreading death and desolation wherever it touched.

Yet Mungo had never seen anything like this. The magnitude of it challenged the imagination. It reached in a great arc around half the horizon, and even as he watched, it swept toward the sun which stood near its noon zenith.

Far north Mungo had seen the khamsin winds raise the mighty sandstorms over the Sahara, yet he realized there was not a sand desert within a thousand miles which could generate such a phenomenon. This was beyond his experience, and his puzzlement turned to alarm as he realized the speed at which this thing was bearing down upon him.

The fringes of the dark veil touched the rim of the sun, and the white noon light altered. The mare fidgeted uncomfortably under Mungo, and a troop of guinea fowl that had been chittering in the grass beside the track fell silent. Swiftly the murky tide flooded the heavens, and the sun turned a sullen orange, like a disk of heated metal from the smithy's forge, and a vast shadow fell upon the land.

A silence had fallen upon the world. The murmurous insect chorus from the forest was stilled, the tinking and cheeping of small birds in the scrub had died away, sounds that were the background song of Africa, unnoticed until they were gone.

Now the stillness was oppressive. The mare nodded her head, and the tinkle of her curb chain sounded jarringly loud. The spreading curtain thickened and smothered the sky, the shadow deepened.

Now there was a sound. A faint and distant sibilance like the wind shifting the sugary white sands of the desert dunes. The sun glowed dully as the ashes of a dying campfire.

The faint hissing sound gathered strength, like the hollow echo in a seashell held to the ear, and the filtered sunlight was a weird purplish glow. Mungo shivered with a kind of religious awe, though the heat of noon seemed even more oppressive in the gloom.

The strange rustling sound mounted swiftly, became a deep humming flutter, and then the rush of high winds; and the sun was gone, blotted out completely. Out of the half-light, he saw it coming low across the forest, sweeping toward him in twisting columns like some monstrous fogbank.

With a low roar of millions upon millions of wings, it was upon him. It struck like a volley of grapeshot from a cannon, driving into his face, the impact of each horny-winged body striking with a numbing shock that broke his skin and drew blood.

He flung up his hands to protect his face, and the startled mare reared, and it was a miracle of horsemanship that he kept his seat. He was half blinded and dazed by the rushing torrent of wings about his head, and he snatched at the air, and they were so thick that he caught one of the flying insects.

It was almost twice as long as his forefinger, wings a glaring orange slashed with intricate designs of black. The thorax was covered in horny armor, and from the helmeted head stared the bulging multiple eyes, yellow as polished topaz, and the long back legs were fanged with red-tipped thorns. It kicked convulsively in his hand, piercing the skin and leaving a fine line of blood droplets upon it.

He crushed it and it crackled and exploded in a burst of yellow juice. "Locusts!" He looked up again, marveling at their multitudes. "The third plague of Egypt," he spoke aloud, then swung the mare away from the onrushing wall of flying bodies and put his heels into her, driving her at a gallop back down the hill toward the mission. The locust cloud flew faster than the mare could go at a full gallop, so he rode in semidarkness, surrounded by the great drumming roar of wings.

A dozen times he almost lost the track, so dense was the swarm in the air around him. They settled on his back and crawled over him, the sharp feet needling his exposed skin. As soon as he struck them away, others took their place, and he had a sense of horror, of being overwhelmed and drowned in a seething cauldron of living organisms.

Ahead of him the buildings of Khami Mission loomed out of the darkened noonday. The twins and servants were gathered on the veranda, paralyzed with astonishment, and he flung himself off the mare and ran toward them.

"Get every person who can walk down into the fields. Take pots, drums—anything they can bang to make a noise, blankets to wave—"

The twins recovered swiftly. Elizabeth pulled a shawl over her head to protect it and ran out into the swirling storm of locusts toward the church and the wards, while Vicky disappeared into the kitchen and came out carrying a nest of iron pots.

"Good girl." Mungo gave her a quick hug. "When this is over, I want a word about you and Harry." He snatched the largest pot from her. "Come on."

With a suddenness that brought them up short from a dead run, the air cleared, and the sunlight was so white and blinding that they had to shield their eyes against it.

It was no release, for the entire heaven-high cloud of locusts had sunk to the earth, and though the sky was blue and high, the fields and the forest were transformed. The tallest trees looked like grotesquely colored haystacks, seething heaps of orange and black. The branches swayed and sagged to the unbearable weight of tiny bodies, and every few seconds there was a sharp crack as a branch snapped and came crashing down. Before their eyes the standing corn flattened under the onslaught, and the very earth crawled with the myriad clicking, rustling bodies.

They ran into the fields, a hundred frantic human figures, banging the metal pots and flapping the coarse gray hospital blankets, and in front of each of them the insects rose in a brief puff of wings and resettled as they passed.

Now the air was raucous with a new sound. The excited shrieks of thousands of birds gorging upon the swarm. There were squadrons of jet black drongos with long forked tails, starlings of iridescent malachite green, rollers and bee-eaters in jeweled colors of turquoise and sunlight yellow, carmine and purple, jinking and whirling in full flight, ecstatic with greed. The storks strode knee-deep through the living carpet, marabous with horrific scaly heads, woolly-necked storks with scarves of fluffy white, saddle-bills with yellow medallions decorating their long red and black beaks, all of them pecking hungrily at the living banquet.

It did not last long, less than an hour. Then, as abruptly as it had settled, the great swarm roared spontaneously into the air as though it were a single creature. Once again an unnatural dusk fell across the earth as the sun was obliterated, and a false dawn followed as the clouds thinned and winged away southward. In the empty fields, the human figures seemed tiny and insignificant as they stared about them in horror. They did not recognize their home.

The maize fields were reduced to bare brown earth; even the coarse, pithy stalks of the corn had been devoured. The rose bushes around the homestead were merely brown sticks. The peach and apple blossoms in the orchards were gone, and bare twisted branches seemed to be an echo of winter; even the indigenous forests on the hills and the thick riverine bush along the banks of the Khami River had been devastated.

There was no trace of green, no leaf or blade of grass untouched in the wide brown swath of destruction that the swarm had blazed through the heart of Matabeleland.

♦ ♦ ♦

Juba traveled with two female attendants. It was a symptom of the decline that had come upon the Matabele nation. There was a time, before the occupation by the company, when a senior wife of one of the great indunas of the House of Kumalo would have had an entourage of forty women in waiting and fifty plumed and armed *amadoda* to see her safely to her husband's kraal. Now Juba carried her own sleeping mat balanced upon her head, and despite her great and abundant flesh, she moved with an extraordinary lightness and grace, her back straight and her head high.

She had shed the woolen vest now that she was away from the mission, although she still wore the crucifix around her neck. Her huge, naked breasts swung and bounced with youthful elasticity. They had been anointed with fat and shone in the sunlight, and her legs flashed under the short cowhide apron as she moved at a gait between a trot and a glide that covered the dusty track at surprising speed.

The two attendants, both newly married young women from Juba's kraal, followed her closely, but they were silent, not singing or laughing. Instead they turned their heads from side to side under their burdens to stare in awe at the bleak and denuded land around them. The locust swarms had passed this way also. The bare, crippled trees were devoid of insect or bird life. The sun had already scorched the exposed earth, and it was crumbling into dust and blowing away on the little eddies of wind.

They came up over a low rise and involuntarily stopped and drew closer together, not even laying down their bundles, so complete was their horrified fascination at what lay ahead of them. Once it had been the great regimental kraal of the Inyati impi which Gandang commanded. Then, by the decree of the new Native Commissioner at Bulawayo, the impi had been disbanded and scattered. The kraal had been destroyed by fire. However, when the women had last seen it, a new growth of grass had begun to cover the scars, but now it had been stripped away by the locust swarms, and the circular black banks of ash lay exposed once again. They invoked memories of a past grandeur, and the new kraal built to house Gandang and his close family was tiny and insignificant in comparison.

It lay a mile down the bank of the Inyati River, and the pasture in between was destroyed. The spring rains had not yet filled the river, and the sandbanks were silvery white; the polished, water-worn boulders glittered like reptile scales in the sunlight. The new kraal itself seemed deserted, and the cattle pens were empty.

"They have taken the cattle again," said Ruth, the handsome young woman who stood beside Juba. She was not yet twenty years of age, and although she had already worn the headdress of the married woman for two seasons, she had not yet conceived. It was the secret terror that she was barren that had driven her to convert to Christianity—three gods as omnipotent as the ones which Juba had described to her would certainly not allow one of their own to remain childless. She had been baptized by Nomusa almost a full moon previously, and her name had been changed by her new gods and Nomusa from Kampu to Ruth. Now she was most anxious to rejoin her husband, one of Gandang's nephews, and to put to the test the efficacy of her new religion.

"No," Juba told her shortly. "Gandang will have sent the herds eastward to find new pasture."

"The *amadoda*—where are the men?"

"Perhaps they have gone with the cattle."

"That is work for boys, not men."

Juba snorted. "Since One-Bright-Eye has taken their shields, our men are merely *mujiba*."

The *mujiba* were the herdboys, not yet initiated into their fighting regiments, and Juba's companions were shamed by the truth of her words. It was true that their men had been disarmed and that the cattle and slave raids which had been the main activity and diversion of the *amadoda* had been forbidden. At least their own husbands were blooded warriors, they had washed their spears in the blood of Wilson's troopers on the banks of the Shangani River in the one beautiful killing, the one small Matabele victory of that war, but what would become of the younger men now that a whole way of life had been denied them? Would they ever be able to win on the battlefield the right to go in to the women and take a wife? Or would the customs and laws under which they had lived all their lives fall into disregard and disuse? And if they did, then what would become of the nation?

"The women are still here." Juba pointed out the rows of workers in the brown, denuded cornfields. They swayed in rhythm to the swing of the hoes.

"They are replanting the fields," Ruth said.

"It is too late," Juba muttered. "There will be no harvest to celebrate at the dance of the first fruits this season." Then she roused herself. "Let us go down."

At one of the shallow pools between the sandbanks, they laid aside their headloads and shed their aprons. In the cool green water, they washed away the sweat and dust of the road. Ruth found a buffalo creeper that had escaped the locusts, and she picked yellow flowers to twine into head-pieces for all of them.

The women in the fields saw them as they came up the bank and ran shrieking with delight to greet them, jostling each other in their eagerness to make obeisance to Juba.

"Mamewethu," they called her as they bowed and clapped their hands in deep respect. They took her load from her and two of her grandchildren came forward shyly to hold each of her hands. Then, singing the songs of welcome, the little procession filed up to the kraal.

Not all the men had left. Gandang sat under the bare branches of the wild fig tree on his carved stool of chiefship, and Juba hurried to kneel before him.

He smiled down at her fondly, nodding comfortably at her protestations of duty and devotion. Then, as an extraordinary mark of his feeling for her, he lifted her with his own hand and seated her on the mat which one of his junior wives spread beside him. He waited while she refreshed herself form the big clay beerpot that another wife knelt to hand her.

Then he waved the women and children away, and alone at last, the two of them leaned their heads together and talked like the beloved companions that they were.

"Nomusa is well?" Gandang asked. He did not share Juba's deep love for the woman doctor at Khami Mission; in fact he viewed with deep suspicion this alien religion that his senior wife had adopted. It was Gandang's impi that had caught Wilson's little patrol on the banks of the Shangani

River during the war and slain them to a man. Among the corpses, stripped naked by his warriors so that the shocking mulberry-colored assegai wounds in their white flesh were exposed, had lain the body of the woman missionary's first husband. There could never be love where there had been blood. However, Gandang respected the white woman. He had known her as long as he had known Juba, and he had watched her unflagging efforts to champion and protect the Matabele people. She had been friend and adviser to the old King Lobengula, and she had brought comfort to thousands of sick and dying Matabele, so now his concern was genuine. "Has she thrown aside the evil spirits that she brought upon herself by drinking the girl's blood?"

It was inevitable that the accounts of Robyn's experiment with the transference of malaria would become garbled and take on the aura of witchcraft.

"She did not drink the girl's blood." Juba tried to explain that the taking of blood had been for the good of the Matabele nation, but because she did not understand it completely herself, her explanation was unconvincing. She saw the doubt in Gandang's eyes, and she abandoned the effort.

"Bazo, the Ax?" she asked instead. "Where is he?" Her firstborn son was also her favorite.

"In the hills with all the other young men," Gandang answered.

The Matopo Hills were always the refuge of the Matabele in time of danger and trouble, and Juba leaned forward anxiously to ask, "There has been trouble?"

Gandang shrugged in reply. "In these times there is always trouble."

"From whence does it come?"

"One-Bright-Eye sent word with his *kanka*—with his jackals— that we must provide two hundred young men to work on the new gold mine in the south that belongs to Henshaw, the Hawk."

"You did not send the men?"

"I told his *kanka*"—the derogatory name for the company native police likened them to the little scavengers that followed the lion for the scraps and expressed the hatred that the Matabele felt for these traitors—"I told them that the white men had deprived me of my shield and assegai and my honor as an induna, therefore I had lost the right to command my young men to dig the white men's holes for them or to build their roads."

"And now One-Bright-Eye comes?"

Juba spoke with resignation. She knew all the moves that must be made: the command, the defiance, the confrontation. She had watched it all before, and now she was sick of men's pride and men's wars and the death and maiming and starvation and suffering.

"Yes," Gandang agreed. "Not all the *kanka* are traitors, and one has sent word that One-Bright-Eye is on the road with fifty men— and so the young men have gone into the hills."

"But you stay here to meet him?" Juba asked. "Unarmed and alone, you wait for One-Bright-Eye and fifty armed men?"

"I have never run from any man," Gandang said simply, "never in my life."

And Juba felt her pride and her love choke her as she looked into the stern, handsome face and noticed as if for the first time the hoarfrost sparkling on the dark cap of his hair above the headring.

"Gandang, my Lord, the old times have passed. Things change. The sons of Lobengula work as houseboys in the kraal of Lodzi far away in the south beside the great water. The impis are scattered, and there is a new and gentle god in the land, the god Jesus. Everything has changed, and we must change with it."

Gandang was silent a long time, staring out across the river as though he had not heard her speak. Then he sighed and took a little red snuff from the buckhorn that hung on a thong around his neck. He sneezed and wiped his eyes and looked at her.

"Your body is part of my body," he said. "Your first-born son is my son. If I do not trust you, then I cannot trust myself. So I tell you that the old times will come again."

"What is this, Lord?" Juba asked. "What strange words are these?"

"The words of the Umlimo. She has called forth an oracle. The nation will be free and great again—"

"The Umlimo sent the impis onto the guns at Shangani and Bembesi," Juba whispered bitterly. "The Umlimo preaches war and death and pestilence. There is a new god now. The god Jesus of peace."

"Peace?" Gandang asked bitterly. "If that is the word of this god, then the white men do not listen very well to their own. Ask the Zulu of the peace they found at Ulundi, ask the shade of Lobengula of the peace they brought with them to Matabeleland."

Juba could not reply, for again she had not fully understood when Nomusa explained, and she bowed her head in resignation. After a while, when Gandang was certain that she had accepted what he had said, he went on:

"The oracle of the Umlimo is in three parts—and already the first has come to pass. The darkness at noon, the wings of the locust, and the trees bare of leaves in the springtime. It is happening and we must look to our steel."

"The white men have broken the assegais."

"In the hills there has been a new birthing of steel." Involuntarily Gandang lowered his voice to a whisper. "The forges of the Rozwi smiths burn day and night, and the molten iron runs as the waters of the Zambezi."

Juba stared at him. "Who has done this?"

"Bazo, your own son."

"The wounds of the guns are still fresh and bright upon his body."

"But he is an induna of Kumalo," Gandang whispered proudly, "and he is a man."

"One man," Juba replied. "One man only—where are the impis?"

"Preparing in secret, in the wild places, relearning the skills and arts which they have not yet forgotten."

"Gandang, my Lord, I feel my heart beginning to break again, I feel my tears gathering like the rainstorms of summer. Must there always be war?"

"You are a daughter of Matabele, of pure Zanzi blood from the south. Your father's father followed Mzilikazi, your father spilled his blood for him, as your own son did for Lobengula—do you have to ask that question?"

She was silent, knowing how futile it was to argue with him when there was that glitter in his eyes. When the fighting madness was in him, there was no room for reason.

"Juba, my little Dove, there will be work for you when the prophecy of the Umlimo comes to full term."

"Lord?" she asked.

"The women must carry the blades. They will be bound up in rolls of sleeping mats and in bundles of thatching grass and carried on the heads of the women to where the impis are waiting.''

"Lord." Her voice was neutral, and she dropped her eyes from his hard, glittering gaze.

"The white men and their *kanka* will not suspect the women; they will let them pass freely upon the road," Gandang went on. "You are the mother of the nation now that the king's wives are dead and scattered. It will be your duty to assemble the young women, to train them in their duty, and to see them place the steel in the hands of the warriors at the time that the Umlimo has foreseen, the time when the hornless cattle are eaten up by the cross.''

Juba was reluctant to reply, afraid to conjure up his wrath. He had to demand her answer.

"You have heard my word, woman, and you know your duty to your husband and your people.''

Then only, Juba lifted her head and looked deeply into his dark fierce eyes.

"Forgive me, Lord. This time I cannot obey you. I cannot help to bring fresh sorrow upon the land. I cannot bear to hear again the wails of the widows and orphans. You must find another to carry the bloody steel.''

She had expected his anger. She could have weathered that as she had a hundred times before, but she saw in his eyes something that had never been there before. It was contempt, and she did not know how she could bear it. When Gandang stood up without another word and stalked away toward the river, she wanted to run after him and throw herself at his feet, but then she remembered the words of Nomusa.

"He is a gentle God, but the way he sets for us is hard beyond the telling of it.''

And Juba found that she could not move. She was trapped between two worlds and two duties, and she felt as though it was tearing her soul down the middle.

♦ ♦ ♦

Juba sat alone under the bare wild fig tree the rest of the day. She sat with her arms folded across her great glossy breasts, and she rocked herself silently, as though the movement might comfort her as it would a fretful child, but there was no surcease in either movement or thought, so it was with relief that at last she looked up and saw her two attendants kneeling before her. She did not know how long they had been there. She had not even heard them come up, so rapt had she been in her sorrow and confusion.

"I see you, Ruth," she said, nodding at the Christian girl and her companion, "and you, too, Imbali, my little Flower. What is it that makes you look so sad?"

"The men have gone into the hills," whispered Ruth.

"And your hearts have gone with them." Juba smiled at the two young women. It was a fond yet sad smile, as though she remembered her own youthful bodily passions and regretted that the flames had burned so low.

"I have dreamed of nothing but my beautiful man every lonely night we have been away," murmured Ruth.

"And of the fine son he will make with you," Juba chuckled. She knew the girl's desperate need and teased her lovingly. "Lelesa, the Lightning Stroke—your man is well named."

Ruth hung her head. "Do not mock me, Mamewethu," she murmured pitifully, and Juba turned to Imbali.

"And you, little Flower, is there no bee to tickle your petals either?"

The girl giggled and covered her mouth and squirmed with embarrassment.

"If you need us, Mamewethu," Ruth said earnestly, "then we will stay with you."

Juba kept them in an agony of suspense for a few seconds longer.

How firm and nubile was their young flesh, how sweetly shaped their young bodies, how eager were their great dark eyes, how vast their hunger for all that life had to offer. Juba smiled again and clapped her hands.

"Be gone," she said, "both of you. There are those that need you more than I do. Away with you both, follow your men into the hills."

The girls squealed with delight, and throwing aside all ceremony, they embraced Juba joyously.

"You are the sunshine and the moon," they told her, and then they fled to their huts to prepare for the journey, and for a little while Juba's own sorrow was lightened. But at the fall of night when no young wife came to summon her to Gandang's hut, it returned in full strength, and she wept alone on her sleeping mat until at last sleep came over her, but then there were dreams—dreams full of the glow of flames and the smell of rotting flesh, and she cried out in her sleep, but there was no one to hear and awaken her.

◆ ◆ ◆

General Mungo St. John reined in and looked around him at the devastated forests. There was no cover, the locusts had seen to that, and it would make his task more difficult.

He lifted the slouch hat from his head and mopped his forehead. This was the suicide month. The great cumulus cloud banks heaved up heaven-high along the horizon, and the heat shivered and wavered in mirage above the bare baked earth. Mungo carefully readjusted the patch over his empty eye socket and turned in the saddle to look back at the file of men that followed him.

There were fifty of them, all Matabele, but wearing a bizarre motley of traditional and European dress. Some wore patched moleskin breeches and others tasseled fur aprons. Some were barefoot, others wore rawhide sandals, and a few even sported hobnailed boots without socks or puttees. Most of them were bare-chested, though a few wore cast-off tunics or tattered shirts. There was, however, one single item of uniform that was common to them all. It was worn on a chain around the left arm above the elbow, a polished brass disk engraved with the words "BSA Co. Police."

They were each of them armed with a new repeating Winchester rifle and a bandolier of brass cartridges. Their legs were dusty to the knees, for they had made a hard, fast march southward, keeping up easily with Mungo St. John's trotting mount. Mungo looked them over with grim satisfaction. Despite the lack of cover, he believed that the speed of their advance must take the kraals by surprise.

It was like one of his slaving expeditions on the west coast, so long ago, before that damned Lincoln and the Royal bloody Navy had cut off the multimillion-dollar trade. By God, those had been the days. The swift approach march, the encirclement of the village, and the dawn rush with the slavers' clubs cracking against woolly black skulls. Mungo roused himself. Was it a sign of age to hark back so often to the long ago? he wondered.

"Ezra," he called his sergeant to come up to him. He

was the only other mounted man in the column. He rode a swaybacked gray with a rough coat.

Ezra was a hulking Matabele with a scarred cheek, memento of a mining accident in the great diamond pit at Kimberley, six hundred miles to the south. It was there that he had adopted his new name and learned his English.

"How far ahead is Gandang's kraal?" Mungo asked him in that language.

"That far." Ezra swept his arm through an arc of the sky, indicating two hours or so of the sun's passage.

"All right," Mungo nodded. "Send the scouts out. But I want no mistakes. Explain to them again that they must cross the Inyati River upstream of the kraal and circle out to wait in the foothills."

"Nkosi," Ezra nodded.

"Tell them they must seize anybody who runs from the kraal and bring them in."

The business of translating every command irked Mungo, and for the hundredth time since he had crossed the Limpopo, he resolved to study the Sindebele language.

Ezra saluted Mungo with an exaggerated flourish, an imitation of the British soldiers he had watched from the barred window of his cell while he was serving his sentence for diamond theft, and turned in the saddle to shout the orders to the men who followed the two horsemen.

"Warn them that they must be in position before dawn. That is when we will ride in."

Mungo unstrapped the felt-covered water bottle from the pommel of his saddle and unscrewed the stopper.

"They are ready, Nkosi," the sergeant reported.

"Very well, Sergeant, send them away," said Mungo, and raised the water bottle to his lips.

◆ ◆ ◆

For many seconds after waking, Juba believed that the screams of the women and the whimpering of the children were all part of her nightmares, and she pulled the fur kaross over her head.

Then there was a crash as the door to the hut was broken open, a rush of bodies into the dark interior, and Juba came fully awake and threw off the kaross. Rough hands seized her and though she screamed and struggled, she was dragged naked into the open. The sky was paling with the dawn,

121

and the constables had piled fresh logs on the fire, so that Juba recognized the white man immediately, and she shrank back into the safety of the crowd of sobbing, wailing women before he could notice her.

Mungo St. John was in a fury, bellowing at his sergeant, striding back and forth beyond the fire, slapping his riding whip against his glossy boot. His face was flushed a dark crimson like the wattles of the waddling black *singisi*, the grotesque turkey buzzard of the veld, and his single eye blazed in the firelight.

"Where are the men? I want to know where the men have gone!"

Sergeant Ezra came hurrying down the rank of cringing women, peering into their faces. He stopped in front of Juba, recognizing her instantly, one of the *grandes dames* of the tribe; as she drew herself to her full height, even in her total and massive nudity she was dignified and queenly. She expected some mark of respect, some gesture of courtesy from him, but instead the sergeant seized her wrist and twisted her arm up so viciously that she was forced to her knees.

"Where are the *amadoda*?" he hissed at her. "Where have the men gone?"

Juba choked down the sob of agony in her throat and croaked, "It is true there are no men here, for certainly the ones who wear the little brass bangles of Lodzi on their arms are not men—"

"Cow," hissed the sergeant, "fat black cow." And he jerked her arm upward, forcing her face into the dirt.

"Enough, *kanka!*" A voice cut through the hubbub, and the tone and power of it commanded instant silence. "Let the woman be."

Involuntarily the sergeant released Juba and stepped back, and even Mungo St. John halted his furious pacing.

Gandang stalked into the firelight, and though he wore only his headring and a short loincloth, he was as menacing as a prowling lion, and the sergeant fell back in front of him. Juba struggled to her feet, rubbing her wrist, but Gandang did not even glance at her. He strode to Mungo St. John and asked, "What is it that you seek, white man, coming into my kraal like a thief in the night?"

Mungo looked to the sergeant for a translation.

"He says you are a thief," the sergeant told him, and Mungo jerked up his chin and glared at Gandang.

"Tell him he knows what I come for; tell him I want two hundred strong young men."

And Gandang retreated immediately into the studied, defensive obtuseness of Africa, which few Europeans know how to counter and which infuriated a man like St. John who could not even understand the language and who had to submit to the laborious process of translation. The sun was well up when Gandang repeated the question he had first asked almost an hour before.

"Why does he want my young men to come to him? They are content here."

And Mungo's clenched fists shook with the effort of restraint.

"All men must work," the sergeant translated, "it is the law of the white men."

"Tell him," Gandang retorted, "that it is not the way of the Matabele. The *amadoda* see no dignity or great virtue in digging in the dirt. That is for women and *amaholi*."

"The induna says that his men will not work," the sergeant translated maliciously, and Mungo St. John could endure no more of it. He took a swift pace forward and slashed the riding whip into the induna's face.

Gandang blinked, but he neither flinched nor raised his hand to touch the shining, tumescent welt that rose swiftly across his cheek. He made no effort to stanch the thin trickle of blood from his crushed lip that snaked down his chin, but he let it drip onto his naked chest.

"My hands are empty now, white man," he said in a whisper that was more penetrating than a bellow, "but they will not always be so." And he turned toward his hut.

"Gandang," Mungo St. John shouted after him. "Your men will work if I have to hunt them down and chain them like animals."

◆ ◆ ◆

The two girls followed the path at a smooth swinging trot that did not disturb the balance of the large bundles they carried upon their heads. In the bundles there were special gifts for their men, salt and stamped corn, snuff and beads and lengths of trade calico for loincloths that they had wheedled out of Nomusa's store at Khami Mission. They were both in high spirits, for they had passed out of the swath of destruction left by the locust swarms, and the acacia forests were a golden yellow haze of spring bloom murmurous with bees.

Ahead of them rose the first pearly granite domes, and among them they would find the men, so they called gaily to each other, silly girlish banter, and their laughter was sweet as the tinkle of bells. It carried far ahead of them. They skirted the base of a tall cliff and, without pausing to rest, started up the natural steps of gray stone. It led them upward into a steep ravine which would eventually take them to the summit.

Imbali was leading, her round, hard haunches swaying under the short skirt as she skipped over the uneven footing, and Ruth, who was every bit as eager, followed her closely into the angle where the path turned sharply between two huge, round boulders that had rolled down from above.

Imbali stopped so abruptly that Ruth almost ran into her, and then she hissed with alarm.

A man stood in the center of the path. Although he was unmistakably a Matabele, the girls had never seen him before. The stranger wore a blue shirt, and on his upper arm sparkled a round brass disk. In his hand he carried a rifle. Quickly Ruth glanced behind her and hissed again. Another armed man had stepped out from the shaded angle of the boulder and cut off their retreat. He was smiling, but there was nothing in that smile to reassure the girls. They lowered the bundles from their heads and shrank closer to each other.

"Where are you going, pretty little kittens?" asked the smiling *kanka*. "Are you going to search for a tomcat?"

Neither of the girls answered. They stared at him with big, frightened eyes.

"We will go with you." The smiling *kanka* was so broad across the chest, his legs so muscular, that he appeared to be deformed. His teeth were very white and big as those of a horse, but the smile never reached his eyes. His eyes were small and cold and dead-looking.

"Lift your bundles, kittens, and lead us to the cats."

Ruth shook her head. "We go only to search for medicine roots; we do not understand what you want of us."

The *kanka* came closer. His thick legs were bowed, and

they gave him a peculiar rolling gait. Suddenly he kicked over Ruth's bundle, and it burst open.

"Ah!" He smiled coldly. "Why do you carry such gifts, if you go to search for *muti?*"

Ruth dropped to her knees and scrabbled among the rocks to retrieve the spilled corn and scattered beads. The *kanka* dropped his hand onto her back and stroked her lustrous black skin.

"Purr, little kitten," he grinned, and Ruth froze, crouched at his feet with her hands filled with spilled grain.

The *kanka* ran his fingers lightly up and placed his hand upon the nape of her neck. His hand was huge, the knuckles enlarged, the fingers thick and powerful. Ruth began to tremble as the fingers encircled her neck.

The *kanka* looked up at his companion, who still guarded the pathway, and the two of them exchanged a glance. Imbali saw and understood.

"She is a bride," she whispered. "Her husband is the nephew of Gandang. Take care, *kanka.*"

The man ignored her. He lifted Ruth to her feet by the neck and twisted her face toward him.

"Take us to where the men are hiding."

Ruth stared at him silently for a second, and then suddenly and explosively she spat into his face. The frothy spittle spattered his cheeks and dripped from his chin.

"*Kanka!*" she hissed. "Traitor jackal!"

The man never stopped smiling. "That is what I wanted you to do," he told her, and hooked his finger into the string of her skirt and snapped it. The skirt fell around her ankles.

He held her by the scruff and she struggled and covered her groin with both hands. The *kanka* looked at her naked body and his breathing changed.

"Watch the other," he told his companion, and tossed his Winchester rifle to him. The second constable caught it by the stock and prodded Imbali with the barrel until she backed up against the high granite boulder.

"Our time will come very soon," he assured her, and turned his head to watch the other couple, at the same time holding Imbali pinned against the rock.

The *kanka* dragged Ruth off the path, but for only a few paces, and the scrub that screened them was thin and leafless.

"My man will kill you," cried Ruth. They could hear everything on the path, even the sound of the *kanka's* ragged breathing.

"Then give me good value, if I must pay with my life," he chuckled, and then gasped with pain. "So, kitten, you have sharp claws." And there was the clap of a blow on soft flesh, the sound of struggling, the bushes heaved and loose pebbles rolled away down the slope.

The constable guarding Imbali strained for a glimpse of what was happening. His lips were open and he licked them. He could make out blurred movement through the leafless branches, and then there was the sound of a body falling heavily to earth and the breath being driven violently from Ruth's lungs by a crushing weight.

"Hold still, kitten," the *kanka* panted. "You make me angry. Lie still." And abruptly Ruth screamed. It was the shrill ringing cry of an animal in mortal agony, repeated again and again, and the *kanka* grunted. "Yes. There, yes." And then he snuffed like a boar at the trough, and there was a soft, rhythmic slapping sound, and Ruth kept screaming.

The man guarding Imbali propped the spare rifle against the boulder and stepped off the path, and with the barrel of his own Winchester parted the branches and stared. His face seemed to swell and darken with passion, his whole attention concentrated on what he was watching.

With the second constable's attention so distracted, Imbali sidled along the granite and then paused for an instant to gather herself before darting away. She had reached the angle of the pathway before the man turned and saw her.

"Come back!" he shouted.

"What is it?" the *kanka* demanded from behind the bushes in a thick, tortured voice.

"The other one, she is running."

"Stop her," the *kanka* bellowed, and his companion ran to the corner.

Imbali was fifty paces down the hillside, flying like a gazelle over the rough ground, driven by her terror. The man thumbed back the hammer of his Winchester, flung the butt to his shoulder, and fired wildly, without aiming. It was a fluke shot. It caught the girl in the small of the back, and the big soft lead slug tore out through her belly. She collapsed and rolled down the steep pathway, her limbs tumbling about loosely.

The constable lowered the rifle. His expression was shocked and unbelieving. Slowly, hesitantly, he went down to where the girl lay. She was on her back. Her eyes were open, and the exit wound in her flat young stomach gaped hideously, her torn entrails bulged from it. The girl's eyes switched to his face, the terror in them flared up for an instant, and then slowly faded into utter blankness.

"She is dead." The *kanka* had left Ruth, and come down the path. He had left his apron in the bushes. His blue shirttails flapped around his bare legs.

Both of them stared down at the dead girl.

"I did not mean it," said the *kanka* with the hot rifle in his hands.

"We cannot let the other one go back to tell what has happened," his companion replied, and turned back up the pathway. As he passed, he picked up his own rifle from where it leaned against the rock. He stepped off the path, behind the thin screen of bushes.

The other man was still staring into Imbali's blank eyes when the second shot rang out. He flinched to the crack of it and lifted his head. As the echoes lapped away among the granite cliffs, the *kanka* stepped back onto the path. He ejected the spent cartridge case from the breech and it pinged against the rock.

"Now we must find a story for One-Bright-Eye and for the indunas," he said quietly, and strapped the fur apron back around his thick waist.

◆ ◆ ◆

They brought the two girls back to Gandang's kraal on the back of the police sergeant's gray horse. Their legs dangled down one side and their arms down the other. They had wrapped a gray blanket around their naked bodies, as though ashamed of the wounds upon them, but the blood had soaked through and dried black upon it, and the big metallic green flies swarmed joyously upon the stains.

In the center of the kraal, the sergeant gestured to the *kanka* who led the gray, and he turned back and cut the line that secured the girls' ankles. The corpses were immediately unbalanced and slid headfirst to the swept bare earth. They fell without dignity in an untidy tumble of bare limbs, like game brought in from the hunting veld for skinning and dressing out.

The women had been silent until then, but now they began the haunting ululation of mourning, and one of them scooped a handful of dust and poured it over her own head. The others followed her example, and their cries brought out the gooseflesh down the arms of the sergeant, though his expression remained neutral and his voice level as he spoke to Gandang.

"You have brought this sadness on your people, old man. If you had obeyed the wishes of Lodzi and sent in your young men, as is your duty, these women would have lived to bear sons."

"What crime did they commit?" Gandang asked, and watched his senior wife come forward to kneel beside the bloody, dust-smeared bodies.

"They tried to kill two of my police."

"Hau!" Gandang expressed his scornful disbelief, and the sergeant's voice rasped with anger for the first time.

"My men caught them and forced them to lead them to where the *amadoda* are hiding. At last night's camp, when my men were asleep, they would have thrust sharpened sticks into their earholes to the brain, but my men sleep lightly, and when they awoke, the women ran into the night and my men had to stop them."

For a long moment, Gandang stared at the sergeant, and his eyes were so terrible that Ezra turned away to watch the senior wife as she knelt beside one of the girls. Juba closed the slack jaws and then gently wiped the congealed blood from Ruth's lips and nostrils.

"Yes," Gandang advised Ezra. "Look well, white man's jackal, remember this thing for all the days that are left to you."

"Dare you threaten me, old man?" the sergeant blustered.

"All men must die"—Gandang shrugged—"but some die sooner and more painfully than others." And Gandang turned and walked back to his hut.

◆ ◆ ◆

Gandang sat alone by the small, smoky fire in his hut. Neither the broiled beef nor white maize cakes in the platter at his side had been touched. He stared into the flames and listened to the wailing of the women and the beat of the drums.

He knew that Juba would come to tell him when the girls' bodies had been bathed and wrapped in the green skin of the freshly slaughtered ox. As soon as it was light, it would be his duty to supervise the digging of the grave in the center of the cattle kraal, so he was not surprised when there was a soft scratching at the doorway, and he called softly to Juba to enter.

She came to kneel at his side. "All is ready for the morning, my husband."

He nodded, and they were silent for a while, and then Juba said, "I wish to sing the Christian song that Nomusa has taught me when the girls are put into the earth."

He inclined his head in acquiescence, and she went on.

"I wish also that you would dig their graves in the forest so that I may place crosses over them."

"If that is the way of your new god," he agreed again, and now he rose and crossed to his sleeping mat in the far corner.

"Nkosi," Juba remained kneeling. "Lord, there is something else."

"What is it?" He looked back at her, his beloved features remote and cold.

"I, and my women, will carry the steel as you bid me," she whispered. "I made an oath with my finger in the wound in Ruth's flesh. I will carry the assegais to the *amadoda*."

He did not smile, but the coldness went out of his eyes, and he held out one hand to her. Juba rose and went to him, and he took her hand and led her to the sleeping mat.

◆ ◆ ◆

Bazo came down out of the hills three days after the girls had been placed in the earth under the bare spreading branches of a giant mimosa at a place which overlooked the river. There were two young men with him, and the three of them went directly to the graves with Juba guiding them. After a while, Bazo left the two young bridegrooms to mourn their women, and he went back to where his father waited for him under the fig tree.

After he had made his dutiful greetings, they drank from

the same beerpot, passing it back and forth between them in silence, and when it was empty, Gandang sighed.

"It is a terrible thing."

Bazo looked up at him sharply. "Rejoice, my father. Thank the spirits of your ancestors," he said. "For they have given us a greater bargain than we could ever have wished for."

"I do not understand this." Gandang stared at his son.

"For two lives—lives of no importance, lives that would have been spent in vain and empty-headed frivolity—for this insignificant price, we have kindled a fire in the belly of the nation. We have steeled even the weakest and most cowardly of our *amadoda*. Now when the time comes, we know that there will be no hesitating. Rejoice, my father, at the gift we have been given."

"You have become a ruthless man," Gandang whispered at last.

"I am proud that you should find me so," Bazo replied. "And if I am not ruthless enough for the work, then my son or his son, in their time, will be."

"You do not trust the oracle of the Umlimo?" Gandang demanded. "She has promised us success."

"No, my father." Bazo shook his head. "Think carefully on her words. She has told us only to make the attempt. She promised us nothing. It is with us alone to succeed or fail. That is why we must be hard and relentless, trusting nobody, looking for any advantage, and using it to the full."

Gandang thought about that for a while, then sighed again.

"It was not like this before."

"Nor will it ever be again. It has changed, Baba, and we must change with it."

"Tell me what else there is to be done," Gandang invited. "What way can I help to bring success?"

"You must order the young men to come down out of the hills and to go in to work as the white men are bidding."

Gandang considered the question without speaking.

"From now until the hour, we must become fleas. We must live under the white men's cloak, so close to the skin that he does not see us, so close that he forgets we are there waiting to sting."

Gandang nodded at the sense of it, but there was a

fathomless regret in his eyes. "I liked it better when we formed the bull, with the horns outflung to surround the enemy and the veterans massed in the center to crush them. I loved the closing in when we went in singing the praise song of the regiment, when we made our killing in the sunlight with our plumes flying."

"Never again, Baba," Bazo told him. "Never again will it be like that. In the future we will wait in the grass like the coiled puff-adder. We may have to wait a year or ten, a lifetime or more—perhaps we may never see it, my father. Perhaps it will be our children's children who strike from the shadows with other weapons than the silver steel that you and I love so well, but it is you and I that will open the road for them to follow, the road back to greatness."

Gandang nodded, and there was a new light in his eyes, like the first glow of the dawn. "You see very clearly, Bazo. You know them so well, and you are right. The white man is strong in every way except patience. He wants it all to happen today. While we know how to wait."

They were silent again, sitting with their shoulders just touching, and the fire had burned low before Bazo stirred.

"I will be gone by daylight," he said.

"Where?" Gandang asked.

"East to the Mashona."

"For what reason?"

"They also must prepare for the day."

"You seek aid from Mashona dogs, from the very eaters of dirt?"

"I seek aid wherever it can be found," said Bazo simply. "Tanase says that we will find allies beyond our borders, beyond the great river. She speaks even of allies from a land so cold that the waters there turn hard and white as salt."

"Is there such a land?"

"I do not know. I know only that we must welcome any ally, from wherever they may come. For Lodzi's men are hard, fierce fighters. You and I both have learned that well."

◆　◆　◆

All the windows of the mule coach were open and the shutters were lowered so that Mr. Rhodes could converse freely with the men who rode in close attendance upon

131

each side. They were the aristocracy of this new land, only a dozen or so of them, but between them they owned vast tracts of fertile, virgin country, sprawling herds of native cattle, and blocks of mineral claims beneath which lay dreams of uncountable wealth.

The man in the luxurious carriage, drawn by a team of five matched white mules, was their head. In his capacity as a private citizen, he enjoyed such wealth and power as was usually only commanded by kings. His company owned a land which was bigger than the United Kingdom and Ireland put together, which he administered by decree as a private estate. He controlled the world's production of diamonds through a cartel that he had made as powerful as an elected government. He owned outright the mines that produced ninety-five per cent of the world's diamonds. On the fabulous Witwatersrand goldfields, his influence was not as great as it might have been, for he had passed up many opportunities to acquire claims along the strike, where the gold-rich banket reef had once stood proud above the surrounding grassland, sharp and black as a shark's dorsal fin, before the miners had whittled it away.

"I do not sense the power in this reef," he had said once as he stood on the outcrop, staring at it moodily with those pale messianic blue eyes. "I can sit on the lip of the great hole at Kimberley and I know just how many carats are coming up with each load, but this—" He had shaken his head and gone back to his horse, turning his back on a hundred million pounds in pure gold.

When, finally, he had been forced to accept the true potential of the "Ridge of White Waters" and was on the very point of hurrying back to pick up what few properties were still available, a tragic accident had distracted him. His dearest friend, a fine and beautiful young man named Neville Pickering, his companion and partner of many years, had been thrown from his horse and dragged.

Rhodes had stayed at Kimberley to nurse him, and then when Neville died, to mourn him. The great opportunities had slipped away from Rhodes in those weeks. Yet still he had at last founded his Consolidated Goldfields Company upon the reef, and though it was nothing like his De Beers Consolidated Mines Company, nor the gold empire that his old rival J.B. Robinson had built, yet at the end of the last financial year it had paid a dividend of 125 per cent.

His fortune was such that when, on a whim, he decided to pioneer the farming of deciduous fruit in southern Africa, he had instructed one of his managers to purchase the entire Franschhoek Valley.

"Mr. Rhodes, it will cost a million pounds," the manager had demurred.

"I did not ask for your estimate," Rhodes replied testily. "I simply gave you an order—buy it!"

That was his private life, but his public life was no less spectacular.

He was a privy councillor to the Queen and thus could speak directly to the men who steered the greatest empire the world had ever known. In truth, some of them were less than sympathetic to him. Gladstone had once remarked, "I know only one thing about Mr. Rhodes. He has made a great deal of money in a very short time. This does not fill me with any overwhelming confidence."

The rest of the British nobility were less critical, and whenever he visited London, he was the darling of society; lords and dukes and earls flocked to him, for there were lucrative directorships on the board of the BSA Company to be filled, and a single word from Mr. Rhodes could lead to a killing on the stock exchange.

Added to all this, Mr. Rhodes was the elected Prime Minister of Cape Colony, sure of the vote of every English-speaking citizen and through the good offices of his old friend Hofmeyr and his Afrikander Bond, sure of most of the Dutch-speaking votes as well.

Thus, as he lolled on the green leather seat of his coach, dressed untidily in a rumpled high-buttoned suit, the knot of his Oriel College necktie slipping a little, he was at the very zenith of his wealth and power and influence.

Seated opposite him, Jordan Ballantyne was pretending to study the shorthand notes that Mr. Rhodes had just dictated, but over the pad he was watching his master with a shadow of concern in his sensitive, long-lashed eyes. Although the flat brim of his hat kept Mr. Rhodes's eyes in shadow and prevented Jordan from reading any trace of pain in them, yet his color was high and unhealthy, and though he spoke with all his old force, he was sweating more heavily than the early morning cool warranted.

Now he raised his voice, calling in that high, almost petulant tone, "Ballantyne." And Zouga Ballantyne spurred his horse up beside the window and leaned attentively from the saddle.

"Tell me, my dear fellow," Rhodes demanded. "What is this new building to be?"

He pointed at the freshly opened foundation trenches and the stacks of red burned brick piled on the corner plot at the intersection of two of Bulawayo's wide and dusty streets.

"That's the new synagogue," Zouga told him.

"So my Jews have come to stay!" Mr. Rhodes said with a smile, and Zouga suspected that Mr. Rhodes had known precisely what those foundations were for but had asked the question to pave the way for his own witticism. "Then my new country will be all right, Ballantyne. They are the birds of good omen, who would never roost in a tree marked for felling."

Zouga chuckled dutifully, and they went on talking while Ralph Ballantyne, riding in the bunch, watched them with such interest that he neglected the lady riding beside him, until she tapped him on the forearm with her crop.

"I said, it will be interesting to see what happens when we reach Khami," Louise repeated, and Ralph's attention jerked back to his stepmother. She rode astride, the only woman he knew that did so, and though she wore ankle-length divided skirts, her seat was elegant and sure. Ralph had seen her outride his own father, beating him in a grueling point-to-point race over rough terrain. That had been in Kimberley, before the trek to the north and this land, but the years had treated Louise kindly indeed. Ralph smiled to himself as he recalled the youthful crush he had been smitten with when first he saw her driving her phaeton and pair of golden palominos down Kimberley's crowded main street. That was so many years ago, and though she had married his father since then, he still felt a special affection for her that was definitely neither filial nor dutiful. She was only a few years older than he was, and the Blackfoot Indian blood in her veins gave her beauty a certain timeless element.

"I cannot imagine that even Robyn, my honored aunt and mother-in-law, would use the occasion of her youngest daughter's marriage for political advantage," Ralph said.

"Are you confident enough to wager on that—a guinea,

say?'' Louise asked with a flash of even white teeth, but Ralph threw back his head and laughed.

"I have learned my lesson—I'll never bet against you again.'' Then he dropped his voice. "Besides, I don't really have that much faith in my mother-in-law's restraint.''

"Then why on earth does Mr. Rhodes insist on going to the wedding? He must know what to expect.''

"Well, firstly, he owns the land the mission is built upon, and secondly, he probably feels that the ladies of Khami Mission are depriving him of a valued possession.'' Ralph lifted his chin to indicate the bridegroom, who rode a little ahead of the group. Harry Mellow had a flower in his buttonhole, a gloss on his boots, and a grin upon his lips.

"He hasn't lost him,'' Louise pointed out.

"He fired him as soon as he realized he couldn't talk Harry out of it.''

"But he is such a talented geologist; they say he can smell gold a mile away.''

"Mr. Rhodes does not approve of his young men marrying, no matter how talented.''

"Poor Harry, poor Vicky, what will they do?''

"Oh, it's all arranged.'' Ralph beamed.

"You?'' she hazarded.

"Who else?''

"I should have known. In fact it would not surprise me to learn that you engineered the whole business,'' Louise accused, and Ralph looked pained.

"You do me a grave injustice, Mama.'' He knew she did not like that title and used it deliberately, to tease her. Then Ralph looked ahead, and his expression changed like a bird dog scenting the pheasant.

The wedding party had ridden out past the last new buildings and shanties of the town onto the broad, rutted wagon road. Coming toward them, up from the south, was a convoy of transport wagons. There were ten of them, so strung out that the farthest of them were marked only by columns of fine white dust rising above the flat-topped acacia trees. On the nearest wagon tent, Louise could already read the company name, RHOLANDS, the shortened form of "Rhodesian Lands and Mining Company,'' which Ralph had chosen as the umbrella for his multitudinous business activities.

"Damn me,'' he exclaimed happily. "Old Isazi has brought

them in five days ahead of schedule. That little black devil is a miracle.'' He tipped his hat in apology to Louise. ''Business calls. Excuse me, please, Mama.'' And he galloped ahead, swinging off his horse as he came level with the lead wagon and embracing the diminutive figure in cast-off military-style jacket who skipped at the flank of the bullock team brandishing a thirty-foot-long trek whip.

''What kept you so long, Isazi?'' Ralph demanded. ''Did you meet a pretty Matabele girl on the road?''

The little Zulu driver tried not to grin, but the network of wrinkles that covered his face contracted, and there was a puckish sparkle in his eyes.

''I can still deal with a Matabele girl and her mother and all her sisters in the time it would take you to inspan a single ox.''

It was not only a declaration of virility, but also an oblique reference to Ralph's skill as a teamster. Isazi had taught him all he knew of the open road but still treated Ralph with the indulgent condescension usually reserved for a small boy.

''No, little Hawk, I did not want to rob you of too much bonus money by bringing them in more than five days ahead.''

This was a gentle reminder of what Isazi expected in his next pay packet.

Now the little Zulu, with the headring granted him by King Cetewayo before the battle of Ulundi still upon his snowy head, stood back and looked at Ralph with the speculative eye he usually reserved for a bullock.

''Hau, Henshaw, what finery is this?'' He glanced at Ralph's suit and English boots, and at the sprig of mimosa blossom in Ralph's buttonhole. ''Even flowers, like a simpering maiden at her first dance. And what is that under your coat—surely the Nkosikazi is the one who carries the babies in your family?''

Ralph glanced down at his own midriff. Isazi was being unfair; there was barely a trace of superfluous flesh there, nothing that a week of hard hunting would not remove, but Ralph sustained the banter that they both enjoyed.

''It is the privilege of great men to wear fine apparel and eat good food,'' he said.

''Then fall to, little Hawk with fine feathers.'' Isazi shook his head disapprovingly. ''Eat your fill. While wiser men do the real work, you play like a boy." His tone belied the warmth of his smile, and Ralph clasped his shoulder.

"There was never a driver like you, Isazi, and there probably never will be again."

"Hau, Henshaw, so I have taught you something, even if only to recognize true greatness when you see it," Isazi chuckled at last, and put the long lash up into the air with a report like a shot of cannon and called to his oxen.

"Come, Fransman, you black devil! Come, Sathan, my darling. *Pakamisa,* pick it up!"

Ralph mounted and backed his horse off the road and watched his laden wagons trundle by. There were three thousand pounds of profit in that single convoy for him, and he had two hundred wagons, plying back and forth across the vast subcontinent. Ralph shook his head in awe as he remembered the single elderly eighteen-footer that he and Isazi had driven out of Kimberley that first time. He had purchased it on borrowed money and laden it with trade goods that he did not own.

"A long road and a hard one," he said aloud as he wheeled his horse and kicked it into a gallop in pursuit of the mule coach and the wedding party.

He fell in again beside Louise, and she started from a reverie as though she had not even noticed his absence.

"Dreaming," he accused her, and she spread the fingers of one graceful hand in admission of guilt and then lifted it to point.

"Do look, Ralph. How beautiful it is!"

A bird flitted across the track ahead of the coach. It was a shrike with a shiny black back and a breast of a stunning crimson that burned in the sunlight like a precious ruby.

"How beautiful it all is," she exulted as the bird disappeared into the scrub, and Louise turned in the saddle to take in the whole horizon with a sweep of her arm that made the tassels of her white buckskin jacket flutter. "Do you know, Ralph, that King's Lynn is the very first real home I have ever known." And only then Ralph realized that they were still on his father's land. Zouga Ballantyne had used up the entire fortune he had won from the blue ground of Kimberley's pit to buy the land grants of the drifters and never-contents among Dr. Jameson's troopers who had ridden into Matabeleland in the expeditionary force that had defeated Lobengula. Each of them had been entitled to four thousand acres of his choice, and some of them had sold that right to Zouga Ballantyne for as little as the price of a bottle of whisky.

It would take a rider on a good horse three days to ride around the boundary of King's Lynn. The home that Zouga had built for Louise stood on one of those distant hills, overlooking the wide plain of acacia trees and sweet grass, its thick golden thatch and burned brick blending with the shading grove of tall trees as though it had always been there.

"This beautiful land will be so good to us," she whispered, her voice husky and her eyes brimming with an almost religious joy. "Vicky will be married today, and her children will grow strong here. Perhaps—" She broke off and a little cloud passed behind her eyes. She had not yet given up all hope of bearing Zouga's child. Every night, after his gentle loving, she would lie with her hands clasped over her stomach and her thighs clenched as if to hold his seed within her, and she would pray, while he slept quietly beside her. "Perhaps—" But it would be ill-omened to even mention it and she changed it. "Perhaps one day Jonathan or one of your sons yet unborn will be the master of King's Lynn." She reached across and laid her hand on his forearm. "Ralph, I have this strange premonition that our descendants will live here forever."

Ralph smiled fondly at her and covered her hand with his. "Well now, my dear Louise, even Mr. Rhodes himself only gives it four thousand years. Will you not settle for that?"

"Oh, you!" She struck him playfully on the shoulder. "Will you never be serious!" she exclaimed, and turned her horse out of the procession.

Under one of the flat-topped acacias beside the track stood a pair of Matabele boys, neither of them older than ten years. They wore only the little *mutsha* loincloths, and hung their heads shyly as Louise greeted them in fluent, rippling Sindebele. King's Lynn employed dozens of these *mujiba* to tend the vast herds of native cattle and the fine breeding bulls that Zouga had brought up from the south. These were but two of them, yet Louise knew them by name, and their faces shone with genuine affection as they returned her greeting.

"I see you also, Balela." The praise name the Matabele

servants of King's Lynn had given her meant the One Who Brings Clear and Sunny Skies, and the two children waited expectantly, answering her questions dutifully, until Louise at last reached into the pocket of her skirt and dropped a morsel of candy into each of their cupped pink palms.

They scampered back to their herds, cheeks bulging like those of squirrels and their eyes huge with delight.

"You spoil them," Ralph chided her as she rejoined him.

"They are our people," she said simply. And then almost regretfully: "Here is the boundary. I hate to leave our own land."

And the wedding procession passed the simple roadside peg and rode onto the land of Khami Mission Station. However, it was almost an hour later that the mules hauled the coach up the steep track, through thick bush, and paused to blow on the level neck of ground high above the whitewashed church and its attendant buildings.

It seemed as though an army was encamped in the valley.

Jordan jumped down from the coach, shrugging off the cotton dustcoat that had protected his beautiful dove-gray suit and smoothing his dense golden curls as he crossed to his brother.

"What on earth is going on, Ralph?" he demanded. "I never expected anything like this."

"Robyn has invited half the Matabele nation to the wedding, and the other half invited themselves." Ralph smiled down at his brother. "Some of them have trekked a hundred miles to be here. Every patient she has ever treated, every convert she ever turned, every man, woman and child who ever came to beg a favor or advice, everyone who ever called her 'Nomusa'—they are all there, and they have all brought their families and friends. It's going to be the greatest jollification since Lobengula held the last *Chawala* ceremony back in ninety-three."

"But who is going to feed them all?" Jordan went immediately to the logistics.

"Oh, Robyn can afford to blow a few of her royalties, and I sent her a gift of fifty head of slaughter-bullocks. Then they do say that Gandang's wife, old fat Juba, has brewed a thousand gallons of her famous *twala*. They will be bloated as pythons and overflowing with good cheer." Ralph punched his brother's arm affectionately. "Which reminds me that I have worked up a fair old thirst myself—let's get on with it."

The road was lined on both sides with hundreds of singing maidens, all of them decked with beads and flowers; their skin was anointed with fat and clay so that it shone like cast bronze in the sunlight. Their short aprons swirled about their thighs as they stamped and swayed, and their naked bosoms bounced and joggled.

"By God, Jordan, have you ever seen such a fine display?" Ralph teased his brother, well aware of his prudish and reserved attitude to all women. "That pair over there would keep your ears warm in a blizzard, I warrant!"

Jordan blushed and quickly made his way back to join his master as the girls crowded about the carriage and the mules were reduced to a walk.

One of the girls recognized Mr. Rhodes.

"Lodzi!" she called, and her cry was taken up by the others. "Lodzi! Lodzi!"

Then they saw Louise. "Balela, we see you. Welcome, Balela," they sang, clapping and swaying. "Welcome, the One Who Brings Clear and Sunny Skies."

Then she recognized Zouga, and they cried, "Come in peace, the Fist." And then to Ralph, "We see you, little Hawk, and our eyes are white with joy."

Zouga lifted his hat and waved it over his head. "By God," he murmured to Louise," I wish Labouchère and the damned Aborigine Protection Society could be here to see this."

"They are happy and secure as they never were under Lobengula's bloody rule," Louise agreed. "This land will be kind to us—I feel it deep in my heart."

From the back of his horse, Ralph could look over the heads of the girls. There were very few men in the crowd, and they hung back at the fringe of the press of black bodies. However, a face caught Ralph's attention, a single solemn face among all the smiles.

"Bazo!" Ralph called and waved, and the young induna looked at him steadily, still without smiling.

"We will talk later," Ralph shouted, and then he was past, swept along by the throng down the avenue of tall, dark green spathodea trees with their flaming orange blossoms.

When they reached the lawns, the dancing black girls fell

back, for, by unspoken accord, these were reserved for the white guests. There were a hundred or so gathered below the wide, thatched veranda. Cathy was there, for she had ridden out three days before to help with the preparations. She was slender and cool in a dress of yellow muslin, and the straw hat upon her dark head was wide as a wagon wheel and loaded with artificial flowers of bright-colored silk that Ralph had ordered from London.

Jonathan let out a shriek when he saw Ralph, but Cathy held his hand firmly to prevent him being trampled in the crowd that surged forward to engulf the bridegroom in a storm of greetings and good cheer. Ralph left his horse and came through the crowd, and Cathy almost lost her hat in the violence of his embrace. She had to snatch desperately at it, and then she froze and the color drained from her face.

The door of the mule coach had opened; Jordan jumped down and set the step.

"Ralph," Cathy blurted, clinging to his arm. "It's him! What's he doing here?"

Mr. Rhodes's bulk had appeared in the doorway of the carriage, and a shocked hush fell upon them all.

"Oh, Ralph, what will Mama say? Couldn't you have stopped him?"

"Nobody stops him," Ralph murmured without releasing her. "Besides, this is going to be better than a cockfight, any day."

As he said it, Robyn St. John, drawn by the commotion, came out onto the step of the homestead. Her face, still flushed from the heat of the stove, was radiant with a smile of welcome for her latest guests, but the smile shriveled when she recognized the man in the doorway of the carriage. She stiffened, and the flush receded from her face, leaving it icily pale.

"Mr. Rhodes," she said clearly in the silence. "I am delighted that you have come to Khami Mission."

Mr. Rhodes's eyes flickered as though she had slapped him across the face. He had expected anything but that, and he inclined his head with cautious gallantry, but Robyn went on:

"Because it gives me a heaven-sent opportunity to order you not to set a foot over my threshold."

Mr. Rhodes bowed with relief; he did not like unresolved positions over which he had no control.

"Let us grant that your jurisdiction reaches that far," he agreed. "But this side of that threshold, the ground on which I stand belongs to the BSA Company of which I am chairman—"

"No, sir," Robyn denied hotly, "the company has granted me the usufruct—"

"A fine legal point." Mr. Rhodes shook his head gravely. "I will ask my Administrator to give us a ruling on that." The Administrator was Dr. Leander Starr Jameson. "But in the meantime, I should like to raise a glass to the happiness of the young couple."

"I assure you, Mr. Rhodes, that you will not be served refreshment at Khami."

Mr. Rhodes nodded at Jordan, and he hurried back to the mule coach. In a flurry of activity, he supervised the uniformed servants who unpacked the camp chairs and tables and placed them in the shade of the tender growth that the spathodea trees had put out since the locust plague.

As Mr. Rhodes and his party settled themselves, Jordan fired the cork from the first bottle of champagne and spilled a frothy deluge into a crystal glass, and Robyn St. John disappeared abruptly from the veranda.

Ralph placed Jonathan in Cathy's arms. "She's up to something," he said, and sprinted across the lawns. He vaulted over the low veranda wall and burst into the living room just as Robyn lifted the shotgun down from its rack above the fireplace.

"Aunt Robyn, what are you doing?"

"Changing the cartridges—taking out the bird shot and putting in big loopers!"

"My darling mother-in-law, you cannot do that," Ralph protested, and edged toward her.

"Not use big loopers?" Robyn circled him warily, keeping out of reach, holding the shotgun with its ornate curly hammers at the level of her chest.

"You cannot shoot him."

"Why not?"

"Think of the scandal."

"Scandal and I have been traveling companions as long as I can remember."

"Then think of the mess," Ralph urged her.

"I'll do it on the lawn," Robyn said, and Ralph knew that she meant it. He sought desperately for inspiration and found it.

"Number Six!" he cried, and Robyn froze and stared at him. "Number Six, 'Thou shalt not kill.' "

"God was not speaking of Cecil Rhodes," Robyn said, but her eyes wavered.

"If the Almighty was allowing open season on specified targets, I'm sure he would have put in a footnote." Ralph pursued his advantage, and Robyn sighed and turned back to the leather cartridge bag on its hook.

"Now what are you doing?" Ralph demanded suspiciously.

"Changing back to bird shot," Robyn muttered. "God didn't say anything about flesh wounds." But Ralph seized the stock of the shotgun and with only a token of resistance Robyn relinquished it.

"Oh, Ralph," she whispered. "The effrontery of that man. I wish I was allowed to swear."

"God will understand," Ralph encouraged her.

"Damn him to bloody hell!" she said.

"Better?"

"Not much."

"Here," he said, and slipped the silver flask from his back pocket.

She took a swallow and blinked at the tears of anger that stung her eyes.

"Better?"

"A little," she admitted. "What must I do, Ralph?"

"Conduct yourself with frosty dignity."

"Right." She lifted her chin determinedly and marched back onto the veranda.

Under the spathodea trees, Jordan had donned a crisp white apron and tall chef's cap and was serving champagne and huge golden Cornish pasties to whomever wanted them. The veranda, which had been crowded with guests before the arrival of the mule coach, was now deserted, and there was a jovial throng around Mr. Rhodes.

"We will start cooking the sausage," Robyn told Juba. "Get your girls busy."

"They aren't even married yet, Nomusa," Juba protested. "The wedding is not until five o'clock—"

"Feed them," Robyn ordered. "I'll back my sausage against Jordan Ballantyne's pasties to bring 'em back."

"And I'll put my money on Mr. Rhodes's champagne to keep 'em there," Ralph told her. "Can you match it?"

"I haven't a drop, Ralph," Robyn admitted. "I have beer and brandy, but not champagne."

With a single glance, Ralph caught the eye of one of the younger guests on the lawn. He was the manager of Ralph's General Dealer's Shop in Bulawayo. He read Ralph's expression, and hurried up the steps to his side, listened intently to his instructions for a few seconds, and then ran to his horse.

"Where did you send him?" Robyn demanded.

"A convoy of my wagons arrived today. They will not have unloaded yet. We'll have a wagon full of bubbly out here within a few hours."

"I'll never be able to repay you for this, Ralph."

For a moment Robyn considered him, and then for the first time ever, she stood on tiptoe and gave him a light, dry kiss on the lips before hurrying back to her kitchen.

Ralph's wagon hove over the hill at a dramatic moment. Jordan was down to his last bottle of champagne, the empty green bottles formed an untidy hillock behind his stall, and the crowd had already begun to drift across to the barbecue pits on which Robyn's celebrated spiced beef sausage was sizzling in clouds of aromatic steam.

Isazi brought the wagon to a halt below the veranda and, like a conjuror, drew back the canvas hood to reveal the contents. The crowd flocked away to leave Mr. Rhodes sitting alone beside his fancy coach.

Within minutes Jordan sidled up beside his brother.

"Ralph, Mr. Rhodes would like to purchase a few cases of your best champagne."

"I'm not selling in job lots. Tell him it's a full wagon or nothing." Ralph smiled genially. "At twenty pounds a bottle."

"That's piracy," Jordan gasped.

"It's also the only available champagne in Matabeleland."

"Mr. Rhodes will not be pleased."

"I'll be pleased enough for both of us," Ralph assured him. "Tell him it's cash, in advance."

While Jordan went with the bad news to his master, Ralph sauntered across to the bridegroom and put one arm around his shoulder.

"Be grateful to me, Harry, my boy. Your wedding is

going to be a hundred-year legend, but have you told the lovely Victoria about her honeymoon yet?"

"Not yet," Harry Mellow admitted.

"Wise decision, laddie. Wankie's country does not have the appeal of the bridal suite at the Mount Nelson Hotel in Cape Town."

"She will understand," Harry said with more force than belief.

"Of course she will," Ralph agreed, and turned to meet Jordan, who returned brandishing the check which Mr. Rhodes had scribbled on a tattered champagne label.

"How charmingly appropriate," Ralph murmured, and tucked it into his top pocket. "I'll send Isazi back to fetch the next wagon."

The rumor of wagonloads of free champagne for all at Khami Mission turned Bulawayo into a ghost town. Unable to compete with these prices, the barman of the Grand Hotel closed down his deserted premises and joined the exodus southward. As soon as the news reached them, the umpires called "stumps" on the cricket match being played on the police parade ground, and the twenty-two players still in their flannels formed a guard of honor for Isazi's wagon, while behind them followed what remained of the town's population on horse, cycle or foot.

The little mission church could hold only a fraction of the invited and uninvited; the rest of them overflowed into the grounds, though the heaviest concentrations were always to be found around the two widely separated champagne wagons. Copious drafts of warm champagne had made the men sentimentally boisterous and many of the women loudly weepy, so a thunderous acclaim greeted the bride when she at last made her appearance on the mission veranda.

On her brother-in-law's arm, and attended by her sisters, Victoria made her way down the alley that opened for her across the lawn.

She was pretty enough to begin with, with her green eyes shining and the vivid coppery mass of her hair upon the white satin of her dress, but when she returned the same way, this time on the arm of her new husband, she was truly beautiful.

"All right," Ralph announced. "It's all legal—now the party can truly begin."

He signaled to the band, a hastily assembled quartet led

145

by Matabeleland's only undertaker on the fiddle, and they launched into a spirited Gilbert and Sullivan. This was the only sheet music available north of the Limpopo. Each member of the quartet provided his own interpretation of *The Mikado*, so that the dancers could waltz or polka to it as the inclination and the champagne dictated.

By dawn of the following day, the party had started to warm up, and the first fistfight broke out behind the church. However, Ralph settled it by announcing to the shirt-sleeved contestants, "This will never do, gentlemen, it is an occasion of joy and goodwill toward all mankind." And then before they realized his intention, he dropped them on their backs in quick succession with a left and right swing that neither of them saw coming. Then he helped them solicitously back onto their feet and led them weaving groggily to the nearest drink wagon.

By dawn on the second day, the party was in full swing. The bride and bridegroom, reluctant to miss a moment of the fun, had not yet left on their honeymoon and were leading the dancing under the spathodea trees. Mr. Rhodes, who had rested during the night in the mule coach, now emerged and ate a hearty breakfast of bacon and eggs cooked by Jordan over the open fire, washed it down with a tumbler of champagne, and was moved to oratory. He stood on the driver's seat of the coach and spoke with all his usual eloquence and charisma honed to an edge by a sense of occasion and his own burning belief in his subject.

"My Rhodesians," he addressed his audience, and they took it as an endearment rather than a claim to ownership, and loved him for it. "Together you and I have made a great leap forward toward the day when the map of Africa will be painted pink from Cape Town to Cairo, when this fair continent will be set beside India, a great diamond beside a lustrous ruby, in the crown of our beloved Queen—"

They cheered him, the Americans and Greeks and Italians and Irish, as loudly as the subjects of the "beloved Queen" herself.

Robyn St. John endured half an hour of these sentiments before she lost control of the frosty dignity that Ralph had counseled, and from the veranda of the homestead, she began a counter reading of her own, as yet unpublished, poetry:

"Mild melancholy and sedate he stands
   Tending another's herds upon the field.
   His father's once, where now the white man builds
   His home and issues forth his proud commands.
   His dark eyes flash not, his listless hand
   Leans on the shepherd staff, no more he wields
   The gleaming steel, but to the oppressor yields—"

Her high, clear voice rang over Mr. Rhodes's; heads
turned back and forth between the two of them like the
spectators at tennis.

"This is only a beginning"—Mr. Rhodes raised his
volume—"a great beginning, yes, but a beginning nonetheless.
There are ignorant and arrogant men, not all of them
black"—and even the dullest listener recognized that the
allusion was to old Kruger, the Boer president of the South
African Republic in the Transvaal—"who must be allowed
the opportunity to come beneath the shield of the *pax
britannica* of their own freewill, rather than be driven to it
by force of arms."

His audience was once again entranced, until Robyn
selected another of her works in matching warlike mood
and let fly with:

"He scorns the hurt, nor regards the scar
   Of recent wound, but burnishes for war
   His assegai and targe of buffalo hide.
   Is he a rebel? Yes, it is a strife
   Between the black-skinned raptor and the white.
   A savage? Yes, though loath to aim at life
   Evil for evil fierce he doth requite.
   A heathen? Teach him then thy better creed,
   Christian! If thou deserv'st that name indeed!"

The audience's critical faculty was dulled by two days
and two nights of revelry, and they applauded Robyn's
impassioned delivery with matching fervor, though the sense
of it was thankfully lost upon them.

"The Lord save us," Ralph groaned, "from emetic jingo-
ism and aperient scansion!" And he wandered away down
the valley to get out of earshot of the competing orators,
carrying a bottle of Mr. Rhodes's champagne in one hand
and with his son perched upon his shoulder. Jonathan wore

a sailor suit with Jack Tar collar, and a straw boater on his head; the ribbon hung down his back, and he clucked and urged his father on with his heels as though he were astride a pony.

There were fifty head of slaughter-oxen and a thousand gallon pots of Juba's beer to account for, and the black wedding guests were giving the task their dedicated attention. Down here the dancing was even more energetic than that under the spathodea trees, the young men leaping and twisting and stamping until the dusk swirled waist-high about them and the sweat cut runnels down their naked backs and chests. The girls swayed and shuffled and sang, and the drummers hammered out their frenetic rhythms until they dropped exhausted, and others snatched up the wooden clubs to beat the booming hollowed-out tree trunks. While Jonathan, on Ralph's back, squealed with delight, one of the slaughter-oxen, a heavy humpbacked red beast, was dragged out of the kraal. A spearsman ran forward and stabbed it through the carotid and jugular. With a mournful bellow, the animal collapsed, kicking spasmodically. The butchers swarmed over the carcass, flaying off the hide in a single sheet, delving for the tidbits, the kidneys and liver and tripe, throwing them wet and shiny onto the live coals, hacking through the rack of ribs, slicing off thick steaks and heaping them on the racks over the cooking fire.

Half raw, running with fat and juice, the meat was stuffed into eager mouths and the beerpots tilted to the hot blue summer sky. One of the cooks tossed Ralph a ribbon of tripe, scorched from the fierce flames and with the contents still adhering to the stomach lining. Without a visible qualm, Ralph stripped away the lining and bit off a chunk of the sweet white flesh beneath.

"*Mushle!*" he told the cook. "Good! Very good." And passed up a sliver to the child on his back. "Eat it, Jon-Jon, what doesn't kill you makes you fat," and his son obeyed with noisy relish and agreed with his father's verdict.

"*Mushle*, it's really *mush*, Papa."

Then the dancers surrounded them, prancing and whirling, challenging Ralph. Ralph sat Jonathan on the fence of the cattle kraal, where he had a grandstand view. Then he strode into the center and set himself in the heroic posture of the Nguni dancer. Bazo had taught him well when they were striplings, and now he raised his right knee as high as his shoulder and brought his booted foot down on the hard earth with a crash, and the other dancers hummed in encouragement and approbation.

"Jee! Jee!"

Ralph leaped and stamped and postured, and the other dancers were pressed to match him; the women clapped and sang, and on the kraal fence, Jonathan howled with excitement and pride.

"Look at my Daddy!"

His shirt soaked with sweat, his chest heaving, and chuckling breathlessly, Ralph dropped out at last and lifted Jonathan back onto his shoulder. The two of them went on, greeting by name those they recognized in the throng, accepting a proffered morsel of beef or a swallow of tart, gruel-thick beer, until at last on the rise beyond the kraal, seated on a log, aloof from the dancers and revelers, Ralph found the man he was seeking.

"I see you, Bazo, the Ax," he said, and sat down on the log beside him, set the champagne bottle between them, and passed Bazo one of the cheroots for which he had developed a taste so long ago on the diamond fields. They smoked in silence, watching the dancers and the feasting, until Jonathan grew restless and edged away to seek more exciting occupation, and found it immediately.

He was confronted by a child a year or so younger than he was. Tungata, son of Bazo, son of Gandang, son of great Mzilikazi, was stark naked except for the string of bright ceramic beads around his hips. His navel popped out in the center of his fat little belly, his limbs were sturdy, and he had dimpled knees and bracelets of healthy fat at his wrists. His face was round and smooth and glossy, his eyes huge and solemn as he examined Jonathan with total fascination.

Jonathan returned his scrutiny with equal candor and made no attempt to pull away as Tungata reached and touched the collar of his sailor suit.

"What is your son's name?" Bazo asked, watching the children with an inscrutable expression.

"Jonathan."

"What is the meaning of that name?"

"The gift of God," Ralph told him.

Jonathan suddenly took the straw hat from his own head and placed it upon that of the Matabele princeling. It made such an incongruous picture, the beribboned boater on the head of the naked black boy with his pot belly and little uncircumcised penis sticking out under it at a jaunty angle, that both men smiled involuntarily. Tungata gurgled with glee, seized Jonathan's hand and dragged him away unprotestingly into the throng of dancers.

The lingering warmth of that magicial moment between the children thawed the stiffness between the two men. Fleetingly they recaptured the rapport of their young manhood. They passed the champagne bottle back and forth, and when it was empty, Bazo clapped his hands and Tanase came to kneel dutifully before him and offered a clay pot of bubbling brew. She never looked up at Ralph's face, and she withdrew as silently as she had come.

At noon she returned to where the two men were still deep in conversation. Tanase led Jonathan by one hand and Tungata, still with the straw hat on his head, by the other. Ralph, who had forgotten all about him, started violently when he saw his son. The child's beatific grin was almost masked by layers of grime and beef fat. His sailor suit was the victim of the marvelous games which he and his newfound companion had invented. The collar hung by a thread, the knees were worn through, and Ralph recognized some of the stains as ash and ox blood and mud and fresh cow dung. He was less certain of the others.''

"Oh my God," Ralph groaned, "your mother will strangle us both." He picked up his son gingerly. "When will I see you again, old friend?" he asked Bazo.

"Sooner than you think," Bazo replied softly. "I told you I would work for you again when I was ready."

"Yes," Ralph nodded.

"I am ready now," said Bazo simply.

◆ ◆ ◆

Victoria was amazingly gracious in her acceptance of the change of honeymoon venue when Harry Mellow explained shamefacedly, "Ralph has this idea. He wants to follow up one of the African legends, at a place called Wankie's country, near the great falls that Dr. Livingstone discovered on the Zambezi River. Vicky, I know how you looked forward to Cape Town and to seeing the sea for the first time, but—"

"I've lived without the sea for twenty years; a little

longer won't hurt much.'' And she took Harry's hand. ''Wherever thou goest, my love—Wankie's country, Cape Town or the North Pole—just as long as we are together.''

The expedition was conducted in Ralph Ballantyne's usual style, six wagons and forty servants to convey the two families northward through the magnificent forests of northern Matabeleland toward the great Zambezi River. The weather was mild and the pace leisurely. The country teemed with wild game, and the newlyweds billed and cooed and made such languorous eyes at each other that it was infectious.

''Just whose honeymoon is this?'' Cathy mumbled in Ralph's ear one lazy, loving morning.

''Action first, questions later,'' Ralph replied, and Cathy chuckled in a throaty, self-satisfied way and cuddled back down in the feather mattress of the wagon bed.

At evening and mealtimes, Jonathan had to be forcibly removed from the back of the pony that Ralph had given him for his fifth birthday, and Cathy anointed the saddle sores on his buttocks with Zambuk.

They reached Wankie's village on the twenty-second day, and for the first time since leaving Bulawayo, the idyllic mood of the caravan bumped back to earth.

Under the reign of King Lobengula, Wankie had been a renegade and outlaw. Lobengula had sent four separate punitive impis to bring his severed head back to GuBulawayo, but Wankie had been as cunning as he was insolent, as slippery as he was mendacious, and the impis had all returned empty-handed to face the king's wrath.

After Lobengula's defeat and death, Wankie had brazenly set himself up as chieftain of the land between the Zambezi and the Gwaai rivers, and he demanded tribute of those who came to trade or hunt the elephant herds that had been driven into the badlands along the escarpment of the Zambezi Valley, where the tsetse fly turned back the horsemen and only the hardiest would go in on foot to chase the great animals.

Wankie was a handsome man in his middle age, open-faced and tall, with the air of the chief he claimed to be, and he accepted the gift of blankets and beads that Ralph presented to him with no effusive gratitude, inquired politely after Ralph's health and that of his father and brother

151

and son, and then waited like a crocodile at the drinking place for Ralph to come to the real purpose of his visit.

"The stones that burn?" he repeated vaguely, his eyes hooded as he pondered, seeming to search his memory for such an extraordinary subject, and then quite artlessly he remarked that he had always wanted a wagon. Lobengula had owned a wagon, and therefore Wankie believed that every great chief should have one, and he turned on his stool and glanced pointedly at Ralph's six magnificent Capebuilt eighteen-footers outspanned in the glade below the kraal.

"That damned rogue has the cheek of a white man," Ralph protested bitterly to Harry Mellow across the campfire. "A wagon, no less. Three hundred pounds of any man's money."

"But, darling, if Wankie can guide you, won't it be a bargain price?" Cathy asked mildly.

"No. I'm damned if I'll give in to him. A couple of blankets, a case of brandy, but not a wagon worth three hundred pounds."

"Damned right, Ralph," Harry chuckled. "I mean, we got Long Island for that price—"

He was interrupted by a discreet cough behind him. Bazo had come across silently from the other fire where the drivers and servants were bivouacked.

"Henshaw," he started when Ralph acknowledged him. "You told me that we had come here to hunt buffalo in order to make trek riems from their hides," he accused. "Did you not trust me?"

"Bazo, you are my brother."

"You lie to your brothers?"

"If I had spoken of the stones that burn in Bulawayo, we would have a hundred wagons following us when we left town."

"Did I not tell you that I had led my impi over these hills, chasing the same hairless baboon upon whom you now shower gifts?"

"You did not tell me," Ralph replied, and Bazo moved on hastily from that subject. He was not proud of his campaign against Wankie, the only one during all the years that he had been induna of the Moles which had not ended in complete success. He still recalled the old king's recriminations—would that he could ever forget them.

"Henshaw, if you had spoken to me, we would not have had to waste our time and demean ourselves by parleying with this son of thirty fathers, this unsavory jackal casting, this—"

Ralph cut short Bazo's opinion of their host by standing up and seizing Bazo's shoulders. "Bazo, can you lead us there? Is that what you mean? Can you take us to the stones that burn?"

Bazo inclined his head in assent. "And it will not cost you a wagon, either," he replied.

They rode into a red and smoky dawn through the open glades in the forest. Ahead of them the buffalo herds opened to give them passage and closed behind them as they passed. The huge black beasts held their wet muzzles high, the massive slaty bosses of horn giving them a ponderous dignity, and they stared in stolid astonishment as the horsemen passed within a few hundred paces, and then returned unalarmed to graze. The riders barely glanced at them; their attention was fastened instead on Bazo's broad bullet-scarred back as he led them at an easy trot toward the low line of flat-topped hills that rose out of the forest ahead.

On the first slope, they tethered the horses and climbed, while above them the furry little brown klipspringer, swift as chamois, flew surefooted up the cliffs, and from the summit an old dog baboon barked his challenge down at them. Though they ran at the slope, they could not keep up with Bazo, and he was waiting for them halfway up on a ledge above which the cliff rose sheer to the summit. He made no dramatic announcement, but merely pointed with his chin. Ralph and Harry stared, unable to speak, their chests heaving and their shirts plastered to their backs with sweat from the climb.

There was a horizontal seam, twenty feet thick, sandwiched in the cliff face. It ran along the cliff as far as they could see in each direction, black as the darkest night and yet glittering with a strange greenish iridescence in the slanted rays of the early sun.

"This was the only thing we lacked in this land," Ralph said quietly. "The stones that burn, black gold—now we have it all."

Harry Mellow went forward and laid his hand upon it reverently, as though he were a worshiper touching the relic of a saint in some holy place.

"I have never seen coal of this quality in a seam so deep, not even in the Kentucky hills."

Suddenly he snatched his hat off his head and with a wild Indian whoop threw it far out down the slope.

"We are rich!" he shouted. "Rich! Rich! Rich!"

"Better than working for Mr. Rhodes?" Ralph asked, and Harry grabbed his shoulders and the two of them spun together in a yelling, stomping dance of jubilation on the narrow ledge, while Bazo leaned against the seam of black coal and watched them unsmilingly.

It took them two weeks to survey and peg their claims, covering all the ground beneath which the seams of coal might be buried. Harry shot the lines with his theodolite, and Bazo and Ralph worked behind him with a gang of axmen driving in the pegs and marking the corners with cairns of loose stones.

While they worked, they discovered a dozen other places in the hills where the deep, rich seams of glittering coal were exposed at the surface.

"Coal for a thousand years," Harry predicted. "Coal for the railways and the blast furnaces, coal to power a new nation."

On the fifteenth day, the two of them traipsed back to camp at the head of their bone-weary gang of Matabele. Victoria, deprived of her new husband for two weeks, was as palely forlorn as a young widow in mourning, but by breakfast the following day she had regained her fine high color and the sparkle in her eyes as she hovered over Harry, replenishing his coffee cup and heaping his plate with slices of smoked warthog and piles of yellow scrambled ostrich egg.

Sitting at the head of the breakfast table set under the giant msasa trees, Ralph called to Cathy: "Break out a bottle of champagne, Katie my sweeting, we have something to celebrate," and he saluted them with a brimming mug. "Ladies and gentlemen, I give you a toast to the gold of the Harkness Mine and the coal of the Wankie field, and to the riches of both!"

They laughed and clinked their mugs and drank the toast.

"Let's stay here forever," said Vicky. "I'm so happy. I don't want it to end."

"We'll stay a little longer," Ralph agreed, with his arm about Cathy's waist. "I told Dr. Jim we were coming up here to hunt buffalo. If we don't bring a few wagonloads of hides back with us, the little doctor is going to start wondering.''

◆ ◆ ◆

The evening wind came softly out of the east. Ralph knew that at this season it would hold steadily during the night and increase with the warmth of the sun.

He sent out two teams of his Matabele, each team leading a span of trek oxen. They moved out eastward, and by dawn they had reached the bank of the Gwaai River. Here they felled two big, dried-out thorn trees and hooked the trek chains onto the trunks.

When they put fire into the branches, the dried wood burned like a torch and the oxen panicked. The drivers ran beside each span, keeping them galloping in opposite directions, heading across the wind, dragging the blazing trees behind them and spreading a trail of sparks and flaring twigs through the tall, dry grass. Within an hour there was a forest fire burning across a front of many miles, with the wind behind it roaring down toward the long open vlei where Ralph's wagons were outspanned. The smoke billowed heaven-high, a vast dun pall.

Ralph had roused the camp before first light, and he supervised the back-burn while the dew on the vlei subdued the flames and made them manageable. The Matabele put fire into the grass on the windward side of the open vlei and let it burn to the forest line on the far side. Here they beat it out before it could take hold of the trees.

Isazi rolled his wagons out onto the blackened, still-hot earth and formed them into a square with his precious oxen penned in the center. Then, for the first time, they had a chance to pause and look eastward. The dark smoke cloud of the forest fire blotted out the dawn, and their island of safety seemed suddenly very small in the path of that terrible conflagration. Even the mood of the usually cheerful Matabele was subdued, and they kept glancing uneasily at the boiling smoke line as they honed their skinning knives.

"We will be covered with soot," Cathy complained. "Everything will be filthy."

"And a little singed, like as not," Ralph laughed as he

and Bazo checked the spare horses and slipped the rifles into their scabbards.

Then he came to Cathy and with an arm about her shoulders told her, "You and Vicky are to stay in the wagons. Don't leave them, whatever happens. If you get a little warm, splash water on yourselves, but don't leave the wagons."

Then he sniffed the wind and caught the first whiff of smoke. He winked at Harry, who had Vicky in his arms in a lingering farewell.

"I'll bet my share of the Wankie field against yours."

"None of your crazy bets, Ralph Ballantyne," Vicky cut in quickly. "Harry has a wife to support now!"

"A guinea, then!" Ralph moderated the wager.

"Done!" agreed Harry.

They shook hands on it and swung up into the saddles.

Bazo led up Ralph's spare horse, which had a rifle in the scabbard and a bandolier of bright brass cartridges looped to the pommel.

"Keep close, Bazo," Ralph told him, and looked across at Harry. He had his own Matabele outrider and spare horse close behind him.

"Ready?" Ralph asked, and Harry nodded, and they trotted out of the laager.

The acrid stink of smoke was strong on the wind now, and the horses flared their nostrils nervously and stepped like cats over the hot ash of the back-burn.

"Just look at them!" Harry's voice was awed.

The herds of buffalo had begun moving downwind ahead of the bushfire. Gradually one herd had merged with another, a hundred becoming five hundred, then a thousand. Then the thousand began multiplying, the westward movement becoming faster, black bodies packing closer, the earth beginning to tremble faintly under the ironblack hooves. Now every few minutes one of the herd bulls, an animal so black and solid that he seemed to be hewn from rock, would stop and turn back, stemming the moving tide of breeding cows. He would lift his mighty horned head with its crenellated bosses and snuffle the east wind into his wet nostrils, blink at the sting of the smoke, turn again and break into a heavy swinging trot; and his cows would be infected by his agitation, while the red calves bawled in bewilderment and pressed to the flanks of their dams.

Now the herds were being compressed against each other. The huge beasts, the largest of them a ton and a half of flesh and bone, were moving shoulder to shoulder and muzzle to tail across a front almost a mile wide. The leaders came cascading out of the forest onto the edge of the vlei, while the serried ranks reached back into the looming dust and were hidden by the twisted silver trunks of the msasa trees.

Ralph knotted the scarf up over his nose and mouth and pulled his hat low over his eyes.

"Harry, my lad, every one that falls this side of the wagons"—he made a wide gesture—"is mine. Everything that side is yours."

"And a guinea on the bag," Harry agreed. He levered a cartridge into the breech of his Lee Enfield rifle and with one of his wild Indian whoops clapped his heels into his horse's flanks and drove straight at the nearest beasts.

Ralph let him go, and held his own horse down to a trot. Gently he angled in toward the rolling herds, careful not to spook them prematurely, letting them concentrate on the flames behind rather than the hunter ahead. This way he got in really close and picked out a good bull in the front rank. He leaned into the rifle and aimed into the barrel of the thick neck, just where the bald, scabby hide creased at the front of the shoulder.

The shot was almost drowned by the din of pounding hooves and bawling calves, but the bull dropped his nose to the earth and somersaulted over it, sliding on his back, kicking convulsively in his death agony, and bellowing as mournfully as a foghorn in a winter gale. The herds plunged into full gallop.

Steering his mount with his heels and toes, leaving both hands free to load and aim and fire, Ralph pressed in against the wall of dark bodies in gargantuan flight. Sometimes he was so close that the rifle muzzle was merely inches from a monstrous neck or shoulder, and the muzzle flash was quick and bright as a lance as it buried itself in the thick black hide. At each crash of the rifle, another beast went down, for at that range an experienced huntsman could make a butchery of it. He fired until the hammer fell on an empty chamber, and then crammed fresh rounds into the magazine and fired again as fast as he could pump the loading handle, not lifting the butt from his shoulder nor his eye from the sights.

The barrel was smoking hot, each shot now recoiling viciously into his shoulder, so that his teeth cracked together in his jaws and the forefinger of his right hand was bleeding, a flap of loose skin torn from the second joint by the trigger guard, so he was seconds slow on the reload, and then he was firing again. Deafened by gunfire, each shot was a muted popping in his abused eardrums, and the uproar of the galloping, bawling, bellowing herd was dreamlike and far away. His vision was dulled by the head-high bank of dust and, as they tore once more into the forest, by the somber shadows of the treetops that met overhead. He was bleeding from chin and lip and forehead where stones as big as acorns had been thrown into his face by the flying hooves ahead of him. Still he loaded and fired and reloaded. He had long ago lost all count of the bag, and the endless herd still pressed close on both flanks of his floundering horse.

Suddenly one bandolier was empty, a hundred rounds fired, he realized with surprise, and Ralph pulled a fresh one from his saddlebag, instinctively ducking under a long branch and straightening up to find an enormous bull galloping half a length ahead of him.

It seemed to Ralph's distorted vision to be the monarch of all buffalo, with a spread of horns wider than a man could reach, heavy as one of the granite boulders of the Matopos, so old that the points were worn blunt and rounded. His rump and back were gray and bald with age, the bush ticks hanging in blue, grapelike bunches in the deep folds of skin on each side of his huge swinging testicles.

Ralph's horse, almost blown now, could not hold him, and the bull was pulling away strongly, his huge quarters bunching and contracting, cloven hooves driving almost hock-deep into the soft, sandy earth under the immense weight of his body. Ralph stood in the stirrups and aimed for the spine at the base of the bull's long tufted tail as it lashed his own sides in the fury of his run.

At the instant that Ralph fired, a branch snatched at his shoulder, and the shot flew wide, socking meatily into the round black haunch. The bull tripped and checked, catching himself before he went down, swinging abruptly aside with blood spurting down his hind legs. Ralph gathered his exhausted horse to follow him, but another thick gray tree trunk sprang out of the dust clouds ahead and forced him to turn hard the other way to avoid it. Rough bark grazed his knee, and the bull was lost in the ranks of racing animals and the billowing dust.

"Let him go," Ralph shouted aloud. There was no chance that he could find a single animal again in this multitude. He cranked another cartridge into the scorching breech of his rifle and shot a sleek red queen through the back of the skull, and an instant later knocked her half-grown calf down with a bullet through the shoulder.

The rifle was empty, and he began to reload, concentrating all his attention on the task until suddenly some instinct warned him and he glanced up.

The wounded bull had turned back to hunt him.

It came out of the gloom like a black avalanche, goring the laggards out of its way to cut a path for itself through the racing black river of animals. Its nose was high, the muzzle glistening wetly, and long silver strings of mucus dangled from the flaring nostrils. It came quartering in, and the dusty earth exploded in pale puffs under the savagely driving hooves.

"Come, boy!" Ralph yelled desperately at his tired gelding, gathering him with knees and reins, turning him away from the bull's charge and at the same time cramming a cartridge into the loading slot of the Winchester.

The bull closed in a crabbing rush, and Ralph swiveled the rifle and fired point-blank into the gigantic head, knowing there would be no time for another shot. The bull's head flinched, and a splinter of slaty gray horn tore from the huge round bosses, and then the bull steadied himself, moving with the grace of a gazelle on his huge front legs. His head dropped. Ralph could have reached out and touched the crest of shaggy hide between his shoulders; instead he jerked his near leg from the stirrup and lifted his knee as high as his chin just as the bull hooked the massive horns at the gelding's flank. At the place where Ralph's knee had been a moment before, the blunt tip of a black horn crashed into the horse's chest.

Ralph heard the ribs crackle and snap like dry sticks, and the air from the gelding's lungs was driven out of his throat in a whistling scream. Horse and rider were lifted high. The gelding was still screaming at the agony of his collapsed chest as Ralph was thrown clear. The rifle spun from his hands, and he landed on his hip and shoulder and rolled to his knees. His right leg was numbed by the shock; it pinned him for precious seconds.

The buffalo was braced over the fallen gelding, front legs splayed, armored head low, blood dribbling and trickling down its massive, muscled quarters, and now it hooked at the horse, catching him in the soft of his belly and splitting him open like a cod on a fishwife's block. Soft, wet entrails, slippery as cooked spaghetti, were wrapped around the blunt point, and as the bull tossed his head, he stripped them out of the gaping belly cavity. The horse kicked once more and then was still.

Dragging his right leg, Ralph crawled toward the base of a wild teak.

"Bazo!" he screamed. "Bring the rifle! Bring the horse! Bazo!"

He could hear the shrill of panic and terror in his own voice, and the bull heard it also. It left the horse, and Ralph heard the splayed hooves thudding into the sandy earth, heard the snort of its breath and smelled the rank bovine reek of the animal. He howled again and dragged himself to his feet, hopping on his good leg. He knew he was not going to reach the mopani, and he whirled to face the enraged bull.

It was so close that he could see the wet trail of tears from the corners of its pink-shot little eyes running down the shaggy black cheeks and the spongy tongue lolling from its jaws as it bellowed at him. The head went down to hook him and split him, as it had the horse, but at that instant another voice bellowed in Sindebele:

"Hau! Thou uglier than death!" The bull checked, and pivoted on his stubby forelegs. "Come, thou witches' curse!"

Bazo was taking the bull off him; he galloped in out of the rolling dust, dragging the spare horse on its lead rein, and he angled in now across the bull's front, taunting it with his voice and flapping his monkey-skin cloak in its face. The bull accepted the lure of the cloak, put his nose down, and went after it. The horse that Bazo rode was still fresh, and it skittered out of the arc of the great swinging head, and the bull's polished horn glinted at the top of its lunge.

"Henshaw," Bazo yelled, "take the spare horse." And

160

he dropped the lead rein, sending the free horse down on Ralph, still at full gallop.

Ralph crouched in its path, and the gray mare saw him and swerved at the last moment, but Ralph leaped for the saddle and got a hold on the pommel. For a dozen strides, he hopped beside the mare, his feet skimming the ground as she carried him away. Then he gathered himself and swung his weight up across her back. His buttocks thumped onto the saddle, and he did not waste time groping for the stirrups. He yanked the spare rifle from the scabbard under his knee and kicked the mare around after the great black bull.

The beast was intent on Bazo still, chasing him in a grotesque, lumbering charge which covered the ground with uncanny speed. At that moment a low branch caught the half-naked Matabele induna a ringing crack across the shoulder and side of the head.

He was thrown sideways, the monkey-skin cloak flew away, flapping like an overfed black crow, and Bazo slid further until he was hanging upside down, his head almost brushing the ground between his mount's slashing hooves.

Coming up on the bull's blood-splattered quarters, Ralph fired into its back, probing for the spine in the mountain of black hide and bulging muscle. He fired with a mechanical action, cranking the loading handle, and the recoil dinned in upon his ears, so he could barely hear the heavy lead bullets slapping into the bull's body with a sound like a housewife beating a carpet. One of his bullets found the pumping lungs, for there was a sudden torrent of frothy blood blown from both the bull's nostrils, and the wild charge broke down into a short, hampered trot.

Ralph came up alongside it, and it turned the great head and looked at him through eyes that swam with the tears of its death agony. Ralph reached across and almost touched the broad forehead under the beetling horns with the muzzle of the rifle. The bull flung its head back from the brain shot, and it dropped silently onto its knees. It never moved again.

Ralph galloped on and caught the bridle of Bazo's running horse. He yanked it down to a halt.

"Only a Matabele rides with his head in the stirrups and his feet in the saddle," he gasped, and pulled Bazo upright.

The dark skin was smeared from Bazo's forehead by the

rough bark of the branch; the raw flesh was pale pink, and droplets of clear lymph welled up out of it like seed pearls.

"Henshaw, my little Hawk," he replied thickly. "You screamed so loudly I thought you were losing your virginity—with a horn, from behind."

Ralph spluttered with shaky laughter, almost hysterical with the relief from terror and mortal danger. Bazo shook his head to clear it, his eyes came back into focus, and his grin was wicked.

"Go back to the women, Henshaw, for you cry like a maiden. Give me your gun and I will win your guinea for you."

"See if you can keep up," Ralph told him, and booted his horse into a run. The reaction from terror came upon him in a kind of atavistic madness, the wild, soaring passion of the hunter, and he fell upon the galloping herds in a murderous frenzy.

The bushfire overtook them and put an end to the slaughter at last. Ralph and Bazo were almost caught between the enveloping arms of flame, but they broke through with the manes of their horses frizzled and stinking from the heat and Ralph's shirt scorched in brown patches. Then, from the sanctuary of the back-burn, they watched in awe as the fire swept by on either side. It was a gale of heat that whirled burning branches aloft and crashed from tree to tree, leaping a gap a hundred feet wide with a deep whooshing roar and bursting the next tree asunder.

The flames sucked the air away so that they gasped for breath, and the heat went deep into their lungs, so they coughed like hemp smokers. It seared the exposed skin of their faces, seemed to dry the moisture from their eyeballs and dazzle their vision as though they were staring into the fierce orb of the sun itself.

Then the fire was gone, burning away into the west, and they were silent and shaken, awed by the grandeur of its passing and by their own insignificance in the face of such elemental power.

It was the following morning before the earth had cooled sufficiently for the skinners to go out to work. The carcasses of the buffalo were half-roasted, the hair burned away on the upper side yet untouched on the side where they had lain against the earth. The skinners worked in a landscape like a hellish vision of Hieronymus Bosch, a desolate and blackened earth, grotesquely twisted bare trees, with the hideous shapes of the vultures crouched in the upper branches.

One team of skinners rolled the huge carcasses and made the shallow incisions around the neck, down the limbs and swollen bellies, then the next team hooked on the bullock teams and stripped off the skin in a single slab, while the third team scooped the coarse white rock salt over the wet hides and spread them in the sun.

By the second day, the air was thick with the reek of hundreds of rotting carcasses, and the chorus of cries and howls and croakings of the scavengers was a fitting accompaniment to the scene. Although the dun palls of smoke had cleared, the sky was dark once again with wings—the glossy sable pinions of the crows, the quick, sharp, stabbing wings of the little kites, and the great majestic spread of the vultures.

Around each naked carcass, stripped of its hide and with the obscene pink bellies massively swollen with gases, the hyena whooped and chuckled and the little doglike jackal darted in nervously to snatch up a tidbit of offal. The vultures hopped and flapped and squabbled, pecking at each other with steely hooked beaks, forcing their way through the enlarged anus of the cadaver into the belly cavern.

The tall black and white marabou storks, solemn as undertakers, stalked in with their bright, greedy eyes set in the naked face mask. Their crops were naked of feathers also; pink and scalded-looking, they dangled down in front of the throat. With their long and powerful bills, they would rip off a strip of flesh on which the greenish iridescent sheen of putrefaction was already blooming. Then they pointed the bill at the sky, gaping and straining with the effort of gobbling the morsel down on top of their already gorged crop.

The stink of rotting, scorched flesh and the smell of the scavengers wafted down on the little circle of wagons and kept the women from sleep.

"Ralph, can we leave here tomorrow?" Cathy whispered.

"Why?" he asked sleepily. "You like it here, you said so."

"Not any more," she answered. And then after a while:

"Ralph, if we go on burning and killing like this, how long will it last?"

He was so startled that he heaved himself on one elbow and peered at her in the candlelight.

"What on earth are you talking about, girl?"

"When the animals are all gone, this will no longer be the land I know and love."

"Gone?" He shook his head in sympathy, as though for an idiot child. "Gone? By God, Katie, you saw the herds out there. They are countless, limitless. They are as thick as that all the way north to Khartoum. We could hunt like that every day and not scratch the surface. No, Katie, they will never go."

"How many did you kill?" she asked quietly.

"Me? Two hundred and fourteen, thirty-two more than your esteemed brother-in-law." Ralph lay back comfortably and pulled her head down onto his chest. "And that cost the cocky bastard a guinea of his ill-gotten loot."

"Between you, almost four hundred—in a single day's hunting, Ralph." Her voice was so low that he barely heard it, but his own became rough with impatience.

"Damn it, Katie, I need the skins. They are mine to take if I want them. That's all there is to it. Now go to sleep, silly girl."

◆ ◆ ◆

If anything, Ralph Ballantyne's estimate of the buffalo herds was conservative. Probably never had any large mammal been so prolifically massed upon the earth's face in all of its history. From the great Sudd, where the infant Nile weaves its way through fathomless swamps of floating papyrus, southward over the wide savannas of eastern and central Africa, down to the Zambezi and beyond to the golden glades and forests of Matabeleland, the vast black herds roamed.

They were very seldom hunted by the primitive tribes. They were too swift and fierce and powerful for their bows and spears. The digging of a pitfall large and deep enough to trap such an enormous beast was a labor that few of the tribesmen thought about seriously enough to interrupt their dancing and beer drinking and cattle raidings. The Arab travelers into the interior were not interested in such coarse game, rather they were intent on capturing and chaining the tender young black maidens and youths for the markets at Malindi and Zanzibar, or in hunting the wrinkled gray elephant for their curved ivory tusks. Very few European travelers, bearing their sophisticated weapons, had yet ventured into these remote lands, and even the huge prides of lion which followed the herds could not check their natural multiplication.

The grasslands were blackened by the huge bovine beasts. Some herds, twenty or thirty thousand strong, were so dense that the animals in the rear literally starved, for the pasturage was destroyed by the forerunners before they could reach it. Weakened by their own vast multitudes, they were ripe for the pestilence that came out of the north.

It came out of Egypt. It was the same plague that Moses' God Jehovah had inflicted on the Pharaoh of Egypt. It was the *Peste bovine*, the rinderpest, a virus disease which attacks all the ruminants, but of those the most susceptible are the bovines: buffalo and domestic cattle. The stricken animals are blinded and choked by the discharge from the mucous membranes. Mucus pours in thick ropes from their nostrils and jaws. The discharge is highly infectious and contagious, and it persists on the pasturage over which the animal has passed long after its host has perished.

The course of the disease is rapid and irreversible. The mucous discharges are swiftly followed by profuse diarrhea and dysentery, with the beasts straining to evacuate even after their bowels are purged of all but bloody slime. Then when at last the animal goes down and no longer has the strength to rise, the convulsions twist the horned head back and around, until the nose touches the flank. That is the position in which they die.

The rinderpest passed with the speed of a gale wind across the continent, so that in places where the concentrations of buffalo were heaviest, a herd of ten thousand great horned animals was wiped out between the dawn and the sunset of a single day. The carcasses lay so thickly on the denuded savanna that they were touching each other like shoals of poisoned sardine washed up on a beach. Over this carnage hung the characteristic fetid odor of the disease with which soon mingled the stench of putrefaction, for even the teeming flocks of vultures and packs of gluttonous hyenas could not devour one thousandth part of this awful windfall.

165

This gale of disease and death blew southward, swallowing up the blundering, bellowing herds—southward until at last it reached the Zambezi. Even that wide stretch of swirling green water could not check the pestilence. It was carried to the far bank in the bulging crops of the vultures and carrion storks, and was scattered upon the pasture in the feces that they voided in flight.

The dreadful gale began again, southward it moved, ever southward.

♦ ♦ ♦

Isazi, the little Zulu driver, was always the first awake in the laager. It gave him satisfaction to be alert and aware when others half his age still slept.

He left his mat and he went to the watch fire. It was nothing but a pile of fluffy white ash, but Isazi moved the blackened tips of the logs together, crushed a few dry leaves of the ilala palm between them, and leaned close to blow upon it. The ash flew away, and a coal glowed sullenly before the palm leaf popped into a cheery little flame. The logs took, and Isazi warmed his palms for a moment and then left the circle of wagons and wandered down to where the oxen were penned.

Isazi loved his bullocks as some men love their children or their dogs. He knew each by name. He knew their separate natures, their strengths and their weaknesses. He knew which of them would try to turn out of the span when the going got tough or the footing soft, and he knew those with great hearts and special intelligence. Of course he had his favorites, like the huge red wheeler he had christened Dark Moon for his huge soft eyes, an ox who had held a loaded eighteen-footer against the flood of the Shashi when the mud bank was crumbling under his hooves, or Dutchman, the black and white dappled lead ox that he had trained to come like a dog to his whistle and lead the others to their place in the span.

Isazi chuckled lovingly as he opened the thornbush gate of the temporary kraal and whistled for Dutchman. In the predawn gloom, a beast coughed, and the sound had a peculiarly harrowing quality that struck a chill into Isazi's guts. A healthy bullock did not cough that way.

He stood in the opening of the kraal, hesitating to go in, then he smelled something that he had never smelled before.

Faint though the whiff of it was, it made his gorge rise. It smelled like a beggar's breath or a leper's sores. He had to force himself to go forward against the smell and his own dread.

"Dutchman," he called. "Where are you, my beauty?"

There was the explosive spluttering sound of a beast racked by dysentery, and Isazi ran toward it. Even in the bad light, he recognized the bulky, dappled shape. The bullock was lying down.

Isazi ran to it. "Up," he called. "*Vusa, thandwa!* Get up, my darling." For a beast only lies down when it has given up hope.

The bullock heaved convulsively, but did not come to its feet. Isazi dropped to his knees and placed his arm around its neck. The neck was twisted back at an awkward, unnatural angle. The velvety muzzle pressed into the beast's flank. The muscles under the sleek skin were as rigid as cast iron.

Isazi ran his hands down the beast's neck, feeling the fierce heat of fever. He touched the cheek, and it was slick and wet. Isazi lifted his hand to his own nose. It was coated with a thick slime, and the little Zulu gagged at the smell of it. He scrambled to his feet and backed away fearfully until he reached the gate. Then he whirled and ran to the wagons.

"Henshaw," he yelled wildly. "Come quickly, little Hawk."

◆ ◆ ◆

"Flame lilies," Ralph Ballantyne growled. His face was congested with black, angry blood as he strode through the kraal. The lily was a lovely flower of crimson edged with gold that grew on a bright green bush that tempted any grazing animal that did not know them.

"Where are the herdboys? Bring those bloody *mujiba* here." He stopped beside the twisted carcass of Dark Moon; a trained wheeler like this was worth fifty pounds. It was not the only dead ox—eight others were down and as many more were sickening.

Isazi and the other drivers dragged in the herders. They were terrified children, the eldest on the verge of puberty, the youngest ten years old, their immature groins covered only by a scrap of *mutsha* cloth, their little round buttocks naked.

"Don't you know what a flame lily is?" Ralph shouted at them. "It's your job to watch for poison plants and keep the oxen off them. I'm going to thrash the skin off your black backsides to teach you."

"We saw no lilies," the eldest boy declared stoutly, and Ralph rounded on him.

"You cocky little bastard."

In Ralph's hand was a sjambok of hippo hide. It was almost five feet long, thicker than a man's thumb at the butt and tapering to whipcord at the tip. It had been cured to the lovely amber color of a meerschaum pipe.

"I'll teach you to look to the oxen instead of sleeping under the nearest tree."

Ralph swung the lash around the back of the child's legs. It hissed like a puff adder, and the boy screamed at the cut of it. Ralph seized his wrist and held him up for a dozen more strokes across the legs and buttocks. Then he let him go and grabbed the next *mujiba*. The child danced to the tune of the sjambok, howling at each cut.

"All right," Ralph was satisfied at last. "Get the healthy animals into the span."

There were only sufficient oxen left to make up three teams. Ralph was forced to abandon half of the wagons with their loads of salted buffalo hides, and they trekked on southward as the sun came up over the horizon.

Within an hour another ox had fallen in the traces with its nose twisted back against its side. They cut it loose and left it lying beside the track. Half a mile further two more bullocks went down. Then they began dropping so regularly that by noon Ralph was forced to abandon two more wagons, and the last one rolled on with a depleted span dragging it. Long ago Ralph's rage had given way to bewilderment. It was clear that this was no ordinary case of veld poisoning. None of his drivers had seen anything to equal it, and there was not even a precedent in the whole vast body of African folklore.

"It is a *tagati*," Isazi gave his opinion. He had seemed to shrink with grief for his beloved bullocks, so now he was a mournful little black gnome of a man. "This is a terrible witchcraft."

"By God, Harry." Ralph led his new brother-in-law out of earshot of the women. "We'll be lucky to get even the one wagon home. There are a few bad river drifts to cross yet. We had better ride ahead and try to pick an easier crossing on the Lupani River.''

The river was only a few miles ahead; they could already make out the dark green of the forest along its course. Ralph and Harry rode side by side, both of them worried and anxious.

"Five wagons lying out here," Ralph muttered moodily. "At three hundred pounds each, to say nothing of the cattle I've lost—" He broke off and sat up very straight in the saddle.

They had come out onto another open glade beside the river, and Ralph was staring across it at the three huge, dappled giraffes. With the stilt legs of herons and the long graceful necks of swans, they were the strangest looking of all Africa's mammals. Their huge eyes were soft and sorrowful, their heads, strangely ugly-beautiful, were topped not by true horns but by outgrowths of bone covered with skin and hair. Their gait had the same deliberate slow motion of a chameleon, and yet a big bull would weigh a ton and stand eighteen feet tall. They were mute; no extremity of pain or passion could induce a whisper of sound from their swanlike throats. Their heart was large as a drum to pump as high as that head, and the arteries of the neck were fitted with valves to prevent the brain exploding under the pressure when the giraffe stooped, splay-legged, to drink.

These three animals were moving in single file across the vlei. The old stink-bull leading them was almost black with age, the cow that followed was splotched with reddish-fawn, and the half-grown calf was a lovely soft beige.

The calf was dancing. Ralph had never seen anything like it. It was swaying, and turning in slow and elegant pirouettes, the neck twisting and untwisting, swinging first to one side, then to the other. Every few paces the mother turned back anxiously to watch its offspring and then, torn between duty and maternal love, swung again to follow the old bull. At last, quite slowly, with a kind of weary grace, the calf slumped to the grassy earth and lay in a tangle of long limbs. The mother hovered for a minute or two, and then, in the way of the wilderness, deserted the weak and went on after her mate.

Ralph and Harry rode up slowly, almost reluctantly, to where the calf lay. Only when they reached it were they aware of the fatal mucous discharge from jaws and nostrils and the diarrhea painting the dappled hindquarters. They stared at the corpse in disbelief until suddenly Harry wrinkled his nose and sniffed.

"That smell, the same as the oxen—" he started, and suddenly realization dawned upon him. "A murrain," he whispered. "By the sweet name of the Virgin, Harry, it's some kind of plague. It is wiping out everything, game and oxen." Under his deep tan, Ralph had turned a muddy color. "Two hundred wagons, Harry," he whispered, "almost four thousand bullocks. If this thing goes on spreading, I'm going to lose them all." He reeled in the saddle so that he had to clutch at the pommel for his balance. "I'll be finished. Wiped out—all of it." His voice trembled with self-pity, and then a moment later he shook himself like a wet spaniel, sloughing off despair, and color rushed back into his darkly handsome face.

"No, I'm not," he said fiercely. "I'm not finished yet, not without a fight anyway." And he whirled to face Harry. "You'll have to bring the women back to Bulawayo alone," he ordered. "I'm taking the four best horses."

"Where are you going?" Harry asked.

"Kimberley."

"What for?"

But Ralph had pivoted his horse like a polo pony and was lying along its neck as he raced back toward the single wagon that had just come out of the forest behind them. Even as he reached it, one of the lead oxen collapsed and lay convulsed in the traces.

◆ ◆ ◆

Isazi did not go to the kraal the following dawn. He was afraid of what he would find. Bazo went in his place.

They were all dead. Every single bullock. They were already stiff and cold as statues, locked in that dreadful final convulsion. Bazo shivered and pulled his monkey-skin cloak more closely around his shoulders. It was not the dawn chill but the icy finger of superstitious awe that had touched him.

"When the cattle lie with their heads twisted to touch their flank, and cannot rise—" He repeated aloud the exact words of the Umlimo, and his dread was carried away by the jubilant rush of his warlike spirits. "It is happening, just as it was prophesied."

Never before had the Chosen One's words been so unequivocal. He should have seen it immediately, but the whirlwind of events had confused him so that it was only now that the true significance of this fatal plague had come upon him. Now he wanted to leave the laager and run southward, day and night, without stopping until he reached that secret cavern in the sacred hills.

He wanted to stand before the assembled indunas and tell them: "You who doubted, believe now the words of the Umlimo. You with milk and beer in your bellies, put a stone in their place."

He wanted to go from mine to farm to the new villages the white men were building where his comrades now labored with pick and shovel instead of the silver blade, wearing the ragged castoffs of their masters rather than the plumes and kilts of the regiment.

He wanted to ask them, "Do you remember the war song of the *Izimvukuzane Ezembintaba*, the Moles That Burrow Under a Mountain? Come, you diggers of other men's dirt, come rehearse the war song of the Moles with me."

But it was not yet full term; there was the third and final act of the Umlimo's prophecy to unfold, and until then Bazo, like his old comrades, must play the white man's servant. With an effort he masked his savage joy, withdrawing behind the inscrutable face of Africa. Bazo left the kraal of dead bullocks and went to the remaining wagon. The white women and the child were asleep within the body of the vehicle, and Harry Mellow was lying wrapped in his blanket under the chassis where the dew could not wet him.

Henshaw had deserted them late the previous afternoon before they had even reached the bank of the Lupani River. He had chosen four horses, the swiftest and strongest. He had charged Bazo most strictly with the task of leading the little party back to Bulawayo on foot, then he had kissed his wife and son, shaken hands briefly with Harry Mellow, and galloped away southward toward the drift on the Lupani, leading the three spare horses on a long rein and riding like a man chased by wild dogs.

Now Bazo stooped beside the wagon and spoke slowly

and clearly to the blanket-wrapped figure beneath it. Though Harry Mellow's grasp of Sindebele improved each day, it was still equivalent to that of a five-year-old and Bazo had to be sure he understood.

"The last of the oxen is dead. One horse was killed by the buffalo, and Henshaw has taken four."

Harry Mellow sat up quickly and made the decision. "That leaves one mount each for the women, and Jon-Jon can ride up behind one of them. The rest of us will walk. How long back to Bulawayo, Bazo?"

Bazo shrugged eloquently. "If we were an impi, fast and fit, five days. But at the pace of a white man in boots—"

They looked like refugees, each servant carrying bundles of only the most essential stores upon his head, and strung out in a long straggling line behind the two horses. The women were hampered by their long skirts whenever they walked to rest the horses, and Bazo could not contain himself to this pace. He ranged far ahead of the others, and once he was out of sight and well beyond earshot, he pranced and stamped, stabbing with an imaginary assegai at a nonexistent adversary and accompanying the *giya*, the challenge dance, with the fighting chant of his old impi.

> "Like a mole in the earth's gut
> Bazo found the secret way—"

The first verse of the song commemorated the impi's assault on the mountain stronghold of Pemba, the wizard, when so long ago Bazo had climbed the subterranean passage to the top of the cliff. It was as a reward for this feat that Lobengula had promoted Bazo to induna, had given him the headring and allowed him to "go in to the women" and choose Tanase as his wife.

Dancing alone in the forest, Bazo sang the other verses. Each of them had been composed after a famous victory, all except the last. That verse was the only one that had never been sung by the full regiment in battle array. It was the verse for the last charge of the Moles, when, with Bazo at their head, they had run onto the laager on the banks of the Shangani River. Bazo had composed it himself as he lay in the cave of the Matopos, near unto death with the mortification of the bullet wounds in his body.

"Why do you weep, widows of Shangani,
  When the three-legged guns laugh so loudly?
  Why do you weep, little sons of the Moles,
  When your fathers did the king's bidding?"

Now suddenly there was another verse. It came into
Bazo's head complete and perfect, as though it had been
sung ten thousand times before.

"The Moles are beneath the earth,
  'Are they dead?' asked the daughters of Mashobane.
  Listen, pretty maids, do you not hear
  Something stirring, in the darkness?"

And Bazo, the Ax, shouted it to the msasa trees in their
soft mantles of red leaves, and the trees bowed slightly to
the east wind as though they, too, were listening.

◆ ◆ ◆

Ralph Ballantyne stopped at King's Lynn. He threw the
reins to Jan Cheroot, the old Hottentot hunter.

"Water them, old man, and fill the grain bags for me. I
will be away again in an hour."

Then he ran up onto the veranda of the sprawling, thatched
homestead, and his stepmother came out to meet him, her
consternation turning to delight when she recognized him.

"Oh, Ralph, you startled me—"

"Where is my father?" Ralph demanded as he kissed her
cheek, and Louise's expression changed to match the grav-
ity of his.

"In the north section, they are branding the calves—but
what is it, Ralph? I haven't seen you like this."

He ignored the question. "The north section, that's six
hours' ride. I cannot spare the time to go to him."

"It's serious," she decided. "Don't torture me, Ralph."

"I'm sorry." He laid his hand on her arm. "There is
some dreadful murrain sweeping down out of the north. It
hit my cattle on the Gwaai River, and we lost them all,
over one hundred head in twelve hours."

Louise stared at him. "Perhaps—" she whispered, but
he cut across her brusquely.

"It's killing everything—giraffe and buffalo and oxen;
only the horses have not been touched yet. But, by God,

Louise, I saw buffalo lying dead and stinking on each side of the track as I rode southward yesterday. Animals that had been strong and healthy the day before.''

"What must we do, Ralph?"

"Sell," he answered. "Sell all the cattle at any price, before it reaches us." He turned and shouted to Jan Cheroot. "Bring the notebook from my saddlebag."

While he scribbled a note for his father, Louise asked, "When did you last eat?"

"I cannot remember."

He ate the slabs of cold venison and raw onion and strong cheese on slices of stone-ground bread and washed it down with a jug of beer while he gave Jan Cheroot his instructions. "Speak to nobody else but my father. Tell nobody else of this thing. Go swiftly, Jan Cheroot." But Ralph was up in the saddle and away before the little Hottentot was ready to ride.

Ralph circled wide of the town of Bulawayo to avoid meeting an acquaintance and to reach the telegraph line at a lonely place, well away from the main road. Ralph's own construction gangs had laid the telegraph line, so he knew every mile of it, every vulnerable point, and how most effectively to cut off Bulawayo and Matabeleland from Kimberley and the rest of the world.

He tethered his horses at the foot of one of the telegraph poles and shinned up it to the cluster of porcelain insulators and the gleaming copper wires. He used a magnus hitch on a leather thong to hold the ends of the wire and prevent them from falling to earth, and then cut between the knots. The wire parted with a singing twang, but the thong held, and when he climbed down to the horses and looked up, he knew it would need a skilled linesman to detect the break.

He flung himself back into the saddle and booted the horse into a gallop. At noon he intersected the road and turned southward along it. He changed horses every hour and rode until it was too dark to see the tracks. Then he knee-haltered the horses and slept like a dead man on the hard ground. Before dawn he ate a hunk of cheese and a slice of the rough bread Louise had put into his saddlebag and was away again with the first softening of the eastern sky.

At midmorning he turned out of the track and found the telegraph line where it ran behind a flat-topped kopje. He knew the company linesmen hunting for the first break in the line would be getting close to it by now, and there might be somebody in the telegraph office in Bulawayo anxious to send a report to Mr. Rhodes about the terrible plague that was ravaging the herds.

Ralph cut the line in two places and went on. In the late afternoon, one of his horses broke down. It had been ridden too hard, and he turned it loose beside the road. If a lion did not get it, then perhaps one of his drivers would recognize the brand.

The next day, fifty miles from the Shashi River, he met one of his own convoys coming up from the south. There were twenty-six wagons in the charge of a white overseer. Ralph stopped only long enough to commandeer the man's horses, leave his own exhausted animals with him, and then he rode on. He cut the telegraph lines twice more, once on each side of the Shashi River, before he reached the railhead.

He came upon his surveyor first, a red-haired Scot. With a gang of blacks, they were working five miles ahead of the main crews and cutting the lines for the rails. Ralph did not even dismount.

"Did you get the telegraph I sent you from Bulawayo, Mac?" he demanded without wasting time on greetings.

"Nowt, Mr. Ballantyne." The Scot shook his dusty curls. "Not a word from the north in five days—they say the lines are down. Longest break I've heard of."

"Damn it to hell," Ralph swore furiously to cover his relief. "I wanted you to hold a truck for me."

"If you hurry, Mr. Ballantyne, sir, there is an empty string of trucks going back today."

Five miles further on Ralph reached the railhead. It was crossing a wide, flat plain dotted with thorn scrub. The boil of activity seemed incongruous in this bleak, desolate land on the edge of the Kalahari Desert. A green locomotive huffed columns of silver steam high into the empty sky, shunting the string of flat-topped bogies to the end of the glistening silver rails. Teams of singing black men, dressed only in loincloths but armed with crowbars, levered the steel rails over the side of the trucks, and as they fell in a cloud of pale dust, another team ran forward to lift and set the tracks onto the teak ties.

The foremen leveled them with cast-iron wedges, and the

175

hammer boy followed them, driving in the steel spikes with ringing blows. Half a mile back was the construction headquarters, a square sweatbox of wood and corrugated iron that could be moved up each day. The chief engineer was in his shirt sleeves, sweating over a desk made of condensed-milk cases nailed together.

"What is your mileage?" Ralph demanded from the door of the shack.

"Mr. Ballantyne, sir." The engineer jumped up. He was an inch taller than Ralph, bull-necked and with thick, hairy forearms, but he was afraid of Ralph. You could see it in his eyes. It gave Ralph a flicker of satisfaction; he was not trying to be the most popular man in Africa. There was no prize for that. "We didn't expect you, not until the end of the month."

"I know. What's your mileage?"

"We have had a few snags, sir."

"By God, man, do I have to kick it out of you?"

"Since the first of the month—" The engineer hesitated. He had proved to himself that there was no profit in lying to Ralph Ballantyne. "Sixteen miles."

Ralph crossed to the survey map and checked the figures. He had noted the beacon numbers of the railhead as he passed.

"Fifteen miles and six hundred yards isn't sixteen," he said.

"No, sir. Almost sixteen."

"Are you satisfied with that?"

"No, sir."

"Nor am I." That was enough, Ralph told himself; any more would decrease the man's usefulness, and there wasn't a better man to replace him, not between here and the Orange River.

"Did you get my telegraph from Bulawayo?"

"No, Mr. Ballantyne. The lines have been down for days."

"The line to Kimberley?"

"That is open."

"Good. Get your operator to send this."

Ralph stooped over the message pad and scribbled quickly.

"For Aaron Fagan, attorney-at-law, De Beers Road, Kimberley. Arriving early tomorrow 6th. Arrange urgent noon meeting with Rough Rider from Rholand."

176

Rough Rider was the private code for Roelof Zeederberg, Ralph's chief rival in the transport business. Zeederberg's express coaches plied from Delagoa Bay to Algoa Bay, from the goldfields of Pilgrims Rest to Witwatersrand to the railhead at Kimberley.

While his telegraph operator tapped it out on the brass and teak instrument, Ralph turned back to his engineer.

"All right, what were the snags that held you up, and how can we beat them?"

"The worst is the bottleneck at Kimberley switching yards."

For an hour they worked, and at the end of it, the locomotive whistled outside the shack. They went out, still arguing and planning. Ralph tossed his saddlebag and blanket roll onto the first flat car and held the train for ten minutes longer while he arranged the final details with his engineer.

"From now on you will get your hardware faster than you can nail it down," he promised grimly as he vaulted up onto the bogie and waved at the driver.

The whistle sent a jet of steam spurting into the dry desert air, and the locomotive wheels spun and then gripped with a jolt, and the long string of empty cars began to trundle southward, building up speed rapidly. Ralph found a corner of the truck out of the wind and rolled into his blanket. Eight days' ride from the Lupani River to the railhead. It had to be some sort of record.

"But there is no prize for that either." He grinned wearily, pulled his hat over his eyes, and settled down to listen to the song of the wheels over the ties. "We have got to hurry. We have got to hurry." And then just before he fell asleep, the song changed: "The cattle are dying. The cattle are dead," sang the wheels over and over again, but even that could not keep him awake one second longer.

♦ ♦ ♦

They pulled into the switching yards at Kimberley sixteen hours later. It was just past four in the morning.

Ralph jumped down off the bogie as the locomotive slowed for the points and, with his saddlebags slung over his shoulder, trudged up the De Beers Road. There was a light on in the telegraph office, and Ralph beat on the wooden hatch until the night operator peered out at him like a barn owl from its nest.

"I want to send an urgent telegraph to Bulawayo."

"Sorry, mate, the line is down."

"When will be it open again?"

"God knows, it's been out for six days already."

Ralph was still grinning as he swaggered into the lobby of Diamond Lil's Hotel.

The night clerk was new. He did not recognize Ralph. He saw a tall, lean, sunburned man whose stained and dusty clothing hung loosely on him. That wild ride had burned off all Ralph's excess flesh. He had not shaved since leaving the Lupani, and his boots were scuffed almost through the uppers by the brushing of the thorn scrub as he had ridden through it. Locomotive soot had darkened his face and reddened his eyes, and the clerk recognized a drifter when he saw one.

"I'm sorry, sir," he said. "The hotel is full."

"Who is in the Blue Diamond Suite?" Ralph asked affably.

"Sir Randolph Charles." The clerk's voice was filled with reverence.

"Get him out," said Ralph.

"I beg your pardon?" The clerk reared back, and his expression was frosty. Ralph reached across the desk, and took him by his watered silk cravat, and drew him closer.

"Get him out of my suite," Ralph repeated, his lips an inch from the man's ear. "Quickly!"

It was at that moment that the day clerk came into the reception office.

"Mr. Ballantyne," he cried with a mixture of alarm and feigned pleasure as he rushed to the rescue of his colleague. "Your permanent suite will be ready in a minute." Then he hissed in the night clerk's other ear. "Clear that suite immediately, or he'll do it for you."

The Blue Diamond had one of the very few bathrooms in Kimberley with laid-on hot water. Two black servants stoked the boiler outside the window to keep steam whistling from the valve while Ralph lay chin-deep and adjusted a trickle of scalding water with his big toe on the tap. At the same time he shaved his jaws with a straight razor, working by touch and scorning the mirror. The day clerk had supervised the removal of Ralph's steamer trunk from the boxroom and hovered over the valets as they pressed the suits and tried to improve upon the perfect shine of the boots that they unpacked from the trunk.

At five minutes before noon, Ralph, smelling of brilliantine and eau de Cologne, marched into Aaron Fagan's office. Aaron was a thin, stooped man, with threadbare hair brushed straight back from a deep, intellectual forehead. His nose was beaked, his mouth full and sensitive, and his sloe eyes aware and bright.

He played a cruel game of kalabrias, giving no quarter, and yet there was a compassionate streak in his nature which Ralph valued as highly as any of his other qualities. If he had known what Ralph intended at this moment, he would have tried to dissuade him, but after having put the case against it, he would then have gone ahead and drawn up a contract as mercilessly as he would have elevated his jasz and menel for a winning coup at kalabrias.

Ralph didn't have time to argue ethics with him now, so as they embraced and patted each other's shoulders affectionately, he forestalled the question by asking, "Are they here?" and then pushing open the door to the inner office.

Roelof and Doel Zeederberg did not rise as he entered, and neither they nor Ralph made any attempt to shake hands. They had clashed viciously, but indecisively, on too many occasions.

"So, Ballantyne, you want to waste our time again?" Roelof's accent was still thick with his Swedish ancestry, but under his pale ginger brows, his eyes were quick with interest.

"My dear Roelof," Ralph protested. "I would never do that. All I want is that we should resolve this tariff on the new Matabeleland route before we put each other out of business."

"Ja!" Doel agreed sarcastically. "That's a good thought, like my mother-in-law should love me."

"We are willing to listen, for a few minutes anyway." Roelof's tone was casual, but his interest was quicker still.

"One of us should buy the other out and set his own tariffs," said Ralph blandly, and the brothers glanced at each other involuntarily. Roelof made a fuss of relighting his dead cigar to hide his astonishment.

"You are asking yourselves why?" Ralph said. "You want to know why Ralph Ballantyne wants to sell out."

Neither brother denied it; they waited quietly as vultures in the treetops.

"The truth is this, I have overextended myself in Matabeleland. The Harkness Mine—"

The lines of tension around Roelof's mouth smoothed out. They had heard about the mine, the talk on the Johannesburg Stock Exchange floor was that it would cost fifty thousand pounds to bring it into production.

"I am behind on the railway contract for Mr. Rhodes," Ralph went on quietly and seriously. "I need cash."

"You had a figure in mind?" Roelof asked, and took a puff on the cigar.

Ralph nodded and gave it to him, and Roelof choked on his smoke. His brother pounded him between his shoulders until he regained his breath, and then Roelof chuckled and shook his head.

"Ja," he said. "That's good. That's a very good one."

"It looks as though you were right," Ralph agreed. "I am wasting your time." He pushed back his chair and stood up.

"Sit down." Roelof stopped laughing. "Sit down and let's talk," he said briskly, and by the following noon Aaron Fagan had drawn up the contract in his own hand.

It was very simple. The purchasers accepted the attached statement of assets as complete and correct. They agreed to take over all existing contracts of carriage and the responsibility of all goods at present in transit. The seller gave no guarantees. The purchase price was in cash, no share transfers were involved, and the effective date was that of the signatures—walk out, walk in.

They signed in the presence of their attorneys, and then both parties, accompanied by their legal counselors, crossed the street to the main branch of the Dominion Colonial and Overseas Bank where the check of Zeederberg Brothers was presented and duly honored by the manager. Ralph swept the bundles of five-pound notes into his carpet bag, tipped his hat to the brothers Zeederberg.

"Good luck to you, gentlemen." And then he took Aaron Fagan's arm and led him in the direction of Diamond Lil's hotel.

Roelof Zeederberg massaged the bald spot on his crown. "I suddenly have this strange feeling," he murmured uneasily as he watched them go.

* * *

The next morning Ralph left Aaron Fagan at the door of his office.

"You'll be hearing from the good brothers Zeederberg again sooner than you expect," he warned him affably. "Try not to bother me with their accusations, there's a good fellow." He sauntered away across the Market Square, leaving Aaron staring after him thoughtfully.

Ralph's progress was slow. Half a dozen acquaintances stopped him to inquire solicitously after his health and then seek confirmation of the sale of his transport company, or to find out if he intended making a public issue of Harkness Mine shares.

"Give me a nod when you decide, Ralph."

"Any help I can give, it will be my pleasure, Mr. Ballantyne."

Rumors of the "payable" values of the Harkness ore put it as high as sixty ounces to the ton, and everybody he met wanted to be let in, so it took him almost an hour to cover the five hundred yards to the offices of the De Beers Consolidated Mines Company.

It was a magnificent edifice, a temple dedicated to the worship of diamonds. The open balconies on all three floors were laced with white grilles of delicate ironwork, the walls were of red brick with corners picked out in worked stone blocks, the windows were of stained glass, and the doors were oiled teak with polished brass fittings.

Ralph signed his name in the visitors' book, and a uniformed janitor with white gloves led him up the spiral staircase to the top floor. There was a brass plate on the teak door, a name only, with no title to accompany it: Mr. Jordan Ballantyne. But the grandeur of the office beyond the door gave some indication of Jordan's importance in the hierarchy of De Beers.

The double windows looked out over the Kimberley Mine. The excavation was almost a mile across, and it was impossible even from this height to see into its depth. It seemed as though a meteor had struck and plowed this crater through the earth's crust. Each day saw it driven deeper and deeper still as the miners followed the fabulous cone of blue kimberlite conglomerate downward. Already that hole had delivered up almost ten million carats of fine diamonds, and Mr. Rhodes's company owned it all.

Ralph merely glanced once at this view of the pit in which he had spent most of his youth groveling and scratching for the elusive stones, and then he surveyed the room appraisingly. The paneling was of seasoned oak, the intricate carving worked by craftsmen, the carpets over the floor were silk Qum, and the books in the shelves were matching sets bound in morocco and stamped in gold leaf.

There was the sound of running water from the open door of the bathroom, and a voice asked, "Who is it?"

Ralph spun his hat onto the stand and turned to face the door as Jordan came through it. He was in his shirt sleeves, with protectors over his cuffs; his shirt was the finest Irish linen, and the cravat under his stock was watered silk. He was drying his hands on a monogrammed towel, but he froze when he saw Ralph, then he threw the towel aside and crossed to him with three long, lithe strides and a cry of delight.

At last Ralph broke the brotherly embrace and held Jordan off at arm's length to study him.

"Always the dandy," Ralph teased him, and ruffled his thick golden curls.

No amount of brotherly familiarity could dim the fact that Jordan was still one of the most handsome men that Ralph had ever met. No, he was more than handsome, he was beautiful, and his evident pleasure at seeing Ralph heightened the glow of his skin and the lively sparkle of green behind his long curved fringe of lashes. As always, his younger brother's charisma and gentle nature recaptivated Ralph.

"And you," Jordan laughed, "you look so hard and brown and lean—what on earth happened to that prosperous paunch?"

"I left it on the road from Matabeleland."

"Matabeleland!" Jordan's expression changed. "Then you'll have brought the terrible news with you." Jordan hurried to the leathertopped desk. "The telegraph line has been down for over a week; this is the first message to come through. I finished decoding it not an hour ago."

He handed Ralph the flimsy, and he scanned it swiftly. The translation was written in Jordan's fair hand between the lines of the teleprinting. The addressee was "Jove,"

Mr. Rhodes's private code name, and it was from General Mungo St. John in his capacity as acting Administrator of Matabeleland in the absence of Dr. Jameson.

Outbreak of cattle disease reported from nothern Matabeleland. Losses sixty per cent repeat sixty per cent. Company veterinarian recognizes symptoms similar to *Peste bovine* epidemic Italy 1880. Disease also known as rinderpest. No known treatment. Possible losses 100 per cent failing isolation and control. Urgently request authority to destroy and burn all cattle in central province to prevent southward spread.

While he feigned astonishment and shock at the first paragraph, Ralph ran his eye swiftly down the remaining text. It was a rare opportunity to read a decoded BSA Company report; the fact that Jordan had handed it to him as a measure of his agitation.

There were lists of police strengths and dispositions, summaries of monies held and dispensed, administrative requisitions, recommendations for trading licenses, and the roster of mineral claims filed in Bulawayo. Ralph passed the sheet back to his brother with a suitably solemn expression.

At the head of the roster of new claims, he had seen a block of forty square miles registered in the name of Wankie Coal Mining Company. That was the name that he and Harry Mellow had agreed upon for their company, and Ralph glowed with satisfaction that did not show on his face. Harry must have got the women and Jonathan safely back to Bulawayo, and he had wasted no time in filing the claims. Once again Ralph congratulated himself on his choice of partner and brother-in-law. The only prickle of uncertainty was the rider to the roster that St. John had sent.

Advise soonest company policy regarding coal and base metals claims—register 198 in favor of Wankie Coal Mining Co. held in abeyance pending clarification.

The claims were filed but not yet confirmed; however, Ralph would have to worry about that later. Right now he had to concentrate on Jordan's apprehensions.

"Papa is right in the path of this thing, this rinderpest.

He has worked so hard all his life, and had such rotten luck—oh, Ralph, it can't happen to him, not again.'' Jordan stopped as another thought occurred to him. ''And you, too. How many bullock teams did you have in Matabeleland, Ralph?''

''None.''

''None? I don't understand.''

''I sold every last ox and wagon to the Zeederbergs.'' Jordan stared at him. ''When?'' he asked at last.

''Yesterday.''

''When did you leave Bulawayo, Ralph?''

''What has that got to do with it?'' Ralph demanded.

''The telegraph lines—they were cut, you know, deliberately. In four places.''

''Extraordinary. Who would have done a thing like that?''

''I don't even dare to ask.'' Jordan shook his head. ''And on second thoughts, I don't want to know when you left Bulawayo or whether or not Papa sold his stock as suddenly as you did yours.''

''Come on, Jordan, I'll take you to lunch at the club. A bottle of bubbly will console you for belonging to a family of rogues and for working for another.''

The Kimberley Club had a most undistinguished facade. Since its foundation, it had been enlarged twice, and the additions were glaringly apparent, unbaked Kimberley brick abutting upon galvanized iron and finally fired red brick. The iron roof was unpainted, but there were strange little touches of pretension: the white picket fence, the front door glazed in Venetian glass.

Until a man had become a member, he could not consider himself truly to have arrived in South Africa. Membership was so prized that Barney Barnato, who despite his millions had been steadfastly blackballed, was finally tempted to sell out his diamond holdings to Mr. Rhodes only after he had been promised the coveted membership as part of the deal. Even then, with the pen in his hand, Barnato had hesitated over signing the contract.

''How do I know they still won't chuck me out again as soon as I've signed?''

''My dear fellow, we will make you a life governor,'' Mr. Rhodes assured him, offering the final plum that was irresistible to the little slum-born cockney.

On his first night as a member of the club, Barnato had

strode up to the long bar dressed like a theatrical impresario and ordered a round of drinks for all, then flashed a magnificent ten-carat blue-white diamond ring on his third finger.

"What do you gents think of that, hey?"

One of the members studied it for a moment and remarked, "Clashes awfully with the color of your fingernails, old boy." Then, ignoring the proffered drink, he sauntered through to the billiard room, and everybody except Barney Barnato and the barman trooped out after him. It was that kind of club.

Ralph's and Jordan's own membership had been assured as soon as they came of age. For not only was their father a founding member and a life governor, but he was also a holder of the Queen's commission and a gentleman. These things counted at the Kimberley Club ahead of vulgar wealth. The porter greeted the brothers by name and put their cards up on the "in" board. The barman behind the long bar poured Jordan a pink gin and Indian tonic without being ordered, though he turned to Ralph apologetically.

"We don't see you often enough, Mr. Ralph. Is it still Glenlivet whisky, sir, water and no ice?"

In the dining room, they both ordered from the carving trolley—juicy young lamb, with the subtle taste of the Karroo herbs on which it had barely been weaned, served with parsleyed baby new potatoes. Jordan declined the champagne that Ralph suggested.

"I am a working man"—he smiled—"my tastes are simpler than yours, something like Château Margaux '73 would suit me better."

The twenty-year-old claret cost four times more than any champagne on the wine list.

"By God!" said Ralph ruefully. "Under that urban veneer, you are a true Ballantyne, after all."

"And you must be neck-deep in filthy lucre after that timely sale. It's my brotherly duty to help you get rid of it."

"Fire sale price," Ralph demurred, but nodded in appreciation of the claret. They ate in contented silence for a few minutes, then Ralph picked up his glass.

"What does Mr. Rhodes think of the coal deposits that Harry and I pegged?" he asked mildly, pretending to study the ruby lights in the wine but watching his brother's reaction.

He saw the corners of Jordan's mouth quiver with surprise, saw his eyes flare with some other emotion which he could not read before it was masked, then Jordan lifted a pink morsel of the lamb on the silver fork, chewed it fastidiously and swallowed before he asked:

"Coal?"

"Yes, coal!" Ralph agreed. "Harry Mellow and I pegged a huge deposit of high-grade coal in northern Matabeleland— haven't you seen the filing yet? Hasn't the Board approved the register? You must know about it, Jordan."

"What a fine wine this is." Jordan inhaled the bouquet. "A big, spicy perfume."

"Oh, of course, the telegraph line has been down. You haven't received it yet?"

"Ralph, I happen to know through my spies," Jordan said carefully, and Ralph leaned closer to him, "that the club secretary has just received a twenty-pound Stilton from Fortnum's. It should be perfect after the voyage."

"Jordan." Ralph stared at him, but Jordan would not look up.

"You know I can't say anything," he whispered miserably, so instead they ate the Stilton on water biscuits and accompanied it with a port from the cask that was not listed on the wine card, its existence known only to the privileged members.

At last Jordan took the gold hunter from his fob pocket.

"I should be getting back; Mr. Rhodes and I are leaving for London at noon tomorrow. There is a great deal to do before we go."

However, as they stepped out of the front door of the club, Ralph took his brother's elbow firmly and steered him into De Beers Road, lulling him with a flow of family gossip until they were opposite a pretty red-brick cottage almost hidden by dog roses, its diamond-paned windows curtained with frilled lace, and a demure little sign on the gate:

French dressmakers. *Haute Couture.*
Continental Seamstresses. Specialities for individual tastes.

Before Jordan had realized what his brother was about, Ralph had lifted the latch of the gate and was leading him down the walk. Ralph felt that on top of good food and wine, the company of one of the young ladies whom Diamond Lil chose with such taste and care to ornament Rose Cottage could not fail to soften and relax the tongue of even such a loyal servant as Jordan into indiscreet comment on his master's affairs.

Jordan took one pace beyond the gate before he pulled back from Ralph's grasp with unnecessary violence.

"Where are you going?" he demanded. He had gone as pale as though a mamba had crossed the path at his feet. "Do you know what this place is?"

"Yes, I do," Ralph nodded. "It's the only whorehouse I know of where a doctor checks the goods on offer at least once a week."

"Ralph, you can't go in there."

"Oh, come now, Jordie." Ralph smiled and took his arm again. "It's me, your brother Ralph. You don't have to put on a show. A salty young bachelor like you, by God, I'll bet there is a plaque on the wall above every bed in there with your name on it—" He stopped as he recognized Jordan's real consternation. "What is it, Jordie?" For once Ralph was uncertain of himself. "Don't tell me you have never had your cuff turned back for you by one of Lil's seamstresses?"

"I have never set foot in that place." Jordan shook his head vehemently. He had gone pale and his lips trembled. "Nor should you, Ralph. You are a married man!"

"Oh Lord, Jordie, don't be daft, lad. Even a solid diet of caviar and champagne can pall after a while. A hunk of country ham and a jug of rough cider makes a nice change."

"That's your business," Jordan flashed at him. "And I don't propose to stand in the street in front of this—this institution, discussing it."

He turned on his heel and strode away down the sidewalk a half-dozen paces before looking back over his shoulder.

"You would do better to consult your lawyer about your damned coal than—" Jordan broke off with a stricken expression, clearly horrified by his indiscretion, then he hurried away toward Market Square.

Ralph's jaw hardened, his eyes went cold and hard as polished emeralds. He had got his hint from Jordan, and it hadn't cost him the price of one of Diamond Lil's fancy girls either. The lace curtain in the front window of Rose Cottage lifted, and a pretty, dark-eyed lass with a creamy oval face and soft red mouth smiled out at him, shaking her ringlets in invitation to enter.

"Sit on it, dearie," Ralph told her grimly. "And keep it warm for me. I'll be back later."

He ground out the half-smoked Romeo y Julieta under his heel and strode away toward Aaron Fagan's office building.

♦ ♦ ♦

Aaron Fagan called them the "wolf pack."

"Mr. Rhodes keeps them chained in specially constructed kennels but lets them run every now and then, just to get a little taste of human flesh."

They did not look particularly lupine. There were four of them, soberly dressed men whose ages ranged from late thirties to mid-fifties.

Aaron introduced each of them individually, and then the group collectively. "These gentlemen are the De Beers Company permanent legal advisers. I think I am correct in saying that they also act on behalf of the British South Africa Company?"

"That is correct, Mr. Fagan," said the senior counselor, and his colleagues arranged themselves down the opposite side of the long table. Each of them placed his pigskin folder of papers neatly in front of him, and then, like a rehearsed vaudeville team, they looked up in unison. It was only then that Ralph recognized the wolflike glitter in their eyes.

"In what way can we be of assistance?"

"My client is seeking clarification of the mining laws promulgated by the BSA Company," Aaron replied, and two hours later Ralph was groping desperately through a maze of jargon and convoluted legal side roads as he tried to follow the discussion, and his irritation was becoming increasingly obvious.

Aaron made a silent plea for patience, and with an effort Ralph stopped the angry words reaching his lips; instead he hunched further down in his chair, and in a deliberately boorish gesture of defiance, he placed one boot on the polished tabletop among the scattered legal papers and crossed his other ankle on top of it.

For another hour he listened, sinking lower and still lower in his chair and scowling at the lawyers opposite him until Aaron Fagan asked humbly: "Does that mean that in your opinion my client has not fulfilled the requirements of Section 27 B Clause Five read in conjunction with Section 7 Bis?"

"Well, Mr. Fagan, we would first have to examine the question of due performance as set out in Section 31," replied the pack leader carefully, smoothing his mustache and glancing at his assistants, who nodded brightly again in concert. "In terms of that section—"

Abruptly Ralph reached the far frontier of his patience. He brought his boots down off the table onto the floor with a crash that startled the four gray-suited men across the table. One of them knocked his folder onto the floor, and papers flew like the feathers when a red caracal cat gets into the hen house.

"I may not know the difference between 'due performance' and the aperture between your buttocks," announced Ralph in a voice that made the leader pale and shrink in size. Like all men of words, he had a horror of violence, and that was what he sensed in the gaze with which Ralph fixed him. "However, I do know a wagonload of horse manure when I see one. And this, gentlemen, is grade-one horse manure you are giving me."

"Mr. Ballantyne." One of the younger assistants was bolder than his chief. "I must protest your use of language! Your insinuation—"

"It is not an insinuation," Ralph rounded on him. "I am telling you outright that you are a bunch of bandits—is that still not clear enough? How about robbers then, or pirates?"

"Sir—" The assistant sprang to his feet, flushed with indignation, and Ralph reached across the table and caught him by the front of his stock. He twisted it sharply, cutting off the man's protest before it emerged.

"Pray be silent, my good fellow, I am speaking," Ralph admonished him, and then went on, "I am sick of dealing with little thieves. I want to speak to the head bandit. Where is Mr. Rhodes?"

At that moment a locomotive down in the switching yards whistled. The sound only just carried even in the silence which followed Ralph's question, and Ralph remembered Jordan's excuse for ending lunch the previous day.

He released the struggling lawyer so abruptly that the man collapsed back into his chair, fighting for breath.

"Aaron," Ralph demanded. "What time is it?"

"Eight minutes of noon."

"He was fobbing me off—the cunning bastard was fobbing me off!"

Ralph whirled and ran from the boardroom.

♦ ♦ ♦

There were half a dozen horses at the hitching rack outside the front of the De Beers Building. Without checking his speed, Ralph decided on a big, strong-looking bay and ran to it. He clinched the girth, unhitched the reins and turned its head out into the road.

"Hey, you," shouted the janitor, "that's Sir Randolph's mount!"

"Tell Sir Randolph he can have his suite back," Ralph called, and vaulted to the saddle. It had been a good choice; the bay drove strongly between his knees. They galloped past the mine stagings, through the gap between the hillocks formed by the high tailing dumps, and Ralph saw Mr. Rhodes's private train.

It was already crossing the points at the southern end of the yards and running out into the open country. The locomotive was hauling four coaches; steam spurted from the pistons of the driving wheels with each stroke. The signal arm was down and the lights were green. The locomotive was picking up speed swiftly.

"Come, boy," Ralph encouraged the bay, swinging it toward the barbed-wire fence beside the track. The horse steadied himself, pricking his ears forward as he judged the wire. Then he went for it boldly. "Oh, good boy." Ralph lifted him with hands and knees.

They flew over it with two feet to spare and landed neatly. There was flat, open ground ahead, and the railway tracks curved slightly. Ralph aimed to cut the curve. He lay against the horse's neck, watching the stony ground for holes. Five hundred yards ahead the train was pulling gradually away from them, but the bay ran on gamely.

Then the locomotive hit the gradient of the Magersfontein hills, and the huffing of the boil rechanged its beat and slowed. They caught it a quarter of a mile from the crest, and Ralph pushed the bay in close enough for him to lean from the saddle and grab the handrail of the rear balcony on the last coach. Ralph swung across the gap and scrambled up onto the balcony. He looked back. The bay was already grazing contentedly on the Karroo bush beside the tracks.

"Somehow, I knew you were coming." Ralph turned quickly. Jordan was standing in the door of the coach. "I even had a bed made up for you in one of the guest compartments."

"Where is he?" Ralph demanded.

"Waiting for you in the saloon. He watched your daredevil riding with interest. I won a guinea on you."

Ostensibly the train was for the use of all the directors of De Beers, though none of them, apart from the Chairman of the Board, had yet shown the temerity to exercise that right.

The exteriors of the coaches and the locomotive were varnished in chocolate brown and gold. The interiors were as luxurious as unlimited expenditure could make them, from the fitted Wilton carpets and cut-glass chandeliers in the saloon to the solid gold and onyx fittings in the bathrooms.

Mr. Rhodes was slumped in a buttoned calf-leather chair beside the wide picture window in his private car. There were sheaves of paper on the Italian gold-embossed leather top of his bureau and a crystal glass of whisky at his elbow. He looked tired and ill. His face was bloated and blotched with livid purple. There was more silver than ruddy gold in his mustache and wavy hair now, but his eyes were still that pale fanatical blue and his voice was high and sharp.

"Sit down, Ballantyne," he said. "Jordan, get your brother a drink."

Jordan placed a silver tray with a ship's decanter, a Stuart crystal glass, and a matching claret jug of water on the table beside Ralph. While he did so, Mr. Rhodes addressed himself once more to the papers in front of him.

"What is the most important asset of any nation, Ballantyne?" he demanded suddenly without looking up again.

"Diamonds?" suggested Ralph mockingly, and he heard Jordan draw breath sharply behind him.

"Men," said Mr. Rhodes as though he had not heard. "Young, bright men, imbued during the most susceptible period of their lives with the grand design. Young men like you, Ralph, Englishmen with all the manly virtues." Mr. Rhodes paused. "I am endowing a series of scholarships in my will. I want these young men to be chosen carefully and sent to Oxford University." For the first time he looked up at Ralph. "You see, it is utterly unacceptable that a man's noblest thoughts should cease merely because the man dies. These will be my living thoughts. Through these young men, I shall live forever."

"How will you select them?" Ralph asked, intrigued despite himself by this design for immortality, devised by a giant with a crippled heart.

"I am working on that now." Rhodes rearranged the papers on his bureau. "Literary and scholastic achievement, of course, success at manly sports, powers of leadership."

"Where would you find them?" For the moment Ralph had set aside his anger and frustration. "From England, all of them?"

"No, no." Mr. Rhodes shook his shaggy leonine head. "From every corner of the Empire—Africa, Canada, Australia, New Zealand, even from America. Thirteen from America each year, one for every state."

Ralph suppressed a smile. The colossus of Africa, of whom Mark Twain had written, "When he stands on Table Mountain, his shadow falls on the Zambezi," had blind spots in his vast, scheming mind. He still believed that America consisted of the original thirteen states. Such small imperfections gave Ralph courage to face him, to oppose him. He did not touch the decanter at his elbow. He would need all his wits to find any other weakness to exploit.

"And after men?" Rhodes asked. "What is the next most precious asset of a new land? Diamonds, as you suggest, or gold perhaps?" He shook his head. "It is the power that drives the railways, that turns the mine headgears, that fuels the blast furnaces, the power that makes all the wheels go round. Coal."

Then they were both silent, staring at each other. Ralph felt every muscle in his body under stress, the hackles at the back of his neck rising in an atavistic passion. The young bull facing up to the herd bull in their first trial of strength.

"It is very simple, Ralph—the coal deposits in Wankie's country must be retained in responsible hands."

"The hands of the British South Africa Company?" Ralph asked grimly.

Mr. Rhodes did not have to reply. He merely went on staring into Ralph's eyes.

"By what means will you take them?" Ralph broke the silence.

"By any means that are necessary?"

"Legal or otherwise?"

"Come on, Ralph, you know it is totally within my power to legalize anything I do in Rhodesia." Not Matabeleland or Mashonaland, Ralph noted, but Rhodesia. The megalomanic dream of grandeur was complete. "Of course you will be compensated—land, gold claims—whatever you choose. What will it be, Ralph?"

Ralph shook his head. "I want the coal deposits that I discovered and that I pegged. They are mine. I will fight you for them."

Rhodes sighed and pinched the bridge of his nose. "Very well, I withdraw my offer of compensation. Instead let me point out a few facts to you of which you are probably unaware. There are two company linesmen who have sworn an affidavit before the Administrator in Bulawayo that they saw you personally cutting telegraph lines south of the town on Monday the fourth at four P.M."

"They are lying," said Ralph, and turned to look at his brother. Only he could have made the deduction and pointed it out to Mr. Rhodes. Jordan sat quietly in an armchair at the end of the saloon. He did not look up from the shorthand pad on his lap, and his beautiful face was serene. Ralph tasted the sourness of treachery on the back of his tongue, and he turned back to face his adversary.

"They may be lying," Mr. Rhodes agreed softly. "But they are prepared to testify under oath."

"Malicious damage to company property." Ralph raised an eyebrow. "Is that a capital offense now?"

"You still do not understand, do you? Any contract made under a deliberate misrepresentation can be set aside by a court of law. If Roelof Zeederberg could prove that when you and he signed your little agreement, you were fully aware of the epidemic of rinderpest which is sweeping Rhodesia," (that name again) "and that you had committed a criminal act to keep that fact from him—" Mr. Rhodes did not finish. Instead he sighed again and rubbed his chin;

the silver stubble rasped under his thumb. "On the fourth, your father, Major Zouga Ballantyne, sold five thousand head of breeding stock to Gwaai Cattle Ranches, one of my own companies. Three days later half of them were dead of rinderpest, and the rest will soon be destroyed by the company antirinderpest measures. Already Zeederberg Brothers have lost sixty per cent of the bullocks you sold them; they have two hundred wagons and their loads stranded on the great north road. Don't you see, Ralph, both your contract of sale and your father's could be declared null and void. Both of you forced to refund the purchase monies you received and to take back thousands of dead and dying animals."

Ralph's face was stony, but his skin had yellowed like a man five days in fever. Now with a jerky movement he poured the crystal tumbler half full of whisky, and he swallowed a mouthful as though it were broken glass. Mr. Rhodes let the subject of rinderpest lie between them like a coiled adder, and he seemed to go off in another direction.

"I hope that my legal advisers followed my instructions and apprised you of the mining and prospecting laws that have been adopted for the Charter territories. We have decided to apply the American law, as opposed to the Transvaal law." Mr. Rhodes sipped from his glass and then twisted it between his fingers. The base had left a wet circle on the expensive Italian leather. "There are some peculiar features of these American laws. I doubt that you have had an opportunity to study all of them, so I will take the liberty of pointing one out to you. In terms of Section 23, any mineral claim pegged between sunset of one day and sunrise of the following day shall be void and the title in those claims liable to be set aside by an order of the mining commissioner. Did you know that?"

Ralph nodded his head. "They told me."

"There is an affidavit on the Administrator's desk at this moment, made in the presence of a Justice of the Peace by one Jan Cheroot, a Hottentot in the domestic service of Major Zouga Ballantyne, to the effect that certain claims registered by the Rhodesian Lands and Mining Company, of which you are the major shareholder, which claims are known as the Harkness Mine, were pegged during the hours of darkness, and therefore liable to be declared void."

194

Ralph started so that his glass rattled against the silver tray, and whisky slopped over the rim.

"Before you chastise this unfortunate Hottentot, let me hasten to assure you that he believed he was acting in the best interests of you and his master when he swore this affidavit."

This time the silence drew out for many minutes while Mr. Rhodes peered out of the window at the bleak, treeless, sun-bleached spaces of the Karroo under a milky blue sky.

Then quite suddenly Mr. Rhodes spoke again. "I understand that you have already committed yourself to the purchase of mining machinery for the Harkness Mine and that you have signed personal sureties for over thirty thousand pounds. The choice before you is simple enough then. Give up all claim to the Wankie coal deposits, or lose not only them but the Zeederberg contract and the Harkness claims. Walk away still a rich man by any standards, or—"

Ralph let the unfinished statement rest for ten beats of his racing heart, and then he asked, "Or?"

"Or else I will destroy you, utterly," said Mr. Rhodes. Calmly he met the ferocious hatred in the eyes of the young man before him. He was inured by now both to adulation and to hatred; such things were meaningless when measured against the grand design of his destiny. Yet he could afford a placating word.

"You must understand that there is nothing personal in this, Ralph," he said. "I have nothing but admiration for your courage and determination. As I said earlier, it is in young men like you that I place my hope for the future. No, Ralph, it is not personal. I simply cannot allow anything or anybody to stand in my way. I know what has to be done, and there is so little time left in which to do it."

The instinct to kill came upon Ralph in a black, unholy rage. He could clearly imagine his fingers locked into the swollen throat, feel his thumbs crushing the larynx from which that shrill, cruel voice rose. Ralph closed his eyes and fought off his rage. He threw it off the way a man throws off a sodden cloak when he comes in from the storm, and when he opened his eyes again, he felt as though his whole life had changed. He was icily calm, the tremor gone from his hands, and his voice was level.

"I understand." He nodded. "In your place I would probably do the same thing. Shall we ask Jordan to draw up the contract making over any rights I or my partners might have in the Wankie coalfields to the BSA Company, and in consideration thereof the BSA Company irrevocably confirms my rights in the claims known as the Harkness Mine.''

Mr. Rhodes nodded approvingly. ''You will go far, young man. You are a fighter.'' Then he looked up at Jordan. ''Do it!'' he said.

◆ ◆ ◆

The locomotive roared on into the night, and despite the tons of lead that had been placed over the axles to soften the ride for Mr. Rhodes, the carriages lurched rhythmically and the ties clattered harshly under the steel wheels.

Ralph sat by the window in his stateroom. The goose down coverlet was drawn back invitingly on the double bed behind the green velvet curtains, but it had no attraction for him. He was still fully dressed, though the ormolu clock on the bedside table showed the time as three o'clock in the morning. He was drunk, yet unnaturally clearheaded, as though his rage had burned up the alcohol as soon as he swallowed it.

He stared out of the window. There was a full moon standing over the strangely shaped purple kopjes along the horizon, and every once in a while, the beat of the wheels changed to a ringing gong as they crossed another low steel bridge over a dry river course in which the sugary sand glowed like molten silver in the moonlight.

Ralph had sat through dinner at Mr. Rhodes's board, listening to his high, jarring voice parading a succession of weird and grandiose ideas, interspersed with sudden startling truths or shopworn old maids' platitudes that spilled endlessly out of the big man with the lumpy, ungainly body.

The only reason why Ralph managed to control his emotions and keep a good face, the reason why he even managed to nod in agreement or smile at one of Mr. Rhodes's sallies, was the realization that he had uncovered another of his adversary's weaknesses. Mr. Rhodes lived in a strata so high above other men, he was so cushioned by his vast wealth, so blinded by his own visions, that he did not seem even to realize that he had made a mortal enemy. If he did think at all of Ralph's feelings, it was to suppose that he had already discounted the loss of the Wankie coalfields and accepted it as philosophically and impersonally as Mr. Rhodes himself had.

Even so, the choice food and noble wines were tasteless as sawdust, and Ralph swallowed them with difficulty and experienced a surge of relief when Mr. Rhodes finally declared the evening ended in his usual abrupt manner by pushing back his chair without warning and rising to his feet. Only then he paused for a moment to examine Ralph's face.

"I measure a man by the style in which he faces adversity," he said. "You will do, young Ballantyne."

In that moment Ralph had come close, once again, to losing control, but then Mr. Rhodes had left the saloon with his bearlike gait, leaving the two brothers together at the table.

"I am sorry, Ralph," Jordan had said simply. "I tried to warn you once. You should not have challenged him. You should not have forced me to choose between you and him. I have put a bottle of whisky in your stateroom. We will reach the village of Matjiesfontein in the morning. There is a first-rate hotel run by a fellow called Logan. You can wait there for the northbound train to take you back to Kimberley tomorrow evening."

Now the whisky bottle was empty, Ralph looked at it with astonishment. He should have been comatose from the amount that he had drunk. It was only when he tried to stand that his legs cheated him, and he fell against the washstand. He steadied himself and peered into his own image in the mirror.

It was not the face of a drunkard. His jaw was hard-edged, his mouth firm, his eyes dark and angry. He pulled back from the mirror, glanced at the bed and knew that he could not sleep, not even now when he was almost burned out with rage and hatred. Suddenly he wanted surcease, a short oblivion, and he knew where to find it. At the far end of the saloon, behind the tall double doors of intricate marquetry work, was an array of bottles, the finest and most exotic liquors gathered from every civilized land— that was where he could find oblivion.

Ralph crossed his stateroom, fumbled with the door catch, and stepped out. The cold Karroo night air flicked his hair, and he shivered in his shirt sleeves and then weaved down the narrow corridor toward the saloon. He bumped first one shoulder and then the other against the polished teak bulkheads and cursed his own clumsiness. He crossed the open balcony between coaches, clutching at the handrail to steady himself, eager to get out of the wind. As he entered the corridor of the second coach, one of the doors slid open ahead of him, and a shaft of yellow light outlined the slim and graceful figure that stepped through.

Jordan had not seen his brother. He paused in the doorway and looked back into the stateroom beyond. His expression was as soft and as loving as that of a mother leaving her sleeping infant. Gently, with exaggerated care, he closed the sliding door so as not to make the least sound. Then he turned and found himself face to face with Ralph.

Like his brother, Jordan was coatless, but his shirt was unbuttoned down to the silver buckle of his breeches; the cuffs of his sleeves were not linked, as though the garment had been thrown on carelessly, and Jordan's feet were bare, very white and elegantly shaped against the dark-toned carpet.

None of this surprised Ralph. He expected that, like himself, Jordan was hungry or visiting the heads. He was too fuddled to ponder on it and was about to invite Jordan to come with him to find another bottle when he saw the expression on Jordan's face.

He was instantly transported back fifteen years in time, to the thatched bungalow of his father's camp near the great pit of the Kimberley Mine, where he and Jordan had passed most of their youth. One night, that long ago, Ralph had surprised his brother in a childish act of onanism and had seen that same expression, that stricken dread and guilt, upon his lovely face.

Now again Jordan was transfixed, rigid and pale, staring at Ralph with huge, terrified eyes, one hand raised as though to shield his throat. Suddenly Ralph understood. He recoiled in horror and found the door onto the balcony closed behind him. He flattened his back against it, unable to speak for infinite seconds while they stared at each other. When at last Ralph regained his voice, it was rough, as though he had run a hard race.

"By God, now I know why you have no use for whores, for you are one yourself."

Ralph turned and tore open the door, he ran out onto the balcony and looked about him wildly, like a creature in a trap, and saw the clean, moon-washed spaces of the open veld. He kicked open the gate of the balcony, swung down the steps, and let himself drop into the night.

The earth hit him with crushing force, and he rolled down the ballasting and came to rest face down in the harsh scrub beside the tracks. When he lifted his head, the red running lights of the caboose were dwindling away into the south and the sound of the wheels was already muted by distance.

Ralph pushed himself up and limped and staggered away into the empty veld. Half a mile from the tracks, he fell to his knees again and gagged and retched as he vomited up the whisky and his own disgust. The dawn was an unearthly orange wash behind a crisp black cutout of flat-topped hills. Ralph lifted his face to it, and he spoke aloud.

"I swear I will have him. I swear that I will destroy this monster, or destroy myself in the attempt."

At that moment the rim of the sun pushed up above the hills and hurled a brazen dart of light into Ralph's face as though a god had been listening and had sealed the pact with flame.

◆　◆　◆

"My father killed a great elephant upon this spot. The tusks stand on the stoep at King's Lynn," Ralph said quietly. "And I shot a fine lion here myself. It seems strange that things like that will never happen again at this place."

Beside him Harry Mellow straightened up from the theodolite, and for a moment his face was grave.

"We have come to conquer the wilderness," he said. "Soon there will be a high headgear reaching up into the sky, and if the Harkness reef runs true, one day a town with schools and churches—hundreds, perhaps thousands, of families. Isn't that what we both want?"

Ralph shook his head. "I would be getting soft if I did not. It just seems strange when you look at it now."

The low valleys were still blowing with the soft grasses, the timber along the ridges was tall, the tree trunks silver in the sunlight, but even as they watched, one of them shivered against the sky and then toppled with a rending, crackling roar. The Matabele axmen swarmed over the fallen giant to lop off the branches, and for a moment longer the shadow of regret lingered in Ralph's eyes, then he turned away.

"You have picked a good site," he said, and Harry followed the direction of his gaze.

"Knobs Hill," he laughed.

The thatch and daub hut was sited so that it would not overlook the compound for the black laborers. Instead it had a breathtaking view over the forest to where the southern escarpment dipped away into infinite blue distances. A tiny feminine figure came out of the hut, her apron a merry spot of tulip yellow against the raw red earth which Vicky hoped would one day be a garden. She saw the two men below her and waved.

"By God, that girl has done wonders." Harry lifted his hat above his head to acknowledge the greeting, his expression fondly besotted. "She copes so well. Nothing upsets her—not even the cobra in the toilet this morning. She just up and blasted it with a shotgun. Of course I'll have to fix the seat."

"It's her life," Ralph pointed out. "Put her in a city and she'd probably be in tears in ten minutes."

"Not my girl," said Harry proudly.

"All right, you made a good choice," Ralph agreed, "but it's bad form to boost your own wife."

"Bad form?" Harry shook his head wonderingly. "You limeys!" he said, and stooped to put his eye back to the lens of the theodolite.

"Leave that damn thing for a minute." Ralph pinched his shoulder lightly. "I didn't ride three hundred miles to look at your backside."

"Fine." Harry straightened. "I'll let the work lie. What do you want to talk about?"

"Show me how you decided on the site of your number one shaft," Ralph invited, and they went down the valley while Harry pointed out the factors which had led him to choose the spot.

"The ancient trenches are inclined at just over forty degrees, and we have three layers of schists overrunning. Now I extended out the strike of the ancient reef, and we put in the potholes here—"

The exploratory potholes were narrow vertical shafts,

each under a gantry of raw native timber, spaced out in a straight line along the slope of the hill.

"We went down a hundred feet on five of them, down through the friable levels, and we picked up the upper schist layer again—"

"Schist isn't going to make us rich."

"No, but the reef's still under it."

"How do you know?"

"You hired me for my nose," Harry chuckled. "I can smell it." He led Ralph on. "So you see this is the only logical spot for the main shaft. I reckon to intersect the reef again at three hundred feet, and once we are on it, we can stope it out."

A small gang of black men were clearing the collar area of the reef, and Ralph recognized the tallest of them.

"Bazo," he cried, and the induna straightened up and rested on his pick handle.

"Henshaw," he greeted Ralph gravely. "Have you come to watch the real men at work."

Bazo's flat, hard muscle shone like wet anthracite, and running sweat had left snaking trails down it.

"Real men?" Ralph asked. "You promised me two hundred, and you have brought me twenty."

"The others are waiting," Bazo promised. "But they will not come if they cannot bring their women with them. One-Bright-Eye wants the women to stay in the villages."

"They can bring their women, as many as they wish. I will speak to One-Bright-Eye. Go to them. Choose the strongest and the best. Bring me your old comrades from the Moles impi, and tell them I will pay them well and feed them better, and they can bring their women and breed strong sons to work my mines."

"I will leave in the morning," Bazo decided. "And be back before the moon shows its horns again."

When the two white men moved on down the survey line, Bazo watched them for a while, his face expressionless and his eyes inscrutable, then he looked at his gang and nodded.

They spat on their palms, hefted their pickaxes and Bazo sang out the opening chorus of the work chant.

"*Ubunyonyo bu ginye entudhla*. The little black ants can eat up the giraffe."

Bazo had composed the line beside the corpse of a giraffe

struck down by the rinderpest and untouched by all the gorged scavengers of the veld except a colony of the black safari ants which had cleaned the cadaver down to the bone. The significance of it had stayed with Bazo—how by persistence even the greatest are overcome—and the seemingly innocent line of gibberish was now insidiously preparing the minds of the *amadoda* who labored under him. At the invocation they swung the picks on high, standing shoulder to shoulder, the crescent-headed tools silhouetted against the blue of the sky.

"*Guga mzimba!*" they replied in soaring chorus. "*Sala nhliziyo.* Though our bodies are worn out, our hearts are constant."

And then together the humming "Jee!" as the pick heads hissed downward in unison and with a crash buried themselves in the iron earth.

Each man levered his pick head free, took one step forward, and braced himself as Bazo sang: "The little black ants can eat up the giraffe."

And again the act was repeated, and again, and a hundred times more, while the sweat was flung from their bodies and the red dust flew.

◆ ◆ ◆

Bazo loped along at a deceptively easy gait that never varied, though the hills were steep and the valleys abrupt. His spirits were joyous; he had not truly realized how much the labors of the last weeks had galled until he was released from them. Once long ago he had worked with pick and shovel in the yellow diamond pit at Kimberley. Henshaw had been his companion then, and the two of them had made a game of the brutal, endless labor. It had built their muscles and made them strong but had caged and cramped their spirits, until neither of them could suffer it longer, and they had escaped together.

Since those days Bazo had known the savage joy and the divine madness of that terrible moment that the Matabele call the "closing in." He had stood against the king's enemies and killed in the sunlight with his regimental plumes flying. He had won honors and the respect of his peers. He had sat on the king's council with the iduna's headring on his brow, and he had come to the brink of the black river and briefly looked beyond it into the forbidden land that men call death, and now he had learned a new truth. It was more painful for a man to go backward than it is for him to go forward. The drudgery of menial labor rankled the more now for the glories that had preceded it.

The path dropped away toward the river and disappeared into the dense, dark green vegetation like a serpent into its hole. Bazo followed it down and stooped into the gloomy tunnel and then froze. Instinctively his right hand reached for the nonexistent assegai on its leather thong under the grip of the long shield that also was not there—so hard do old habits die. The shield had long ago been burned on the bonfires with ten thousand other shields, and the steel snapped in half on the anvils of the BSA Company blacksmiths.

Then he saw this was no enemy that came toward him down the narrow tunnel of the riverine bush, and his heart bounded almost painfully against his ribs.

"I see you, Lord," Tanase greeted him softly.

She was as slim and upright as the young girl he had captured at the stronghold of Pemba, the wizard—the same long, graceful legs and clinched-in waist, the same heron's neck like the stem of a lovely black lily.

"Why are you so far from the village?" he demanded as she knelt dutifully before him and clapped her hands softly at the level of her waist.

"I saw you on the road, Bazo, son of Gandang."

And he opened his mouth to question her further, for he had come swiftly, then he changed his mind and felt the little superstitious prickle of insect feet along the nape of his neck. Sometimes still there were things about this woman that disquieted him, for she had not been stripped of all her occult powers in the cave of the Umlimo.

"I see you, Lord," Tanase repeated. "And my body calls to yours the way a hungry infant fresh roused from sleep frets for the breast."

He lifted her up and held her face between his hands to examine it as though he had picked a rare and beautiful flower in the forest. It had taken much to accustom himself to the way she spoke of their secret bodily desires. He had been taught that it was unseemly for a Matabele wife to show pleasure in the act of generation and to speak of it the way a man does. Instead she should be merely a pliant and unprotesting vessel for her husband's seed, ready whenever he was and unobtrusive and self-effacing when he was not.

Tanase was none of these things. At first she had shocked and horrified him with some of the things she had learned in her apprenticeship for the dark mysteries. However, shock had turned to fascination as she had unfolded each skill before him.

She had potions and perfumes that could rouse a man even when he was exhausted and wounded from the battlefield; she had tricks of voice and eyes that bit like an arrowhead. Her fingers could find unerringly the spots beneath his skin at places on his body of which even he was unaware, upon which she played like the keys of the marimba, making him more man than he had ever dreamed was possible. She could make each separate muscle of her own body move and tighten in complete freedom from the muscles around it. At will she could bring him to precipitous rushing release or keep him hovering high.

"We have been too long apart," she whispered with that combination of voice and slant of wide Egyptian eyes that tripped his breath and made his heart race. "I came to meet you alone, so we could be free for a while of your son's clamorous adoration and the eyes of the villagers." And she led him off the track and unclasped her leather cloak to spread it on the soft bed of fallen leaves.

Long after the storm had passed and the aching tension had left his body, when his breathing was deep and even again and his eyelids drooped with the deeply contented lassitude that follows the act of love, she raised herself on her elbow above him and, with a kind of reverential wonder, traced out the planes of his face with the tip of one finger, and then said softly, "Bayete!"

It was the greeting that is made only to a king, and he stirred uncomfortably and his eyes opened wide. He looked at her and knew that expression. Their loving had not softened her and made her sleepy as it had done him. That royal greeting had not been a jest.

"Bayete!" she said again. "The sound of it troubles you, my fine sharp-bladed ax. But why should it do so?"

Suddenly Bazo felt the insects of fear and superstition crawling on his skin again, and he was angry and afraid. "Do not talk like this, woman. Do not offend the spirits with your silly girlish prattlings."

She smiled, but it was a cruel, catlike smile, and she continued, "Oh, Bazo, the bravest and the strongest, why do you then start so at my girlish words? You in whose veins runs the purest blood of Zanzi? Son of Gandang, the son of Mzilikazi, do you dream perchance of the little redwood spear that Lobengula carried in his hand? Son of Juba, whose great-grandfather was mighty Diniswayo, who was nobler even than his protégé Chaka, who became King of Zulu, do you not feel the royal blood coursing in your veins, does it make you itch for things you dare not even speak aloud?"

"You are mad, woman, the mopani bees have entered your head and driven you mad."

But Tanase smiled still with her lips close to his ear, and she touched his eyelids with her fingertip.

"Do you not hear the widows of Shangani and Bembesi crying aloud, 'Our father Lobengula is gone, we are orphans with no one to protect us.' Do you not see the men of Matabeleland with empty hands entreat the spirits? 'Give us a king,' they cry. 'We must have a king.' "

"Babiaan," whispered Bazo. "Somabula and Gandang. They are Lobengula's brothers."

"They are old men, and the stone has fallen out of their bellies, the fire has gone out in their eyes."

"Tanase, do not speak so."

"Bazo, my husband, my king, do you not see to whom the eyes of all the indunas turn when the nation is in council?"

"Madness." Bazo shook his head.

"Do you not know whose word they wait upon now, do you not see how even Babiaan and Somabula listen when Bazo speaks?"

She laid the palm of her hand over his mouth to still his protests, and then in one swift movement she had mounted and straddled him again, and miraculously he was ready and more than ready for her, and she cried out fiercely: "Bayete, son of kings! Bayete, father of kings, whose seed will rule when the white men have been swallowed again by the ocean which spewed them up."

And with a shuddering cry, he felt as though she had drawn the very life force from his guts and left in its place a dreadful haunting longing, a fire in his blood that would not be assuaged until he held in his hand the little redwood spear that was the symbol of the Nguni monarch.

They went side by side, hand in hand, which was a curious thing, for a Matabele wife always walks behind her husband with the roll of the sleeping mat balanced upon her head. But they were like children caught up in a kind of delirious dream, and when they reached the crest of the pass, Bazo took her in his arms and held her to his breast in an embrace that he had never used before.

"If I am the ax, then you are the cutting edge, for you are a part of me, but the sharpest part."

"Together, Lord, we will hack through anything that stands in our way," she answered fiercely, and then she pulled out from the circle of his arms and lifted the flap of the beaded pouch upon her belt.

"I have a gift to make your brave heart braver and your will as hard as your steel." She took something soft and gray and fluffy from her pouch and stood before him on tiptoe, reaching high with both arms to bind the strip of fur around his forehead. "Wear this moleskin for the glory that was and that shall be again, induna of the Moles That Burrow Under a Mountain. One day soon we will change it for a headband of spotted gold leopard skin with royal blue heron feathers set upon it."

She took his hand and they started down from the hilltop, but they did not reach the grassy plain before Bazo stopped again and inclined his head to listen. There was a faint popping sound on the small dry breeze, like the bubbles bursting in a pot of boiling porridge.

"Guns," he said. "Still far away, but many of them."

"It is so, Lord," Tanase replied. "Since you left, the guns of One-Bright-Eye's *kanka* have been busy as the tongues of the old women at a beer-drink."

✦ ✦ ✦

"There is a terrible pestilence sweeping through the land." General Mungo St. John had selected a clay anthill as a rostrum from which to address his audience. "It passes from one animal to the next as a bushfire jumps from tree to tree. Unless we can contain it, all the cattle will die."

Below the anthill, Sergeant Ezra was translating loudly, while the listening tribesmen squatted silently facing them. There were almost two thousand of them, the occupants of all the villages that had been built along both banks of the Inyati River to replace the regimental kraals of Lobengula's impi.

The men were in the foremost ranks, their faces expressionless but their eyes watchful; behind them were the youths and boys not yet admitted to the rank of warrior. These were the *mujiba*, the herdboys, whose daily life was intimately interwoven with the herds of the tribe. The present *indaba* concerned them as much as it did the elders. There were no women present, for it was a matter of cattle, of the nation's wealth.

"It is a great sin to try to hide your cattle as you have done, to drive them into the hills or the thick forest. These cattle carry with them the seeds of the pestilence," Mungo St. John explained, and waited for his sergeant to translate before going on. "Lodzi and I are very angry with these deceptions. There will be heavy fines for those villages which hide their cattle, and as further punishment I will double the work quotas for the men, so that you will work like *amaholi*, like slaves you will toil if you attempt to defy the word of Lodzi." Mungo St. John paused again and lifted the black eye patch to wipe away the sweat that trickled down from under the wide-brimmed slouch hat. Drawn by the lowing herds in the thornbush kraal, the big shiny green flies swarmed, and the place stank of cow dung and unwashed humanity. Mungo found himself impatient with the necessity of trying to explain his actions to this silent, unresponsive throng of half-naked savages, for he had already repeated this same warning at thirty other *indabas* across Matabeleland. His sergeant finished the translation and glanced up at him expectantly.

Mungo St. John pointed to the mass of cattle penned in the thorn kraal behind him. "As you have seen, it is of no avail to try to hide the herds. The native police track them down." Mungo stopped again and frowned in annoyance. In the second row, a Matabele buck had risen and was facing him quietly.

He was a tall man, finely muscled, although one arm seemed deformed, for it was twisted from the shoulder at an awkward angle. Though the body was that of a man in his full prime, the face was eroded and ravaged, as though by grief or pain, and was aged before its time. On the neat cap of dense curls, the man wore the headring of an induna, and around his forehead a headband of gray fur.

"Baba, my Father," said the induna. "We hear your words, but like children we do not understand them."

"Who is this fellow?" Mungo demanded of Sergeant Ezra, and nodded when he heard the reply. "I know about him. He is a troublemaker." Then to Bazo, raising his voice, "What is so strange about what I say? What is it that puzzles you?"

"You say, Baba, that the sickness will kill the cattle—so before it does you will shoot them dead. You say, Baba, that to save our cattle you must kill them for us."

The quiet ranks of Matabele stirred for the first time. Though their expressions were still impassive, here a man coughed and there another shuffled his bare feet in the dust or yet another flicked his switch at the circling flies. No man laughed, not one mocked with word or smile, but it was mockery nonetheless, and Mungo St. John sensed it. Behind those inscrutable black African faces, they were gleefully following the mock humble questions of the young induna with the old, worn face.

"We do not understand such deep wisdom, Baba. Please be kind and patient with your children and explain it to us. You say that if we try to hide our cattle, then you will confiscate them from us to pay the heavy fines that Lodzi demands. You say in the same breath, Baba, that if we are obedient children and bring the cattle to you, then you will shoot them and burn them up."

In the packed ranks, an elderly whitebeard who had taken snuff sneezed loudly, and there was immediately an epidemic of sneezing and coughing. Mungo St. John knew they were encouraging the young induna in this sly impudence.

"Baba, gentle Father, you warn us that you will double our work quotas and we will be as slaves. This is another matter which escapes from us, for is a man who works one day at another's command less a slave than he who works two days? Is not a slave merely a slave—and is not a free man truly free? Baba, explain to us the degrees of slavery."

There was a faint humming sound now, like the sound of a hive at noon, and though the lips of the Matabele facing Mungo St. John did not move, he saw that their throats trembled slightly. They were beginning to drum; it was the prelude, and, unchecked, it would be followed by the deep ringing "Jee! Jee!" of the chant.

"I know you, Bazo," Mungo St. John shouted. "I hear and mark your words. Be sure that Lodzi also will hear them."

"I am honored, little Father, that my humble words will be carried to the great white father, Lodzi."

This time there were cunning and wicked grins on the faces of the men around Bazo.

"Sergeant," Mungo St. John shouted. "Bring that man to me!"

The big sergeant leaped forward with the brass badge of his rank glittering on his upper arm, but as he did so the ranks of silent Matabele rose to their feet and closed up. No man raised a hand, but the sergeant's forward rush was smothered, and he struggled in the crowd as though in living black quicksand, and when he reached the place where Bazo had been, the induna was gone.

"Very well." Mungo St. John nodded grimly when the sergeant reported back to him. "Let him go. It will wait for another day, but now we have work to do. Get your men into position."

A dozen armed black police trotted forward and formed a line facing the throng of tribesmen, holding their rifles at high port. At the same time, the rest of the contingent climbed up onto the thorny walls of the kraal, and at the command they pumped cartridges into the breeches of the repeating Winchester rifles.

"Let it begin," Mungo nodded, and the first volley of rifle fire thundered out.

The black constables were firing down into the milling mass of cattle in the kraal, and at each shot a beast would fling its horned head high and collapse, to be hidden at once by the others. The smell of fresh blood maddened the herd, and it surged wildly against the thorn barrier; the din of the blood-bellow was deafening, and from the ranks of watching Matabele went up a mourning howl of sympathy.

These animals were their wealth and their very reason for existence. As *mujiba* they had attended the birthings in the veld and helped to beat off the hyena and the other predators. They knew each animal by name and loved them with that special type of love that will make the pastoral man lay down his own life to protect his herds.

In the front rank was a warrior so old that his legs were thin as those of the marabou stork and whose skin was the color of a tobacco pouch and puckered in a network of fine wrinkles. It seemed there was no moisture left in his dried-out, ancient frame, and yet fat heavy tears rolled down his withered cheeks as he watched the cattle shot down. The crash of rifle fire went on until sunset, and when it at last was silent, the kraal was filled with carcasses. They lay upon each other in deep windrows like the wheat after the scythes have passed. Not a single Matabele had left the scene; they watched in silence now, their mourning long ago silenced.

"The carcasses must be burned." Mungo St. John strode down the front rank of warriors. "I want the carcasses covered with wood. No man is spared this labor, neither the sick nor the old. Every man will wield an ax, and when they are covered, I will put the fire to it myself."

♦ ♦ ♦

"What is the mood of the people?" Bazo asked softly, and Babiaan, the senior of all the old king's councillors, answered him. It was not lost on the others in the packed beehive thatched hut that Babiaan's tone was respectful.

"They are sick with grief," said Babiaan. "Not since the death of the old king has there been such despair in their hearts as now that the cattle are being killed."

"It is almost as though the white men wish to plunge the assegai in their own breast," Bazo nodded. "Each cruel deed strengthens us and confirms the prophecy of the Umlimo. Can there be one among you who still has doubts?"

"There are no doubts. We are ready now," replied Gandang, his father, and yet he also looked to Bazo for confirmation and waited for his reply.

"We are not ready." Bazo shook his head. "We will not be ready until the third prophecy of the Umlimo has come to pass."

" 'When the hornless cattle are eaten up by the cross,' " Somabula whispered. "We saw the cattle destroyed today, those that the pestilence has spared."

"That is not the prophecy," Bazo told them. "When it comes, there will be no doubt in our minds. Until that time we must continue with the preparations. What is the number of the spears, and where are they held?"

One by one the other indunas stood, and each made his report. They listed the numbers of warriors that were trained and ready, where each group was situated, and how soon they could be armed and in the field. When the last one had finished, Bazo went through the form of consulting the senior indunas and then gave the field commanders their objectives.

"Suku, induna of the Imbezu impi. Your men will sweep the road from the Malundi drift southward to Gwanda Mine. Kill anybody you find upon the road, cut the copper wires at each pole. The *amadoda* working at the mine will be ready to join you when you reach there. There are twenty-eight whites at Gwanda, including the women and the family at the trading post. Afterward, count the bodies to make certain that none have escaped."

Suku repeated the orders, word-perfectly, displaying the phenomenal recall of the illiterate who cannot rely on written notes, and Bazo nodded and turned to the next commander to give him his instructions and to hear them recited back to him.

It was long after midnight before all of them had received and repeated their orders, and then Bazo addressed them again.

"Stealth and speed are our only allies. No warrior will carry a shield, for the temptation to drum upon it in the old way would be too strong. Steel alone, silent steel. There will be no singing the war songs when you run, for the leopard does not growl before he springs. The leopard hunts in darkness, and when he enters the goat shed he spares nothing—as easily as he rips the throat from the billy, he kills also the nanny and the kids."

"Women?" asked Babiaan somberly.

"Even as they shot down Ruth and Imbali." Bazo nodded.

"Children?" asked another induna.

"Little white girls grow up to bear little white boys, and little white boys in their turn grow up to carry guns. When a wise man finds a mamba's lair, he kills the snake and crushes the eggs under foot."

"Will we spare none?"

"None," Bazo confirmed quietly, but there was something in his voice that made Gandang, his father, shiver. He recognized the moment when the real power shifted from the old bull to the younger. Indisputably, Bazo was now their leader.

So it was Bazo who said at last, "*Indaba pelile!* The meeting is finished!" And one by one the indunas saluted him and left the hut and slipped away into the night, and when the last was gone, the screen of goatskins at the back was pushed aside and Tanase stepped out and came to Bazo.

"I am so proud," she whispered, "that I want to weep like a silly girl."

◆ ◆ ◆

It was a long column, counting the women and children, almost a thousand human beings. It was strung out over a mile, winding like a maimed adder down out of the hills. Again custom was being flouted, for although the men led, they were burdened with grain bags and cooking pots. Of old, they would have carried only their shield and weapons. There were more than the two hundred strong men that Bazo had promised Henshaw.

The women came after them. Many of the men had brought more than one wife and some as many as four. Even the very young girls, those not yet in puberty, carried rolls of sleeping mats balanced upon their heads, and the mothers had their infants slung upon their hips so that they could suckle from a fat black breast while on the march. Juba's roll of matting was as heavy as any of them. However, despite her great bulk, the younger women had to step out to keep pace with her. Her high, clear soprano led the singing.

Bazo came back along the column at an easy lope; unmarried girls turned their heads, careful not to unbalance their burdens, to watch him as he passed, and then they whispered and giggled among themselves, for though he was ravaged and scarred, the aura of power and purpose that surrounded him was intensely attractive to even the youngest and flightiest of them.

Bazo came level with Juba and fell in at her side.

"Mamewethu." He greeted her respectfully. "The burdens of your young girls will be a little lighter after we cross the river. We will leave three hundred assegais concealed in the millet bins and buried under the goat shed of Suku's people."

"And the rest of them?" Juba asked.

"Those we will take with us to the Harkness Mine. A place of concealment has been prepared. From there your girls will take them out a few at a time to the outlying villages."

Bazo started back toward the head of the column, but Juba called him back.

"My son, I am troubled, deeply troubled."

"It grieves me, little Mother. What troubles you?"

"Tanase tells me that all the white folk are to be kissed with steel."

"All of them," Bazo nodded.

"Nomusa, who is more than a mother to me, must she die also, my son? She is so good and kind to our people."

Gently Bazo took her by the arm and led her off the path, where they could not be overheard.

"That very kindness which you speak of makes her the most dangerous of all of them," Bazo explained. "The love that you bear for her weakens us all. If I say to you, 'We will spare this one,' then you will ask, 'Can we not also spare her little son, and her daughters and their children?' " Bazo shook his head. "No, I tell you truly, if I were to spare one of them, it would be One-Bright-Eye himself."

"One-Bright-Eye!" Juba started. "I do not understand. He is cruel and fierce, without understanding."

"When our warriors look on his face and hear his voice, they are reminded once again of all the wrongs we have suffered, and they become strong and angry. When they look upon Nomusa, they become soft and hesitant. She must be among the very first to die, and I will send a good man to do that work."

"You say they must all die?" Juba asked. "This one that comes now. Will he die also?" Juba pointed ahead, where the path wound lazily beneath the spreading flat-topped acacia trees. There was a horseman cantering toward them from the direction of the Harkness Mine, and even at this distance there was no mistaking the set of his powerful shoulders and his easy and yet arrogant seat in the saddle. "Look at him!" Juba went on. "It was you who gave him the praise name of 'little Hawk.' You have often told me how as youths you worked shoulder to shoulder and ate from the same pot. You were proud when you described the wild falcon that you caught and trained together."

Juba's voice sank lower. "Will you kill this man that you call your brother, my son?"

"I will let no other do it," Bazo affirmed. "I will do it with my own hand, to make sure it is swift and clean. And after him I will kill his woman and his son. When that is done, there will be no turning back."

"You have become a hard man, my son," Juba whispered with terrible shadows of regret in her eyes and an ache in her voice.

Bazo turned away from her and stepped back onto the path. Ralph Ballantyne saw him and waved his hat above his head.

"Bazo," he laughed as he rode up. "Will I ever learn never to doubt you? You bring me more than the two hundred you promised."

◆ ◆ ◆

Ralph Ballantyne crossed the southern boundary of King's Lynn, but it was another two hours' riding before he made out the milky gray loom of the homestead kopjes on the horizon.

The veld through which he rode was silent now and almost empty. It chilled Ralph so that his expression was gloomy and his thoughts dark. Where several months ago his father's herds of plump multicolored cattle had grazed, the new grass was springing up again, dense and green and untrodden, as though to veil the white bones with which the earth was strewn so thickly.

Only Ralph's warning had saved Zouga Ballantyne from complete financial disaster. He had managed to sell off some small portion of his herds to Gwaai Cattle Ranches, a BSA Company subsidiary, before the rinderpest struck King's Lynn, but he had lost the rest of his cattle, and their bones gleamed like strings of pearls amid the new green grass.

Ahead of Ralph among the mimosa trees was one of his father's cattle posts, and Ralph stood in the saddle and shaded his eyes, puzzled by the haze of pink dust which hung over the old stockade. The dust had been raised by hooves, and there was the sharp crack of a trek whip, a sound that had not been heard in Matabeleland for many months.

Even at a distance, he recognized the figures silhouett

214

upon the railing of the stockade like a pair of scraggly old crows.

"Jan Cheroot!" he called as he rode up. "Isazi! What are you two old rogues playing at?"

They grinned at him delightedly and scrambled down to greet him.

"Good Lord!" Ralph's astonishment was unfeigned as he realized what the animals in the stockade were. The curtains of thick dust had hidden them until this minute. "Is this how you spend your time when I am away, Isazi? Whose idea is this?"

"Bakela, your father's." Isazi's expression instantly became melancholy. "And it is a stupid idea."

The fat, sleek animals were striped in vivid black and white, their manes stiff as the bristles in a chimney sweep's broom.

"Zebras, by God!" Ralph shook his head. "How did you round them up?"

"We used up a dozen good horses chasing them," Jan Cheroot explained, his leathery yellow features wrinkled with disapproval.

"Your father hopes to replace the trek oxen with these dumb donkeys. They are as wild and unreasonable as a Venda virgin. They bite and kick until you get them in the traces, and then they lie down and refuse to pull." Isazi spat with disgust.

It was manifest folly to try to bridge in a few short months the vast gap between wild animal and domesticated beast of burden. It had taken millennia of selection and breeding to develop the doughty courage, the willing heart and strong back of the draft bullock. It was a measure of the settlers' desperate need for transport that Zouga should even make the attempt.

"Isazi"—Ralph shook his head—"when you have finished this boy's game, I have man's work for you at the railhead camp."

"I will be ready to go with you when you return," Isazi promised enthusiastically. "I am sick to the stomach with striped donkeys."

Ralph turned to Jan Cheroot. "I want to talk to you, old friend." When they were well beyond the stockade, he asked the little Hottentot, "Did you put your mark on a company paper saying that we had pegged the Harkness claims in darkness?''

"I would never let you down," Jan Cheroot declared proudly. "General St. John explained to me, and I put my mark on the paper to save the claims for you and the major." He saw Ralph's expression and demanded anxiously, "I did the right thing?''

Ralph leaned out of the saddle and clasped the bony old shoulder. "You have been a good and loyal friend to me all my life.''

"From the day you were born," Jan Cheroot declared. "When your mama died, I fed you and held you on my knee.''

Ralph opened his saddlebag, and the old Hottentot's eyes gleamed when he saw the bottle of Cape brandy.

"Give a dram to Isazi," Ralph told him, but Jan Cheroot clasped the bottle to his bosom as though it were a first-born son.

"I wouldn't waste good brandy on a black savage," he declared indignantly, and Ralph laughed and rode on toward the homestead of King's Lynn.

Here there was all the bustle and excitement that he had expected. There were horses that Ralph did not recognize in the paddock below the big thatched house, and among them the unmistakable matched white mules of Mr. Rhodes's equipage. The coach itself stood under the trees in the yard, its paintwork asparkle and harness-wear carefully stacked on the racks in the saddle room beside the stables. Ralph felt his anger flare up when he saw it. His hatred burned, and he could taste the acid of it at the back of his throat. He swallowed hard to control it as he dismounted.

Two black grooms ran to take his horse. One of them unstrapped his blanket roll, his saddlebags and rifle scabbard, and ran with them up toward the big house. Ralph followed him, and he was halfway across the lawns when Zouga Ballantyne came out onto the wide stoep and with a linen table napkin shaded his eyes against the glare. He was still chewing from the luncheon table.

"Ralph, my boy. I didn't expect you until evening.''

Ralph ran up the steps and they embraced, and then Zouga took his arm and led him down the veranda. The walls were hung with trophies of the chase, the long, twisted horns of kudu and eland, the gleaming black scimitars of sable and roan antelope, and guarding each side of the double doors that led into the dining room were the immense tusks of the great bull elephant that Zouga Ballantyne had shot on the site of the Harkness Mine. These heavy, curved shafts of ivory were as tall as a man standing on tiptoe could reach and thicker than a fat lady's thigh.

Zouga and Ralph passed between them into the dining room. Under the thatch it was cool and dark after the brilliant white glare of noon. The floor was of hand-sawn wild teak, and the roof beams of the same material. Jan Cheroot had made the long refectory table and the chairs with seats of leather thonging from timber cut on the estate, but the glinting silver was from the Ballantyne family home at King's Lynn in England, a tenuous link between two places of the same name and yet of such dissimilar aspect.

Zouga's empty chair was at the far end of the long table, and facing it down the long board was the familiar massive, brooding figure that raised his shaggy head as Ralph came in from the stoep.

"Ah, Ralph, it's good to see you." It amazed Ralph that there was no rancor in either. Mr. Rhodes's voice or eyes. Could he have truly put the dispute over the Wankie coalfields out of his mind, as though it had never happened? With an effort Ralph matched his own reaction to the other man's.

"How are you, sir?" Ralph actually smiled as he gripped the broad hand with its hard, prominent knuckles. The skin was cool, like that of a reptile, the effect of the poor circulation of the damaged heart. Ralph was pleased to release it and pass on down the length of the long table. He was not certain that he could long conceal his true feelings from the close scrutiny of those hypnotic eyes.

They were all there. The suave little doctor at Mr. Rhodes's right hand, his appropriate station.

"Young Ballantyne," he said coldly, offering his hand without rising.

"Jameson!" Ralph nodded familiarly, knowing that the deliberate omission of the title would rankle him as much as the condescending "young" had annoyed Ralph.

At Mr. Rhodes's other hand was a surprising guest. It was the first time that Ralph had ever seen General Mungo St. John at King's Lynn. There had once been a relationship between the lean, grizzled soldier with the wicked single eye and Louise Ballantyne, Ralph's stepmother. That had been many years ago, long before Ralph had left Kimberley for the north.

Ralph had never entirely fathomed that relationship, nor somehow the breath of scandal clouding it. But it was significant that Louise Ballantyne was not in the room and that there was no place set at the table for her. If Mr. Rhodes had insisted that St. John be present at this gathering and Zouga Ballantyne had agreed to invite him, then there was a compelling reason for it. Mungo St. John flashed that wolfish smile at Ralph as they shook hands. Despite the family complications, Ralph had always had a sneaking admiration for this romantically piratical figure, and his answering smile was genuine.

The stature of the other men at the table confirmed the importance and significance of this gathering. Ralph guessed that the meeting was being held here to preserve the absolute secrecy that they could not have assumed in the town of Bulawayo. He guessed also that every guest had been personally selected and invited by Mr. Rhodes rather than by his father.

Apart from Jameson and St. John, there was Percy Fitzpatrick, a partner of the Corner House mining group, and prominent representative of the Witwatersrand Chamber of Mines, the organ of the gold barons of Johannesburg. He was a lively and personable young man with a fair complexion and ruddy hair and mustache, whose checkered career had included bank clerk, transport rider, citrus farmer, guide to Lord Randolph Churchill's Africa expedition, author and mining magnate. Many years later Ralph would reflect on the irony of this extraordinary man's claim to immortality being founded on a sentimental book about a dog called Jock.

Beyond Fitzpatrick sat the Honorable Bobbie White, who had just visited Johannesburg at Mr. Rhodes's suggestion. He was a handsome and pleasant young aristocrat, the type of Englishman that Mr. Rhodes preferred. He was also a staff officer and a career soldier as his mess tunic revealed.

Next to him sat John Willoughby, second-in-command of the original pioneer column which had taken occupation of Fort Salisbury and Mashonaland. He had also ridden with Jameson's column that had destroyed Lobengula, and his

Willoughby's Consolidated Company owned almost one million acres of prime pastoral land in Rhodesia, a rival to Ralph's Rholands Company, so their greetings were guarded.

Then there was Dr. Rutherford Harris, the first secretary of the British South Africa Company and a member of Mr. Rhodes's political party, in which he represented the Kimberley constituency in the Cape Parliament. He was a taciturn gray man with a sinister cast of eye, and Ralph mistrusted him as one of Mr. Rhodes's slavish minions.

At the end of the table, Ralph came face to face with his brother Jordan, and he hesitated for just a fraction of a second, until he saw the desperate appeal in Jordan's gentle eyes. Then he gripped his brother's hand briefly, but he did not smile, and his voice was cool and impersonal as he greeted him like a mere acquaintance and then took the place that a servant in a white Kanza uniform and scarlet sash had hurriedly laid beside Zouga at the head of the table.

The animated conversation that Ralph had interrupted was resumed, with Mr. Rhodes orchestrating and directing it.

"What about your trained zebras?" he demanded of Zouga, who shook his golden beard.

"It was a desperate measure and doomed from the outset. But when you consider that out of the hundred thousand head of cattle that we had in Matabeleland before the rinderpest, only five hundred or so have survived, any chance seemed worth taking."

"They say that the Cape buffalo have been wiped out utterly and completely by the disease," Dr. Jameson suggested. "What do you think, Major?"

"Their losses have been catastrophic. Two weeks ago, I rode as far north as the Pandamatenga River, where a year ago I counted herds of over five thousand together. This time I saw not a single living beast. Yet I cannot believe they are now extinct. I suspect that somewhere out there are scattered survivors, the ones that had a natural immunity, and I believe that they will breed."

Mr. Rhodes was not a sportsman; he had once said of his own brother Frank, "Yes, he's a good fellow, he hunts and he fishes—in other words, he is a perfect loafer," and this conversation about wild game bored him almost immediately. He changed it by turning to Ralph."

"Your railway line—what is the latest position, Ralph?"

"We are still almost two months ahead of our schedule," Ralph told him with a touch of defiance. "We crossed the Matabeleland border fifteen days ago—I expect as we sit here that the railhead has reached the trading post at Plumtree already."

"It's as well," Rhodes nodded. "We shall have urgent need of your line in a very short while." And he and Dr. Jim exchanged a conspiratorial glance.

When they had all relished Louise's bread-and-butter pudding, thick with nuts and raisins and running with wild honey, Zouga dismissed the servants and poured the Cognac himself while Jordan carried around the cigars. As they settled back in their seats, Mr. Rhodes made one of his startlingly abrupt changes of subject and pace, and Ralph was immediately aware that the true purpose for which he had been summoned to King's Lynn was about to be revealed.

"There is not one of you who does not know that my life's task is to see the map of Africa painted red from Cape Town to Cairo. To deliver this continent to our Queen as another jewel in her crown." His voice, which had been irritable and carping up until now, took on a strange mesmeric quality. "We men of the English-speaking Anglo-Saxon race are the first among nations, and destiny has imposed a sacred duty upon us—to bring the world to peace under one flag and one great monarch. We must have Africa, all of it, to add to our Queen's dominions. Already my emissaries have gone north to the land between the Zambezi and the Congo rivers to prepare the way." Rhodes broke off and shook his head angrily. "But all this will be of no avail if the southern tip of the continent eludes us."

"The South African Republic," said Jameson. "Paul Kruger and his little banana republic in the Transvaal." His voice was low but bitter.

"Do not be emotive, Dr. Jim," Rhodes remonstrated mildly. "Let us concern ourselves merely with the facts."

"And what are the facts, Mr. Rhodes?" Zouga Ballantyne leaned forward eagerly from the head of the table.

"The facts are that an ignorant old bigot, who believes that the rabble of illiterate Dutch nomads that he leads are the new Israelites, specifically chosen by their Old Testament God—this extraordinary personage sits astride a vast stretch of the richest part of the African continent like an unkempt and savage hound with a bone and growls at all efforts at progress and enlightenment.''

They were all silenced by this bitter invective, and Mr. Rhodes looked around at their faces before he went on.

''There are thirty-eight thousand Englishmen on the goldfields of Witwatersrand, Englishmen who pay nineteen of every twenty pounds of the revenue that flows into Kruger's coffers, Englishmen who are responsible for every bit of civilization in that benighted little republic, and yet Kruger denies them the franchise—they are taxed mercilessly and denied representation. Their petitions for the vote are greeted in the Volksraad by the contemptuous derision of a motley assembly of untutored oafs.'' Rhodes glanced at Fitzpatrick. ''Am I being unfair, Percy? You know these people, you live with them on a day-to-day basis. Is my description of the Transvaal Boer accurate?''

Percy Fitzpatrick shrugged. ''Mr. Rhodes is correct. The transvaal Boer is a different animal from his Cape cousins. The Cape Dutch have had the opportunity of absorbing some of the qualities of the English way of life. By comparison they are an urbane and civilized people, while the Transvaaler has unfortunately lost none of the traits of his Dutch ancestry: he is slow, obstinate, hostile, suspicious, cunning and malevolent. It galls a man to be told to go to hell by that ilk, especially when we ask only for our rights as free men, the right to vote.''

Mr. Rhodes, not long to be denied the floor, went on.

''Not only does Kruger insult our countrymen, but he plays other more dangerous games. He has discriminated against British goods with punitive tariffs. He has given trade monopolies in all essential mining goods, even dynamite, to members of his family and government. He is blatantly arming his burghers with German guns and building a corps of German Krupp artillery, and he is openly flirting with the Kaiser.'' Rhodes paused. ''A German sphere of influence in the midst of Her Majesty's domains would forever damn our dreams of a British Africa. The Germans do not have our altruism.''

''All that good yellow gold going to Berlin,'' Ralph mused softly, and immediately regretted having spoken, but Mr. Rhodes did not seem to have heard, for he went on.

"How to reason with a man like Kruger? How can one even talk to a man who still believes implicitly that the earth is flat?"

Mr. Rhodes was sweating again, although it was cool in the room. His hand shook so that as he reached for his glass, he knocked it over, and the golden Cognac spread across the polished tabletop. Jordan rose quickly and mopped it up before it could cascade into Mr. Rhodes's lap, and then he took a silver pillbox from his fob pocket and from it took a white tablet and placed it close to Mr. Rhodes's right hand. The big man took it, and still breathing heavily, placed it under his tongue. After a few moments, his breathing eased and he could speak again.

"I went to him, gentlemen. I went to Pretoria to see Kruger at his own home. He sent a message with a servant that he could not see me that day."

They had all of them heard this story; their surprise was only that Mr. Rhodes could recount such a humiliating incident. President Kruger had sent a black servant to one of the richest and influential men in the world with this message: "I am rather busy at the moment. One of my burghers has come to discuss a sick ox with me. Come back on Tuesday."

"God knows"—Dr. Jim intervened to break the embarrassed silence—"Mr. Rhodes has done everything a reasonable man could. To risk further insult from this old Boer could bring discredit not only on Mr. Rhodes personally, but on our Queen and her Empire." The little doctor paused and looked at each of his listeners in turn. Their faces were rapt; they waited intently for his next words. "What can we do about it? What *must* we do about it?"

Mr. Rhodes shook himself and looked at the young staff officer in his resplendent mess tunic.

"Bobbie?" he said in invitation.

"Gentlemen, you may be aware that I have just returned from the Transvaal." Bobbie White lifted a leather briefcase from the floor beside his chair to the table and from it produced a sheaf of crisp white paper. He passed a sheet to every man at the table.

Ralph glanced at his copy and started slightly. It was the order of battle of the army of the South African Republic. His surprise was so intense that he missed the first part of what Bobbie White was saying.

"The fort at Pretoria is under repair and extension. The walls have been breached for this purpose and will be entirely vulnerable to a small, determined force." Ralph had to force himself to believe what he was hearing. "Apart from the corps of artillery, there is no regular standing army. As you can see from the paper before you, the Transvaal depends upon its citizen commandos for defense. It requires four to six weeks for them to assemble into an effective force."

Bobbie White finished his recital, and Mr. Rhodes turned from him to Percy Fitzpatrick.

"Percy?" he invited.

"You know what Kruger calls those of us whose capital and resources have developed his gold mining industry for him? He calls us the 'Uitlanders,' the 'Outlanders,' the 'Foreigners.' You know also that we Outlanders have elected our own representatives, which we call the 'Johannesburg Reform Committee.' I have the honor to be one of the elected members of that committee, and so I speak for every Englishman in the Transvaal." He paused and carefully dressed his mustache with his forefinger, and then went on. "I bring you two messages. The first is short and simple. It is: 'We are determined and united in the cause. You may rely upon us to the utmost.' "

The men about the table nodded, but Ralph felt his skin tingle. They were taking this seriously—it was not some boyish nonsense. They were plotting one of the most audacious acts of piracy in history. He kept his expression serious and calm with an enormous effort as Fitzpatrick went on.

"The second message is in the form of a letter signed by all the members of the Reform Committee. With your permission I shall read it to you. It is addressed to Dr. Jameson in his capacity as Administrator of Rhodesia, and it reads as follows:

Johannesburg.

"Dear Sir,
The position of matters in this state has become so critical that we are assured that at no distant period there will be a conflict between the Transvaal Government and the Uitlander population" . . .

As the letter unfolded, Ralph recognized that it was a justification for armed insurrection.

"A foreign corporation of Germans and Hollanders is controlling our destinies and in conjunction with the Boer Leaders endeavouring to cast them in a mould which is wholly alien to the genius of the British peoples" . . .

They were going to try to take by force of arms the richest gold reef in existence. Ralph sat bemused.

"When our petition for franchise was debated in the Transvaal Volksraad, one member challenged the Uit-landers to fight for the rights they asked for, and not a single member spoke against him. The Transvaal Government has called into existence all the elements necessary for armed conflict.

"It is under these circumstances that we feel constrained to call upon you, as an Englishman, to come to our aid should a disturbance arise. We guarantee any expense you may incur by helping us, and we ask you to believe that nothing but the sternest necessity has prompted this appeal."

Percy Fitzpatrick looked up at Dr. Jim and then finished. "It is signed by all the members of the committee: Leonard, Phillips, Mr. Rhodes's brother Frank, John Hays Hammond, Farrar and myself. We have not dated it."

At the head of the table, Zouga Ballantyne let out his breath in a low whistle, but nobody else spoke while Jordan rose and passed down the table refilling each glass from the crystal decanter. Mr. Rhodes was slumped forward over the table, his chin resting on the heel of his hand, staring out of the windows down across the lawns toward the far blue line of hills, the Hills of the Indunas, where once the Matabele king's kraal had stood. Everybody at the table waited for him, until at last he sighed heavily.

"I much prefer to find a man's price, and pay it, rather than to fight him, but we are not dealing with a normal man here. God save us all from saints and fanatics; give me a solid rogue every time." His head turned toward Dr.

Jameson, and the dreaming blue eyes focused. "Dr. Jim," he invited, and the little doctor rode his chair back on its hind legs and thrust his hands deep into his pockets.

"We will need to send five thousand rifles and a million rounds of ammunition into Johannesburg."

Intrigued and fascinated despite himself, Ralph interrupted to ask, "Where will you—where will we get those? They are not common trade goods."

Dr. Jim nodded. "That's a good question, Ballantyne. The rifles and ammunition are already in the mine stores of De Beers at Kimberley."

Ralph blinked; the plot was far advanced, further than he had believed possible. Then he recalled the little doctor's suspicious behavior at the base camp from which they had discovered the Harkness reef. They must have been busy for months. He must find out all the details.

"How will we get them into Johannesburg? They'll have to be smuggled in, and it's a bulky shipment—"

"Ralph," Mr. Rhodes smiled. "You didn't really believe you were invited here for a social luncheon. Who would you judge to be the most experienced of us in shipping weapons? Who carried the Martini rifles to Lobengula? Who is the shrewdest transport operator on the subcontinent?"

"Me?" Ralph was startled.

"You," agreed Mr. Rhodes, and as Ralph stared at him, he felt a sudden unholy excitement welling up within him. He was to be at the center of this fantastic conspiracy, privy to every detail. His mind began to race; he knew intuitively that this was one of the opportunities that comes a man's way once in a lifetime, and he had to wring from it every last advantage.

"You will do it, of course?" A small shadow passed across the penetrating blue eyes.

"Of course," said Ralph, but the shadow persisted. "I am an Englishman. I know my duty," Ralph went on quietly and sincerely, and he saw the shadow clear from Mr. Rhodes's eyes. That was something he could believe in, something he could trust. He turned back to Dr. Jameson.

"I'm sorry," Mr. Rhodes said. "We interrupted you."

And Jameson went on: "We will raise a mounted force of around six hundred picked men here—" and he looked at John Willoughby and Zouga Ballantyne, both of them proven soldiers. "I will rely heavily on you two."

Willoughby nodded, but Zouga frowned and said, "Six hundred men will take weeks to ride from Bulawayo to Johannesburg."

"We will not start from Bulawayo," Jameson replied evenly. "I have the approval of the British Government to maintain a mobile armed force in Bechuanaland, on the railway concession strip which runs down the border of the Transvaal. The force is for the protection of the railway, but it will be based at Pitsani, a mere one hundred eighty miles from Johannesburg. We can be there in fifty hours' hard riding, long before the Boers could raise any kind of resistance."

It was at that moment that Ralph realized that it was feasible. Given Dr. Leander Starr Jameson's legendary luck, they could pull it off. They could take the Transvaal with the same ease as they had seized Matabeleland from Lobengula.

By God, what a prize that would be! A billion pounds sterling in gold annexed to Rhodes's own land, Rhodesia. After that everything else was possible—British Africa, a whole continent. Ralph was stunned at the magnitude of the design.

It was Zouga Ballantyne again who unerringly identified the fatal flaw in the scheme. "What is the position of Her Majesty's Government? Will they support us?" he asked. "Without them it will all be in vain."

"I have just returned from London," Mr. Rhodes replied. "While I was there, I dined with the colonial secretary, Mr. Joseph Chamberlain. As you know, he has instilled a new spirit of vigor and determination into Downing Street. He is in complete sympathy with the plight of our subjects in Johannesburg. He is also fully aware of the dangers of German intervention in southern Africa. Let me just assure you all that Mr. Chamberlain and I understand each other. I can say no more at this stage; you must trust me."

If that is true, Ralph thought, then the chances of complete success were better than even. The swift thrust to the heart of the unprepared enemy, the uprising of armed citizenry, the appeal to a magnanimous British Government, and finally the annexation.

As he listened to the planning, Ralph was swiftly calculating the consequences of the successful outcome of the plot. The chief of these were that the British South Africa Company and De Beers Consolidated Mines Company would become the richest and most powerful commercial enterprises on the face of the earth, and they were Mr. Rhodes's alter ego. Ralph's anger and hatred returned so fiercely that his hands trembled, and he had to place them carefully in his lap, but still he could not prevent himself glancing at his younger brother.

Jordan was staring at Mr. Rhodes with such an expression of naked adoration that Ralph was certain that every other man at the table must see it too, and he was sickened with shame. He need not have concerned himself; they were all caught up in the glory and grandeur of one man's dream, carried forward by the charisma and compelling leadership of the shaggy colossus at the head of the table.

Yet it was still Zouga the pragmatic soldier who probed for flaws and faults.

"Dr. Jim, will you be raising all six hundred men here in Rhodesia?" he asked.

"For reasons of secrecy and expediency, we cannot raise them in Cape Colony, or anywhere else, for that matter." Jameson nodded. "With the rinderpest scourge having swept away their fortunes, there will be that number and more of young Rhodesians eager to enlist if only for the pay and the rations, and all of them will be good fighting men who rode against the Matabele."

"Do you think it wise to leave this country stripped bare of its able-bodied men?"

Mr. Rhodes frowned quickly as he intervened. "It would be only for a few short months, and we do not have an enemy to fear, do we?"

"Don't we?" Zouga asked. "There are tens of thousands of Matabele—"

"Oh, come now, Major," Jameson cut in. "The Matabele are a defeated and disorganized rabble. General St. John will be acting Administrator of the territory in my absence; perhaps he is the best person to set your fears at rest."

They all looked to the tall man at Jameson's side, and Mungo St. John removed the long cheroot from his mouth and smiled, crinkling the corner of his single eye.

"I have two hundred armed native police whose loyalty is unquestioned. I have informers placed in every large

Matabele village who will give me warning of any stirrings. No, Major, I give you my assurance that the only enemy we need take into account is the obstinate old Boer in Pretoria.''

"I accept that from a soldier of General St. John's caliber,'' said Zouga simply, and turned back to Mr. Rhodes. ''Can we discuss the details of raising this force—how much money do we have at our disposal?''

Ralph watched their faces as they planned and argued and with surprise saw that his own father's was as greedy and eager as any of them. Whatever words came from their mouths, Ralph thought, whatever they seem to be talking about, what they are actually talking about is money.

Suddenly Ralph remembered that dawn over the barren Karroo when he had knelt alone in the desert and sworn an oath, calling on God to witness it, and he now had to use all his willpower to prevent himself from looking up at Mr. Rhodes. He knew that this time he could not conceal it from him, so he kept his eyes on the crystal glass of Cognac in front of him while he strove for self-control and forced himself to think dispassionately.

If it was possible to destroy this giant of a man, was it not also possible to destroy his company, to wrest from it the powers of government and the land rights and the mineral rights that it held over all Rhodesia?

Ralph felt the thrill of it humming through his blood as he realized that this might be not only the chance for fierce vengeance but also for vast fortune within his grasp. If the plot failed, then the shares of the gold mining companies involved—Corner House mining group, Rand Mines, Consolidated Goldfields—would all crash with it. A simple bear coup on the Johannesburg Stock Exchange could net millions of pounds.

Ralph Ballantyne felt a sense of awe at the magnitude of the prospect that faced him, a prospect of power and wealth such as he had never dreamed of until this moment. He almost missed the question, and looked up when Mr. Rhodes repeated it.

''I said, how soon can you leave for Kimberley to take charge of the shipments, Ralph?''

''Tomorrow,'' Ralph replied evenly.

Mr. Rhodes nodded. ''I knew we could rely upon you.''

Ralph had lingered deliberately to be the last to leave King's Lynn. Now he and his father stood on the veranda and watched the dust column raised by Mr. Rhodes's mule coach dwindling away down the hill. Ralph leaned against one of the whitewashed pillars that supported the roof, with his sunbrowned, muscular arms folded across his chest and his eyes crinkled against the spiraling smoke of the cheroot between his teeth.

"You aren't naïve enough to accept young Percy's estimate of the Boers, are you, Papa?"

Zouga chuckled. "Slow, suspicious, malevolent and all that nonsense." He shook his head. "They ride hard and shoot straight, they have fought every black tribe south of the Limpopo—"

"Not to mention our own soldiers," Ralph reminded him. "Majuba Hill, 1881. General Colley and ninety of his men are buried on the peak; the Boers didn't lose a single man."

"They are good soldiers," Zouga admitted, "but we will have surprise on our side."

"However, you do agree that it will be an act of international banditry, Papa?" Ralph removed the cheroot from his mouth and tapped off the ash. "We won't have one shred of moral justification for it."

Ralph watched the scar on Zouga's cheek turn white as bone china. It was an infallible barometer of his mood.

"I do not understand," Zouga said, but they both knew he understood perfectly.

"It's robbery," Ralph persisted. "Not just a little footpaddery, but robbery on the grand scale. We are plotting to steal a country."

"Did we then steal this land from the Matabele?" Zouga demanded.

"That was different." Ralph smiled. "They were pagan savages, but here we are planning to overthrow a government of fellow Christians."

"When we consider the greater good of the Empire—" Zouga's scar had turned from icy white to crimson.

"Empire, Papa?" Ralph was still smiling. "If there are two people who should be entirely honest with each other, they are you and me. Look at me and tell me straight that there will be no profit in it for us—other than the satisfaction of having done our duty to the Empire."

But Zouga did not look at him. "I am a soldier—"

"Yes." Ralph cut him short. "But you are also a rancher who has just come through the rinderpest. You managed to sell five thousand head of cattle, but we both know that was not enough. How much do you owe, Papa?"

After a moment's hesitation, Zouga told him grudgingly. "Thirty thousand pounds."

"Do you have any expectation of paying off those debts?"

"No."

"Not unless we take the Transvaal?"

Zouga did not reply, but the scar faded and he sighed.

"All right," Ralph told him. "I just wanted to be certain that I was not alone in my motives."

"You will go through with it?" Zouga asked.

"Don't worry, Papa. We'll come out of it, I promise you that." Ralph pushed himself away from the pillar and called to the grooms to bring his horse.

From the saddle he looked down at his father and for the first time noticed how the weariness of age had faded the green of his eyes.

"My boy, just because some of us will be rewarded for our endeavors, it does not mean that the enterprise is not a noble one. We are the servants of the Empire, and faithful servants are entitled to a fair wage."

Ralph reached down and clasped his shoulder, then he picked up the reins and rode down the hill through the acacia forests.

◆ ◆ ◆

The railhead was feeling its way up the escarpment like a cautious adder, often following the ancient elephant roads, for these huge beasts had pioneered the easiest gradients and the gentlest passes. It had left the swollen baobabs and yellow fever trees of the Limpopo basin far below, and the forests were lovelier, the air sweeter, and the streams clearer and colder.

Ralph's base camp had moved up with the railhead into one of the secluded valleys, just out of earshot of the hammers of the gangs driving the steel spikes into the teak railway ties. The spot had many of the charms of the remote wilderness. In the evenings a herd of sable antelope came down to feed in the grass glade below the camp, and the barking of baboons from the hills roused them each dawn. Yet the telegraph hut at the railhead was ten minutes' stroll away, around the foot of the wooded hill, and the locomotive bringing up the rails and ties from Kimberley delivered as well the latest copy of the *Diamond Fields Advertiser* and any other small luxuries that the camp required.

In an emergency Cathy would have the railway overseer and any men of his gang to call upon, while the camp itself was protected by twenty loyal Matabele servants and Isazi, the little Zulu driver, who pointed out modestly that he alone was worth twenty more of the bravest Matabele. In the unlikely event of Cathy becoming lonely or bored, the Harkness Mine was only thirty miles away, and Harry and Vicky promised to ride across every weekend.

"Can't we come with you, Daddy?" Jonathan pleaded. "I could help you, really I could."

Ralph lifted him into his lap. "One of us has to stay and look after Mama," he explained. "You are the only one I can trust."

"We can take her with us," Jonathan suggested eagerly, and Ralph had a vision of his wife and child in the midst of an armed revolution, with barricades in the streets and Boer commandos ravaging the countryside.

"That would be very nice, Jon-Jon," Ralph agreed, "but what about the new baby? What happens if the stork arrives here while we are all away and there is nobody to sign for your little sister?"

Jonathan scowled. He was already developing a healthy dislike for this not yet arrived but eternally present female personage. She seemed to stand squarely in the way of every pleasant prospect or exciting plan; both parents managed to introduce his darling sister into almost every conversation, and his mother spent much of the time formerly devoted to Master Jonathan's interests in knitting and sewing or just sitting smiling to herself. She no longer went out riding with him each morning and evening, nor indulged in those rowdy romps which he enjoyed so heartily. Jonathan had in fact already consulted Isazi on the possibility of getting a message to the stork and telling him not to bother, that they had changed their minds. However, Isazi had not been very encouraging, although he had promised to have a word with the local witch doctor on Jonathan's behalf.

Now confronted once more with that ubiquitous female, Jonathan capitulated with poor grace.

"Well, can I come with you when my baby sister is here to look after Mama?"

"I tell you what, old fellow, I'll do better than that. How would you like to go on a big boat across the sea?" This was the kind of talk Jonathan preferred, and his face lit up.

"Can I sail it?" he demanded.

"I'm sure the captain will let you help him," Ralph chuckled. "And when we get to London, we will stay in a big hotel and we will buy all sorts of presents for your mama."

Cathy dropped her knitting into her lap and stared at him in the lamplight.

"What about me?" Jonathan demanded. "Can we buy all sorts of presents for me, too?"

"And for your baby sister," Ralph agreed. "Then when we come back, we will go to Johannesburg, and we will buy a big house with shining chandeliers and marble floors."

"And stables for my pony." Jonathan clapped his hands.

"And a kennel for Chaka." Ralph ruffled his curls. "And you will go to a fine brick school with lots of other little boys." Jonathan's grin wavered slightly; that was perhaps carrying things a little too far, but Ralph stood him on his feet again, slapped his backside lightly and told him, "Now go and kiss your mother goodnight, and ask her to tuck you up in your cot."

Cathy hurried back from the nursery tent, moving with the appealing awkwardness of her pregnancy into the firelight, and she came to where Ralph sat in the canvas folding chair with his boots stretched to the blaze and the whisky glass in his hand. She stopped behind his chair, put both arms around his neck and, with her lips pressed to his cheek, whispered, "Is it true, or are you just teasing me?"

"You have been a good, brave girl for long enough. I'm going to buy you a home that you didn't dare even dream about."

"With chandeliers?"

"And a carriage to take you to the opera."

"I don't know if I like opera—I've never been to one."

"We'll find out in London, won't we?"

"Oh, Ralph, I'm so happy I think I could cry. But why now? What has happened to make it all change?"

"Something is going to happen before Christmas that is going to change our lives. We are going to be rich."

"I thought we were already rich?"

"I mean really rich, the way Robinson and Rhodes are rich."

"Can you tell me what it is?"

"No," he said simply. "But you only have a few short weeks to wait, just until Christmas."

"Oh, darling," she sighed. "Will you be away that long? I miss you so."

"Then let's waste no more precious time talking." He stood up, picked her up in his arms, and carried her carefully to the bell tent under the spreading wild fig tree.

In the morning Cathy stood with Jonathan beside her, holding his hand to restrain him, and they looked up at Ralph on the footplate of the big green locomotive.

"We always seem to be saying good-bye." She had to raise her voice above the hiss of steam from the driving wheels and the roar of the flames in the firebox.

"It's the last time," Ralph promised her.

How handsome and gay he was; it made her heart swell until it threatened to choke her.

"Come back to me as soon as you can."

"I will, just as soon as I can." The engine driver pulled down the brass throttle handle, and the huff of steam drowned Ralph's next words.

"What? What did you say?" Cathy trotted heavily beside the locomotive as it began to trundle down the steel tracks.

"Don't lose the letter," he repeated.

"I won't," she promised, and then the effort of keeping level with the rolling locomotive became too much. She came up short and waved with the white lace handkerchief until the curve in the southbound tracks carried the train out of sight beyond the heel of a kopje and the last mournful sob of its steam whistle died on the air. Then she turned back to where Isazi waited with the trap. Jonathan wrested his hand from hers and raced ahead to scramble up onto the seat.

"Can I drive them, Isazi?" he pleaded, and Cathy felt a prick of anger at the fickleness of boyhood—one moment tearful and bereft, the next shrieking with the prospect of handling the reins.

As she settled onto the buttoned leather rear seat of the trap, she slipped her hand into the pocket of her apron to check that the sealed envelope that Ralph had left with her was still safe. She drew it out and read the tantalizing instruction he had written upon the face: "Open only when you receive my telegraph."

She was about to return it to her pocket; then she bit her lip, fighting the temptation, and at last ran her fingernail under the flap, splitting it open, and drew out the folded sheet.

Upon receiving my telegraph, you must send the following telegraph immediately and urgently: "To Major Zouga Ballantyne. Headquarters of Rhodesian Horse Regiment at Pitsani Bechuanaland: Your wife Mrs. Louise Ballantyne gravely ill. Return immediately Kings Lynn."

Cathy read the instruction twice and suddenly she was deadly afraid.

"Oh, my mad darling, what are you going to do?" she whispered, and Jonathan urged the horses into a trot back along the track toward the camp.

◆ ◆ ◆

The workshops of the Simmer and Jack Gold Mine stood below the steel headgear on the crest of the ridge. The town of Johannesburg sprawled away in the low valley and over the farther rounded hills. The workshop was roofed and walled with corrugated iron, and the concrete floor was stained with black puddles of spilled engine oil. It was oven-hot under the iron, and beyond the big double sliding doors at the end of the shed, the sunlight of early summer was blinding.

"Close the doors," Ralph Ballantyne ordered, and two of the small group went to struggle with the heavy wood and iron structures, grunting and sweating with unaccustomed physical effort. With the doors closed, it was gloomy as a Gothic cathedral, and the white beams of sunlight through chinks in the iron walls were filled with swirling dust motes.

Down the center of the floor stood a row of fifty yellow drums. Stenciled on each lid in black paint were the words "Heavy Duty Engine Oil. 44 gals."

Ralph slipped off his beige linen jacket, pulled down the knot of his necktie and rolled up his shirt sleeves. He selected a two-pound hammer and a cold chisel from the nearest workbench and started to hack open the lid of the nearest drum. The four other men crowded closer to watch. The hammer strokes echoed hollowly about the long shed. The yellow paint flew off in tiny flakes beneath the chisel, and the raw metal was bright as newly minted shillings.

At last Ralph prized open the half-severed lid and bent it back. The surface of the oil glimmered glutinous and coal-black in the poor light; Ralph thrust his right arm into it as far as the elbow and drew out a long oilskin-wrapped bundle dripping with the thick oil. He carried it to the workbench and slit the binding with the chisel, and there were exclamations of satisfaction as he stripped away the covering.

"The very latest Lee Metford bolt-action rifles firing the new smokeless cordite load. There is no other rifle in the world to match it."

They passed the weapon from hand to hand, and when it reached Percy Fitzpatrick, he rattled the bolt, opening and closing it rapidly.

"How many?"

"Ten to a drum," Ralph answered. "Fifty drums."

"And the rest of them?" demanded Frank Rhodes. He was as unlike his younger brother as Ralph was to Jordan. A tall, lean man with deepset eyes and high cheekbones, his graying hair receded from a deep, bony forehead.

"I can bring through a shipment every week for the next five weeks," Ralph told him, wiping his greasy hands on a ball of cotton waste.

"Can you do it quicker than that?"

"Can you clean and distribute them quicker than that?" Ralph countered, and without waiting for a reply, turned to John Hays Hammond, the brilliant American mining engineer whom he trusted more than Mr. Rhodes's effete brother.

"Have you decided on the final plan of action?" he asked. "Mr. Rhodes will want to know when I return to Kimberley."

"We will seize the Pretoria fort and the arsenal as our first objective," Hays Hammond told him, and they fell

235

into a detailed discussion with Ralph scribbling notes on the back of a cigarette packet. When at last Ralph nodded and stuffed the packet into his back pocket, Frank Rhodes demanded:

"What is the news from Bulawayo?"

"Jameson has his men, over six hundred of them. They are mounted and armed. He will be ready to move southward to Pitsani on the last day of the month; that's his latest report." Ralph shrugged on his jacket again. "It will be wiser if we are not seen together."

He returned to shake hands with each of them, but when he reached Colonel Frank Rhodes, he could not resist the temptation to add, "It would also be wiser, Colonel, if you could limit your telegraph messages to essentials only. The code you are using, the daily references to this fictitious gold mine flotation of yours, is enough to attract the attention of even the most dim-witted of the Transvaal police agents, and we know for certain that there is one in the Johannesburg telegraph office."

"Sir, we have indulged in no unnecessary traffic," Frank Rhodes replied stiffly.

"Then how do you rate your latest effort? *'Are the six hundred northern shareholders in a position to take up their debentures?'*" Ralph mimicked his prim, old-maidish diction, then nodded farewell and went out to where his horse was tethered and rode down the road to Fordsberg Dip and the city.

◆　◆　◆

Elizabeth rose at a glance from her mother and began to gather up the soup bowls.

"You haven't finished, Bobby," she told her young brother.

"I'm not hungry, Lizzie," the child protested. "It tastes funny."

"You always have an excuse not to eat, Master Robert," Elizabeth scolded him. "No wonder you are so skinny; you'll never grow up strong and tall like your Papa."

"That's enough, Elizabeth," Robyn spoke sharply. "Leave the boy if he's not hungry. You know he isn't well."

Elizabeth glanced at her mother, then dutifully stacked Robert's bowl with the others. None of the girls had ever been allowed to leave food, not even when they were giddy

236

with malaria, but she had learned not to protest the unfairness of Robyn's indulgence of her only son. With the kerosene lantern in her other hand, Elizabeth went out of the back door and crossed to the thatched kitchen hut.

"It is time she had a husband." Juba shook her head mournfully. "She needs a man in her bed and a baby at her breast to make her smile."

"Don't talk nonsense, Juba," snapped Robyn. "There will be time for that later. She is doing important work here; I could not let her go. She is as good as a trained doctor."

"The young men come out from Bulawayo one after the other, and she sends them all away," Juba went on, ignoring Robyn's injunction.

"She's a sensible, serious girl," Robyn agreed.

"She is a sad girl—with a secret."

"Oh, Juba, not every woman wants to spend her life as some man's chattel," Robyn scoffed.

"Do you remember when she was a girl?" Juba went on, unperturbed. "How bright she was, how she shone with joy, how she sparkled like a drop of morning dew."

"She has grown up."

"I thought it was the tall young rock finder, the man from across the sea who took Vicky away." Juba shook her head. "It was not him. She laughed at Vicky's wedding, and it was not the laughter of a girl who has lost her love. It is something else," Juba decided portentously, "or somebody else."

Robyn was about to protest further, but she was interrupted by the sound of excited voices in the darkness outside the door, and she stood up quickly.

"What is it?" she called. "What is happening out there, Elizabeth?" And the flame of the lantern came bobbing back across the yard, lighting Elizabeth's flying feet but leaving her face in darkness.

"Mama! Mama! Come quickly!" Her voice rang with excitement. Elizabeth burst in through the door.

"Control yourself, girl." Robyn shook her shoulder, and Elizabeth took a deep breath.

"Old Moses has come up from the village—he says that there are soldiers, hundreds of soldiers riding past the church."

"Juba, get Bobby's coat." Robyn took her woolen shawl

and her cane down from behind the door. "Elizabeth, give me the lantern!"

Robyn led the family down the driveway under the dark spathodea trees, past the godowns of the hospital, toward the church. They went in a small, tight group, with Bobby bundled up in a woolen coat riding on Juba's fat hip, but before they reached the church, there were many other dark figures hurrying along in the darkness around them.

"They are coming out of the hospital." Juba was righteously indignant. "And tomorrow they will all be sick again."

"You'll never stop them," Elizabeth sighed with resignation. "Curiosity killed the cat." And then she exclaimed, "There they are! Moses was right—just look at them!"

The starlight was bright enough to reveal the torrent of dark horsemen pouring down the road from the neck of the hills. They rode two abreast and a length between each rank. It was too dark to see their faces under the broad brims of their slouch hats, but a rifle barrel stuck up like an accuser's finger behind each man's shoulder, silhouetted against the frosty fields of stars that filled the heavens. The deep dust of the track muffled the hooves to a soft, floury puffing sound, but the saddles squeaked with the rub of dubbined leather and a curb chain tinkled as a horse snorted softly and tossed its head.

Yet the quiet was uncanny for such a multitude. No voice raised above a whisper, no orders to close up, not even the usual low warning, " 'Ware hole!" of massed horsemen moving in formation across unfamiliar terrain in darkness. The head of the column reached the fork in the road below the church, but took the lefthand turning, the old wagon road toward the south.

"Who are they?" Juba asked with a thrill of superstitious awe in her voice. "They look like ghosts."

"Those aren't ghosts," Robyn said flatly. "Those are Jameson's tin soldiers; that's his new Rhodesian Horse Regiment."

"Why are they taking the old road?" Elizabeth, too, spoke in a whisper, infected by Juba and by the unnatural quiet. "And why are they riding in the dark?"

"This stinks of Jameson—and his master." Robyn stepped forward to the edge of the road, lifting the lantern above her head. "Where are you going?" she called loudly.

A low voice from the column answered her: "There and back to see how far it is, missus!" and there were a few low chuckles, but the column flowed on past the church without a check.

In the center of the column were the transports, seven wagons drawn by mules, for the rinderpest had left no draft-oxen. After the wagons came eight two-wheeled carts with canvas covers over the Maxim machine guns, and then three light field guns, relics of Jameson's expeditionary force that had captured Bulawayo a few short years ago. The tail of the column was again made up of mounted men, two abreast.

It took almost twenty minutes for them all to pass the church, and then the silence was complete, with just the taint of dust in the air as a reminder of their going. The patients from the hospital began to slip away from the roadside, back into the darker shadows beneath the spathodea trees, but the little family group stayed on silently, waiting for Robyn to move.

"Mummy, I am cold," Bobby whined at last, and Robyn roused herself.

"I wonder what devilry they are up to now," she murmured, and led them back up the hill toward the homestead.

"The beans will be cold by now," Elizabeth complained as she hurried back into the kitchen hut, while Robyn and Juba climbed up the steps onto the stoep.

Juba let Bobby down from her hip, and he scampered back into the warm lamplight of the dining room. Juba was about to follow him, but Robyn stopped her with a hand upon her forearm. The two women stood together, close and secure in the love and companionship they bore each other. They looked out across the valley in the direction in which the dark and silent horsemen had disappeared.

"How beautiful it is!" Robyn murmured. "I always think of the stars as my friends, they are so constant, so well remembered, and tonight they are so close." She lifted her hand as though to pluck them from the firmament. "There is Orion, and there is the bull."

"And there Manatassi's four sons," Juba said, "the poor murdered babes."

"The same stars." Robyn hugged Juba closer to her. "The same stars shine upon us all, even though we know them by different names. You call those four white stars Manatassi's Sons—but we call them the Cross. The Southern Cross."

She felt Juba start and then began to shiver, and Robyn's voice was instantly concerned. "What is it, my little Dove?" she asked.

"Bobby was right," whispered Juba. "It is cold; we should go in now." She sat silent during the rest of the meal, but when Elizabeth took Bobby through to his bedroom, she said simply, "Nomusa, I must go back to the village."

"Oh, Juba, you have only just returned—whatever is the matter?"

"I have a feeling, Nomusa, a feeling in my heart that my husband needs me."

"Men," said Robyn bitterly. "If we could only be shot of all of them—life would be so much simpler if we women ran the world."

◆ ◆ ◆

"It is the sign," whispered Tanase, holding her son to her bosom, and the light from the smoky little fire in the center of the hut left her eyes in shadow like those of a skull. "It is always the way with the prophecy of the Umlimo—the meaning becomes clear only when the events come to pass."

"The wings in the dark noon"—Bazo nodded—"and the cattle with their heads twisted to touch their flanks, and now—"

"And now the cross has eaten up the hornless cattle, the horsemen have gone south in the night. It is the third, the last sign for which we waited," Tanase exulted softly. "The spirits of our ancestors urge us on. The time of waiting is over."

"Little Mother, the spirits have chosen you to make their meaning clear. Without you we would never have known what the white men call those four great stars. Now the spirits have other work for you. You are the one who knows where they are, you know how many are at Khami Mission."

Juba looked at her husband, and her lips trembled, her

great dark eyes were swimming with tears. Gandang nodded to her to speak.

"There is Nomusa," she whispered. "Nomusa, who is more than a mother and a sister to me. Nomusa, who cut the chain that held me in the slave ship—"

"Put those thoughts from your mind," counseled Tanase gently. "There is no place for them now. Tell us who else is at the mission."

"There is Elizabeth, my gentle, sad Lizzie, and Bobby, who I carry upon my hip."

"Who else?" Tanase insisted.

"There are no others," Juba whispered.

Bazo looked at his father.

"They are yours, all of them at Khami Mission. You know what must be done."

Gandang nodded, and Bazo turned back to his mother.

"Tell me, sweet little Mother." His voice sank to a soothing rumble. "Tell me about Bakela, the Fist, and his woman. What news do you have of him?"

"Last week he was in the big house at King's Lynn, he and Balela, the One Who Brings Clear and Sunny Skies."

Bazo turned to one of the other indunas who sat in the rank behind Gandang.

"Suku!"

The induna rose on one knee.

"Baba?" he asked.

"Bakela is yours, and his woman," Bazo told him. "And when you have done that work, go on to Hartley Hills and take the miners there; there are three men, and a woman with four whelps."

"Nkosi Nkulu," the induna acknowledged the order, and no one queried or demurred when he called Bazo, "Nkosi Nkulu! King!"

"Little Mother, where is Henshaw and his woman, who is the daughter of Nomusa?"

"Nomusa had a letter from her three days ago. She is at the railhead, she and the boy. She carries an infant, which will be born about the time of the *Chawala* festival. She wrote of her great joy and happiness."

"And Henshaw?" Bazo asked patiently. "What of Henshaw?"

"In the letter she said he was with her, the source of her happiness. He may still be with her."

241

"They are mine," Bazo said. "They and the five white men who are at the railhead. Afterward we will sweep up the wagon road and take the two men and the woman and three children at Antelope Mine." He went on quietly allocating a task to each of his commanders. Each farm and lonely mine was given to one of them with a recountal of the victims to be expected there. The telegraph lines were to be cut, the native police were to be executed, the drifts were to be guarded; all the wagon roads had to be swept for travelers, firearms collected and livestock carried off and hidden. When he had finished, he turned to the women.

"Tanase, you will see to it that all our own women and children go into the ancient place of sanctuary; you yourself will lead them into the sacred hills of the Matopos. You will make certain that they stay in small groups, each well separated from the others, and the *mujiba*, the young boys not yet initiated, will watch from the hilltops against the coming of the white men. The women will have the potions and the *muti* ready for those of our men who are wounded."

"Nkosi Nkulu," said Tanase after each instruction, and she watched his face, trying not to let her pride and her wild exultation show. "King!" she called him, as the other indunas had done.

Then the telling of it was over, and they waited for one thing more. The silence in the hut was strained and intense, the white of eyes gleaming in faces of polished ebony as they waited, and at last Bazo spoke.

"By tradition, on the night of the *Chawala* moon, the sons and daughters of Mashobane, of Mzilikazi and of Lobengula, should celebrate the Festival of the First Fruits. This season there will be no cobs of corn to reap, for the locusts have reaped them for us. This season there will be no black bull for the young warriors to kill with their bare hands, for the rinderpest has done their work for them."

Bazo slowly looked about the circle of their faces.

"So on the night of this *Chawala* moon, let it begin. Let the storm rage. Let the eyes turn red. Let the young men of Matabele run!"

"Jee!" hummed Suku in the second rank of indunas, and "Jee!" old Babiaan took up the war chant, and then they were all swaying together with their throats straining and their eyes bulging redly in the firelight with the divine fighting madness coming down upon them.

The ammunition was the most time-consuming of the stores to handle, and Ralph was limited to twenty trusted men to do the work for him.

There were ten thousand rounds in each iron case, with the "W.D." and arrow impressed upon its lid. They were secured with a simple clip that could be knocked open with a rifle butt. The British Army always learned its lessons the hard way. They had learned this one at Isandhlwana, the Hill of the Little Hand, on the frontier of Zululand, when Lord Chelmsford left a thousand men at his base camp while he took a flying column to bring the Zulu indunas to battle. Avoiding contact with the column, the indunas doubled back and stormed the base camp. Only when the swarming impis broke through the perimeter did the quartermasters realize that Chelmsford had taken the keys for the ammunition chests with him. Isazi, Ralph's little Zulu driver, had given him an eyewitness account of the end.

"They were tearing at the boxes with axes, with bayonets and with their bare hands. They were swearing and screaming with rage and chagrin when we brought the assegais to them, and at the last they tried to defend themselves with their empty rifles." Isazi's eyes had gone misty with the memory, the way an old man recalls a lost love. "I tell you, little Hawk, they were brave men, and it was a beautiful stabbing."

Nobody could be certain how many Englishmen had died at the Little Hand, for it was almost a year before Chelmsford retook the field, but it was one of the most terrible disasters of British military history, and immediately after it the War Office redesigned their ammunition chests.

Now the fact that the .303 ammunition was packed in these W.D. chests was some indication of how deep was the understanding between Mr. Rhodes and the colonial secretary in Whitehall. However, the bulk packets had to be broken down and repacked in waxed paper, one hundred rounds to the packet, then these had to be soldered into tin sheets before going into the oil drums. It was an onerous task, and Ralph was pleased to escape for a few hours from the workshops of the De Beers Consolidated Mines Company where it was being done.

Aaron Fagan was waiting for him in his office, with his coat on and his derby hat in his hand.

"You are becoming a secretive fellow, Ralph," he accused. "Couldn't you have given me some idea of what you expect?"

"You will learn that soon enough," Ralph promised, and put a cheroot between his lips. "All I want to know from you is that this fellow is trustworthy, and discreet."

"He is the eldest son of my own sister," Aaron bridled, and Ralph struck a match to the end of the cheroot to calm him.

"That is all very well, but can he keep his mouth shut?"

"I will stake my life on it."

"You may have to," Ralph told him dryly. "Well, let us go to visit this paragon."

David Silver was a plump young man with a scrubbed complexion, gold-rimmed pince-nez and his hair glossy with brilliantine and parted down the center so that his scalp gleamed in the division. He deferred courteously to his Uncle Aaron and went to pains to make certain that both his guests were comfortable, that their chairs were arranged with the light from the windows falling from behind, and that each of them had an ashtray beside him and a cup of tea in his hand.

"It's orange pekoe," he pointed out modestly as he settled beside his desk. Then he placed his fingertips together, pursed his lips primly, and looked expectantly at Ralph.

While Ralph briefly explained his requirements, he nodded his head brightly and made little sucking sounds of encouragement.

"Mr. Ballantyne"—he kept nodding like a mandarin doll when Ralph had finished—"that is what we stockbrokers"—he spread his hand deprecatingly—"in our jargon call a 'bear position' or 'selling short.' It is quite a commonplace transaction."

Aaron Fagan squirmed a little in his chair and glanced apologetically at Ralph. "David, I think Mr. Ballantyne knows—"

"No, no"—Ralph raised a hand to Aaron—"please let Mr. Silver continue. I am sure his discourse will be enlightening." His expression was solemn, but his eyes twinkled with amusement. The irony was lost on David Silver and he accepted Ralph's invitation.

"It is an entirely short-term speculative contract. I always make a point of mentioning this to any of my clients who contemplate entering into one. To be entirely truthful, Mr. Ballantyne, I do not approve of this speculation. I always feel that the stock exchange is a venue for legitimate investment, a market where capital can meet and mate with legitimate enterprise. It should not have been made into a bookmakers' turf, where sportsmen bet on dark horses."

"That is a very noble thought," Ralph agreed.

"I am glad you see it that way." David Silver puffed out his cheeks pompously. "However, to return to the operation of selling shares short. The client enters the market and offers to sell shares of a specified company which he does not possess, at a price below the current market price, for delivery at some future date, usually one to three months ahead."

"Yes," Ralph nodded solemnly. "I think I follow so far."

"Naturally the expectation of the bear operator is that the shares will fall considerably in value before he is obliged to deliver them to the purchaser. From his point of view, the larger the fall in value the greater will be his profit."

"Ah!" said Ralph. "An easy way to make money."

"On the other hand"—David Silver's plump features became stern—"should the shares rise in value, the bear operator will incur considerable losses. He will be forced to re-enter the market and buy shares at the inflated prices to make good his delivery to the purchaser, and naturally he will be paid only the previously agreed price."

"Naturally!"

"Now you can see why I try to discourage my clients from engaging in these dealings."

"Your uncle assured me that you were a prudent man."

David Silver looked smug. "Mr. Ballantyne, I think you should know that there is a buoyant mood in the market. I have heard it rumored that some of the Witwatersrand companies will be reporting highly elevated profits this quarter. In my view this is the time to buy gold shares, not to sell them."

"Mr. Silver, I am a terrible pessimist."

"Very well." David Silver sighed with the air of a superior being inured to the intractability of the common man.

"Will you tell me exactly what you have in mind, please, Mr. Ballantyne?"

"I want to sell the shares of two companies short," Ralph told him. "Consolidated Goldfields and the British South Africa Company."

An air of vast melancholy came over David Silver. "You have chosen the strongest companies on the board—those are Mr. Rhodes's enterprises. Did you have a figure in mind, Mr. Ballantyne? The minimum lot that can be traded is one hundred shares—"

"Two hundred thousand," said Ralph mildly.

"Two hundred thousand pounds!" gasped David Silver.

"Shares," Ralph corrected him.

"Mr. Ballantyne." Silver had paled. "BSA is standing at twelve pounds and Consolidated at eight. If you sell two hundred thousand shares—well, that is a transaction of two million pounds."

"No, no!" Ralph shook his head. "You misunderstand me."

"Thank the good Lord for that." A little color flowed back into David Silver's chubby cheeks.

"I meant not two hundred thousand in total, but two hundred thousand in each company. That is four million pounds' worth altogether."

David Silver sprang to his feet with such alacrity that his chair flew back against the wall with a crash, and for a moment it seemed that he might try to escape out into the street.

"But," he blubbered, "but—" And then he could think of no further protest. His pince-nez misted, and his lower lip stuck out like a sulky child's.

"Sit down," Ralph ordered gently, and he sank back miserably into his chair.

"I will have to ask you to make a deposit." Silver made one last effort.

"How much will you need?"

"Forty thousand pounds."

Ralph opened his checkbook on the edge of the desk and took one of David Silver's pens from the rack. The squeak of the nib was the only sound in the little hot office until Ralph sat back and fanned the check to dry the ink.

"There is just one thing more," he said. "Nobody outside these four walls—nobody—is ever to know that I am the principal in this transaction."

"You have my word."

"Or your testicles," Ralph warned him as he leaned close to hand him the check, and though he smiled, his eyes were such a cold green that David Silver shivered, and he felt a sharp pang of anticipation in his threatened parts.

◆ ◆ ◆

It was a typical highveld Boer homestead set on a rocky ridge above an undulating treeless plain of silver grass. The roof was of galvanized corrugated iron which had begun to rust through in patches. The house was surrounded by wide verandas, and the whitewash was discolored and flaking from the wall. There was a windmill on a skeletal tower behind the house. The vanes blurred against the pale, cloudless sky, spinning in the dusty wind, and at each weary crank of the plunger, a cupful of cloudy green water spilled into the circular concrete cistern beside the kitchen door.

There was no attempt at a garden or lawn. A dozen scrawny speckled fowls scratched at the bare baked earth or perched disconsolately on the derelict Cape wagon and the other ruined equipment that always seemed to ornament the yard of every Boer homestead. On the side of the prevailing wind stood a tall Australian eucalyptus tree with the old bark hanging in tatters from the silver trunk like the skin of a molting serpent. In its scant shade were tethered eight sturdy brown ponies.

As Ralph dismounted below the veranda, a pack of mongrel hounds came snapping and snarling about his boots, and he scattered them yelping and howling with a few kicks and a hissing cut from his hippo-hide sjambok.

"*U kom 'n bietjie laat, meneer.*" A man had come out onto the veranda. He was in shirt sleeves, with suspenders holding up the baggy brown trousers that left his bare ankles exposed. On his feet, he wore rawhide velskoen without socks.

"*Jammer.*" Ralph apologized for being late, using the simplified form of Dutch, which the Boer called the *taal*, the language.

The man held the door open for Ralph, and he stooped through it into the windowless living room. It smelled of stale smoke and dead ash from the open fireplace. The floor was covered with rush mats and animal skins. There was a single table down the center of the room, of heavy, crudely fashioned dark wood. There was a single hanging on the wall opposite the fireplace, an embroidered copy of the ten commandments in High Dutch script. The only book in the room lay open on the bare tabletop. It was an enormous Dutch Bible with leather cover and bindings of brass.

On leather-thonged chairs, eight men sat along the length of both sides of the table. They all looked up at Ralph as he entered. There was not a man among them younger than fifty years old, for the Boers valued experience and acquired wisdom in their leaders. Most of them were bearded, and all of them wore rough, hard-worn clothing and were solemn and unsmiling. The man who had greeted Ralph followed him in and silently indicated an empty chair. Ralph sat down, and every shaggy, bearded head turned away from him toward the figure at the end of the table.

He was the biggest man in the room, monumentally ugly, as a bulldog or one of the great anthropoids is ugly. His beard was a gray, scraggly fringe, but his upper lip was shaven. His face hung in folds and bags; the skin was darkly burned by ten thousand fierce African suns, and it was lumped and stained with warts and with the speckles of benign skin cancer. One eyelid drooped, giving him a crafty, suspicious expression. His brown eyes had also been affected by the white sun glare of Africa, and by the scouring dust of the hunting veld and the battlefield, so they were now perpetually bloodshot, sore and inflamed-looking. His people called him Oom Paul, Uncle Paul, and held him in only slightly less veneration than they did their Old Testament God.

Paul Kruger began to read aloud again from the open Bible before him. He read slowly, following the text with his finger. The thumb was missing from his hand. It had been blown off by a bursting gun barrel thirty years before. His voice was a rumbling basso profundo.

"Nevertheless the people be strong that dwell in the land, and the cities are walled and very great: and moreover we saw the children of the Anak there . . .

248

And Caleb stilled the people, and said; Let us go up at once and possess it, for we are well able to overcome it."

Ralph watched him intently, studying the huge, slumped body, the shoulders so wide that the ugly head seemed to perch upon them like a bedraggled bird on a mountaintop, and he thought of the legend that surrounded this strange man.

Paul Kruger had been nine years old when his father and uncles had packed their wagons and gathered their herds and trekked northward, away from British rule, driven on by the memory of their folk heroes hanged at Slachters Nek by the redcoats. The Krugers trekked from the injustice of having their slaves turned free, from the English black circuit courts, from judges who did not speak their language, from taxes levied on land that was theirs, and from the foreign troops who seized their beloved herds to pay those taxes.

The year had been 1835, and on that hard trek, Paul Kruger became a man at an age when most boys are still playing with kites and marbles. Each day he was given a single bullet and a charge of powder and sent out to provide meat for the family. If he failed to bring back a buck, his father beat him. He became, by necessity, an expert marksman.

It was one of his duties to scout ahead for water and good grazing and to lead the caravan to it. He became a skilled horseman and developed an almost mystical affinity for the veld and the herds of fat-tailed sheep and multihued cattle that were his family's wealth. Like a Matabele *mujiba*, he knew every beast by name and could pick out an ailing animal from the herd at a mile distant.

When Mzilikazi, the Matabele emperor, sent his impis with their long shields swarming down upon the little caravan of wagons, little Paul took his place with the other men at the barricades. There were thirty-three Boer fighting men inside the circle of wagons. The wagon trucks were lashed together with trek chains and the openings between the wheels latticed with woven thorn branches.

The Matabele *amadoda* were uncountable. Regiment after regiment they charged, hissing their deep ringing "Jee!" They attacked for six hours without respite, and when the bullets ran low, the Boer women smelted and cast lead in the midst of the battle. When the Matabele fell back at last, their dead lay chest-deep around the wagons and little Paul had become a man, for he had killed a man—many men.

Strangely, it was another four years before he killed his first lion, sending a hardened ball through its heart as it sprang upon his horse's back. By now he was able to test a new horse by galloping it over broken ground. If it fell, young Paul would land catlike, on his feet, shake his head with disapproval, and walk away. When hunting buffalo he would mount facing his horse's tail so as to have a steadier shot when the beasts chased his horse, as they invariably did. This unusual seat in no way hampered his control of the horse, and he could change to face ahead so swiftly and smoothly as not to upset his mount's stride in full gallop.

About this time he showed a gift of extrasensory powers. Before a hunt, standing at his horse's head, he would go into a self-induced trance and begin describing the surrounding countryside and the wild animals in it. "One hour's ride to the north, there is a small muddy pan. A herd of quaggas are drinking there, and five fat eland are coming down the path to the water. On the hill above it, under a camel thorn tree, a pride of lions are resting—'n ou swart maanhaar, an old blackmane, and two lionesses. In the valleys beyond, three giraffes." The hunters would find the animals, or the signs they had left, exactly as young Paul described them.

At sixteen, he was entitled, as a man, to ride off two farms, as much land as a horseman could encircle in a day. Each of them was approximately sixteen thousand acres. They were the first of the vast land holdings he acquired and held during his lifetime, sometimes bartering sixteen thousand acres of prime pasture for a plow or a bag of sugar.

At twenty he was a field cornet, an elected office which was something between magistrate and sheriff; at such tender years to be chosen by men who venerated age marked him as somebody unusual. About this time he ran a footrace against a horseman on a picked steed over a course of a mile, and won by a length. Then during a battle against the black chief Sekukuni, the Boer general was shot through the head and tumbled over the edge of the kopje. The general was a big, bulky man, two hundred and forty pounds weight, but Paul Kruger leaped down the krantz, picked up the body, and ran back up the hillside under the musket fire of Sekukuni's men.

When he set off to claim his bride, he found his way blocked by the wide Vaal River in raging spate, the carcasses of cattle and wild game rolling by in the flood. Despite cries of warning from the ferryman, and without even removing his boots, he urged his horse into the brown waters and swam across. Flooded rivers would not stop a man like Paul Kruger.

After having fought Moshesh and Mzilikazi and every other warlike tribe south of the Limpopo River, after having burned Dr. David Livingstone's mission on the suspicion that he was supplying arms to the tribes, after having fought even his own people, the rebellious Boers of the Orange Free State, he was made Commandant-in-Chief of the Army, and still later the President of the South African Republic.

It was this indomitable, courageous, immensely physically powerful, ugly, obstinate, devout and cantankerous old man, rich in land and herds, who now lifted his head from the Bible and finished his reading with a simple injunction to the men who waited upon him attentively.

"Fear God, and distrust the English," he said, and closed the Bible.

Then still without taking his bloodshot eyes from Ralph's face, he bellowed with shocking force, "Bring coffee!" and a colored maid bustled in with a tin tray loaded with steaming mugs. The men around the table exchanged pouches of black Magaliesberg shag and charged their pipes, watching Ralph with closed and guarded expressions. Once the oily blue smoke had veiled the air, Kruger spoke again.

"You asked to see me, *mijn heer?*"

"Alone," said Ralph.

"These men I trust."

"Very well."

They used the *taal*. Ralph knew that Kruger could speak English with some fluency, and that he would not do so as a matter of principle. Ralph had learned to speak the *taal* on the diamond diggings. It was the simplest of all European languages, suited to the everyday life of an uncomplicated society of hunters and farmers, though even they, for the purposes of political discussion or worship, fell back upon the sophistication of High Dutch.

"My name is Ballantyne."

"I know who you are. Your father was the elephant hunter. A strong man, they say, and straight—but you"—and now a world of loathing entered the old man's tone—"you belong to that heathen, Rhodes." And though Ralph shook his head, he went on, "Do not think I have not heard his blasphemies. I know that when he was asked if he believed there was a God, he replied"—and here he broke into heavily accented English for the first time—" 'I give God a fifty-fifty chance of existing.' " Kruger shook his head slowly. "He will pay for that one day, for the Lord has commanded, 'Thou shalt not take My name in vain.' "

"Perhaps that day of payment is already at hand," said Ralph softly. "And perhaps you are God's chosen instrument."

"Do you dare to blaspheme, also?" the old man demanded sharply.

"No." Ralph shook his head. "I come to deliver the blasphemer into your hands." And he laid an envelope on the dark wood, then with a flick slid it down the length of the table until it lay in front of the President. "A list of the arms he has sent secretly into Johannesburg and where they are held. The names of the rebels who intend to use them. The size and force of the commando gathered on your borders at Pitsani, the route they will take to join the rebels in Johannesburg, and the date on which they intend to ride."

Every man at the table had stiffened with shock; only the old man still puffed calmly at his pipe. He made no effort to touch the envelope.

"Why do you come to me with this?"

"When I see a thief about to break into a neighbor's home, I take it as my duty to warn him."

Kruger removed the pipe from his mouth and flicked a spurt of yellow tobacco juice from the stem onto the dung-floor beside his chair.

"We are neighbors," Ralph explained. "We are white men living in Africa. We have a common destiny. We have many enemies, and one day we may be required to fight them together."

Kruger's pipe gurgled softly, but nobody spoke again for fully two minutes until Ralph broke the silence.

"Very well then," he said. "If Rhodes fails, I will make a great deal of money."

Kruger sighed and nodded. "All right, now I believe you at last, for that is an Englishman's reason for treachery." And he picked up the envelope in his brown, gnarled old hand. "Good-bye, *mijn heer*," he said softly.

◆ ◆ ◆

Cathy had taken to her paint box again. She had put it away when Jon-Jon was born, but now there was time for it once more. However, this time she was determined to make a more serious work of it, instead of sugary family portraits and pretty landscapes.

She had begun a study of the trees of Rhodesia and already had a considerable portfolio of them. First she painted the entire tree, making as many as twenty studies of typical specimens before settling on a representative example, and then to the master painting she added detailed drawings of the leaves, the flowers and the fruits, which she rendered faithfully in watercolors; finally she pressed actual leaves and blooms and gathered the seeds, then wrote a detailed description of the plant.

Very soon she had realized her own ignorance, and had written to Cape Town and London for books on botany and for Linnaeus' *Systema Naturae* for plants. Using these, she was training herself to become a competent botanist. Already she had isolated eight trees that had not been previously described, and she had named one for Ralph—*Terminalia ralphii*—and another for Jonathan, who had climbed to the upper branches to bring down its pretty pink flowers for her.

When she diffidently sent some of her dried specimens and a folio of drawings to Sir Joseph Hooker at Kew Gardens, she received an encouraging letter, complimenting her on the standard of her artwork and confirming her classifications of the new species. With the letter was an autographed copy of his *Genera Plantarum*—"to a fellow student of nature's wonders"—and it had become the start of a fascinating correspondence. The new hobby was one that could be practiced side by side with Jon-Jon's bird nesting activities, and it helped fill the dreary days when

253

Ralph was away, although now she had difficulty keeping up with Jon-Jon, her swollen belly reducing her to an undignified waddle. She had to leave all the climbing and rock scrambling to him.

This morning they were working one of the kloofs of the hills above the camp where they had found a beautiful spreading tree with strange candelabra of fruit on the upper branches. Jonathan was twenty feet above ground, edging out to snatch a laden branch when Cathy heard voices calling in the thick bush that clogged the mouth of the kloof. She swiftly rebuttoned her blouse and dropped her skirts down over her bare legs—the heat was oppressive in the confined gully between the hills, and she had been sitting on the bank and dabbling her feet in the trickle of the stream.

"Yoo hoo!" she yodeled, and the telegraph operator came sweating and scrambling up the steep side.

He was a dismal shrimp of a man, with a bald head and protruding eyes, but he was also one of Cathy's most fervent admirers. The arrival of a telegraph for her was an excuse for him to leave his hut and seek her out. He waited adoringly with his hat in his hands and she read the message.

PASSAGE RESERVED UNION CASTLE LEAVING CAPE TOWN FOR LONDON MARCH 20TH STOP OPEN ENVELOPE AND FOL-LOW INSTRUCTIONS CAREFULLY STOP HOME SOON LOVE RALPH.

"Will you send a telegraph for me, Mr. Braithwaite?"

"Of course, Mrs. Ballantyne, it will be a great pleasure." The little man blushed like a girl and hung his head bashfully.

Cathy wrote out the message recalling Zouga Ballantyne to King's Lynn on a sheet of her sketch pad, and Mr. Braithwaite clutched it to his concave chest like a holy talisman.

"Happy Christmas, Mrs. Ballantyne," he said, and Cathy started. The days had gone by so swiftly, she had not realized that the year 1895 was so far gone. Suddenly the prospect of Christmas alone in the wilderness, another Christmas without Ralph, appalled her.

"Happy Christmas, Mr. Braithwaite," she said, hoping

he would leave before she began to cry. Her pregnancy made her so weak and weepy—if only Ralph would come back. If only . . .

◆ ◆ ◆

Pitsani was not a town, nor even a village. It was a single trading store standing forlornly in the flat sand veld on the edge of the Kalahari Desert that stretched away fifteen hundred miles to the west. However, it was only a few miles to the frontier of the Transvaal, but no fence or border post marked the division. The country was so flat and featureless and the scrub so low that the rider could see the trading store from a distance of seven miles, and around it, shimmering like ghosts in the heat mirage, the little cone-shaped white tents of an army encamped.

The rider had pushed his horse mercilessly along the thirty miles from the railway at Mafeking, for he bore an urgent message. He was an unlikely choice for a peace messenger, for he was a soldier and a man of action. His name was Captain Maurice Heany, a handsome man with dark hair and mustaches and flashing eyes. He had served with Carrington's horse and the Bechuana police, and in the Matabele war he had commanded a troop of mounted infantry. He was a hawk, and he bore the message of a dove. The sentries picked up his dust from two miles out, and there was a small bustle as the guard was called out.

When Heany trotted into the camp, all its senior officers were already gathered at the command tent, and Dr. Jameson himself came forward to shake his hand and lead him into the tent, where they were screened from curious eyes. Zouga Ballantyne poured Indian tonic onto a dram of gin and brought it to him.

"Sorry, Maurice, this is not the Kimberley Club; I'm afraid we have no ice."

"Ice or not, you have saved my life."

They knew each other well. Maurice Heany had been one of Ralph Ballantyne's and Harry Johnston's junior partners when they had contracted to bring the original pioneer column into Mashonaland.

Heany drank and wiped his mustache before looking up at John Willoughby and the little doctor. He was in a quandary as to whom he should address his message to, for although Willoughby was the regimental commander and

Zouga Ballantyne his second-in-command, and although Dr. Jameson was officially only a civilian observer, they all knew with whom the ultimate decision making and authority lay.

Jameson smoothed his embarrassment by ordering directly, "Well, then, out with it, man."

"It's not good news, Dr. Jim. Mr. Rhodes is utterly determined that you must remain here until after the Reform Committee has captured Johannesburg."

"When will that be?" Jameson demanded bitterly. "Just look at these!" He picked up a sheaf of telegraph flimsies from the camp table. "A new telegraph every few hours, in Frank Rhodes's execrable code. Take this one, yesterday." Jameson read aloud: " *'It is absolutely necessary to delay floating until company letterhead agreed upon.'* " Jameson dropped the telegraphs back on the table with disgust. "This ridiculous quibbling over what flag to fly. Damn me, but if we aren't doing this for the Union Jack, then what are we doing it for?"

"It is rather like the timorous bride who, having set the date, views the approach of the wedding day with delicious confusion," Zouga Ballantyne smiled. "You must remember that our friends on the Reform Committee in Johannesburg are more used to stock deals and financial speculation than the use of steel. Like the blushing virgin, they may need a little judicial forcing."

"That's it exactly," Dr. Jameson nodded. "And yet Mr. Rhodes is concerned that we should not move ahead of them."

"There is one other thing that you should know." Heany hesitated. "It does seem that the gentlemen in Pretoria are aware that something is afoot. There is even talk that there is a traitor among us."

"That is unthinkable," snapped Zouga.

"I agree with you, Zouga," Dr. Jim nodded. "It is much more likely that these damned puerile telegraphs of Frank Rhodes's have come to old Kruger's notice."

"Be that as it may, gentlemen. The Boers are making certain preparations—it is even possible that they have already called out their commandos in the Rustenburg and Zeerust divisions."

"If that is the case," Zouga said softly, "then we have a

choice. We can either move immediately, or we can all go home to Bulawayo."

Dr. Jameson could not remain seated any longer; he jumped up from his canvas chair and began pacing up and down the tent with quick, jerky little strides. They all watched in silence until he stopped in the opening of the tent and stared out across the sun-scorched plain toward the eastern horizon beneath which lay the great golden prize of the Witwatersrand. When at last he turned to face them, they could see that he had reached his decision.

"I am going," he said.

"Thought you would," murmured Zouga.

"What are you going to do?" Jameson asked as softly.

"Going with you," said Zouga.

"Thought you would," said Jameson, and then glanced at Willoughby, who nodded.

"Good! Johnny, will you call the men out? I would like to speak to them before we ride—and Zouga, will you see to it that the telegraph lines are all cut? I don't want ever to see another one of those communications from Frankie. Anything more he has to say, he can tell me face to face when we reach Johannesburg."

◆ ◆ ◆

"They've got Jameson!" The cry echoed through the elegant hush of the Kimberley Club like a Hun war cry at the gates of Rome.

The consternation was immediate and overwhelming. Members boiled out of the long bar into the marbled lobby and surrounded the news crier. Others, from the reading room, lined the banisters, shouting their queries down the stairwell. In the dining room, someone bumped into the carving wagon in his haste to reach the lobby and sent it crashing on its side, while the joint rolled across the floor with roast potatoes preceding it like a squad of footmen.

The bearer of the news was one of the prosperous Kimberley diamond buyers, a profession no longer referred to as "kopje walloping," and such was his agitation that he had forgotten to remove his straw boater when entering the club portals, an offense that at another time would have merited a reprimand from the committee.

Now he stood in the center of the lobby, hat firmly on his head and reading spectacles sliding to the end of his empurpled nose, a symptom of his excitement and agitation. He was reading from a copy of the *Diamond Fields Advertiser,* the ink of which was so fresh that it smeared his fingers: "Jameson raises White Flag at Doornkop after sixteen killed in fierce fighting. Dr. Jameson, I have the honor to meet you. General Cronje accepts surrender."

Ralph Ballantyne had not left his seat at the head of the corner table, although his guests had deserted him to join the rush into the lobby. He signaled the distracted wine waiter to refill his glass and then helped himself to another spoonful of the *sole bonne femme* while he waited for his guests to return. They came trooping back, led by Aaron Fagan, like a funeral party returning from the cemetery.

"The Boers must have been waiting for them—"

"Dr. Jim walked straight into it—"

"What on earth did the man think he was doing?"

Chairs rasped, and every one of them reached for his glass the moment he was seated.

"He had six hundred sixty men and guns. By God, it was a carefully planned thing then."

"There will be a few tales to tell."

"And heads to roll, no doubt."

"Dr. Jim's luck has run out at last."

"Ralph, your father is among the prisoners!" Aaron was reading the newsprint.

For the first time, Ralph showed emotion. "That's not possible." He snatched the paper from Aaron's hand and stared at it in agony.

"What happened?" he muttered. "Oh God, what has happened?" But somebody else was yelling in the lobby.

"Kruger has arrested all the members of the Reform Committee—he has promised to have them tried for their lives."

"The gold mines!" another said clearly in the ensuing silence, and instinctively every head lifted to the clock on the wall above the dining-room entrance. It was twenty minutes to two. The stock exchange reopened on the hour. There was another rush, this time out of the club doors. On the sidewalk hatless members shouted impatiently for their carriages while others set out at a determined trot toward the stock exchange buildings.

The club was almost deserted; not more than ten diners were left at the tables. Aaron and Ralph were alone at the corner table. Ralph still held the list of prisoners in his hand.

"I cannot believe it," he whispered.

"It's a catastrophe. What can possibly have possessed Jameson?" Aaron agreed.

It seemed that the worst had happened—nothing could match the dreadful tidings that they had received so far— but then the club secretary came out of his office ashen-faced and stood in the doorway of the dining room.

"Gentlemen," he croaked. "I have some more terrible news. It has just come through on the wire. Mr. Rhodes has offered his resignation as Prime Minister of Cape Colony. He has also offered to resign from the chairmanship of the Charter Company, of De Beers and of Consolidated Gold-fields."

"Rhodes," Aaron whispered. "Mr. Rhodes was in it. It's a conspiracy—the Lord only knows what will be the final consequences of this thing and who Mr. Rhodes will bring down with him."

"I think we should order a decanter of port," said Ralph as he pushed his plate away from him. "I'm not hungry anymore."

He thought about his father in a Boer prison, and suddenly an image came into his mind of Zouga Ballantyne in a white shirt, his hands bound behind his back, his gold- and silver-laced beard sparkling in the sunlight, the whitewashed wall at his back, regarding the rank of riflemen in front of him with those calm green eyes of his. Ralph felt nauseated, and the rare old port tasted like quinine on his tongue. He set the glass down.

"Ralph." Aaron was staring at him across the table. "The bear transaction—you sold the shares of Charter and Consolidated short, and your position is still open."

◆ ◆ ◆

"I have closed all your transactions," said David Silver. "I averaged out BSA shares at a little over seven pounds; that gives you a profit, after commission and levy, of almost four pounds a share. You did even better on the Consolidated Goldfields transactions; they were the worst hit in the crash—from eight pounds when you began selling them short, they dropped to almost two pounds when it looked as though Kruger was going to seize the mining companies of the Witwatersrand in retaliation.'' David Silver broke off and looked at Ralph with awe. "It is the kind of killing which becomes a legend on the floor, Mr. Ballantyne. The frightful risk you took." He shook his head in admiration. "What courage! What foresight!"

"What luck!" said Ralph impatiently. "Do you have my difference check?"

"I have." David Silver opened the black leather valise in his lap and brought from it a snowy white envelope sealed with a rosette of scarlet wax.

"It is countersigned and guaranteed by my bank." David laid it reverently upon his Uncle Aaron's desk top. "The total is"—and he breathed it like a lover—"one million and fifty-eight pounds eight shillings and sixpence. After the one that Mr. Rhodes paid to Barney Barnato for his claims in the Kimberley Mine, it is the largest check ever drawn in Africa south of the equator—what do you say to that, Mr. Ballantyne!"

Ralph looked at Aaron in the chair behind the desk. "You know what to do with it. Just be certain it can never be traced back to me."

"I understand," Aaron nodded, and Ralph changed the subject.

"Has there been an answer to my telegraph yet? My wife is not usually so slow in replying." And because Aaron was an old friend who loved the gentle Cathy as much as any of her many admirers, Ralph went on to explain. "She is within two months of her time. Now that the dust of Jameson's little adventure has begun to settle and there is no longer any danger of war, I must get Cathy down here where she can have expert medical attention."

"I'll send my clerk to the telegraph office." Aaron rose and crossed to the door of the outer office to give his instructions. Then he looked back at his nephew. "Was there anything else, David?" The little stockbroker started. He had been staring at Ralph Ballantyne with the glow of hero worship in his eyes. Now he hastily assembled his papers and stuffed them into his valise before coming and offering his soft white hand to Ralph.

"I cannot tell you what an honor it has been to be associated with you, Mr. Ballantyne. If there is ever anything at all I can do for you—"

Aaron had to shoo him out of the door.

"Poor David," he murmured as he came back to the desk. "His very first millionaire; it's a watershed in any young stockbroker's life."

"My father—" Ralph did not even smile.

"I'm sorry, Ralph. There is nothing more we can do. He will go back to England in chains with Jameson and the others. They are to be imprisoned in Wormwood Scrubs until they are called to answer the charge." Aaron selected a sheet of paper from the pile on his desk. " *'That they, with certain other persons in the month of December 1895, in South Africa, within Her Majesty's dominions, did unlawfully prepare and fit out a military expedition to proceed against the dominions of a certain friendly state, to wit, the South African Republic, contrary to the provisions of the Foreign Enlistment Act of 1870.'* "

Aaron laid down the paper and shook his head. "There is nothing any of us can do now."

"What will happen to them? It's a capital offense—"

"Oh no, Ralph, I am sure it won't come to that."

Ralph sank down in his chair and stared moodily out of the window, for the hundredth time castigating himself for not having anticipated that Jameson would cut the telegraph lines before marching on Johannesburg. The recall that Cathy had sent to Zouga Ballantyne, the fiction that Louise was gravely ill, had never reached him, and Zouga had ridden into the waiting Boer commandos with the rest of them.

If only, Ralph thought, and then his thoughts were interrupted. He looked up expectantly as the clerk came hesitantly into the office.

"Has there been a reply from my wife?" Ralph demanded, and the man shook his head.

"Begging your pardon, Mr. Ballantyne, sir, but there has not."

He hesitated, and Ralph urged him: "Well, man, what is it? Spit it out, there's a good fellow."

"It seems that all the telegraph lines to Rhodesia have been down since noon on Monday."

"Oh, so that is it."

"No, Mr. Ballantyne, that's not all. There has been a message from Tati on the Rhodesian border. It seems a rider got through this morning." The clerk gulped. "This messenger seems to have been the only survivor."

"Survivor!" Ralph stared at him. "What does that mean? What on earth are you talking about?"

"The Matabele have risen. They are murdering all the whites in Rhodesia—man, woman and child, they are being slaughtered!"

◆ ◆ ◆

"Mummy, Douglas and Suss aren't here. There is nobody to get me breakfast." Jon-Jon came into the tent while Cathy was still brushing out her hair and twisting it up into thick braids.

"Did you call for them?"

"I called and called."

"Tell one of the grooms to go down and fetch them, darling."

"The grooms aren't here also."

"The grooms aren't here either," Cathy corrected him, and stood up. "All right, then, let's go and see about your breakfast."

Cathy stepped out into the dawn. Overhead the sky was a lovely, dark rose color shaded to ripe orange in the east, and the bird chorus in the trees above the camp was like the tinkle of silver bells. The campfire had died to a puddle of powdery ash and had not been replenished.

"Put some wood on, Jon-Jon," Cathy told him, and crossed to the kitchen hut. She frowned with annoyance. It was deserted. She took down a tin from the gauzed meat safe and then looked up as the doorway darkened.

"Oh, Isazi," she greeted the little Zulu. "Where are the other servants?"

"Who knows where a Matabele dog will hide himself when he is needed?" Isazi asked contemptuously. "They have most likely spent the night dancing and drinking beer, and now their heads are too heavy to carry."

"You'll have to help me," said Cathy. "Until the cook gets here."

After breakfast in the dining tent, Cathy called Isazi from the fire again.

"Have any of them come back yet?"

"Not yet, Nkosikazi."

"I want to go down to the railhead. I hope there is a telegraph from Henshaw. Will you put the ponies into the trap, Isazi."

262

Then, for the first time, she noticed the little frown of concern on the old Zulu's wrinkled features.

"What is it?"

"The horses—they are not in the kraal."

"Where are they then?"

"Perhaps one of the *mujiba* took them out early; I will go to find them."

"Oh, it doesn't matter." Cathy shook her head. "It's only a short walk to the telegraph office. The exercise will be good for me," and she called to Jonathan. "Fetch my bonnet for me, Jon-Jon."

"Nkosikazi, it is perhaps not wise, the little one—"

"Oh, don't fuss," Cathy told him fondly, and took Jonathan's hand. "If you find the ponies in time, you can come and fetch us." Then swinging her bonnet by its ribbon and with Jonathan skipping beside her, she started along the track that led around the side of the wooded hill toward the railhead.

There was no clangor of hammers on steel. Jonathan noticed it first.

"It's so quiet, Mama." And they stopped to listen.

"It's not Friday," Cathy murmured. "Mr. Mac can't be paying the gangs." She shook her head, still not alarmed. "That's strange." And they went on.

At the corner of the hill, they stopped again, and Cathy held her bonnet up to shade her eyes from the low sun. The railway lines ran away southward, glistening like the silken threads of a spider's web, but below them they ended abruptly at the raw gash of the cut line through the bush. There was a pile of teak ties at the railhead and a smaller bundle of steel rails; the service locomotive was due up from Kimberley this afternoon to replenish those materials. The sledgehammers and shovels were in neat stacks where the shift had left them at dusk the night before. There was no human movement around the railhead.

"That's even stranger," said Cathy.

"Where is Mr. Henderson, Mama?" Jonathan asked. His voice was unusually subdued. "Where are Mr. Mac and Mr. Braithwaite?"

"I don't know. They must still be in their tents."

The tents of the white surveyor and the engineer and his supervisors were grouped just beyond the square galvanized iron shack of the telegraph. There was no sign of life around the hut or between the neat pyramids of canvas, except for a single black crow which sat on the peak of one of them. Its hoarse cawing reached them faintly, and as Cathy watched, it spread its black wings and flapped heavily to earth at the entrance of the tent.

"Where are all the hammer boys?" Jonathan piped, and suddenly Cathy shivered.

"I don't know, darling." Her voice cracked and she cleared her throat. "We will go and find out." She realized she had spoken too loudly, and Jonathan shrank against her legs.

"Mummy, I'm frightened."

"Don't be a silly boy," Cathy told him firmly, and dragging him by the hand, she started down the hill.

By the time she reached the telegraph hut, she was moving as fast as her big, round belly would allow, and her breathing in her own ears was deafening.

"Stay here." She did not know what prompted her to leave Jonathan at the steps of the veranda, but she went up alone to the door of the telegraph hut.

The door was ajar. She pushed it fully open.

Mr. Braithwaite sat beside his table facing the doorway. He was staring at her with those pale, popping eyes, and his mouth hung open.

"Mr. Braithwaite," Cathy said, and at the sound of her voice, there was a hum like a swarm of bees taking flight, and the big cobalt-blue flies that had covered his shirtfront rose in a cloud into the air, and Cathy saw that his belly was a gaping, mushy red pit and that his entrails hung in ropes down between his knees into a tangle on the floor under the desk.

Cathy shrank back against the door. She felt her legs turn rubbery under her, and black shadows wheeled through her vision like the wings of bats at sundown. One of the metallic blue flies settled on her cheek and crawled sluggishly down toward the corner of her mouth.

Cathy leaned forward slowly and retched explosively, and her breakfast spattered on the wooden floor between her feet. She backed away slowly out of the door, shaking her head and trying to wipe the sickly sweet taste of vomit from her lips. She almost tripped on the steps, and sat down heavily. Jonathan ran to her and clung to her arm.

"What happened, Mummy?"

"I want you to be a brave little man," she whispered.

"Are you sick, Mummy?" The child shook her arm with agitation, and Cathy found it difficult to think.

She realized what had caused the hideous mutilation of the corpse in the hut. The Matabele always disemboweled their victims. It was a ritual that released the spirit of the dead man and allowed it to go on to its Valhalla. To leave the belly pouch was to trap the victim's shade upon the earth and have it return to haunt the slayer.

Mr. Braithwaite had been split by the razor-sharp edge of a Matabele assegai, and his hot entrails had been plucked from him like those of a chicken. It was the work of a Matabele war party.

"Where is Mr. Henderson, Mummy?" Jon-Jon demanded shrilly. "I am going to his tent."

The big, burly engineer was one of Jonathan's favorite friends, and Cathy caught his arm.

"No, Jon-Jon—don't go!"

"Why not?"

The crow had screwed up its courage at last, and now it hopped into the opening of the engineer's tent and disappeared. Cathy knew what had attracted it.

"Please be quiet, Jon-Jon," Cathy pleaded. "Let Mummy think."

The missing servants. They had been warned, of course, as had the Matabele construction gangs. They knew that a war party was out, and they had faded away—and a horrifying thought struck Cathy. Perhaps the servants, her own people, were part of the war party. She shook her head violently. No, not them. These must be some small band of renegades, not her own people.

They would have struck at dawn, of course, for it was the favorite hour. They had caught Henderson and his foreman asleep in the tents. Only the faithful little Braithwaite had been at his machine. The telegraph machine—Cathy started up—the telegraph was her one link with the outside world.

"Jon-Jon, stay here," she ordered, and crept back toward the door of the hut.

She steeled herself and then glanced into the interior, trying not to look at the little man in the chair. One quick glance was enough. The telegraph machine had been ripped from the wall and smashed into pieces on the floor of the hut. She reeled back and leaned against the iron wall beside the door, clutching her swollen stomach with both hands, forcing herself to think again.

The war party had struck the railhead and then disappeared back into the forest—and then she remembered the missing servants. The camp—they had not disappeared, they would be circling up through the trees toward the camp. She looked around her desperately, expecting at any moment to see the silent black files of plumed warriors come padding out of the thick bush.

The service train from Kimberley was due late that afternoon, ten hours from now, and she was alone except for Jonathan. Cathy sank down on her knees, reached for him and clung to him with the strength of despair, and only then realized that the boy was staring through the open doorway.

"Mr. Braithwaite is dead!" Jonathan said matter-of-factly. Forcibly, she turned his head away. "They are going to kill us, too, aren't they, Mummy?"

"Oh, Jon-Jon!"

"We need a gun. I can shoot. Papa taught me."

A gun—Cathy looked toward the silent tents. She did not think she had the courage to go into one of them, not even to find a weapon. She knew what carnage to expect there.

A shadow fell over her and she screamed.

"Nkosikazi. It is me."

Isazi had come down the hill as silently as a panther.

"The horses are gone," he said, and she motioned him to look into the telegraph hut.

Isazi's expression did not change.

"So," he said quietly, "the Matabele jackals can still bite."

"The tents," Cathy whispered. "See if you can find a weapon."

Isazi went with the lithe, swinging run of a man half his age, ducking from one tent opening to another, and when he came back to her, he carried an assegai with a broken shaft.

"The big one fought well. He was still alive, with his guts torn out of him, and the crows were eating them. He could no longer speak, but he looked at me. I have given him peace. But there are no guns—the Matabele have taken them."

"There are guns at the camp," Cathy whispered.

"Come, Nkosikazi." He lifted her tenderly to her feet, and Jonathan manfully took her other arm, though he did not reach to her armpit.

The first pain hit Cathy before they reached the thick bush at the edge of the cut line, and it doubled her over. They held her while the paroxysm lasted, Jonathan not understanding what was happening, but the little Zulu was grave and silent.

"All right." Cathy straightened up at last and tried to wipe the long tendrils of her hair off her face, but they were plastered there by her own sweat.

They went up on the track at Cathy's pace. Isazi was watching the forest on both sides for the dark movement of warriors, and he carried the broken assegai in his free hand with an underhand stabbing grip.

Cathy gasped and staggered as the next pain caught her. This time they could not hold her and she went down on her knees in the dust. When it passed, she looked up at Isazi.

"They are too close together. It is happening."

He did not have to reply.

"Take Jonathan to the Harkness Mine."

"Nkosikazi, the train—"

"The train will be too late. You must go."

"Nkosikazi—you, what will become of you?"

"Without a horse, I could never reach the Harkness. It is almost thirty miles. Every moment you waste now wastes the boy's life."

He did not move.

"If you can save him, Isazi, then you save part of me. If you stay here, we will all die. Go, go quickly!" she urged.

Isazi reached for Jonathan's hand, but he jerked away.

"I won't leave my Mummy." His voice rose hysterically. "My Daddy said I must look after my Mummy."

Cathy gathered herself. It took all her determination to perform the most difficult task of her young life. She hit Jonathan openhanded across the face, back and forth, with all her strength. The child staggered away from her, the vivid crimson outlines of her fingers rising on the pale skin of his cheeks. She had never struck his face before.

"Do as I tell you," Cathy blazed at him furiously. "Go with Isazi this very instant."

The Zulu snatched up the child and looked down at her for a moment longer.

"You have the heart of a lioness. I salute you, Nkosikazi." And he went bounding away into the forest, carrying Jonathan with him. In seconds he had disappeared, and then only did she let the sobs come shaking and choking up her throat.

She thought then that being entirely alone is the hardest thing in life to bear. She thought of Ralph, and she had never loved or wanted him the way she did at that moment. It seemed for a time that she had used the last grain of her courage to strike her only child and to send him away for a faint chance of salvation. She would be content to stay here kneeling in the dust in the early sunlight until they came for her with the cruel steel.

Then from somewhere deep within her, she found the strength to rise and hobble on up the path. At the heel of the hill, she looked down at the camp. It looked so quiet and orderly. Her home. The smoke from the campfire rose like a pale feather into the still morning air, so welcoming, so safe; illogically she felt that if she could only reach her tent, then it would be all right.

She started, and she had not gone a dozen paces before she felt something burst deep within her, and then the abrupt, hot rush down the inside of her legs as her waters broke and poured from her. She struggled on, hampered by her sodden skirts, and then, unbelievably, she had reached her own tent.

It was so cool and dark within, like a church, she thought, and again her legs gave way beneath her. She crawled painfully across the floor, and her hair came tumbling down and blinded her. She groped her way to the wagon chest set at the foot of the big camp cot and threw the hair out of her eyes as she rested against it.

The lid was so heavy that it took all her strength, but at last it fell open with a crash. The pistol was tucked under the crocheted white bedcovers that she had hoarded for the home that Ralph would one day build for her. It was a big service Webley revolver. She had only fired it once, with Ralph steadying her from behind, holding her wrists against the recoil.

Now it needed both her hands to lift it out of the chest. She was too tired to climb onto the cot. She sat with her back against the chest, both her legs straight out in front of her flat against the floor, and she held the pistol with both hands in her lap.

She must have dozed, for when she started awake, it was to hear the whisper of feet against the bare earth. She looked up. There was the shadow of a man silhouetted by the slanting rays of the sun against the white canvas of the tent like a figure in a magic lantern show. She lifted the pistol and aimed at the entrance. The ugly black weapon wavered uncertainly in her grip, and a man stepped through the flap.

"Oh, thank God." Cathy let the pistol fall into her lap. "Oh, thank God, it's you," she whispered, and let her head fall forward. The thick curtain of her hair fell open, splitting down the back of her head, exposing the pale skin at the tender nape of her neck. Bazo looked down at it. He saw a soft pulse throbbing beneath the skin.

Bazo wore only a kilt of civet tails, and about his forehead a band of moleskin—no feathers or tassels. His feet were bare. In his left hand he held a broad stabbing assegai. In his right, he carried a knobkerrie like the mace of a medieval knight. The handle was of polished rhinoceros horn, three feet long, and the head was a ball of heavy leadwood studded with hand-forged nails of native iron.

When he swung the knobkerrie, all the strength of his wide shoulders was behind the blow, and his point of aim was the pulse in the pale nape of Cathy's neck.

Two of his warriors came into the tent and flanked Bazo; their eyes were still glazed with the killing madness. They also wore the moleskin headbands, and they looked down at the crumpled body on the floor of the tent. One of the warriors changed his grip on the assegai, ready for the cutting stroke.

"The woman's spirit must fly," he said.

"Do it!" Bazo said, and the warrior stooped and worked quickly, expertly.

"There is life within her," he said. "See! It moves yet."

"Still it!" Bazo ordered, and left the tent, striding out into the sunlight.

"Find the boy," he ordered his men who waited there. "Find the white cub."

◆　◆　◆

The driver of the locomotive was terrified. They had stopped for a few minutes at the trading post beside the tracks at Plumtree siding, and he had seen the bodies of the storekeeper and his family lying in the front yard.

Ralph Ballantyne thrust the muzzle of the rifle between his shoulder blades and marched him back to the cab, forcing him to go on northward, deeper and deeper into Matabeleland.

They had come all the way from the Kimberley switching yards with the loco throttle wide open, and Ralph had spelled the stoker on the footplate, shoveling the lumpy black coal into the firebox with a monotonous rhythm, bare-chested and sweating in the furnace glare, the coal dust blackening his face and arms like those of a chimney sweep, his palms wet and raw from the burst blisters.

They had clipped almost two hours off the record run to the railhead. As they came roaring around the bend between the hills and saw the iron roof of the telegraph shack, Ralph hurled the shovel aside and clambered onto the side of the cab to peer ahead.

His heart leaped joyfully against his ribs; there was movement around the hut and between the tents, there was life here! Then his heart dropped as swiftly as it had risen as he recognized the skulking, doglike shapes.

The hyenas were so intent on squabbling over the things they had dragged out of the tents that they were totally unafraid. It was only when Ralph started shooting that they scattered. He knocked down half a dozen of the loathsome beasts before the rifle was empty. He ran from the hut to each tent in turn and then back to the locomotive. Neither the driver nor the fireman had left the cab.

"Mr. Ballantyne, these murdering, bloody 'eathen will be back at any minute—"

"Wait!" Ralph shouted at him, and scrambled up the side of the cattle car behind the coal buggy. He knocked out the locking pins, and the door came crashing down to form a drawbridge.

Ralph led the horses out of the car. There were four of them, one already saddled, the best mounts he had been able to find. He paused only long enough to clinch the girth, and then swung up into the saddle with the rifle still in his hand.

"I'm not going to wait here," the driver yelled. "Christ Almighty, those niggers are animals, man, animals."

"If my wife and son are here, I'll need to get them back. Give me one hour," Ralph asked.

"I'm not waiting another minute. I'm going back." The driver shook his head.

"You can go to hell then," Ralph told him coldly.

He kicked his horse into a gallop and dragging the spare mounts on the lead rein behind him, took the track up the side of the kopje toward the camp.

As he rode, he thought once more that perhaps he should have listened to Aaron Fagan, perhaps he should have recruited a dozen other horsemen in Kimberley to go with him. But he knew that he would never have been able to abide the few hours that he would have needed to find good men. As it was, he had left Kimberley less than half an hour after he had received the telegraph from Tati—just long enough to fetch his Winchester, fill the saddlebags with ammunition, and take the horses from Aaron's stables to the switching yard.

Before he turned the angle of the hill, he glanced back over his shoulder. The locomotive was already huffing back along the curve of the rails toward the south. Now, as far as he knew, he might be the only white man left alive in Matabeleland.

Ralph galloped into the camp. They had been there already. The camp had been looted; Jonathan's tent had collapsed; his clothing was scattered and trampled into the dust.

"Cathy," Ralph shouted as he dismounted. "Jon-Jon! Where are you?"

Paper rustled under his feet, and Ralph looked down. Cathy's portfolio of drawings had been thrown down and had burst open; the paintings of which she was so proud were torn and crumpled. Ralph picked up one of them; it was of the lovely, dark scarlet trumpet flowers of *Kigelia africana*, the African sausage tree. He tried to smooth out the rumpled sheet and then realized the futility of that gesture.

He ran on to their living tent and ripped open the flap.

Cathy lay on her back with her unborn child beside her. She had promised Ralph a daughter—and she had kept her promise.

He fell on his knees beside her and tried to lift her head, but her body had set into an awful rigidity; she was stiff as a carven statue in marble. As he lifted her, he saw the great cup-shaped depression in the back of her skull.

Ralph backed away and then flung himself out of the tent.

"Jonathan," he screamed. "Jon-Jon! Where are you?"

He ran through the camp like a madman.

"Jonathan! Please, Jonathan!"

When he found no living thing, he stumbled into the forest up onto the slope of the kopje.

"Jonathan! It's Daddy. Where are you, my darling!"

Dimly in his anguish he realized that his cries might bring the *amadoda,* as the bleat of the goat brings the leopard, and suddenly he wanted that to happen with all his soul.

"Come!" he yelled into the silent forest. "Come on. Come and find me also!" And he stopped to fire the Winchester into the air and listen to the echoes go bounding away down the valley.

At last he could run and scream no more, and he came up panting against the bole of one of the forest trees.

"Jonathan," he croaked. "Where are you, my baby?"

Slowly he turned and went down the hill. He moved like a very old man.

At the edge of the camp, he stopped and peered short-sightedly at something that lay in the grass, then he stopped and picked it up. He turned it over and over in his hands, and then balled it into his fist. His knuckles turned white with the strength of his grip. What he held was a headband of softly tanned moleskin.

Still holding the scrap of fur in his hand, he went into the camp to prepare his dead for burial.

♦　♦　♦

Robyn St. John woke to the soft scratching on the shutter of her bedroom, and she raised herself on one elbow.

"Who is it?" she called.

"It is me, Nomusa."

"Juba, my little Dove, I did not expect you!"

Robyn slipped out of bed and crossed to the window. When she opened the shutter, the night was opalescent with moonlight, and Juba was huddled below the sill.

"You are so cold." Robyn took her arm. "You'll catch your death. Come inside immediately. I'll fetch a blanket."

"Nomusa, wait." Juba caught her wrist. "I must go."

"But you have only just arrived."

"Nobody must know that I was here—please tell nobody, Nomusa."

"What is it? You are shaking—"

"Listen, Nomusa. I could not leave you—you are my mother and sister and friend, I could not leave you."

"Juba—"

"Do not speak. Listen for a minute," Juba pleaded. "I have so little time."

It was only then that Robyn realized that it was not the chill of night that shook Juba's vast frame. She was racked with sobs of fear and of dread.

"You must go, Nomusa. You and Elizabeth and the baby. Take nothing with you, leave this very minute. Go into Bulawayo, perhaps you will be safe there. It is your best chance."

"I don't understand you, Juba. What nonsense is this?"

"They are coming, Nomusa. They are coming. Please hurry."

Then she was gone. She moved swiftly and silently for such a big woman, and she seemed to melt into the moon shadows under the spathodea trees. By the time Robyn had found her shawl and run down the veranda, there was no sign of her.

Robyn hurried down toward the hospital bungalows, stumbling once on the verge of the path, calling with increasing exasperation.

"Juba, come back here! Do you hear me? I won't stand any more of this nonsense!"

She stopped at the church, uncertain which path to take.

"Juba! Where are you?"

The silence was broken only by the yipping of a jackal up on the hillside above the mission. It was answered by another on the peak of the pass where the road to Bulawayo crossed the hills.

"Juba!"

The watch fire by the hospital bungalow had burned out. She crossed to it and threw onto it a log from the woodpile. The silence was unnatural. The log caught and flared. In its light she climbed the steps of the nearest bungalow.

The sleeping mats of the patients were in two rows facing each other down each wall, but they were deserted. Even the most desperately ill had gone. They must have been carried away, for some of them had been past walking.

Robyn hugged the shawl around her shoulders. "Poor ignorant heathen," she said aloud. "Another witchcraft scare—they will run from their own shadows."

She turned sorrowfully away and walked through the darkness back toward the house. There was a light burning in Elizabeth's room, and as Robyn climbed the steps of the veranda, the door opened.

"Mama! Is that you?"

"What are you doing, Elizabeth?"

"I thought I heard voices."

Robyn hesitated; she did not want to alarm Elizabeth, but then she was a sensible child and unlikely to go into hysteria over a bit of Matabele superstition.

"Juba was here. There must be another witchcraft scare. She ran off again."

"What did she say?"

"Oh, just that we should go into Bulawayo to escape some sort of danger."

Elizabeth came out onto the veranda in her nightdress carrying the candle.

"Juba is a Christian, she doesn't dabble in witchcraft." Elizabeth's tone was concerned. "What else did she say?"

"Just that," Robyn yawned. "I'm going back to bed." She started along the veranda and then stopped. "Oh, the others have all run off. The hospital is empty. It's most annoying."

"Mama, I think we should do as Juba says."

"What do you mean by that?"

"I think we should go into Bulawayo immediately."

"Elizabeth, I thought better of you."

"I have an awful feeling. I think we should go. Perhaps there is real danger."

"This is my home. Your father and I built it with our own hands. There is no power on earth that will force me to leave it," Robyn said firmly. "Now go back to bed. With no help, we are going to have a busy day tomorrow."

◆ ◆ ◆

They squatted in long, silent ranks in the long grass below the crest of the hills. Gandang moved quietly down the ranks, stopping occasionally to exchange a word with an old comrade in arms, to revive a memory of another waiting before a battle of long ago.

It was strange to sit upon the bare earth during the waiting time. In the old days they would have sat on their shields, the long dappled shields of iron-hard oxhide, squatting upon them not for comfort but to hide their distinctive shape from a watchful enemy until the moment came to strike terror into his belly and steel into his heart; squatting upon them also to prevent some young buck in the throes of the divine madness from prematurely drumming upon the rawhide with his assegai and giving warning of the waiting impi.

It was strange also not to be decked out in the full regimentals of the Inyati impi: the plumes and furs and tassels of cow tails, the war rattles at ankle and wrist, the tall headdress that turned a man into a giant. They were dressed like neophytes, like unblooded boys, with only their kilts about their waists, but the scars upon their dark bodies and the fire in their eyes gave the lie to that impression.

Gandang felt himself choking with a pride that he once thought he would never experience again. He loved them, he loved their fierceness and their valor, and though his face was quiet and expressionless, the love shone through in his eyes.

They picked it up and gave it back to him a hundred times. "Baba!" they called him in their soft, deep voices. "Father, we thought we would never fight at your shoulder again," they said. "Father, those of your sons who die today will be forever young."

Across the neck of the hills, a jackal wailed mournfully and was answered from close at hand. The impi was in position, lying across the Khami Hills like a coiled mamba, waiting and watchful and ready.

There was a glow in the sky now. The false dawn that would be followed by the deeper darkness before the true dawn. The deep darkness that the *amadoda* loved and used so well.

They stirred quietly and grounded the shaft of assegai

275

between their heels, ready for the order: "Up, my children. It is the time of the spears."

This time the order did not come, and the true dawn flushed the sky with blood. In its light the *amadoda* looked at each other.

One of the senior warriors, who had won Gandang's respect on fifty battlefields, spoke for all of them. He went to where Gandang sat alone to one side of the impi.

"Baba, your children are confused. Tell us why we wait."

"Old friend, are your spears so thirsty for the blood of women and babes that they cannot wait for richer fare?"

"We can wait as long as you command it, Baba. But it is hard."

"Old friend, I am baiting for a leopard with a tender goat," Gandang told him, and let his chin sink back on the great muscles of his chest.

The sun pushed up and gilded the treetops along the hills, and still Gandang did not move, and the silent ranks waited behind him in the grass.

A young warrior whispered to another. "Already the storm has begun. Everywhere else our brethren are busy. They will mock us when they hear how we sat on the hilltop—"

One of the older men hissed a rebuke at him, and the young warrior fell silent, but further down the ranks another youngster shifted on his haunches and his assegai tapped against that of his neighbor. Gandang did not raise his head.

Then from the hilltop a wild francolin called. "*Qwaali! Qwaali!*" The sharp penetrating cry was a characteristic sound of the veld; only a sharp ear would have detected anything strange about this one.

Gandang rose to his feet. "The leopard comes," he said quietly, and stalked up to the vantage point from which he could look down the full length of road that led to the town of Bulawayo. The sentry who had sounded the call of the wild pheasant pointed wordlessly with the hilt of his assegai.

There was an open coach and a troop of horsemen upon the road. Gandang counted them, eleven riding hard, coming directly out toward the Khami Hills. The figure that led them was unmistakable even at this distance. The height in the saddle, the alert set of head, the long stirrups.

"Hau! One-Bright-Eye!" Gandang greeted him softly. "I have waited many long moons for you."

◆ ◆ ◆

General Mungo St. John had been awakened in the middle of the night. In his nightshirt he had listened to the hysterical outpourings of a colored servant who had escaped from the trading store on the Ten-Mile Drift. It was a wild tale of slaughter and burning, and the man's breath smelled of good Cape brandy.

"He's drunk," said Mungo St. John flatly. "Take him away, and give him a good thrashing."

The first white man got into town three hours before dawn. He had been stabbed through the thigh, and his left arm was broken in two places by blows from a knobkerrie. He was clinging to his horse's neck with his good arm.

"The Matabele are out!" he screamed. "They are burning the farms—" And he slid out of the saddle in a dead faint.

By first light there were fifty wagons formed into a laager in the Market Square; without oxen to draw them, they had been manhandled into position. All the town's women and children had been brought into the laager and put to work making bandages, reloading ammunition, and baking hard bread against a siege. The few able-bodied men that Dr. Jameson had not taken with him into captivity in the Transvaal were swiftly formed into troops, and horses and rifles were found for those who lacked them.

In the midst of the bustle and confusion, Mungo St. John had commandeered a fast open coach with a colored driver, picked out the most likely and best-mounted troop of horsemen, and, using his authority as acting Administrator, given them the order, "Follow me!"

Now he reined in on the crest of the hills above Khami Mission, at the point where the track was narrowest and the tall yellow grass and the forest hemmed it in like a wall on each side, and he shaded his single eye.

"Thank God!" he whispered. The thatched roofs of the mission that he expected to see billowing with smoke and flame stood serenely in the quiet green valley beyond.

The horses were sweating and blowing from the pull up the hills, and the coach had lagged two hundred paces behind Mungo. As soon as it came up, without giving a moment's rest to the mules, Mungo shouted, "Troop, forward!" and spurred away down the track, with his troopers clattering behind him.

Robyn St. John came out of the thatched rondavel that was her laboratory, and as soon as she recognized the man that led the column, she placed her hands upon her boyish hips and lifted her chin angrily.

"What is the meaning of this intrusion, sir?" she demanded.

"Madam, the Matabele tribe is in full rebellion. They are murdering women and children, burning the homesteads."

Robyn took a step backward protectively, for Robert had come pale-faced from the clinic to hang onto her skirts.

"I have come to take you and your children to safety."

"The Matabele are my friends," said Robyn. "I have nothing to fear from them. This is my home. I do not intend leaving it."

"I do not have time to indulge your predilection for obstructive disputation, madam," he said grimly, and stood in the stirrups.

"Elizabeth!" he bellowed, and she came onto the veranda of the homestead. "The Matabele are in revolt. We are all in mortal danger. You have two minutes to gather what personal items your family may need—"

"Take no heed of him, Elizabeth," Robyn shouted angrily. "We are staying here."

Before she realized his intention, Mungo had pricked his horse with a spur, backing it up toward the laboratory doorway; then he stooped from the saddle and caught Robyn about the waist. He swung her up over the pommel of the saddle, with her backside in the air and her skirts around her hips. She kicked and yelled with outrage, but he walked his horse alongside the open coach and with a heave of his shoulder dumped her in another flurry of petticoats onto the back seat.

"If you do not stay there, madam, I will not hesitate to have you bound. It will be most undignified."

"I will never forgive you for this!" she panted through white lips, but she could see he meant the threat seriously.

"Robert," Mungo St. John ordered his son, "go to your mother. Immediately!"

The child scampered to the coach and climbed into it.

"Elizabeth!" Mungo St. John bellowed again. "Hurry, girl. All our lives depend on haste now."

Elizabeth ran out onto the veranda with a bundle over her shoulder.

"Good girl!" Mungo St. John smiled at her. So pretty and brave and level-headed, she had always been one of his favorites. He jumped down to boost her into the coach and then vaulted back into the saddle.

"Troop, walk. March! Trot!" he ordered, and they wheeled out of the yard.

The coach was in the rear of the column, the ten troopers in double ranks ahead of it, and five lengths out in front of them again rode Mungo St. John. Despite herself, Elizabeth was thrilled and deliciously fearful. It was all so different from the quiet, monotonous round of life at Khami Mission: the armed men, the urgency and tension in each of them, the dark threat of the unknown surrounding them, the romance of the faithful husband riding through the valley of the shadow of death to save his beloved woman. How noble and dashing he looked at the head of the column, how easily he sat his horse, and when he turned to look back at the coach, how reckless was his smile—there was only one other man in all the world to match him. If only it had been Ralph Ballantyne come to save her alone! The thought was sinful, and she put it away quickly and, to distract herself, looked back down the hill.

"Oh, Mama!" she cried, jumping up in the swaying coach, pointing wildly. "Look!"

The mission was burning. The thatch of the church stood in a tall beacon of leaping flame. Smoke was curling out of the homestead, and as they stared in horror, they saw tiny, dark human figures running down the pathway under the spathodea trees, carrying torches of dry grass. One of them stopped to hurl his torch onto the roof of the clinic.

"My books," whispered Robyn. "All my papers. My life's work."

"Don't look, Mama." Elizabeth sank down beside her on the seat, and they clung to each other like lost children.

The little column reached the crest of the pass; without a pause the weary horses plunged down the far side—and the Matabele came simultaneously from both sides of the track. They rose out of the grass in two black waves, and the humming roar of their war chant swelled like the sound of an avalanche gathering momentum down a steep mountainside.

The troopers had been riding with their carbines cocked, the butts resting on their right thighs, but so swift was the rush of Matabele that only a single volley rippled down the column. It made no impression upon the black wave of humanity, and then as the horses reared and whinnied with terror, the troopers were dragged from their saddles and stabbed through and through, ten and twenty times. The warriors were mad with bloodlust. They swarmed over the bodies, snarling and howling, like the hounds tearing the carcass of the fox.

A huge sweat-shining warrior seized the colored driver by the leg and plucked him off the driver's seat of the coach, and while he was still in the air, another warrior transfixed him on the broad silver blade of an assegai.

Only Mungo St. John, five lengths ahead of the column, broke clear. He had taken a single assegai thrust through the side, and the blood streamed down one leg of his breeches, down his riding boot, and dripped from the heel.

He still sat high in the saddle, and he looked back over his shoulder. He looked over the heads of the Matabele straight into Robyn's eyes. It was only for an instant, and then he had wheeled his horse, and he drove back into the mass of black warriors, riding for the coach. He fired his service pistol into the face of a warrior who leaped to catch his horse's head, but from the other side, another Matabele stabbed upward overhanded, deep into his armpit. Mungo St. John grunted and spurred onward.

"I'm here!" he shouted to Robyn. "Don't worry, my darling—" And a warrior stabbed him through the belly. He doubled over. His horse went down, sharp steel driven through its heart, and it seemed that it was all over, but miraculously Mungo St. John rose to his feet and stood foursquare with the pistol in his hand. His eye patch had been torn from his head, and the empty eye socket glared so demoniacally-that for a moment the warriors fell back, and he stood in their midst with the terrible spear wounds in his chest and belly running red.

Gandang stepped out of the press, and a silence fell upon them all. The two men stood face to face for a long second. Mungo tried to lift the pistol, but his strength failed him, and then Gandang drove the silver blade through the center of Mungo St. John's chest, and it shot a hand's span out of his back.

Gandang stood over the body and placed one foot upon Mungo St. John's chest and pulled the blade free. It made a sucking sound like a boot in thick mud. It was the only sound, and after it was silence. The silence was even more terrible than the war chant and the screams of dying men.

The dense press of black bodies hemmed in the coach and hid the corpses of the dead troopers. The *amadoda* formed a ring around where Mungo St. John lay upon his back, his features still twisted into a grimace of rage and agony, his one eye glaring at the enemy he could no longer see.

One at a time, the warriors lifted their heads and stared at the huddle of women and a child in the open body of the coach. The very air was charged with menace, their eyes were glazed with the killing madness, and blood still splattered their arms and chests and speckled their faces like a macabre war paint. The ranks swayed like prairie grass touched by a little breeze. In the rear a single voice began to hum, but before it could spread, Robyn St. John rose to her feet and from the height of the coach looked down upon them. The hum died out into silence.

Robyn reached forward and picked up the reins. The Matabele watched her and still not one of them moved. Robyn flicked the reins, and the mules started forward at a walk.

Gandang, son of Mzilikazi, senior induna of the Matabele, stepped off the track, and behind him the ranks of his *amadoda* opened. The mules passed slowly down the lane between them, stepping daintily over the mutilated corpses of the troopers. Robyn stared straight ahead, holding the reins stiffly. Just once as she drew level with where Mungo St. John lay, she glanced down at him, and then looked ahead again.

Slowly the coach rolled on down the hill, and when Elizabeth looked back again, the road was deserted.

"They have gone, Mama," she whispered, and only then did she realize that Robyn was shaking with silent sobs.

Elizabeth put her arm around her shoulders, and for a moment Robyn leaned against her.

"He was a terrible man, but, oh God forgive me, I loved him so," she whispered, and then she straightened up and urged the mules into a trot toward Bulawayo.

* * *

Ralph Ballantyne rode through the night, taking the difficult and direct path through the hills rather than the broad wagon road. The spare horses were loaded with food and blankets that he had salvaged from the railhead camp. He led them at a walk over the rocky terrain, husbanding them for whatever efforts lay ahead of them.

He rode with his rifle across his lap, loaded and cocked. Every half hour or so he halted his horse and fired three spaced rifle shots into the starry sky. Three shots, the universal recall signal. When the echoes had muttered and rumbled away down the hills, he listened carefully, twisting slowly in the saddle to cover every direction, and then he called, yelling his despair into the silences of the wilderness.

"Jonathan! Jonathan!"

Again he rode on slowly through the darkness, and when the dawn came, he watered the horses at a stream and let them graze for a few hours, sitting on an ant heap to guard them, munching biscuit and bully, and listening.

It was strange how many of the sounds of the bush could seem like the cries of a human child to someone who listened wishfully. The mournful "quay" of a gray lourie brought Ralph to his feet with his heart hammering; the screech of a meercat, even the wail of the wind in the treetops, disturbed him.

In midmorning he saddled up and rode again. He knew that in daylight there was greater danger of running into a Matabele patrol, but the prospect had no terrors. He found himself welcoming it. Deep inside him was a cold, dark area, a place that he had never visited before, and now as he rode on, he explored it and found there such hatred and anger as he had never believed was possible. Riding slowly through the lovely forests in the clean white sunshine, he discovered that he was a stranger to himself; until this day he had never known what he was, but now he was beginning to find out.

He reined in his horse on the crest of a high, bare ridge where watching Matabele eyes could have seen him from afar silhouetted against the blue, and deliberately he fired another three single shots. When no file of running warriors came to the summons, his hatred and anger were stronger still.

An hour after noon he climbed the ridge of the ancients where Zouga had killed the great elephant and looked down onto the Harkness Mine.

The buildings had been burned. On the far ridge, the walls that Harry Mellow had built for Vicky were still standing, but the empty windows were like the eyes of a skull. The roof beams were stark and blackened, some of them collapsed beneath the weight of charred thatch. The gardens were trampled, and the lawns were strewn with the debris of two young lives—the brass bedstead with stuffing bursting out of the torn mattress, the chests of Vicky's dowry broken open and the contents scorched and scattered.

Further down the valley, the mine store and office had been burned also. The stacks of blackened goods still smoldered, and there was the stink of burning rubber and leather on the air. There was another smell mingled with it, a smell like greasy pork cooking, the first time Ralph had smelled human flesh roasting, but instinctively he knew what it was, and he felt his stomach heave.

In the trees about the burned-out buildings roosted the hunch-backed vultures. There were hundreds of these disgusting birds, from the big black vultures with their bald red heads to the dirty brown birds with obscene woolen caps covering their long necks. Among the vultures were the carrion storks, the raucous crows and the little wheeling black kites. It must be a rich banquet to attract such a gathering.

Ralph rode down off the crest and almost immediately found the first bodies. Matabele warriors, he saw with grim satisfaction, they had crawled away to die of their wounds. Harry Mellow had held out better than the construction gang at the railhead.

"That he should have taken a thousand of the black butchers with him," Ralph hoped aloud, and rode on cautiously with his rifle at the ready.

He dismounted behind the ruins of the mine store and tethered the horses with a slippery hitch, ready for a quick run. Here there were more dead Matabele, lying amid their own broken and discarded weapons. The ash was still hot, and three or four corpses lay within the shell of the store. They had been burned to unrecognizable black mounds, and the smell of pork was overpowering.

Holding his rifle at high port, Ralph stepped carefully

through the ash and debris toward the corner of the building. The squawk and flap of the vultures and the scavengers covered any small sounds he might make, and he was ready to meet the sudden charge of warriors that might be lying in ambush for him. He steeled himself also to the discovery of the corpses of Harry and pretty blond little Vicky. Burying his own mutilated loved ones had not hardened him to the horror of what he knew he would find here.

He reached the corner of the building, removed his hat and carefully peeked around the wall.

There were two hundred yards of open ground between the burned-out store and the open mouth of the No. 1 adit shaft that Harry had driven into the side of the hill. The open ground was heaped with dead warriors. There were piles and skeins of them, drifts and windrows of them. Some were twisted into agonized sculptures of black limbs, and some of them lay singly, as though resting, curled into the fetal position. Most of them had been ripped and gnawed by the birds and the jackals, but others were untouched.

This killing ground gave Ralph a bitter feeling of pleasure.

"Good for you, Harry, my boy," he whispered.

Ralph was about to step into the open when his eardrums cracked with the brutal disruption of passing shot, so close that he felt his own hair flap against his forehead. He reeled back behind the shelter of the wall, shaking his head to clear the insect humming in his ears. That bullet must have missed by an inch or less, good shooting for a Matabele sniper. They were notoriously poor marksmen.

He had been careless. The piles of dead warriors had distracted him; he had presumed that the impi had finished its bloody business and gone on, a stupid presumption.

He crouched low and ran back down the length of the burned building, sweeping his open flank with an eye sharpened by the hot rush of adrenaline through his veins. The Matabele loved the encircling movement: if they were out front, then they would soon be in his rear, up there among the trees.

He reached the horses, slipped the tether and led them over the hot ash into the shelter of the walls. From the saddlebag he took a fresh bandolier of ammunition and slung it over his other shoulder, crisscrossing his chest like a Mexican bandit and muttering to himself, "All right, you black bastards, let's burn some powder."

One corner of the stone wall had collapsed where the unbaked Kimberley brick had not been able to withstand the heat. The opening was jagged; it would break the silhouette of his head, and the rear wall would prevent back lighting. Carefully he peered out over the bloody ground. They were well concealed, probably in the bush above the mine shaft.

Then with a start of surprise, he realized that the mouth of the adit shaft had been barricaded; it was blocked with balks of timber and what looked like sacks of maize.

They were in the mine shaft—but that didn't make sense, he puzzled. Yet it was confirmed immediately. There was a vague, shadowy movement beyond the barricade in the throat of the shaft, and another bullet sang off the lip of the wall under Ralph's nose, blinding him with brick dust.

He ducked down and wiped his swimming eyes. Then he filled his lungs and bellowed.

"Harry! Harry Mellow!"

There was silence, even the vultures and the jackals quieted by the shocking burst of gunfire.

"Harry—it's me, Ralph."

There was a faint answering shout, and Ralph jumped up, vaulted over the broken wall, and ran toward the shaft. Harry Mellow was racing toward him, jumping over the piles of dead Matabele, a wide grin on his face. They met halfway and embraced with the violence of relief, wordlessly pounding each other's backs, and then before he could speak, Ralph looked over the big American's shoulder.

Other figures had emerged from behind the rude barricade. Vicky dressed in men's breeches and shirt, with a rifle in her hand and coppery hair tangled around her shoulders. At her side Isazi, the diminutive Zulu driver, and another even smaller figure ran ahead of them both. The child ran with both arms pumping and face screwed up.

Ralph caught him up and hugged him to his chest, pressing his haggard, unshaven cheek against the boy's velvet skin.

"Jonathan," he croaked and then his voice failed. The feel of the child's warm little body and the milky puppy smell of his sweat was almost too painful to be borne.

"Daddy." Jon-Jon pulled back his head, and his face

was pale and stricken. "I couldn't look after Mummy. She wouldn't let me."

"That's all right, Jon-Jon," Ralph whispered. "You did your best—"

And then he was crying. The terrible, dry, hacking sobs of a man driven to the far frontiers of his love.

◆ ◆ ◆

Though he hated to let the child out of his arms for a moment, Ralph sent Jonathan to help Isazi feed the horses at the entrance to the shaft. Then he drew Vicky and Harry Mellow aside, and in the gloom of the tunnel where they could not see his face, he told them simply, "Cathy is dead."

"How?" Harry broke the stunned silence. "How did she die?"

"Badly," Ralph told them. "Very badly. I don't want to say any more."

Harry held Vicky while she wept, and when her first sharp grief was over, Ralph went on. "We can't stay here. We have a choice—the railhead or Bulawayo."

"Bulawayo may be burned and sacked by now," Harry pointed out.

"And there may be an impi between here and the railhead," said Ralph. "But if Vicky wants to try and reach the railhead, we can send her and Jon-Jon south on the first train that gets through."

"Then?" Harry asked. "What then?"

"Then I am riding to Bulawayo. If they are still alive, then they'll need fighting men to stay that way."

"Vicky?" Harry hugged his wife.

"My mother and my family are at Bulawayo. This is the land of my birth—I'm not running away." She wiped the wetness off her cheeks with her thumbs. "I'm coming with you to Bulawayo."

Ralph nodded. He would have been surprised if she had agreed to go south.

"We will ride as soon as we have eaten."

They took the wagon road northward, and it was a dismal route. The derelict wagons abandoned during the rinderpest were as regular as milestones. The wagon canvas was already rotted to tatters, the cargoes looted and scattered on the grass—shattered cases and broken boxes and rusting tins. In the traces of some of the wagons, the mummified remains of the oxen lay where they had fallen, heads twisted back in the convulsions that had killed them.

Then at intervals they came upon death and destruction that was fresher and more poignant. One of the Zeederbergs' express coaches in the middle of the track, with the mules speared to death and, festooned from the branches of a thorn tree, the disemboweled bodies of the driver and his passengers.

At the drift of the Inyati River, the blackened walls of the trading post were all that was left standing. Here there was a macabre twist to the usual mutilation of the dead. The naked bodies of the Greek shopkeeper's wife and her three daughters had been laid in a neat row in the front yard with the shafts of the knobkerries thrust up into their private parts. The shopkeeper himself had been beheaded and his trunk thrown onto the fire. His head, fixed on an assegai, leered at them in the center of the road. Ralph covered Jon-Jon's face with his coat and held him close as they rode past.

Ralph sent Isazi ahead to scout the drift, and he found it defended. Ralph closed up the little party, and they took it at a gallop, catching the dozen or so Matabele *amadoda* by surprise, shooting four of them down as they ran to their weapons and thundering up the far bank together in the dust and gunsmoke. They were not followed, though Ralph, hoping they might be, turned back and lay in ambush beside the road.

Ralph held Jonathan in his lap during the night, starting awake every few minutes from nightmares in which Cathy screamed and pleaded for mercy. In the dawn he found that without realizing it he had taken the moleskin headband from his jacket and held it balled in his fist. He put it back in his pocket and buttoned the flap, as though it was something rare and precious.

They rode on northward all that day, past the little one-man gold mines and the homesteads where men and their families had begun to carve a life out of the wilderness. Some of them had been taken completely by surprise. They were still clad in the remnants of their nightclothes. One little boy even clutched his teddy bear, while his dead mother reached out to him with fingers that did not quite touch his sodden curls.

Others had sold their lives dearly, and the dead Matabele were flung like wood chips from a sawmill in a wide circle around the burned-out homesteads. Once they found dead *amadoda* but no white bodies. There were tracks of horses and a vehicle heading out northward.

"The Andersons. They got away," Ralph said. "Please God, they are in Bulawayo by now."

Vicky wanted to take the old wagon road, past Khami Mission, but Ralph would not do so.

"If they are there, it's too late. You've seen enough. If they got away, we'll find them in Bulawayo."

So they rode into the town of Bulawayo in the early morning of the third day. The barricades opened to let them pass into the huge central laager in the town square, and the townspeople thronged around the horses, shouting questions.

"Are the soldiers coming?"

"When are the soldiers coming?"

"Did you see my brother? He was at the Antelope Mine—"

"Have you any news?"

When she saw Robyn waving to her from the top of one of the wagons in the Market Square, Vicky wept for the first time since leaving the Harkness Mine. Elizabeth jumped down from the wagon and pushed her way through the crowd to Ralph's horse.

"Cathy?" she asked.

Ralph shook his head and saw his own sorrow reflected in her clear honey-colored eyes. Elizabeth reached up and lifted Jon-Jon down from the front of the saddle.

"I'll look after him, Ralph," she said softly.

◆ ◆ ◆

The family was installed in a corner of the central laager. Under Robyn and Louise's direction, the single wagon had been turned into a crowded but adequate home.

On the first day of the rising, Louise and Jan Cheroot, the little Hottentot, had brought the wagon in from King's Lynn. One of the survivors from the Matabele attack at Victoria Mine had galloped past the homestead, shouting a barely coherent warning as he went by.

Louise and Jan Cheroot, already alerted by the desertion of the Matabele laborers and servants, had taken time to pack the wagon with a load of essentials—tinned food and blankets and ammunition—and they had driven into Bulawayo, Jan Cheroot handling the traces and Louise sitting on top of the load with a rifle in her hands. Twice they had seen small war parties of Matabele at a distance, but a few warning shots had kept them there, and they reached the town among the very first refugees.

Thus the family did not have to rely on the charity of the townsfolk, like so many others who had arrived in Bulawayo with only a lathered horse and an empty rifle.

Robyn had set up a clinic under a canvas awning beside the wagon and had been asked by the Siege Committee to supervise the health and sanitation of the laager. While Louise had quite naturally taken charge of the other women in the laager, setting up a system by which all food stocks and other essential supplies were pooled and rationed, delegating the care of the half-dozen orphans to foster mothers, and organizing the other activities, from an entertainment committee to lessons in loading ammunition and handling firearms for those gentlewomen who did not already have those skills.

Ralph left Vicky to break the news of Cathy's death to her mother, gave Jon-Jon into Elizabeth's care, and set off across the laager to find a member of the Siege Committee.

It was after dark when Ralph got back to the wagon. Surprisingly, there was a brittle air of festivity upon the town. Despite the terrible bereavements that most families had suffered, despite the threat of dark impis gathering just beyond the walls of the laager, yet the cries of the children playing hide-and-go-seek among the wagons, the merry notes of a concertina, the laughter of women, and the cheerful blaze of the watch fires might have been those of a picnic in happier times.

Elizabeth had bathed both Jonathan and Robert, so they glowed and smelled of carbolic soap; and now as they ate their dinner at the camp table, she was telling them a story that made their eyes big as marbles in the lamplight.

Ralph smiled his thanks at her and summoned Harry Mellow with an inclination of his head.

The two men sauntered off on a seemingly casual circuit of the darkening laager. They walked with their heads close together while Ralph told Harry quietly, "The Siege Committee seem to be doing a good job. They have held a census of the laager already, and they reckon there are six hundred thirty-two women and children and nine hundred fifteen men. The defense of the town seems to be on good footing, but nobody has yet thought of anything but defense. They were delighted to hear that their plight is known in Kimberley and Cape Town. I gave them the first news that they have had from outside the territory since the rising began''—Ralph drew on his cheroot—''and they seemed to think it was as good as a couple of regiments of cavalry on their way already. We both know that isn't so.''

"It will take months to get troops up here."

"Jameson and his officers are on their way to England for trial, and Rhodes has been summoned to a court of inquiry." Ralph shook his head. "And there is worse news. The Mashona tribes have risen in concert with the Matabele."

"Good God." Harry stopped dead and seized Ralph's arm. "The whole territory—all at the same time? This thing has been carefully planned."

"There has been heavy fighting in the Mazoe Valley and in the Charter and Lomagundi districts around Fort Salisbury."

"Ralph, how many have these savages murdered?"

"Nobody knows. There are hundreds of scattered farms and mines out there. We have to reckon on at least five hundred men, women and children dead."

They walked on in silence for a while. Once a sentry challenged them but recognized Ralph.

"Heard you got through, Mr. Ballantyne—are the soldiers coming?"

"Are the soldiers coming?" Ralph muttered when they were past. "That's what they all ask, from the Siege Committee downward." They reached the far end of the laager, and Ralph spoke quietly to the guard there.

"All right, Mr. Ballantyne, but keep your eyes open. Those murdering heathen are all over."

Ralph and Harry passed through the gateway into the town. It was utterly deserted. Everyone had been moved into the central laager. The thatch and daub shanties were dark and silent, and the two men walked down the center of the broad, dusty main street until the buildings petered out on either hand; they stopped and stood staring out into the scrubland.

"Listen!" said Ralph. A jackal yipped down near the

Umguza River and was answered from the shadows of the acacia forest out in the south.

"Jackal," said Harry, but Ralph shook his head.

"Matabele!"

"Will they attack the town?"

Ralph did not reply immediately. He was staring out into the veld, and he had something in his hands that he was teasing like a string of Greek worry beads. "There are probably twenty thousand fighting bucks out there. They have got us bottled up here, and sooner or later, when they have massed their impis and plucked up their courage, they will come. They will come long before the soldiers can get here."

"What are our chances?"

Ralph wrapped the thing he held in his hand around one finger, and Harry saw it was a strip of drab fur. "We have got four Maxim guns, but there are six hundred women and children, and out of the nine hundred men, half are not fit to hold a rifle. The best way to defend Bulawayo is not to sit in the laager and wait for them—"

Ralph turned away and they went back along the silent street. "They wanted me to join the Siege Committee, and I told them I did not like sieges."

"What are you going to do, Ralph?"

"I am going to get together a small group of men. Those who know the tribe and the land, those who can shoot straight and talk Sindebele well enough to pass as natives—and we are going to go out there in the Matopo Hills, or wherever else they are hiding, and we are going to start killing Matabele."

◆ ◆ ◆

Isazi brought in fourteen men. They were all Zulus from the south, drivers and wagon boys from the Zeederberg Company who had once worked for Rholands Transport but had been stranded in Bulawayo by the rinderpest.

"I know you can drive an eighteen-ox span." Ralph nodded at the circle of their faces as they squatted around the fire passing from hand to hand the red tin of Wrights No. 1 Best Stuff that Ralph had provided. "I also know that any one of you can eat his own weight in *sadza* maize porridge in one sitting and wash it down with enough beer to stun a rhinoceros, but can you fight?"

And Isazi answered for them all, using the patient tone usually reserved for an obtuse child.

"We are Zulu." It was the only reply necessary.

◆ ◆ ◆

Jan Cheroot brought in six more, all of them Cape boys, with mixed Bushman and Hottentot blood, like Jan Cheroot himself.

"This one is named Grootboom, the Big Tree," and Ralph thought he looked more like a Kalahari Desert thornbush—dark, dry and thorny. "He was a corporal in the Fifty-second Foot at Cape Town Fort. He is my nephew."

"Why did he leave Cape Town?"

Jan Cheroot looked pained. "There was a dispute over a lady. A man had his gizzard slit. They accused my dear nephew of the dastardly deed."

"Did he do it?"

"Of course he did. He is the best man with a knife that I know—after me," Jan Cheroot declared modestly.

"Why do you want to kill Matabele?" Ralph asked him in Sindebele, and the Hottentot answered him fluently in the same language.

"It is work I understand and enjoy."

Ralph nodded and turned to the next man.

"It is possible that this one is even more closely related to me," Jan Cheroot introduced him. "His name is Taas, and his mother was a great beauty. She owned a famous bar at the foot of Signal Hill above Cape Town docks. At one time she and I were dear and intimate friends, but then the lady had many friends."

The prospective recruit had the flat nose and high cheekbones, the oriental eyes and the same waxen smooth skin as Jan Cheroot—if he was one of Jan Cheroot's bastards and had spent his boyhood in Cape Town's notorious dockland, then he should be a good man in a fight. Ralph nodded.

"Five shillings a day," he said. "And a free box to bury you in if the Matabele catch you."

◆ ◆ ◆

Jameson had taken many hundreds of horses south with him, and the Matabele had swept the horses off the farms. Maurice Gifford had already taken 160 mounted men down toward Gwanda to bring in any survivors who might be cut off on the outlying farms and mines and still be holding out, while Captain George Grey had formed a troop of mounted infantry, "Grey's Scouts," with most of the mounts that remained. The four mounts that Ralph had brought in with him were fine beasts, and he had managed to buy six more at exorbitant prices—a hundred pounds for an animal that would have fetched fifteen on a good day at Kimberley Market—but there were no others. He lay awake long after midnight under the wagon worrying about it while above him Robyn and Louise slept with the twins and the children on the wagon truck under the canvas tent.

Ralph's eyes were closed, and a few feet away Harry Mellow was breathing deeply and regularly, drowning out any small sounds. Yet even in his preoccupation, Ralph became aware of another presence near him in the darkness. He smelled it first, the taint of woodsmoke and cured animal furs and the odor of the fat with which a Matabele warrior anoints his body.

Ralph slipped his right hand up under the saddle he was using for a pillow, and his fingers touched the checkered walnut butt of his Webley pistol.

"Henshaw," whispered a voice he did not recognize, and Ralph whipped his left arm around a thick-corded neck and at the same moment thrust the muzzle of the pistol into the man's body.

"Quickly," he grated. "Who are you, before I kill you?"

"They told me you were quick and strong." The man was speaking Sindebele. "Now I believe it."

"Who are you?"

"I have brought you good men and the promise of horses."

Neither of them had spoken above a whisper.

"Why do you come like a thief?"

"Because I am Matabele; the white men will kill me if they find me here. I have come to take you to these men."

Ralph released him carefully and reached for his boots.

They left the laager and slipped through the silent, deserted town. Ralph had spoken only once more.

"You know that I will kill you if this is treachery."

"I know it," replied the Matabele.

He was tall, as tall as Ralph but even heavier built, and once when he glanced back at Ralph, the moonlight showed the silky sheen of scar tissue slashed across his cheek beneath his right eye.

In the yard of one of the last houses of the town, close to the open veld, yet screened from it by the wall that some houseproud citizen had erected to protect his garden, there were twelve more Matabele *amadoda* waiting. Some of them wore fur kilts, while others were dressed in ragged western castoffs.

"Who are these men?" Ralph demanded. "Who are you?"

"My name is Ezra, Sergeant Ezra. I was sergeant to One-Bright-Eye who the impis killed at Khami Hills. These men are all company police." -

"The company police have been disbanded and disarmed," Ralph said.

"Yes, they have taken away our guns. They say they do not trust us. That we may go over to the rebels."

"Why do you not?" Ralph said. "Some of your brothers have. They say a hundred of the company police have gone over, and taken their rifles with them."

"We cannot—even if we had wished to." Ezra shook his head. "Have you heard of the killing of two Matabele women near the Inyati River? A woman called Ruth and another called Flower, Imbali?"

Ralph frowned. "Yes, I remember."

"It was these men, and I was their sergeant. The induna named Gandang has asked that we be taken to him alive. He wishes personally to supervise the manner of our deaths."

"I want men who can kill the women of the Matabele as easily as they killed ours," said Ralph. "Now what of these horses?"

"The horses captured by the Matabele at Essexvale and Belingwe are being held in the hills at a place I know of."

♦ ♦ ♦

Long before the curfew bell, they had all slipped out of the central laager singly and in pairs, Jan Cheroot and his Cape boys taking the horses with them; and by the time Ralph and Harry Mellow strolled down the main street as though they were taking the evening air before returning to the laager for dinner, the others were all gathered in the walled garden at the end of the street.

Sergeant Ezra had brought the kilts and spears and knobkerries, and Jan Cheroot had the big black three-

294

legged pot of beef fat and lampblack boiled to a paste. Ralph and Harry and the Hottentots stripped naked and smeared each other with the rancid mixture, taking care to work it in around the back of the ears, the knees and elbows, and below the eyes where pale skin might show.

By the time the curfew bell in the Anglican Church began to toll, they were all dressed in the kilts of Matabele *amadoda*. Ralph and Harry covered their hair, which would have betrayed them, with headdresses of black widow bird feathers. Isazi and Jan Cheroot strapped the rawhide bootees over the hooves of the horses while Ralph gave his final orders, speaking in Sindebele, the only language they would use during the entire raid.

They left the town in the sudden darkness between sunset and moonrise, the hoofbeats of the horses deadened by the rawhides, and Ezra's Matabele running at the stirrups on silent bare feet. After the first hour, Ralph muttered a curt order to the Matabele, and they took a stirrup leather and hung from it, a man on each side of the horses. The pace of the march never slackened below a canter. They swept south and eastward, until the crenellated crests of the Matopo Hills were outlined against the moon-pale sky.

A little after midnight Ezra grunted.

"This is the place!"

Ralph rose in the stirrups and raised his right arm. The column bunched up and dismounted. Jan Cheroot's reputed bastard, Taas, came to take the horses while Jan Cheroot himself checked his men's weapons.

"I will put them against the firelight for you," Ralph whispered to him. "Watch for my signal."

Then Ralph smiled at Isazi, his teeth glinting in the shiny black mask of his daubed face. "There will be no prisoners. Lie close, but beware of Jan Cheroot's bullets."

"Henshaw, I want to go in with you."

Harry Mellow spoke in Sindebele, and Ralph answered him in the same language.

"You shoot better than you talk. Go with Jan Cheroot."

Another order from Ralph, every one of them reached into the leather pouch on his hip and brought out a white cow tail tassel necklace. They were the recognition insignia that might prevent them killing each other in the press of the fighting. Only Ralph added another ornament to his dress. From his hip pouch he brought the strip of moleskin and bound it around his upper arm; then he hefted the heavy assegai and leadwood knobkerrie and nodded at Ezra.

"Lead!"

The line of Matabele, with Ralph running in second place, trotted at a traverse across the slope of the hill. As they turned the southern buttress, they saw the red glow of a watch fire in the valley below. Ralph sprinted past Ezra to the front of the line. He filled his lungs and began to sing.

"Lift the rock under which sleeps the serpent.
Lift the rock and let the Mamba loose.
The Mamba of Mashobane has silver fangs of steel."

It was one of the fighting songs of the Insukamini impi, and behind him the line of Matabele picked up the refrain in their deep melodious voices. It resounded from the hills and woke the camp in the valley. Naked figures, risen from their sleeping mats, threw wood on the fires, and the red glow lit the underside of the acacia trees so they formed a canopy like a circus tent overhead.

Ezra had estimated there were forty *amadoda* guarding the horses, but there were more than that already gathered around the fires, and every second more flocked into the bivouac, the outposts coming in to see what was causing the commotion. Ralph had planned for that. He wanted no stragglers. They must be concentrated, so that his riflemen could fire into the bunch, making one bullet do the work of three or four. Ralph trotted into the Matabele encampment.

"Who commands here?" Ralph broke off the battle song and demanded in a bellow. "Let the commander stand forth to hear the word I bring from Gandang." He knew from the account that Robyn had given him of the massacre on the Khami Hills that the old induna was one of the leaders of the uprising. His choice of name had the effect he had hoped for.

"I am Mazui." A warrior stepped forward respectfully. "I wait for the word of Gandang, son of Mzilikazi."

"The horses are no longer safe in this place. The white men have learned where they are. At the rise of the sun we will take them deeper into the hills," Ralph told him. "To a place that I shall show you."

"It shall be done."

"Where are the horses?"

"They are in the kraal, guarded by my *amadoda*, safe from the lions."

"Bring in all your pickets," Ralph ordered, and the commander shouted an order and then turned back to Ralph eagerly.

"What news is there of the fighting?"

"There has been a great battle." Ralph launched into a fanciful account, miming the fighting in the traditional way, leaping and shouting and stabbing in the air with his assegai.

"Thus we came upon the rear of the horsemen, and thus and thus we stabbed them—" His own Matabele gave him a chorus of long drawn-out "Jee" and leaped and postured with him.

The audience was enraptured, beginning to stamp and sway in sympathy with Ralph and his Matabele. The sentries and pickets had come in from the periphery of the camp. No more hurrying black figures emerged from the shadows. They were all here—a hundred, perhaps a hundred and twenty, not more, Ralph estimated, against his forty men. Not unfair odds; Jan Cheroot's Cape boys were all first-rate marksmen, and Harry Mellow with a rifle was worth five ordinary men.

From close at hand, on the first slope of the hill, a nightjar called. It was a musical, quavering cry that sounded like "Good Lord, deliver us"; this pious sentiment gave the bird its popular name, the litany bird. It was the signal which Ralph had been listening for. He felt a bleak satisfaction that Jan Cheroot had followed his orders so strictly. From the position on the slope, Jan Cheroot would have the crowd of *amadoda* silhouetted against the firelight.

Making it all part of the dance, Ralph whirled away, still prancing and stamping, opening a distance of twenty paces between himself and the nearest Matabele. Here Ralph ended his dance abruptly with his arms spread like a crucifix. He stood deathly still staring at his audience with wild eyes, and a silence fell upon them all.

Slowly Ralph raised his arms above his head. He stood like that for a moment, a heroic figure glistening with fat, every muscle in his arms and chest standing proud, the kilt of civet tails hanging to his knees, the collar of white cow tails around his neck, his charm against the death that lurked in the darkness beyond the firelight. His blackened features were twisted into a ferocious grimace that held the watchers spellbound. The dancing and singing had served its purpose well. It had distracted the *amadoda* and masked any noise that the Zulus and Hottentots might have made while moving into position around the bivouac.

Now suddenly Ralph let out a demoniacal howl that made the *amadoda* shudder, and he dropped his arms—the signal for which Harry and Jan Cheroot were waiting.

The curtains of darkness were torn aside by the blast of massed rifle fire. The range was point-blank, the muzzles almost touching the press of dark, naked bodies. It smashed into them, a single bullet churning through belly and chest and spine, bringing down four men, stopping only when the slug broke up against one of the heavy bones of pelvis or femur.

So unexpected was the assault that the mass of warriors milled aimlessly, receiving three volleys from the repeating Winchesters before they broke and ran. More than half of them were down already, and many of those still on their feet were wounded. They ran on top of Isazi's Zulus and piled up against them like water on a dam wall. Ralph heard the great shouts of "*Ngidla!* I have eaten!" as the Zulus put in the steel, and heard the screams of the dying men.

Now at last the Matabele were rallying, closing up shoulder to shoulder to meet the thin line of Zulus and overrun it. It was the moment Ralph had waited for. He led his own Matabele racing across their rear and flung them at the naked undefended backs of the struggling warriors.

Long ago, as boys on the Kimberley diamond workings, Bazo had taught Ralph the art of spearsmanship. Ralph had been as skillful with the broad blade as any of the Matabele youths who were his companions. However, it was one thing to practice the long, underhanded killing stroke and another actually to send the point into living flesh.

Ralph was unprepared for the sensation of the steel in his hand running in and slowing against the sucking resistance, feeling the steel touch and grate on bone, and the haft kick in his hand as his victims bucked and convulsed at the agony. It felt like the butt of the rod when a salmon makes its first run.

Instinctively Ralph twisted the blade in the man's body, the way Bazo had taught him, maximizing the tissue damage and breaking the vacuum that held the steel—then he jerked it clear, and for the first time felt the fine hot spray of blood from the wound fly into his face and splatter his right arm and chest.

He stepped over the dying man who thrashed on the earth, and sank the steel again and then again. The smell of blood and the screams maddened him, but it was a cold, fierce madness that magnified his vision and slowed down the microseconds of mortal combat, so that he saw the counterthrust and turned his adversary's blade aside with contemptuous ease, using the momentum of his shoulders to drive his own point through the Matabele guard and into the notch formed by the joint of his collarbones at the base of his throat. The man's breath whistled over his severed vocal cords, and he dropped his assegai and seized Ralph's blade with his bare hands. Ralph pulled it back, and the razor edges cut to the bone of the man's fingers, and his hands fell open nervelessly as the Matabele dropped to his knees.

Ralph leaped over him and poised to thrust again.

"Henshaw!" a voice screamed in his face. "It is me!" And through his madness Ralph saw the white cow tail tassels about the neck and held the stroke; the two lines of attackers had met.

"It is over," Isazi panted, and Ralph looked about him in bewilderment. It had happened so swiftly. He shook his head to free the cold vice of fighting madness that gripped it.

They were all down, though a few of them still twisted and twitched and groaned.

"Isazi, finish them!" Ralph ordered, and watched the Zulus begin the grim work, passing quickly from body to body, feeling for the pulse below the ear and if they found it, stilling it with a quick thrust.

"Ralph." Harry came scrambling down the slope at the head of the Cape boys. "By God, that was one—"

"No English," Ralph warned him. Then raising his voice, "We will take the horses now. Bring the spare bridles and lead reins."

There were fifty-three fine horses in the thornbush kraal. Most of them carried the BSA Company brand. Each of the unmounted Zulus and Matabele selected a mount, and the remaining animals were put onto lead reins.

In the meantime the Cape boys were going over the field with the speed and precision of born footpads, selecting the rifles that could be used and throwing the ancient Martini-Henrys and muzzle-loaders and knobkerries onto the fire, snapping the assegai blades in the fork of a tree. The loot they discovered, cutlery and crockery and clothing of European manufacture, proved that this impi had taken part in the depredations of the first few days of the rising. That, too, was thrown upon the flames. Within an hour of the first rifle shot, they were moving out again. This time every man was well mounted, and the spare horses followed at a canter on the lead reins.

They rode down the main street of Bulawayo in the uncertain gray light of predawn. In the front rank, Ralph and Harry had scrubbed most of the blackening from their faces, but to make certain they did not draw the fire of a jittery sentry, they carried a flag made from Harry Mellow's white flannel undershirt.

The inhabitants of the laager tumbled out of their beds to gape and question, and then as they began to realize that this little cavalcade heralded the first retaliation against the slaughter and arson committed by the tribes, the cheering began and rose into joyous hysteria.

While Vicky and Elizabeth proudly served them a double ration breakfast under the wagon awning, Ralph and Harry received an endless string of well-wishers—tearful windows whose husbands had perished under the Matabele assegais, bringing thanks and a half-dozen eggs or a freshly baked cake, wistful boys come merely to stare at the heroes, and keen young men demanding eagerly, "Is this where we sign up to join Ballantyne's Scouts?"

◆ ◆ ◆

There were shrieks of delight as Judy set about her long-suffering husband with her baton. The children in the front row clapped their hands as the blows cracked upon Punch's wooden head and his grotesquely humped back, and the bells on his cap jingled.

Swimming valiantly against the mainstream of sentiment, Jon-Jon's face was red as Punch's hooked nose and screwed up with outrage. "Hit her back!" he howled, bouncing up and down. "She's only a girl!"

"Spoken like a true Ballantyne," Ralph laughed, at the

same time forcibly restraining his son from leaping into the fray on the side of downtrodden mankind.

Elizabeth sat beyond Jon-Jon with Robert on her lap. The child's sickly face was solemn, and he sucked dedicatedly upon his thumb like an elderly gnome upon his pipe. In contrast, Elizabeth was radiant with a childlike joy, her cheeks flushed and her eyes shining as she egged Judy on to further excesses.

A shining lock of her hair had come loose from the tortoiseshell comb and lay against the tender, velvety skin of her temple, half curled around the lobe of her ear. Her ear was so thin and delicately shaped that the sunlight shone through it as though it were made from some rare bone china. The same sunlight made the Burgundy sparks flare like electricity in her thick, dark tresses.

It drew Ralph's attention from the marionettes, and he watched her covertly over Jonathan's curly head. Her laughter was a throaty purr, natural and unashamed, and Ralph laughed again in sympathy. She turned her head, and for a moment Ralph looked deeply into her eyes. It was like looking into a bowl of hot honey. He seemed to be able to see into limitless depths that were flecked with gold. Then Elizabeth dropped the veil of dark, curved lashes over them and looked back at the tiny stage, but she was no longer laughing. Instead her lower lip trembled and a dark flush of blood washed up her throat.

Feeling strangely guilty and shaken, Ralph quickly fastened his own eyes, if not his attention, on the squawking, battling marionettes. The sketch ended, to Jonathan's vast satisfaction, with Judy being led away to some nameless but richly deserved fate by a policeman in Mr. Peel's blue helmet, and the mild, bespectacled little bookkeeper of Meikles Store came out from behind his candy-striped screen with the glove puppets still upon his hands, to take his bows.

"He looks just like Mr. Kipling," Elizabeth whispered, "and he has the same bloodthirsty and violent imagination."

Ralph felt a rush of gratitude toward her that she should gloss over that unexpected moment of awkwardness so gracefully. He picked up the boys, sat one upon each shoulder, and they followed the dispersing audience across the laager.

Upon his father's shoulder, Jonathan chattered like a

flock of starlings, explaining to Bobby the finer points of the play, which were clearly too subtle for any lesser intelligence than his own to follow. However, both Ralph and Elizabeth walked in silence.

When they reached the wagon, Ralph slid both children to the ground, and they scampered away. Halfheartedly, Elizabeth made to follow them but stopped and turned back to him when Ralph spoke.

"I don't know what I would have done without you— you've been wonderfully kind—" he hesitated. "Without Cathy—" He saw the pain in her eyes and broke off. "I just wanted to thank you."

"You don't have to do that, Ralph," she answered quietly. "Anything you need—I'll always be here to help." Then her reserve cracked, she started to speak again, but her lips trembled and she turned away sharply and followed the two boys into the wagon.

◆ ◆ ◆

Ralph had paid siege prices for the bottle of whisky by scrawling a check on the label from a bully beef tin for twenty pounds. He took it hidden under his coat to where Isazi and Jan Cheroot and Sergeant Ezra sat together beside a fire away from their men.

They swilled the coffee grounds out of their enamel mugs and proffered them for a good dram of the whisky and sipped in silence for a while, all of them staring into the campfire flames, letting the warmth of the spirit spread out through their bodies.

At last Ralph nodded at Sergeant Ezra, and the big Matabele began to speak quietly.

"Gandang and his Inyati impi are still waiting in the Khami Hills—he has twelve hundred men. They are all blooded warriors. Babiaan is bivouacked below the Hills of the Indunas with six hundred. He could be here in an hour—" Quickly Ezra recounted the positions of the impis, the names of their indunas, and the mood and mettle of their warriors.

"What of Bazo and his Moles?" At last Ralph asked the question that concerned him most, and Ezra shrugged.

"We do not have word of them. I have my best men in the hills, searching for them. Nobody knows where the Moles have gone."

"Where will we strike next?" Ralph asked the question rhetorically, musing as he stared in the fire. "Will it be at Babiaan in the Hills of the Indunas, or Zama with his thousand lying across the Mangiwe Road?"

Isazi coughed in polite disagreement, and when Ralph glanced up at him, he said, "Last night I sat at one of Babiaan's campfires, eating his meat and listening to his men talk. They spoke of our attack upon the camp of the horses and how the indunas had warned them in future to be on their guard against all strangers, even though they wore the furs and feathers of the fighting impis. We will not work the same trick twice."

Jan Cheroot and Ezra grunted in agreement, and the little Hottentot inverted his mug to prove it empty and glanced significantly at the bottle between Ralph's feet. Ralph poured again, and as he cupped the mug in his hands and inhaled the pungent perfume of the spirit, his mind went back to that afternoon—to the laughter of the children and a lovely young girl whose hair burned with soft fires in the sunlight.

His voice was rough and ugly. "Their women and children," he said. "They will be hidden in the caves and the secret valleys of the Matopos. Find them!"

◆ ◆ ◆

There were five small boys under the bank of the stream. They were all stark naked, and their legs were coated to above the knees with slick yellow clay. They laughed and squabbled good-naturedly as they dug the clay out of the bank with sharpened sticks and packed it into crudely woven reed baskets.

Tungata Zebiwe, The Seeker After What Has Been Stolen, was the first to climb out of the stream, lugging the heavy basket to a shady place where he squatted and set to work. The others straggled up the bank after him and seated themselves in a circle.

Tungata took a handful of clay from his basket and rolled it into a thick soft sausage between his pink palms. Then he molded it with practiced skill, forming the humped back and sturdy legs. When it was complete, he set the body carefully between his knees on a slab of dried bark, then turned his attention to sculpturing the head separately with curved red devil thorns for the horns and chips of water-worn rock crystal for the eyes. He attached the head to the thick neck, sticking out his tongue with concentration as he adjusted it to a proud angle, and then he sat back and studied it with a critical eye.

"Inkunzi Nkulu!" he hailed his creation. "Great Bull!"

Grinning with delight, he carried the clay beast to the ant heap and set it on its bark base to dry in the sun. Then he hurried back to begin making the cows and calves for his herd. As he worked, he mocked the creations of the other boys, comparing them to his own great herd bull and grinning cheekily at their retorts.

Tanase watched him from the shadows. She had come silently down the path through the thick riverine bush, led on by the tinkling of child laughter and the happy banter. Now she was reluctant to interrupt this magical moment.

In the sadness and striving, in the menace and smoke of war, it seemed that all joy and laughter had been forgotten. It needed the resilience and vision of a child to remind her of what had once been—and what might be again. She felt a suffocating weight of love overwhelm her, followed almost immediately by a formless dread. She wanted to rush to the child and take him in her arms, to hold him tightly to her bosom and protect him from—she was not sure what.

Then Tungata looked up and saw her and came to her carrying the clay bull with shy pride.

"See what I have made."

"It is beautiful."

"It is for you, Umame, I made it for you."

Tanase took the offering. "He is a fine bull, and he will breed many calves," she said, and her love was so strong that the tears scalded her eyelids. She did not want the child to see.

"Wash the clay off your legs and arms," she told him. "We must go up to the cave."

He skipped beside her on the path, his body still wet from the river, his skin glistening with a velvety black sheen, laughing delightedly when Tanase set the clay bull upon her head, walking straight-backed and with hips swinging, to balance the load.

They came up the path to the base of the cliff. It was not truly a cave, but a long, low overhang of the cliff face. They were not the first to use it as a home. The rocky roof was blackened with the soot of innumerable cooking fires, and the back wall was decorated with the ancient paintings and engravings of the little yellow Bushmen who had hunted here long before Mzilikazi led his impis into these hills. They were wonderful pictures of rhinoceroses and giraffes and gazelles, and of the little stick figures, armed with bows and outsized genitalia, who hunted them.

There were almost five hundred persons living in this place, one of the secret safe places of the tribe, where the women and the children were sent when war or some other catastrophe threatened the Matabele. Though the valley was steep and narrow, there were five escape routes, hidden paths scaling the cliffs or narrow clefts through the granite, which made it impossible for an enemy to trap them in the gut of the valley.

The stream provided fresh, clear water for drinking; thirty milch cows that had survived the rinderpest provided *maas*, the soured milk which was one of the tribe's staples. And when they marched in, every woman had borne upon her head a leather grain bag. The locusts had depleted the harvest, but with careful planning they could exist here for many months.

The women were spread out down the length of the rock shelter, busy with their separate tasks. Some of them were stamping the corn in mortars carved from a dried tree trunk, using a heavy wooden pestle that they swung up with both hands above their head and then let drop of its own weight into the cup of the mortar, clapping their hands and then seizing the club to lift it for the next stroke. Others were plaiting bark cloth for sleeping mats, or tanning wild animals' skins, or stringing ceramic beads. Over it all hung the faint blue mist of the cooking fires and the sweet hum of women's voices, interspersed with the gurgling and chirping of black babes who crawled naked on the rocky floor or hung like fat limpets from their mothers' breasts.

Juba was at the far end of the shelter, imparting to two of her daughters and the new wife of one of her middle sons the delicate secrets of beer brewing. The sorghum grain had been soaked and had germinated; now came the drying and grinding of the yeast. It was an absorbing task, and Juba did not become aware of the presence of her senior daughter-in-law and her eldest grandson until they stood over her. Then she looked up and her smile split the great round of her face.

"My mother," Tanase knelt before her respectfully. "I must speak with you."

Juba struggled to rise but was pinned by her own vast weight. Her daughters took an elbow each and heaved her upright. Once she was on her feet, she moved with surprising agility, swept Tungata onto her hip, and carried him easily along the pathway. Tanase fell in beside her.

"Bazo has sent for me," Tanase told her. "There is dissension among the indunas; Bazo needs the words of the Umlimo made clear. Without that the struggle will fall into vacillation and talk. We will lose all that we have won so dearly."

"Then you must go, my child."

"I must go swiftly. I cannot take Tungata with me."

"He is safe here—I will look after him. When do you leave?"

"Immediately."

Juba sighed and nodded. "So be it."

Tanase touched the child's cheek. "Obey your grandmother," she said softly, and like a shadow was gone around the bend of the narrow pathway.

♦ ♦ ♦

Tanase passed through the granite portals that guarded the valley of the Umlimo. She had only her memories of this place for traveling companions, and they were not good company. Yet when she went down the path, she walked straight, with a kind of antelope grace, her long limbs swinging freely and her head held high on the long heron's neck.

As soon as she entered the little cluster of huts in the bottom of the valley, her trained senses were immediately aware of the tensions and angers that hung over the place like a sickly miasma over a fever swamp. She could feel the anger and frustration in Bazo when she knelt before him and made her dutiful obeisance. She knew so well what those knots of tense muscle at the points of his clenched jaw and the reddish glaze in his eyes meant.

Before she rose, she had noted how the indunas had drawn into two separate groups. On one side were the elders, and facing them, the young and headstrong were ranged about Bazo. She crossed the space between them and knelt before Gandang and his white-headed brothers, Somabula and Babiaan.

"I see you, my child." Gravely Gandang acknowledged her greeting, and then the abruptness with which he broached the real reason for her summons warned Tanase of its dire import.

"We wish you to speak to us on the meaning of the Umlimo's latest prophecy."

"My Lord and Father, I am no longer an intimate of the mysteries—"

Impatiently Gandang brushed aside her disclaimer. "You understand more than anyone outside that dreadful cave. Listen to the words of the Umlimo, and discourse faithfully upon them."

She bowed her head in acquiescence, but at the same time turned slightly so that she had Bazo at the very edge of her vision.

"The Umlimo spake thus: 'Only a foolish hunter blocks the opening of the cave from which the wounded leopard seeks to escape.' " Gandang repeated the prophecy, and his brothers nodded at the accuracy of his rendition.

Veiling her eyes behind thick black lashes, Tanase turned her head the breadth of a finger. Now she could see Bazo's right hand as it rested on his bare thigh. She had taught him the rudiments of the secret sign language of the initiates. His forefinger curled and touched the first joint of his thumb. It was a command.

'Remain silent!" said that gesture. "Speak not!" She made the signal of comprehension and acknowledgment with the hand that hung at her side. Then she raised her head.

"Was that all, Lord?" she asked of Gandang.

"There is more," he answered. "The Umlimo spake a second time: 'The hot wind from the north will scorch the weeds in the fields before the new corn can be planted. Wait for the north wind.' " All the indunas leaned forward eagerly, and Gandang told her, "Speak to us of the meaning."

"The meaning of the Umlimo's words is never clear at once. I must ponder on it."

"When will you tell us?"

"When I have an answer."

"Tomorrow morning?" Gandang insisted.

"Perhaps."

"Then you will spend the night alone, that your meditation be not disturbed," Gandang ordered.

"My husband," Tanase demurred.

"Alone," Gandang repeated sharply. "With a guard on the door of your hut."

The guard that was set upon her hut was a young warrior, not yet married, and because of it he was that more susceptible to the wiles of a beautiful woman. When he brought the bowl of food to Tanase, she smiled in such a way that he lingered at the door of the hut. When she offered him a choice morsel, he glanced outside guiltily and then came to take it from her hand.

The food had a strange bitter taste, but he did not want to give offense, so he swallowed it manfully. The woman's smile promised things that the young warrior could barely believe possible, but when he tried to answer her provocative sallies, his voice slurred strangely in his own ears, and he was overcome with a lassitude such that he had to close his eyes for a moment.

Tanase replaced the stopper on the buckhorn bottle she had concealed in her palm and stepped quietly over the guard's sleeping form. When she whistled, Bazo came swiftly and silently to where she waited by the stream.

"Tell me, Lord," she whispered, "that which you require of me."

When she returned to the hut, the guard still slept deeply. She propped him in the doorway with his weapon across his lap. In the morning his head would ache, but he would not be eager to tell the indunas how he had spent the night.

◆ ◆ ◆

"I have thought deeply on the words of the Umlimo" Tanase knelt before the indunas—"and I read meaning into the parable of the foolish hunter who hesitates in the entrance of the cave."

Gandang frowned as he guessed the slant of her reply, but she went on calmly.

"Would not the brave and skilled hunter go boldly into the cave where the animal lurks and slay it?" One of the elder indunas hissed with disagreement and sprang to his feet.

"I say that the Umlimo has warned us to leave the road

to the south open, so that the white men with all their women and chattels may leave this land forever," he shouted, and immediately Bazo was on his feet facing him.

"The white men will never leave. The only way to rid ourselves of them is to bury them." There was a roar of approval from the younger indunas grouped around Bazo, but he lifted his hand to silence them.

"If you leave the south road open, it will certainly be used—by the soldiers who march up it with their little three-legged guns."

There were angry cries of denial and encouragement.

"I say to you that we are the hot wind from the north that the Umlimo prophesied, we are the ones who will scorch the weeds—"

The shouts that drowned him out showed just how deeply the nation's leaders were divided, and Tanase felt the blackness of despair come down upon her. Gandang rose to his feet, and such was the weight of tradition and custom that even the wildest and fiercest of the young indunas fell silent.

"We must give the white men a chance to leave with their women. We will leave the road open for them to go, and we will wait in patience for the hot wind, the miraculous wind from the north that the Umlimo promises to blow our enemies away—"

Bazo alone had not squatted respectfully to the senior induna, and now he did something that was without precedent. He interrupted his father, and his voice was full of scorn.

"You have given them chance enough," said Bazo. "You have let the woman from Khami and all her brats go free. I ask you one question, my father, is what you propose kindness or is it cowardice?"

They gasped, for when a son could speak thus to his father, then the world that once they all had known and understood was now changed. Gandang looked at Bazo across the small space that separated them, which was a gulf neither of them would ever be able once again to bridge. Through he was still tall and erect, there was such sorrow in Gandang's eyes that it made him seem as old as the granite hills that surrounded them.

"You are no longer my son," he said simply.

"And you are no longer my father," Bazo said, and

turning on his heel, strode from the hut. First Tanase, and then, one after another, the young indunas stood up and followed Bazo out into the sunlight.

◆ ◆ ◆

An outrider came in at full gallop and brought his horse up so sharply that it reared and sawed its head against the bit.

"Sir, there is a large party of rebels coming up the road ahead," he shouted urgently.

"Very well, trooper." The Honorable Maurice Gifford, officer commanding troops B and D of the Bulawayo field force, touched the brim of his slouch hat with a gloved hand in acknowledgment. "Go forward and keep them under observation." Then he turned in the saddle. "Captain Dawson, we will put the wagons into laager under those trees—there will be a good field of fire for the Maxim from there. I will take out fifty mounted men to engage the enemy."

It really was a piece of astonishing good luck to run into a group of rebels so close to Bulawayo. After weeks of scouring the countryside, Gifford and his 160 troopers had managed to gather in thirty or so survivors from the isolated villages and trading posts, but so far they had not had even a chance of a scrap with the Matabele. Leaving Dawson to prepare the laager, Gifford spurred down the Bulawayo road at the head of fifty of his best men.

Gifford was the youngest son of an earl, a handsome young aristocrat and junior officer in a famous guards regiment. He had been spending his leave on a spot of shooting in Africa and had been fortunate enough to have his holiday enlivened by a native uprising. The general opinion of the Honorable M. Gifford was that he was frightfully keen, and a damned fine young fellow, bound to go a long way.

He reined his horse at the crest of the rise and held up his gloved right hand to halt the troop.

"There they are, sir," cried the outrider. "Bold as brass."

The Honorable Maurice Gifford polished the lenses of his binoculars on the tail of his yellow silk scarf and then held the glasses to his eyes.

"They are all mounted," he said, "and jolly well mounted

at that. But, I say, what a murderous-looking bunch of ruffians."

The approaching horsemen were half a mile away, a straggling mob, dressed in war kilts and headdresses, armed with a weird assortment of modern and primitive weapons.

"Troop, into extended order, left and right wheel," Gifford ordered. "Sergeant, we will use the slope to charge them, and then disengage and attempt to draw them within range of the Maxim."

"Begging your pardon, sir," the sergeant mumbled, "but isn't that a white man leading them?"

Gifford lifted the binoculars and peered through them again. "The devil it is!" he muttered. "But the fellow is dressed in furs and things."

The fellow gave him a cheery wave, as he rode up at the head of his motley gang.

"Morning. You aren't Maurice Gifford by any chance?"

"I am, sir," Gifford replied frostily. "And who are you, if I may be so bold as to ask?"

"The name's Ballantyne, Ralph Ballantyne." The fellow gave him an engaging grin. "And these gentlemen"—with his thumb he indicated those who followed him—"are Ballantyne's Scouts."

Maurice Gifford looked them over with distaste. It was impossible to tell their racial origins, for they were all painted with fat and clay to look like Matabele, and they wore castoffs and tribal dress. Only this fellow Ballantyne had left his face its natural color, probably to identify himself to the Bulawayo field force, but it was equally probable that he would blacken it as soon as he had what he wanted from them. He was not shy about making his wants known, either.

"A requisition, Mr. Gifford," he said, and handed over a folded and sealed note from his belt pouch.

Gifford bit on the finger of his glove and drew it off his right hand before he accepted the note and broke the seal.

"I cannot let you have my Maxim, sir," he exclaimed as he read. "I have a duty to protect the civilians in my care."

"You are only four miles from the laager at Bulawayo, and the road is clear of Matabele. We have just swept it for you. There is no longer any danger to your people."

"But—" said Gifford.

"The requisition is signed by Colonel William Napier, officer commanding the Bulawayo field force. I suggest you take the matter up with him when you reach Bulawayo." Ralph was still smiling. "In the meantime, we are rather pressed for time. We will just relieve you of the Maxim, and trouble you no further."

Gifford crumpled the note and glared impotently at Ralph, then shifted his ground.

"You and your men appear to be wearing enemy uniforms," he accused. "That is in contravention of the articles of war, sir."

"Read the articles to the indunas, Mr. Gifford, particularly those dealing with the murder and torture of noncombatants."

"There is no call for an Englishman to descend to the level of the savages he is fighting," said Gifford loftily. "I have had the honor to meet your father, Major Zouga Ballantyne. He is a gentleman. I wonder what he would say about your conduct."

"My father and his fellow conspirators, all of them English gentlemen, are presently standing trial on charges of having waged war against a friendly government. However, I will certainly solicit his opinion of my conduct at the first available opportunity. Now if you will send your sergeant back with us to hand over the Maxim, I will bid you good day, Mr. Gifford."

They unloaded the Maxim from its cart, removed the tripod and ammunition boxes, and loaded them onto three packhorses.

"How did you get Napier to sign away one of his precious Maxims?" Harry Mellow demanded as he clinched the straps on the packsaddles.

"Sleight of hand." Ralph winked at him. "The pen is mightier—"

"You forged the requisition." Harry stared at him. "They'll shoot you."

"They'll have to catch me first." Ralph turned and bellowed to his Scouts, "Troop, mount! Walk march, forward!"

♦ ♦ ♦

There was no doubt that he was a wizard. A wizened little fellow, not much taller than Tungata or any of his companions, but he was painted in the most marvelous colors, zigzags of crimson and white and black across his face and chest.

When he first appeared out of the bush beside the stream in the secret valley, the children were frozen with terror. But before they could recover their wits sufficiently to run, the little painted wizard uttered such a string of cries and grunts, imitating horse and eagle and chacma baboon, at the same time prancing and flapping and scratching, that their terror turned to fascination.

Then, from the sack over his shoulder, the wizard dug out a huge lump of rock sugar candy. He sucked it noisily, and the children who had not tasted sugar in weeks drew closer and watched him with glistening dark eyes. He proffered the lump of sugar to Tungata, who edged forward, snatched it and scampered back. The little wizard laughed in such an infectious manner that the other children laughed with him and swarmed forward to grab at the fresh lumps of candy he offered. Surrounded by laughing, clapping children, the little wizard climbed the path up the side of the valley to the rock shelter.

The women, lulled and reassured by the sounds of happy children, came to crowd about the little wizard, to stare and giggle, and the boldest to ask him:

"Who are you?"

"Where do you come from?"

"What is in the sack?"

In reply to the last question, the wizard drew out a handful of colored ribbons, and the younger women shrieked with feminine vanity and tied them at their wrists and throats.

"I bring gifts and happy things," the wizard cackled. "Look what I bring you."

There were steel combs and small, round mirrors, a little box that played sweet, tinkling music—they crowded about him, utterly enchanted. "Gifts and happy tidings," sang the wizard.

"Tell us! Tell us!" they chanted.

"The spirits of our forefathers have come to aid us. They have sent a divine wind to eat up the white men as the rinderpest ate up the cattle. All the white men are dead!"

"The *amakiwa* are dead!"

"They have left behind them all these wonderful gifts. The town of Bulawayo is empty of white men, but these things are there for all to take. As much as you will—but hurry, all the men and women of the Matabele are going there. There will be nothing left for those who come after. Look, look at these beautiful pieces of cloth—there are thousands of them. Who wants these pretty buttons, these sharp knives? Those who want them must follow me!" sang the wizard. "For the fighting is over! The white men are dead! The Matabele have triumphed! Who wants to follow me?"

"Lead us, little Father," they begged him. "We will follow you."

Still digging out gewgaws and trifles from the sack, the painted wizard started down toward the end of the narrow valley, and the women snatched up their little ones, strapped them to their backs with strips of cloth, called to the older children, and hurried after the wizard.

"Follow me, people of Mashobane!" he chirped. "Your time of greatness has come. The prophecy of the Umlimo is fulfilled. The divine wind from the north has blown the *amakiwa* away."

Tungata, almost hysterical with excitement and dread that he would be left behind, hurried down the length of the rock shelter until he saw the huge, beloved figure squatting against the back wall of rock.

"Grandmother," he squeaked. "The wizard has pretty things for us all. We must hurry!"

♦ ♦ ♦

Over the millennia the stream had cut a narrow, twisted exit from the bowel of the valley, with high cliffs on each side. The granite was painted with rich orange and yellow lichens. Compressed into this chasm, the steam fell in smoking cascades of white water before debouching into a shallower, wider valley in the lower foothills.

The valley was filled with fine grass the color of a ripening wheat field. The pathway clung to the edge of the chasm, with a perilous drop to foaming white water on one hand and with the cliff rising sheer on the other. Then the gradient became more gentle, and the path emerged into the quiet valley below. Rainwater had scarred the side of the lower valley with deep dongas, natural entrenchments, and one of these afforded an ideal emplacement for the Maxim.

Ralph had two of his troopers set it up with the thick, water-jacketed barrel just clearing the lip of the donga. There were two thousand rounds of ammunition in the oblong boxes stacked beside the weapon. While Harry Mellow cut branches of thornbush to screen the Maxim, Ralph paced off the ranges in front of the donga and set up a cairn of loose stones beside the footpath.

He came scrambling back up the slope and told Harry, "Set the sights for three hundred yards."

Then he went down the length of the donga, giving his orders to each man and making him repeat them to insure there was no misunderstanding.

"When Jan Cheroot reaches the cairn, the Maxim will fire. Wait for the Maxim, then open up on the back of the column and move your fire forward."

Sergeant Ezra nodded and levered a cartridge into the breech of the Winchester. He screwed up his eyes, judging the wind deflection by the swaying of the grass tops and the feel of it against his face. Then he settled his elbow on the earthen parapet of the gully and laid his scarred cheek against the butt.

Ralph returned along the donga to where Harry Mellow was preparing the Maxim. He watched while Harry twisted the elevation screw to raise the barrel slightly to the three-hundred-yard setting and then swung the gun left and right on its tripod to make certain that the traverse was free and clear.

"Load one," Ralph ordered, and Taas, who was loading, fed the brass tag of the cartridge belt into the open breech. Harry let the loading handle fly back, and the mechanism clattered harshly.

"Load two!" He pumped the handle a second time, pulling the belt through, and the first round was extracted from the belt and fed smoothly into the breech.

"Ready!" Harry looked up at Ralph.

"Now all we have to do is wait."

Ralph nodded and opened the pouch on his hip. From it he took the strip of brown moleskin and bound it carefully about his right arm above the elbow. Then they settled down to wait.

They waited in the sunlight, and it beat down upon their greasy, naked backs, until their sweat oozed from clogged pores and the flies came swarming gleefully to it. They waited while the sun made its noon and then began to slip down the farther side of the sky.

Abruptly Ralph raised his head, and at the movement a little stirring rippled down the row of marksmen lining the lip of the donga. There was a sound of many voices at a distance, and they woke echoes from the lichen-stained cliffs that guarded the entrance to the gorge. Then there was singing, sweet children's voices; the sound of it rose and fell with each fluke of the wind and each turn in the rocky passage.

From the entrance to the gorge, a diminutive figure came dancing. The weird pattern of red and black and white paints disguised Jan Cheroot's flat puglike features and the buttery yellow of his skin, but there was no mistaking his sprightly step and the way he carried his head at a birdlike angle. The sack of pretties that he had used as bait was long ago empty and had been discarded.

He scampered down the path toward the stone cairn which Ralph had built, and behind him came the Matabele. So eager were they that they crowded three or four abreast and jostled each other to keep pace with the Pied Piper that led them.

"More than I had hoped," Ralph whispered, but Harry Mellow did not look at him. The coating of black fat covered the pallor of his face, but his eyes were stricken as he stared fixedly over the sights of the Maxim.

The long column of Matabele was still emerging from the gorge, but Jan Cheroot was almost level with the cairn.

"Ready," Ralph grated.

Jan Cheroot reached the cairn, and then with a miraculous twinkling movement, he disappeared as though a pitfall had sucked him in.

"Now!" said Ralph.

Not a man in the long line of riflemen moved. They were all staring down into the valley.

"Now!" Ralph repeated.

The head of the column had stopped in bewilderment at Jan Cheroot's abrupt disappearance, and those behind pushed forward.

"Open fire!" Ralph ordered.

"I can't do it," whispered Harry, sitting behind the gun with both hands on the grips.

"Damn you!" Ralph's voice shook. "They slit Cathy's

belly open and tore my daughter out of her womb. Kill them, damn you!"

"I can't," Harry choked, and Ralph seized his shoulder and dragged him backward.

He dropped down behind the gun in his place and grabbed the double pistol grips. With his forefingers he hooked the safety locks open and then pressed his thumbs down on the checkered firing button. The Maxim gun began its hellish, fluttering roar, and the empty brass cartridge cases spewed in a bright stream from the breech.

Peering through the drifts of blue gunsmoke, Ralph slowly traversed the gun from left to right, sweeping the pathway from the mouth of the gorge to the stone cairn, and from the donga on each side of him the repeating Winchesters added their thunder to the din. The gunfire almost, but not quite, drowned out the sounds from the valley below.

♦ ♦ ♦

Juba could not keep pace with the younger women, nor with the racing children. She lagged farther and farther behind, with Tungata urging her on anxiously.

"We will be too late, Grandmother. We must hurry."

Before they reached the gorge at the end of the valley, Juba was wheezing and staggering, all her rolls of shining fat wobbling at each heavy pace, and she was seeing patches of darkness before her eyes.

"I must rest," she panted, and sank down beside the path. The stragglers streamed past her, laughing and joshing her as they entered the gorge.

"Ah, little Mother, do you want to climb up on my back?"

Tungata waited beside her, hopping from one foot to the other, wringing his hands with impatience.

"Oh, Grandmother, just a little farther—"

When at last the patches of darkness cleared from her vision, she nodded at him, and he seized her hands and threw all the weight of his tiny body into levering her upright.

Now, as Juba hobbled along the path, they were the very last in the file, but they could hear the laughter and chanting far ahead, magnified by the funnel of the gorge. Tungata ran forward, and then drawn by his duty, skipped back to seize Juba's hand again.

"Please, Grandmother—oh, please!"

Twice more Juba was forced to stop. They were all alone now, and the sunlight did not penetrate the depths of the narrow gorge. It was shadowy, and the cold coming up from the dashing white waters chilled even Tungata's high spirits.

The two of them came around the bend and looked out between the high granite portals into the open, sunlit grassy bowl beyond.

"There they are!" Tungata cried with relief.

The pathway through the yellow grassland was thick with people, but like a column of safari ants on the march that had come against an impossible obstacle, the head of the line was bunching and milling.

"Hurry, Grandmother, we can catch up!"

Juba heaved her bulk upright and hobbled toward the welcoming, warm sunlight.

At that moment the air around her head began to flutter as though a bird had been trapped within her skull. For a moment she thought that it was a symptom of her exhaustion, but then she saw the masses of human figures ahead of her begin to swirl and tumble and boil like dust motes in a whirlwind.

Although she had never heard it before, she had listened when the warriors who had fought at Shangani and the Bembesi Crossing described the little three-legged guns that chattered like old women. Armed suddenly by reserves of strength that she never believed she possessed, Juba seized Tungata and blundered back up the gorge like a great cow elephant in flight.

◆ ◆ ◆

Ralph Ballantyne sat on the edge of his camp cot. There was a lighted candle set in its own wax on the upturned tea chest that served as a table, and a half-filled whisky bottle and enamel mug beside it.

Ralph frowned at the open page of his journal, trying to focus in the flickering yellow candlelight. He was drunk. The bottle had been full half an hour before. He picked up the mug and drained it, set it down and poured from the bottle again. A few drops spilled onto the empty page of his journal. He wiped them away with his thumb and studied the wet mark it left with a drunkard's ponderous concentration. He shook his head to try and clear it, then he picked up his pen, dipped it and carefully wiped off the excess ink from the nib.

He wrote laboriously, and where the ink touched the wetness left by the spilled whisky, it spread in a soft blue fan shape on the paper. That annoyed him inordinately, and he flung the pen down and deliberately filled the enamel mug to the brim. He drank it, pausing twice for breath, and when the mug was empty, he held it between his knees, with his head bowed over it.

After a long time, and with an obvious effort, he lifted his head again and reread what he had written, his lips forming the words, like a schoolboy with his first reader.

"War makes monsters of us all."

He reached for the bottle again but knocked it on its side, and the golden brown spirit glugged into a puddle on the lid of the tea chest. He fell back on the cot and closed his eyes, his legs dangling to the floor and one arm thrown over his face protectively.

Elizabeth had put the boys to bed in the wagon and crawled into the cot below theirs, careful not to disturb her own mother. Ralph had not eaten dinner with the family, and he had sent Jonathan back with a rough word when he had gone across to the tent to fetch his father to the meal.

Elizabeth lay on her side under the woolen blanket, and her eye was level with the laced-up opening in the canvas hood, so she could see out. The candle was still burning in Ralph's tent, but, in the corner of the laager, the tent that Harry and Vicky shared had been in darkness for an hour. She closed her eyes and tried to force herself to sleep, but she was so restless that beside her Robyn St. John sighed petulantly and rolled over. Elizabeth opened her eyes again and peered surreptitiously through the canvas slit. The candle was still burning in Ralph's tent.

Gently she eased herself out from under the blanket, watching her mother the while. She picked up her shawl from the lid of the chest and clambered silently down to the ground.

With the shawl about her shoulders, she sat on the disselboom of the wagon. There was still only a sheet of canvas between her and where her mother lay. She could clearly hear the rhythm of Robyn's breathing. She judged when she sank deeply below the level of consciousness, for her breathing made a soft, glottal rattle in the back of her throat.

The night was warm and the laager almost silent; a puppy yapped unhappily from the far end, and closer at hand a baby's hungry wail was swiftly gagged by a mother's teat. Two of the sentries met at the nearest corner of the laager, and their voices murmured for a while. Then they parted, and she saw the silhouette of a slouch hat against the night sky as one of them passed close to where she sat.

The candle still burned in the tent, and it must be past midnight by now. The flame drew her as though she were a moth. She rose and crossed to the tent. Silently, almost furtively, she lifted the flap and slipped in, letting it drop closed behind her.

Ralph lay on his back on the steel cot; his booted feet dangled to the ground, and one arm covered his face. He was making an unhappy little whimpering sound in his sleep. The candle was guttering, burned down into a puddle of its own molten wax, and the smell of spilled whisky was sharp and pungent. Elizabeth crossed to the tea chest and set the fallen bottle upright. Then the open page of the journal caught her attention, and she read the big, uneven scrawl: "War makes monsters of us all."

It gave her a pang of pity so sharp that she closed the leather-bound journal quickly and looked at the man who had written that agonized heart cry. She wanted to reach across and touch his unshaven cheek, but instead she hitched her nightdress in a businesslike fashion and squatted beside the cot. She undid the straps of his riding boots, and then, taking them one at a time between her knees, she pulled them off his feet. Ralph muttered and flung the arm off his face, rolling away from the candlelight. Gently Elizabeth lifted his legs and swung them up onto the cot. He groaned and curled into a fetal position.

"Big baby," she whispered, and smiled to herself. Then she could resist no longer, and she stroked the thick, dark lock of hair off his forehead. His skin was fever-hot, moist with sweat, and she laid her palm against his cheek. His dark new beard was stiff and harsh; the feel of it sent electric prickles shooting up her arm. She pulled her hand away and, once more businesslike, unfolded the blanket from the foot of the cot and drew it up over his body.

She leaned over him to settle it under his chin, but he

320

rolled over again, and before she could jump back, one hard, muscular arm wrapped over her shoulder. She lost her balance and fell against his chest, and the arm pinned her helplessly.

She lay very still, her heart pounding wildly. After a minute the grip of his arm relaxed, and gently she tried to free herself. At her first movement, the arm locked about her with such savage strength that her breath was driven from her lungs with a gasp.

Ralph mumbled and brought his other hand over, and she convulsed with shock as it settled high up on the back of her thigh. She dared not move. She knew she could not break the grip of his restraining arm. She had never expected him to be so powerful; she felt as helpless as an unweaned infant, totally in his power. She felt the heat of his body soaking through her nightdress, felt the hand behind her begin to fumble and grope upward—and then she sensed the moment when he became conscious.

The hand slid up to the nape of her neck, and her head was pulled forward with a gentle but irresistible force until she felt the heat and the wetness of his mouth spread over hers. He tasted of whisky and something else, a yeasty, musky man taste, and without her volition her own lips melted and spread to meet his.

Her senses spun like wheels of flame behind her closed eyelids; the sensations were so tumultuous that for long moments she did not realize that he had swept her nightdress up to the level of her shoulder blades, and now his fingers, hard as bone and hot as fire, ran in a long, slow caress down the cleft of her naked buttocks and then settled into the soft curve where they joined her thighs. It galvanized her.

Her breath sobbed in her throat, and she struggled to be free, to escape from the torture of her own wild wanting, of her cruel need for him, and from his skillful, insistent fingers. He held her easily, his mouth against the soft of her throat, and his voice was hoarse and rough.

"Cathy!" he said. "My Katie! I missed you so!"

Elizabeth stopped struggling. She lay against him like a dead woman. No longer fighting, no longer even breathing.

"Katie!" His hands were desperate to find her, but she was dead, dead.

He was fully awake now. His hands left Elizabeth's body

and came up to her face. He cupped her head in his hands and lifted it. He looked at her uncomprehendingly for a long moment, and then she saw the green change in his eyes.

"Not Cathy!" he whispered.

She opened his fingers gently and stood up beside the cot.

"Not Cathy," she said softly. "Cathy has gone, Ralph."

She stooped over the guttering candle, cupped one hand behind it, and blew it out. Then she stood upright again in the sudden total darkness. She unfastened the bodice of her nightdress, shrugged it over her shoulders, and let it fall around her ankles. She stepped out of it and lay down on the cot beside Ralph. She took his unresisting hand and placed it where it had been before.

"Not Cathy," she whispered. "Tonight it's Elizabeth. Tonight and forever more." And she placed her mouth over his.

When at last she felt him fill all the sad and lonely places within her, her joy was so intense that it seemed to crush and bruise her soul, and she said: "I love you. I have always loved you—I will always love you."

◆ ◆ ◆

Jordan Ballantyne stood beside his father on the platform of the Cape Town railway station. They were both stiff and awkward in the moment of parting.

"Please don't forget to give my"—Jordan hesitated over the choice of words—"my very warmest regards to Louise."

"I am sure she will be pleased," said Zouga. "I have not seen her for so long—" Zouga broke off.

The separation from his wife had drawn out over the long months of his trial in the Queen's Bench Division of the High Court before the Lord Chief Justice, Baron Pollock, Mr. Justice Hawkins, and a special jury. The Lord Chief Justice had shepherded a reluctant jury toward the inevitable verdict.

"I direct you that, in accordance with the evidence and your answers to the specific questions I have put to you, you ought to find a verdict of guilty against all the defendants." And he had his way.

"The sentence of the Court, therefore, is that as to you, Leander Starr Jameson, and as to you, John Willoughby, that you be confined for a period of fifteen months' imprisonment without hard labor. That you, Major Zouga Ballantyne, have three months' imprisonment without hard labor.''

Zouga had served four weeks of his sentence in Holloway and, with the balance remitted, had been released to the dreadful news that in Rhodesia the Matabele had risen and that Bulawayo was under siege.

The voyage southward down the Atlantic had been agonizing; he had had no word of Louise or of King's Lynn, and his imagination conjured up horrors that were nourished by tales of slaughter and mutilation. Only when the *Union Castle* mail boat had docked that morning in Cape Town Harbor were his terrible anxieties relieved.

''She is safe in Bulawayo,'' Jordan had answered his first question. Overcome with emotion, Zouga had embraced his youngest son, repeating, ''Thank God, oh, thank God!'' over and over again.

They had lunched together in the dining room of the Mount Nelson Hotel, and Jordan had given his father the latest intelligence from the north.

''Napier and the Siege Committee seem to have stabilized the situation. They have got the survivors into Bulawayo, and Grey and Selous and Ralph with their irregulars have given the rebels a few bloody knocks to keep them at a wary distance.

''Of course the Matabele have an absolutely free run of the territory outside the laagers at Bulawayo and Gwelo and Belingwe. They do as they please, though strangely enough they do not seem to have closed the road to the southern drifts. If you can reach Kimberley in time to join the relief column that Spreckley is taking through, you should be in Bulawayo by the end of the month—and Mr. Rhodes and I will not be long in joining you.

''Spreckley will be taking through only essential supplies, and a few hundred men to stiffen the defense of Bulawayo until the imperial troops can get there. As you probably know, Major General Sir Frederick Carrington has been chosen to command, and Mr. Rhodes and I will be going up with his staff. I have no doubt we will bring the rebels to book very swiftly.''

Jordan kept up a monologue during the entire meal to cover the embarrassment caused by the stares and the whispers of the other diners, who were deliciously scandalized by the presence of one of Jameson's freebooters in their midst. Zouga ignored the stir he was creating and addressed himself to the meal and the conversation with Jordan until a young journalist from the *Cape Times*, clutching his shorthand pad, approached the table.

"I wonder if you would care to comment on the leniency of the sentences passed by the Lord Chief Justice."

Only then did Zouga raise his head, and his expression was bleak.

"In the years ahead, they will give medals and knighthoods to men who achieve exactly the same task that we attempted," he said quietly. "Now will you be kind enough to let us finish our lunch in peace."

At the railway station, Jordan fussed over making certain that Zouga's trunk was in the goods van and that he had a forward-facing seat in the last carriage. Then they faced each other awkwardly as the guard blew his warning whistle.

"Mr. Rhodes asked me to inquire whether you would still be good enough to act as his agent at Bulawayo?"

"Tell Mr. Rhodes that I am honored by his continued confidence."

They shook hands and Zouga climbed into the coach.

"If you see Ralph—"

"Yes?" Zouga asked.

"Never mind." Jordan shook his head. "I hope you have a safe journey, Papa."

Leaning from the carriage window as the train pulled out from the platform, Zouga studied the receding figure of his youngest son. He was a fine-looking young fellow, Zouga decided, tall and athletic, his gray three-piece suit in fashion yet also in perfect understated taste—and yet there was something incongruous about him, an air of the lost waif, an aura of uncertainty and deep-rooted unhappiness.

"Damned nonsense," Zouga told himself, and drew his head in and pulled up the window by its leather strap.

The locomotive built up speed across the Cape flats for its assault on the rampart of mountains that guarded the African continental shield.

◆ ◆ ◆

Jordan Ballantyne cantered up the driveway toward the great white house that crouched among its oaks and stone pines on the lower slopes of the flat-topped mountain. He was pursued by a feeling of guilt. It was many years since he had neglected his duties for an entire day. Even a year ago it would have been unthinkable for him to do so. Every day, Sunday and public holidays notwithstanding, Mr. Rhodes needed him close at hand.

The subtle change in their relationship was something that increased his feelings of guilt and introduced a more corrosive emotion. It had not been entirely necessary for him to spend the whole day with his father, from when the mail ship worked her way into Table Bay, with the furious red dawn and the southeaster raging about her, until the northern express pulled out from under the glassed dome of Cape Town Station. He could have slipped away and been back at his desk within a few hours, but he had tried to force a refusal out of Mr. Rhodes, an acknowledgment of his own indispensability.

"Take a few days if you like, Jordan—Arnold will be able to handle anything that might come up." Mr. Rhodes had barely glanced up from the London papers.

"There is that new draft of Clause Twenty-seven of your will—" Jordan had tried to provoke him, and instead received the reply he most dreaded.

"Oh, give that to Arnold. It's time he understood about the scholarships. Anyway it will give him a chance to use that newfangled Remington machine of his."

Mr. Rhodes's childlike pleasure in having his correspondence printed out swiftly and neatly on the calligraph was another source of disquiet to Jordan. Jordan had not yet mastered the calligraph's noisy keyboard, chiefly because Arnold's jealousy monopolized the machine. Jordan had ordered his own model shipped out to him, but it had to come from New York, and it would be months yet before he could expect it to arrive.

Now Jordan reined in the big, glossy bay at the steps to Groote Schuur's back stoep, and as he dismounted, he tossed the reins to the groom and hurried into the house. He took the back stairs to the second floor and went directly to his own room, unbuttoning his shirt and pulling the tails from his breeches as he kicked the door closed behind him.

He poured water from the Delft jug into the basin and splashed it onto his face. Then he dried on a fluffy white towel, tossed it aside and picked up the silver-handled brushes and ran them over his crisp golden curls. He was about to turn away from the mirror and find a fresh shirt when he stopped and stared thoughtfully at his own image.

Slowly he leaned closer to the glass and touched his face with his fingertips. There were crows' feet at the outer corners of his eyes; he stretched the skin between his fingers but the lines persisted. He turned his head slightly; the light from the tall window showed up the pouches beneath his eyes.

"You only see them at that angle," he thought, and then flattened his hair back from the peak of his forehead with the palm of his hand. There was the pearly gleam of his scalp through the thinning strands, and quickly he fluffed his hair up again.

He wanted to turn away, but the mirror had a dreadful fascination. He smiled: it was a grimace that lifted his upper lip. His left canine tooth was darker, definitely a darker gray than it had been a month before when the dentist had drilled out the nerve, and suddenly Jordan was overwhelmed by a cold, penetrating despair.

"In less than two weeks' time, I will be thirty years old—oh God, I'm getting old, so old and ugly. How can anyone still like me?"

He bore down hard on the sob that threatened to choke him and turned away from the cruel glass.

In his office there was a note in the center of the tooled morocco leather top of his desk, weighted down with the silver inkwell.

"See me as soon as possible. C. J. R."

It was in that familiar spiky scrawl, and Jordan felt a leap of his spirits. He picked up his shorthand pad and knocked on the communicating door.

"Come!" the high-pitched voice commanded, and Jordan went through.

"Good evening, Mr. Rhodes, you wanted to see me?"

Mr. Rhodes did not reply at once but went on making corrections to the typed sheet in front of him, crossing out a word and scrawling a substitute above it, changing a comma to a semicolon, and while he worked Jordan studied his face.

The deterioration was shocking. He was almost totally gray now, and the pouches below his eyes were a deep purple color. His jowl had thickened, and it hung in a dewlap under his jawbone. His eyes were red-rimmed, and their messianic blue was blurred and diluted. All this in the six months or so since Jameson's disastrous raid, and Jordan's thoughts jumped back to that day that the news had come. Jordan had brought it to him in this same library.

There had been three telegrams. One from Jameson himself was addressed to Mr. Rhodes's Cape Town office, not to the mansion at Groote Schuur, and so it had lain all weekend in the letterbox of the deserted building. It began, "As I do not hear from you to the contrary—"

The second telegram was from the magistrate at Mafeking, Mr. Boyes. It read in part, "Colonel Grey has ridden with police detachments to reinforce Dr. Jameson—"

The last telegram was from the commissioner of police at Kimberley. "I deem it my duty to inform you that Dr. Jameson, at the head of a body of armed men, has crossed the Transvaal border—"

Mr. Rhodes had read the telegrams, meticulously arranging them on the top of his desk before him as he finished each.

"I thought I had stopped him," he had kept muttering as he read. "I thought he understood that he must wait."

By the time he had finished reading, he had been pale as candle wax and the flesh seemed to have sagged from the bones of his face.

"Poor old Jameson," he had whispered at last. "Twenty years we have been friends, and now he goes and destroys me." Mr. Rhodes had leaned his elbows on the desk and placed his face in his hands. He had sat like that for many minutes and then said clearly, "Well, Jordan, now I will see who my true friends are."

Mr. Rhodes had not slept for five nights after that. Jordan had lain awake in his own room down the passage and listened to the heavy tread back and forth across the yellowwood floor, and then, long before the first light of dawn, Mr. Rhodes would ring for him, and they would ride together for hours upon the slopes of Table Mountain before returning to the great white mansion to face the latest renunciations and rejections, to watch with a kind of helpless fascination his life and his work crumbling inexorably into dust about them.

Then Arnold had arrived to take his place as Jordan's

assistant. His official title was second secretary, and Jordan had welcomed his assistance with the more mundane details of running the complex household. He had accompanied them on their visit to London in the aftermath of Jameson's misadventure and remained firmly by Rhodes's side on the long return journey via the Suez Canal, Beira and Salisbury.

Now Arnold stood attentively beside Mr. Rhodes's desk, handing him a sheet typed upon the calligraph, waiting while he read and corrected it, and then replacing it with a fresh sheet. With the rancid taste of envy, Jordan recognized, not for the first time, that Arnold possessed the clean blond good looks that Mr. Rhodes so much admired. His demeanor was modest and frank, yet when he laughed, his entire being seemed to glow with some inner illumination. He had been up at Oriel, Mr. Rhodes's old Oxford college, and it was more and more obvious that Mr. Rhodes took pleasure and comfort in having him nearby, as he had once taken from Jordan's presence.

Jordan waited quietly by the door, feeling strangely out of place in what he had come to think of as his own home, until Mr. Rhodes handed the last corrected sheet to Arnold and looked up.

"Ah, Jordan," he said. "I wanted to warn you that I am advancing the date of my departure for Bulawayo. I think my Rhodesians need me. I must go to them."

"I will see to it immediately," Jordan nodded. "Have you decided on a date, Mr. Rhodes?"

"Next Monday."

"We will take the express to Kimberley, of course?"

"You will not be accompanying me," said Mr. Rhodes flatly.

"I do not understand, Mr. Rhodes." Jordan made a helpless little gesture of incomprehension.

"I require utter loyalty and honesty in my employees."

"Yes, Mr. Rhodes, I know that." Jordan nodded, and then slowly his expression became uncertain and disbelieving. "You are not suggesting that I have ever been disloyal or dishonest—"

"Get that file, please, Arnold," Mr. Rhodes ordered, and when he fetched it from the library table, he added, "Give it to him."

Arnold silently came across the thick silk and wool car-

328

pet and offered the box file to Jordan. As he reached for it, Jordan was aware, for the first time ever, of something other than openness and friendly concern in Arnold's eyes; it was a flash of vindictive triumph so vicious as to sting like the lash of a riding whip across the face. It lasted for only a blink of time and was gone so swiftly that it might never have been, but it left Jordan feeling utterly vulnerable and in dreadful danger.

He placed the folder on the table beside him and opened the cover. There were at least fifty sheets in the folder. Most of them had been typed on the calligraph, and each was headed "Copy of original."

There were stockbrokers' buy and sell orders for shares in De Beers and Consolidated Goldfields. The quantities of shares in the transactions were enormous, involving millions of pounds sterling. The broking firm was Silver & Co., of whom Jordan had never heard, though they purported to conduct business in Johannesburg, Kimberley and London.

Then there were copies of statements from half a dozen banks, in the different centers where Silver & Co. had offices. A dozen or so entries on the statements had been underlined in red ink: "Transfer to Rholands—£86,321-7s-9d. Transfer to Rholands— 146,821-9s-11d."

The name shocked him, Ralph's company, and though he did not understand why, it increased his sense of peril.

"I don't understand what this has to do with me—" He looked up at Mr. Rhodes.

"Your brother entered into a series of large bear transactions in those companies most drastically affected by the failure of Jameson's enterprise."

"It would appear—" Jordan began uncertainly, and was interrupted by Mr. Rhodes.

"It would appear that he has made profits in excess of a million pounds, and that he and his agents have gone to extreme lengths to disguise and conceal these machinations."

"Mr. Rhodes, why do you tell me this, why do you adopt that tone? He is my brother, but I cannot be held responsible—"

Mr. Rhodes held up one hand to silence him. "Nobody has accused you of anything yet—your eagerness to justify yourself is unbecoming."

Then he opened the leather-bound copy of Plutarch's

329

Lives which lay on one corner of his desk. There were three sheets of writing paper lying between the pages. Mr. Rhodes took out the sheets and proffered the top one to Jordan.

"Do you recognize this?"

Jordan felt himself blushing agonizingly. At that moment he hated himself for ever having written this letter. He had done so in the terrible spiritual travail following the night of Ralph's discoveries and brutal accusation in the private pullman coach from Kimberley.

"It is the copy of a private letter that I wrote to my brother—" Jordan could not lift his eyes to meet those of Mr. Rhodes. "I do not know what possessed me to keep a copy of it."

A paragraph caught his eye, and he could not prevent himself rereading his own words.

"There is nothing I would not do to convince you of my continued affection, for only now, when I seem to have forfeited it, am I truly conscious of how much your regard means to me."

He held the sheet possessively. "This is a private and intimate communication," he said in a low voice which shook with shame and outrage. "Apart from my brother, to whom it is addressed, nobody has the right to read it."

"You do not deny that you are the author, then?"

"It would be vain of me to do so."

"Indeed it would," Mr. Rhodes agreed, and passed him the second sheet.

Jordan read on down the page in mounting bewilderment. The handwriting was his, but the words were not. So skillfully and naturally did they continue from the sentiments of the first page, however, that he found himself almost doubting his own recall. What he was reading was his own acquiescence to pass on to Ralph confidential and privileged information related to the planning and timing of Jameson's intervention in the Transvaal. *"I do agree that the contemplated venture is totally outside civilized law, and this has convinced me to give you my assistance—this and the moral debt that I feel that I owe to you."*

Only then he noticed the slant and form of a letter that was not in his hand. The entire page was a skillful forgery. He shook his head wordlessly. He felt as though the fabric of his existence had been ripped through and through.

330

"That your conspiracy was successful, we know from the rich fruits your brother harvested," said Mr. Rhodes wearily, the voice of a man so often betrayed that this no longer had the power to wound him. "I congratulate you, Jordan."

"Where did this come from?" The page shook in Jordan's hand. "Where—" He broke off and looked up at Arnold, standing behind his master's shoulder. There was no trace of that vindictive triumph remaining; Arnold was grave and concerned—and unbearably handsome.

"I see." Jordan nodded. "It is a forgery, of course."

Mr. Rhodes made an impatient gesture. "Really, Jordan. Who would go to the trouble of forging bank statements that can readily be verified?"

"Not the bank statements, the letter."

"You agreed it was yours."

"Not this page, not this—"

Mr. Rhodes's expression was remote, his eyes cold and unfeeling.

"I will have the bookkeeper come up from the town office to go over the household accounts with you and to make an inventory. You will, of course, hand over your keys to Arnold. As soon as all that has been done, I will instruct the bookkeeper to issue you a check for three months' salary in lieu of notice, though I am certain you will understand my reluctance to provide you with a letter of recommendation. I would be obliged if you could remove yourself and your belongings from these premises before my return from Rhodesia."

"Mr. Rhodes—"

"There is nothing further that we have to discuss."

◆　◆　◆

Mr. Rhodes and his entourage, Arnold among them, had left on the northern express for Kimberley and the Matabeleland railhead three weeks before. It had taken that long for Jordan to wind up the inventories and complete the household accounts.

Mr. Rhodes had not spoken to Jordan again after that final confrontation. Arnold had relayed two brief instructions, and Jordan had retained his dignity and resisted the temptation to hurl bootless recriminations at his triumphant rival. He had only seen Mr. Rhodes three times since that fateful evening, twice from his office window as he returned from those long, aimless rides through the pine forests on the lower slopes of the mountain, and the third and final time as he climbed into the coach for the railway station.

Now, as he had been for three long weeks, Jordan was alone in the great, deserted mansion. He had ordered the servants to leave early and had personally checked the kitchens and rear areas before locking up the doors. He moved slowly through the carpeted passageways carrying the oil lamp in both hands. He wore the Chinese silk brocade dressing gown that had been Mr. Rhodes's personal gift to him on his twenty-fifth birthday. He felt burned out, blackened like a forest tree after the fire has passed, leaving the hollowed-out trunk continuing to smolder within.

He was on a pilgrimage of farewell about the great house and the memories that it contained. He had been present from the very first days of the planning to renovate and redecorate the old building. He had spent so many hours listening to Herbert Baker and Mr. Rhodes, taking notes of their conversations and occasionally, at Mr. Rhodes's invitation, making a suggestion.

It was Jordan who had suggested the motif for the mansion, a stylized representation of the stone bird from the ancient ruins of Rhodesia, the falcon of Zimbabwe. The great raptor, the pedestal on which it perched decorated with a shark's tooth pattern, adorned the banisters of the main staircase. It was worked into the polished granite of the huge bath in Mr. Rhodes's suite, it formed a fresco around the walls of the dining room, and four replicas of the strange bird supported the corners of Mr. Rhodes's desk.

The bird had been a part of Jordan's life from as far back as his earliest memories reached. The original statue had been taken by Zouga Ballantyne from the ancient temple, one of seven identical statues that he had discovered there. He had only been able to carry one of them. He had left the other birds lying in the ancient temple enclosure and taken the best-preserved example.

Almost thirty years later, Ralph Ballantyne had returned to Great Zimbabwe, guided by his father's journal and the map he had drawn. Ralph had found the six remaining statues lying in the temple enclosure of the ruins just as his father had left them, but Ralph had come prepared. He had loaded the statues onto the draft-oxen he had brought with him and, despite the attempts of the Matabele guardians to prevent him, had escaped southward across the Shashi River with his treasure. In Cape Town a syndicate of businessmen headed by the multimillionaire Barney Barnato had purchased the relics from Ralph for a substantial sum and had presented them to the South African Museum in Cape Town. The six statues were still on display to the public there. Jordan had visited the premises and spent an hour standing transfixed before them.

However, his own personal magic was embodied in the original statue that his father had discovered and which throughout his childhood had ridden as ballast over the rear wheel-truck of the family wagon during their wanderings and travels across the vast African veld. Jordan had slept a thousand nights above the bird, and somehow its spirit had pervaded his own and taken possession of him.

When Zouga at last led the family to the Kimberley diamond diggings, the bird statue had been unloaded from the wagon and placed under the camel thorn tree which marked their last camp. When Jordan's mother, Aletta Ballantyne, had fallen sick with the deadly camp fever and finally succumbed to the disease, the statue had come to play an even larger part in Jordan's life.

He had christened the bird Panes, after the goddess of the North American Indian tribes, and later he had avidly studied the lore of the great goddess Panes that Frazer had detailed in his *Golden Bough: A Study in Magic and Religion*. He learned how Panes was a beautiful woman who had been taken up into the mountains. To the adolescent Jordan, Panes and the bird statue became confused with the image of his dead mother. Secretly he had developed a form of invocation to the goddess, and in the dead of night when all the other members of his family slept, he would creep out to make a small sacrifice of hoarded food to Panes and worship her with his own rituals.

When Zouga, financially reduced, had been forced to sell the bird to Mr. Rhodes, the boy had been desolated— until the opportunity to enter Mr. Rhodes's service and follow the goddess replaced the emptiness of his existence with not one but two deities: the goddess Panes and Mr. Rhodes. Even after he had grown to manhood in Mr. Rhodes's service, the statue continued to bulk large in Jordan's consciousness, though it was only very occasionally, in times of deep turmoil of the spirit, that he actually resorted to the childish rituals of worship.

Now he had lost the lodestone of his life, and irresistibly he was drawn toward the statue for the last time. Slowly he descended the curve of the main staircase. As he passed, he caressed the carved balustrades which were worked into faithful copies of the ancient bird.

The lofty entrance hallway below was floored with black and white marble slabs arranged in a checkerboard pattern. The main doors were in massive red teak, and the fittings were of burnished brass. The light of the lantern that Jordan carried sent grotesquely misshapen shadows flowing across the marble or fluttering like gigantic bats against the high, carved ceiling. In the center of the marble floor stood a heavy table upon which were the silver trays for visiting cards and mail. Between them was a tall decoration of dried protea blooms which Jordan had arranged with his own hands.

Jordan set the lamp of Sèvres porcelain upon the table like a ritual lantern upon a pagan altar. He stepped back from it and slowly raised his head. The original stone falcon of Zimbabwe stood in its high niche, guarding the entrance to Groote Schuur. Seeing it thus, it was not possible to doubt the aura of magical power that invested the graven image. It seemed that the prayers and incantations of the long-dead priests of Zimbabwe still shimmered in the air about it, that the blood of the sacrifices steamed from the wavering shadows upon the marble floor, and that the prophecies of the Umlimo, the Chosen One of the ancient spirits, invested it with separate life.

Zouga Ballantyne had heard the prophecies from the Umlimo's lips and had faithfully recorded them in his journal. Jordan had reread them a hundred times and could repeat them by rote, he had made them part of his own personal ritual and invocation to the goddess.

"There shall be no peace in the kingdom of the Mambos or the Monomotapas until they return. For the white eagle will war with the black bull until the stone falcons return to roost."

Jordan looked up at the bird's proud, cruel head, at the sightless eyes which stared blankly toward the north, toward the land of the Mambos and the Monomotapas which men now called Rhodesia, and where the white eagle and the black bull were again locked in mortal conflict, and Jordan felt a sense of helplessness and emptiness, as though he were caught up in the coils of destiny and was unable to break free.

"Have pity on me, great Panes," and he dropped to his knees. "I cannot go. I cannot leave you or him. I have no place to go."

In the lamplight his face was tinged with a faint greenish sheen, as though it had been carved from glacial ice. He lifted the procelain lamp from the table and held it high above his head with both hands.

"Forgive me, great Panes," he whispered, and hurled the lamp against the paneled woodwork of the wall.

The lobby was plunged into darkness for a moment as the flame of the shattered lamp fluttered to the very edge of extinction. Then it sent a ghostly blue light skittering across the surface of the spreading pool of oil. Suddenly the flames burned up strongly and touched the trailing edges of the long velvet drapes that covered the windows.

Still kneeling before the stone statue, Jordan coughed as the first wisps of smoke enveloped him. He was mildly surprised that, after the first burning sting of it in his lungs, there was so very little pain. The image of the falcon high above him slowly receded, dimmed by the tears that filled Jordan's eyes and by the dense swirling curtains of smoke.

The flames made a low drumming roar as they caught on the wooden paneling and shot to the ceiling. One of the heavy drapes burned through, and as it fell it spread open like the wings of an immense vulture. The fiery wings of thick velvet covered Jordan's kneeling figure and their weight bore him face down to the marble floor.

Already asphyxiated by the dense blue smoke, he did not even struggle, and within seconds the mound of crumpled velvet was transformed into a funeral pyre, and the flames reached up joyously to lick against the base of the stone falcon in its high niche.

◆　◆　◆

"Bazo has come down from the place of the Umlimo at last," Isazi said quietly, and Ralph could not contain himself.

"Are you sure of this?" he demanded eagerly, and Isazi nodded.

"I have sat at the campfires of his impi and with my own

eyes have seen him, with the bullet scars shining like medals of silver upon his chest; with my own ears I have heard him harangue his *amadoda*, steeling them for the fighting which lies ahead."

"Where is he, Isazi? Tell me where I can find him."

"He is not alone." Isazi was not about to spoil the dramatic impact of his report by prematurely divulging the bare bones of fact. "Bazo has with him the witch who is his woman. If Bazo is warlike, then this woman, Tanase, the favorite of the dark spirits, is bold and ruthless, driven by such bloody cruelty that the *amadoda* when they look upon her beauty shudder as though it is an unspeakable ugliness."

"Where are they?" Ralph repeated.

"Bazo has with him the wildest and most reckless of the young indunas, Zama and Kamuza, and they have brought their *amadoda*, three thousand of the fiercest and finest. With Bazo and Tanase at their head, these impis are as dangerous as the gut-stabbed lion, as deadly as the old bull buffalo circling in thick cover to lay for the unwary hunter—"

"Goddamn you, Isazi, we have waited long enough," Ralph snarled at him. "Tell me where he is."

Isazi looked pained and deliberately took a little snuff. His eyes watered, then he sneezed delectably and wiped his nostrils on the palm of his hand.

"Gandang and Babiaan and Somabula are not with him." Isazi took up his recital precisely at the point where Ralph had so boorishly interrupted him. "I listened while the *amadoda* spoke of an *indaba* held many weeks back at the Valley of the Umlimo. They say that the old indunas decided to wait for the divine intervention of the spirits, to leave the road southward open for the white men to leave Matabeleland and to sit upon their shields until these things come to pass."

Ralph made a gesture of disgusted resignation. "Do not hurry in your telling of it, wise one," he encouraged Isazi with weighted sarcasm. "Do not spare us the smallest detail."

Isazi nodded seriously, but his dark eyes sparkled, and he tugged at his little goatee beard to prevent himself grinning.

"The bellies of the old indunas are cooling—they recall the Shangani and Bembesi battlefields. Their spies report that the laager here at Bulawayo is guarded by the three-legged guns. I tell you, Henshaw, that Bazo is the serpent's head. Cut it off and the body dies." Isazi nodded sagely.

"Now will you tell me where Bazo is, my brave and wise old friend?"

Isazi nodded again in appreciation of Ralph's change of tone.

"He is very close," Isazi said. "Not two hours' march from where we sit." Isazi made a wide gesture that took in the darkened laager about them. "He lies with his three thousand *amadoda* in the Valley of the Goats."

Ralph looked up at the segment of old moon that hung low down in the sky.

"Four days to new moon," he murmured. "If Bazo plans to attack the laager here, then it will be in the dark of the moon."

"Three thousand men," Harry Mellow murmured. "There are fifty of us."

"Three thousand. The Moles and the Insukamini and the Swimmers." Sergeant Ezra shook his head. "As Isazi has said, the fiercest and the finest."

"We will take them," said Ralph Ballantyne calmly. "We will take them in the Valley of the Goats, two nights from now, and here is the way we will do it—"

♦ ♦ ♦

Bazo, son of Gandang, who had denied his father and defied the greater indunas of Kumalo, passed from one watch fire to the next, and beside him moved the slim and exquisitely graceful figure of his woman, Tanase.

Bazo reached the fire and stood tall above it. The flames lit his features from below, so that the cavities of his eyes were black caverns in the depths of which his eyes glinted like the coils of a deadly reptile. The light of the campfire picked out in harsh detail every line and crease that suffering had riven into his face. Around his forehead was bound the simple strip of moleskin; he did not need the feathers of heron and paradise widow birds to place the seal upon his majesty. The firelight glinted upon the great muscles of his chest and arms, and his scars were the only regalia of honor that he wore.

Tanase's beauty was even more poignant when seen beside his ravaged features. Her naked breasts were strangely incongruous in these warlike councils, but beneath their satiny swelling they were hard as battle-forged muscle, and the sudden thrust of her nipples puckered and dark, large as the first joint of a man's little finger, were like the bosses in the center of a war shield.

As she stood at Bazo's shoulder in the firelight, her gaze was as fierce as any warrior there, and she looked up at her husband with a ferocious pride as he began to speak.

"I offer you a choice," Bazo said. "You can remain as you are, the dogs of the white men. You can stay as *amaholi*, the lowliest of slaves, or you can become once again *amadoda*—"

His voice was not raised, nor strained; it seemed to rumble up out of his throat, but it rang clearly to the highest part of the natural rocky amphitheater, and the dark masses of warriors that filled the bowl stirred and sighed at the words.

"The choice is yours, but it must be made swiftly. This morning I have received runners from the south." Bazo paused, and his listeners craned forward. There were three thousand of them squatting in massed ranks, but there was no sound from them as they waited for Bazo's next words.

"You have heard the fainthearted tell you that if we do not dispute the southern road, then the white men that are in Bulawayo will pack their wagons, take their women and go meekly down that road to the sea." Still not a sound from the listening warriors.

"They were wrong—and now they are proven so. Lodzi has come," said Bazo, and there was a sigh like the wind in the grass.

"Lodzi has come," Bazo repeated. "And with him the soldiers and the guns. They gather now at the head of the iron road that Henshaw built. Soon, very soon, they will begin the march up the road which we have left open for them. Before the new moon is half grown to its full, they will be in Bulawayo, and then you will truly be *amaholi*. You and your sons and their sons will toil in the white men's mines and herd the white men's herds."

There was a growl, like a leopard when first it is roused, and it shook the dark ranks until Bazo lifted high the hand that held his silver assegai.

"That is not to be. The Umlimo has promised us that this land will once again belong to us, but it is our task to make this prophecy into reality. The gods do not favor those who wait for fruit to fall from the tree into their open mouths. My children, we will shake the tree."

"Jee!" said a single voice from the massed ranks, and immediately the humming war chant was taken up by them all.

"Jee!" sang Bazo, stamping his right foot and stabbing the broad blade toward the moonless sky, and his men sang with him.

Tanase stood still as an ebony carving beside him, but her lips were parted softly, and her huge slanted eyes glowed like moons in the firelight.

At last Bazo spread his arm again and waited for their silence. "Thus it will be," he said, and again the waiting warriors strained for every word. "First we will eat up the laager at Bulawayo. It has always been the way of the Matabele to fall upon their enemy at that hour before the dawn, just before the first light of day"—the warriors hummed softly in assent—"and the white men know this is our way," Bazo went on. "Every morning, in the last deep darkness, they stand to their guns, waiting for the leopard to walk into their trap. *The Matabele always come before the dawn*, they tell each other. *Always!* they say, but I tell you that this time it will be different, my children."

Bazo paused and looked carefully into the faces of the men who squatted in the front rank.

"This time it will be in the hour before midnight, at the rise of the white star from the east."

Standing before them in the old way, Bazo gave them their order of battle; and squatting in the black mass of half-naked bodies, his bare shoulders touching those of the *amadoda* on each side of him, his hair covered by the feather headdress and his face and body plastered with the mixture of fat and soot, Ralph Ballantyne listened to the detailed instructions.

"At this season, the wind will rise with the rise of the white star. It will come from the east, so from the east we will come also. Each one of you will carry upon his head a bundle of thatch grass and the green leaves of the msasa trees," Bazo told them, and anticipating what was to come, Ralph felt the nerve ends in his fingertips tingle with the shock.

"A smoke screen," he thought. "That's a naval tactic!"

"As soon as the wind rises, we will build a great fire."
Bazo confirmed it immediately. "Each of you will throw
his bundle upon it as he passes, and we will go forward in
the darkness and the smoke. It will avail them not at all to
shoot their rockets into the sky, for our smoke will blind
the gunners."

Ralph imagined how it might be, the warriors emerging
from the impenetrable rolling bank of smoke, not visible
until they were within stabbing range, swarming over the
wall of wagons or creeping between the wheels. Three
thousand of them coming in silently and relentlessly—even
if the laager were warned and alerted, it would be almost
impossible to stop them. The Maxims would be almost
useless in the smoke, and the broad-bladed assegais the
more effective weapon at such close range.

A vivid image of the slaughter burned into his brain, and
he remembered Cathy's corpse and imagined beside it the
mutilated remains of Jonathan and of Elizabeth, her white,
smooth flesh as cruelly desecrated. His rage came strongly
to arm him, and he stared down into the amphitheater at
the tall, heroic figure with the ravaged face laying out the
terrible details of the massacre.

"We must leave not a single one of them. We must
destroy the last reason why Lodzi should bring his soldiers.
We will offer him only dead bodies, burned buildings and
silver steel if he makes the attempt."

Then in his rage Ralph shouted with the other *amadoda*
and hummed the wild war chant, his features as contorted
as theirs and his eyes as wild.

"The *indaba* is ended," Bazo told them at last. "Go now
to your sleeping mats to refresh yourself for the morrow.
When you rise with the sun, let your first task be to cut,
each of you, a bundle of dry grass and green leaves as
heavy as you can carry."

◆ ◆ ◆

Ralph Ballantyne lay beneath his fur kaross on a sleeping
mat of woven reeds and listened to the camp settling into
sleep about him. They had withdrawn into the narrower
reaches of the valley. He saw the watch fires dwindle and
the circles of their orange light shrink in upon them. He
listened to the murmur of voices subside and the breathing

of the warriors near him changing, becoming deeper and more regular.

Here the Valley of the Goats was broken, rocky defile, choked with thick thorn scrub, so that the impis could not concentrate in one place. They were spread out in pockets, down the length of the valley, fifty men or so in each small clearing, the narrow, twisted paths through the thorn scrub overshadowed by the taller trees, which formed a canopy overhead.

The darkness became more menacing as the last fires died into powdery gray ash, and Ralph, lying beneath the fur blanket, gripped the haft of his assegai and judged his moment.

It came at last, and Ralph drew back the kaross stealthily. On all fours he crept to where the nearest warrior lay, groping gently for him. His fingers touched the bare skin of an arm. The warrior started awake at the touch and sat bolt upright.

"Who is it?" he asked in a thick, guttural voice, rough with sleep, and Ralph stabbed him in the stomach.

The man screamed. It was a cry of ringing, mortal agony that bounded from the rocky sides of the valley, cutting through the silences of the night watch, and Ralph bellowed with him.

"Devils! Devils are killing me!" He rolled over and stabbed another warrior, wounding him so he yelled with surprise and pain.

"There are devils here!"

At fifty other watch fires down the valley, the men of Ballantyne's Scouts were stabbing and screaming with Ralph.

"Defend yourselves, there are ghosts at work!"

"*Tagati!* Witchcraft! Beware the witches!"

"Kill the witches!"

"Witchcraft! Defend yourselves!"

"Run! Run! The devils are among us."

Three thousand warriors, every one of them steeped from childhood in superstition and witch lore, awakened to the screams and wild cries of dying men and the panic-stricken warnings yelled by men come face to face with the devil's legions. They awakened in blinding, suffocating darkness, and seized their weapons and struck out in terror, yelling with fright, and the comrades they wounded shrieked and struck back at them.

"I am wounded. Defend yourselves from the devils. Hah! Hah! The devils are killing me!"

The night was filled with running figures that collided and stabbed and cried.

"The valley is haunted!"

"The devils will kill us all!"

"Run! Run!"

Then from the head of the valley rose such a monstrous iron-lunged braying, such a cacophony, that it could only be the voice of the great demon himself. Tokoloshe, the eater of men. It was a sound that drove terrified men over the last frontier of reason into the realms of witless, insensate pandemonium.

On his hands and knees, Ralph crawled down the narrow pathway, keeping below the level of the slashing spears, silhouetting the frantic figures of running men against the faint light of the stars, and when he stabbed up at them, he aimed for the groin and belly rather than the killing stroke, so that the men that he maimed added their cries to the uproar.

From the head of the valley, Harry Mellow blew another blaring blundering up the sides of the valley and escaping into the open blast on the brass foghorn, and it was echoed by the screams of men grassland beyond.

Ralph crept forward, listening for a single voice in the thousands. In the first few minutes, hundreds of fleeing warriors, most of them unarmed, had escaped from the valley. In every direction they were disappearing into the night, and each second they were followed by others, men who would have unflinchingly charged into the smoking muzzles of the Maxim machine guns but who were reduced by fear of the supernatural to mindless, panic-stricken children. Their cries faded with distance, and now at last Ralph heard the voice for which he had waited.

"Stand fast, Moles," it roared. "Stand with Bazo. These are not demons." And Ralph crept toward the sound.

In the clearing ahead of him, a campfire fed with fresh logs flared up sullenly, and Ralph recognized the tall figure with wide, gaunt shoulders and the slim woman at his side.

"This is white men's trickery," she cried beside her lord. "Wait, my children."

Ralph sprang up and ran through the dense scrub to them. "Nkosi," he cried. He did not have to disguise his voice; it was rough and hoarse with dust and tension and battle lust. "Lord Bazo, I am with you! Let us stand together against this treachery."

"Brave comrade!" Bazo greeted him with relief as Ralph loomed out of the dark. "Stand back to back, form a ring in which each of us will guard the other, and call out to other brave men to join us."

Bazo turned his back to Ralph, and drew the woman Tanase to his side. It was she who glanced back and recognized Ralph as he stooped.

"It is Henshaw," she screamed, but her warning came too late. Before Bazo could turn back to face him, Ralph had changed his grip on the assegai, using it like a butcher's cleaver, and with a single stroke he hacked across the back of Bazo's legs, just above the ankles, and the Achilles tendons parted with a soft, rubbery popping sound. Bazo collapsed onto his knees, both legs crippled, pinned like a beetle to a board.

Ralph seized Tanase's wrist, jerked her out of the circle of firelight, and hurled her headlong to earth. Holding her easily, he tore off her short leather skirt and placed the point of the assegai in her groin.

"Bazo," he whispered. "Throw your spear upon the fire, or I will open your woman's secret parts as you opened those of mine."

◆ ◆ ◆

The Scouts used the first glimmerings of the new day to move slowly down the valley in an extended line, finishing the wounded Matabele. While they worked, Ralph sent Jan Cheroot back to where they had left the horses to fetch the ropes. He was back within minutes with the heavy coils of new yellow manila over the saddles of the horses that he led.

"The Matabele have scattered back into the hills," he reported grimly. "It will take a week for them to find each other and regroup."

"We won't wait that long."

Ralph took the ropes and began making the knots. The Scouts came in as he worked. They were scrubbing their assegai blades with handfuls of dried grass, and Sergeant Ezra told Ralph, "We lost four men, but we found Kamuza, the induna of the Swimmers, and we counted over two hundred bodies."

"Get ready to pull out," Ralph ordered. "What remains to be done will not take long."

Bazo sat beside the remains of the fire. His arms were bound behind him with thongs of rawhide, and his legs were thrust straight out in front of him. He had no control over his feet, they flopped nervelessly like dying fish stranded on a receding tide, and the slow, watery blood oozed from the deep gashes above his heels.

Tanase sat beside him. She was stark naked, and bound like him with her arms behind her back.

Sergeant Ezra stared at her body, and he murmured, "We have worked hard all night. We have earned a little sport. Let me and my *kanka* take this woman into the bushes for a short while."

Ralph did not bother to reply, but turned to Jan Cheroot instead. "Bring the horses," he ordered.

Tanase spoke to Bazo without moving her lips, in the way of the initiates.

"What is the business of the ropes, Lord? Why do they not shoot us, and have done?"

"It is the white man's way, the way that conveys the deepest disrespect. They shoot honored enemies and use the ropes on criminals."

"Lord, on the day I first met this one you call Henshaw, I dreamed that you were high upon a tree and he looked up at you and smiled," she whispered. "It is strange that in that dream I did not see myself beside you upon that tree."

"They are ready now," said Bazo, and turned his head to her. "With my heart I embrace you. You have been the fountainhead of my life."

"I embrace you, my husband. I embrace you, Bazo, who will be the father of kings."

She went on staring into his ravaged, ugly-beautiful face, and she did not turn her head when Henshaw stood tall over them and said in a harsh, tortured voice, "I give you a better death than you gave to the ones I loved."

◆ ◆ ◆

The ropes were of different lengths, so that Tanase hung slightly lower than her lord. The soles of her bare feet, suspended at the height of a man's head, were very white, and her toes pointed straight at the earth like those of a little girl standing on tiptoe. Her long heron neck was twisted sharply to one side, so that she still seemed to listen for Bazo's voice.

Bazo's swollen face was lifted toward the yellow dawn sky, for the knot had ridden around under his chin. Ralph Ballantyne's face was lifted also as he stood at the base of the tall acacia tree in the bottom of the Valley of the Goats looking up at them.

In one other respect, Tanase's vision was unfulfilled— Ralph Ballantyne did not smile.

◆ ◆ ◆

So Lodzi came and with him came Major General Carrington and Major Robert Stephenson Smyth Baden-Powell, who would one day coin the motto "Be Prepared," and behind them came the guns and the soldiers. The women and children danced out from the laager at Bulawayo with bouquets of wild flowers for them, and they sang "For they are jolly good fellows" and wept with joy.

The senior indunas of Kumalo, betrayed by the Umlimo's promises of divine intervention, uncertain and with the fire in their bellies swiftly cooling, squabbling among themselves and awed by the massive show of military force that they had provoked, withdrew slowly with their impis from the vicinity of Bulawayo.

The imperial troops sortied in great, lumbering columns and swept the valleys and the open land. They burned the deserted villages and the standing crops and they drove away the few cattle that the rinderpest had spared. They shelled the hills where they suspected the Matabele might be hiding, and they rode their horses to exhaustion chasing the elusive black shadows that flittered through the forest ahead of them. The Maxims fired until the water in the cooling jackets boiled, but the range was nine hundred yards or more and the targets were as fleet as rabbits.

So the weeks dragged on and became months, and the soldiers tried to starve the Matabele and force them into a set piece battle, but the indunas sulked in the broken ground and took refuge in the Matopo Hills, where the guns and the soldiers dared not follow them.

Occasionally the Matabele caught an isolated patrol or a man on his own, once even the legendary Frederick Selous, elephant hunter and adventurer extraordinary. Selous had dismounted to "pot" one of the rebels that were disappearing over the ridge ahead, when a stray bullet grazed his pony, and his usually impeccably behaved animal bolted and left him stranded. Only then he realized that he had outridden the main body of his Scouts and that the Matabele were instantly aware of his predicament. They turned back and coursed him like dogs on a hare.

It was a race the likes of which Selous had not run since his elephant-hunting days. The barefooted and lightly equipped *amadoda* gained swiftly, so close at last that they freed their blades from the thongs and began that terrible, humming war chant. Only then Lieutenant Windley, Selous' second-in-command, spurred in and pulling his foot from the left stirrup, gave Selous the leather and galloped with him into the ranks of the oncoming Scouts.

At other times the swing of fortune was toward the soldiers, and they would surprise a foraging patrol of Matabele at a drift or in thick bush and hang them from the nearest trees that would bear the weight.

It was an inconclusive, cruel little war that drew on and on. The military officers who were conducting the campaign were not businessmen, they did not think in terms of cost-efficiency, and the bill for the first three months was a million pounds of sterling, a cost of five thousand pounds per head of Matabele killed. The bill was for the account of Mr. Cecil John Rhodes and his British South Africa Company.

In the Matopo Hills, the indunas were forced toward starvation, and in Bulawayo Mr. Rhodes was forced just as inexorably toward bankruptcy.

◆ ◆ ◆

The three riders moved in a cautious, mutually protective spread. They kept to the center of the track; their rifles were loaded and cocked and carried at high port.

Jan Cheroot rode point, fifty yards ahead. His little woolly head turned tirelessly from side to side as he searched the bush on each side. Behind him came Louise Ballantyne, delighting in her escape from the confinements of the Bulawayo laager after these weary months. She rode astride, with all the élan of a natural horsewoman, and there was a feather in her little green cap; and when she turned to look

346

back every few minutes, her lips parted in a loving smile. She was not yet accustomed to having Zouga with her once again, and she had constantly to reassure herself.

Zouga was fifty yards behind her, and he answered her smile in a way that wrenched something deep inside her. He sat easy and straight in the saddle, the wide-brimmed slouch hat slanted over one eye. The sun had gilded away the pallor of Holloway jail, and the silver and gold of his beard gave him the air of a Viking chieftain.

In that extended order, they rode up from the grassy plains, under the high arched branches of the msasa trees, up the first slope of the hills, and as he reached the false crest, Jan Cheroot stood in his stirrups and shouted with relief and delight. Unable to contain themselves, Louise and Zouga cantered forward and reined in beside him.

"Oh, thank you, Lord," Louise whispered huskily, and reached across for Zouga's hand.

"It's a miracle," he said softly, and squeezed her fingers.

Ahead of them the mellow thatch of King's Lynn basked comfortably in the sunlight. It seemed to be the most beautiful sight either of them had ever looked upon.

"Untouched." Louise shook her head in wonder.

"Must be the only homestead in Matabeleland that wasn't burned."

"Oh, come on, my darling," she cried with sudden ecstasy. "Let's go back to our home."

Zouga restrained her at the steps of the wide front porch and made her stay in the saddle, her rifle at the ready, holding the reins of their horses while he and Jan Cheroot searched the homestead for any sign of Matabele treachery.

When Zouga came out onto the stoep again, he smiled at her.

"It's safe!"

He helped her down from the saddle, and while Jan Cheroot led the horses away to stall feed them in the stables from the grain bags he had brought, Zouga and Louise went up the front steps hand in hand.

The thick ivory curves of the old bull elephant's tusks still framed the doorway to the dining room, and Zouga stroked one of them as he passed.

"Your good luck charms," Louise chuckled indulgently.

"The household gods," he corrected her, and they passed between them into the house.

The house had been looted. They could not have expected less, but the books were still there, thrown from the shelves, some with their spines broken or with the leather boards damaged or gnawed by rats, but they were all there.

Zouga retrieved his journals and dusted them superficially with his silk scarf. There were dozens of them, the record of his life, meticulously handwritten and illustrated with ink drawings and colored maps.

"It would have truly broken my heart to have lost these," he murmured, piling them carefully on the library table and stroking one of the red morocco covers. The silver was lying on the dining-room floor, some of it battered, but most of it intact. It had no value to a Matabele.

They wandered through the rambling homestead, through the rooms that Zouga had added haphazardly to the original structure, and they found small treasures among the litter: a silver comb he had given her on their first Christmas together, the diamond and enamel dress studs which had been her birthday present to him. She handed them back to him and went up on tiptoe to offer her face to his kiss.

There was still crockery and glassware on the kitchen shelves, though all the pots and knives had been stolen and the doors to the pantry and storerooms had been broken off their hinges.

"It won't take much to fix," Zouga told her. "I can't believe how lucky we've been."

Louise went out into the kitchen yard and found four of her red Rhode Island hens scratching in the dust. She called Jan Cheroot from the stable and begged a few handfuls of grain from the horses' feed bags. When she clucked at the hens, they came in a flutter of wings to be fed.

The glass in the windows of the main bedroom was smashed, and wild birds had come through to roost in the rafters. The bedspread was stained with their excrement, but when Louise stripped it off, the linen and mattress beneath it were clean and dry.

Zouga put an arm around her waist, squeezed it and looked down at her in the way she knew so well.

"You are a wicked man, Major Ballantyne," she breathed huskily. "But there are no curtains on the windows."

"Fortunately there are still shutters." He went to close them while Louise folded back the sheet and then unfastened the top button of her blouse. Zouga returned in time to assist her with the others.

An hour later when they came out again onto the front stoep, they found Jan Cheroot had dusted off the chairs and table and unpacked the picnic basket they had brought from Bulawayo. They drank fine Constantia wine and ate cold Cornish pasties, while Jan Cheroot waited upon them and regaled them with anecdotes and reminiscences of the exploits of Ballantyne's Scouts.

"There were none like us," he declared modestly. "Ballantyne's Scouts! The Matabele learned to know us well."

"Oh, don't let's talk about war," Louise pleaded.

But Zouga asked with good-natured sarcasm, "What happened to all your heroes? The war still goes on, and we need men like you."

"Master Ralph changed," said Jan Cheroot darkly. "He changed just like that." He snapped his fingers. "From the day we caught Bazo at the Valley of the Goats, he wasn't interested any more. He never rode with the Scouts again, and within a week he had gone back to the railhead to finish building his railway. They say he will drive the first train into Bulawayo before Christmas, that's what they say."

"Enough!" Louise declared. "It's our first day at King's Lynn in almost a year. I will not have another word of war. Pour some wine, Jan Cheroot, and take a little sip for yourself." Then she turned to Zouga. "Darling, can't we leave Bulawayo and come back here?"

Zouga shook his head regretfully. "I'm sorry, my love. I could not risk your precious life. The Matabele are still in rebellion, and this is so isolated—"

From the back of the house came the sudden shriek and cackle of alarmed poultry. Zouga broke off and jumped to his feet. As he reached for his rifle propped against the wall, he said softly but urgently, "Jan Cheroot, go around the back of the stables. I'll come from the other side." Then to Louise, "Wait here, but be ready to run for the horses if you hear a shot." And the two men slipped silently away down the veranda.

Zouga reached the corner of the wall below the main bedroom just as there was another storm of squawks and cackles and the beating of wings. He ducked around the corner, sprinted down the thick, white-washed wall that protected the kitchen yard, and flattened himself beside the gate. Above the cacophony of terrified chickens and the flapping of wings, he heard a voice say, "Hold that one! Do not let it go!"

The voice was Matabele, and almost immediately a half-naked figure ducked through the doorway beside Zouga, carrying a chicken in each hand.

One thing only prevented Zouga firing. The pendulant bare breasts that flapped against the Matabele's ribs as she ran. Zouga smashed the butt of his rifle between the woman's shoulders, knocking her to the earth, and he leaped over her body into the kitchen yard.

Beside the kitchen door stood Jan Cheroot. He held his rifle in one hand and in the other the skinny, naked, struggling body of a small black boy.

"Shall I knock his head in?" Jan Cheroot asked.

"You are no longer a member of Ballantyne's Scouts," Zouga told him. "Just keep a hold on him, but don't hurt him." And he turned back to examine his own prisoner.

She was an elderly Matabele woman, almost on the point of starvation. She must once have been a big, heavily fleshed woman, for her skin hung loosely upon her in folds and wrinkles. Once those breasts must have been the size of watermelons and almost bursting with fat, but now they were empty pouches that dangled almost to her navel. Zouga caught her wrist and hauled her to her feet. He marched her back into the kitchen yard, and he could clearly feel the bones of her arm through the wasted flesh.

Jan Cheroot was still holding the boy, and now Zouga studied him briefly. He also was skeletally thin; each rib and each knob of his spine poked through the skin, and his head seemed too big for his body and his eyes too big for his head.

"Little bugger is starving," said Zouga.

"That's one way of getting rid of them," Jan Cheroot agreed, and at that moment Louise stepped into the kitchen doorway with the rifle still in her hand, and her expression changed the instant she saw the black woman.

"Juba," she said. "Is that you, Juba?"

"Oh, Balela," the Matabele woman whimpered. "I had thought never to see the sunshine of your face again."

"What now!" said Zouga grimly. "We have caught ourselves a pretty prize, Jan Cheroot. The senior wife of the great and noble induna Gandang, and this puppy must be his grandson! I didn't recognize either of them—they are on their last legs."

Tungata Zebiwe sat in his grandmother's bony lap and ate with a quiet frenzy, the total dedication of a starving animal. He ate the extra Cornish pasties from the picnic basket, then he ate the crusts that Zouga had left. Louise searched the saddlebags and found a battered tin of bully, and the child ate that also, stuffing the rich fatty meat into his mouth with both hands.

"That's right," said Jan Cheroot sourly. "Fatten him up now, so we have to shoot him later." And he went off sulkily to saddle the horses for the return to Bulawayo.

"Juba, little Dove," Louise asked, "are all the children like this?"

"The food is finished," Juba nodded. "All the children are like this, though some of the little ones are dead already."

"Juba—is it not time that we women put an end to the foolishness of our men, before all the children are dead?"

"It is time, Balela," Juba agreed. "Time and past time."

◆ ◆ ◆

"Who is this woman?" Mr. Rhodes asked in that exasperated high-pitched voice that betrayed his agitation, and he peered at Zouga. His eyes seemed to have taken a new prominence, as though they were being squeezed out of his skull.

"She is the senior wife of Gandang."

"Gandang—he commanded the impi that massacred Wilson's patrol on the Shangani?"

"He was a half brother to Lobengula. With Babiaan and Somabula, he is the senior of all the indunas."

"I don't suppose there is anything to lose by talking to them." Mr. Rhodes shrugged. "This business will destroy us all if it goes on much longer. Tell this woman to take a message back that the indunas must lay down their arms and come in to Bulawayo."

"I'm sorry, Mr. Rhodes," Zouga told him. "They won't do that. They have had an *indaba* in the hills, all the indunas have spoken, and there is only one way."

"What is that, Ballantyne?"

"They want you to go to them."

"Me—personally?" Mr. Rhodes asked softly.

"We will speak only to Lodzi, and he must come to us unarmed. He must come into the Matopos without the soldiers. He may bring three other men with him, but none of them must carry a weapon. If they do, we kill them immediately." Zouga repeated the message that Juba had brought out of the hills for him, and Mr. Rhodes closed his eyes and covered them with the palm of his hand. His voice wheezed painfully in his chest, so that Zouga had to lean forward to catch his words.

"In their power," he said. "Alone and unarmed, completely in their power."

Mr. Rhodes dropped his hand and stood up. He moved heavily to the opening of the tent. He clasped his hands behind his back and rocked back on his heels. Outside in the hot, dusty noon, a bugle sang the advance, and there was the distant sound of a cavalry troop leaving the laager—hooves and the rattle of the lance butts in their hard leather boots.

Mr. Rhodes turned back to Zouga. "Can we afford to trust them?" he asked.

"Can we afford not to, Mr. Rhodes?"

◆　◆　◆

They left the horses at the place that had been agreed, in one of the myriad valleys in the granite hills that reared into broken crests and dropped into deep troughs like the frozen surf whipped up by a wild Atlantic gale. Zouga Ballantyne led from there, taking the twisted, narrow footpath through dense brush, moving slowly and looking back every few paces at the shambling bearlike figure that followed him.

When the path began to climb, Zouga stopped and waited for him to regain his breath. Mr. Rhodes's face had taken on a bluish, mottled appearance, and he was sweating heavily. However, after only a few minutes, he waved Zouga onward impatiently.

Close behind Mr. Rhodes followed the two others that the indunas had stipulated. One was a journalist—Mr. Rhodes was too much of a showman to miss an opportunity such as this—and the other was a doctor, for he realized that the assegais of the Matabele were not the only threat he faced on this grueling journey.

The shimmering heat of the Matopo Hills made the air above the granite surfaces dance and waver as though they were the plates of a wood-fired iron stove. The silence had a cloying, suffocating texture that seemed almost tangible, and the sudden, sharp bird calls that cut through it every few minutes served only to emphasize its intensity.

The scrub pressed in closely on each side of the track, and once Zouga saw a branch tremble and stir when there was no breeze. He strode on upward with a measured pace, as though he were leading the guard of honor at a military funeral. The path turned sharply into a vertical crack in the highest point of the granite wall, and here Zouga waited again.

Mr. Rhodes reached him and leaned against the heated granite with his shoulder while he wiped his face and neck with a white handkerchief. He could not speak for many minutes, and then he gasped, "Do you think they will come, Ballantyne?"

Farther down the valley, from the thickest bush, a robin called, and Zouga inclined his head to listen. It was almost convincing mimicry.

"They are here before us, Mr. Rhodes. The hills are alive with Matabele," and he looked for fear in the pale blue eyes. When he found none, he murmured quietly, almost shyly, "You are a brave man, sir."

"A pragmatic one, Ballantyne." And a smile twisted the swollen, disease-ravaged face. "It's always better to talk than to fight."

"I hope the Matabele agree." Zouga returned his smile, and they went on into the vertical crack in the granite, passing swiftly through shadow into the sunlight once more, and below them was a basin in the granite. It was ringed by high ramparts of broken granite and bare of any cover.

Zouga looked down into the little circular valley and all his soldier's instincts were offended.

"It's a trap," he said. "A natural killing ground from which there is no escape."

"Let us go down," said Mr. Rhodes.

In the middle of the basin was a low anthill, a raised platform of hard yellow clay, and instinctively the little group of white men made their way toward it.

"We might as well make ourselves comfortable," Mr. Rhodes panted, and sank down upon it. The other members of the party sat on each side of him—only Zouga remained upon his feet.

Though he kept his face impassive, his skin itched as the insects of dread crawled over it. This was the heart of the Matopo Hills, the sacred hills of the Matabele, their stronghold in which they would be at their bravest and most reckless. It was folly to come unarmed into this place, to throw themselves upon the mercy of the most savage and bloodthirsty tribe of a cruel, wild continent. Zouga stood with his empty hands clasped behind his back, and turned slowly upon his heel, surveying the wall of rock that hemmed them in. He had not completed his circle before he said quietly: "Well, gentlemen. Here they are!"

Without a word, with no spoken command, the impis rose from their concealment and formed a living barricade along the skyline. They stood in rank upon rank and shoulder to shoulder, completely encompassing the rocky valley. It was impossible to count their multitude, impossible even to guess at their thousands, but still the silence persisted as though their eardrums were filled with wax.

"Do not move, gentlemen," Zouga cautioned them, and they waited in the sunlight. They waited while the silent, impassive impis stood guard about them. Now no bird called and not the lightest breeze stirred the forest of feather headdresses and the kilts of fur.

At last the ranks opened and a group of men came through. The ranks closed behind them, and the little group came on down the path. These were the great princes of Kumalo, the Zanzi of royal blood—but how they were reduced.

They were all of them old men, with the hoarfrost of the years sparkling in their hair and beards. They were starved to the thinness of pariah dogs, with their warriors' muscles stringy and wasted and their old bones showing through. Some of them had blood-soaked bandages bound over their wounds, while the limbs and faces of others were scabbed with the sores that starvation and deprivation breed.

Gandang led them, and a pace behind him on either hand came his half brothers Babiaan and Somabula, and behind them again the other sons of Mashobane, wearing the headrings of honor and carrying every one of them the broad silver killing blades and the tall rawhide shields that gave them their name, Matabele, the People of the Long Shields.

Ten paces in front of Zouga, Gandang stopped and grounded his shield, and the two men stared deeply into each other's eyes, and both of them were thinking of the day they had first met thirty years and more before.

"I see you, Gandang, son of Mzilikazi," Zouga said at last.

"I see you, Bakela, the One Who Strikes with the Fist."

And behind Zouga Mr. Rhodes ordered calmly, "Ask him if it is to be war or peace."

Zouga did not take his eyes from those of the tall, emaciated induna.

"Are the eyes still red for war?" he asked.

Gandang's reply was a deep rumble, but it carried clearly to every induna who followed him, and it rose up to the massed ranks of warriors upon the heights.

"Tell Lodzi that the eyes are white," he said, and he stooped and laid his shield and his assegai upon the ground at his feet.

◆ ◆ ◆

Two Matabele, dressed only in loincloths, pushed the steel cocopan along the narrow-gauge railway tracks. When they reached the tip, one of them knocked out the retaining pin and the steel pan swiveled and spilled its five-ton load of sugary blue quartz into the funnel-shaped chute. The rock tumbled and rolled into the sizing box and piled onto the steel grating, where another dozen Matabele fell upon it with ten-pound sledgehammers and broke it up so that it could fall through the grating into the stamp boxes below.

The stamps were of massive cast iron; hissing steam drove them in a monotonous see-saw rhythm, pounding the ore to the consistency of talcum powder. The roar of the stamps was ear-numbing. A continuous stream of water, piped up from the stream in the valley below, sluiced the powdered ore out of the stamp boxes and carried it down the wooden gutters to the James tables.

In the low, open-sided hut, Harry Mellow stood over the No. 1 table and watched the flow of thick, mud-laden water washing across the heavy copper sheet that was the tabletop. The top was inclined to allow the worthless mud to run to waste, and eccentric cams agitated the table gently to spread the flow and insure that every particle of ore touched the coated surface of the table. Harry closed off the screw valve and diverted the flow of mud to the No. 2 table. Then he threw the lever and the agitation of the table ceased.

Harry glanced up at Ralph Ballantyne and Vicky, who were watching him avidly, and he cocked a thumb to reassure them—the thunderous roar of the stamps drowned all conversation here—and then Harry stooped over the table once more. The tabletop was coated with a thick layer of quicksilver, and, using a wide spatula, Harry began scraping it off the copper and squeezing it into a heavy dark ball. One of the unique properties of mercury is its ability to mop up particles of gold the way that blotting paper sucks up ink.

When Harry had finished, he had a ball of amalgamated mercury twice the size of a baseball and which weighed almost forty pounds. He needed both hands to lift it. He carried it across to the thatched rondavel that served as laboratory and refinery for the Harkness Mine, and Ralph and Vicky hurried after him and crowded into the tiny room behind him.

The three of them watched with utter fascination as the ball of amalgam began to dissolve and bubble in the retort over the intense blue flame of the Primus stove.

"We cook off the mercury," Harry explained, "and condense it again, but what we have left behind is this."

The boiling silver liquid reduced in quantity, and began to change in color. They caught the first reddish-yellow promise, the gleam that has enchanted man for more than six thousand years.

"Just look at it!" Vicky clapped her hands with excitement, shaking out her thick coppery tresses, and her eyes shone as though with a reflection of the luster of the precious liquid that she was watching. The last of the mercury boiled away and left behind a deep, glowing puddle of pure gold.

"Gold," said Ralph Ballantyne. "The first gold of the Harkness Mine." And then he threw back his head and laughed. The sound startled them. They had not heard Ralph laugh since he had left Bulawayo, and while they stared at him, he seized both of them, Vicky in one arm and Harry in the other, and danced them out into the sunlight.

They danced in a circle, and the two men whooped and howled, Ralph like a highlander and Harry like a plains Indian, while the Matabele hammer boys broke off their labors and watched them, first with astonishment, and then chuckling in sympathy.

Vicky broke out of the circle first, panting and holding the first bulge of her pregnant tummy in both hands.

"You are mad!" she laughed breathlessly. "Mad! Both of you! And I love you for it."

♦ ♦ ♦

The mix was fifty-fifty, half river clay dug from the banks of the Khami and half yellow anthill clay, the adhesive qualities of which had been enhanced by the saliva of the termites which had carried it up through their subterranean tunnels to the surface. The clays were puddled in a pit beside the bottom well, the same well that Clinton Codrington, Robyn's first husband, and Jordan Ballantyne had dug together so long ago, even before the Charter Company's pioneers had first ridden into Matabeleland.

Two of the mission converts cranked up each bucketful from the well and spilled it into the mixing pit, another two shoveled in the clay, and a dozen naked black children, led by Robert St. John, made a game out of trampling the clay to the correct consistency. Robyn St. John was helping pack the clay into the oblong wooden molds, each eighteen inches by nine. A line of mission boys and girls carried the filled molds away to the drying ground, where they carefully turned out the wet bricks onto the beds of dry grass, and then hurried back with the empty molds to have them refilled.

There were thousands of yellow bricks lying in long lines in the sun, but Robyn had calculated that they needed at least twenty thousand for the new church alone. Then of course they would have to cut all the timber and cure it, and in a month's time the thatch grass in the vleis would be tall enough to begin cutting.

Robyn straightened and placed her muddied yellow hand in the small of her back to ease the cramping muscles. A lock of gray-flecked hair had escaped from under the scarf she had knotted over her head, and there was a smear of mud down her cheek and neck, but the little runnels of her own sweat were eroding this away and staining the high collar of her blouse with it.

She looked up at the burned-out ruins of the mission; the charred roof beams had fallen in, and the heavy rains of the last wet season had dissolved the unbaked brick walls into a shapeless hillock. They would have to re-lay every brick and lift every rafter into place again, and the prospect of all that grinding, unremitting labor gave Robyn St. John a deep and exciting sense of anticipation. She felt as strong and alive as the young medical missionary who had first stepped onto this unforgiving African soil almost forty years before.

"Thy will be done, dear Lord," she said aloud, and the Matabele girl beside her cried happily, "Amen, Nomusa!"

Robyn smiled at her and was about to bend once more to the brick molds, when she started, shaded her eyes and then picked up her skirts and rushed down the track toward the river, running like a young girl.

"Juba!" she cried. "Where have you been? I have waited so long for you to come home."

Juba set down the heavy load she carried balanced on her head and came lumbering to meet her.

"Nomusa!" She was weeping as she hugged Robyn to her. Great, fat, oily tears slid down her cheeks and mingled with the sweat and mud on Robyn's face.

"Stop crying, you silly girl," Robyn scolded her lovingly. "You will make me start. Just look at you! How skinny you are—we will have to feed you up! And who is this?"

The black boy dressed only in a soiled loincloth came forward shyly.

"This is my grandson, Tungata Zebiwe."

"I did not recognize him, he has grown so big."

"Nomusa, I have brought him to you so that you can teach him to read and to write."

"Well, the first thing we will have to do is give him a civilized name. We shall call him Gideon and forget that horrible, vengeful name."

"Gideon," Juba repeated. "Gideon Kumalo. And you will teach him to write?"

"We have got a lot of work to do first," Robyn said firmly. "Gideon can go into the mud puddle with the other children, and you can help me pack the molds. We have to start all over, Juba, and build it all up from the beginning again."

"I admire the grandeur and loneliness of the Matopos, and therefore I desire to be buried in the Matopos on the hill which I used to visit and which I called the 'View of the World,' in a square to be cut in the rock on the top of the hill and covered with a plain brass plate with these words thereon: 'Here lie the remains of CECIL JOHN RHODES.' "

So when at last the pumping of his diseased heart ceased, he came to Bulawayo once more along the railroad that Ralph Ballantyne had laid. The special saloon coach in which his coffin rode was draped with purple and black, and at each town and siding along the way, those whom he had called "my Rhodesians" brought wreaths to pile upon the casket. From Bulawayo the coffin was taken on a gun carriage into the Matopo Hills, and the pure black bullocks that drew it plodded slowly up the rounded, egg-shaped dome of granite that he had chosen.

Above the open sepulcher stood a tripod gantry, with block and chain at the peak, and around it a dense throng of humanity: elegant gentlemen, uniformed officers and ladies with black ribbons on their hats. Then farther out there stretched a vast black sea of half-naked Matabele, twenty thousand come to see him go down into the earth. At their head were the indunas who had met him near this same hill to treat for peace. There were Gandang and Babiaan and Somabula, all of them very old men now.

Gathered at the head of the grave were the men who had replaced them in real power, the administrators of the Charter Company, Milton and Lawley, and the members of the first Rhodesian Council. Ralph Ballantyne was among them with his young wife beside him.

Ralph's expression remained grave and tragic as the coffin was lowered on its chains into the gaping tomb, and the bishop read aloud the obituary that Mr. Rudyard Kipling had composed:

> "It is his will that he look forth
> Across the world he won,
> The granite of the ancient north,
> Great spaces washed with sun.
> There shall he patient take his seat

(As when the death he dared)
And there await a people's feet
In the paths that he prepared."

As the heavy brass plaque was lowered into position, Gandang stepped out of the ranks of the Matabele and lifted one hand.

"The father is dead," he cried, and then in a single blast of sound, like the thunder of a tropical storm, the Matabele nation gave the salute they had never given to a white man before.

"Bayete!" they shouted as one man. "Bayete!"

The salute to a king.

♦ ♦ ♦

The funeral crowds dispersed slowly, seemingly reluctantly. The Matabele drifted away like smoke among the valleys of their sacred hills, and the white folk followed the path down the face of the granite dome. Ralph helped Elizabeth over the uneven footing, and he smiled down at her.

"The man was a rogue, and you weep for him," he teased her gently.

"It was all so moving." Elizabeth dabbed at her eyes. "When Gandang did that—"

"Yes. He fooled them all, even those he led into captivity. Damn me, but it's a good thing they buried him in solid rock and put a lid on him, or he would have squared the devil and got out of it at the last moment."

Ralph turned her out of the stream of people, of mourners who were following the path.

"I told Isazi to bring the carriage around to the back of the hill; we don't want to be caught in the crush."

Under their feet the granite was painted a vivid orange with lichen, and the little blue-headed lizards scuttled for cover in the crevices and then glared at them with their throats throbbing and the cockscomb crests of their monstrous heads fully erect. Ralph paused on the lower slope of the dome, where a twisted and deformed msasa tree had found precarious purchase in one of the crevices, and he looked back up at the peak.

"So he's dead at long last, but his company still governs

us. I have work to do yet, work that may take the rest of my life."

Then abruptly and uncharacteristically, Ralph shivered, although the sun was blazing hot.

"What is it, my dear?" Elizabeth turned to him with quick concern.

"Nothing," he said. "Perhaps I just walked over my own grave." Then he chuckled. "We'd best go down now before Jon-Jon drives poor Isazi completely out of his mind."

He took her arm and led her down to where Isazi had parked the carriage in the shade, and from a hundred paces they picked up the piping of Jonathan's questions and speculations, each punctuated with a demanding:

"*Uthini*, Isazi? What do you say, Isazi?"

And the patient reply: "Eh-heh, Bawu. Yes, yes, little Gadfly."

PART II
-◆- 1977 -◆-

PART II
1977

THE LAND ROVER TURNED OFF THE BLACKTOPPED ROAD, AND AS soon as it hit the dirt track, the pale dust boiled out from under its back wheels. It was an elderly vehicle; the desert-colored paintwork was scored and scratched by thorn and branch down to the bare metal. Rock and sharp shale had bitten chunks of rubber out of the heavily lugged tires.

The doors and the top were off and the cracked windshield lay flat on the hood, so that the wind swept over the two men in the front seat. Behind their heads stood the gun rack. The forks, lined with foam rubber, held a formidable battery of weapons: two semiautomatic FN rifles, sprayed with dun and green camouflage paint, a short 9mm Uzi submachine gun with the extra long magazine clipped on ready for instant use, and, still in its canvas slipcover, a heavy Colt Sauer "Grand African" whose .458 magnum cartridge could knock a bull elephant off its feet. From the uprights of the gun rack dangled haversacks containing the spare clips and magazines and a damp canvas water bottle. They swung harmoniously with each jolt and lurch of the Land Rover.

Craig Mellow drove with his foot jamming the accelerator to the floorboards. Though the vehicle's body clattered and banged loosely, he had always serviced and tuned the engine himself, and the speedometer needle pressed against the stop pin at the end of the dial. There is only one way to go into an ambush, and that is flat out. Get through it as fast as possible, remembering always that they usually laid it out at least half a kilometer deep. Even at 150 kilometers an hour, that meant receiving fire for twelve seconds. In that time a good man with an AK 47 can get off three magazines of thirty rounds each.

Yes, the way to go in was fast—but of course a land

mine was a beast of an entirely different color. When they boosted one of those sweethearts with ten kilos of plastic, it kicked you and your vehicle fifty feet in the air and shot your spine out through the top of your skull.

So although Craig lounged comfortably on the hard leather seat, his eyes scoured the road ahead. This late in the day there had been traffic through ahead of him, and he drove for the diamond tracks in the dust, but he watched for an extraneous tuft of grass, an old cigarette packet, or even a pat of dried cow dung that could conceal the marks of a dig in the road. Of course this close to Bulawayo he was in more danger from a drunken driver than from terrorist activity, but it was wise to nurture the habit.

Craig glanced sideways at his passenger and jerked his thumb over his shoulder. The man swiveled in his seat and reached into the cooler in the back. He brought out two cans of Lion beer with the dew on them, and while he did so, Craig flicked his attention back to the road.

Craig Mellow was twenty-nine years old, although the floppy thatch of dark hair blowing all over his forehead, the innocent candor of his hazel eyes, and the vulnerable slant to his wide, gentle mouth gave him the air of a small boy who expects to be unjustly reprimanded at any moment. He still wore the embroidered green shoulder patches of a ranger in the Department of Wildlife and Nature Conservation on his khaki bush shirt.

Beside him Samson Kumalo pulled the tabs off the beer cans. He wore the same uniform, but he was a tall Matabele with a deep, intelligent forehead and a hard, smooth-shaven lantern jaw. He ducked as a spurt of froth flew from the cans, and then handed one of them to Craig and kept one for himself. Craig saluted him with his can and swigged a mouthful, then licked the white mustache from his upper lip and put the Land Rover to the twisting road up the Khami Hills.

Before they reached the crest, Craig dropped the empty can into the plastic trash bag that hung from the dash and slowed the Land Rover, looking for the turnoff.

Tall yellow grass hid the small faded sign.

KHAMI ANGLICAN MISSION
Staff Cottages. No through road.

It was at least a year since Craig had last driven this road, and he almost missed it.

"Here it is!" Samson warned him, and he swung sharply onto the secondary track. It jinked through the forest, then came abruptly to the long, straight avenue of spathodea trees that led down to the staff village. The trunks were thicker than a man's chest, and the dark green branches met overhead. At the head of the avenue, almost screened by the trees and the long grass, was a low, whitewashed wall with a rusty wrought-iron gate. Craig pulled onto the shoulder and switched off the engine.

"Why are we stopping here?" Samson asked.

They always spoke English when they were alone; just as they always spoke Sindebele when anyone else was listening; just as Samson called him "Craig" in private and "Nkosi" or "Mambo" at all other times. It was a tacit understanding between them, for in this tortured, war-torn land, there were those who had taken Samson's fluent English as the mark of a "cheeky mission boy," and recognized by the easy intimacy between the two men that Craig was that thing of doubtful loyalties, a *kaffir lover*.*

"Why are we stopping at the old cemetery?" Samson repeated.

"All that beer." Craig climbed out of the Land Rover and stretched. "I have to pump ship."

He relieved himself against the battered front wheel, then went to sit on the low wall of the graveyard, swinging his long, bare, sun-browned legs. He wore khaki shorts and suede desert boots without socks, for the barbed seeds of arrow grass stick in knitted wool.

Craig looked down onto the roofs of Khami Mission Station that lay below the wooded hills. Some of the older buildings, dating back to before the turn of the century, were thatched, although the new school and hospital were tiled with red terra-cotta. However, the rows of low-cost housing in the compound were covered with unpainted corrugated asbestos. They made an unsightly gray huddle

---

*"Kaffir" is derived from the Arabic word for an infidel. During the nineteenth century, it denoted members of the southern African tribes. Without any derogatory bias, it was employed by statesmen, eminent authors, missionaries and champions of the native peoples. Nowadays its use is the sure mark of the racial bigot.

beside the lovely green of the irrigated fields. They offended Craig's aesthetic sense, and he looked away.

"Come on, Sam, let's get cracking—" Craig broke off and frowned. "What the hell are you doing?"

Samson had gone through the wrought-iron gate into the walled cemetery and was urinating casually on one of the gravestones.

"Jesus, Sam, that's desecration."

"An old family custom." Samson shook himself and zipped up. "My grandpa Gideon taught it to me," he explained, and then switched into Sindebele. "Giving water to make the flower grow again," he said.

"What the hell is that supposed to mean?"

"The man that lies down there killed a Matabele girl called Imbali, the Flower," said Samson. "My grandfather always pees on his grave whenever he passes this way."

Craig's shock was gradually replaced by curiosity. He swung his legs over the wall and went to stand beside Samson.

"Sacred to the memory of General Mungo St. John, Killed during the Matabele Rebellion of 1896."

Craig read the inscription aloud:

> "Man hath no greater love than this that he
> lay down his life for another.
> Intrepid sailor, brave soldier, faithful
> husband and devoted father.
> Always remembered by his widow Robyn and
> his son Robert."

Craig combed the hair out of his eyes with his fingers. "Judging by his advertising, he was one hell of a guy."

"He was a bloody murderer—he, as much as any one man could, provoked the rebellion."

"Is that so?"

Craig passed on to the next grave—and read that inscription.

> "Here lie the mortal remains of
> DOCTOR ROBYN ST. JOHN, Née BALLANTYNE
> Founder of Khami Mission,
> Departed this life April 16th 1931, aged 94 years.
> Well done thou good and faithful servant."

He glanced back at Samson. "Do you know who she was?"

"My grandfather calls her Nomusa, the Girl-Child of Mercy. She was one of the most beautiful people who ever lived."

"Never heard of her either."

"You should have—she was your great-great-grandmother."

"I have never bothered much with the family history. Mother and Father were second cousins, that's all I know. Mellow and Ballantynes for generations back—I've never sorted them all out."

" 'A man without a past, is a man without a future,' " Samson quoted.

"You know, Sam, sometimes you get up my nose." Craig grinned at him. "You've got an answer for everything."

He walked on down the row of old graves, some of them with elaborate headstones, doves and groups of mourning angels, and they were decked with faded artificial flowers in domes of clear glass. Others were covered with simple concrete slabs in which the lettering had eroded to the point of illegibility. Craig read those he could.

> "ROBERT ST. JOHN. Aged 54 years.
>   Son of Mungo and Robyn."

> "JUBA KUMALO. Aged 83 years.
>   Fly little Dove."

And then he stopped as he saw his own surname.

> VICTORIA MELLOW, Née CODRINGTON
> Died 8th April 1936, aged 63 years.
> Daughter of Clinton and Robyn, wife of Harold.

"Hey, Sam, if you were right about the others, then this must have been my great-grandmother."

There was a tuft of grass growing out of a crack through the slab, and Craig stooped and plucked it out. And as he did so, he felt a bond of affinity with the dust beneath that stone. It had laughed and loved and given birth that he might live.

"Hi there, Gran," he whispered. "I wonder what you were really like?"

"Craig, it's almost one o'clock," Sam interrupted him.

"Okay, I'm coming." But Craig lingered a few moments longer, held by that unaccustomed nostalgia. "I'll ask Bawu," he decided, and went back to the Land Rover.

He stopped again outside the first cottage of the village. The small yard was freshly raked, and there were petunias in tubs on the veranda.

"Look here, Sam," Craig began awkwardly. "I don't know what you're going to do now. You could join the police, like I am doing. Perhaps we could work it that we were together again."

"Perhaps," Sam agreed expressionlessly.

"Or I could talk to Bawu about getting you a job at King's Lynn."

"Clerk in the pay office?" Sam asked.

"Yea! I know." Craig scratched his ear. "Still, it's something."

"I'll think about it," Sam murmured.

"Hell, I feel bad, but you didn't have to come with me, you know. You could have stayed in the department."

"Not after what they did to you." Sam shook his head.

"Thanks, Sam."

They sat silently for a while, then Sam climbed down and lugged his bag out of the back of the Land Rover.

"I'll come out and see you as soon as I'm fixed up. We'll work something out," Craig promised. "Keep in touch, Sam."

"Sure." Sam held out his hand, and they shook briefly.

"*Hamba gashle,* go in peace," Sam said.

"*Shala gashle.* Stay in peace."

Craig started the Land Rover and swung back the way they had come. As he drove up the avenue of spathodea, he glanced in the rearview mirror. Sam was standing in the center of the road with his bag on one shoulder, watching him go. There was a hollow feeling of bereavement in Craig's chest. The two of them had been together for so long.

"I'll work something out," he repeated determinedly.

◆ ◆ ◆

Craig slowed at the top of the rise as he always did here, anticipating his first glimpse of the homestead, but when it came it was with that little shock of disappointment.

Bawu had stripped the thatch off the roof and replaced it with dull gray corrugated asbestos sheet. It had to be done, of course, an RPG-7 rocket fired into the thatch from outside the perimeter—and the whole building would have gone up like the Fifth of November. Still Craig resented the change, just as he did the loss of the beautiful jacaranda trees. They had been planted by Bawu's grandfather, old Zouga Ballantyne, who built King's Lynn back in the early 1890s. In spring their gentle rain of blue petals had carpeted the lawns, but they had been cut down to open a field of defensive fire around the house, and in their place now stood the ten-foot security fence of diamond mesh and barbed wire.

Craig drove down into the shallow dip below the main homestead toward the complex of offices, storerooms and tractor workshops which were the heart of the vast, sprawling ranch. Before he was halfway down, a lanky figure appeared in the high doorway of the workshop and stood with arms akimbo watching him approach.

"Hello, Grandpa." Craig climbed out of the Land Rover, and the old man frowned to cover his pleasure.

"How many times have I got to tell you, 'Don't call me that!' You want people to think I'm old?" Jonathan Ballantyne was burned and desiccated by the sun to the consistency of biltong, the dark strips of dried venison that were such a Rhodesian delicacy.

It seemed that if you were to cut him, dust and not blood would pour from the wound, but his eyes were still a brilliant, twinkling green, and his hair was a dense white shock that fell to his collar at the back of his neck. It was one of his many conceits. He shampooed it every day, and brushed it with a pair of silver-backed brushes that stood on the table beside his bed.

"Sorry, Bawu." Craig reverted to his Matabele name, the Gadfly, and seized the old man's hand. It was mere bone covered by cool, dry skin, but the grip was startlingly strong.

"So you got yourself fired again," Jonathan accused. Although his teeth were artificial, they were a neat fit, filling out the wizened cheeks, and he kept them so spar-

kling white as to match his hair and silvery mustache.
Another of his conceits.

"I resigned," Craig denied.

"You got fired."

"It was close," Craig admitted. "But I beat them to it. I
resigned."

Craig was not really surprised that Jonathan already knew
of his latest misfortune. Nobody knew how old Jonathan
Ballantyne was for certain—the outside estimate was a
hundred years, though eighty-plus was Craig's guess—but
still nothing got by him.

"You can give me a lift up to the house." Jonathan
swung up easily onto the high passenger seat and with
relish began pointing out the additions to the defense of the
homestead.

"I have put in twenty more Claymores on the front
lawn." Jonathan's Claymore mines were ten kilos of plastic
explosive packed inside a drum of scrap iron suspended on
a pipe tripod. He could fire them electrically from his
bedroom.

Jonathan was a chronic insomniac, and Craig had a bizarre mental picture of the old man spending every night
sitting bolt upright in his nightshirt with his finger on the
button praying for a terrorist to come within range. The
war had added twenty years to his life. Jonathan hadn't had
such a good time since the first battle of the Somme, where
he had won his Military Cross one lovely autumn morning
by grenading three German machine-gun nests in quick
succession. Secretly Craig believed that the first thing any
ZIPRA* guerrilla recruit was taught when he began his
basic training was to give King's Lynn and the crazy old
man who lived there the widest possible berth.

As they drove up through the gates in the security fence
and were surrounded by a mixed pack of fearsome Rottweilers and Doberman pinschers, Jonathan explained the latest
refinements to his battle plan.

"If they come from behind the kopje, I'll let them get
into the minefield, then take them in enfilade—"

He was still explaining and gesticulating as they climbed
the steps to the wide veranda, and he finished the briefing
by adding darkly and mysteriously: "I have just invented a

*Zimbabwe People's Revolutionary Army.

secret weapon—I'm going to test it tomorrow morning. You can watch."

"I'd enjoy that, Bawu," Craig thanked him doubtfully. The last tests that Jonathan had conducted had blown all the windows out of the kitchens and flesh-wounded the Matabele cook.

Craig followed Jonathan down the wide, shady veranda. The wall was hung with hunting trophies, the horns of buffalo and kudus and eland, and on each side of the double glass doors leading to the old dining room, now the library, stood a pair of enormous elephant tusks, so long and curved that their tips almost met at the level of the ceiling above the doorway.

As he went through the door, Jonathan absentmindedly stroked one of them. There was a spot on the thick yellow curve that had been polished shiny by the touch of his fingers over the decades.

"Pour us each a gin, my boy," he ordered. Jonathan had stopped drinking whisky on the day that Harold Wilson's government had imposed sanctions on Rhodesia. It was Jonathan's single-handed retaliatory attempt at disrupting the economy of the British Isles.

"By God, you've drowned it," he complained as he tasted the concoction, and dutifully Craig took his glass back to the imbuia cocktail cabinet and stiffened the gin component.

"That's a little better." Jonathan settled himself behind his desk and placed the Stuart crystal tumbler in the center of his leather-and-brass-bound blotter.

"Now," he said. "Tell me what happened this time." And he fixed Craig with those bright green eyes.

"Well, Bawu, it's a long story. I don't want to bore you." Craig sank down into the deep leather armchair and became intensely interested in the furnishings of the room, which he had known since childhood. He read the titles on the spines of the morocco-bound books on the shelves and studied the massed display of blue silk rosettes which the prize Afrikander bulls of King's Lynn had won at every agricultural show south of the Zambezi River.

"Shall I tell you what I heard? I heard you refused to obey the legitimate order of your superior, to wit the head game warden, and that thereafter you perpetrated a violence upon that worthy, or more specifically that you punched him in the head. Giving him the excuse to dismiss you for which he had probably been searching desperately since the first day you arrived in the park."

"The reports are exaggerated."

"Don't give me that little-boy grin of yours, young man. This is not a matter of levity," Jonathan told him sternly. "Did you refuse to partake in the elephant cull, or did you not?"

"Have you ever been on a cull, Jon-Jon?" Craig asked softly. He only used his grandfather's pet name in moments of deep sincerity. "The spotter plane picks a likely herd, say fifty animals, and radio talks us onto them. We go in the last mile or so on foot at a dead run. We get in very close, ten paces, so we are shooting uphill. We use the four fifty-eights to cannon them. What we do is pick out the old queens of the herd, because the younger animals love and respect them so much that they won't leave them. We hit the queens first, head shots, of course; that gives us plenty of time to work on the others. We are pretty good at it by now. We drop them so fast that the heaps have to be pulled apart by tractors afterward. That leaves the calves. It's interesting to watch a calf trying to lift its dead mother back onto her feet again with its tiny trunk."

"It has to be done, Craig," said Jonathan quietly. "The parks are overstocked by thousands of animals." But Craig seemed not to have heard.

"If the orphan calves are too young to survive, we hit them also, but if they are the right age, we round them up and sell them to a nice old man who takes them away and resells them to a zoo to Tokyo or Amsterdam, where they will stand behind bars with a chain around the foot and eat the peanuts that the tourists throw them."

"It has to be done," Jonathan repeated.

"He was taking kickbacks from the animal dealers," Craig said. "So that we were ordered to leave orphans that were so young they only had a fifty-fifty chance of survival. So that we looked for herds with high percentages of small calves. He was taking bribes from the dealers."

"Who? Not Tomkins, the head warden?" Jonathan exclaimed.

"Yes, Tomkins." Craig stood up and took both their glasses to refill.

"Have you got proof?"

374

"No, of course I haven't," Craig replied irritably. "If I had I would have taken it straight to the minister."

"So you just refused to cull."

Craig flopped back in the chair—long, bare legs sprawled and hair hanging in his eyes.

"That's not all. They are stealing the ivory from the cull. We are supposed to leave the big bulls, but Tomkins ordered us to hit anything with good ivory, and the tusks disappear."

"No proof on that either, I suppose?" Jonathan asked dryly.

"I saw the helicopter making the pickup."

"And you got the registration letters?"

"They were masked"—Craig shook his head—"but it was a military machine. It's organized."

"So you punched Tomkins?"

"It was beautiful," said Craig dreamily. "He was on his hands and knees trying to pick up his teeth that were scattered all over the floor of his office. I never worked out what he was going to do with them."

"Craig, my boy, what did you hope to achieve? Do you think it will stop them, even if your suspicions are correct."

"No, but it made me feel a lot better. Those elephants are almost human. I became pretty fond of them."

They were both silent for a while and then Jonathan sighed. "How many jobs is that now, Craig?"

"I wasn't keeping score, Bawu."

"I cannot believe that anybody with Ballantyne blood in his veins is totally lacking in either talent or ambition. Christ, boy, we Ballantynes are winners—look at Douglas, look at Roland—"

"I'm a Mellow, only half a Ballantyne."

"Yes, I suppose that accounts for it. Your grandfather frittered away his share in the Harkness Mine, so when your father married my Jean he was almost a pauper. Good God, those shares would be worth ten million pounds today."

"That was during the Great Depression of the thirties—a lot of people lost money then."

"We didn't—the Ballantynes didn't."

Craig shrugged. "No, the Ballantynes doubled up during the depression."

"We are winners," Jonathan repeated. "But what happens to you now? You know my rule, you don't get a penny more from me.''

"Yes, I know that rule, Jon-Jon.''

"You want to try working here again? It didn't pan out so well last time, did it?''

"You are an impossible old bastard," said Craig fondly. "I love you, but I'd rather work for Idi Amin than for you again.''

Jonathan looked immensely pleased with himself. His image of himself as tough, ruthless and ready to kill was another of his conceits. He would have been deeply insulted if anybody had called him easygoing or generous. The large, anonymous donations he made to every charity, deserving or otherwise, were always accompanied by blood-curdling threats to anybody revealing his identity.

"So what are you going to do with yourself this time?''

"Well, I was trained as an armorer when I did my national service, and there is an armorer's berth open in the police. The way I see it, I'm going to be called up again anyway, so I might as well beat them to it and enlist.''

"The police," Jonathan mused. "That does have the virtue of being one of the few things you haven't tried yet. Get me another drink.''

While Craig poured gin and tonic, Jonathan put on his fiercest expression to cover his embarrassment and growled, "Look here, boy, if you are really short, I'll bend the rule this once and lend you a few dollars to tide you over. Strictly a loan though.''

"That's very decent of you, Bawu, but a rule is a rule.''

"I make 'em, I break 'em.'' Jonathan glared at him. "How much do you need?''

"You know those old books you wanted?'' Craig murmured as he put the old man's glass back in front of him, and an expression of intense cunning came into Jonathan's eyes which he tried in vain to conceal.

"What books?'' His innocence was loaded.

"Those old journals.''

"Oh, those!'' And despite himself Jonathan glanced at the bookshelves beside his desk upon which were displayed his collection of family journals. They stretched back over a hundred years, from the arrival of his grandfather, Zouga Ballantyne, in Africa in 1860 up to the death of Jonathan's father, Sir Ralph Ballantyne, in 1929; but the sequence was broken by a few missing years, three volumes which had come down on Craig's side of the family through old Harry Mellow, who had been Sir Ralph's partner and dearest friend.

For some perverse reason that Craig could not even understand himself, he had up until now resisted all the old man's blandishments and attempts to get his hands on them. It was probably because they were the one small lever he had on Jonathan that he had held out since they had come into his possession on his twenty-first birthday, the only item of any value in the inheritance from his long-dead father.

"Yes, those," Craig nodded. "I thought I might let you have them."

"You must be hard-pressed." The old man tried not to let his glee shine through.

"Even more than usual," Craig admitted.

"You waste—"

"Okay, Bawu. We've been that road before." Craig stopped him hurriedly. "Do you want them?"

"How much?" Jonathan demanded suspiciously.

"Last time you offered me a thousand each."

"I must have been soft."

"Since then there has been one hundred per cent inflation—"

Jonathan loved to haggle. It enhanced his image of himself as hard and ruthless. Craig reckoned he was worth ten million. He owned King's Lynn and four other ranches. He owned the Harkness Mine, which after eighty years in production was still producing fifty thousand ounces of gold a year, and he had assets outside this beleaguered country, prudently stashed away over the years in Johannesburg, London and New York. Ten million was probably conservative, Craig realized, and set himself to bargain as hard as the old man.

At last they reached a figure with Jonathan grumbling. "They're worth half of that."

"There are two other conditions, Bawu," and immediately Jonathan was suspicious again.

"Number one, you leave them to me in your will, the whole set, Zouga Ballantyne's and Sir Ralph's journals, all of them."

"Roland and Douglas—"

"They are going to get King's Lynn and the Harkness and all the rest—that's what you told me."

"Damn right," he growled. "They won't blow it all out the window like you would."

"They can have it." Craig grinned easily. "They are Ballantynes as you say, but I want the journals."

"What is your second condition?" Jonathan demanded.

"I want access to them now."

"What do you mean?"

"I want to be able to read and study any of them whenever I want to."

"What the hell, Craig, you have never given a damn about them before. I doubt you have even read the three you own."

"I've glanced through them," Craig admitted shamefacedly.

"And now?"

"I was up at Khami Mission this morning, in the old cemetery. There is a grave there, Victoria Mellow—"

Jonathan nodded. "Aunty Vicky, Harry's wife—go on."

"I had this strange feeling as I was standing there. Almost as though she was calling to me." Craig plucked at the thick forelock over his eyes and could not look at his grandfather. "And suddenly I wanted to find out more about her, and the others."

They were both silent for a while, and then Jonathan nodded.

"All right, my boy, I accept your conditions. Both sets will be yours one day, and until then you can read them whenever you wish to."

Jonathan had seldom been so pleased with a bargain. He had completed his sets after thirty years, and if the boy was serious about reading them, he had found a good home for them. The Lord knew, neither Douglas nor Roland were interested, and in the meantime perhaps the journals might draw Craig back to King's Lynn more often. He wrote out the check and signed it with a flourish while Craig went out to the Land Rover and dug the three leather-bound manuscripts from the bottom of his kit bag.

"I suppose you will spend it all on that boat," Jonathan accused as he came in from the veranda.

"Some of it," Craig admitted. He placed the books in front of the old man.

"You are a dreamer." Jonathan slid the check across the desk.

"Sometimes I prefer dreams to reality." Craig scrutinized the figures briefly, then buttoned the pink check into his top pocket.

"That's your trouble," said Jonathan.

"Bawu, if you start lecturing me, I'm going to head straight back to town."

Jonathan held up both hands in capitulation. "All right," he chuckled. "Your old room is the way you left it, if you want to use it."

"I have an appointment with the police recruiting officer on Monday, but I'll stay the weekend, if that's okay?"

"I'll ring Trevor this evening and fix the interview."

Trevor Pennington was the assistant commissioner of police. Jonathan believed in starting at the top.

"I wish you wouldn't, Jon-Jon."

"Don't be daft," Jonathan snapped. "You must learn to use every advantage, my boy, that's the way life works."

Jonathan picked up the first of the three volumes of manuscript and gloatingly stroked it with his gnarled brown fingers.

"Now, you can leave me alone for a while," he ordered as he unfolded his wire-framed reading glasses and perched them on his nose. "They are playing tennis across at Queen's Lynn. I will see you back here for sundowners."

Craig glanced back from the doorway, but Jonathan Ballantyne was hunched over the book, transported by the entries in yellow, faded ink back to his childhood.

♦ ♦ ♦

Although it shared a common seven-mile boundary with King's Lynn, Queen's Lynn was a separate ranch. Jonathan Ballantyne had added it to his holdings during the Great Depression of the 1930s, paying five cents on the dollar of its real worth. Now it formed the eastern spread of the Rholands Ranching Company.

It was the home of Jonathan's only surviving son, Douglas Ballantyne, and his wife Valerie. Douglas was the managing director of both Rholands and the Harkness Mine. He was also Minister of Agriculture in Ian Smith's UDI Government, and with any luck he might be away on mysterious government or company business.

Douglas Ballantyne had once given Craig his honest appraisal. "At heart you are a bloody hippie, Craig. You should get your hair cut and start bracing up—you can't go on dawdling through life and expecting Bawu and the rest of the family to carry you forever."

Craig pulled a sour face at the memory as he drove down past the stockyards of Queen's Lynn and smelled the ammoniacal tang of cow dung.

The huge Afrikander beasts were a uniform deep chocolate red, the bulls humpbacked and with swinging dewlaps that almost brushed the earth. This breed had made Rhodesian beef almost as renowned as the marbled beef of Kobe. As Minister of Agriculture it was Douglas Ballantyne's duty to see that, despite sanctions, the world was not deprived of this delicacy. The route that it took to the tables of the great restaurants of the world was via Johannesburg and Cape Town, where it perforce changed its name, but the connoisseurs recognized it and asked for it by its nom de guerre, their taste buds probably piqued by the knowledge that they were eating forbidden fruits. Rhodesian tobacco and nickel and copper and gold all went out the same way, while petrol and diesel oil made the return trip. The popular bumper sticker said simply, "Thank you, South Africa."

Beyond the stock pens and veterinary block, once again protected by the diamond mesh and barbed-wire security fence, lay the green lawns and banks of flowering shrubs and the blazing Pride-of-India trees of the gardens of Queen's Lynn. The windows had been covered with grenade screens and the servants would drop steel bulletproof shutters into their slots before sunset, but here the defenses had not been built with the same gusto as Bawu had shown at King's Lynn. They fitted unobtrusively into the gracious surroundings.

The lovely old house was very much as Craig remembered it from before the war—rosy red brick and wide, cool verandas. The jacaranda trees that lined the long, curved driveway were in full flower, like a mist bank of pale, ethereal blue, and there were at least two dozen cars parked beneath them, Mercedes and Jaguars, Cadillacs and BMW's, their paintwork hazed with the red dust of Matabeleland. Craig concealed his venerable Land Rover behind the tumble of red and purple bougainvillea creeper, so as not to lower the tone of a Queen's Lynn Saturday. From habit he slung an FN rifle over his shoulder and wandered around the side of the house.

◆ ◆ ◆

From ahead there came the sound of children's voices, gay as songbirds, and the genial scolding of their black nannies, punctuated by the sharp "pock! pock!" of a long rally from the tennis courts.

Craig paused at the head of the terraced lawns. Children spilled and tumbled and chased each other in circles like puppies over the green grass. Nearer the yellow clay courts, their parents sprawled on spread rugs or sat at the shaded white tea tables under the brightly colored umbrellas. They were bronzed young men and women in tennis whites, sipping tea or drinking beer from tall, frosted glasses, calling ribald comment and advice to the players upon the courts. The only incongruous note was the row of machine pistols and automatic rifles beside the silver tea set and cream scones.

Someone recognized Craig and shouted, "Hi, Craig, long time no see," and others waved, but there was just that faint edge of condescension in their manner reserved for the poor relative. These were the families with great estates, a closed club of the wealthy in which, for all their geniality, Craig would never have full membership.

Valerie Ballantyne came to meet him, slim-hipped and girlishly graceful in her short white tennis skirt. "Craig, you are as thin as a bean pole." He always brought out the maternal instincts in any female between eight and eighty.

"Hello, Aunty Val."

She offered him a smooth cheek that smelled of violets. Despite her delicate air, Valerie was president of the Women's Institute, served on the committees of a dozen schools, charities and hospitals, and was a gracious, accomplished hostess.

"Uncle Douglas is in Salisbury. Smithy sent for him yesterday. He will be sorry to have missed you." She took his arm. "How is the game department?"

"It will probably survive without me."

"Oh, no, Craig, not again!"

" 'Fraid so, Aunty Val." He didn't really feel up to a

discussion of his career at that moment. "Do you mind if I get myself a beer?"

There was a group of men around the long trestle table that did service as a bar. The group opened to let him in, but the conversation went straight back to a discussion of the latest raid that the Rhodesian security forces had made on the terrorists in Mozambique.

"I tell you, when we hit the camp, there was food still cooking on the fires, but they had run for it. We caught a few stragglers, but the others had been warned."

"Bill is right. I had it from a colonel in intelligence—no names, no pack drill, but there is a bad security leak. A traitor near the top, the terrs are getting up to twelve hours' warning."

"We haven't had a really good kill since last August when we took six hundred."

The eternal war talk bored Craig. He sipped his beer and watched the play on the nearest court.

It was mixed doubles, and at that moment they changed ends.

Roland Ballantyne came around the net with his arm around his partner's waist. He was laughing, and his teeth were startlingly white and even in the deep tan of his face. His eyes were that peculiar Ballantyne green, like crème de menthe in a crystal glass, and although he wore his hair short, it was thick and wavy, bleached to honey gold by the sun.

He moved like a leopard, with a lazy, gliding gait, and the superb physical condition that was a prerequisite of any member of the Scouts glossed the muscles of his forearms and bare legs. He was only a year older than Craig, but his assurance always made Craig feel gawky and callow in comparison. Craig had once heard a girl he admired, a young lady usually blasé and affectedly unimpressed, describe Roland Ballantyne as the most magnificent stud on show.

Now Roland saw him, and waved his racquet. "Don't be vague, call for Craig!" he greeted him across the court, and then said something inaudible to the girl beside him. She chuckled and looked at Craig.

Craig felt the shock begin in the pit of his stomach and ripple outward like a stone dropped into a still pool. He stared at her, petrified, unable to drag his eyes off her face.

She stopped laughing, and for a moment longer returned his gaze, then she broke out of the circle of Roland's arm and went to the base line, bouncing the ball lightly off her racquet, and Craig was certain that her cheeks had flushed a shade pinker than the game had previously rouged them.

Still he could not take his eyes off her. She was the most perfect thing he had ever seen. She was tall; she reached almost to Roland's shoulder, and he was six one. Her hair was cropped into a glossy cap of curls that changed color as the sunlight played upon it, from the burnished iridescence of obsidian to the rich, dark glow of a noble Burgundy wine held to the candlelight.

Her face was squarish, with a firm, perhaps stubborn, line to the jaw, but her mouth was wide and tender and humorous. Her eyes were wide-spaced and slanted to such a degree that they seemed just a touch squint. It gave her a vulnerable, appealing air, but when she glanced at Roland, they took on a wicked, taunting glint.

"Let's blast them, pardner," she called, and the lilt of her voice raised little goose bumps on Craig's forearms.

The girl turned her shoulders and hips away, tossed the yellow ball high as she went up on tiptoe and then swung back into the overhead stroke. The racquet spranged sharply, and the ball blurred low across the net and spurted white chalk from the center line.

She crossed the court with quick, dainty steps and caught the return on the volley. She tucked it away in the corner and then glanced at Craig.

"Shot!" he called, his voice ringing hollowly in his own ears, and a little satisfied smile puckered the corner of her mouth.

She turned away and stooped to recover a loose ball. Her back was turned toward Craig, her feet slightly apart, and she did not bend her knees. Her legs were long and shapely, and as her short pleated skirt popped up, he had a fleeting glimpse of thin, lacy panties and the buttocks in them so neat and hard and symmetrical that he was reminded of a pair of ostrich eggs gleaming in the Kalahari sunlight.

Craig dropped his eyes guiltily as if he had played the peeping Tom. He felt light-headed and strangely breathless. He forced himself not to look back at the court, but his heart was pounding as though he had just run a cross-country, and the conversation around him seemed to be in a foreign language, relayed through a faulty transmitter. It did not make sense.

It seemed hours later that a hard, muscular arm was thrown around his shoulders and Roland's voice in his ear.

"You're looking well, old son." At last Craig allowed himself to look around.

"The terrs haven't caught you yet, Roly?"

"No way, Sonny." Roland hugged him. "Let me introduce you to a girl who loves me." Only Roland could make a remark like that sound witty and sophisticated. "This is Bugsy. Bugsy, this is my favorite cousin, Craig, the well-known sex maniac."

"Bugsy?" Craig looked into those strangely tilted eyes. "It doesn't suit you." He realized that they were not black, but an indigo blue.

"Janine," she said. "Janine Carpenter." She held out her hand. It was slim and warm and moist from the game. He did not want to release it.

"I warned you," Roland laughed. "Stop molesting the girl and come and have a set with me, Sonny."

"I haven't got togs."

"All you need is shoes. We are the same size, I'll send a servant for a spare pair."

◆ ◆ ◆

Craig hadn't played for over a year. The layoff seemed to have worked wonders. He had never played so well. The ball came off the sweet spot of his racquet so fast and clean that it felt as though he had clean missed it, and the top spin pulled it down onto the base line as though it were a magnet.

Effortlessly he passed Roland on either side and then dropped the ball so short that it left him stranded in midcourt. He hit first-time serves that nicked the line, and returned shots that usually he would not have bothered to chase, then he rushed the net and slaughtered Roland's best forehand.

He was loving it, so involved with the marvelous, unaccustomed sense of power and of his own invincibility that he had not even noticed that the stream of Roland Ballantyne's easy banter had long ago dried up—until he won another game and Roland said, "Five games to love."

384

Something in his tone reached Craig at last, and for the first time since they had begun playing, he really looked at Roland's face. It was a swollen, ugly red. His jaw clenched so that there were lumps of muscle below his ears. His eyes were murderous green, and he was dangerous as a wounded leopard.

Craig looked away from him as they changed sides, and he saw that their game had fascinated everybody. Even the older women had left the tea tables and come down to the fence. He saw Aunty Val, with a nervous little smile on her lips. From hard experience she recognized her son's mood. Craig saw the sniggering smiles on the faces of the men. Roland had won his tennis half-blue at Oxford, and he had been Matabeleland singles champion three years running. They were enjoying this as much as Craig had been up until then.

Suddenly Craig felt appalled at his own success. He had never beaten Roland at anything, not a single contest of any sort, not even monopoly or darts; not once in twenty-nine years. The elasticity and strength went out of his legs, and he stood on the base line, just a long-legged gangling boy again, dressed in faded khaki shorts and worn tennis shoes without socks. He gulped miserably, pushed the hair out of his eyes, and crouched to receive service.

Across the net Roland Ballantyne was a tall, athletic figure. He glared at Craig. Craig knew he was not seeing him, he was seeing an adversary, something to be destroyed.

"We Ballantynes are winners," Bawu had said. "We have got the instinct for the jugular."

Roland seemed, impossibly, to grow even taller, and then he served. Craig began to move left, saw it was the wrong side and tried to change. His long legs tangled and he sprawled on the yellow clay. He stood up, retrieved his racquet, and went across to the other court. There was a bloody smear on his knee. Roland's next service crashed in, and he did not get a touch of his racquet to it.

When his turn came, he hit one into the net, and the next one off the wood. Roland broke his service three times in a row, and it went on like that.

"Match point," Roland said. He was smiling again, gay and handsome and genial as he bounced the ball at his feet and lined up for his final service. Craig felt that old, heavy feeling in his limbs, the despair of the born loser.

He glanced off court. Janine Carpenter was looking directly at him, and in the instant before she smiled encouragingly, Craig saw the pity in those indigo eyes, and abruptly he was angry.

He socked Roland's service, double-handed, into the corner, and had it come back as hard. He crossed with his forehand, and Roland was grinning as he drove it back. Again Craig caught it perfectly, and even Roland was forced to lob. It came down from on high, floating helplessly, and Craig was under it, poised and coldly angry, and he hit it with all his weight and strength and despair. It was his best shot. After that he had nothing to follow. Roland trapped it on the bounce, before it could rise, and he punched it tantalizingly past Craig's right hip while he was twisted hopelessly off balance by the power of his own stroke.

Roland laughed and vaulted easily over the net.

"Not bad, Sonny." He put his arm patronizingly around Craig's shoulders. "I'll know not to give you a start in future," he said, and led Craig off the court.

Those who had been gloatingly anticipating Roland's humiliation a few minutes before now crowded slavishly around him.

"Well played, Roly."

"Great stuff."

And Craig slipped away from them. He picked a clean white towel off the pile and wiped his neck and face. Trying not to look as miserable as he felt, he went to the deserted bar and fished a beer out of the bath of crushed ice. He swallowed a mouthful, and it was so tart that it made his eyes swim. Through the tears he realized suddenly that Janine Carpenter was standing beside him.

"You could have done it," she said softly. "But you just gave up."

"Story of my life." He tried to sound gay and witty, like Roland, but it came out flat and self-pityingly.

She seemed about to speak again, then shook her head and walked away.

◆   ◆   ◆

Craig used Roland's shower, and when he came out with the towel around his waist, Roland was in front of the full-length mirror adjusting the angle of his beret.

The beret was dark maroon with a brass cap-badge above

the left ear. The badge was a brutish human head, with the forehead of a gorilla and the same broad, flattened nose. The eyes were crossed grotesquely and the tongue protruded from between negroid lips, like a Maori carving of a war idol.

"When old great-grandpa Ralph recruited the Scouts during the rebellion," Roland had once explained to Craig, "one of his better-known exploits was to catch the leader of the rebels and to hang him from the top of an acacia tree. We have taken that as our regimental emblem—Bazo's hanged head. How do you like it?"

"Charming," Craig had given his opinion. "You always did have such exquisite taste, Roly."

Roland had conceived the Scouts three years previously when the sporadic warfare of the earlier days had begun to intensify into the merciless internecine conflict of the present time. His original idea had been to gather a force of young white Rhodesians who could speak fluent Sindebele and reinforce them with young Matabele who had been with their white employers since childhood, men whose loyalty was unquestionable. He would train black and white elements into an elite strike force that could move easily through the tribal trust areas among the peasant farmers, speaking their language and understanding their ways, able to impersonate innocent tribesmen or ZIPRA terrorists at will, able to meet the enemy at the border or drop onto him from the sky and take him on at the most favorable terms.

He had gone to General Peter Walls at Combined Operations Headquarters. Of course Bawu had made the usual phone calls to clear the way, and Uncle Douglas had put a word in Smithy's ear during a cabinet meeting. They had given Roland the go-ahead, and so Ballantyne's Scouts had been reborn, seventy years after the original troop was disbanded.

In the three years since then, Ballantyne's Scouts had cut their way into legend. Six hundred men who had been officially credited with two thousand kills, who had been five hundred miles over the border into Zambia to hit a ZIPRA training base; men who had sat at the village fires in the tribal trust lands listening to the chatter of the women who had just returned from carrying baskets of grain to the ZIPRA cadres in the hills, men who laid their ambushes and maintained them for five straight days, burying their

own excrement beside them, waiting patiently and as un-
moving as a leopard beside the waterhole, waiting for yet
another good kill.

Roland turned from the mirror as Craig came into the
bedroom. The stars of a full colonel sparkled on his
shoulders, and over his heart the cluster of the Silver Cross
was pinned below his dog tag on the crisply ironed khaki
bush shirt.

"Help yourself to what you need, Sonny," he invited,
and Craig went to the built-in cupboard and selected a pair
of flannels and a white cricket sweater with the colors of
Oriel College around the neck. It seemed like coming home
to be wearing Roland's castoffs again; he had always been
a year behind him.

"Mom tells me you've been fired again."

"That's right." Craig's voice was muffled by the sweater
over his head.

"There's a billet for you with the Scouts."

"Roly, I don't fancy the idea of putting piano wire around
somebody's neck and plucking his head off."

"We don't do that every day." Roland grinned. "Personally I much prefer a knife—you can also use it to slice
biltong when you aren't slitting throats. But seriously, Sonny,
we could use you. You talk the lingo like one of them, and
you are a real buff at blowing things up. We are short of
blast bunnies."

"When I left King's Lynn, I swore an oath that I would
never work for anyone in the family again."

"The Scouts aren't family."

"You are the Scouts, Roly."

"I could have you seconded, you know that?"

"That wouldn't work."

"No," Roland agreed. "You always were a stubborn
blighter. Well, if you change your mind, let me know." He
knocked a cigarette half out of its soft pack and then pulled
it the rest of the way with his lips. "What do you think of
Bugsy?" The cigarette waggled as he asked the question,
and he flicked his gold Ronson to it.

"She's all right," Craig said cautiously.

"Only all right?" Roland protested. "Try magnificent,
try sensational, wonderful, supergreat—wax lyrical, for
you're talking about the woman I love."

"Number one thousand and ten on the list of the women you have loved," Craig corrected.

"Steady, old son, this one I am going to marry."

Craig felt a coldness come over his soul, and he turned away to comb his damp hair in the mirror.

"Did you hear what I said? I'm going to marry her."

"Does she know?"

"I'm letting her ripen a little before I tell her."

" 'Ask her,' don't you mean 'ask her'?"

"Old Roly tells 'em, he doesn't ask 'em. You are supposed to say, 'Congratulations, I hope you will be very happy."

"Congratulations, I hope you will be very happy."

"That's my boy. Come on, I'll buy you a drink."

They went down the long central corridor that bisected the house, but before they reached the veranda, a telephone rang in the lobby, and they heard Aunty Val's voice:

"I'll fetch him. Hold the line, please"—and then louder—"Roland, darling, it's Cheetah for you."

Cheetah was the call sign of Scout base. "I'm coming, Mom." Roland strode into the lobby, and Craig heard him say, "Ballantyne," and then after a short silence, "are you sure it's him? By Christ, this is the chance we have been waiting for. How soon can you get a chopper here? On its way? Good! Throw a net around the place, but don't go in until I get there. I want this baby myself."

When he came back into the corridor, he was transformed. It was the same look as he had given Craig across the net, cold and dangerous and without mercy.

"Can you get Bugsy back to town for me, Sonny? We are going into a contact."

"I'll look after her."

Roland strode out onto the veranda. The last of the tennis guests were dispersing toward their vehicles, gathering up nannies and children as they went, shouting farewells and last-minute invitations for the coming week. There was a time when a gathering like this would not have broken up until after midnight, but now nobody drove the country roads after 4 P.M., the new witching hour.

Janine Carpenter was shaking hands and laughing with a couple from the neighboring ranch.

"I'd love to come over," she said, and then she looked up and saw Roland's expression. She hurried to him.

"What is it?"

"We are going in. Sonny will look after you. I'll call you." He was searching the sky, already remote and detached, and then there was the whack, whack, whacking of helicopter rotors in the air, and the machine came bustling in low over the kopje. She was painted in dull battle brown, and there were two Scouts standing in the open belly port, one white and one black, both in bush camouflage and full webbing.

Roland ran down the lawns to meet her as she sank, and before she touched he jumped to link arms with his Matabele sergeant, and swung up into the cabin of the helicopter. As the machine rose and beat away, nose low over the kopje, Craig caught a last glimpse of Roland. He had already replaced the beret with a soft bush hat, and his sergeant was helping him into his camouflage fatigues.

"Roly said I was to see you home. I take it you live in Bulawayo?" Craig asked as the helicopter disappeared and the sound of its rotors dwindled. It seemed to take an effort for her to bring her attention back to him.

"Yes, Bulawayo. Thanks."

"We won't make it this evening, not before ambush hour. I was going to stay over at my grandpa's place."

"Bawu?"

"You know him?"

"No, but I'd love to. Roly has kept me in fits with stories about him. Do you think there'd be a bed for me also?"

"There are twenty-two beds at King's Lynn."

She perched on the seat of the old Land Rover beside him, and the wind made her hair shimmer and flutter.

"Why does he call you Bugsy?" Craig had to raise his voice above the engine noise.

"I'm an entomologist," she shouted back. "You know, bugs and things."

"Where do you work?" The cool evening air flattened her blouse against her chest, and she was very obviously not wearing a bra. She had small, finely shaped breasts, and the cold made her nipples stand out in little dark lumps under the thin cloth. It was difficult not to gawk.

"At the museum. Did you know that we have the finest collection of tropical and subtropical insects in existence,

390

better than the Smithsonian or the Kensington Natural History Museum?''

''Bully for you.''

''Sorry, I can be a bore.''

''Never.''

She smiled her thanks but changed the subject. ''How long have you known Roland?''

''Twenty-nine years.''

''How old are you?''

''Twenty-nine.''

''Tell me about him.''

''What's to tell about somebody who is perfect?''

''Try to think of something,'' she encouraged him.

''Head boy at Michaelhouse. Captain of rugger and cricket. Rhodes scholarship to Oxford, Oriel scholar. Blues for rowing and cricket, half-blue for tennis, colonel in the Scouts, Silver Cross for valor, heir to twenty-million-plus dollars. You know, all the usual things.'' Craig shrugged.

''You don't like him,'' she accused.

''I love him,'' he said. ''In a funny sort of way.''

''You don't want to talk about him any more?''

''I'd rather talk about you.''

''That suits me. What do you want to know?''

He wanted to make her smile again. ''Start at the time you were born and don't leave anything out.''

''I was born in a little village in Yorkshire. My daddy is the local veterinarian.''

''When? I said not to miss anything.''

She slanted her eyes mischievously. ''What is the local expression for an indeterminate date—some time before the rinderpest?''

''That was in the eighteen nineties.''

''Okay.'' She smiled again. ''I was born some time after the rinderpest.''

It was working, Craig realized. She liked him. She smiled more readily, and their banter was light and easy. Perhaps it was just wistful imagination, but he thought he detected the first sexual awareness in her manner, the way she held her head and moved her body, the way she—then abruptly he thought of Roland and felt the cold slide of despair.

♦ ♦ ♦

Jonathan Ballantyne came out onto the veranda of King's Lynn, took one look at her, and went immediately into his role of the lustful roué.

He kissed her hand. "You are the prettiest young lady that Craig has ever come up with—by a street."

Some perverse streak made Craig deny it. "Janine is Roly's friend, Bawu."

"Ah," the old man nodded. "I should have known. Too much class for your taste, boy."

Craig's marriage had lasted a little longer than one of his jobs, just over a year, but Bawu had not approved of Craig's choice, had said so before the wedding and after it, before the divorce and after it—and at every opportunity since then.

"Thank you, Mr. Ballantyne." Janine slanted her eyes at Jonathan.

"You may call me Bawu." Jonathan gave her his ultimate accolade, made an arm for her and said, "Come and see my Claymore mines, my dear."

Craig watched them go off on a tour of the defenses, another sure sign of Bawu's high favor.

"He has three wives buried up on the kopje," Craig muttered ruefully, "and is still as randy as an old goat."

◆ ◆ ◆

Craig woke to his bedroom door cracking back on its hinges and Jonathan Ballantyne's cry: "Are you going to sleep all day? It's four-thirty already."

"Just because you haven't slept for twenty years, Bawu."

"Enough of your lip, boy—today's the big day. Get that pretty little filly of Roland's, and we'll all go down to test my secret weapon."

"Before breakfast?" Craig protested, but excited as a child invited to a picnic, the old man had gone already.

It was parked at a prudent distance from the nearest building. The cook had threatened to resign if there were any more experiments conducted within blast range of his kitchen. It stood on the edge of a field of ripening seed maize, and it was surrounded by a small crowd of laborers and tractor drivers and clerks.

"What on earth is it?" Janine puzzled as they crossed the plowed land toward it, but before anyone could reply a figure in greasy blue overalls detached itself from the crowd and hurried toward them.

"Mr. Craig, thank goodness you are here. You've got to stop him."

"Don't be a blithering old idiot, Okky," Jonathan ordered. Okky van Rensburg had been chief mechanic on King's Lynn for twenty years. Behind his back Jonathan boasted that Okky could strip down a John Deere tractor, and build up a Cadillac and two Rolls Royce Silver Clouds out of the spare parts. He was a wiry, grease-stained little monkey of a man. He ignored Jonathan's injunction to silence.

"Bawu's going to kill himself unless somebody stops him." He wrung his scarred, blackened hands pitifully.

But already Jonathan was donning his helmet and fastening the strap under his chin. It was the same tin helmet that he had worn on that day in 1916 that he won his Military Cross, and the dent in the side had been made by a shard of German shrapnel. There was an unholy gleam in his eyes as he advanced upon the monstrous vehicle.

"Okky has converted a three-ton Ford truck," he explained to Janine, "lifted the chassis"—as though it were on stilts, the vehicle's body stood high above the huge, lugged tires—"put in deflectors here"—he pointed out the heavy steel vee-shaped plates under the cab that would split the blast of a land mine—"armored the cab"—the body looked like a tiger tank, with steel hatches, a driver's slit and gunports for a heavy Browning machine gun—"but look what we have got on top!" At a glance it could have been mistaken for the conning tower of a nuclear submarine, and Okky was still wringing his hands.

"He's got twenty galvanized steel pipes filled with plastic explosive and thirty pounds of ball bearings each."

"Good Lord, Bawu." Even Craig was horrified. "The damn things will explode!"

"He has set them in blocks of concrete," Okky moaned, "and aimed them out on each side just like the cannons on one of Nelson's ships of the line. Ten on each side."

"A twenty-gun Ford," Craig breathed with awe.

"When I run into an ambush, I just press the button—a boom, a broadside of three hundred pounds of ball bearings into the bastards." Jonathan gloated openly. "A whiff of grape, as old Bonaparte said."

"He's going to blow himself to hell," Okky moaned.

"Oh, do stop being an old woman," Jonathan told him. "And give me a leg up."

"Bawu, this time I really do agree with Okky." Craig tried to stop him, but the old man went up the steel ladder with the agility of a vervet monkey and posed dramatically in the hatchway, like the commander of a panzer division.

"I'll let off one broadside at a time, the starboard side first." Then his eyes lit on Janine. "Would you like to be my copilot, my dear?"

"That is astonishingly civil of you, Bawu, but I think I'll get a better view from the irrigation ditch over there."

"Then stand back everyone." Jonathan made a wide, imperious gesture of dismissal, and the Matabele laborers and drivers who had been witnesses to Jonathan's previous test took off like a brigade of Egyptian infantry departing from the Six-Day War. Some of them were still running as they crossed the ridge of the kopje.

Okky reached the irrigation ditch half a dozen paces ahead of Craig and Janine, and then the three of them cautiously lifted their heads above the bank. Three hundred yards away, the grotesque Ford stood in monumental isolation in the middle of the plowed land, and from the hatchway Jonathan gave them a cheery wave and then disappeared.

They covered their ears with both hands and waited. Nothing happened.

"He's chickened out," Craig said hopefully, and the hatch opened again. Jonathan's helmeted head reappeared, his face red with outrage.

"Okky, you son of a bitch, you disconnected the wiring," he roared. "You are fired, do you hear me? Fired!"

"Third time he has fired me this week," Okky muttered morosely. "It was the only way I could think of to stop him."

"Hold on, my dear," Jonathan addressed himself to Janine. "I'll have it connected up in a jiffy."

"Don't worry on my account, Bawu," she yelled back, but he had disappeared again.

The minutes passed, each one a separate eternity, and their hopes gradually rose again.

"It's not going to work."

"Let's get him out of there."

Craig cupped his hands and bellowed, "Bawu, we are coming to get you, and you'd better come quietly."

He rose slowly out of the ditch, and at that moment the armored Ford disappeared in a huge, boiling cloud of smoke and dust. A sheet of white flame licked over the field of standing maize, scything it flat, as though some monstrous combine harvester had swept across it, and they were enveloped by such an appalling blast of sound that Craig lost his balance and fell back into the ditch on top of the other two.

Frantically they scrambled to untangle themselves in the bottom of the ditch and then looked out fearfully again across the plowed field. The dreadful silence was broken only by the ringing in their own ears and the dwindling yelps of the old man's pack of savage Rottweilers and Doberman pinschers as they fled in utter panic back up the road toward the homestead. The field was obscured by a dense curtain of drifting blue smoke and dust.

They climbed up out of the ditch and stared into the smoke and dust, and the breeze blew it gently aside. The Ford lay upon its back. All four of its massive, lugged tires were pointing to the heavens as though in abject surrender.

"Bawu!" Craig cried and raced toward it. The gaping mouths of the pipe cannons were still oozing oily wreaths of smoke, but there was no other movement.

Craig wrestled the steel hatch open and crawled into it on his hands and knees. The dark interior stank of acrid plastic explosive burn.

"Bawu!" He found him crumpled in the bottom of the cab, and he knew instantly that the old man was in extremis. The whole shape of his face had altered, and his voice was an unintelligible blur.

Craig caught him up in his arms and tried to drag him toward the hatch, but the old man fought him off with desperate strength, and at last Craig understood what he was saying.

"My teeth, blown my bloody teeth out!" He was back on his hands and knees searching desperately. "Mustn't let her see me. Find them, boy, find them."

Craig found the missing plates under the driver's seat, and with them once more in place, Jonathan shot out of the hatchway and confronted Okky van Rensburg furiously.

"You made it top-heavy, you blithering old idiot."

"You can't talk to me like that, Bawu, I don't work for you any longer. You fired me."

"You're hired," bellowed Jonathan. "Now get that thing right way up again."

Twenty sweating, singing Matabele heaved the Ford slowly upright and at last it flopped over onto its wheels again.

"Looks like a banana," Okky remarked with obvious satisfaction. "The recoil of your cannons has bent it almost double. You'll never get that chassis straight again."

"There is only one way to straighten it," Jonathan announced, and began tightening the strap of his tin helmet again.

"What are you going to do, Jon-Jon?" Craig demanded anxiously.

"Fire the other broadside, of course," said Jonathan grimly. "That will knock it straight again." But Craig seized one of his arms, Okky the other, and Janine murmured soothingly to him as they led him away to the waiting Land Rover.

◆ ◆ ◆

"Can you imagine Bawu reaching for the cigarette lighter and hitting the wrong button while driving down Main Street," Craig chortled, "and letting that lot go through the front doors of the City Hall?"

They giggled over it the whole way back to town, and as they drove in past the lovely lawns of the municipal gardens, Craig suggested easily, "Sunday evening in Bulawayo, you could suffer a nervous breakdown from the mad gaiety of it. Let me cook you one of my famous dinners on the yacht and save you from it."

"The yacht?" Janine was instantly intrigued. "Here? Fifteen hundred miles from the nearest salt water?"

"I will say no more," Craig declared. "Either you come with me, or you will forever be consumed by unsatisfied curiosity."

"A fate worse than death," she agreed. "And I have always been a good sailor. Let's go!"

Craig took the airport road, but before they left the built-up area, he turned into one of the older sections of the town. Between two run-down cottages was an empty plot. It was screened from the road by the dense greenery of a row of ancient mango trees. Craig parked the Land Rover under one of the mango trees and led her deeper into an unkempt jungle of bougainvillea and acacia trees, until she stopped abruptly and exclaimed: "You weren't kidding. It's a real yacht."

"They don't come any realer than that," Craig agreed proudly. "Livranos-designed, forty-five feet overall length, and every plank laid by my own lily-whites."

"Craig, she's beautiful!"

"She will be one day when I finish her."

The vessel stood on a wooden cradle, with balks of timber chocking the sides. The deep keel and ocean-going hull lifted the stainless steel deck railings fifteen feet above Janine's head as she ran forward eagerly.

"How do I get up?"

"There is a ladder round the other side."

She scrambled up onto the deck and called down. "What is her name?"

"She hasn't got one yet."

He climbed up into the cockpit beside her. "When will you launch her, Craig?"

"The good Lord knows." He smiled. "There is a mountain of work to be done on her yet, and every time I run out of money, everything comes to a grinding halt."

He was unlocking the hatch as he spoke, and the moment he swung it open Janine ducked down the companionway.

"It's cozy down here."

"This is where I live." He climbed down into the saloon after her and dropped his kit bag on the deck. "I've finished her off below decks—the galley is through there. Two cabins each with double bunks, a shower and a chemical toilet."

"It's beautiful," Janine repeated, running her fingers over the varnished teak joinery and then bouncing experimentally on the couches.

"Beats paying rent," he agreed.

"What remains to be done?"

"Not much—engine, winches, rigging, sails, only about twenty thousand dollars' worth. However, I have just soaked Bawu for almost half of that." He lit the gas refrigerator and then selected a tape and put it on the player.

Janine listened to the liquid purling piano for a few moments and then said, "Ludwig van B., of course?"

"Of course, who else?"

Then with slightly less assurance, she said, "The Pathétique Sonata?"

"Oh, very good"—he grinned as he found a bottle of Zonnebloem Riesling in one of the cupboards—"and the *artiste?*"

"Oh, come on!"

"Give it a shot."

"Kentner?"

"Not bad, but it's Pressler." She pulled a face to show her mortification, and he drew the cork and half filled the glasses with pale golden wine.

"Here's looking at you, kid."

She sipped and murmured, "Mmm! That's good."

"Dinner!" Craig dived back into the cupboard. "Rice and canned stuff. The potatoes and onions are three months old, growing sprouts already."

"Macrobiotic," she said. "Good for you. Can I help?"

They worked happily shoulder to shoulder in the tiny gallery, and every time they moved, they brushed against each other. She smelled of scented soap, and when he looked down on top of her head, her curly hair was so dense and lustrous that he had an almost uncontrollable urge to bury his face in it. Instead he went to look for another bottle of wine.

He emptied four assorted cans into the pot, chopped onions and potatoes over the mixture, and spooned in curry powder. He served it on a bed of rice.

"Delicious," Janine declared. "What do you call it?"

"Don't ask embarrassing questions."

"When you launch her, where will you sail her?"

Craig reached over her head and brought down a chart and an Indian Ocean pilot from the bookshelves.

"All right." He pointed out a position on the chart. "Here we are anchored in a secluded little cove on an island in the Seychelles. If you look out the porthole, you will see the palm trees and the beaches whiter than sugar. Under us the water is so clear that we seem to be floating in air."

Janine looked out of the porthole. "You know what— you are right! There are the palm trees and I can hear guitars."

398

When they finished eating, they pushed the dishes aside and pored over the books and charts.

"Where next? How about the Greek islands?"

"Too touristy." She shook her head.

"Australia and the Great Barrier Reef?"

"Beauty!" She mimicked an Aussie accent. "Can I go topless, sport?"

"Bottomless, too, if you want."

"Rude boy."

The wine had flushed her cheeks and put a sparkle in her eyes. She slapped his cheek lightly, and he knew he could kiss her then, but before he moved, she said, "Roland told me you were a dreamer."

The name stopped him dead. He felt the coldness in his chest, and suddenly he was angry with her for spoiling the mood of the moment. He wanted to hurt her as she had just hurt him.

"Are you sleeping with him?" he asked, and she swayed back and stared at him with shock. Then her eyes slanted like those of a cat, and the rims of her nostrils turned bone-white with fury.

"What did you say?"

His own perversity would not let him turn back from the precipice, and he stepped out over it.

"I asked if you were sleeping with him."

"Are you sure you want to know?"

"Yes."

"All right, the answer is yes, and it's bloody marvelous. Okay?"

"Okay," he said miserably.

"Now you can take me home, please."

They drove in complete silence except for her terse directions, and when he parked outside the three-story block of apartments, he noticed that they were called Beau Vallon, the same as the Seychelles beach over which they had fantasized.

She climbed out of the Land Rover. "I'm grateful for the lift," she said, and walked up the paved path toward the entrance of the building.

Before she reached it, she turned and came back. "Do you know that you are a spoiled little boy?" she asked. "And that you give up on everything, just like you did on the tennis court."

This time she disappeared into the entrance of the building without looking back.

When he got back to the yacht, Craig put the charts and books away, then he cleaned the dishes, dried them, and stacked them in their racks. He thought he had left a bottle of gin in one of the cupboards, but he couldn't find it. There wasn't even any of the wine left. He sat in the saloon with the gaslight hissing softly over his head, and he felt numb and empty. There was no point in going to his bunk. He knew he would not sleep.

He unlaced the kit bag; the leather-bound journal that Jonathan had loaned him was on top. He opened it and began to read. It had been written in 1860. The writer was Zouga Ballantyne, Craig's great-great-grandfather.

After a while Craig no longer felt numb and empty, for he was on the quarterdeck of a tall ship, running southward down the green Atlantic toward a savage, enchanted continent.

◆ ◆ ◆

Samson Kumalo stood in the center of the dusty track and watched Craig's beaten-up old Land Rover growl away up the avenue of spathodea trees. When it took the turn past the old cemetery and disappeared, he picked up his bag and opened the garden gate of the staff cottage. He walked around the side of the building and stopped below the back porch.

His grandfather, Gideon Kumalo, sat on a straight-backed kitchen chair. The walking stick, carved like a twisted serpent, was propped between his feet, and both his hands rested on the head. He was asleep, sitting upright in the uncomfortable chair in the blaze of the white sunlight.

"It is the only way I can get warm," he had told Samson.

His hair was white and fluffy; the little goatee beard on the tip of his chin trembled with each gentle snore of his breathing. His skin seemed so thin and delicate that it might tear like ancient parchment, and it was the same very dark amber color. The network of wrinkles that covered it were cruelly exposed by the direct glare of the sun.

Careful not to block the old man's sunlight, Samson climbed the steps, set his bag aside and sat on the half wall in front of him. He studied his face and felt again that gentle, suffocating feeling of love. It was more than the duty that any Matabele boy was taught to show to his elders; it went beyond the conventions of parental affection, for between the two of them was an almost mystical bond.

For almost sixty years, Gideon Kumalo had been the assistant headmaster at Khami Mission School. Thousands of young Matabele boys and girls had grown up under his guidance, but none had been as special to him as his own grandson.

Suddenly the old man started and opened his eyes. They were milky-blue and sightless as those of a newborn puppy. He tilted his head at a blind listening angle. Samson held his breath and sat motionless, fearful that Gideon might have at last lost the sense of perception which was almost miraculous. The old man turned his head slowly the other way and listened again. Samson saw his nostrils flare slightly as he sniffed the air.

"Is it you?" he asked in a rusty voice, like the squeak of an unoiled hinge. "Yes, it is you, Vundla." The hare has always played a prominent place in African folklore, the original of the legend of Br'er Rabbit that the slaves took to America with them. Gideon had nicknamed Samson after the lively, clever little animal. "Yes, it is you, my little Hare!"

"Baba!" Samson let his breath out and went down on one knee before him. Gideon groped for his head and caressed it.

"You have never been away," he said. "For you live always in my heart."

Samson thought he might choke if he tried to speak. Silently he reached and took the thin, fragile hands and held them to his lips.

"We should have a little tea," Gideon murmured. "You are the only one who can make it to my taste."

The old man had a sweet tooth, and Samson placed six heaped teaspoons of brown sugar into the enamel mug before he poured the brew from the blackened tin kettle into it. Gideon cupped his hands around the mug, sipped noisily, and then smiled and nodded.

"Now tell me, little Hare, what has happened to you? I feel something in you, an uncertainty, like a man who has lost the path and seeks to find it again."

He listened while Samson spoke, sipping and nodding. Then when he finished talking, he said: "It is time you came back to the mission to teach. You told me once that you could not teach the young people about life until you learned yourself. Have you learned yet?"

"I do not know, Baba. What can I teach them? That death stalks the land, that life is as cheap as a single bullet?"

"Will you always live with doubts, my dear grandson? Must you always look for the questions that have no answers? If a man doubts everything, then he will attempt nothing. The strong men of this world are the ones who are always certain of their own rightness."

"Then perhaps I will never be strong, Grandfather."

They finished the pot of tea and Samson brewed another. Even the melancholy of their conversation could not dim their pleasure in each other, and they basked in it until at last Gideon asked, "What time is it?"

"Past four o'clock."

"Constance will be off duty at five. Will you go down to the hospital to meet her?"

Samson changed into jeans and a light blue shirt and left the old man on the porch. He went down the hill. At the gate of the high security fence that enclosed the hospital, he submitted to the body search by the uniformed guards, and then went up past the postoperative wards, outside which the convalescent patients in blue dressing gowns sat on the lawn in the sunlight. Many of them had limbs missing, for the Khami Hospital received many of the victims of land mine explosions and other war injuries. All the patients were black. Khami Hospital was graded as African only.

At the reception desk in the main entrance hall, the two little Matabele nurses recognized him and chittered like sparrows with pleasure. Gently Samson tapped them for the current gossip of the Mission Station, the marriages and births, the deaths and courtships of this close-knit little community. He was interrupted by a sharp, authoritative voice.

"Samson, Samson Kumalo!" and he turned to see the hospital superintendent striding purposefully down the wide corridor toward him.

Dr. Leila St. John wore a white laboratory coat with a row of ballpoint pens in the top pocket and a stethoscope dangling from her neck. Under the open coat was a shapeless maroon sweater and a long skirt of crumpled Indian cotton in a gaudy ethnic design. Her feet were in thick green men's socks and open sandals which buckled at the side. Her dark hair was stringy and lank, tied with leather thongs into two tails that stuck out on each side of her head above her prominent ears.

Her skin was unnaturally pale, inherited from her father, Robert St. John. It was pock-marked with the cicatrices of ancient acne. Her horn-rimmed spectacles were square and mannish, and a cigarette dangled from the corner of her thin lips. She had a prim, serious, old-fashioned face, but the gaze of her green eyes was direct and intense as she stopped in front of Samson and took his hand firmly.

"So the prodigal returns—to run off with one of my best operating-room nurses, I have no doubt."

"Good evening, Dr. Leila."

"Are you still playing 'boy' to your white settler?" she demanded. Leila St. John had spent five years in detention in Gwelo political prison at the pleasure of the Rhodesian Government. She had been there at the same time as Robert Mugabe who, from exile, now led the ZANU wing of the liberation army.

"Craig Mellow is a fourth-generation Rhodesian on both sides of his family. He is also my friend. He is not a settler."

"Samson, you are an educated and highly capable man. All around you the world is melting in the crucible of change; history is being forged on the anvil of war. Are you content to waste the talents that God gave you and let other, lesser men snatch the future from you?"

"I do not like war, Dr. Leila. Your father made me a Christian."

"Only mad men do, but what other way is there to destroy the insensate violence of the capitalist-imperialist system? What other way to meet the noble and legitimate aspirations of the poor, the weak and the politically oppressed?"

Samson glanced swiftly around the entrance hall, and she smiled.

"Don't worry, Samson. You are among friends here. True friends." Leila St. John glanced at her wristwatch. "I must go. I will tell Constance to bring you to dinner. We will talk again." She turned abruptly away, and the heels of her scuffed brown sandals clacked on the tiled floor as she hurried toward the double swing doors marked "Outpatients."

Samson found a seat on one of the long benches outside these doors, and waited among the sick and lame, the coughing and sniffing, the bandaged and the bleeding. The sharp, antiseptic smell of the hospital seemed to permeate his clothes and skin.

Constance came at last. One of the nurses must have warned her, for her head turned eagerly from side to side and her dark eyes shone excitedly as she searched for him. He savored the pleasure of seeing her for a moment or two longer before standing up from his seat on the bench.

Her uniform was crisply starched and ironed, the white apron stark upon the pink candy stripes, and her cap was perched at a jaunty angle. The badges of her grades— operating-room nurse, midwife and the others—gleamed on her breast. Her hair was pulled up tightly and plaited into intricate patterns over her scalp, an arrangement which took many patient hours to perfect. Her face was round and smooth as a dark moon, the classical Nguni beauty, with huge black eyes and sparkling white teeth in her welcoming smile.

Her back was straight, her shoulders narrow but strong. Her breasts under the white apron were good, her waist narrow and her hips broad and fecund. She moved with that peculiar African grace, as though she danced to music that she alone could hear.

She stopped in front of him. "I see you, Samson," she murmured. Suddenly shy, she dropped her eyes.

"I see you, my heart," he replied as softly. They did not touch each other, for a display of passion in public was against custom and would have been distasteful to both of them.

They walked slowly up the hill together toward the cottage. Although she was not a blood relative of Gideon Kumalo, Constance had been one of his favorite students before his failing eyesight drove him into retirement. When his wife died, Constance had gone to live with him, to care for him and keep his house. It was there she had met Samson.

Though she chattered easily enough, relating the small happenings that had taken place in his absence, Samson sensed some reserve in her, and twice she glanced back along the path with something of fear in her eyes.

"What is it that troubles you?" he asked as they paused at the garden gate.

"How did you know—" she began, and then answered herself. "Of course you know. You know everything about me."

"What is it that troubles you?"

"The 'boys' are here," Constance said simply, and Samson felt the chill on his skin so that the goose pimples rose upon his forearms.

The "boys" and the "girls" were the guerrilla fighters of the Zimbabwe People's Revolutionary Army.

"Here?" he asked. "Here at the mission?"

She nodded.

"They bring danger and the threat of death upon everybody here," he said bitterly.

"Samson, my heart," she whispered. "I have to tell you. I could shirk my duty no longer. I have joined them at last. I am one of the 'girls' now."

◆ ◆ ◆

They ate the evening meal in the central room of the cottage, which was kitchen, dining room and sitting room in one.

In place of a tablecloth, Constance covered the scrubbed deal table with sheets of the *Rhodesian Herald* newspaper. The columns of newsprint were interspersed with columns of blank paper, the editors' silent protest against the draconian decrees of the government censors. In the center of it she placed a large pot of maize meal, cooked stiff and fluffy white, and beside it a small bowl of tripes and sugar beans. Then she filled the old man's bowl, placed it in front of him, and put his spoon in his hand; sitting beside him throughout the meal, she tenderly directed his hand and wiped up his spillage.

From the wall the small black and white television set gave them a fuzzy image of the newscaster.

"In four separate contacts in Mashonaland and Matabeleland, twenty-six terrorists have been killed by the security forces in the past twenty-four hours. In addition sixteen civilians were killed in crossfire and eight others were reported killed in a land mine explosion on the Mrewa road. Combined Operations Headquarters regrets to announce the death in action of two members of the security forces. The dead were Sergeant John Sinclair of the Ballantyne Scouts—''

Constance stood up and switched off the television set, then sat down again and spooned a little more meat and beans into Gideon's bowl.

''It is like a soccer match,'' she said with a bitterness that Samson had never heard in her voice. ''Each evening they give us the score. Terrorists—two: security forces—twenty-six; we should fill in the coupons for the pools.'' Samson saw that she was crying and could think of nothing to say for her comfort.

''They give us the names and ages of the white soldiers, how many children they leave, but the others are only 'terrorists,' or 'black civilians.' Yet they have mothers and fathers and wives and children also.'' She sniffed up her tears. ''They are Matabele as we are, they are our people. Death has become so easy, so commonplace in this land, but the ones that do not die, those will come to us here— our people, with their legs torn from their bodies or their brains damaged so that they become drooling idiots.''

''War is always crueler when the women and children are in it,'' Gideon said in his dusty old voice. ''We kill their women, they kill ours.''

There was a soft scratching at the door, and Constance stood up and went quickly to it. She switched out the electric light before she opened it. Outside it was night, but Samson saw the silhouettes of two men in the darkened doorway. They slipped into the room, and there was the sound of the door closing. Then Constance switched on the light.

Two men stood against the wall. One glance was enough for Samson to know who they were. They were dressed in jeans and denim shirts, but there was an animal alertness about them, in the way they moved, in their quick, bright, restless eyes.

The elder of the two nodded at the other, who went quickly into the bedrooms, searched them swiftly and then came back to check the curtains over the windows, to make certain there was no chink between them. Then he nodded at the other man and slipped out of the door again. The elder man sat down on the bench opposite Gideon

Kumalo. He had finely boned features, with an Arab beakiness to his nose, but his skin was almost purple-black and his head was shaven bald.

"My name is Comrade Tebe," he said quietly. "What is your name, old Father?"

"My name is Gideon Kumalo." The blind man looked past his shoulder, his head cocked slightly.

"That is not the name your mother gave you; that is not how your father knew you."

The old man began to tremble, and he tried three times to speak before the words came out.

"Who are you?" he whispered.

"That is not important," the man said. "We are trying to find who you are. Tell me, old man, have you ever heard the name Tungata Zebiwe? The Seeker After What Has Been Stolen, the Seeker After Justice?"

Now the old man began to shake so that he knocked the bowl from the table and it rang in narrowing circles on the concrete floor at his feet.

"How do you know that name?" he whispered. "How do you know these things?"

"I know everything, old Father. I even know a song. We will sing it together, you and I."

And the visitor began to sing in soft but thrilling baritone:

> "Like a mole in the earth's gut,
> Bazo found the secret way—"

It was the ancient battle hymn of the Moles impi, and the memories came crashing back upon Gideon Kumalo. In the way of very old men, he could remember in crystal detail the days of his childhood, while the events of the previous week were already becoming hazy. He remembered a cave in the Matopo Hills and his father's never-forgotten face in the firelight, and the words of the song came back to him:

> "The moles are beneath the earth.
> 'Are they dead?' asked the daughters of Mashobane."

Gideon sang in his scratchy, old man's voice, and as he sang, the tears welled up out of his milky blind eyes and ran unheeded down his cheeks.

"Listen pretty maids, do you not hear
Something stirring, in the darkness?"

When the song was ended, the visitor sat in silence while Gideon wiped away his tears. Then he said softly, "The spirits of your ancestors call you, Comrade Tungata Zebiwe."

"I am an old man, blind and feeble—I cannot respond to them."

"Then you must send somebody in your place," said the stranger. "Someone in whose veins runs the blood of Bazo, the Ax, and Tanase, the witch." Then the stranger turned slowly toward Samson Kumalo, who sat at the head of the table, and he looked directly into Samson's eyes.

Samson stared back at him flatly. He was angry. He had known instinctively why the stranger had come. There were few Matabele who were university graduates or who had his other obvious gifts. He had known for a long time now how badly they wanted him, and it had taken all his ingenuity to avoid them. Now at last they had found him, and he was angry at them and at Constance. She had led them to him. He had noticed the way she had kept glancing up at the door during the meal. He knew now that she had told them that he was here.

On top of his anger, he felt a weight of weary resignation. He knew that he could no longer resist them. He knew the risks that it would involve, not for himself alone. These were hard men, tempered in blood to a cruelty that was hard to imagine. He understood why the stranger had spoken first to Gideon Kumalo. It was to mark him. If now Samson refused to bend to them, then the old man was in terrible peril.

"You must send someone in your place."

It was the age-old bargain, a life for a life. If Samson refused the bargain, he knew the old man's life was forfeit and that even then that would not end the affair. They wanted him; they would have him.

"My name is Samson Kumalo," he said. "I am a Christian, and I abhor war and cruelty."

"We know who you are," said the stranger. "And we know that in these times there is no place for softness."

The stranger broke off as the door was pushed open a slit, and the second stranger, who had been on watch outside in the night, put his head into the room and said urgently,

"*Kanka!*" Just the one word, "Jackals!" and he was gone.

Swiftly the elder stranger stood up, drew a 7.62mm Tokarev pistol from the waistband of his jeans, and at the same time switched out the light. In the darkness he whispered close to Samson's ear. "The Bulawayo bus station. Two days from today at eight o'clock in the morning."

Then Samson heard the latch of the door click, and the three of them were alone. They waited in the darkness for five minutes before Constance said, "They have gone." She switched on the light and began collecting the dishes and balling up the newsprint that had served as a tablecloth. "Whatever alarmed the 'boys' must have been a false alarm. The village is quiet. There is no sign of security forces."

Neither of the men answered, and she made mugs of cocoa for them.

"There is a film on television at nine o'clock, *The Railway Children.*"

"I am tired," Samson said. He was still angry with her.

"I am tired also," Gideon whispered, and Samson helped him toward the front bedroom. He looked back from the doorway, and Constance gave him such a pathetically appealing glance that he felt his anger toward her falter.

He lay in the narrow iron bed across from the old man, and in the darkness listened to the small sounds from the kitchen as Constance cleaned up and set out the breakfast for the next morning. Then the door to her small back bedroom closed.

Samson waited until the old man began to snore before he rose silently. He draped the rough woolen blanket over his naked shoulders, left the bedroom and went to Constance's room. The door was unlocked. It swung open to his touch, and he heard her sit up quickly in the bed.

"It is me," he said quietly,

"Oh, I was so afraid you would not come."

He reached out and touched her naked skin. It was cool and velvety soft. She took his fingers and drew him down toward her, and he felt the last vestige of his resentment shrivel away.

"I am sorry," she whispered.

"It does not matter," he said. "I could not have hidden forever."

"You will go?"

"If I do not, then they will take my grandfather, and that will not satisfy them."

"That is not the reason you will go. You will go for the same reason that I did. Because I had to."

The smooth length of her body was as naked as his own. When she moved, her breasts jostled against his chest, and he felt the heat beginning to flow through her.

"Are they taking you into the bush?" he asked.

"No. Not yet. I am ordered to remain here. There is to be work for me here."

"I am glad." He brushed her throat with his lips. In the bush her chances would be very slim. The security forces were maintaining a kill ratio of over thirty to one.

"I heard Comrade Tebe give you an hour and a place. Do you think they will use you in the bush?"

"I do not know. I think they will take me for training first."

"This may be our last night together for a long time," she whispered, and he did not reply but traced her spine in its valley of velvety pliant muscle down to the deep cleft of her buttocks.

"I want you to place a son in my womb," she whispered. "I want you to give me something to cherish while we are apart."

"It is an offense against law and custom."

"There is no law in this land except the gun, there is no custom except that which we care to observe." Constance rolled under him and clasped him with her long, hard limbs. "Yet in the midst of all this death we must preserve life. Give me your child, my heart, give him to me tonight, for there may be no other nights for us."

Samson woke in a blaze of nightmare. Light flooded the tiny room, striking through the threadbare curtain over the single window and casting harsh moving shadows on the bare, whitewashed wall. Constance clung to him, her body still hot and moist from their loving and her eyes soft with sleep. From outside a monstrous distorted voice blared orders.

"This is the Rhodesian Army. All people are to come out of their houses immediately. Do not run. Do not hide. No

410

innocent person will be harmed. Come out of your houses immediately. Hold up your hands. Do not run. Do not attempt to hide."

"Get dressed," Samson told Constance. "Then help me with the old man."

She staggered, still half-asleep, to the corner cupboard and pulled a plain pink cotton shift down over her nude body. Then, barefoot, she followed Samson to the front bedroom. He was dressed only in a pair of khaki shorts, and he was helping Gideon to rise. Outside the cottage the bullhorns were screeching in their metallic, stentorian voices.

"Come out immediately. Innocent people will not be harmed. Do not run."

Constance spread a woolen blanket over the old man's shoulders, then between them they led him through the living room to the front porch. Samson unlocked the door and stepped out, holding both hands high, palms forward, and the blinding white beam of a searchlight fixed on him, so that he was forced to protect his face with one hand.

"Bring Grandfather."

Constance led the old man out of the front door, and the three of them stood close together in a pathetic huddle, blinded by the light and confused by the repeated bellow of the bullhorn.

"Do not run. Do not attempt to hide."

The row of staff cottages had been surrounded. The searchlights beamed out of the darkness and picked out the little family groups of the teachers and nursing staff and their families as they clung together for comfort, most of them covered only with flimsy nightclothes or hastily draped blankets.

From the impenetrable darkness behind the searchlight, figures emerged, moving like panthers, alert and predatory. One of them vaulted over the veranda railing and flattened against the wall, using Samson's body to shield himself from the doorway and windows.

"Three of you. Is that all?" he demanded in Sindebele. He was a lean, powerful-looking man in fatigues and jungle hat. His face and hands were painted with night camouflage, so it was impossible to tell whether he was black or white.

"Only three," Samson replied.

The man had an FN rifle on his hip, the barrel swinging slightly to cover them all.

"If there is anybody in the building, say so quickly, otherwise they will be killed."

"There is nobody."

The soldier called an order, and his troopers went in simultaneously through the back and front doors and side windows. They swept through the cottage in seconds, working as a skilled team, covering each other. Satisfied that it was clear, they scattered back into the darkness and left the three on the veranda.

"Do not move," screeched the bullhorns. "Stay where you are."

In the darkness under the spathodea trees, Colonel Roland Ballantyne took the unit reports as they came in. With each negative show, his frustration increased. Their information had been good and the scent hot. It was a scent he had followed often before. Comrade Tebe was one of their prime targets. He was a ZIPRA commissar who had been operating within Matabeleland for almost seven months now. They had been as close to him as this on three other occasions. It always seemed to be the same. The tip from one of the informers or from a member of the Scouts operating under civilian cover. *Tebe was in such and such a village.* They would move up silently and surround it, methodically closing every bolt-hole. Then in the bleakest hour of the night, they would go in and sweep. Once they had taken two of his lieutenants, but Tebe was not with them. The regimental sergeant major of the Scouts, Esau Gondele, had questioned the two terrorists while Roland watched. By dawn neither of them were able to stand up any longer, but they had not spoken.

"Use the chopper," Roland ordered.

They hovered at two thousand feet while Sergeant Major Gondele hung the most defiant terrorist from the belly hatch, holding him by the webbing belt looped under his armpits.

"Tell me, my friend, where we will find your Comrade Tebe."

The man had twisted his head up sideways and tried to spit at Esau Gondele, but the downdraft of the spinning rotors had blown his spittle away. The sergeant major had glanced at Roland, and when he nodded, opened his fist.

The terrorist had fallen two thousand feet, turning slowly end over end. Perhaps he was past screaming or perhaps it was his final defiance, but he was utterly silent during the drop.

Sergeant Major Gondele had reached for the second terrorist and looped a webbing under his armpits. As he lowered him out of the hatch, his bound feet dangling two thousand feet above the golden Matabele grasslands, the man had looked up and said, "I will tell you."

However, they had held out for just thirty minutes too long. When the Scouts hit the safe house in Hillside Location, Comrade Tebe had moved again.

Roland Ballantyne's frustration was corrosive. The week before, Comrade Tebe had left an explosive device in a supermarket pushcart. It had killed seven people, all of them female, two of them under ten years of age. Roland wanted him very badly, so badly that when he realized that once again he had escaped, a kind of heavy black feeling closed down over half his mind.

"Bring the informer," he ordered, and Esau Gondele spoke softly into the portable radio. Within minutes they heard the Land Rover coming up the hill, and its headlights flickered through the trees of the forest.

"All right, Sergeant Major. Get these people lined up."

There were sixty or so of them lined up along the shoulder of the road in front of the long row of staff cottages. The searchlights trapped them in a stark and merciless glare. Colonel Roland Ballantyne vaulted up onto the back of the Land Rover and held the bullhorn to his lips. He spoke in perfect colloquial Sindebele.

"The evil ones have been among you. They have left the stink of death on this village. They have come here to plan destruction, to kill and cripple you and your children. You should have come to us that we might protect you. Because you were afraid to ask for our help, you have brought even greater hardship upon yourselves."

The long line of black people, men and women and children still in their nightclothes, stood stolidly and stoically as cattle in the crush. They were caught between the millstones of the guerrillas on one side and the security forces on the other. They stood in the white searchlights and listened.

"The government is your father. Like a good father it

seeks to protect its children. However, there are stupid children among you. Those who conspire with the evil ones, those who feed them and give them news and warn them when we come. We know these things. We know who warned them.''

At Roland's feet, sitting on the crossbench of the Land Rover, was a human figure. It was draped from head to foot in a single sheet of cloth so that it was impossible to tell whether it was a man or a woman. There were eye holes cut in the hood of the cloth.

''We will now smell out the evil ones among you, those who give comfort to the death bringers,'' Roland told them.

The Land Rover rolled slowly along the line of villagers, and as it drew even with each man or woman, the soldier shone his flashlight into the person's face at a range of only a few feet. In the open back of the vehicle, the mysteriously robed and masked figure stared out of the eye holes in the sheet. The dark eyes gleamed in the reflected light of the flashlight as they examined each face.

The veiled informer sat unmovingly as the Land Rover came on at a walking pace down toward where Samson and Constance supported the old man between them.

Without moving his lips, Samson asked her, ''Is it safe—do they know you?''

''I do not know,'' she answered him.

''What can we do—'' But by that time the Land Rover was drawing even with where they stood, and Constance did not have time to reply.

In the rear of the vehicle, the masked figure moved for the first time. A long black arm shot out from under the sheet and pointed directly into Constance's upturned face. Not a word was spoken, but two of the camouflaged Scouts stepped out of the darkness behind her and seized her arms.

''Constance!'' Samson ran forward and reached for her. A rifle butt smashed into his back at the level of his kidneys, and flaming agony tore up his spine and burst against the roof of his skull. He dropped to his knees.

Pain distorted his vision, and the flashlight shone into his face, blinding him. He pushed himself upright with a violent effort but found that the muzzle of an FN rifle was pressed into his stomach.

"We don't want you, my friend. Do not interfere in what does not concern you."

The Scouts were leading Constance away. She went docilely. She seemed very small and helpless between the two tall soldiers in full battle dress. She turned and looked back at Samson. Her great, soft eyes clung to his face and her lips moved.

Then for an instant the body of the Land Rover blocked the beam of the searchlight. Darkness enveloped the group, and a second later when the searchlight caught them again, Constance had broken away from her captors and she was running.

"No!" screamed Samson in terrible agony. He knew what was about to happen. "Stop, Constance, stop."

She flew like a lovely moth in the light, the pink of her dress flitting between the trunks of the spathodea trees, and then the bullets ripped chunks of white, wet wood from the trees about her, and she was no longer swift and graceful; it was as though the moth's wings had been shredded by a spiteful child.

Four soldiers carried her body back, each of them holding a leg or an arm. Constance's head hung back almost to touch the ground, and the blood from her nostrils and mouth running down her cheeks was thick and black as treacle in the searchlights. They tossed her up into the back of the Land Rover, where she lay in a tangle of dark limbs like a gazelle shot on the hunting veld.

◆ ◆ ◆

Samson Kumalo walked down the main street of Bulawayo. The cool of the night still lingered, and the shadows of the jacaranda trees threw tiger stripes across the blue macadam surface. He mingled easily with the lazy flow of humanity along the sidewalk, and he made no effort to avert his face as he passed a BSA police constable in his blue and khaki uniform and pith helmet at the corner of the park.

While he waited for the traffic lights, he watched the faces about him: the flat, incurious expression of the Matabele, their eyes veiled defensively, the bright young white matrons in pretty floral dresses, going about their shopping with a handbag on one shoulder and a machine pistol on the other. There were very few white men in the streets, and most of those too old for military service—the others were all uniformed and armed.

The traffic that crossed the intersection in front of him was mostly military. Since the imposition of economic sanctions, the gasoline ration had been reduced to a few liters a month. The farmers coming into town for the day drove the ungainly mine-proofed machines with blast deflectors and armored bodies.

Samson was aware for the first time since Constance's death of the true extent of his hatred as he watched their white faces. Before today there had been a numbness in him that was anesthetic, but that was fading.

He carried no luggage, for a parcel would immediately have attracted attention and invited a body search. He wore jeans and a short-sleeved shirt and gym shoes—no jacket that might have concealed a weapon; and like the other Matabele around him, his face was blank and expressionless. He was armed only with his hatred.

The lights changed, and he crossed the road unhurriedly and turned down toward the bus station. Even this early it was crowded. There were patient queues of peasants waiting to make the journey back to the tribal trust lands. All of them were loaded with their purchases: bags of meal and salt, tins of cooking oil or paraffin, bundles of material and cardboard boxes of other luxuries, of matches and soap and candles. They squatted under the iron roofs of the shelters, chattering and laughing, chewing roasted maize cobs, drinking Coca-Cola, some of the mothers feeding their infants from the breast or scolding their toddlers.

Every few minutes a bus would draw up in greasy clouds of diesel exhaust to discharge a horde of passengers, and immediately they were replaced from the endless queues. Samson leaned against the wall of the public latrines. It was the most central position, and he settled himself to wait.

He did not at first recognize Comrade Tebe. He wore a filthy, tattered blue overall with "Cohen's Butchery" embroidered across the back in red letters. His careless stoop disguised his height, and an expression of moronic goodwill made him appear harmless.

He passed Samson without a glance in his direction and entered the latrine. Samson waited a few seconds before he followed him. The toilet reeked of cheap tobacco smoke and stale urine. It was crowded, and Comrade Tebe jostled against Samson and slipped a blue cardboard ticket into his hand.

In one of the cubicles, Samson examined it. It was a single third-class ticket, Bulawayo to Victoria Falls. He took his place in the Victoria Falls queue five places behind Tebe. The bus was thirty-five minutes late, and there was the usual rush to heave luggage up onto the roof racks and find a seat.

Tebe was in a window seat three rows ahead of Samson. He never looked around while the heavily loaded red bus lumbered out through the northern suburbs. They passed the long avenue of jacaranda trees that Cecil Rhodes had planted and which led up to the gabled State House on the hill above the town where once the royal kraal of Lobengula, King of the Matabele, had stood. They passed the turnoff to the airport and reached the first roadblock.

Every passenger was forced to dismount and identify his luggage. It was opened and searched by the constables manning the roadblock, and then a random selection of men and women was made for body searching. Neither Samson nor Tebe was among those selected, and fifteen minutes later the bus was reloaded and allowed to pass.

As they roared on northward, the acacia and savanna swiftly gave way to stately forest. Samson crouched on the hard bench and watched it pass. Ahead of him Tebe appeared to be sleeping. A little before noon they reached the stop for St. Matthew's Mission on the Gwaai River at the edge of the Sikumi Forest Reserve. Most of the passengers fetched their luggage down from the roof racks and trudged away along the web of footpaths that led into the forest.

"We will stop here one hour," the uniformed driver told the others. "You can make a fire and cook your meal."

Tebe caught Samson's eye and sauntered away toward the little general dealer's store at the crossroads. When Samson followed him into the building, he did not at first find Tebe. Then he saw the door behind the counter was ajar, and the proprietor made a small gesture of invitation toward it. Tebe was waiting for him in the back room among the piles of maize sacks and dried skins, the cartons of carbolic soap and the crates of cold drinks.

He had shed the ragged overalls and, with them, the character of the indolent laborer.

"I see you, Comrade Samson," he said quietly.

"That is my name no longer," Samson answered.

"What is your name?"

"Tungata Zebiwe."

"I see you, Comrade Tungata." Tebe nodded with satisfaction. "You worked in the game department. You understand guns, do you not?"

Tebe did not wait for an answer. He opened one of the metal bins of ground meal that stood against the rear wall. He brought out a long bundle wrapped in a green plastic agricultural fertilizer bag and dusted off the powdery white meal. He undid the twine that secured it and handed the weapon that it contained to Tungata Zebiwe, who recognized it instantly. In the early days of the bush war, the security forces had mounted a publicity campaign to tempt informers to report the presence of guerrilla weapons in their villages. They had used television spots and newspaper advertisements. In the remote tribal trust areas, they had made massive aerial drops of illustrated pamphlets, all offering a five-thousand-dollar reward for information leading to the recovery of a single one of these.

It was a 7.62mm automatic Kalashnikov (AK) assault rifle. Tungata took it in his hands and found it surprisingly heavy for its size. Unlike most NATO weapons, it was made not of metal-stamped components but of milled steel. The butt and stock were of laminated wood.

"These are the magazines." The Rhodesians called it the "Banana gun" because of these characteristic curved magazines. "Loading the mags." Tebe demonstrated, pushing the short, light, brass cartridges down into the mouth with his thumb. "Try it." Tungata was immediately competent; he had the second magazine loaded with its full thirty rounds in as many seconds.

"Good." Tebe nodded again, the wisdom of his choice confirmed. "Now to load the rifle. Like this." He pressed the forward end of the magazine into the receiver slot and then tilted the rear end upward. There was a click as the catch engaged.

In less than three minutes, Tebe had demonstrated why the AK was the preferred weapon of guerrilla troops the world around. Its ease of operation and its robust construction made it ideal for the task. With a racial sneer, the

Rhodesians called it the only "kaffir-proof" weapon in the shop.

"Selector up as far as it will and it's safe." Tebe finished the demonstration. "Fully down is semiautomatic. In between is fully automatic." He showed Tungata the two Cyrillic letters stamped in the block. "AB," he said, "Russian for 'Automatic.' Take it." He handed it to Tungata, and he watched while he loaded and cocked and unloaded swiftly and neatly. "Yes, good. Remember the gun is heavy, but it climbs quickly in automatic. Take a firm grip."

Tebe rolled the weapon into a cheap gray blanket from which it could be freed instantly.

"The owner of this store is one of us," Tebe said. "He is even now loading supplies for us onto the bus. It is time for me to tell you why we are here and where we are going."

When Tungata and Tebe left the general dealer's store and sauntered toward the parked bus, the children had already arrived. There were almost sixty of them, the boys in khaki shirts and short pants, and the girls in blue gymslips with the green sash of St. Matthew's Mission School around their waists. All of them were barefooted. They were chattering and giggling with excitement at this unexpected outing, this delightful release from the tedium of the schoolroom. Tebe had said they were the Standard VIII pupils, which meant their average age would be fifteen years. All the girls appeared to be pubescent, full-breasted under the coarse cloth of their school uniforms. Under the direction of their class teacher, a young bespectacled Matabele, they were lining up beside the dusty red bus in an obedient and orderly manner. As soon as he saw Tebe, the teacher hurried to meet him.

"It is as you ordered, comrade."

"What did you tell the fathers at the mission?"

"That it was a field trip. That we would not return until after dark, comrade."

"Get the children into the bus."

"Immediately, comrade."

The bus driver, with his peaked cap perched authoritatively on his head, began to protest the influx of young passengers, none of them with a ticket, until Tebe stepped up behind him and pressed the Tokarev pistol into his ribs. Then he turned the pale gray of last night's campfire ashes and subsided into his seat. The children scrambled for seats beside the windows, and then looked up with expectant, shining faces.

"We are going on an exciting journey," the bespectacled teacher told them. "You must do exactly as you are told. Do you understand?"

"We understand," they replied in dutiful chorus.

Tebe touched the bus driver on the shoulder with the barrel of the pistol.

"Drive northward toward the Zambezi River and the Victoria Falls," he ordered softly. "If we should meet a security roadblock, stop immediately and behave as you always do. Do you hear?"

"Yes," mumbled the driver.

"I hear you, comrade, and I will obey," Tebe prompted him.

"I hear you, comrade, and I will obey."

"If you do not, then you will be the very first to die. I give you my word on it."

Tungata sat on the bench seat at the very rear of the bus, with the blanket-wrapped AK on the floorboards at his feet. He had counted the children and made a list. There were fifty-seven of them, of which twenty-seven were girls. As he asked their names, he made his estimate of each one's brightness and leadership potential and marked the best on the list with a star. He was pleased that the bespectacled teacher confirmed his choice. He had selected four of the boys and a girl. She was fifteen years old, her name was Miriam, and she was a slim, pretty child with a quick smile and a bright, intelligent gaze. There was something in her that reminded him of Constance, and she sat beside him on the bench seat so that he could watch her respond to the first session of indoctrination.

While the bus roared on northward beneath the marvelous vaulted roof of the forest, along the straight, smooth, macadamized highway, Comrade Tebe stood beside the driver's seat facing the upturned fresh young faces.

"What is my name?" he asked, and then he told them, "I am Comrade Tebe. What is my name?"

"Comrade Tebe," they cried.

"Who is Comrade Tebe? Comrade Tebe is your friend and your leader."

"Comrade Tebe is our friend and our leader."

Question and answer repeated again and again.

420

"Who is Comrade Tungata?"

"Comrade Tungata is our friend and our leader."

The children's voices took on a strident fervor, and there was a mesmeric glitter in their eyes.

"What is the revolution?"

"The revolution is power to the people," they shrieked, like Western children of the same age at a rock concert.

"Who are the people?"

"We are the people."

"Who is the power?"

"We are the power."

They swayed in their seats, transported into a state of ecstasy. By this time most of the girls were crying with wild joy.

"Who is Comrade Inkunzi?"

"Comrade Inkunzi is father of the revolution."

"What is the revolution?"

"The revolution is power to the people."

The catechism began again, and impossibly they were carried even higher on the wings of political fanaticism.

Tungata, himself strangely roused, wondered at the skill and ease with which it was orchestrated. Higher still and higher Tebe carried them, until Tungata found himself shrieking with them in a wonderful catharsis of the hatred and grief which had festered within him since Constance's murder. He was shaking like a man in fever, and when the bus lurched and threw Miriam's slim, barely matured body against him, he found himself instantly and painfully sexually aroused. It was a strange, almost religious, madness that overwhelmed them all, and at the end Comrade Tebe gave them the song.

"This is the song which you will sing as you go into battle; it is the song of your glory; it is the song of the revolution."

They sang it, the girls harmonizing and clapping in spontaneous rhythm:

"There are guns across the border
And your murdered fathers stir.
There are guns across the river
And your slave-born children weep.
There is a bloody moon arising
How long will freedom sleep?"

Now at last Tungata felt the tears break from his own eyes and pour in scalding streams down his face.

"There are guns in Angola
And a whisper on the wind.
There are guns in Maputo
And a rich red crop to reap.
There's a bloody moon arising
How long will freedom sleep?"

It left them stunned and exhausted, like the survivors of some terrible ordeal. Comrade Tebe spoke quietly to the bus driver, and they turned off the main road onto a barely noticeable track into the forest. The bus was forced to slow down to a crawl, as it followed the serpentine track that jinked around the bigger trees and dipped through dry riverbeds. It was dark by the time they stopped. The track had petered out and most of the children were asleep. Tungata went down the bus waking them and moving them out.

The boys were sent to find firewood and the girls set to preparing a simple meal of maize meal and sweet tea. Tebe led Tungata aside and explained to him.

"We have entered the liberated area—the Rhodesians no longer patrol this strip of territory. From here we go on foot. It will be two days to the drifts. You will march in the rear of the column—be alert for deserters. Until we reach the river, there is always the danger from the fainthearted. Now I will deal with the driver."

Tebe led the subdued and terrified man away from the camp with an arm around his shoulders. He returned alone twenty minutes later, by which time most of the children had eaten and had curled up like puppies on the bare earth beside the fires.

The girl Miriam came to them shyly with a bowl of maize cake, and the two men sat close together while they ate. Tebe spoke with his mouth full. "You think them babes." He indicated the sleeping schoolchildren. "Yet they learn swiftly and believe what they are taught without question. They have no concept of death, therefore they know no fear. They obey, and when they die there is no loss of trained men who cannot be replaced. The Simbas used them in the Congo; the Viet Cong used them against the

Americans; they are the perfect fodder on which the revolution is nurtured." He scraped out the bowl. "If any of the girls is to your liking, you may use her. That is one of their duties."

Tebe stood up. "You will take the first watch. I will relieve you at midnight." Still chewing, he walked away. At the nearest fire, he squatted down beside where Miriam lay and whispered something to her. She stood up immediately, and followed him trustingly out of the firelight.

Later, while Tungata patrolled the perimeter of the sleeping camp, he heard a strangled little wail of pain from the darkness where Tebe and the girl lay. Then there was a sound of a blow, and the cry choked off into gentle sobbing. Tungata moved around to the opposite side of the camp, where he did not have to listen.

Before dawn Tungata drove the bus to the brink of the steep watercourse, and then, yelling with delight, the boys pushed it over the edge. The girls helped them gather branches and heap them over the vehicle until it was hidden from even a low-flying helicopter.

They moved out northward at first light. Tebe took the point, keeping half a kilometer ahead of the column. The schoolmaster stayed with the children, enforcing the complete silence Tebe had ordered. Before they had covered a mile, he was sweating through the back of his shirt and his spectacles were misted over. Tungata camp up behind them, carrying the AK at the trail, avoiding the footpath, staying in the dappled forest shade, stopping every few minutes to listen, and once every hour doubling back to lie beside the path and make certain they were not followed.

None of the skills of the game ranger had deserted him. He found himself completely at ease, and in a strange sort of way he was happy. The future had taken care of itself. He was committed at last. There were no longer any doubts, no guilty sense of duty neglected, and the warrior blood of Gandang and Brazo flowed strongly in his veins.

At noon they rested for an hour. There were no fires, and they ate cold maize cake and washed it down with muddy water from a water hole in the mopani. The water tasted of the urine of the elephants who had bathed in it during the night. When Miriam brought his ration to Tungata, she could not look into his face, and when she walked away, she moved carefully, as though favoring an injury.

In the afternoon they began to descend toward the Zambezi River, and the character of the bush altered. The grand forests gave way to more open savanna, and there were profuse signs of wild game. Circling out behind the column, Tungata surprised a solitary old sable antelope bull, with ebony and salt-white body and elegant backswept horns. He stood noble and proud. Tungata felt a strange affinity with him, and when he took the wind and went away at a gallop, he left Tungata feeling enriched and strengthened.

Tebe halted the column in the middle of the afternoon and told them, "We will be marching all night. You must rest now."

Then for Tungata he drew a sketch map in the dust with a twig.

"This is the Zambezi. Beyond it is Zambia. They are our allies. That is where we go. To the west is Botswana and the waterless land. We are moving parallel to its border, but before we reach the Zambezi we must cross the road between Victoria Falls and Kazungula. The Rhodesians patrol it. We must cross it in darkness. Then beyond it, along this bank of river, the Rhodesians have laid their *cordon sanitaire*. It is a minefield to prevent us using the drifts. It is necessary to reach it at dawn."

"How do we cross the minefield?"

"Our people will be waiting for us there to take us through. Now rest."

◆　◆　◆

Tungata woke with a hand on his shoulder, and was instantly alert.

"The girl," Tebe whispered. "The girl Miriam, she has run."

"Did the schoolteacher not stop her?"

"She told him she was going to relieve herself."

"She is not important," Tungata suggested. "Let her go."

"She is not important," Tebe agreed. "But the example to the others is important. Take the spoor," he ordered.

Miriam must have known the geography of this extreme northwestern corner of Matabeleland. Instead of going back, she had struck boldly northward on the line of their march; clearly she was hoping to reach the Kazungula road while it was still light, and then she would go in to one of the Rhodesian patrols.

"How wise we were to follow her," Tebe whispered as soon as the line of the spoor was evident. "The bitch would have called the *kanka* down on us within an hour."

The girl had made no attempt to hide her spoor, and Tungata followed it at a run. He was superbly fit, for he had worked beside Craig Mellow in the bloody elephant culls, and ten miles was barely far enough to roughen his breathing. Comrade Tebe matched him stride for stride, leopard-quick and with cruel, bleak eyes searching ahead.

They caught Miriam two miles before she reached the road. When she saw them behind her, she simply gave up. She sank onto her knees and trembled so uncontrollably that her teeth rattled in her jaw. They stood over her, and she could not look up at them.

"Kill her," Tebe ordered softly.

Tungata had known instinctively that it would happen this way, and yet his soul turned leaden and icy.

"We never give an order twice," Tebe said, and Tungata changed his grip on the stock of the AK.

"Not with the rifle," Tebe said. "The road lies just beyond those trees. The Rhodesians could be here in minutes."

He took a clasp knife from his pocket and handed it to Tungata. Tungata propped his rifle against a mopani trunk and opened the knife. He saw that the point of the blade had been snapped off, and when he tested the edge with his thumb, he found that Tebe had deliberately dulled the edge by rubbing it against a stone.

He felt appalled and sickened by what he was expected to do, and the manner in which he was expected to do it. He tried to hide his emotions, for Tebe was watching him curiously. He understood that he had been set a test, trial by cruelty, and Tungata knew that if he failed it, then he was as doomed as was the child, Miriam. Still stony-faced, Tungata pulled the leather belt from the loops of his jeans and used it to strap the girl's wrists together behind her back.

He stood behind her so that he did not have to look into the dark terrified eyes. He placed his knee between her shoulder blades and pulled her chin back to expose the slender throat. Then he glanced once more at Tebe for a reprieve. There was no mercy there, and he began to work.

It took some minutes, with the damaged blade and the

child struggling wildly, but at last the carotid artery erupted and he let her fall forward on her face. He was panting and bathed in his own rancid-smelling sweat, but the last vestiges of his previous existence as Samson Kumalo were burned away. At last he was truly Tungata Zebiwe, the Seeker After What Has Been Stolen—the Seeker After Vengeance.

He broke a bunch of leaves off the nearest mopani sapling and scrubbed his hands with it. Then he cleansed the blade by stabbing it into the earth. When he handed the knife back to Comrade Tebe, he met his eyes unflinchingly and saw in them a spark of compassion and understanding.

"There is no going back now," Tebe said softly. "At last you are truly one of us."

◆ ◆ ◆

They reached the road a little after midnight, and while the schoolmaster held the children in a quiet group in a copse beside it, Tebe and Tungata swept the shoulders for a kilometer in both directions in case the Rhodesians had laid an ambush. When they found it clear, they took the children across at the point which Tungata had chosen, where hard gravel approaches would hold no signs. Then Tungata went back and carefully swept the road surface with a broom of grass.

They reached the *cordon sanitaire* before the light. The minefield was forty miles long and one hundred yards deep. It contained over three million explosive devices of various types, from the Claymores on trip wires to the plastic antipersonnel mines, which would take off a limb but would seldom kill outright. The object was to leave the enemy with a casualty to succor and nurse, a casualty who would never again be a fighting warrior.

The edge of the minefield was marked by a line of enamel disks set on stakes or nailed to the trunks of tree. They bore a red skull and crossbones device and the words "Danger—Minefield." Tebe ordered the children to lie flat in the dense brown grass and to draw the stalks over them as concealment from the air.

Then they settled to wait, and Tebe explained to Tungata: "The AP mines are laid in a certain pattern. There is a key to the pattern, but it is very difficult to discover, and often there are deliberate flaws in it. It requires great skill and iron courage to enter the field and pick up the pattern, to identify exactly at which point one has come in and to anticipate the sequence. The Claymores are different and need other tricks."

"What tricks are those?"

"You will see when our guide comes." But he did not come at dawn.

At noon Tebe said, "We can only wait. It is certain death to go into the field alone." There was no food or water, but he would not let the children move. "It is something they would have had to learn anyway." He shrugged. "Patience is our weapon."

The guide came in the late afternoon. Even Tungata did not know he was close until he was among them.

"How did you find us?"

"I cast along the edge of the road until I found where you had crossed." The guide was not much older than any of the hijacked schoolchildren, but his eyes were those of an old man for whom life had no surprises left.

"You are late," Tebe accused.

"There is a Rhodesian ambush on the drifts." The guide shrugged. "I had to go around."

"When can you take us through?"

"Not until the dew falls." The guide lay down beside Tungata. "Not until the morning."

"Will you explain to me the pattern of the mines?" Tungata asked, and the boy glanced across at Tebe. He nodded his permission.

"Think of the veins in the leaf of the mopani," the guide began, and drew the lines in the dust. He talked for almost an hour with Tungata nodding and asking an occasional question.

When he had finished speaking, the boy laid his head on his folded arms and did not move again until dawn the following morning. It was a trick that they all learned, the trick of instant sleep and instant awakening. Those who did not learn it never lasted very long.

As soon as the light was strong enough, the guide crawled to the edge of the field. Tungata followed him closely. In his right hand the guide carried a sharpened spoke from a bicycle wheel, in the other a bunch of yellow plastic strips cut from a cheap shopping bag. He crouched low against the earth, his head cocked like a sparrow.

"The dew," he whispered. "Do you see it?" And Tungata started. Just a few paces in front of them a string of sparkling diamond drops seemed suspended in the air a few inches above the earth.

The almost invisible trip wire of a Claymore was lit up for them by its necklace of dew and by the first low rays of the sun. The guide marked it with a yellow strip and began to probe with the bicycle spoke. Within seconds he hit something in the loose, friable earth and, with gentle fingers, swept clear the gray, circular top of an AP mine. He stood with it between his toes and reached out to probe again. He worked with amazing speed and found three more mines.

"So, we have found the key," he called to Tungata, who lay at the edge of the field. "Now we must be quick, before the dew dries."

The young guide crawled boldly down the passageway to which he had discovered the entrance. He marked two more Claymore trip wires before he reached the invisible turn in the passage. Here he probed again and, as soon as he confirmed the pattern, turned into the next zigzag.

It took him twenty-six minutes to open and mark the passage through to the far edge of the field. Then he came back and grinned at Tungata. "Do you think you can do it now?"

"Yes," Tungata replied without conceit, and the boy's cocky grin faded.

"Yes, I think you could—but always watch for the wild one. They put it there on purpose. There is no way to guard against it, except care."

He and Tungata took the children through in groups of five, making them hold hands. At each Claymore, Tungata or the guide stood with a foot on each side of the trip wires to make certain not one of them touched it as they passed.

On the last journey through, when Tungata was less than a dozen paces from safety, but while he was straddling the final trip wire, they all heard the throb of an aircraft engine. It was coming upriver from the direction of the Victoria Falls, and it grew rapidly in volume. Tungata and the last three children were in the open. The temptation to run was almost irresistible.

"Do not move," the young guide called desperately. "Stay still, crouch down." So they knelt in the middle of the open minefield, and the fine steel wire with its single plastic strip marker ran through the crotch of Tungata's legs. He was an inch away from violent death.

The aircraft noise built up swiftly, and then it roared over the treetops between them and the river. It was a silver-painted Beechcraft Baron with the letters "RUAC" in black upon the fuselage.

"Rhodesian United Air Carriers," the guide identified it. "They take rich capitalist pig tourists to see the Smoke That Thunders."

The machine was so slow and close that they could see the pilot chatting to the woman passenger beside him, and then the plane banked away and was hidden again by the fronds of the ivory-nut palms growing along the banks of the Zambezi River. Slowly Tungata straightened up. He found his shirt was sticking to his body with perspiration.

"Move," he said to the child beside him. "But carefully."

At the Victoria Falls the entire Zambezi River plunges over a precipitous ledge and falls in a turmoil of thundering spray into the narrow gorge far below, giving it the African name the "Smoke That Thunders."

A few miles upriver from this incredible phenomenon, the drifts begin. For forty miles, up as far as the little border post at Kazungula, the wide river tumbles through rapids and then spreads into dawdling shallows. There are twelve places at which oxen can drag a wagon through to the north bank, or a man can wade across if he is willing to chance the Zambezi crocodiles, some of which weigh a ton and can tear the leg off a buffalo and swallow it whole.

"They have an ambush on the drifts," the skinny little guide told Tungata. "But they cannot guard them all. I know where they were this morning, but they may have moved. We will see."

"Go with him," Tebe ordered, and Tungata accepted it as a mark of trust.

That morning he learned from the little guide that to survive it was necessary to use all the senses, not merely the ears and the eyes. The two of them moved in on the approaches to the nearest drift. They moved an inch at a time, searching and listening, sweeping the dense riverine scrub and the tangled lianas beneath the water-fattened trunks of the forest.

The guide's touch alerted Tungata, and they lay shoulder to shoulder on a bed of damp leaf mold, utterly still but tense as coiled adders. It was only minutes later that Tungata realized that beside him the guide was snuffling the air. When he placed his lips on Tungata's ear, his whisper was a breath only.

"They are here." Gently he drew Tungata back, and when they were clear he asked, "Did you smell them?"

Tungata shook his head, and the guide grinned. "Spearmint. The white officers cannot understand that the smell of toothpaste lingers for days."

They found the next drift unguarded and waited for darkness to take the children across, making them hold hands to form a living chain. On the far bank, the guide would not let them rest. Although the children were shivering with cold in their sodden clothing, he forced them on.

"We are in Zambia at last, but we are not yet safe," he warned. "The danger is as great here as it is on the south bank. The *kanka* cross at will, and if they suspect us, they will come in hot pursuit."

He kept them marching all that night and half the following day, by which time the children were dragging and whining with hunger and fatigue. In the afternoon the path brought them suddenly out of the forest to the wide cut of the main railway line, and beside the track were half a dozen crude huts of canvas and rough-hewn poles. In the siding stood two cattle trucks.

"This is the ZIPRA recruiting post," the guide explained. "For the moment you are safe."

In the morning, while the children were embarking into one of the cattle trucks, the skinny guide came to Tungata.

"Go in peace, comrade. I have an instinct for those who will survive and for those who will die in the bush. I think you will live to see the dream of glory fulfilled." And he shook hands, the alternate grip of palm and thumb which was the sign of respect. "I think we will meet again, Comrade Tungata."

He was wrong. Months later Tungata heard that the skinny little guide had walked into an ambush at the drifts. With half his stomach shot away, he had crept into an ant bear hole and kept them off until his last round was fired. Then he had pulled the pin of a grenade and held it to his own chest.

◆ ◆ ◆

The camp was two hundred miles north of the Zambezi. There were fifteen hundred recruits housed in the thatched barracks. Most of the instructors were Chinese. Tungata's instructor was a young woman named Wan Lok. She was short and broad, with the sturdy limbs of a peasant. Her face was flat and sallow, her eyes slitted and bright as those of a mamba, and she wore a cloth cap over her hair and a baggy cotton uniform like a suit of pajamas.

On the first day she made them run forty kilometers in the heat carrying a forty-kilo pack. Equally burdened, she kept easily ahead of the strongest runners, except when she doubled back to harangue and chivy on the stragglers. By that evening Tungata was no longer supercilious and scornful of being taught by a woman.

They ran every day after that, then they drilled with heavy wooden poles, and learned the discipline of Chinese shadow boxing. They worked with the AK assault rifles until they could field-strip them while blindfolded and reassemble them in under fifteen seconds. They worked with the RPG-7 rocket launchers and the grenades. They worked with bayonet and trench knife. They learned to lay a land mine and how to boost it with plastic explosive to destroy even a mine-proofed vehicle. They learned how to set a mine under the blacktop of a macadamized highway by tunneling in from the shoulder. They learned to lay out an ambush on a forest path or along a main road. They learned how to make a running defense in front of a superior fire force while delaying and harassing it, and they did all this on a daily ration of a scoop of maize meal and a handful of dried kapenta, the smelly little fish from Lake Kariba that looked like English whitebait.

Zambia, their host country, had paid a high price for supporting their cause. The railway line to the south that crossed the bridge over the Victoria Falls had been closed since 1973, and Rhodesian task forces had attacked and destroyed the bridges into Tanzania and Maputo, which were landlocked Zambia's only remaining lifeline to the outside world. The rations offered the guerrillas were sumptuous fare compared to those of the average Zambian citizen.

Starved to the leanness of greyhounds and worked to the hardness of iron, half their nights were spent in the political rallies, the endless chanting and singing and shouted massed responses to the commissar's catechism.

"What is the revolution?"

"The revolution is power to the people."

"Who are the people?"

"Who is the power?"

After midnight they were allowed to stagger away to the thatched barracks and sleep—until the instructors woke them again at four o'clock in the morning.

After three weeks Tungata was taken to the sinister isolated hut beyond the camp periphery. Surrounded by instructors and political commissars, he was stripped naked and forced to "struggle." While they shrieked the foulest abuse at him, calling him "running dog of the racist capitalists" and "counterrevolutionary" and "imperialist reactionary," Tungata was driven to strip his soul as bare as his body.

He shouted aloud his confessions: he told them how he had worked with the capitalist tyrants, how he had denied his brethren, how he had doubted and backslid and harbored reactionary and counterrevolutionary thoughts, how he had lusted for food and sleep and had betrayed the trust of his comrades. They left him utterly exhausted and broken on the floor of the hut. Then Wan Lok took him by the hand, as though she were his mother and he her child, and led him stumbling and weeping back to the barracks.

The next day he was allowed to sleep until noon and awoke feeling serene and strong. In the evening at the political rally, he was called to take his place in the front rank among the section leaders.

A month later Wan Lok summoned him to her sleeping hut in the instructors' compound. She stood before him, a dumpy, squat figure in her rumpled cotton uniform.

"Tomorrow you are going in," she said, and took the cloth cap from her head.

He had never seen her hair before. It fell to her waist, as thick and black and liquid as a spill of crude oil.

"You will not see me again," she said, and unbuttoned the front of her uniform. Her body was the color of butter, hard and immensely powerful, but what startled and intrigued Tungata was that her pubic hair was as straight as that upon her head, without any kinking or curling. It excited him inordinately.

"Come," she said, and led him to the thin mattress on the dirt floor of the hut.

432

◆ ◆ ◆

They did not use the drifts on the return, but they crossed the Zambezi in dugout canoes at the point where the river flowed into the immensity of Lake Kariba. In the moonlight the stark silhouettes of the drowned trees were as silver and tortured as the limbs of lepers against the starry sky.

There were forty-eight of them in the cadre, under a political commissar and two young but battle-tempered captains. Tungata was one of the four section leaders with ten men under him. Each of them, even the commissar, carried a sixty-kilo load beneath which they toiled like pregnant hunchbacks. There was no place for food in their packs, so they lived on lizards and bush rats and the half-incubated eggs of wild birds. They competed with the hyena and vulture at lion kills for the putrefying scraps, and at night they visited the kraals of the black peasant farmers and emptied the grain bins.

They crossed the Chizarira Hills and struck southward through trackless forest and waterless wilderness until they hit the Shangani River. They followed it southward still, passing within a few kilometers of the lonely monument in the mopani forest which marks the spot where Allan Wilson and his patrol made their last heroic but futile stand against the impi of Gandang, son of Mzilikazi, brother of the last Matabele king, Lobengula.

When they came to the lands of the white farmers, their work began. On the dirt roads, they laid the heavy land mines that they had carried so far upon their backs. Freed of this onerous burden, they attacked the isolated white homesteads.

They hit four farmhouses in a single week, secure in the knowledge that the security forces were no longer moving to the rescue of a beleaguered homestead during the hours of darkness, because they were aware that the attackers mined all the approach roads before commencing an attack. So the guerillas had all night to finish the job and escape.

The technique was highly developed by this time. At dusk they poisoned the dogs and cut the telephone wire. Then they fired rockets into the windows and doorways and rushed the breaches they had made. At two farms they were held off by a dogged defense, but at the other two they penetrated. The horrors that they left behind them were a deliberate provocation to the rescuers who would come in at first light. What they found might drive the security forces to take out their shock and rage and frustration on the local black population, and in doing so drive them into the ZIPRA camp.

At last, after six weeks in the field, low on ammunition and explosives, they began to pull back, laying ambushes as they withdrew. They abandoned the first ambush after two fruitless days. However, at the second ambush on a remote country road, they were lucky.

They trapped a white farmer who was rushing his wife, suffering from peritonitis following a burst appendix, to the local hospital. The farmer had his two teenage daughters in the vehicle with him. He almost broke through the ambush, but as the armored vehicle passed Tungata's position, he jumped up and ran into the road behind it. He hit it in the soft rear section with an armor-piercing RPG-7 rocket at point-blank range.

The farmer and his eldest daughter were killed in the blast, but his sick wife and the younger daughter were still alive. The political commissar let the ''boys'' have the dying women. They queued up and took them in the road beside the shattered vehicle, one after the other.

When Tungata did not join the line, the commissar condescended to explain, ''When a honey guide leads you to the hive, you must leave him a piece of the comb. Since the beginning of history, rape has always been one of the rewards of the conquerors. It makes them fight better, and it will madden the enemy.''

They left the road that night and moved back into the hills, back toward the lake and sanctuary. Ballantyne's Scouts caught them in the middle of the following afternoon. There was very little warning— just a tiny Cessna 210 spotter plane circling high overhead. And while the commissars and the captains were still shouting the orders to deploy and set up a perimeter, the Scouts came in.

The delivery vehicle was an ancient twin-engined Dakota that had seen service in the Western Desert during World War II. It was painted with gray, nonreflective paint to thwart the infrared seekers of SAM-7 missiles. It flew so low that it seemed to scrape the ragged, rocky crests of the kopjes, and as its shadow momentarily blotted out the sun, the fighting men spewed out of the gaping belly port.

The olive-green umbrellas of their parachutes popped open only seconds before they hit the ground. As the silk flared, they were down. They landed on their feet, and even before the parachutes settled softly in billowing folds, they had snapped their harnesses and were running forward, firing.

The commissar and both veteran captains were killed within the first three minutes, and the Scouts swept forward, rolling up the green panic-stricken guerrillas against the foot of the kopje. Tungata, acting without conscious thought, gathered the men closest to him and led them in a desperate counterattack down a shallow donga that bisected the line of Scouts.

He heard the Scout commander give the order on the bullhorn. "Green and red, hold on your position; blue, clean out that gully." The distorted voice echoed against the hills, but Tungata recognized it. He had last heard it at Khami Mission on the night Constance was murdered. It turned him cold and clear thinking.

He judged his moment finely and then pulled out of the donga under the whipping crackle of the FNs. His calm steadied the men with him, and he started the running defense as Wan Lok had taught him. They were in contact for three hours, in contact with élite, battle-hardened troops, and Tungata kept his little band in hand as they counterattacked and laid AP mines behind them and held at every natural strongpoint until it was dark. Then Tungata broke off the contact and pulled his men out. By that time there were only eight of them left, and three of these were wounded.

Seven days later, in the morning before the dew dried, Tungata opened a passage through the *cordon sanitaire*, probing with a bayonet until he found the key to the pattern, and he took his men across the drifts. There were only five of them left. None of the wounded had been able to stand the pace, and Tungata had personally finished them with the commissar's Tokarev pistol to save them being interrogated by the pursuers.

In the town of Livingstone, on the north bank of the Zambezi opposite the Victoria Falls, Tungata reported to ZIPRA headquarters, and the commissar was astonished.

"But you were all killed. The Rhodesians claimed on the television—"

A driver in a black Mercedes with the party flag fluttering on the hood took Tungata up to the Zambian capital of Lusaka, and there in a safe house on a quiet street, he was ushered into a sparsely furnished room where a man sat alone at a cheap pine desk.

"Baba!" Tungata recognized him immediately. "Nikosi Nkulu! Great Chief!"

The man laughed, a throaty bellow of sound. "You may call me that when we are alone, but at other times you must call me Comrade Inkunzi."

Inkunzi was the Sindebele word for a bull. It suited the man admirably. He was huge, with a chest like a beer keg and a belly like a sack of grain, and his hair was thick and white—all the things that the Matabele venerate: physical size and strength and the hair of age and wisdom.

"I have watched you with interest, Comrade Tungata. Indeed, it was I that sent to fetch you."

"I am honored, Baba."

"You have richly repaid my faith."

The big man settled lower in his chair and linked his fingers over the bulk of his stomach. He was silent for a while, studying Tungata's face, then abruptly he asked, "What is the revolution?"

The reply, so often repeated, came instantly to Tungata's lips.

"The revolution is power to the people."

Comrade Inkunzi's delighted bull bellow crashed out again.

"The people are mindless cattle," he laughed. "They would not know what to do with power if anyone was fool enough to let them have it! No, no! It is time you learned the true answer." He paused, and he was no longer smiling. "The truth is that the revolution is power to the chosen few. The truth is that I am the head of those few, and that you, Comrade Commissar Tungata, are now one of them."

◆ ◆ ◆

Craig Mellow parked the Land Rover and switched off the engine. He twisted the rearview mirror on its gooseneck and used it to adjust the angle of his peaked uniform cap. Then he looked around at the elegant new building that housed the museum. It stood in the middle of the botanical gardens, surrounded by tall palms and green lawns and bright beds of geraniums and sweet peas.

Craig realized that he was putting off the moment and clenched his jaw determinedly. He left the Land Rover in the car park and climbed the front steps of the museum.

"Good morning, Sergeant." The girl at the inquiries desk recognized the three stripes on the sleeve of his khaki and navy blue police uniform. Craig still felt vaguely ashamed of his rapid promotion.

"Don't be damned silly, boy," Bawu had growled when he protested at the family influence. "It's a technical appointment— Sergeant Armorer."

"Hi!" Craig gave the girl his boyish grin, and her expression warmed instantly. "I'm looking for Miss Carpenter."

"I'm sorry, I don't know her." The girl looked unhappy at having to disappoint him.

"But she works here," Craig protested. "Janine Carpenter."

"Oh!" she brightened. "You mean Dr. Carpenter. Is she expecting you?"

"Oh, I'm sure she knows I'm coming," Craig assured her.

"She is in Room 211. Up the stairs, turn left, through the door that says 'Staff Only,' and it's the third door on the right."

Craig pushed the door open at the invitation of "Enter!" that greeted his knock. It was a long, narrow room with skylights and fluorescent tubes overhead and the walls lined as high as the ceiling with shallow drawers, each with a pair of bright brass handles.

Janine stood at the bench table which ran down the center of the room. She was dressed in blue jeans and a brightly checked lumberjack's woolen shirt.

"I didn't know you wore glasses," Craig said. They gave her an air of owlish erudition, and she whipped them off her face and hid them behind her back.

"Well!" she greeted him. "What do you want?"

"Look," he said, "I just had to find out what an entomologist does. I had this bizarre picture of you wrestling with tsetse flies and beating locusts to death with a club." He closed the door quietly behind him and kept talking as he sidled up to the table beside her. "I say, that looks interesting!"

She was like an affronted cat, back arched and every hair upon it erect, but slowly she relaxed.

"Slides," she explained reluctantly. "I am setting up microscopic slides." And then with fresh irritation in her voice, "You know, you show the typical prejudice of the ignorant and uninformed layman. As soon as anyone mentions insects, you immediately think of pests like locusts and disease carriers like tsetse flies."

"Is that wrong?"

"Hexapoda is the largest class of the largest animal phylum, Arthropoda. It has literally hundreds of thousands of members, most of which are beneficial to man, and the pests are in the vast minority."

He wanted to take her up on the "vast minority" as a contradiction in terms, but his good sense for once prevailed. Instead he said, "I never thought of that. How do you mean 'beneficial to man'?"

"They pollinate plants, they scavenge and control pests, and they serve as food—" She was away, and after a few minutes, Craig's interest was no longer feigned. Like any dedicated specialist, she was fascinating while talking in her chosen field. Once she realized that he was a receptive and sympathetic audience, she became even more articulate.

The banks of shallow drawers contained the collection which she had boasted on their first meeting was the finest in the world. She showed Craig microscopic, feather-winged beetles of the family Ptiliidae which were a mere one hundredth of an inch long and compared them to the monstrous African Goliath beetles. She showed him insects of exquisite jeweled beauty and others of repulsive ugliness. She showed him insects that imitated orchids and flowers and sticks and tree bark and snakes. There was a wasp that used a pebble as a tool, and a fly that, like a cuckoo, placed its eggs in the nest of another. There were ants that kept aphids as milch cows and farmed crops of fungus. She showed him insects that lived in glaciers and others that lived in the depths of the Sahara, some that lived in seawater and even larvae that existed in pools of crude petroleum where they devoured other insects trapped in the glutinous liquid.

She showed him dragonflies with twenty thousand eyes and ants that could lift a thousand times their own body weight; she explained bizarre forms of nutrition and reproduction, and such was her rapture that she forgot her vanity and put the horn-rimmed spectacles back on her nose. She looked so cute that Craig wanted to hug her.

At the end of two hours, she removed the spectacles and faced him defiantly. "Okay," she said. "So I am primarily the curator of the collection of Hexapoda, but at the same time I am also a consultant to the Departments of Agriculture, Wildlife and Nature Conservation and Public Health. That's what entomologists do, mister—now what the hell do you do?"

"What I do is I go around inviting entomologists to lunch."

"Lunch?" She looked vague. "What is the time? My God, you've wasted my entire Saturday morning!"

"T-bone steaks," he wheedled. "I have just been paid."

"Perhaps I am lunching with Roly," she told him cruelly.

"Roly is in the bush."

"How do you know that?"

"I phoned Aunty Val at Queen's Lynn to check."

"You crafty blighter." She laughed for the first time. "Okay, I give up. Take me to lunch."

The steaks were thick and juicy, and the beer was icy cold, with dew running down the glass. They laughed a lot, and at the end of the meal he asked, "What do entomologists do on Saturday afternoons?"

"What do police sergeants do?" she countered.

"They go sleuthing up their family antecedents in weird and wonderful places—want to come along?"

She knew all about the Land Rover by now, so she put a silk scarf around her head and dark glasses over her eyes to protect them from the wind, and Craig restocked the cooler with crushed ice and beer. They drove out into the Rhodes Matopos National Park, into the enchanted hills where once the Umlimo had held sway and the Matabele had come for succor and sanctuary in the times of tribal disasters. The beauty of the place struck Janine to the heart.

"The hills look like those wonderful fairy castles along the banks of the Rhine."

In the valleys there were herds of wild antelope, sables and kudus, as tame as sheep. They barely lifted their heads as the Land Rover passed and then returned to graze.

It seemed that they had the hills to themselves, for few others would risk being alone on these dirt-surfaced roads

439

in the very stronghold of Matabele tradition, but when Craig parked the Land Rover in a shady grove beneath a massive bald dome of granite, an old Matabele guardian in the suntans and slouch hat of the Park Board came down to meet them and escort them as far as the gates that bore the inscription, "Here are buried men who deserve well of their country."

They climbed to the summit of the hill and there, guarded by stone sentinels of natural granite and covered by a heavy bronze plaque, they found the grave of Cecil John Rhodes.

"I know so little about him," Janine confessed.

"I don't think anybody knew much about him," Craig said. "He was a very strange man, but when they buried him, the Matebele gave him the royal salute. He had some incredible power over other men."

They went down the far side of the hill to the square mausoleum of stone blocks with its bronze frieze of heroic figures.

"Allan Wilson and his men," Craig explained, "they exhumed their bodies from the battlefield on the Shangani and reburied them here."

On the north wall of the memorial were the names of the dead, and Craig ran his finger down the graven roll of honor and stopped at one name.

"The Rev. Clinton Codrington." He read it aloud. "He was my great-great-grandfather, a strange man, and his wife, my great-great-grandmother, was a remarkable woman indeed. The two of them, Clinton and Robyn, founded the mission station at Khami. A few months after he was killed by the Matabele, she married the column commander who had ordered Clinton to his death, an American chap called St. John. I bet there was some interesting hanky-panky there! A bit of hithering and thithering, a touch of toing and froing."

"They used to do it even in those days?" Janine asked. "I thought it was a recent invention."

They wandered on around the side of the hill and came to another grave. Over the grave stood a misshapen and dwarfed msasa tree that had taken precarious hold in a fault in the solid granite. Like the one on the summit, this grave also was covered by a heavy plate of weathered bronze, but the inscription read:

Here lies the body of
SIR RALPH BALLANTYNE.
FIRST PRIME MINISTER OF SOUTHERN RHODESIA.
He deserves well of his country.

"Ballantyne," she said. "Must be an ancestor of Roly's."

"A mutual ancestor of both of ours," Craig agreed.
"Our great-grandfather, Bawu's papa. This is the real reason why we have driven out here."

"What do you know about him?"

"A great deal, actually. I have just finished reading his
personal journals. He was quite a lad. If they hadn't knighted
him, they would probably have had to hang him. By his
own secret confessions, he was an unqualified rogue, but a
colorful one."

"So that is where you get it from," she laughed. "Tell
me more."

"Funny thing, he was a sworn enemy of that other old
rogue up there." Craig pointed up the hill toward Cecil
Rhodes's grave. "And here they are buried almost side by
side. Great-grandpa Ralph writes in his journal that he
discovered the Wankie coalfield, but Rhodes cheated him
out of it. He swore an oath to destroy Rhodes and his
company—he actually wrote that down! I'll show you! And
he boasts that he succeeded. In 1923 the rule of Rhodes's
British South Africa Company came to an end. Southern
Rhodesia became a British colony; old Sir Ralph was its
prime minister. He had made good his threat."

They sat down side by side on the curbstone of the
grave, and he told her the funniest and most interesting of
the stories that he had read in the secret journals, and she
listened with fascination.

"It's strange to think that they are a part of us and we a
part of them," she whispered. "That everything that is
happening now had its roots in what they did and said."

"Without a past there is no future." Craig repeated the
words of Samson Kumalo, then went on, "That reminds
me, I have something else I want to do before we go back
to town."

This time Craig did not have to be warned of the hidden
turnoff, and he swung onto the track that led past the
cemetery, down the avenues of spathodea trees to the
whitewashed staff cottages of Khami Mission. The first

cottage in the row was deserted. There were no curtains in the windows, and when Craig climbed up onto the porch and peered in, he saw the rooms were bare.

"Who are you looking for?" Janine asked when he came back to the Land Rover.

"A friend."

"A good friend?"

"The best friend I ever had."

He drove on down the hill to the hospital and parked again. He left Janine in the Land Rover and went into the lobby. A woman came striding to meet him. She wore a white laboratory coat, and her unnaturally pale face was set in a belligerent frown.

"I hope you haven't come here to harass and frighten our people," she began. "Here police mean trouble."

"I'm sorry," Craig glanced down at his uniform. "It's a private matter. I am looking for a friend of mine. His family lived here. Samson Kumalo—"

"Oh," the woman nodded. "I recognize you now. You were Sam's employer. Well, he's gone."

"Gone? Do you know where?"

"No," she said flatly and unhelpfully.

"His grandfather, Gideon—"

"He's dead."

"Dead?" Craig was appalled. "How?"

"He died of a broken heart—when your people murdered someone who was dear to him. Now, if there is nothing more you want to know, we don't like uniforms here."

♦ ♦ ♦

By the time they reached town, it was late afternoon. Craig drove directly to his yacht without asking her permission, and when he parked under the mango trees, Janine made no comment but climbed out and walked beside him to the ladderway.

Craig put a tape on the recorder and opened a bottle of wine, then he brought down Sir Ralph's leather-bound journal that Bawu had loaned him, and they sat side by side on the bench in the saloon and pored over it. The faded ink and pencil drawings that decorated the margins delighted Janine, and when she came to a description of the locust plagues of the 1890s, she was captivated.

"The old geezer had a good eye." She studied his drawing of a locust. "He might have been a trained naturalist—just look at the detail."

She glanced up at him sitting close beside her. He looked like a puppy, an adoring puppy. She deliberately closed the leather-bound book without taking her eyes from his. He leaned closer to her, and she made no effort to pull away. He covered her lips with his own, and felt them soften and part. Her huge, slanted eyes closed, and the lashes were long and delicate as butterflies' wings.

After a long time she whispered huskily, "For God's sake, don't say anything stupid. Just keep right on doing what you are doing at the moment."

He obeyed, and it was she who broke the silence. Her voice was shaky.

"I hope you had enough forethought to make the bunk wide enough for two."

Still he said nothing, but lifted her up in his arms and took her to see for herself.

"Do you know, I didn't realize it could be like that." There was wonder in his voice as he stared down at her, leaning on one elbow. "It was so good and natural and easy."

She traced a fingertip over his bare chest, drawing little circles around his nipples. "I like a hairy chest," she purred.

"I mean—you know, I always felt it was such a solemn thing to do—after vows and declarations."

"The sound of organ music?" she giggled. "If you'll excuse the expression."

"That's the only time I have ever heard you giggle," he said.

"That's the only time I ever felt like giggling," she agreed, and giggled again. "Do be a pet and get the wineglasses."

"Now what is so funny?" he demanded from the companionway.

"Your bottom is white and baby smooth—no, don't cover it."

While he hunted in the galley cupboard, she called from the cabin, "Do you have a tape of the 'Pastoral.' "

"I think so."

"Put it on, pet."

"Why?"

"I will tell you when you come back to bed."

She was sitting at the head of the bunk, stark naked in the lotus position. He put one of the wineglasses in her hand and, after a short struggle, managed to twist his own long legs into the lotus and sat facing her.

"So tell me," he invited.

"Don't be dense, Craig—I mean isn't that just a perfect accompaniment?"

Another great storm of music and love swept over them, leaving them clinging helplessly to each other, and in the aching silence that followed, she tenderly stroked back the sweat-damp hair that had fallen into his eyes.

It was too much for him. "I love you," he blurted out. "Oh God, I love you so!"

Almost roughly she pushed him aside and sat up.

"You are a sweet, funny boy and a gentle, considerate lover, but you do have an ungodly talent for saying stupid things at the wrong time."

In the morning she said, "You made dinner, so I'll make breakfast," and went to the galley wearing one of his old shirts. She had to roll the sleeves up, and the tails dangled below her knees.

"You've got enough eggs and bacon to open your own restaurant—were you expecting a visitor?"

"Not expecting, but hoping," he called back from the shower. "Make mine sunny-side up!"

After breakfast she helped him install the big, glittering stainless steel winches on the main deck. He needed someone to hold the gusset plates in position while he drilled and bolted through from the other side.

"You are very handy, aren't you?" she said. They had to shout at each other, for he was working belowdecks while she was perched on the edge of the cockpit.

"It's kind of you to notice."

"So I suppose you are a first-class armorer."

"I'm pretty good."

"Do you do what I suspect—fix up guns?"

"One of my duties."

"How can you bring yourself to do it? Guns are so evil."

"That is the typical prejudice of the ignorant and uninformed layman." He turned her own words against her. "Firearms are on one level highly functional and useful

444

tools, and on another level they can be magnificent works of art. Man has always lavished some of his most creative instincts on his weapons."

"But the way men use them!" she protested.

"For instance, they were used to prevent Adolf Hitler gassing the entire Jewish nation," he pointed out.

"Oh, come on, Craig. What are they being used for out there in the bush at this very moment?"

"Guns aren't evil, but some of the men who use them are. You could say the same about wrenches."

He tightened the bolts on the winch and stuck his head out of the hatch. "That's enough for today—on the seventh day He rested— how about a beer?"

Craig had rigged a speaker in the cockpit and they lolled in the sun and drank beer and listened to the music.

"Look, Jan, I don't know a tactful way to put this, but I don't want you seeing anyone else, do you know what I mean?"

"There you go again." Her eyes slanted and crackled like blue ice. "Do shut up, Craig!"

"I mean after what has happened between us," he plowed on doggedly. "I think we should—"

"Look, dear boy, you have a choice—make me mad again, or make me giggle again. What's it going to be?"

At lunchtime on Monday, she came up to police headquarters, and they ate his ham sandwiches while he showed her around the armory, and despite herself she was intrigued by the exhibits of captured weapons and explosives. He explained the operation of the various types of mines and how they could be detected and disarmed.

"You have to hand it to the terrs," Craig admitted. "The swine carry those things in on their backs, two hundred miles or so through the bush. Just try and pick that up, and you'll see what I mean."

At last he took her through to a small back room. "This is my special project. It's called T & I, trace and identify." He gestured at the charts that covered the walls and the big boxes of empty cartridge cases piled beside the workbench. "After each contact with terrs, our armorers sweep the area and pick up every used cartridge. Firstly they are checked for fingerprints. So if the terr has a record, then we can identify him immediately. If he has polished his rounds before loading or if we have no record of his fingerprints—we can still trace exactly which rifle fired the cartridge.''

He led her to the bench and let her look into the low-power microscope that stood on it. ''The firing pin in each rifle strikes an indentation into the cap of the cartridge which is as individual as a fingerprint. We can follow the career of each active terr in the field. We can make accurate estimates of how many there are and which are the hot ones.''

''The hot ones?'' She looked up from the microscope.

''Out of every hundred terrs in the field, ninety or so of them hole up in good cover near a village which can supply them with food and young girls, and they try to keep out of danger and contact with our forces. But the hot ones are different. They are the tigers, the fanatics, the killers; these charts show their first team.''

He led her to the wall.

''Look at this one. We call him Primrose because his firing pin leaves a mark like a flower. He has been in the bush for three years and been in contact ninety-six times. That is almost once every ten days—he must be made of steel.''

Craig ran his finger down the chart.

''Here is another. We call him Leopard Paw; you can see why by the print of his rifle. He is a newcomer, his first time across the river, but he hit four farms and ran an ambush, then he went into contact with Roly's Scouts. Not many of them survive that; Roly's boys are incredible. They wiped out most of the cadre, but Leopard Paw fought like a veteran and got away with a bunch of his men. Roly's combat report says he lost four men to AP mines that Leopard Paw put down as he ran, and another six in the actual fighting—ten men. That's the heaviest casualties the Scouts have ever taken in any one contact.'' Craig tapped the name on the chart. ''He is a hot one. We are going to hear more of this lad.''

Janine shuddered. ''It's awful—all this death and suffering. When will it ever end?''

''It started when man first stood up on his hind legs; it's not going to end tomorrow. Now let's talk about dinner tonight. I'll pick you up at your flat at seven, okay?''

She telephoned him at the armory a little before five o'clock.

"Craig, don't come for me this evening."

"Why not?"

"I won't be there."

"What has happened?"

"Roly is back from the bush."

Craig did a little work on the foredeck of the yacht, placing the cleats for the jib sheets, but when it was too dark, he went below and wandered around disconsolately. She had left her dark glasses on the table beside the bunk, and a lipstick on the edge of the washbasin. The saloon still smelled of her perfume, and the two wineglasses stood together in the sink.

"I think I will get drunk," he decided, but he had no tonic, and gin with plain water tasted awful. He poured it into the sink, and put the "Pastoral" on the tape, but the images it conjured up were too painful. He hit the "stop" button.

He picked Sir Ralph's leather-bound journal off the table and flicked through it. He had read it twice. He should have gone out to King's Lynn at the weekend; Bawu would have been expecting him to come for the next journal in the series. He started to read it again, and it was an immediate opiate for the loneliness.

After a while he searched in the drawer of the chart table and found the ruled exercise book which he had used for drawing the layout of the cabins and galley. He tore out the used pages, and there were still over a hundred unused sheets. He sat down at the saloon table with an HB pencil from the navigation set and stared at the first empty sheet for almost five minutes. Then he wrote:

"Africa crouched low on the horizon, like a lion in ambush, tawny and gold in the early sunlight, seared by the cold of the Benguela Current.

"Robyn Ballantyne stood by the ship's rail and stared toward it—"

Craig reread what he had written and felt a strange excitement, something he had never experienced before. He could actually see the young woman. He could see the way she stood with her chin lifted eagerly and the wind snapping and tangling her hair.

The pencil started to race across the empty page, and the woman moved in his mind and spoke aloud in his ears. He turned the page and wrote on, then, almost before he realized it, the exercise book was filled with his pointed, peaky handwriting, and outside the porthole by his head, the day was lightening.

♦ ♦ ♦

Ever since Janine Carpenter could remember, there had always been horses in her father's stables at the back of the veterinary dispensary. When she was eight, her father had taken her out for the first time with the local hunt. Just after her twenty-second birthday, a few months before she had left home for Africa, she had been awarded her hunt buttons.

The mount that Roland Ballantyne had given her was a beautiful chestnut filly without any other markings. She was curried to a gloss so that she shone in the sunlight like red silk. Janine had ridden her often before. She was fleet and strong, and there was an accord between them.

Roland rode his stallion. It was an enormous black beast he called "Mzilikazi" after the old king. The veins stood out under the skin of his shoulders and belly like living serpents. The great black bunch of his testicles was crudely and overpoweringly masculine. When he laid back his ears and bared his teeth, the mucous membrane in the corners of his savage eyes was the color of blood. There was an arrogance and menace in him that frightened Janine and yet excited her also. Horse and rider were of a pair.

Roland Ballantyne wore brown whipcord breeches and high boots boned to glossy perfection. The short sleeves of the crisp white shirt were stretched tightly across the hard, smooth muscle of his upper arms. Janine was certain that he always wore white to contrast against the deep tan of his face and arms. She thought he was impossibly handsome, and that cruel and ruthless streak in him made him all the more attractive than mere good looks alone could ever do.

Last night in the bed in her bachelor flat she had asked him, "How many men have you killed?"

"As many as necessary," he had replied, and though she thought that she hated war and death and suffering, it excited her in a way she could not control. Afterward he had laughed easily and said, "You are a kinky little bitch, did you know that?" She had hated him for understanding, and she had been desperately ashamed and so angry that she had gone for his eyes with her nails. He had held her down effortlessly, and still chuckling, he had whispered in her ear until she lost control again.

Now when she looked up at him riding beside her, she felt the lingering fear of him and the gooseflesh on her arms and the hard ball of excitement in the pit of her stomach.

They rode up to the top of the hills, and he reined the stallion down. It danced in a tight little circle, picking up its hooves delicately, and tried to nuzzle her filly, but Roland pulled its head away and pointed at the horizons that fell away into blue distances in every direction.

"Everything you can see from here—every blade of grass, every grain of earth—all of it belongs to the Ballantynes. We fought for it, we won it—it's ours, and anyone who wants to take it from us will have to kill me first." The idea of anyone or anything doing that was ludicrous. He was a young god, one of the immortals.

He dismounted and led the horses to one of the tall msasa trees. He tied them and then reached up and lifted her down from the saddle. He walked her to the edge of the precipice and held her against him, her back to his chest, so that she could look out and see it all.

"There it is!" he said. "Just look at it."

It was beautiful—rich, golden grasslands and graceful trees; waters that flowed in the small, clear streams or shone like mirrors where the dam walls held them back; the tranquil herds of cattle as red as the earth beneath their hooves; and arched above it all, the high cloud-dappled blue of the African sky.

"It needs a woman to love it as I love it," he said. "A woman to breed fine sons to cherish it, to hold it as I will hold it."

She knew what he was going to say then, and now that it was about to happen, she felt numbed and confused. She felt herself beginning to tremble against him.

"I want you to be that woman," Roland Ballantyne said, and she began to weep uncontrollably.

◆ ◆ ◆

The NCOs of Ballantyne's Scouts clubbed together to give their colonel and his new lady an engagement party.

They held it in the sergeants' mess at the Thabas Indunas barracks. The officers and the wives of the regiment were all invited, so that when Roland and Janine drove up in the

449

Mercedes, there was a packed crowd waiting on the front veranda to greet them. Led by Sergeant Major Gondele, they launched into a rollicking but untuneful rendition of "For They Are Jolly Good Fellows."

"Damn good thing you don't fight like you sing," Roland told them. "Your backsides would have more holes than a sieve by now."

He treated them with a rough, paternal severity and affection, the total easy assurance of the dominant male, and they worshiped him openly. Janine understood that. She would have been surprised if it were otherwise. What did surprise her was the brotherhood of the Scouts. The way that officers and men, black and white, were held together by an almost tangible bond of trust and accord.

She sensed that it was something stronger than even the strongest family ties, and later when she spoke to Roland about it, he replied simply, "When your life depends on another man, you come to love him."

They treated Janine with enormous respect, almost awe. They called her "Donna" if they were Matabele and "Ma'am" if they were white, and she responded immediately to them.

Sergeant Major Gondele personally fetched her a gin that would have stunned an elephant and looked hurt when she asked for a little more tonic. He introduced her to his wife. She was a pretty, plump daughter of a senior Matabele tribal chief, "which makes her a sort of princess," Roly explained. She had five sons, the exact number that Janine and Roly had decided upon, and she spoke excellent English, so she and Janine were immediately in deep and earnest conversation from which Janine was at last distracted by a voice at her elbow.

"Dr. Carpenter, may I apologize for being late." It was said in the perfectly modulated tones and classless accents of a BBC announcer or a graduate of the Royal Academy of Dramatic Art. Janine turned to face an elegant figure in the uniform of a wing commander of the Rhodesian Air Force.

"Douglas Hunt-Jeffreys," he said, and offered her a narrow, almost femininely smooth hand. "I was desolated by the prospect of not meeting the lovely lady of the gallant colonel." He had the cultured, vacuous features of a dilettante, and the uniform, no matter that it was perfectly tailored, looked out of place on his narrow shoulders. "The whole regiment has been in a complete tizzy since we heard the monumental tidings."

She knew instinctively that despite his appearance and his choice of words, he was not gay. If she needed confirmation of his heterosexuality, it was the way he held her hand, and the subtle glance that dropped down her body like a silken robe and then came back to her face. She found her interest titillated; he was like a razor blade wrapped in velvet.

"Dougie, my old fruit." Roland's smile had a white, sharkish quality.

"Bon soir, mon brave." The wing commander took the ivory cigarette holder from between his teeth. "I must say I didn't expect you to show such exquisite taste. Dr. Carpenter is utterly ravishing. I do approve, dear boy. I truly do."

"Dougie has to approve everything we do," Roland explained: "He's our liaison with Combined Ops."

"Dr. Carpenter and I have just discovered that we were almost neighbors, we are members of the same hunt, and she was at school with my little sister. I cannot understand how we haven't met before."

Janine realized then, almost with disbelief, that Roland Ballantyne was jealous of her and this man. He took her arm just above the elbow and with a light pressure steered her away.

"You will excuse us, Douglas. I want Bugsy to meet some of the lads—"

"Bugsy, forsooth!" Douglas Hunt-Jeffreys shook his head in pained disbelief. "These colonials are all of them barbarians." And he wandered away to find another gin and tonic.

"You don't like him?" Janine could not resist stirring Roland's jealousy a little.

"He's good at his job," Roland said shortly.

"I thought he was rather cute."

"Perfidious Albion," he replied.

"What does that mean?"

"He is a greenhorn."

"So am I," she said with a slight edge beneath her smile. "And if you go back just a little, so are you, Roland Ballantyne. So we shall get on very well together, you and

I." She hugged his arm in a gesture of reconciliation, and he led her to a group of young men at the end of the bar. With their cropped heads and fresh faces, they looked like undergraduates; only their eyes held that flat, pebbly look. She remembered Hemingway had called them "machine-gunners' eyes."

"Nigel Taylor, Nandele Zama, Peter Sinclair," Roland introduced them. "These lads almost missed the party. They only got back from the bush two hours ago. This morning they had a good contact near the Gwaai—twenty-six kills."

Janine hesitated over her choice of words, and then said faintly, "That's nice," rather than "Congratulations," both of which seemed grossly inappropriate for the passing of twenty-six human lives. It seemed to suffice, however.

"Will you be riding the colonel this evening, Donna?" the young Matabele sergeant asked eagerly, and Janine looked hurriedly to Roland for clarification. Even in such a close family environment, it seemed a rather personal inquiry.

"Mess tradition." Roland grinned at her discomfort. "At midnight Sergeant Major and I race down to the main gates and back. Princess Gondele will be his jockey, and I am afraid you will be rather expected to do the honors for me."

"You are not as fat as Princess." The young Matabele ran an appraising eye over Janine. "I'm going to bet ten dollars on you, Donna."

"Oh, goodness. I do hope we don't let you down."

By midnight the excitement was frenetic—of the peculiar quality that grips men who live their daily lives in mortal danger and who know that this stolen hour of joyous existence may be their last. They thrust bunches of bank notes into the hands of the adjutant who was official holder of bets, and crowded around their fancies to bolster them with raucous encouragement.

Princess and Janine were in stockinged feet, with their skirts rucked up and tucked into their panties like little girls at the seaside, standing on a chair on each side of the main doors to the mess. Outside, the tarmac road down to the main gates was lit by the headlights of army vehicles parked along the shoulder, and lined with the overflow from the mess bar, all of them full of gin and rowdy enthusiasm.

On the bar Sergeant Major Gondele and Roland were

stripped down to breeches and jungle boots. Esau Gondele was a black giant, his shaven head like a cannon ball and his shoulders lumpy with muscle. Beside him even Roland looked like a boy; his chest, untouched by the sun, was very smooth and white.

"You trip me this time, S'arn Major, and I'll tear your head off," he warned, and Esau patted his shoulder soothingly.

"Sorry, boss. You ain't ever going to get close enough to trip."

The adjutant took the last bets and then mounted to the bar top rather unsteadily, with a service pistol in one hand and a glass in the other.

"Shut up, all of you. At the gun the two competitors will each consume a quart bottle of beer. When the bottle is empty, they will be free to take up one of these beautiful young ladies."

There was a storm of wolf whistles and clapping.

"Do shut up, chaps!" The adjutant, swaying precariously on the bar top, tried to look stern.

"We all know the rules."

"Get on with it!"

The adjutant made a gesture of resignation, pointed the pistol at the ceiling, and pulled the trigger. There was a crash of shot, and one of the roof lights went out. The adjutant's bald head was showered with fragments of the shattered bulb.

"I say, I forgot to change to blanks," he murmured distractedly, but nobody took any further interest in him.

Sergeant Major Gondele and Roland both had their heads thrown back, the base of the black bottles pointed at the roof, and their throats pulsed regularly as the frothing beer gushed down them. Gondele finished a second before Roland, leaped from the counter, emitted a great beer belch, and swept a squealing Princess up onto his shoulders. He was out of the doors before Janine could wrap her bare legs around Roland's neck.

Roland scorned the veranda stairs and vaulted over the far railing. It was a four-foot drop to the lawn below, and Janine, a veteran of the hunt, only stayed on his shoulders by a fierce grip in his hair and a miracle of balance, but they had cut two yards off the big Matatele's lead. They stayed close behind him down the long, curving drive, jungle boots pounding on the black tarmac with Roland grunting at each stride and Janine bouncing and swaying on his shoulders. The spectators howled and leaned on the horns of the parked trucks, so the noise was pandemonium.

They reached the main gates, and the black sentry recognized Roland and gave him a flourishing salute.

"At ease!" Roland told him as he turned in Gondele's wake.

"If you get a chance, pull Princess off," he panted to Janine.

"That's cheating," she protested breathlessly.

"This is war, baby."

Gondele was breathing like a bull, lumbering up the hill with the headlights glistening on his burnished muscles, and still two paces behind him, Roland ran with quick, light steps. Janine could feel the strength flowing out of his body like electricity, but it was not that alone that started whittling the inches off Gondele's lead. It was that same rage to win that she had seen grip him on the courts at Queen's Lynn.

Then suddenly they were running side by side, straining their hearts and their bodies beyond mere physical strength. It was at the end a contest of wills, a trial of who could bear the agony longest.

Janine looked across at Princess and saw in her set expression that she expected Janine to foul her; both knew it was within the rules, and she had heard Roland order Janine to do so.

"Don't worry," Janine called to her, and got a flashing smile as a reward.

Shoulder to shoulder the two men came around the bend of the driveway; the lawn stretched to meet them, and beneath her Janine felt Roland make some almost mystical call on reserves that should not have existed. It was to her unthinkable that anyone could make such an effort to win a childish contest—a normal man could not have done it; a totally sane man would not have done it. There was a wildness, a madness in Roland Ballantyne that frightened and at the same time elated her.

In the glare of headlights and the roar of the crowd, Roland Ballantyne simply burned off the bigger, stronger man and left him floundering half a dozen yards behind him as he leaped up the stairs, crashed through the mess doors, and dropped Janine onto the bar top.

His face was swollen and ugly red as he thrust it inches from hers. "I told you to do something," he snarled hoarsely. "Don't you ever disobey me again, ever!" And in that moment she was truly afraid of him.

Then he went to Esau Gondele, and the two of them threw their arms around each other and sobbed with laughter and exhaustion and staggered in a circle trying to lift each other off their feet. The adjutant thrust a roll of bank notes into Roland's hand. "Your winnings, sir," he said, and Roland slapped it onto the bar counter. "Come on, lads, help me drink it up," he wheezed, still fighting for breath.

Esau Gondele took one sip of his beer and then poured the rest over Roland's head.

"Sorry, Nkosi," he roared. "But I've always wanted to do that."

"This is, my dear, just a typical homely evening with Ballantyne's Scouts." Janine looked around to find Douglas Hunt-Jeffreys beside her, with the ivory cigarette holder between his teeth. "Sometime when the varsity rugger club atmosphere palls and your intended is away in the bush, you might find a little civilized company makes a pleasant change."

"The only thing about you that interests me is what makes you think I might be interested."

"It takes one to recognize one, darling."

"You are impertinent. I could tell Roland."

"You could," he agreed. "But then I always like to live dangerously. Goodnight, Dr. Carpenter. I hope we meet again."

They left the mess after two in the morning. Despite the alcohol he had taken, Roland drove as he always did, very fast and well. When they reached her apartment, he carried her up the stairs, despite her muted protests. "You will wake everybody in the building!"

"If they sleep so lightly—just wait until I get you upstairs. They will be sending you lawyers' letters, or get-well cards."

After he had made love to her, he fell instantly asleep. She lay next to him and watched his face in the orange and red flashes of the neon sign on the roof of the service station across the street. In relaxation he was even more beautiful than awake, but she found herself thinking suddenly of Craig Mellow, of his funniness and his gentleness.

"They are so different," she thought. "And yet I love them both now, each in a different way."

It troubled her so that she fell asleep only as the dawn swamped the neon flashes on the bedroom curtains.

Roland seemed to waken her immediately. "Breakfast, wench," he ordered. "I've got a meeting at nine o'clock at Combined Ops."

They sat on her balcony, amid her miniature forest of pot plants, and ate scrambled eggs and wild mushrooms.

"I know it's usually the bride's prerogative, Bugsy, but can we set a date for around the end of next month?"

"So soon? Can you tell me why?"

"Not all of it—but after that we will be going into quarantine, and I might be out of circulation for a while."

"Quarantine?" She laid down her fork.

"When we start planning and training for a special operation, we go into total isolation. There have been too many security leaks lately. Too often our boys have walked into a sucker punch. We have got a big one coming up, and the whole group will be quarantined in a special camp; nobody, not even myself, will be allowed outside contact, not even with parents or wives, until after the operation."

"Where is this camp?"

"I cannot tell you, but if we spend the honeymoon at Victoria Falls as you wanted, it will suit me just fine. You can fly back here afterward and I can go straight into quarantine."

"Oh, darling, it's so soon. There will be so many arrangements to make. I don't know if Mummy and Daddy can get out here by then."

"Telephone them."

"All right," she agreed. "But I hate the thought of your having to leave so soon afterward."

"I know. It won't always be that way." He looked at his watch. "Time to go. I'll be a little late this evening; I want to talk to Sonny. I hear he's living in that boat of his again."

She tried to cover her shock.

"Sonny? Craig. Why do you want to see him?"

When Roland told her why, she could think of nothing to say. She went on staring at him in appalled silence.

Janine telephoned him at the police armory as soon as she reached the museum.

"Craig, I have to see you."

"Wonderful, I'll make the dinner."

"No, no—immediately. You must get away."

He laughed. "I've only had this job a few months. Even for me it will be a record."

"Tell them your mother is sick."

"I'm an orphan."

"I know, darling, but this is life and death."

"What did you call me?"

"It slipped out."

"Say it again."

"Craig, don't be an idiot."

"Say it."

"Darling."

"Where and when?"

"Half an hour at the bandstand in the gardens, and, Craig, it's bad news." She hung up without letting him talk again.

She saw him first. He came at a lope, like a Saint Bernard puppy, with legs too long and his hair sticking out under the peak of his cap, a frown of worry crumpling up his face, but when he saw her sitting on the steps of the white-painted bandstand, the frown smoothed and his eyes lit with that special, soft look that today she found too painful to bear.

"God," he said. "I had forgotten how lovely you are."

"Let's walk." She couldn't look at him, but when he took her hand, she could not bring herself to pull her fingers out of his.

Neither of them spoke again until they reached the river. They stood on the bank and watched a little girl in a white dress and pink ribbons feeding bread crumbs to the ducks.

"I had to tell you first," she said. "I owed you that at least." She felt him go very still beside her, but still she could not look at him, yet she could not withdraw her hand from his.

"Before you say anything, I want to tell you again what I told you before. I love you, Jan."

"Oh, Craig."

"Do you believe me?"

She nodded and swallowed.

"All right, then, now you tell me what you called me to hear."

"Roland has asked me to marry him."

His hand began to tremble.

"And I said yes."

"Why, Jan?"

She jerked her hand away at last. "Damn you, why do you always have to do it?"

"Why?" he persisted. "I know you love me. Why are you going to do it?"

"Because I love him more," she said, still angry. "If you were me, who would you marry?"

"When you put it that way," he agreed, "I suppose you are right." Now at last she looked at him. He was very pale. "Roly always was the winner. I hope you will be very happy, Jan."

"Oh, Craig, I'm so sorry."

"Yes, I know. So am I. Can we just leave it now, Jan. There is nothing more to say."

"Yes, there is. Roland is coming to see you this evening. He is going to ask you to be his best man."

♦ ♦ ♦

Roland Ballantyne perched on the edge of the operations table. It was an enormous relief map of Matabeleland. The disposition of the security force elements were shown by small, movable counters and their strength by a numbered card set into each counter like a menu in its holder. Every branch of the force had its own color—the Ballantyne Scouts were maroon. They were shown as having 250 in Thabas Indunas barracks, but there was still a patrol of 50 near the Gwaai involved in the hot pursuit of the survivors of the previous day's contact.

On the opposite side of the operations table, Wing Commander Douglas Hunt-Jeffreys slapped the wooden pointer into the palm of the other hand.

"All right," he nodded. "This is for heads of staff only. Let's go over it from the beginning, please."

There were just the two of them in the operations room, and the red security light above the steel door was burning.

"Code name Buffalo," Roland said. "The object of operation is the elimination of Josiah Inkunzi and/or one or all of his chiefs of staff—Tebe, Chitepo and Tungata.''

"Tungata?" Hunt-Jeffreys asked.

"A new one," Roland explained.

"Go on, please."

"We will cull them at the safe house in Lusaka at some date after the fifteenth of November when we expect Inkunzi to return from a visit to Hungary and East Germany."

"You will be able to get intelligence of his return?" Douglas asked. And when Roland nodded: "Can you let me know your source?"

"That is not even for you, Dougie, my boy."

"Very well, as long as you will be certain that Inkunzi is in residence before you move."

"From now on let's call him Buffalo."

"How will you go in?"

"We will go in overland. A column of Land Rovers with Zambian police markings, and all personnel will wear Zambian police uniforms."

Douglas raised an eyebrow. "Geneva Convention?"

"Legitimate ruse of war," Roland countered.

"They'll shoot you if they catch you."

"They would do that anyway, uniforms or not. The answer will be not to let any of our lads get caught."

"All right, you go in by road—which one?"

"Livingstone to Lusaka."

"A long haul through hostile territory, and our air force has blown the bridges at Kaleya."

"There is an alternative route upstream; there will be a guide waiting to take us through the bush to reach it."

"So you have covered that bridge, but how do you cross the Zambezi?"

"There is a drift below Kazungula."

"Which you have checked, of course?"

"On a dummy run. We took a vehicle across, using winch and floats, in nine minutes flat. We will have the entire task force across in under two hours. There is a track that will take us out onto the great north road fifty K's north of Livingstone."

"What about resupply?"

"The guide at Kaleya is a white maize farmer. He has fuel on his farm, and we will back up with helicopters."

"I take it you will use the helicopters to evacuate if you are forced to abort the operation?"

Roland nodded. "That's it, Dougie old bean. Pray it's not necessary."

"Let's go on to personnel then. How many will you use?"

"Forty-five Scouts—that includes S'arn Major and myself—and ten specialists."

"Specialists?"

"We expect to find a pile of documents in Buffalo's HQ. Probably so much that we will not be able to bring it all back. We need at least four intelligence experts to evaluate on the spot what to keep and what to burn. You pick them for us."

"The other specialists?"

"Medicos, two of them. Henderson and his aide. We have used them before."

"Good, who else?"

"Blast bunnies, to clear the house of booby traps, to set our own when we leave, and to blow the bridges behind us on our way home."

"Armorers from Salisbury?"

"I can get two good lads here in Bulawayo; one is a cousin of mine."

"Fine, let me have a list of names." Douglas carefully withdrew the stub of his cigarette from the ivory holder, crushed it out, and replaced it with a fresh tube from the packet of Gold Leaf.

"What about a site for the quarantine camp?" he asked. "Have you given it some thought?"

"There is the Wankie Safari Lodge on the Dett vlei. It's two hours' drive from the Zambezi, and it has been on a caretaker basis since the Wankie strip was abandoned."

"Five-star comfort—the Scouts are getting soft." Douglas grinned mockingly. "Okay, I'll see that you get it." Douglas made a note and then looked up. "Now let's go over the dates. How soon can you be ready to go?"

"Fifteenth of November. That gives us eight weeks to assemble the equipment, and rehearse the raid—"

"It probably also fits in rather well with the date of your wedding, doesn't it?" Douglas tapped the ivory holder against his teeth and delighted in Roland Ballantyne's quick flare of temper.

"The timing of the raid has nothing to do with my private affairs; it will be dictated entirely by Buffalo's movements. In any event, my wedding will take place a week before the start of quarantine. Janine and I will spend our honeymoon at the Victoria Falls Hotel, which is only two hours' drive from the camp at Wankie Safari Lodge. She will fly back to Bulawayo on the airway's scheduled flight, and I will go into quarantine directly from Vic Falls."

Douglas lifted a defensive hand and grinned mockingly. "I say, do keep your hair on, old man. Just a civil inquiry, that's all. By the way, I think my wedding invitation must have been lost in the post—" But Roland had returned to his list and was studying it with all his attention.

◆ ◆ ◆

Douglas Hunt-Jeffreys lay on the ample bed in the cool, shuttered bedroom and examined the naked woman who slept beside him. At first she had seemed a most unpromising subject, with her pale acne-scarred face and disconcerting, staring eyes behind horn-rimmed spectacles; her abrupt, aggressive, almost mannish manner; and the smoldering intensity of the political militant. But stripped of her shapeless sweater and baggy skirts, of her thick woolen socks and crude leather sandals, she had a slim, pale, almost girlish body, with fine, small breasts that Douglas found very much to his taste. When she removed the spectacles, her staring eyes softened into appealing, unfocused myopia, and under Douglas' skillful lips and fingers, she unloosed a tumultuous physical response which had at first astonished and then delighted him. He found he could induce in her an epileptic passion, a state in which she was almost catatonic and totally susceptible to his will, her depravity limited only by the range of Douglas' fertile imagination.

"A murrain on beautiful women." He smiled contentedly to himself. "It's the ugly little ducklings who are the absolute ravers!"

They had met in the middle of the morning, and now it was—careful not to disturb her, Douglas checked his gold Rolex—it was two o'clock in the afternoon. Even for Douglas, a marathon performance.

"Poor lamb is exhausted." He craved a cigarette, but decided to give her ten minutes more. There was no hurry.

He could afford to lie a little longer and leisurely review this case.

Like many good controllers, Douglas had found that a sexual relationship with his female agents, and occasionally even with some of his male agents, was an effective tool of manipulation, a shortcut to the dependencies and loyalties that were so desirable in his trade. This case was a perfect example. Without the physical lever, Dr. Leila St. John would be a difficult and unpredictable subject, whereas with it she had become one of his best agents ever.

Douglas Hunt-Jeffreys by a fluke of war was a born Rhodesian. His father had come out to Africa at the beginning of Hitler's war to command the Royal Air Force training station at Gwelo. He had met and married a local girl, and Douglas had been delivered in 1941 by the Air Force doctor. The family had returned to England at the end of his father's tour of duty, and Douglas had followed the well-worn family path to Eton, and then on to the Royal Air Force.

After that there had been an unusual diversion in his career, and he found himself in British military intelligence. Back in 1964, when Ian Smith came to power in Rhodesia and started making the first threatening noises about breaking with Britain in a unilateral declaration of independence, Douglas Hunt-Jeffreys had been the perfect choice of an agent to place in the field. He had returned to Rhodesia, taken up his Rhodesian nationality, joined the Rhodesian Air Force, and begun immediately to mole his way up the ladder of command.

He was now chief coordinator for British intelligence throughout the territory, and Dr. Leila St. John was one of his recruits. Naturally, she had no idea as to who was her ultimate employer; any suggestion of military intelligence, no matter to which country it belonged, would have sent her scampering up the nearest tree like a frightened cat. Douglas grinned lazily at his own imagery. Leila St. John believed herself to be a member of a small, courageous group of left-wing guerrillas intent on wresting the land of her birth from its racialist, fascist conquerors and delivering it unto the joys of Marxist communism.

On the other hand, the concern of Douglas Hunt-Jeffreys and his government was to arrive at the swiftest settlement acceptable to the United Nations and to the United States,

France, West Germany and their other western allies, and to withdraw from an embarrassing, untidy and costly situation with what dignity and dispatch they could still muster, preferably leaving in charge the least objectionable of the African guerrilla leaders.

British and American intelligence appraisals showed that Josiah Inkunzi, despite all his extreme left-wing rhetoric and the military assistance which he had solicited and received from communist China and the Soviet bloc countries, was a pragmatist. From the western viewpoint, he was far and away the least of several possible evils; his elimination would clear the way for a horde of truly vicious Marxist monsters to take over and lead the future Zimbabwe into the clutches of the big red bear.

A secondary consideration was that a successful Rhodesian assassination coup on Inkunzi would bolster the slowly flagging fighting resolve of the Rhodesian UDI Government, and would render Ian Smith and his gang of right-wing cabinet ministers even less amenable to reason than he had been to date. No, it was absolutely essential that Josiah Inkunzi's life be protected at all costs, and Douglas Hunt-Jeffreys tickled the sleeping woman gently.

"Wake up, pussy cat," he said. "It's time to talk."

She sat up and stretched, and then groaned softly and touched herself cautiously. "Ah!" she murmured huskily. "I ache all over, inside and out, and it feels good."

"Light each of us a cigarette," he ordered, and she fitted one into his ivory holder with practiced dexterity, lit it and placed it between his lips.

"When do you expect the next courier from Lusaka?" He blew a spinning smoke ring that broke on her bosom like mist on a hilltop.

"Overdue," she said. "I told you about the Umlimo."

"Oh yes," Douglas nodded. "The spirit medium."

"The arrangements to move her are all in hand, and Lusaka is sending a high party official, probably a commissar, to take charge of the transfer. He will arrive at any time."

"It seems a lot of trouble to go to for a senile old witch doctor."

"She is the spiritual leader of the Matabele people," Leila told him fiercely. "Her presence with the guerrilla army would be of incalculable value to their morale."

"Yes, I understand; you explained the superstitions to

me." Douglas stroked her cheek soothingly and she subsided gradually. "So they are sending a commissar. That's good, though it always puzzles me how they move back and forth across the border, in and out of the towns, and from one end of the country to the other, with so little trouble."

"To the average white man, one black face looks the same as every other," Leila explained. "There is no system of passes or passports; every village is a base, nearly every black person an ally. As long as they do not carry arms or explosives, they can use the buses and railways and pass through the roadblocks with impunity."

"All right," Douglas agreed. "Just as long as what I have for you gets back to Lusaka as soon as possible."

"By next week at the latest," Leila promised.

"The Ballantyne Scouts are setting up a full-scale operation to cull Inkunzi and his staff at the safe house in Lusaka."

"Oh my God, no!" Leila gasped with shock.

"Yes, I'm afraid so, unless we can warn him. Now here are the details. Memorize them, please."

◆ ◆ ◆

The rackety old bus came down the winding road through the hills, leaving behind it a long smear of diesel fumes which drifted sluggishly aside on the small breeze. The roof racks were piled with bundles tied with rope and pieces of string, with cardboard boxes and cheap suitcases, with squawking chickens in cages of plaited bark and bent twigs, and with other less readily identifiable packages.

The driver slammed on his brakes when he saw the roadblock ahead, and the chattering and laughter of his passengers died into an uneasy silence. As soon as the bus stopped, the black passengers poured out of the forward entrance and, under the direction of the waiting armed police, separated into groups according to their sex, men to one side, women and their children to the other. In the meantime, two black constables climbed aboard to search the empty bus for fugitives hiding under the seats or for hidden weapons.

Comrade Tungata Zebiwe was among the huddle of male passengers. He was dressed in a floppy hat, a ragged shirt and short khaki trousers; on his feet were filthy tennis shoes, and his big toes protruded through the stained canvas uppers. He seemed typical of the unskilled itinerant laborers who made up the great bulk of the country's labor force; he was safe, just as long as the police check was cursory, but he had every reason to believe that this one would not be.

After crossing the Zambezi drifts in darkness and negotiating the *cordon sanitaire*, he had made his way south through the abandoned strip and reached the main road near the collieries at Wankie. He was traveling alone and carrying forged employment papers to show that he had been discharged two days previously from employment as a laborer at the collieries. It should have been enough to take him through any ordinary roadblock.

However, two hours after he had boarded the crowded bus and when they were approaching the outskirts of Bulawayo, he realized suddenly that there was another ZIPRA courier among the passengers. She was a Matabele woman in her late twenties who had been in the training camp with him in Zambia. She was also dressed like a peasant girl, and had an infant strapped upon her back in the traditional fashion. Tungata studied her surreptitiously as the bus roared southward, hoping that she might not be carrying incriminating material. If she was, and if she was picked up at a roadblock, then every other passenger in the bus would be subjected to full security scrutiny, which included fingerprints, and as a former Rhodesian Government employee, Tungata's fingerprints were on the files.

The woman, although his ally and comrade, was a deadly danger to him now. She was a totally unimportant pawn, a mere courier, and she was expendable, but what was she carrying at the moment? He watched her surreptitiously, looking for any indication of her status, and then suddenly his attention focused on the infant strapped to the girl's back. With a swoop of dread in the pit of his stomach, Tungata realized the worst. The woman was active. If they took her, they would almost certainly take Tungata also.

Now he lined up with the other male passengers for the body search by the black police members; on the far side of the bus, the women passengers were forming a separate line. Women police would search them to the skin. The girl courier was in fifth place in the line; she was joggling the sleeping infant on her back, and its tiny head waggled from side to side. Tungata could wait no longer.

Abruptly he pushed his way to the front of the queue and spoke urgently but quietly to the black sergeant in charge of the search. Then Tungata pointed deliberately at the girl in the women's line. The girl saw the accuser's finger pointed at her, she looked about her, and then broke from the line and started to run.

"Stop her!" the sergeant bellowed, and the running girl loosed the strap of cloth that held the infant to her back and let the tiny black body fall to the earth. Freed of her burden, she raced for the line of thick thornbush along the shoulder of the road. However, the roadblock had been laid to prevent just such an escape, and two police constables rose from concealment at the edge of the bush. The girl doubled back, but they had her trapped and a heavy blow with a gun-butt knocked her sprawling in the grass. They dragged her back, struggling and kicking, spitting and snarling like a cat, and as she passed Tungata, she shrieked at him.

"Traitor, we will eat you! Jackal, you will die—"

Tungata stared at her with bovine indifference.

One of the constables picked up the naked infant from where the girl had abandoned it, and he exclaimed immediately, "It's cold." He turned the body gingerly, and the tiny limbs sprawled lifelessly. "It's dead!" The constable's voice was shocked, and then he started again. "Look! Look at this!"

The child's body had been gutted like that of a fish. The cut ran upward from its groin, across its stomach, through the sternum of the chest to the base of the little throat, and the wound had been closed with sacking twine and crude cobbled stitches. The white police captain, with a sickly expression on his face, snipped the stitches, and the body cavity bulged open. It was packed with ropes of brown plastic explosive.

"All right." The captain stood up. "Hold them all. We will run a full check on every one of the bastards."

Then the captain came to Tungata. "Well done, friend." He clapped Tungata's shoulder. "You can claim your reward from the main police station. Five thousand dollars— that's good, hey! You just give them this." He scribbled on his notebook and tore off the sheet. "That's my name and

466

rank. I will witness your claim. One of our Land Rovers will be going into Bulawayo in a few minutes—I'll see you get a lift into town."

Tungata submitted docilely to the customary search by the guards at the gates to Khami Mission Hospital. He was still dressed in his laborer's rags and carrying the forged discharge from the Wankie collieries.

One of the guards glanced at the work papers. "What is wrong with you?"

"I have a snake in my stomach."

Tungata clasped his hands over the offending organ. A snake in the stomach could mean anything from colic to duodenal ulcers.

The guard laughed. "The doctors will cut out your mamba for you; go to the outpatient department." He pointed out the side entrance, and Tungata went up the driveway with an ungainly, sloppy gait.

The Matabele nurse at the outpatient desk recognized him with a flicker of surprise; then her expression went deadpan and she made out a card for him and waved him to one of the crowded benches. A minute or two later the black sister rose from the desk and crossed to the door marked "Duty Doctor." She went in and closed the door behind her.

When she came out again, she pointed at Tungata. "You next!" she said.

Tungata shambled across the hall and went in through the same door. Leila St. John came joyfully to meet him as soon as he closed the door behind him.

"Comrade Commissar!" she whispered, and embraced him. "I was so worried!" She kissed him on each cheek, and as she stepped back, Tungata had changed character from dull-witted peasant to deadly warrior, tall and dangerously cold-faced.

"You have clothes for me?"

Behind the movable screen, Tungata changed swiftly and stepped out again buttoning the white laboratory coat. On his lapel he wore a plastic dog tag that identified him as "Dr. G. J. Kumalo," which placed him immediately above idle suspicion.

"I would like to know what arrangements you have made," he said, and seated himself facing Leila St. John across her desk.

"I have had the Umlimo in our geriatric ward since she was brought in by her followers from the Matapos Reservation about six months ago."

"What is her physical condition?"

"She is a very old lady—'ancient' is perhaps the better word. I see no reason to doubt her claim that she is a hundred and twenty years old. She was already a young woman when Cecil Rhodes's freebooters rode into Bulawayo and hunted King Lobengula to his death."

"Her condition, please."

"She was suffering from malnutrition, but I have had her on a nutritional drip and she is much stronger, though she cannot walk, nor is she in control of her bowels and bladder. She is an albino, and she suffers from a type of skin allergy, but I have been able to prescribe an antihistamine ointment which has given her a great deal of relief. Her hearing and eyesight are failing, but her heart and other vital organs are remarkably strong for her age. Moreover, her brain is sharp and clear. She appears to be totally lucid."

"So she can travel?" Tungata insisted.

"She is eager to do so. It is her own prophecy that she must cross the great waters before the spears of the nation prevail."

Tungata made an impatient gesture, and Leila St. John interpreted it.

"You do not set any store by the Umlimo, and her predictions, do you, comrade?"

"Do you, Doctor?" he asked.

"There are areas which our sciences have not yet penetrated. She is an extraordinary woman. I don't say I believe everything about her, but I am aware of a force within her."

"It is our estimate that she will be extremely valuable as a propaganda weapon. The great majority of our people are still uneducated and superstitious. You still have not answered my question, Doctor. Can she travel?"

"I think she can. I have prepared medications for her to take on the journey. I have also made out medical certificates, which should be sufficient to see her safely through any security checks as far as the border with Zambia. I will provide one of my best medical orderlies, a black male nurse, to travel with her. I would go myself, but it would attract too much attention."

Tungata was silent for a long time, his hard, handsome features rapt in thought. He had such a presence of command and authority that Leila found herself waiting almost timidly for his next words, eager to respond whether they were command or question.

However, when he spoke, it was to muse softly. "The woman is as valuable dead as alive, and dead she would be easier to handle, I presume you could preserve her body in fomaldehyde or something of that nature?"

Despite herself Leila was shocked, and yet strangely awed by the ruthlessness, excited by the man's deadly resolve.

"I pray that won't be necessary," she whispered, staring at him. She had never met a man like this.

"I will see her first, then I will decide," Tungata said quietly. "I wish to do so immediately."

There were three weird crones squatting outside the door of the private ward on the top floor in the south wing of the hospital. They were dressed in the dried skins of wild cat and jackals and pythons, and hung about the neck and waist with bottles and gourds and stoppered buckhorns, with dried goat bladders and bone rattles, with phials and the leather bags that contained their divining bones.

"These are the old woman's followers," Leila St. John explained. "They will not leave her."

"They will," said Tungata softly, "when I decide that they will."

One of them hopped toward him, whining and sniveling, reaching out to touch his leg with filth-encrusted fingers, and Tungata spurned her aside with his foot and opened the door to the private ward. He went in, and Leila followed him and closed the door behind them. It was a small room with bare tiled floor, and the walls were painted with a white gloss paint. There was a bedside locker with a stainless steel tray of medicines and instruments upon it. The bed was on casters, with an adjustable handle and screw at the foot. The head of the bed frame was raised, and the frail figure under the single sheet seemed no larger than a child. There was the glass bowl of a drip suspended above the bed, and a transparent plastic tube snaked down from it.

The Umlimo was asleep. Her unpigmented skin was a dusty gray, crusted with dark scabs that extended up over the bald scalp. The skin that covered her skull was so thin and fragile that the bone seemed to shine through it like a water-worn pebble beneath the surface of a mountain stream; but from her brow down to the edge of the white sheet beneath her chin, the skin was impossibly wrinkled and folded, like that of some prehistoric relic from the age of the great reptiles. Her mouth was open, the scabbed lips trembled with each breath, and there was a single yellow worn tooth left in the desiccated gray gums. She opened her eyes. They were pink as those of a white rabbit, sunk deeply in folds of gray skin, swimming in their own gummy mucus.

"Greetings, old Mother." Leila went to her and touched the age-ravaged cheek. "I have a visitor for you," she said in perfect Sindebele.

The old woman made a small keening sound in her throat, and she began to shake, her entire body taken by convulsions as she stared at Tungata.

"Calm yourself, old Mother." Leila was concerned. "He will not harm you."

The old woman lifted one arm from under the sheet. It was skeletal, the elbow joint enlarged and distorted by arthritic processes; the hand was a claw, with lumpy knuckles and twisted fingers. She pointed them at Tungata.

"Son of kings," she wailed, her voice surprisingly clear and strong, "father of kings. King that will be, when the falcons return. Bayete, he that will be king, Bayete!" It was the royal salute, and Tungata went rigid with shock. His own skin-tone changed to dark gray, and little blisters of sweat burst out upon his brow. Leila St. John fell back until she was against the wall. She stared at the frail old woman in the high steel bed. Spittle frothed on the thin, scabbed lips, and the pink eyes rolled back into the ancient skull, yet the wailing voice rose higher.

"The falcons have flown afar. There will be no peace in the kingdoms of the Mambos or the Monomotapas until they return. He who brings the stone falcons back to roost shall rule the kingdoms." Her voice rose to a shriek. "Bayete, Nkosi Nkulu. Hail, Mambo. Live forever, Mono-motapa." The Umlimo greeted Tungata with all the titles of the ancient rulers and then collapsed against the soft white pillows. Leila hurried back to her side and placed her fingers over the sticklike wrist.

"She's all right," she said after a moment, and looked up at Tungata. "What do you want me to do?"

He shook himself like a man awakening from deep sleep and, with the sleeve of his white coat, wiped the icy sweat of superstitious dread from his forehead.

"Look after her well. Make sure she is ready to leave by morning. We will take her north across the great river," he said.

◆ ◆ ◆

Leila St. John backed up her small Fiat into the ambulance bay beside the casualty department, and, screened from curious eyes, Tungata slipped through the back door and crouched down between the seats. Leila spread a mohair traveling rug over him and drove down to the main gates. She spoke briefly to one of the guards and then swung the Fiat onto the branch road that led to the superintendent's residence.

She spoke without looking back or moving her lips.

"No sign of security forces—not yet. It looks as though your arrival has gone unnoticed, but we will take no chances."

She parked in the lean-to garage which had been added to the old stone-walled building, and while she unloaded her valise and a pile of files from the seat, she made certain they were still not observed. The garden was screened from the road and the thatched church by trellised creepers and flowering shrubs.

She opened the side door to the house and said, "Please keep low, and go in as quickly as you can."

He ducked out of the Fiat, and she followed him into the living room. The shutters and curtains were drawn and it was half-dark.

"My grandmother built this house after the original was burned down during the 1896 troubles. Fortunately she took precautions against the troubles of the future."

Leila crossed the floor of sawn Rhodesian teak, the highly polished surface of which was strewn with tanned animal skins and handwoven rugs in bold patterns and primary colors.

She entered the walk-in stone fireplace and drew aside

the black grate. The floor of the fireplace was of slate flags, and she used the fire irons to prize and lift one of these. When Tungata stepped up beside her, he saw that she had exposed a square vertical shaft into one wall of which were set stone steps.

"This was where Comrade Tebe was hiding that night?" Tungata asked. "When the Scouts, the *kanka*, could not find him?"

"Yes, he was here. It would be best if you went down now."

He dropped nimbly down the shaft and found himself in darkness. Leila closed the slate hatch and came down beside him. She groped along the wall and turned a switch. A bare electric bulb lit on the roof of the tiny stone cell. There was a deal table on which were stacked a few well-thumbed books. Pushed beneath it was a low stool, and there was a narrow truckle bed against the far wall. A chemical toilet stood at its foot.

"Not very comfortable," she apologized. "But nobody will find you here."

"I have had less luxurious accommodations," he assured her. "Now let us go over your arrangements."

She had the medical certificates ready on the table, and she sat on the stool and wrote down his requirements for the transportation of the Umlimo as he dictated them.

When she had finished, he said, "Memorize that and destroy it."

"Very well."

He watched while she went over the list carefully and then looked up.

"Now, there is a message for you to take to Comrade Inkunzi," she said. "It is from our friend in high places."

"Give it to me." He nodded.

"Ballantyne's Scouts, the *kanka*, they are planning a special operation. It is to destroy Comrade Inkunzi and his staff. Your own name is high on their list."

Tungata's expression did not change. "Do you have any details of their plans?"

"All the details," she assured him. "This is what they will do—"

She spoke slowly and deliberately for almost ten minutes, and he did not interrupt her. Even when she had finished, he was silent for many minutes, lying flat on his back on

472

the bed, staring up at the electric bulb. Then she saw that his jaws clenched and that a smoky red tide seemed to have spread over his eyeballs. His voice, when he spoke, was thick with loathing.

"Colonel Roland Ballantyne. If we could get him! He is responsible for the deaths of over three thousand of our people—he and his *kanka*. In the camps they speak his name in whispers, as though he were some sort of demon. His name alone turns our bravest men to cowards. I have seen him and his butchers at work. Oh, if we could only take him." He sat up and glared at her. "Perhaps—" His voice was choked and slurred as though he was drunk with hatred. "Perhaps this is our chance."

He reached out and took Leila by the shoulders. His fingers dug deeply into her flesh, and she winced and tried to draw away. He held her without effort.

"This woman of his. You say that she will fly from Victoria Falls? Can you get me the date, the number of the flight, the exact time?"

She nodded, afraid of him now, terrified by his strength and fury.

"We have somebody in the airway booking office," she whispered, no longer trying to escape the agony of his grip. "I can get it for you."

"The bait," he said, "the tender lamb that will lure the leopard into the trap."

◆ ◆ ◆

She brought him food and drink down the stone shaft and waited while Tungata ate.

For a while he ate in silence, then abruptly he returned to the subject of the Umlimo.

"The stone falcons," he started. "You heard what the old woman said?"

She nodded and he went on. "Tell me what you know of these things."

"Well, the stone falcons are the emblem on the flag. They are minted on the coinage of this country."

"Yes, go on."

"They are ancient carvings of bird figures. They were discovered in the ruins of Zimbabwe by the early white adventurers and stolen by them. There is a legend that Lobengula tried to prevent them, but they were taken south."

"Where are they now?" Tungata demanded.

"One of them was destroyed by fire when Cecil Rhodes's house at Groote Schuur was burned down, but the others, I'm not absolutely certain, but I think they are at Cape Town in South Africa."

"Whereabouts?"

"In the museum there."

He grunted and went on eating steadily. When the bowl and mug were empty, he pushed them aside and stared at her again with those smoky eyes.

"The words of the old woman," he began and then paused.

"The prophecy of the Umlimo," she went on for him, "is that the man who returned the falcons would rule this land, and that you were that man."

"You will tell nobody what she said—do you understand me?"

"I will tell nobody," she promised.

"You know that if you do, I will kill you."

"I know that," she said simply, and gathered the bowl and mug and replaced them on the tray.

She stood before him waiting, and when he did not speak again, she asked, "Is there anything else?"

He went on staring at her, and she dropped her eyes.

"Do you wish me to stay?"

"Yes," he said, and she turned to the light switch.

"Leave the light," he ordered. "I want to see your whiteness."

The first time she cried out, it was in fear and pain, the second time—and the uncounted times after that—was in mindless, incoherent transports of ecstasy.

◆　◆　◆

Douglas Ballantyne had selected a dozen of the finest slaughter-beasts from the herds of King's Lynn and Queen's Lynn. The prime carcasses had hung in the cold room for three weeks until they were perfect. They were being barbecued whole on the open coal pits at the bottom of the gardens. The kitchen servants of Queen's Lynn worked in relays, turning the spits and basting the sizzling, golden carcasses amid clouds of fragrant steam.

There were three bands to provide continuous music. The caterers had been flown in with all their equipment from Johannesburg, and paid suitable danger money for entering the war zone. The gardens of every homestead for fifty miles around had been ransacked for flowers and the marquees were filled with banks of floral decorations, of roses and poinsettia and dahlia in fifty blazing shades of color.

Bawu Ballantyne had chartered a special aircraft to bring the liquor up from South Africa. There was a little over four tons' weight of fine wines and spirits. After searching his political conscience, Bawu had even decided to suspend his personal sanctions against the United Kingdom of Great Britain and Ireland for the duration of the wedding festivities and had included one hundred cases of Chivas Regal whisky in the shipment. This was his most valuable contribution to the preparations, but there had been others.

He had transferred some of his most potent and cherished Claymore mines across from the King's Lynn defenses and added them to the decorations in the Queen's Lynn gardens.

"You can never be too careful," he explained darkly when taxed with it. "If there is a terr attack during the ceremony—" He made the motion of pressing a button, and the entire family shuddered at the thought of a mushroom-shaped cloud hanging over Queen's Lynn. It had taken all their combined powers of persuasion to get him to remove his pets.

He had then sneaked into the kitchens and added an extra six bottles of brandy to the mix for the wedding cake. Fortunately Valerie had made a final tasting and, when she got her breath back, ordered the chef to bury it and start a new batch. From then on Bawu was banned from the kitchens in disgrace, and Douglas had drawn up a roster of family members to keep him under surveillance during the great day.

Craig had the first shift, from nine in the morning when the two thousand invited guests started arriving until eleven when Craig would hand over to a cousin and assume his other duties as Roland's best man. Craig had helped the old man dress in his uniform from the Kaiser's war. A local tailor had been brought out to King's Lynn to make the alterations, and the results were surprising. Bawu looked dapper and spry with his Sam Browne belt and swagger stick, and the double row of colored ribbons on his chest.

Craig was proud of him as he took up his position on the front veranda and looked over the crowded lawns, lifting his swagger stick in acknowledgment of the affectionate cries of "Hello, Uncle Bawu," brushing out his gleaming silver mustaches, and tipping the peak of his cap at a more debonair angle over one eye.

"Damn me, boy," he told Craig. "This whole business makes me feel quite romantic again. I haven't been married myself for nearly twenty years. I have a good mind to give it one last whirl!"

"There is always the widow Angus," Craig suggested, and his grandfather was outraged.

"That old crow!"

"Bawu, she is rich and only fifty."

"That's old, boy. Catch 'em young and train 'em well. That's my motto." Bawu winked at him. "Now how about that one?"

His choice was twenty-five years old, twice divorced already, wearing an unfashionable miniskirt and casting a bold eye about her.

"You can introduce me." Bawu gave his magnanimous permission.

"I think the Prime Minister wants to see you, Bawu." Craig searched desperately for a distraction before the pert little bottom under the miniskirt was soundly pinched. Craig had seen the old man flirting before. He left Bawu, gin and tonic in hand, giving Ian Smith a few tips on international diplomacy.

"You have to remember that these fellows, Callaghan and his friends, are working-class, Ian, my boy; you cannot treat them like gentlemen. They wouldn't understand that—"

And the Prime Minister, worn and tired and wan with his responsibilities, one eyelid drooping, his curly sandy hair receding, tried to hide his smile as he nodded.

"Quite right, Uncle Bawu, I'll remember that."

Craig felt safe to leave him for ten minutes, sure that the old man's opinions of the British Labour Government were good for at least that long, and he made his way swiftly through the crowds to where Janine's parents stood with a small group at the end of the veranda.

He insinuated himself unobtrusively into the circle and studied Janine's mother out of the corner of his eye. It gave him a hollow, aching feeling to recognize the same features, the jawline and deep forehead blurred only marginally by the passage of time. She had the same slanted eyes with the same appealing catlike cast to them. She caught his gaze and smiled at him.

"Mrs. Carpenter, I'm a good friend of Janine's. My name is Craig Mellow."

"Oh yes, Jan wrote about you in her letters." Her smile was warm, and her voice had haunting echoes of her daughter's. Craig found himself babbling away to her and could not prevent it—until softly and compassionately she said:

"She told me you were such a nice person. I am sorry, I truly am."

"I don't understand?" Craig stiffened.

"You love her very much, don't you?"

He stared at her miserably, unable to reply, and she touched his arm in understanding.

"Excuse me," he blurted. "Roland will be ready to dress; I must go." He stumbled and almost fell on the veranda steps.

"By God, Sonny, where have you been? I thought you were going to let me go into contact on my own," Roland shouted from the shower. "Have you got the ring?"

They waited side by side under the bower of fresh flowers in front of the makeshift altar which also was smothered with flowers. Roland wore full-dress uniform: the maroon beret with Bazo's head cap-badge, the colonel's crowns on his shoulders, the Silver Cross for valor on his breast, white gloves on his hands, and the gilt and tasseled sword at his waist.

In his simple police uniform, Craig felt gauche and drab, like a sparrow beside a golden eagle, like a tabby cat beside a leopard, and the waiting seemed to go on forever. Through it all, Craig clung to a hopeless notion that it was still not going to happen—that was the only way he could hold his despair at bay.

Then there was the triumphant swell of the bridal march, and down both sides of the carpeted aisle from the house, the crowds stirred and hummed with excitement and anticipation. Craig felt his soul begin the final plunge into cold and darkness; he could not bring himself to look around. He stared straight ahead at the face of the priest.

He had known him since childhood, but now he seemed a stranger; his face swam and wavered in Craig's vision.

Then he smelled Janine; even over the scent of the altar flowers, he recognized her perfume, and he almost choked on the memories it evoked. He felt the train of her dress brush against his ankle, and he moved back slightly and turned so that he could see her for the last time.

She was on her father's arm. The veil covered her hair and misted her face, but beneath its soft folds, he could see her eyes, those great slanted eyes, the indigo of a tropical sea, shining softly as she looked up at Roland Ballantyne.

"Dearly beloved, we are gathered together here in the sight of God, and in the face of his church, to join together this man and this woman in holy matrimony—"

Now Craig could not take his eyes from her face. She had never looked so lovely. She wore a crown of fresh violets, the exact color of her eyes. He still hoped that it would not happen, that something would prevent it.

"Therefore if any man can show any just cause, why they may not lawfully be joined together, let him now speak—"

He wanted to call out, to stop it. He wanted to shout, "I love her, she is mine," but his throat was so dry and painful that he could not draw breath enough through it. Then it was happening.

"I, Roland Morris, take thee, Janine Elizabeth, to have and to hold from this day forward—" Roly's voice was clear and strong and it raked Craig's soul to its very depths. After that nothing else mattered. Craig seemed to be standing a little away from it all, as though all the laughter and joy was on the other side of a glass partition; the voices were strangely muted, even the light seemed dulled as though a cloud had passed across the sun.

He watched from the back of the crowd, standing under the jacaranda trees, while Janine came out onto the veranda still carrying her bouquet of violets, dressed in her blue going-away ensemble. She and Roland were still hand in hand, but now he lifted her onto a tabletop, and there were feminine shrieks of excitement as Janine poised to toss her bouquet.

In that moment, she looked over their heads and saw Craig. The smile stayed on her lovely wide mouth, but something moved in her eyes, a dark shadow, perhaps of pity, perhaps even regret; then she threw the bouquet, one of her bridesmaids caught it, and Roland swept her down and away. Hand in hand, the two of them ran down the lawns to where the helicopter waited with its rotor already turning. They ran laughing, Janine clutching her wide-brimmed straw hat and Roland trying to shield her from the storm of confetti that swirled around them.

Craig did not wait for the machine to bear them away. He returned to where he had left the old Land Rover at the back of the stables. He drove back to the yacht. He stripped off his uniform, threw it onto the bunk, and pulled on a pair of silk jogging shorts. He went into the galley and from the refrigerator hooked out a can of beer. Sipping the froth, he went back into the saloon. A loner all his life, he had believed himself immune to the tortures of loneliness, and now he knew he had been mistaken.

By this time there was a stack of over fifty exercise books upon the saloon table, each of them filled from cover to cover with his penciled scrawl. He sat down and selected a pencil from the bunch stuck into an empty coffee mug like porcupine quills. He began to write, and slowly the corrosive agony of loneliness receded and became merely a slow, dull ache.

On Monday morning, when Craig walked into police headquarters on his way through to the armory, the member-in-charge called him into his office.

"Craig, I've got movement papers for you. You are being detached on special assignment."

"What is it?"

"Hell, I don't know. I just work here. Nobody tells me anything, but you are ordered to report to the area commander, Wankie, on the twenty-eighth—" The inspector broke off and studied Craig's face. "Are you feeling okay, Craig?"

"Yes, why do you ask?"

"You are looking bloody awful." He considered for a few moments. "I tell you what—if you sneak away from here on the twenty-fifth, you could give yourself a couple of days' break before reporting to your new assignment."

"You are the only star in my firmament, George." Craig grinned lopsidedly and thought to himself, "That's all I need, three days with nothing to do but feel sorry for myself."

♦   ♦   ♦

The Victoria Falls Hotel is one of those magnificent monuments to the great days of Empire. Its walls are as thick as those of a castle, but painted brilliant white. The floors are of marble, with sweeping staircases and colonnaded porticos; the ceilings are cathedral-high, with fancy plaster-work and gently revolving fans. The terraces and lawns stretch down to the very brink of the abyss through which the Zambezi River boils in all its fury and grandeur.

Spanning the gorge is the delicate steel tracery of the arched bridge of which Cecil Rhodes ordered, "I want the spray from the falls to wet my train as it passes on its way to the north." The spray hangs in a perpetual snowy mantle over the chasm, twisting and folding upon itself as the breeze picks at it, and always there is the muted thunder of falling water like the sound of storm surf heard from afar. When David Livingstone, the missionary explorer, first stood on the edge of the gorge and looked down into the somber, sunless depths, he said, "Sights such as these must have been gazed upon by angels in their flight." The Livingstone Suite, which looks out upon this view, was named after him.

One of the black porters who carried up their luggage told Janine proudly, "King Georgey slept here—and Missy Elizabeth, who is now the Queen, with her sister Margaret when they were little girls."

Roly laughed. "Hell, what was good enough for King Georgey!" And he grossly overtipped the grinning porters and fired the cork from the bottle of champagne that waited for them in a silver ice bucket.

They walked hand in hand along the enchanted path beside the Zambezi River, while the timid little spotted bushbuck scuttled away into the tropical undergrowth and the vervet monkeys scolded them from the treetops. They ran laughing hand in hand through the rain forests, under the torrential downpour of falling spray; Janine's hair melted down her face, and their sodden clothing clung to their bodies. When they kissed, standing on the edge of the high cliff, the rock trembled under their feet and the turmoil of air displaced by the volume of tumbling water buffeted them and flung the icy spray into their faces.

They cruised on the placid upper reaches of the river in

480

the sunset, and they chartered a light aircraft to fly over the serpentine gorge in the noon sun, and Janine clung to Roland in delicious vertigo as they skimmed the rocky lip of the gorge. They danced to the African steel band under the stars, and the other guests who recognized Roland's uniform watched them with pride and affection. "One of Ballantyne's Scouts," they told each other, "they are very special, the Scouts," and they sent wine to their table in the manorial dining room to mark their appreciation.

Roland and Janine lay late in bed in the mornings and had their breakfast sent up to them. They played tennis, and Roland lobbed his service and returned to her forehand. They lay in the sunlight beside the Olympic-sized pool and anointed each other with sun cream. In their brief bathing suits, they were magnificently healthy, clean young animals and so obviously in love that they seemed charmed and set apart. In the evenings they sat under the umbrella spread of the great trees on the terrace and drank Pimms No. 1 cup, and experienced a marvelous sense of defiance in flaunting themselves to the full view of their mortal enemies on the far side of the gorge.

Then one evening at dinner the manager stopped at their table.

"I understand that you are leaving us tomorrow, Colonel Ballantyne. We shall miss you both."

"Oh no!" Janine shook her head laughingly. "We are staying until the twenty-sixth."

"Tomorrow is the twenty-sixth, Mrs. Ballantyne."

◆ ◆ ◆

The head porter had all their luggage piled at the hotel entrance, and Roland was settling their bill. Janine waited for him under the portico. Suddenly she started as she recognized the battered old open Land Rover that swung in through the gates and parked in one of the open slots at the end of the lot.

Her first reaction, as she watched the familiar gawky figure untangle his long legs and flick the hair out of his eyes as he climbed out, was quick anger.

"He's come on purpose," she thought. "Just to try and spoil it all."

Craig came ambling toward her with his hands thrust into his pockets, but when he was less than a dozen paces from where she stood, he recognized her and his confusion was obviously unfeigned.

"Jan." He blushed furiously. "Oh my God, I didn't know you'd be here."

She felt her anger recede. "Hello, Craig dear. No, it was a secret, until now."

"I'm so dreadfully sorry—"

"Don't be, we are leaving anyway."

"Sonny boy." Roland came out of the doorway behind Janine and went to throw a brotherly arm around Craig's shoulders. "You are ahead of time. How are you?"

"You knew I was coming?" Craig looked even more confused.

"I knew," Roland admitted, "but not so soon. You were supposed to report on the twenty-eighth."

"George gave me a couple of days." Since that first, startled exchange, Craig had not looked at Janine again. "I thought I would spend them here."

"Good boy, you will need the rest. You and I are going to be doing a bit of work together. I tell you what, Sonny, let's have a quick drink. I'll explain it to you—some of it anyway."

"Oh, darling," Janine cut in swiftly, "we don't have time. I'll miss the flight." She could not bear the hurt and confusion in Craig's eyes another moment.

"Damn it, I suppose you are right." Roland checked his watch. "It will have to keep until I see you the day after tomorrow, Sonny." And at that moment the airways' bus drove into the hotel driveway. Roland and Janine were the only passengers in the minibus out to the airport.

"Darling, when will I see you again?"

"Look, I can't say for sure, Bugsy—that depends on so many things."

"Will you telephone me or write even?"

"You know I can't."

"I know, but I will be at the flat, just in case."

"I wish you would go out to live at Queen's Lynn— that's where you belong now."

"My job—"

"The hell with your job. Ballantyne wives don't work."

"Well, see here, Colonel, sir, this Ballantyne wife is going on working until—"

"Until?" he asked.

482

"Until you give me something better to do."

"Like what?"

"Like a baby."

"Is that a challenge?"

"Oh, please, Colonel, sir, do take it as one."

At the airport there was a cheerfully rowdy young crowd, all the men in uniform, come to see the aircraft leave. Most of them knew Roland, and they plied him and Janine with drinks. It made the last minutes more bearable. Then suddenly they were standing at the gate and the air hostess was calling for boarding.

"I shall miss you so," Janine whispered. "I shall pray for you."

He kissed her and held her so fiercely that she almost lost her breath.

"I love you," Roland said.

"You never said that before."

"No," he agreed. "Not to anybody before. Now go, woman—before I do something stupid."

She was the last in the straggling line of passengers that climbed the boarding ladder into the elderly Viscount aircraft parked on the hardstand. She wore a white blouse with a daffodil-yellow skirt and flat sandals. There was a matching yellow scarf around her hair and a sling bag over her shoulder. In the doorway of the aircraft at the top of the boarding ladder, she looked back, shading her eyes as she searched for Roland, and when she found him, she smiled and waved and then stepped through the fuselage door. The door closed and the boarding ladder wheeled away. The Rolls-Royce Dart turboprop engines whined and fired, and the silver Viscount, with the flying Zimbabwe bird emblem on its tail, taxied downwind to its holding point.

Cleared for takeoff, it lumbered back down the runway and climbed slowly into the air. Roland watched it bank onto its southerly heading for Bulawayo, and then went back into the airport building, showed his pass to the guard at the door, and climbed the steps to the control tower.

"What can we do for you, Colonel?" the assistant controller at the flight-planning desk greeted him.

"I am expecting a helicopter flight coming in from Wankie to pick me up—"

"Oh, you are Colonel Ballantyne—yes, we have your

bird on the plot. They were airborne twelve minutes ago. They will be here in an hour and ten minutes."

While they were talking, the flight controller at the picture windows was speaking quietly with the pilot of the departing Viscount.

"You are cleared to standard departure, unrestricted climb fifteen thousand feet. Over now to Bulawayo approach on one eighteen comma six. Good day!"

"Understand standard departure unrestricted climb to flight level—"

The pilot's calm, almost bored voice broke off, and the side band hummed for a few seconds. Then the voice came back crackling with urgency. Roland spun away from the flight-planning desk and strode to the controller's console. He gripped the back of the controller's chair and through the tall windows, stared up into the sky.

The high fair-weather clouds were already turning pink with the oncoming sunset, but the Viscount was out of sight, somewhere out there in the south. Roland's face was hard and terrible with anger and fear as he listened to the pilot's voice grating out of the radio speakers.

◆　◆　◆

The portable surface-to-air missile launcher, designated SAM-7, is a crude-looking weapon almost indistinguishable from the bazooka anti-tank rocket launcher of World War II. It looks like a five-foot section of ordinary drainpipe, but the exhaust end is slightly flared into the mouth of a funnel. At the point of balance, there is a shoulder plate below the barrel and an aiming and igniting device like a small, portable AM radio set attached to the upper surface of the barrel.

The weapon is operated by two men. The loader simply places the missile in the exhaust breech of the barrel and, making sure the fins engage the slots, pushes it forward until its rim engages the electrical terminals and locks it into the firing position. The missile weighs a little less than ten kilos. It has the conventional rocket shape, but in the front of the nose cone is an opaque glass eye, behind which is located the infrared sensor. The tail fins are steerable, enabling the rocket to lock onto and follow a moving target. The gunner settles the barrel across his shoulder, places the earphones on his head, and switches on the power pack. In the earphones he hears the cyclic tone of his audio warning. He tunes this down below the background infrared count so that it is no longer audible.

The weapon is now loaded and ready to fire. The gunner searches out his target through the crosshatched gunsight. As soon as an infrared source is detected by the missile's sensor, the audio warning begins to sound and a tiny red bulb lights up in the eye piece of the gunsight to confirm that the missile is "locked-on." It remains only for the gunner to press the trigger in the pistol-type grip, and the missile launches itself in relentless pursuit of its prey, steering itself to track it accurately through any turns or changes of altitude.

Tungata Zebiwe had held his cadre in position for four days. Apart from himself there were eight of them, and he had chosen each of them with extreme care. They were all veterans of proven courage and determination, but more importantly, they were all of superior intelligence and capable of operating under their own initiative. Every one of them had been trained in the use of the SAM-7 missile launcher, in both roles of loader and gunner, and each of them carried one of the finned missiles in addition to their AK 47 assault rifles, and the usual complement of grenades and AP mines. Any two of them could make the attack and had been thoroughly briefed to do so.

The wind direction would dictate the departure track of any aircraft leaving the main runway of Victoria Falls Airport. Wind velocity would also affect the aircraft's altitude as it passed over any specific point on the extended center-line and crosswind legs of its outward track. Fortunately for Tungata's calculations, the prevailing northeasterly wind had been blowing at a steady fifteen knots during the entire four days in which they had been in position.

He had chosen a small kopje, thickly wooded enough to give them good cover but not so thick that it impeded the view over the surrounding treetops. From the peak in the early mornings, before the heat haze and dust thickened, Tungata had been able to see the stationary silver cloud of spray that marked the Victoria Falls on the northern horizon.

Each afternoon they had practiced the attack drill. Half an hour before the expected time of departure of the scheduled Viscount flight from Victoria Falls to Bulawayo, Tungata had moved them into position: six men in a ring below the summit to guard against surprise attack by security forces, and three men above them in the actual attack group.

Tungata himself was the gunner, and his loader and backup loader had both been chosen for the acuteness of their hearing and the sharpness of their eyesight. On each of the three preceding afternoon drills, they had been able to hear the turboprop Rolls-Royce Dart engines minutes after takeoff. They were in climb power setting, and the whine was distinctive; it drew the eye to the tiny crucifix shape of the aircraft against the blue.

On the first afternoon, the Viscount had climbed almost directly over their kopje at not more than eight thousand feet in altitude, and Tungata had locked on and tracked it until it passed out of sight and then out of hearing. The second afternoon the aircraft had passed at about the same altitude, but five miles to the east of their position. That was extreme range for the missile. The audio signal had been weak and intermittent, and the lock-on bulb had glowed only fitfully. Tungata had to admit to himself that an attack would probably have failed. The third day the Viscount had been east of them again, three miles out. It would have been a good kill, so that the odds seemed to be about two to one in their favor.

This fourth day he moved the attack team into position on the summit fifteen minutes early and tested the SAM launcher by aiming it at the lowering sun. It howled in his ears at the excitation of that immense infrared source. Tungata switched off the power pack, and they settled down to wait, all their faces lifted to the sky.

His loader glanced at his wristwatch and murmured, "They are late."

Tungata hissed at him viciously. He knew they were late, and already the doubts were crowding in—flight delayed or canceled, even a leak in their own security; the *kanka* might already be on their way.

"Listen!" said his loader, and seconds later he heard it also, the faint whistling whine in the northern sky.

"Ready!" he ordered, and settled the shoulder plate into position and switched on the power pack. The audio warning had been preset, but he checked it again.

"Load!" he said. He felt the missile go into the breech and weight the barrel slightly tail-heavy. He heard the clunk of the rim seating itself against the terminals.

"Loaded!" his No. 2 confirmed, and tapped his shoulder.

He traversed left and right, making certain he was firmly settled, and his loader spoke again, "*Nansi!* There!" He extended his arm over Tungata's left shoulder, and pointed upward with his forefinger. Tungata searched, and then caught the high silver spark as the sunlight reflected off burnished metal.

"Target identified!" he said, and heard his two loaders move aside softly to avoid the backblast of the rocket.

The tiny speck grew swiftly in size, and Tungata saw that it was tracking to pass less than half a mile to the west of the hillock and that it was at least a thousand feet lower than it had been on the preceding afternoons. It was in a perfect position for attack. He picked it up in the cross wires of the gunsight, and the missile howled lustfully in his earphones, a wicked sound like a wolf pack hunting at full moon. The missile had sensed the infrared burn from the exhausts of the Rolls-Royce engines. In the gunsight the lock-on bulb burned like a fiery red Cyclops' eye, and Tungata pressed the trigger.

There was a stunning whoosh of sound, but almost no recoil from the weapon across his shoulder as it exhausted through the funnel vent in the rear. He was enveloped for microseconds in white fumes and whirling dust, but when they were whipped away by their own velocity, he saw the little silver missile going upward into the blue on the feather of its own rocket vapors. It was like a hunting falcon bating from the gloved fist, going up to tower above its quarry. Its speed was dazzling, so that it seemed to dwindle miraculously into nothingness, and there was only the faint, drumming rumble of its rocket burn.

Tungata knew that there was no time for a second launch. By the time they could reload, the Viscount would be well out of range. They stared up at the tiny, shiny aircraft, and the seconds seemed to flow with the slow viscosity of honey.

Then there was a little flick of liquid silver that distorted the perfect cruciform of the aircraft's wing profile. It popped open like a ripe cotton pod, and the Viscount seemed to lurch and yaw, then steady again. Seconds later they heard the crack of the strike to confirm what they had seen, and a hoarse roar of triumph burst up out of Tungata Zebiwe's throat.

As he watched, the Viscount banked into a gentle turn; then abruptly something large and black detached itself from the port wing and fell away toward the earth. The aircraft dropped its nose sharply, and the engine noise rose into a shrill, wild whine.

◆ ◆ ◆

Standing in the control tower, staring out through the floor-to-ceiling nonreflective glass window into the mellow evening sky and listening to the rapid, tense exchanges between the flight controller and the Viscount pilot, Roland Ballantyne was held in a paralyzing vise of helplessness and rage.

"Mayday! Mayday! Mayday! This is Viscount 782. Do you copy, tower?"

"Viscount 782, what is the nature of your emergency?"

"We have taken a missile strike on our port engine housing. We are engine out."

"Viscount 782, I query your assessment."

The pilot's tension and stress flared. "Damn you, tower, I was in 'Nam. It's a SAM hit, I tell you. I have activated the fire extinguishers and we still have control. I am initiating a one-hundred-eighty-degree turn!"

"We will have all emergency standby here, Viscount 782. What is your position?"

"We are eighty nautical miles outbound." The pilot's voice cracked. "Oh God! The port engine has gone. It's fallen clean out of her."

There was a long silence. They knew the pilot was fighting for control of the crippled machine, fighting the asymmetrical thrust of the remaining engine, which was trying to flip the Viscount over into a graveyard spiral, fighting the enormous weight transfer caused by the loss of the port engine. In the control tower, they were all frozen in silent agony, and then the radio speaker crackled and croaked. "Rate of descent three thousand feet a minute. Too fast. I can't hold her. We are going in. Trees. Too fast. Too many trees. This is it! Oh mother, this is it!"

Then there was no more.

◆ ◆ ◆

In the control tower, Roland sprang back to the flight-planning desk and snapped at the assistant controller. "Rescue helicopters!"

"There's only one helicopter within three hundred miles. That's your one coming in from Wankie."

"The only one—are you sure?"

"They have all been pulled out for a special op in the Vumba Mountains. Yours is the only one in this zone."

"Get me in touch with it," he ordered, and took the microphone from the controller as soon as contact was established.

"This is Ballantyne. We have lost a Viscount with forty-six crew and passengers," he said.

"I copied the transmissions," the helicopter pilot answered.

"You are the only rescue vehicle. What is your ETA?"

"I'm fifty minutes out."

"What personnel do you have aboard?"

"I have Sergeant Major Gondele and ten troopers."

Roland had planned to rehearse night jump landings during the return to Wankie. Gondele and his Scouts would be in full combat gear, and they would have Roland's personal pack and weapons aboard.

"I'll be waiting on the tarmac for your pickup. We will have a doctor with us," he said. "This is Cheetah One standing by."

◆ ◆ ◆

Janine Ballantyne had the aisle seat in the second to last row on the port side of the Viscount. In the window seat was a teenage girl with braces on her teeth and pigtails in her hair. The girl's parents were in the seats directly in front of her.

"Did you go to the crocodile farm?" she demanded of Janine.

"We didn't get around to it," Janine admitted.

"They have got a huge big croc there, he's five meters long. They call him Big Daddy," the girl burbled.

The Viscount had stabilized in its climb attitude, and the seat belt lights went out. From the seat behind Janine the blue-uniformed hostess stood up and went forward along the aisle.

Janine glanced across the aisle, across the two empty seats, through the Perspex porthole. The lowering sun was a big sullen red ball, wearing a mustache of purple cloud. The forest roof was a sea of dark green that spread away in all directions below them, its monotony broken by an occasional pimple of higher ground.

"My Daddy bought me a T-shirt with 'Big Daddy' on it, but it's in my case—"

There was a shattering crash, a great swirling silver cloud obscured the portholes, and the Viscount lurched so wildly that Janine was hurled painfully against her safety belt. The air hostess was flung upward against the roof of the cabin, and she fell back like a broken doll and lay twisted across the back of one of the empty seats. There was a cacophony of shrieks and screams from the passengers, and the girl clung desperately to Janine's arm, shrilling incoherently. The cabin tilted sharply but smoothly as the aircraft banked, and then suddenly the Viscount plunged forward and swung viciously from side to side.

The safety belt held Janine in her seat, but it felt like an insane roller coaster ride down the sky. Janine leaned over and hugged the child to try and still her piercing screams. Although her head was being whipped from side to side, Janine got a glimpse out of the porthole and saw the horizon turning like the spokes of a spinning wheel, and it made her feel giddy and nauseated. Then abruptly she focused on the silver wing of the aircraft below her. Where the streamlined engine nacelle had been was a ragged hole. Through it she could see the fluffy roof of the forest. The torn wing was flexing and twisting; she could see the wrinkles appearing in the smooth metal skin. Her ears were popping and creaking with the violent pressure change, and the trees were rushing toward her in a somber green blur.

She tore the child's arms from around her neck and forced her head down into her own lap. "Hold your knees," she shouted. "Keep your face down." And she did herself what she had ordered.

Then they hit, and there was a deafening rending, roaring, crashing tumult. She was flung mercilessly about in her seat, tumbled and battered, blinded and stunned and hammered by flying pieces of debris.

It seemed to go on forever. She saw the roof above her clawed away and blinding sunlight struck her for an instant. Then it was gone, and something hit her across one shin. Clearly, above all the other sounds, she heard her own bone break, and the pain shot up her spine into her skull. End over end she was hurled; and then another blow in the back of the neck, and her vision exploded into shooting sparks of light through a black, singing void.

When she recovered consciousness, she was still in her seat, but hanging upside down from her safety strap. Her face felt engorged with the blood that had flowed into it, and her vision wavered and swam like a heat mirage. Her head ached. It felt as though a red-hot nail was being driven into the center of her forehead with a sledgehammer.

She twisted slowly and saw that her broken leg was hanging down in front of her face, the toe pointing where the heel should have been.

"I will never walk again," she thought, and the horror of it braced her. She reached for the release on the buckle of her safety belt and then remembered how many necks are broken from a release in the upside-down position. She hooked her elbow through the arm of her seat and then lifted the release. Her hold on the seat flipped her as she fell, and she landed on her hip with her broken leg twisted under her. The pain was too much and she lost consciousness again.

It must have been hours later that she awoke again, for it was almost dark. The silence was frightening. It took her many groggy seconds to realize where she was, for she was looking at grass and tree trunks and sandy earth.

Then she realized that the fuselage of the Viscount had been severed just in front of her seat, as though by a guillotine; the tail section was all that was left around her. Over Janine's head the body of the child who had been her seating partner still hung by its strap. Her arms dangled below her head, and her blond pigtails pointed at the earth. Her eyes were wide open and her face contorted with the terror in which she had died.

Janine used her elbows to crawl out of the shattered fuselage, dragging her leg behind her, and she felt the coldness and nausea of shock sweep over her. Still on her stomach, she retched and vomited until she was too weak to do anything else but let herself sink back into the darkness in her head. Then she heard a sound in the silence, faint at first, but growing swiftly in volume.

It was the wackety-wackety-wack of a helicopter's rotors. She looked up at the sky, but it was shrouded by the roof of the forest overhead, and she realized that the last rays of daylight had gone and the swift African night was rushing down upon the earth.

"Oh, please!" she screamed. "Here I am. Please help me!" But the sound of the helicopter grew no louder; it seemed to pass only a few hundred meters from where she lay under the concealing trees, and then the sound of its rotors receded as swiftly as the darkness came on, and at last there was silence.

"A fire," she thought. "I must start a signal fire."

She looked around her wildly, and almost within reach of where she lay was the crumpled body of the blond girl's father, who had been in the seat in front of her. She crawled to him, and touched his face, running her finger lightly over his eyelids. There was no flicker of response. She sobbed and drew back and then steeled herself and returned once more to search the dead man's pockets. The disposable Bic plastic cigarette lighter was in the side pocket of his jacket. At the first flick, it gave her a pretty yellow flame, and she sobbed again—this time with relief.

◆ ◆ ◆

Roland Ballantyne sat in the copilot's seat of the Super Frelon helicopter and peered down at the treetops only two hundred feet below him. It was so dark that the occasional clearing in the forest was a mere pale, leprous patch. There was no definition in the treetops; they were a dark, amorphous mattress. Even when the light had been stronger, the chances of spotting wreckage below the treetops had been remote. Of course there was the possibility that part of a wing or tail section had torn off and been left hanging high up and in easy view. However, they could not trust to that.

At first they were looking for damage to the treetops, a blaze of lopped branches or the telltale white splotches of torn bark and raw, wet wood. They were looking for a signal flare, or for smoke, or the chance reflection of the late sun off bare metal, but then the light started to go. Now they were flying in desperation, waiting for, but not really believing, they would see a signal flare or a torch or even a fire.

Roland turned to the pilot and shouted in the rackety cabin.

"Landing lights. Switch them on!"

"They will overheat and burn out in five minutes," the pilot bellowed back. "No good!"

"One minute on, and one minute off to cool again," Roland told him. "Try it." The pilot reached for the switch, and below them the forest was lit with the cruel bluish-white glare of the phosphorous lamps. The pilot dropped even closer to the earth.

The shadows below the trees were stark and black. In one clearing they trapped a small herd of elephants. The animals were monstrous and unearthly in the flood of light, with their tentlike ears extended in alarm. Then the helicopter bore on and plunged them back into utter darkness.

Back and forth they flew, covering the corridor which the Viscount must have followed on her outward track, but that was one hundred nautical miles long and ten wide— one thousand square miles. It was full night now, and Roland glanced at the luminous dial of his wristwatch. It was nine o'clock, almost four hours since the Viscount had gone down. If there were survivors, they would be dying by now from the cold and shock, from loss of blood and internal injuries, while here in the main cabin of the Super Frelon there was a doctor with twenty quarts of plasma, with blankets— with the chance of life.

Grimly Roland stared down into the brilliant circle of white light as it danced over the treetops like the spotlight over a theatrical stage, and there was a cold and desolate despair in him that seemed slowly to numb his limbs and paralyze his resolve. He knew she was down there, so close, so very close, and yet he was helpless.

Suddenly he bunched his right fist and slammed it into the metal partition at his side. The skin smeared from his knuckles, and the pain shot up his arm to the shoulder, but the pain was a stimulant, and in it he found his anger again. He cupped the anger to him, the way a man shelters a candle flame in a high wind.

In the seat beside him, the pilot checked the time lapse on his stopwatch and then switched off the landing lights to cool them. The blackness that followed was more intense for the brilliance that had preceded it. Roland's night sight was destroyed, his vision filled with wriggling insects of starred light, and he was forced to cover his eyes with his hands for a few seconds to rest them and let them readjust.

So he did not see the tiny dull red spark down below him

that showed through the forest tops for the smallest part of a second and then was left behind as the Super Frelon roared back on the next leg of its search pattern.

◆ ◆ ◆

Janine had gathered a pile of dried grass and twigs and built them up into a cone ready for the flame of the lighter. It had been difficult work. She had dragged herself slowly backward on her buttocks and hands, with her broken leg sliding along after her as she gathered the kindling from the nearest bushes. Each time her leg caught or twisted over an irregularity of the torn earth, she almost fainted again with the pain.

Once she had the fire ready, she had laid the plastic lighter beside it and fallen back to rest. Almost immediately the night cold struck through her thin clothing, and she began to shiver uncontrollably. It required an enormous effort of will to force herself to move again, but she started back toward the shattered tail section of the Viscount. It was still just light enough to make out the trail of devastation that the main forward section of the aircraft had smashed through the forest.

There were pieces of metal and burst luggage and bodies littered down this dreadful pathway, although the main wreckage, carried on by its own weight, was not in sight from where she lay.

Once again Janine called, "Is anybody there, is anybody else alive?" But the night was silent. She dragged herself on.

The lighter tail section in which Janine had been seated must have struck one of the larger trees as the fuselage broadsided, and it had been sheered off neatly. The whiplash of impact had broken the necks of the passengers around her—only the fact that Janine had been leaning forward with her face pressed into her lap had saved her.

Janine reached the severed tail end and raised herself to peer in, avoiding looking at the body of the teenage girl which still hung upside down from her inverted seat. The storage cupboards forward of the aircraft's galley had broken open, and in the gloom she could make out a treasure-house of blankets and canned food and drink. She dragged herself inchingly toward it. The feel of a woolen blanket around her shoulders was a blessed boon, and then thirstily she drank two cans of bitter lemon before searching further through the spilled and jumbled contents of the storage cupboard.

She found the first aid kit and splinted and strapped her leg as best she could. The relief was immediate. There were disposable syringes and a dozen ampules of morphine in the kit. The prospect of a surcease from agony was an acute temptation, but she knew it would dull her, and inactivity or the inability to respond swiftly would be mortally dangerous in the long hours of darkness that lay ahead. She was still playing with the temptation when she heard the helicopter again.

It was coming swiftly toward her—she dropped the syringe and lunged clumsily toward the gaping hole in the fuselage. She tumbled out onto the dusty earth, a fall of almost three feet, and the pain of her leg anchored her for seconds. Then, through it, she heard the whistle and throbbing beat of the helicopter coming toward her.

She clawed her fingers into the earth and bit into her bottom lip until she tasted blood in her mouth to subdue the pain as she dragged herself toward the pile of kindling. By the time she reached it, the helicopter engine was a vast roaring in her head, and the sky above the forest was lightening with a bluish-white glow. She flicked the plastic lighter and held the tiny flame to the dried grass. It flared up swiftly.

She lifted her face to the sky, and in the light of the fire and the growing glare of the landing lights, her cheeks were smeared with dust and dried blood from the cut in her scalp, and wet with the new tears of mingled agony and hope that slid from under her swollen eyelids.

"Please," she prayed. "Oh, sweet, merciful God, please let them see me."

The landing lights grew stronger, dazzling, blinding—and then suddenly went out. Darkness struck her like a club. The sound of the helicopter passed over her, and she felt the buffeting downdraft of air from the rotors. For a brief instant, she saw the black sharklike shape of it silhouetted against the stars—and then it was gone, and the sound of the spinning rotors sank swiftly into silence.

In that silence she heard her own wild shrieks of despair. "Come back! You can't leave me! Please come back!"

She recognized the hysteria in her own voice and thrust

her fist into her mouth to gag it, but still the savage, uncontrollable sobs racked her whole body, and the coldness of the night was made unbearable by the icy grip that despair had upon her.

She crawled closer to the fire. She had been able to gather only a few handfuls of twigs. It would not last long, but the yellow and orange flames gave her a brief warmth and a moment of comfort in which to regain control. She gave one last choking, gasping sob and bit down upon it. She closed her eyes and counted slowly to ten, and felt herself steadying.

She opened her eyes, and across the fire from her, at the level of her own eyes, she saw a pair of canvas jungle boots. Slowly she lifted her eyes and shaded them from the fire with one hand. She made out the form of a man, a tall man, and the flickering light of the fire lit his face. He was looking down at her with an expression she could not fathom—perhaps it was compassion.

"Oh, thank you, God," Janine whispered. "Oh, thank you." She began to drag herself toward the man. "Help me," she croaked. "My leg is broken—please help me."

♦ ♦ ♦

Standing on the peak of the kopje, Tungata Zebiwe watched the stricken aircraft tumble down the sky like a high-flighting duck hit by shot. He threw the empty rocket launcher aside, and he lifted both hands above his head, fists clenched, and shook them in triumph to the heavens.

"It is done," he roared, "they are dead!" His face was swollen with the raging blood of the berserker, and his eyes were smoky like the glow of slag upon the tip when it comes red-hot from the blast furnace.

Behind him his men shook their weapons above their heads, caught up like Tungata in the divine killing madness of the victors, the atavistic instinct come down from their forefathers who had formed the fighting bull and raced in on the horns to the stabbing.

As they watched, the Viscount fell toward the forest top, and then at the very last moment it seemed to check. The nose of the tiny silver machine came up out of its death dive, and for a fleeting few seconds, it seemed to fly parallel with the earth. Then it touched the treetops and was instantly snatched from view, but the crash site was so close that Tungata had been able to hear, if only very faintly, the shattering impact of metal against trees and earth.

"Mark it!" Tungata sobered. "Comrade, the compass! Get a fix on it!" He remeasured the distance with his eye. "About six miles—we can be there by dark."

They moved out from the base of the kopje in their running formation, in the haft and spearhead, the flanks covering the bearers of the heavy equipment and the point breaking trail and clearing for ambush. They moved fast, at a pace just below a jog trot that would carry them seven kilometers to the hour. Tungata was running the point himself, and every fifteen minutes he halted and went down on one knee to check the bearing on the compass. Then he was up and, with an overhead pump of his fist, signaled the advance. They went on, swiftly and relentlessly.

As the light started to fade, they heard the helicopter, and Tungata gave the sidearm cutout signal that dropped them into cover. The helicopter passed a mile to the east, and he got them up and took them on for ten minutes more before stopping again.

He brought in his wing men and told them quietly, "We are here—the machine is lying within a few hundred meters of us."

They looked around them at the forest; the tall, twisted columns of tree trunks seemed to reach as high as the darkening heaven. Through a chink in the leafy roof of the forest, the evening star was a bright white prick of light.

"We will go into extended line," Tungata told them, "and sweep along the line of bearing."

"Comrade Commissar, if we stay too late, we will not be able to reach the river tomorrow. The *kanka* will be here at first light," one of his men pointed out diffidently.

"We will find the wreck," Tungata said. "Do not even think otherwise. That is why we have done this. To lay a trail for the *kanka* to follow. Now let us begin the search."

They moved like gray wolves through the forest, Tungata keeping them in line and on direction with a code of bird whistles like those of a nightjar. They went southward for twenty minutes by his watch, and then he pivoted his line, and they went back, moving silently, bowed under their packs but with the AK 47 rifles held at high port across their chests.

Twice more Tungata pivoted his line, and they searched back and forth, and the minutes drained away. It was past nine o'clock; there was a limit to how much longer he dared remain in the area of the wreck. His man had been right. First light would bring the avengers swarming out of the skies.

"One hour more," he told himself aloud. "We will search one hour more." Yet he knew that to leave without laying a hot scent for the jackals to follow was to abandon the most important part of the operation. He had to entice Ballantyne and his *kanka* to the killing ground that he had chosen so carefully. He had to find the wreck and leave something there for the *kanka* that would madden them, that would bring them rushing after him without regard to any of the consequences.

He heard the helicopter then, still far off, but coming back swiftly. Then he saw the glow of its landing lights on the treetops, and he gave the signal to put his line into cover. The helicopter passed within half a kilometer of where they lay. Its glaring eye confused and jumbled up the shadows beneath the trees, making them run across the forest floor like ghostly fugitives.

Abruptly the light was quenched, but the memory of it left a hot red spot on the retina of Tungata's eyeballs. They listened to the engine beat dwindle, and then Tungata whistled his men to their feet, and they went forward once more. Within two hundred paces, Tungata stopped again and sniffed the dank, cold air of the forest.

Woodsmoke! His heart jumped against his ribs, and he gave the soft, warbling birdcall that presaged danger. He slipped out of the shoulder straps of his heavy backpack and lowered it gently to earth. Then the line went forward again, moving lightly and silently. Ahead of Tungata something large and pale loomed from the darkness. He flicked his flashlight on. It was the nose section of the Viscount, the wings sheared off it, the fuselage shattered. It lay on its side, so that he could flash his beam through the windshield into the cockpit. The dead crew were still strapped into their seats. Their faces were bloodlessly pale, their eyes staring and glassy.

The line of guerrillas moved on quickly down the swath that the machine had hacked from the forest for itself. It was strewn with wreckage and debris—with clothing from the burst luggage hold, with books and newspapers that fluttered aimlessly in the small night breeze. In the litter the corpses seemed strangely peaceful and relaxed. Tungata turned his flashlight into the face of a gray-haired, middle-aged woman. She lay on her back with no visible injury. Her skirts were tucked modestly down below her knees, and her hands relaxed at her sides. However, her false teeth had been flung from her mouth, and it gave her the look of an ancient crone.

He passed her and went on. His men were stopping every few paces to hunt swiftly through the clothing of the dead or to examine an abandoned handbag or briefcase. Tungata wanted a live one. He needed a live one, and the dead were scattered all about him.

"The smoke," he whispered. "I smelled smoke."

And then ahead of him, at the very edge of the forest line, he saw a pretty little flower of flame, flickering and wavering in the gentle movement of air. He changed his grip on the rifle and slipped the selector onto semiautomatic fire. From the shadows he searched the area around the fire carefully and then stepped up to it. His jungle boots made no sound.

There was a woman lying beside the fire. She wore a thin yellow skirt, but it was stained with blood and dirt. The woman lay with her face in her arm. Her whole body was racked with gasping sobs. Her one leg below the skirt was roughly bound up with wooden splints and field bandages. Slowly she raised her head. In the feeble firelight, her eyes were dark as those of a skull, and the pale skin, like her clothing, was smeared with blood and dirt. She raised her head very slowly until she was looking up at him, and then words came tumbling out of her swollen lips.

"Oh, thank you, God," she blurted, and began to crawl toward Tungata, the leg slithering along behind her. "Oh, thank you. Help me!" Her voice was so hoarse and broken that he could barely understand the words. "My leg is broken—please help me!" She reached out and clasped his ankle.

"Please," she blubbered, and he squatted down beside her.

"What is your name?" he asked very gently, and his tone touched her, but she could not think—could not even remember her own name.

He started to stand, but she reached out in dreadful fear of being left alone again. She seized his hand.

"Don't go, please! My name—I'm Janine Ballantyne."

He patted her hand, almost tenderly, and he smiled. The quality of that smile warned her. It was savagely, joyfully triumphant. She snatched her hand away and pushed herself to her knees. She looked wildly about her. Then she saw the other dark figures that crowded out of the night around her. She saw their faces, the white gleam of teeth as they grinned down at her. She saw the guns in their hands and the glittering stare in their eyes.

"You," she gasped. "It's you!"

"Yes, Mrs. Ballantyne," Tungata said softly. "It is us."

He stood up and spoke to the men about him. "I give her to you. She is yours. Use her—but do not kill her. On your own lives, do not kill her—I want to leave her here alive."

Two of the men stepped forward and seized Janine's wrists. They dragged her away from the fire, behind the tail section of the wreckage. The other comrades laid down their rifles and followed them. They were laughing and bickering quietly over the order of preference and beginning to loosen their clothing.

At first the screams from the darkness were so shrill and harrowing that Tungata turned away and squatted over the fire, feeding it with twigs to distract himself, but very soon there were no more screams, only the soft sound of sobbing and the occasional sharper cry immediately muffled.

It went on for a long time, and Tungata's early disquiet was submerged and controlled. There was no passion or lust in this thing. It was an act of violence, of extreme provocation to a deadly enemy, an act of war, without guilt or compassion, and Tungata was a warrior.

One by one his men came back to the fire, adjusting their clothing. Strangely, they were subdued and stony-faced.

"Is it over?" Tungata looked up, and one of them stirred and half rose, looking inquiringly at Tungata. Tungata nodded.

"Be quick then," he said. "It is only seven hours to first light."

Not all of them went back behind the wreckage, but when they were ready to move out, Tungata did so.

Ballantyne's woman's naked white body was curled in the fetal position. She had chewed her lips until they were raw meat, and she blubbered softly and monotonously through them.

Tungata squatted beside her and took her face in his hands and twisted it up until he could look into her eyes. He shone his flashlight into them. They were the eyes of a wounded and terrified animal; perhaps she had already crossed over the line between sanity and madness. He could not be certain, so he spoke slowly, as though to a retarded child.

"Tell them my name is Tungata Zebiwe, the Seeker After What Has Been Stolen—the Seeker After Justice, After Vengeance," he said, and he stood up.

She tried to roll away from him, but pain stopped her, and as she covered her groin with both hands, he saw the thin spurt of fresh blood from between her fingers. He turned from her and picked up her stained yellow skirt from where it had been tossed over a bush. As he strode back to the fire, he stuffed the skirt into his pocket.

"*Lungela!*" he said. "All right, it is done. Move out!"

♦ ♦ ♦

At midnight the pilot yelled across at Roland Ballantyne. "We are almost out of fuel; we must go back. They have a tanker waiting for us on the apron."

For a few moments, Roland did not seem to understand. In the greenish reflection of the instrument panel, his face was expressionless, but his mouth was a thin, cruel slash and his eyes were terrible.

"Go quickly," he said. "And get back here quickly."

On the tarmac the Scouts' own doctor, Paul Henderson, was waiting to take over from the GP that Roland had picked up at Victoria Falls. Once he was aboard, Roland led Sergeant Major Gondele a little apart from the other troopers.

"If only we could know which way the bastards are headed," he murmured. "Are they going south, or are they heading back for the river? Are they going to try the drifts—and if so, which one?"

Esau Gondele recognized in him the need to talk, to say something merely to take his mind off the horror of what awaited them out there in the dark forest.

"We won't be able to follow them with the bird," he

501

said. "The forest is too thick. They would hear us from five miles and disappear."

"We can't follow with the chopper," Roland agreed. "They have got a SAM-7 with them. They would chop us out of the sky. The helicopter could be suicide—only way is to pick up their spoor and go after them on foot."

"They will have a night's start, a full night." Esau Gondele shook the great black cannonball of his head doubtfully.

"The cat cannot resist mauling the dead bird," Roland said. "Perhaps they have not yet started to run; perhaps they are drunk with blood; perhaps we can still take them."

"Ready to go!" the pilot shouted as the fuel tanker started up and backed away from the Super Frelon, and they ran back to the open port in the fuselage and scrambled aboard. The helicopter lifted swiftly, not wasting time in climbing, and roared away low over the dark bush.

At ten minutes to five o'clock the following morning, long before the sun had pushed up above the horizon but when the light was already strong enough to make out shapes and colors, Roland slapped the pilot's shoulder and pointed to port. The pilot banked the Super Frelon sharply in that direction. It was a broken branch; the underside of the leaves were lighter in color than those around it; it had been a flag to catch Roland's eye. Then there was another fleck of white, the raw stump of freshly broken branch sticking into the morning light. The pilot checked the Frelon, and they hovered fifty feet above it. They were staring down through the leafy canopy, and something white fluttered in the downdraft of the rotors.

"Go down!" Roland shouted, and as they sank lower, suddenly it was all there, broken wreckage and the debris of the dead, blowing aimlessly about in the windstorm of the rotors.

"There is a clearing!" Roland pointed, and as the helicopter settled toward it, the Scouts spilled out of her, jumping from fifteen feet to the earth and immediately spreading out into a defensive perimeter. Then Roland deployed them into a line of skirmishers, and they went forward into the swath line in quick rushes, ready to meet enemy fire. Within minutes they had cleared the area.

"Survivors!" Roland snapped. "Search for survivors!"

They went back down the swath, and in the dawn light the carnage was horrific. Beside each corpse a Scout paused briefly, but they were cold and stiff and the men went on. Roland reached the nose section and glanced through the windshield. There was nothing for the crew to do until the long green plastic body bags arrived. He turned back, searching frantically, looking for a scrap of bright yellow, the color of Janine's skirt.

"Colonel!" There was a faint shout from the forest edge.

Roland sprinted toward it. Sergeant Major Gondele was standing by the shattered tail section of the aircraft.

"What is it?" Roland demanded harshly, and then saw her.

Esau Gondele had covered Janine's naked body with a blue airways blanket from the wreck. She lay curled under it like a sleeping child with just her tousled head showing. Roland dropped on his knee and gently lifted the corner of the blanket. Her eyes were closed with swollen purple bruises, and her lips were raw, chewed flesh. For seconds he did not recognize her, and when he did, he believed that she was dead. He laid his open palm upon her cheek, and the skin was moist and warm.

She opened her eyes. They were mere slits in the abused flesh. She looked up at him, and the dull, lifeless eyes were more frightening than her torn and battered flesh. Then the eyes came alive—with terror. Janine screamed, and there was the ring of madness in the sound.

"Darling." Roland caught her up in his arms, but she fought him wildly, still screaming. Her eyes were mad and staring. Fresh blood oozed from the cracked scabs on her lips.

"Doctor!" Roland yelled. "Here! On the double!" And it took all his strength to hold her. She had thrown off the blanket, and, naked, she kicked and lashed out at him.

Paul Henderson came at the run and tore open his pack. He filled a syringe and muttered, "Hold her still!" as he swabbed her skin. He pressed in the needle and squeezed the clear contents of the syringe into her arm. She went on fighting and screaming for almost a minute and then gradually quietened and relaxed.

The doctor took her from Roland's arms and nodded to his assistant. The young medic orderly held up a blanket as a screen, and the doctor laid Janine on another.

"Get out of here," he snapped at Roland, and began his examination.

Roland picked up his rifle and stumbled to the tail section of the Viscount. He leaned against it, and his breathing was hoarse and ragged, but slowly it eased and he pushed himself upright.

"Colonel, sir." Esau Gondele appeared beside him. "We have picked up their spoor, incoming and outgoing."

"How long ago?"

"Five hours at the least, probably longer."

"Be ready to move out. We are going after them." Roland turned away from him. He needed to be alone just a little longer; he was not yet entirely under control.

Two of the Scouts came from the helicopter at a trot, carrying one of the yellow plastic body-molded stretchers between them.

"Colonel!" Paul Henderson tucked the blue blanket carefully around Janine's body, and then he and the orderly lifted her tenderly onto the yellow stretcher and tightened the straps to hold her. While the orderly prepared the plasma drip, the doctor led Roland a little aside.

"It's not very good news," he said softly.

"What did they do to her?" Roland asked, and Paul Henderson told him. Roland gripped the stock of the rifle so hard that his arms began to shudder and the muscles in his forearms stood out in ridges and hard knots.

"She is bleeding internally," Henderson finished. "I have to get her into the hospital very quickly. A unit that can handle this type of surgery—Bulawayo."

"Take the helicopter," Roland ordered brusquely.

They ran with the stretcher to the Super Frelon, the orderly holding the drip bottle high.

"Colonel," Henderson looked back. "She is still conscious. If you want—" He did not finish. The little group waited for Roland beside the fuselage, not certain whether to load the stretcher aboard.

With a strange reluctance, Roland walked heavily toward them. The enemy had used his woman. She was one thing that was sacred. How many of them? The thought made him check, and he had to force himself to go on to where she lay on the stretcher. He looked down at her. Only her face showed above the blanket. It was grotesquely swollen, and her mouth was a raw red ruin. Her once-lustrous hair was stiff with filth and dried blood, but her eyes were clear. The drug had driven back the madness, and now she was looking up at him. Only the eyes were the same, indigo blue.

Painfully her damaged lips framed a word, but no sound came. It was his name she was trying to say.

"Roland!"

And his revulsion rushed upon him; he could not hold it back. How many of them had taken her that way? A dozen? More? She had been his woman, but that had been destroyed. He tried to fight it, but he felt nauseated, and quick, cold sweat chilled his face. He tried to force himself to stoop over her, to kiss that terribly battered face, but he could not. He could not speak or move, and slowly the light of recognition went out in her eyes. It was replaced by that dull, empty look he had seen before, and then she closed the livid, swollen lids over them and rolled her head slowly away from him.

"Take good care of her," Roland muttered hoarsely, and they lifted the stretcher into the helicopter. Paul Henderson turned to him, his face twisted with pity and helpless anger, and he laid his hand on Roland's arm.

"Roly, it wasn't her fault," he said.

"If you say anything more, I might kill you." Roland's voice was thickened and coarsened by disgust and hatred.

Paul Henderson turned from him and clambered into the machine. Roland made a wind-up signal to the pilot in the bubble windshield above him, and the big, clumsy aircraft lifted noisily into the sky.

"Sergeant Major," Roland called. "Take the spoor!" And he did not look back as the helicopter rose high into the pink dawn and then swung away southward.

◆ ◆ ◆

They went in deep formation, so that if they ran into an ambush, the tail could circle and outflank the attackers to free the head. They went at storming speed, much too fast for safety, going hard as marathon runners. Within the first hour, Roland had ordered his Scouts to strip their packs. They abandoned everything but the radio set, their weapons and water bottles and first aid kits, and Roland pushed the pace still harder.

He and Esau Gondele took turns at point, the one dropping back each hour as the other came forward. They lost the spoor twice in stony ground but each time picked it up on the first cast ahead. It was running true and straight, and they had quickly made the number of the chase as nine men. Within two hours Roland knew each of them as individuals by the spoor they left behind them: the one with a nick in his left heel, Flatfoot, Long One with a gap of over a meter in his stride, and each of the others with more subtle characteristics to differentiate them. He knew them, and he hungered for them.

"They are going for the drifts," Esau Gondele grunted as he came up and took over the point from Roland. "We should radio ahead and set a patrol for them."

"There are twelve drifts, forty miles. A thousand men wouldn't do it." Roland wanted them for himself, all nine of them. One look at his face and Esau Gondele realized that. He picked up the run of the spoor. They were crossing an open glade of golden grass. The chase had left a sweep line through the grass, the stems still bent in the direction of their flight, and the sunlight reflected at a different intensity from these. It was like following a highway. They went down it at a swinging, easy run, and ahead of him Esau Gondele saw some of the grass stems springing upright again. They were that close already, and it wasn't yet noon. They had cut at least three hours off the lead that the ZIPRA cadres had upon them.

"We can catch them before the river—we can have them for ourselves," Esau Gondele thought fiercely, and resisted the temptation to lengthen his stride. They could move no faster, an inch more on his stride would put a term on their endurance, whereas at this pace they could run the sun down and the moon up.

At two in the afternoon they lost the spoor again. They were on a long, low ridge of black ironstone, and the ground took no prints. As soon as Esau Gondele lost contact, the line stopped dead and went into a defensive attitude; only Roland moved up and knelt out on his flank, keeping good separation so that a single burst could not take them both.

"How does it look?" Roland brushed the tiny mopani bees from his eyes and nostrils. They were maddeningly persistent in their hunt for moisture.

"I think they are going straight in."

"If they are going to twist, this is the place to do it," Roland answered. He wiped his face on his forearm, and the greasy camouflage paint came away in a dirty brown and green smear.

"If we cast ahead again, we may lose half an hour," Esau Gondele pointed out, "three kilometers."

"If we run blind we may lose more than that—we may never make them again." Roland looked around thoughtfully at the mopani forest along the ridge. "I don't like it," he decided at last. "We will make a cast."

The two of them circled out beyond the ridge, and as Esau Gondele had warned, it cost them half an hour of their gain, but they did not make the cut. There was no spoor on the direct line that they had been following; the chase had turned.

"They can only have followed the ridge. We have a one-on-one choice. East is away from the drifts—I don't believe they would chance it. We will run the western ridge blind," Roland decided, and they turned and went on harder than before, for they were rested and they had the lost half hour to make up. Roland ran with doubt gnawing his guts and rocky black ironstone crunching under his boots.

Esau Gondele was far out on his right flank, on the softer earth below the ridge, watching for the point where the chase left it and turned northward toward the river again—if it ever did.

Roland could not cover the southern edge of the ridge as well—the ironstone belt was too wide. It would mean splitting his meager forces. The south side was his blind side. If they had doubled, or turned eastward, then he had lost them. The thought of that was unbearable. He clenched his jaws until they ached and it felt as though his teeth might splinter, and he checked his watch—they had been on the ridge forty-eight minutes. He was making the conversion of time to distance in his head when he saw the birds.

There were four of them, two brace of sandgrouse, and they were flighting in that peculiar quick-winged slant that made their intention unmistakable.

"They are going down to water," Roland said aloud, and marked their descent below the treetops before signaling to Esau Gondele.

The water was a pothole in the mopani, a relic of the last rains. Twenty meters in diameter, most of it black mud, trampled by the game herds to the consistency of putty. The nine sets of man prints were perfectly cast in it, going

507

directly to the puddle of muddy water in the center and then once again heading directly northward toward the river. They were onto the chase again, and Roland's hatred burned up brightly once more.

"Drain your bottles," he ordered. There was no profit in adulterating what remained of their sweet water with that filthy coffee-colored liquid in the pan. They drank greedily, and then one man collected their bottles and went out across the mud to refill them. Roland would not risk more of his troopers than was necessary out there on the exposed pan.

It was almost four o'clock by the time they were ready to take the spoor again, and by Roland's reckoning, they were still ten miles from the river.

"We can't let them get across, Sergeant Major," he told him quietly. "From now on we won't hold back—push all out."

The pace was too hard, even for superbly trained athletes such as they were. If they ran into contact now, they would be blown almost helpless during the long minutes it would take to recover—but they reached the Kazungula road unchallenged.

There had been no security patrol over the gravel surface for at least four hours. They found where the chase had taken the precaution of reconnoitering the road and sweeping away the signs of their crossing. That had cost them precious minutes, and the Scouts were within an ace of contact. The patch of earth where one of the terrorists had urinated was still wet. The sandy earth had not had time to absorb it, nor the sun to evaporate it. They were minutes behind. It was folly to go in at the run, but as they crossed the road, Roland repeated, "All out!" And when he saw the flicker of Esau Gondele's eyes as he looked back, Roland went on, "Take number two, I will lead."

He led at full run, hurdling the low thorn scrub in his path, relying only on his own speed to survive the first volley when they made the contact, knowing that even if the terrs took him out, he could leave Esau Gondele and his men to finish it for him. Survival no longer was important to Roland; all that mattered was to make the contact and destroy them, as they had destroyed Janine.

Yet when he saw the flash of movement and color in the scrub ahead of him, he went belly-down from full run and made two quick rolls to the side to spoil the aim. He was onto the target an instant later, and fired a short burst; one light touch on the trigger and the FN hammered into his shoulder. Then as the echoes fled, there was complete silence. No return fire; and his Scouts were down in cover behind him, not firing until they had a target.

He signaled Esau Gondele. "Stay and cover me!" And he went up on his feet, keeping low, rushing forward, jinking and twisting,

He dropped to the ground again beside a thornbush. In the thorny branches above his head was the thing that had drawn his fire. It flapped again on the hot little breeze off the river. It was a woman's skirt—soft, fine cotton, bright buttercup yellow, but stained with dried blood and dirt.

Roland reached up and tore the skirt off the thorns; he bundled it in his fist and pressed his face into the cloth. Her perfume still lingered, very faintly but unmistakably. Roland found himself on his feet running forward with all his strength, with all his hatred, driven on by a madness that was at last out of control.

Ahead of him through the trees, he saw the warning markers along the edge of the *cordon sanitaire*. The little red-painted skulls seemed to taunt him, to goad him on. He did not check as he passed them—nothing was going to stop him now. Ahead of him stretched the minefield. Something smashed into the back of Roland's knees, and he was thrown to earth, the wind driven from his lungs, but immediately he was trying to struggle up. Esau Gondele tackled him again, dragged him back from the edge, and they swayed together, straining chest to chest.

"Let me go!" Roland panted. "I have to—"

Esau Gondele got his right arm free and crashed his fist into Roland's face, into his cheek, knocking his head across, half-stunning him, then taking instant advantage of his shock by twisting his arm up between his shoulder blades and dragging him back. Clear of the minefield, he threw Roland to earth again and dropped down beside him, pinning him with one massive black arm.

"You crazy bastard, you'll get us all killed," he snarled into Roland's face. "You were into it already—just one more step—"

Roland stared at him uncomprehendingly, like a sleeper waking from a nightmare.

"They have gone through the *cordon*," Esau hissed at him. "They have got clear. It's finished. They have gone."

"No," Roland shook his head. "They haven't got away. Get the radio up here. We can't let them get away."

Roland used the security network; the calling channel was 129.7 megahertz.

"All units, this is Cheetah One—come in, any station," he called quietly, but with the edge of desperation in his voice. The power on the set was only four watts, and Victoria Falls was thirty miles or so downriver. The only reply was the hum and burr of static.

He switched to the aviation frequencies and tried the Vic Falls approach on 126.9. Still no reply; he clicked over to tower and keyed the microphone.

"Tower, this is Cheetah One. Come in, please."

There was a whisper, scratchy and faint.

"Cheetah One, this is Victoria Falls tower. You are transmitting on a restricted frequency."

"Tower, we are a unit of Ballantyne's Scouts; we are in hot pursuit."

"Cheetah One, is your chase the gang that Sammed the Viscount?"

"Tower, that's affirmative!"

"Cheetah One, you have our full cooperation."

"I need a chopper to lift us over the *cordon sanitaire*. Do you have one on the plot?"

"Negative, Cheetah One. Only fixed-wing aircraft available."

"Stand by."

Roland lowered the microphone and stared out across the minefield. It was so narrow. It would take twenty seconds to cross it, but it might have been the Sahara.

"If they send a vehicle to pick us up—we can fly from Vic Falls and make a parajump on the far bank," Esau Gondele muttered beside his ear.

"No good. It will take two hours—" Roland broke off. "By God, that's it!" He thumbed the key of the microphone.

"Tower, this is Cheetah One."

"Go ahead, Cheetah One."

"There is a police armorer at Victoria Falls Hotel. Name, Sergeant Craig Mellow. I want him dropped on my position soonest possible to open the minefield. Telephone the hotel."

"Stand by, Cheetah One." Tower's thin whisper faded,

and they lay in the sun and sweated, burned up by the heat and their hatred.

"Cheetah One, we have Mellow. He is already en route to the field. We will make the delivery with a silver Beechcraft Baron. RUAC markings. Give us a position and a recognition."

"Tower, we are on the *cordon sanitaire*, estimate thirty miles upstream from the falls. We will give you a white phosphorous grenade."

"Roger, Cheetah One. I understand white smoke marker. In view of SAM danger, we can only make one pass at low level. Expect delivery in twenty minutes."

"Tower, we are running out of daylight. Tell them to hurry it up, for God's sake—those bastards are going to get clean away."

◆ ◆ ◆

Esau Gondele had the grenade launcher fitted to the muzzle of his FN rifle. They heard the faint beat of twin aircraft engines coming from downstream, and Roland touched Esau's arm.

"Ready?" he asked.

The sound of the engines built up swiftly. Roland raised himself into a kneeling position and stared into the east. He saw the flash of silver just on the treetops, and he tapped Esau's shoulder.

"Now!"

There was the crack of the blank cartridge, and the grenade lobbed up and over in a lazy parabola, fired away from the minefield toward the Kazungula road. The grenade exploded, and a column of white smoke leaped above the brown, sun-seared bush. The small twin-engine aircraft banked gently toward the marker, and then steadied again.

The passenger door had been removed, leaving a square opening above the wing root. In the opening crouched a familiar lanky figure with the cross-webbing of the parachute harness coming out of his crotch over his chest and shoulders. The bulky chute package dangled low against the back of his legs. He wore a paratrooper's helmet and goggles, but his legs were brown and bare and his feet were thrust into plain suede velskoen.

The Beechcraft was very low—perhaps too low. Roland felt a stab of anxiety; Sonny was no Scout. He had done his eight jumps for his paratrooper wings, but they were standard jumps from four thousand feet. The Beechcraft was barely two hundred feet above the bush. The pilot was taking no chances with incoming SAM fire.

"Make another pass," Roland shouted. "You are too low."

He crossed his arms overhead, waving them off, but as he did it, the wind-battered figure in the hatch of the Beechcraft dropped headfirst over the trailing edge of the silver wing. The tail seemed to slash at him like an executioner's ax, skimming his back, and the long ribbon of the rip cord flirted out behind him, still attached to the speeding machine like an umbilical cord.

Craig dropped like a stone toward the earth, and watching him, Roland felt his breath jam in his throat. Abruptly the silk streamed from the chute pack, flared open with an audible snap like a whiplash, and Craig was plucked violently erect, his legs rodding out stiffly under him, almost touching the earth. For a long second, he seemed to be suspended there like a man on the gallows, and then he dropped and rolled on his back with his feet together but high above him. Another roll and he was on his feet, sawing the parachute cords to collapse the blooming silk mushroom.

Roland let his breath out. "Bring him in," he ordered.

Two of the Scouts hustled Craig forward with a grip on each arm, forcing him to crouch and run. He dropped beside Roland, who greeted him harshly. "You have to get us through, Sonny, as quick as you can."

"Roly, was Janine on the Viscount?"

"Yes, damn you, now get us through."

Craig had opened his light pack and was assembling his tools: probe and side cutters and rolls of colored tape, steel tape measure and hand compass.

"Is she alive?" Craig could not look at Roland's face for the answer, but he started to tremble as he heard it.

"She's alive, but only just—"

"Thank God, oh, thank God," Craig whispered, and Roland studied his face thoughtfully.

"I didn't realize that you felt that way, Sonny."

"You never were very perceptive." At last Craig looked up at him defiantly. "I loved her from the first moment I saw her."

"All right, then you will want to get these bastards as much as I do. Open that field, and hurry." Roland signaled, and his Scouts moved up quickly and lay along the edge of the minefield, their weapons pointing forward. Roland turned back to Craig.

"Ready?"

Craig nodded.

"You know the pattern?"

"You'd better pray I do."

"Get in there, Sonny," Roland ordered, and Craig stood up and walked into the minefield and started to work with the probe and the tape measure.

Roland contained his impatience for less than five minutes, then he called, "Christ, Sonny, we have two hours of daylight—how long is this going to take?"

Craig did not even look around. He was stooped like a potato harvester, probing the earth gently, and the sweat had soaked through the back of his khaki shirt in a long, dark stain.

"Can't you hurry it up?"

With all the concentration of a surgeon clamping off an artery, Craig snipped the piano-wire trip of a Claymore mine and then laid the colored tape on the earth behind him as he moved forward a pace. It was their thread through the labyrinth that Craig was laying.

Craig probed again. He had chosen an unfortunate point to enter the pattern—on an overlap of two separate systems. Ordinarily he would have retraced his steps along the colored tape and begun again at another point on the perimeter, but that could cost him precious time, perhaps as much as twenty minutes.

"Craig, you are bloody standing still," Roland called. "Christ, man, have you lost your nerve?"

Craig flinched at the accusation. He should have checked the pattern to his left; there should be an AP at a thirty-degree angle from the last one he had found, and a twenty-four-inch gap between them, if he had correctly read the pattern. To check it would mean two minutes' work.

"Move, damn you, Mellow!" Roland's voice lashed him. "Don't just stand there. Move!"

Craig steeled himself; the chance was three-to-one in his favor. He stepped forward one pace and gingerly put his weight onto his left foot. It was firm. He took another pace, placing his right foot with the delicacy of a cat stalking a bird—firm again. Now the left foot. A droplet of sweat fell from his brow into his eye, flooding it and half blinding him. He blinked it away and completed the step. Safe again.

There must be a Claymore mine on his right now. His legs were trembling, but he lowered himself into a squat. The wire—it wasn't there! He had misread the pattern. He was blind in the middle of the field, living on chance. He blinked his eyes rapidly, and then with a surge of relief, he picked up the almost invisible wire exactly where it should have been. It seemed to quiver with tension like his own nerves. He reached out with the side cutters, and had almost touched the wire when Roland's voice spoke just at his shoulder.

"Don't waste time—"

Craig started violently and jerked his hand away from the deadly wire. He looked back. Roland had followed the colored tape marker; he had come out into the minefield, and he was down on one knee with his FN rifle across his thigh only a pace behind Craig. His face was masked with a thick layer of camouflage paint, like some primitive warrior from another time, savage and monstrous.

"I am going as fast as I dare." Craig used his thumb to squeeze the heavy drops of nervous sweat from his eyebrows.

"You aren't," Roland told him flatly. "You have been in here almost twenty minutes, and you haven't moved twenty paces. It will be dark before we get through if you chicken it."

"Damn you!" Craig whispered hoarsely.

"Yes," Roland encouraged. "Get mad. Get fighting mad."

Craig reached forward and snipped the trip wire. It made a tiny quivering spang like a guitar string lightly plucked with a fingernail.

"That's it, Sonny. Move!" Roland's voice was at his back, a low, monotonous litany. "Think of those bastards, Sonny. They are out there, running like rabid jackals. Think of them getting away."

Craig moved forward, taking each pace more firmly.

"They killed everybody on that Viscount, Craig. Everybody—men and women and children. Everybody except her." Roland did not use her name. "They left her alive.

But when I found her, she couldn't speak, Sonny. She could only scream and struggle like a wild animal.''

Craig stopped dead and looked back. His face was drained of color.

"Don't stop, Sonny. Keep going."

Craig stooped and probed quickly. The AP was there, exactly where it should be. He went forward into the corridor with quick, short steps, and Roland's dry, cold whisper was in his ear.

"They had raped her, Sonny, all of them. Her leg was broken in the crash, but that didn't stop them. They got on top of her like rutting animals, one after the other.''

Craig found himself running forward up the invisible corridor, merely counting his paces, not using the tape measure to check the length of it, not using the compass to measure the angle of the turn. At the end he fell flat and stabbed frantically into the earth with the probe, but Roland's voice was there behind him.

"When they had all finished, they started again," he whispered. "But this time they rolled her over and sodomized her, Sonny—''

Craig heard himself sob with each stroke of the probe. He hit the casing of a mine lying just under the surface, and the force of the blow jarred his arm. He dropped the probe and scratched with his fingers into the earth, exposing the circular top of the AP mine. It was the size of one of those old-fashioned tins of fifty Players Navy Cut cigarettes. Craig lifted it out of its cavity, set it aside and went forward, but Roland's whisper followed relentlessly.

"One after the other they did it to her, Sonny, all except the last one. He couldn't manage it twice, so he took his bayonet and pushed that up her instead.''

"Stop it, Roly! For Chrissake, stop it!"

"You say you love her, Sonny—then hurry, for her sake, hurry!''

Craig found the second AP mine and plucked it from the earth; he hurled it away from him down the length of the minefield and it bounced and rolled like a rubber ball before disappearing into a clump of grass. It did not explode. Craig clawed his way forward, stabbing the probe ferociously as though into the heart of one of them, and he found the third mine, the last one in the ninety-degree corner of the corridor.

It was open all the way to the opposite perimeter of the minefield, where there would be two Claymore trip wires. Craig jumped to his feet and ran down the corridor, with violent death only inches on each side of his flying feet. He was almost blinded by his own tears, and he sobbed in time to his run. He reached the end of the corridor and stopped. Only the trip wires now, only the trip wires of the Claymores and they would be through the *cordon sanitaire*.

"Well done, Sonny"—Roland's voice close behind—"well done; you've got us through."

Craig changed the side cutters into his right hand and took one step more. He felt it move under the sole of his right foot, the almost infinitesimal give, as though he had stepped on a subterranean mole run and it had collapsed.

"It shouldn't have been there," he thought despairingly, and time seemed to be suspended.

He heard the click of the primer. It sounded like the release of a camera shutter, but muted by the thin layer of sand over it.

"The wild one," he thought, and still time was frozen. He had time to think. "It's the wild one in the pattern." And nothing happened, just that click. He felt a spring of hope. "It's a dud, it's a misfire." He was going to get away with it.

Then the mine exploded under his right foot. It felt as though someone had hit him with a full swing of a crowbar under the sole. There was no pain, just that stunning slam of shock into his foot, driven up his spine until his jaws clashed and he felt his tongue split between his teeth, bitten clean through.

No pain, just the deafening implosion of the shock wave into his eardrums, as though somebody had held a double-barreled shotgun close to his head and fired both barrels together.

No pain, just the blinding rush of dust and smoke past his face; and then he was flung into the air as though he were the plaything of a callous giant, and he came down again on his belly. The wind was driven from his lungs, so he wheezed for breath; his mouth filled with blood from his bitten tongue. His eyes were stinging from flying grit and smoke. He wiped them clear, and Roland's face was in front of his, hazy and wavering like a heat mirage. Roland's lips were moving, but Craig could not hear the words. His ears buzzed viciously from the blast.

"It's all right, Roly," he said, and his own voice was almost lost in the singing memory of the explosion. "I'm all right," Craig repeated.

He pushed himself up and rolled into a sitting position. His left leg stuck straight out ahead of him. The inside of the calf was lacerated and discolored purple-black from the explosion, and blood oozed from out of the opening of his short khaki pants—shrapnel must have flown up into his buttocks and lower belly. But the velskoen was still on his left foot. He tried to move his foot, and it responded immediately, waggling at him reassuringly.

But there was something wrong. He was dazed and groggy, his ears still dinning, yet through it he realized there was something dreadfully wrong—and then gradually it dawned on him.

There was no right leg, just the short, fat stump of it sticking out of the leg of his pants. The heat of the explosion had cauterized the raw end of the stump and seared it white, the dead bloodless white of frostbite. He stared at it and knew it was a trick of his eyesight, because he could *feel* his leg was still there. He tried to move the missing foot, and he *felt* it move, but there was nothing there.

"Roly." Even through the din in his ears, he heard the high, hysterical tone of his own voice. "Roly, my leg. Oh God, my leg! It's gone!"

Then at last the blood came, bursting through the heat-seared flesh in bright, arterial spurts.

"Roly, help me!"

Roland stepped over him, squatting with a foot on each side of Craig's body, his back to Craig, screening him from his own mutilated lower body. Roland unrolled the canvas wallet that contained his field medical kit and strapped the tourniquet from it around the stump. The hemorrhage shriveled, and he bound the field dressing over the stump. He worked quickly, with the dexterity of practice and experience, and the second that he finished, he swiveled to look into Craig's pale, dusty, sweat-streaked face.

"Sonny, the Claymores. Can you do the Claymores? For her sake, Sonny, try!"

Craig stared at him. "Sonny—for Janine," Roland

whispered, and pulled him up into a sitting position. "Try! For her sake, try!"

"Side cutters!" Craig mumbled, staring with great, hurt eyes at the blood-soaked turban that wrapped his stump. "Find my side cutters!"

Roland pressed the tool into his hand.

"Turn me onto my belly," Craig said.

Roland rolled him carefully, and Craig began to slide himself forward; walking his elbows in the torn, dusty earth, he dragged his one remaining leg over the shallow crater left by the exploding AP mine, and then stopped and reached forward. There was the guitar twang, as the first trip wire parted in the jaws of the cutter, and, laboriously as a maimed insect squashed under a gardener's heel, Craig dragged himself on to the very edge of the minefield. For the last time, he reached out. His hand was shaking wildly, and he seized his own wrist with his left hand to steady it; sobbing with the effort, he guided the open jaws of the cutter over the hair-thin steel wire and bore down. It went with a ping, and Craig dropped the tool.

"Okay, it's open," he sobbed, and Roland pulled the lanyard out of the vee of his shirt and lifted the whistle to his lips. He blew a single crisp blast and pumped his arm over his head.

"Let's go!"

The Scouts came through the minefield at a run, keeping their rigid ten-pace separation, following the zigzag of the tape that Craig had laid down the corridor to guide them. As each one of them came to where Craig still lay on his belly, they jumped lightly over his back and melted away into the open bush, beyond the minefield, spreading out into their running formation. Roland lingered a second longer at Craig's side.

"I can't spare anyone to stay with you, Sonny." He laid the medical kit beside his head. "There is morphine for when it gets too bad." He laid something else beside the medical kit. It was a hand grenade. "The terrs may get to you before our boys do. Don't let them take you. A grenade is messy but effective." Then Roland leaned forward and kissed Craig on the forehead. "Bless you, Sonny!" he said, and then he was on his feet going forward again at a run. Within seconds, the thick riverine Zambezi bush had swallowed him, and slowly Craig lowered his face into the crook of his arm.

Then, at last, the pain came at him like a ravening lion.

♦ ♦ ♦

Commissar Tungata Zebiwe crouched in the bottom of the slit trench and listened to the husky voice speaking from the portable radio.

"They are through the minefield, coming down to the river."

His observers were on the north bank of the Zambezi, in carefully prepared positions from which they could sweep the opposite bank and the small heavily wooded islands that split the shallows of the wide river course.

"How many?" Tungata asked into the microphone.

"No count yet."

Of course they would be mere flickers of movement in the darkening bush, impossible to count as they came forward in overlapping covering rushes. Tungata looked up at the sky. There was less than an hour before dark, he estimated, and felt a fresh onslaught of the doubts that had beset him ever since he had brought his cadre through the drifts almost three hours before.

Could he entice the pursuers into crossing the river? Without that the destruction of the Viscount and all else that he had so far achieved would be halved in propaganda and psychological value against the enemy. He had to bring the Scouts across into the carefully prepared killing ground. He had carried the woman's skirt and left it on the edge of the *cordon sanitaire* for just that purpose, to bring them on.

Yet he recognized that it would be an irrational act for any commander to take a small force across such a natural barrier as the Zambezi at the close of day with darkness only minutes away, into hostile territory against an enemy of unknown strength who must anticipate his arrival and who had been able to prepare for it at leisure. Tungata could not expect them to come—he could only hope.

It would depend chiefly upon who had command of the pursuers. The bait that he had laid to draw them in would be only truly effective on one man; the multiple rape and mutilation of the woman, and the bloodied skirt, would have their full effect only upon Colonel Roland Ballantyne himself. Tungata tried objectively to assess the chances that it was Ballantyne himself commanding the pursuit.

He had been at the Victoria Falls Hotel; ZIPRA agents had made a positive identification. The woman had called herself Ballantyne. The Scouts were the nearest and most effective force in the area. Surely they must be the first to the site of the wreck, and surely Ballantyne would be with them. Tungata had to allow himself a better than even chance that his operation was working as planned.

Tungata's first confirmation that the pursuit was close had been a little before four o'clock that afternoon, when there had been one short burst of automatic fire from the south bank. At that moment Tungata's cadre had just completed the crossing of the drift. They were still soaked and lying panting, like hunting dogs too hard run, and Tungata had been chilled to realize how close the Scouts had been behind them despite the many hours' start they had had and the fierce pace that Tungata had forced on his men. Twenty minutes more and they would have been caught on the south bank at the *cordon sanitaire,* and Tungata cherished no illusions as to what that would have meant. His men were the elite of the ZIPRA forces, but they were no match for Ballantyne's Scouts. On the south bank they would have been doomed, but now that they were across the Zambezi, the advantage had swung dramatically. Tungata's preparations to receive the pursuing force had taken fully ten days and had been carried out with the full cooperation of the Zambian army and police force.

The radio crackled again, and Tungata lifted the microphone to his lips and acknowledged curtly. The observer's voice was lowered, as though he feared it might carry to the dangerous quarry across the river.

"They have not attempted the crossing. Either they are waiting for dark, or they are not coming."

"They must come," Tungata whispered to himself, and then he keyed the microphone.

"Put up the flare," he ordered.

"Stand by!" the observer answered, and Tungata lowered the microphone and looked up expectantly into the purple and rose of the evening sky. It was a risk, but then it had all been a risk—from the very moment they crossed the Zambezi carrying the SAM-7 launcher.

The signal flare streaked up into the sunset, and five

hundred feet above the river it burst into a crimson ball of fire. Tungata watched it begin to sink gracefully toward the earth again. He found that he had driven his fingernails into the flesh of his palms with the strength of his grip upon the radio microphone.

The flare, fired so tantalizingly close to the river bank, from just behind the first line of trees on the north bank, could frighten them off and make them abandon the pursuit, or it could have the effect that Tungata hoped for. It could convince them how close they were to their quarry and precipitate the catlike reflex to follow anything that flees.

Tungata waited and the seconds dragged by. He shook his head, facing at last the prospect of failure, feeling the chill of it begin in the pit of his stomach and beginning to spread. Then the radio crackled, and the observer's voice was strained and hoarse: "They are coming!" he said.

Tungata snatched the microphone to his lips. "All units. Hold your fire. This is Comrade Tungata. Hold your fire."

He had to pause then, his relief mixed with dread that at this last moment one of his nervous guerrillas might spring the trap prematurely. He had six hundred men deployed on the killing ground; only regimental strength was sufficient for a detachment of *kanka*. With his own eyes, Tungata had seen them fight, and anything less than odds of twenty to one in his favor would not be acceptable.

He had achieved his numerical advantage, but in his own great numbers there was a concealed danger. Control was weakened—not all of his men were warriors of quality. Among them there must be many of those who were nervous and susceptible to the mysterious aura, the almost superstitious awe, that surrounded the legend of Ballantyne's Scouts.

"All field commanders," he kept repeating into the microphone, "hold your fire. This is Comrade Commissar Tungata. Hold your fire." Then he lowered the microphone and made one long, last, careful study of the ground in front of him.

The north bank of the river was almost a mile from where he waited. It was marked by a palisade of taller trees—the twisted trunks of great strangler figs and tall mkusi, their branches laden with trailing lianas—and higher even than these were the elegant bottle palms, their spiky fronds silhouetted against the blushing sunset. There was no glimpse of the river through this wall of lush growth.

Then abruptly the line of forest ended on this wide meadowlike opening. It was one of the Zambezi floodplains. In the rainy season, when the river burst its banks, this area would be inundated and transformed into a shallow lagoon filled with water lilies and reeds; but now it had dried out, and the reeds had wilted and fallen, no longer providing cover for a pursuer, or a fugitive.

One of Tungata's main concerns had been to keep the soft surface of this wide pan uncontaminated by spoor and footprints. There had been a regiment encamped along its fringes for almost ten days now, a regiment digging the trench system and batteries for the mortars. Just one man wandering across the pan would have left a warning to the pursuers, but it had been kept clean.

The only spoor out there was that of the wild buffalo herds, of the dainty red puku antelope, and the tracks of nine men, the same tracks that led from the crash site of the Viscount and which Tungata and his cadre had laid only three hours previously. These tracks emerged from the fringe of riverine bush and ran down the center of the open floodplain to the higher forested ground on this side.

The carrier band of Tungata's radio hummed to life, and the whisper of his observer warned, "They are halfway across the drift."

Tungata imagined the line of dark heads above the sunset-pink waters, looking like a string of beads on a bodice of velvet.

"How many?" Tungata asked.

"Twelve."

Tungata felt a quick drop of disappointment. So few? He had hoped for more. He hesitated for a heartbeat before he asked, "Is there a white officer?"

"Only one man in camouflage paint; he is at the head of the line."

"It's Ballantyne," Tungata told himself. "It's the great jackal himself—it must be him."

Again the voice spoke from the radio. "They are across, into the trees. We have lost sight."

Now, would they commit themselves to cross the floodplain? Tungata focused his night glasses on the tree line. The specially ground and coated lenses picked up every available ray of light—but still, even through the lenses, the shapes of the trees and bushes beneath them were becoming indistinct. The sun had gone, and the last colors of the sunset were fading; the first stars were pricking the dark canopy of the night sky.

"They are still in the trees." It was a different voice on the radio, deeper and harsher. One of the second line of observers covering the southernmost fringe of the pan.

Tungata gave another order into the microphone.

"Unscreen the fire!" he said quietly, and seconds later there was a tiny yellow glow of a campfire in the tree line farthest from the river. As Tungata stared at it through the night glasses, a human figure passed in front of the low flames. It gave the perfect illusion of a quiet camp among the trees, where an unsuspecting quarry exhausted from the long chase, but believing themselves safe at last, were resting and preparing the evening meal. But was it too obvious a lure, Tungata wondered anxiously, was he relying too much upon the unbalanced rage of the pursuers?

His self-doubts were answered almost immediately. The gruff voice on the radio said suddenly, "They have left the trees; they are crossing the pan."

It was too dark now to make out anything at that range. He had to rely on the sighting of his forward posts, and he turned the luminous dial of his wristwatch so that he could see the sweep of the second hand. The pan was one and a half kilometers across; at a run the Scouts would take approximately three minutes to cross it.

Without taking his eyes off the dial, Tungata spoke into the microphone. "Mortars, stand by with star shell."

"Mortars, standing by!"

The second hand completed its circuit of the dial and started around again.

"Mortars, fire!" Tungata ordered.

From the forest behind him came that hollow, clunking sound of three-inch mortars, and Tungata heard the flute of the mortar bombs rising swiftly overhead. Then suddenly, at the zenith of their trajectory, the star shells burst.

They hung suspended on their tiny parachutes, and their light was a harsh, electric blue. The open floodplain was illuminated like some gigantic sports stadium. The tiny group of running men in the center were trapped in the naked glare, and their shadows on the earth beneath them seemed black and weighty as solid ironstone.

They went down instantly—but there was no cover. Even though they were flattened against the earth, their bodies formed sharply defined hummocks. But they were almost immediately obliterated by the leaping sheets of dust and flying clods of earth that sprang up around them like a bank of pale, whirling fog. Tungata had six hundred men in the tree line surrounding the pan. All of them were firing now, and the hurricane of automatic fire swept over the huddled figures in the middle of the open pan.

From the mortar batteries set farther back in the forest, the bombs rose high over Tungata's head and then dropped into the open pan. The crack of their explosions added a sharp counterpoint to the background thunder of small-arms fire, and the mortar bursts jumped up like pale dust devils in the light of the star shells.

Nothing could live out there. The Scouts must long ago all be torn to shreds by shot and shrapnel, but still it went on and on, minute after minute, while more star shells crackled into eye-searing, bright, sizzling blue light overhead.

Tungata panned his binoculars slowly over the drifting screen of dust and smoke. He could see no sign of life—and at last he shifted the microphone to order the cease-fire. But before he could speak, he saw movement directly in front of his position, not two hundred paces distant, and out of the curtain of dust came two ghostly figures.

They came at a run, side by side, seeming to wade through the thick swamp of mortar smoke and dust, and they appeared monstrous and inhuman in the stark light of the star shells. One of them was a huge Matabele. He had lost his helmet and his head was round and black as a cannonball, his open mouth was a pink cave lined with ivory teeth, and his bull bellow rose above even that storm of gunfire. The other was a white man, the top of his battle dress torn half off his body, exposing the pale flesh of chest and shoulders, but his face was daubed with fiendish streaks of dark green and brown paint.

The two of them were firing as they came on, and Tungata felt a stir of the superstitious dread that he had despised in his own troops, for they seemed immune to the storm of bullets through which they charged.

"Kill them!" Tungata heard his own voice screaming,

and a burst of FN fire from one of them kicked the top off the bank of loose earth in front of his slit trench.

Tungata ducked and ran to the gunner behind the heavy machine gun at the end of the trench.

"Aim carefully," he shouted, and the gunner fired a long, thunderous burst, but the two figures ran on toward them unscathed.

Tungata pushed the man away from the gun and took his place. For infinite seconds he peered over the sights, making the tiny adjustments to the gun's elevation, and then he fired.

The tall Matabele was driven backward as though he had been hit by a runaway automobile, and then he seemed to disintegrate, breaking up like a straw man in a high wind as the bullets tore him to pieces. He melted into the surface of the pan.

The second man came on, running and firing, screaming an incoherent challenge, and Tungata swung the machine gun onto him. He paused for a microsecond to make certain of his aim, and he saw the flash of hard white flesh through the gunsight and the diabolically painted face above it.

Tungata fired, and the heavy gun pounded briefly in his hand, then jammed and was silent.

Tungata was frozen, completely in the grip of supernatural dread, for the man was still coming on. He had dropped his FN rifle, and half his shoulder was shot away. The shattered arm dangled uselessly at his side, but he was on his feet coming straight at Tungata.

Tungata jumped to his feet and pulled the Tokarev pistol from the webbing holster on his side. The man was almost at the trench now, not ten paces away, and Tungata pointed the pistol at him. He fired and saw the bullet strike in the center of the naked white chest. The man dropped to his knees, no longer able to come forward but straining to do so, reaching out toward his enemy with his one remaining arm, no sound coming out of the open, blood-glutted mouth.

This close, despite the thick mask of camouflage paint, Tungata recognized him from that never-forgotten night at Khami Mission. The two men stared at each other for a second longer, and then Roland Ballantyne fell forward onto his face.

Slowly the great storm of gunfire from around the rim of

the pan shriveled and died away. Tungata Zebiwe climbed stiffly out of the trench and went to where Roland Ballantyne lay. With his foot he rolled him down the bank of earth onto his back, and with a sense of disbelief saw the eyelids quiver and then open slowly. In the light of the star shells, the green eyes that stared up at him still seethed with rage and hatred.

Tungata squatted beside the man and said softly in English, "Colonel Ballantyne, I am very pleased to meet you again."

Then Tungata leaned forward, placed the muzzle of the Tokarev against his temple, just an inch in front of his earhole, and fired a bullet through Roland Ballantyne's brain.

♦ ♦ ♦

The paraplegic section of St. Giles' Hospital was a haven, a sanctuary into which Craig Mellow retreated gratefully.

He was more fortunate than some of the other inmates. He suffered only two journeys along the long, green-painted corridor, the wheels of the trolley on which he lay squeaking unrhythmically, and the masked impersonal faces of the nurses hovering above his, down through the double swing doors at the end, into the stink of asepsis and anesthetic.

The first time they had built him a fine stump, with a thick cushion of flesh and skin around it to take the artificial limb. The second time they had removed most of the larger fragments of shrapnel that had peppered his crotch and buttocks and lower back. They had also searched, unsuccessfully, for some mechanical reason for the complete paralysis of his body below the waist.

His mutilated flesh recovered from the surgery with the rapidity of that of a healthy young animal, but the leg of plastic and stainless steel stood unused beside his bedside locker, and his arms thickened with muscle from lifting himself on the chain handles and from manipulating the wheelchair.

Swiftly he found his special niches in the sprawling old building and gardens. He spent much of his day in the therapeutic workshop working from the wheelchair. He stripped his old Land Rover completely and rebuilt the engine, grinding the crankshaft and reboring the block. Then he converted it to hand controls, fitted handles and adapted the driver's seat to make it easier to swing his paralyzed lower body in and out. He built a rack for the folding wheelchair where once the gun racks had been behind the front seat, and he resprayed the body a lustrous maroon color.

When he finished work on the Land Rover, he began designing and machining stainless steel and bronze fittings for the yacht, working hour after hour on the lathes and drilling presses. While his hands were busy, he found he could crowd out the haunting memories, so he lavished care and total concentration on the task, turning out small masterpieces in wood and metal.

In the evenings he had his reading and his writing, though he never read a newspaper or watched the television set in the hospital common room. He never took part with the other patients in any discussion of the fighting or of the complicated peace negotiations which commenced with such high hopes and broke down so regularly. That way Craig could pretend to himself that the wolves of war were not still hunting across the land.

Only at night he could not control the tricks his mind and memory played upon him, and once again he sweated with terror in an endless minefield, with Roly's voice whispering obscenities in his ears, or he saw the electric glare of star shells in the night sky above the river and heard the storm of gunfire. Then he would wake screaming, with the night nurse beside him, concerned and compassionate.

"It's all right, Craig, it was just one of your nightmares. It's all right." But it was not all right; he knew it would never be all right.

Aunty Valerie wrote to him. The one thing that tortured her and Uncle Douglas was that Roland's body had never been recovered. They had heard a horror story through the security forces' intelligence that Roland's bullet-riddled corpse had been put on public display in Zambia and that the guerrillas in the training camps had been invited to spit and urinate upon it to convince themselves that he was truly dead. Afterward the body had been dumped into one of the pit latrines of the guerrilla training camp.

She hoped Craig would understand that neither she nor Uncle Douglas felt up to visiting him at present, but if there was anything he needed, he had only to write to them.

On the other hand, Jonathan Ballantyne came to visit Craig every Friday. He drove his old silver Bentley and brought a picnic basket with him. It always contained a bottle of gin and half a dozen tonics. He and Craig shared it, in a sheltered nook at the end of the hospital gardens. Like Craig, the old man wanted to avoid the painful present, and they found escape together into the past. Each week Bawu brought one of the old family journals, and they discussed it avidly, Craig trying to glean every one of the old man's memories of those far-off days.

Only twice did they break their accord of forgetfulness and silence. Once Craig asked, "Bawu, what has happened to Janine?"

"Valerie and Douglas wanted her to go and live at Queen's Lynn when she was released from the hospital, but she wouldn't go. As far as I know, she is still working at the museum."

The next week it was Bawu who paused as he was about to climb back into the Bentley and said, "When they killed Roly, that was the first time I realized that we were going to lose this war."

"Are we going to lose, Bawu?"

"Yes," said the old man, and drove away leaving Craig in the wheelchair staring after the Bentley.

At the end of the tenth month at St. Giles', Craig was sent for a series of tests that lasted four days. They X-rayed him and stuck electrodes to his body, they tested his eyesight and his reaction time to various stimuli, they scanned the surface of his skin for heat changes that would show nervous malfunction, they gave him a lumbar puncture and sucked out a sample of his spinal fluid. At the end of it, Craig was nervous and exhausted. That night he had another nightmare. He was lying in the minefield again, and he could hear Janine. She was in the darkness ahead of him. They were doing to her what Roland had described, and she was screaming for him to help her. He could not move. When he woke at last, his sweat had formed a tepid puddle in the red rubber undersheet.

The next day the doctor in charge of his case told him, "You did wonderfully in your tests, Craig; we are really proud of you. Now I am going to start a new course of treatment. I am sending you to Dr. Davis."

Dr. Davis was a young man with an intense manner and a disconcerting directness in his stare. Craig took an immediate dislike to him, sensing that he would seek to destroy the cocoon of peace which Craig had almost succeeded in weaving about himself. It was only after he had been in Davis' office for ten minutes that Craig realized that he was a psychiatrist.

"Look here, Doctor, I'm not a funny bunny."

"No, you are not, but we think you might need a little help, Craig."

"I am fine. I don't need help."

"There is nothing wrong with your body or nervous system; we want to find out why you have no function in your lower body."

"Listen, Doctor, I can save you a lot of trouble. The reason I can't move my stump and my one good kicker is that I stepped on an AP mine and it blew pieces of me all over the scenery."

"Craig, there is a recognized condition; once they used to call it shell shock—"

"Doctor," Craig interrupted him. "You say there is nothing wrong with me?"

"Your body has healed perfectly."

"Fine, why didn't somebody tell me before?"

Craig wheeled his chair down the corridor to his room. It took him five minutes to pack his books and papers, then he wheeled himself out to the shiny maroon Land Rover, slung his valise into the back, dragged himself up into the driver's seat, loaded the wheelchair into the rack behind him, and drove out to the yacht.

In the St. Giles' workshop he had designed and put together a system of pulley and hand winches to lift himself easily up the high side of the hull to deck level. Now the other modifications to the yacht absorbed all his energy and ingenuity. First he had to install grab handles to pull himself around the deck and cockpit and belowdecks. He sewed leather patches on the seat of his trousers and skidded around on his backside as he adapted the galley and the head, lowered the bunk and rebuilt the chart table to his new requirements. He worked with music blaring out from the speakers and a mug of gin within easy reach— music and liquor helped to chase away unwanted memories.

The yacht was a fortress. He left it only once a month, when he went into town to pick up his police pension check, and to stock up his larder and his supply of writing paper.

On one of these trips he found a secondhand typewriter and a "teach yourself to type" paperback. He screwed the base of the machine to a corner of the chart table where it would be secure even in a gale at sea, and he began converting the mess of handwritten exercise books into neat piles of typescript; his speed built up with practice until he could make the keys chatter in time to the music.

Dr. Davis, the psychiatrist, tracked him down at last, and Craig called down to him from the cockpit of the yacht.

"Look here, Doc, I realize now that you were right—I am a raving homicidal psychopath. If I were you, I wouldn't put a foot on that ladder."

After that Craig rigged up a counterbalance so that he could pull the ladder up after him like a drawbridge. He let it down only for Bawu, and each Friday they drank gin and built a little world of fantasy and imagination in which they both could hide.

Then Bawu came on a Tuesday. Craig was up on the foredeck reinforcing the stepping of the mainmast. The old man climbed out of the Bentley, and Craig's happy cry of welcome died on his lips. Bawu seemed to have shriveled up. He looked ancient and fragile, like one of those unwrapped mummies in the Egyptology section of the British Museum. In the back of the Bentley was the Matabele cook from King's Lynn who had worked for the old man for forty years. Under Bawu's direction, the Matabele unloaded two large crates from the trunk of the Bentley and placed them in the goods lift.

Craig winched the crates up, and then lowered the lift for the old man. In the saloon Craig poured gin into the glasses, avoiding looking at his grandfather, embarrassed for his sake.

Bawu was truly an old man at last. His eyes were rheumy and unfocused, his mouth slack so that he mumbled and sucked noisily at his lips. He spilled a dribble of gin down his shirtfront and didn't realize that he had done so. They sat in silence for a long time, the old man nodding to himself and making small, incoherent grunts and burbles. Then suddenly he said: "I've brought you your inheritance." And Craig realized that the crates on the deck must contain the journals that they had haggled over. "Douglas wouldn't know what to do with them anyway."

"Thank you, Bawu."

"Did I ever tell you about the time Mr. Rhodes held me upon his lap?" Bawu asked with a disconcerting change of direction. Craig had heard the story fifty times before.

"No, you never did. I'd love to hear it, Bawu."

"Well, it was during a wedding out at Khami Mission— must have been ninety-five or ninety-six." The old man bumbled on for ten minutes before he lost the thread of the story entirely and lapsed into silence again.

Craig refilled the glasses, and Bawu stared at the opposite bulkhead, and suddenly Craig realized that tears were running down the withered old cheeks.

"What is it, Bawu?" he demanded with quick alarm. Those slow, painful tears were a terrible thing to watch.

"Didn't you hear the news?" the old man asked.

"You know I never listen to the news."

"It's over, my boy, all over. We have lost. Roly, you, all those young men, it was all for nothing—we have lost the war. Everything we and our fathers fought for, everything we won and built, it's all gone. We have lost it all over a table in a place called Lancaster House."

Bawu's shoulders were shaking quietly, the tears still streaming down his face. Craig dragged himself across the saloon and lifted himself onto the bench beside him. He took Bawu's hand and held it. The old man's hand was thin and light and dry, like the dried bones of a dead seabird. The two of them, old and young, sat holding hands like frightened children in an empty house.

◆ ◆ ◆

On the following Friday, Craig crawled out of his bunk early and did his housekeeping in anticipation of Bawu's regular visit. The previous day he had laid in half a dozen bottles of gin, so there was unlikely to be a drought, and he broke the seal on one of them and set it ready with the two glasses polished to a shine. Then he put the first three hundred pages of the typescript next to the bottle.

"It will cheer the old man up." He had taken months to pluck up his courage sufficiently to tell Bawu what he was attempting. Now that another person was about to be allowed to read his typescript, Craig was seized by conflicting emotions; firstly by dread that it would all be judged as valueless, that he had wasted time and hope upon something of little worth, and secondly by a sharp resentment that the private world that he had created upon those blank white sheets was to be invaded by a trespasser, even one as beloved as Bawu.

"Anyway, somebody has to read it sometime," Craig consoled himself, and dragged himself down to the heads.

While he sat on the chemical toilet, he could see his own face in the mirror above the handbasin. For the first time in months he truly looked at himself. He had not shaved in a week, and the gin had left soft putty-colored pouches under his eyes. The eyes themselves were hurt and haunted by terrible memories, and his mouth was twisted like that of a lost child on the verge of tears.

He shaved and then switched on the shower and sat under it— reveling in the almost forgotten sensation of hot suds. Afterward he combed his wet hair over his face and with the scissors trimmed it straight across the line of his eyebrows; then he scrubbed his teeth until the gums bled. He found a clean blue shirt and then slid along the companionway, hoisted himself to deck level, lowered the boarding ladder, and found a place in the sun with his back against the coping of the cabin to wait for Bawu.

He must have dozed, for the sound of an automobile engine made him start awake, but it was not the whisper of the old man's Bentley but the distinctive throb of a Volkswagen Beetle. Craig did not recognize the drab green vehicle, nor the driver who parked it under the mango trees and came hesitantly toward the yacht.

She was a dumpy little figure, of that indeterminate age that plain girls enter in their late twenties and which carries them through to old age. She walked without pride, slumping as though to hide her breasts and the fact that she was a woman. Her skirt was bulky around her thick waist, and the low, sensible shoes almost drew attention away from the surprisingly lovely lines of her calves and the graceful ankles.

She walked with her arms folded across her chest as though she was cold, even in the hot morning sunlight. She peered shortsightedly at the path through horn-rimmed spectacles, and her hair was long and lank, hanging straight and lusterless to hide her face. She stood below the yacht side and looked up at Craig. Her skin was bad, like that of a teenager who was on junk food, and her face was plump, but with an unhealthy soft look and a sickroom pallor.

Then she lifted the horn-rimmed spectacles from her face. The frames left little red indentations on each side of her nose, but the eyes, those huge slanted cat's eyes with the strange little cast in them, those eyes so indigo blue as to be almost black—they were unmistakable.

"Jan," Craig whispered. "Oh God, Jan, is it you?"

She made a heartbreakingly feminine gesture of vanity—pushing the lank, dull hair off her face—and dropped her eyes, standing awkwardly pigeon-toed in the dowdy skirt.

Her voice barely carried up to him. "I'm sorry to bother you. I know how you must feel about me, but can I come up, please?"

"Please, Jan, please do." He dragged himself to the rail and steadied the ladder for her.

"Hello." He grinned at her shyly as she reached the deck level.

"Hello, Craig."

"I'm sorry, I'd like to stand up, but you'll have to get used to talking down to me."

"Yes," she said. "I heard."

"Let's go down to the saloon. I'm expecting Bawu. It will be like old times."

She looked away. "You've done a lot of work, Craig."

"She's almost finished," he told her proudly.

"She's beautiful." Janine went down from the cockpit into the saloon, and he lowered himself after her.

"We could wait for Bawu," Craig said as he placed a tape on the machine, instinctively avoiding Beethoven and selecting Debussy for a lighter, happier sound. "Or we could have a drink right now." He grinned to cover his uneasiness and discomfort. "And quite frankly I *need* one right away."

Janine did not touch her glass but sat staring at it.

"Bawu told me you were still working at the museum."

She nodded, and Craig felt his chest constricted with helpless pity for her.

"Bawu will be here—" He searched desperately for something to say to her.

"Craig, I came to tell you something. The family asked me to come to you; they wanted somebody whom you knew to break the news." Now she looked up from the glass. "Bawu won't be coming today," she said. "He won't be coming ever again."

After a long time, Craig asked softly, "When did it happen?"

"Last night, while he was sleeping. It was his heart."

"Yes," Craig murmured. "His heart. It was broken—I knew that."

"The funeral will be tomorrow at King's Lynn, in the afternoon. They want you to be there. We could go together, if you don't mind?"

♦ ♦ ♦

The weather changed during the night, and the wind went up into the southeast, bringing with it the thin, cold, drizzling *guti* rain.

They laid the old man down among his wives and children and grandchildren in the little cemetery at the back of the hills. The rain on the freshly turned red earth piled beside the open grave made it seem as though the earth were bleeding from a mortal wound.

Afterward Craig and Janine drove back to Bulawayo in the Land Rover.

"I'm staying at the same flat," Janine said as they drove through the park. "Will you drop me there, please?"

"If I am alone now, I'll just get sad drunk," Craig said. "Won't you come back to the yacht, just for a little while, please?" Craig heard the pleading in his own voice.

"I'm not very good around people anymore," she said.

"Nor am I," Craig agreed. "But you and I aren't just people, are we?"

Craig made coffee for both of them and brought it through from the galley. They sat opposite each other, and he found it difficult not to stare at her.

"I must look a sight," she said abruptly, and he did not know how to answer her.

"You will always be the most beautiful woman I have ever known."

"Craig, did they tell you what happened to me?"

"Yes, I know."

"Then you must know that I am not really a woman anymore. I will never be able to let a man, any man, touch me again."

"I can understand that."

"That's one of the reasons that I never tried to see you again."

534

"What are the other reasons?" he asked.

"That you would not wish to see me, to have anything to do with me."

"That I don't understand."

Janine was silent again, huddled on the bench seat, hugging herself with that protective gesture.

"Roly felt that way," she blurted. "After they were finished with me. When he found me there beside the wreck, when he realized what they had done to me, he could not even bear to touch me, not even to speak to me."

"Jan—" Craig started, but she cut him off.

"It's all right, Craig. I didn't tell you to hear you deny it for me. I told you so that you would know about me. So that you would know that I have nothing left to offer a man that way."

"Then I can tell you that, like you, I have nothing to offer a woman—that way."

There was quick and real pain in her eyes. "Oh, Craig, my poor Craig—I didn't realize—I thought it was just one leg—"

"On the other hand, I can offer someone friendship and caring, and just about everything else." He grinned at her. "I can even offer a shot of gin."

"I thought you didn't want to get drunk." She smiled back at him gently.

"I said sad drunk, but we should give Bawu a little wake. He would have liked that."

They sat facing each other across the saloon table, chatting in desultory fashion, both of them beginning to relax as the gin warmed them, and gradually they recaptured some of that long-lost camaraderie that they had once enjoyed.

Janine explained her reasons for not accepting the invitation of Douglas and Valerie to live at Queen's Lynn. "They look at me with such pity that I start to feel it all over again. It would be like going into a state of perpetual mourning."

He told her about St. Giles' and the way he had absconded. "They say it's not my legs but my head that prevents me from walking. Either they are crazy or I am—I prefer to think that it's them."

He had two steaks in the refrigerator, and he grilled them on the gas while she made a dressing for the salad, and while they worked he explained all the modifications that he had made to the layout of the yacht.

"With the roller boom, I would be able to shorten or make sail without leaving the cockpit," he chatted on. "I bet that I could manage her single-handed. It's a pity I'm not ever going to have the chance."

"What do you mean?" She stopped with an onion in one hand and a knife in the other.

"My darling is never going to feel the kiss of salt water on her bottom," he explained. "They have impounded her."

"Craig, I don't understand."

"I applied to the Exchange Control Authority for a permit to ship her to the coast. You know what they are like, don't you?"

"I've heard they are pretty rough," she answered.

"Rough? That's like calling Attila the Hun unkind. If you try to get out of the country, even as a legal emigrant, they allow you to take out only a thousand dollars' worth of goods or cash. Well, they sent an inspector round, and he valued the yacht at two hundred and fifty thousand dollars. If I want to take it out, I have to make a cash deposit of a quarter of a million dollars, a quarter of a million! I have a little over ten thousand dollars between me and prostitution, so until I come up with another two hundred and forty thousand, here I sit."

"Craig, that's cruel. Couldn't you appeal? I mean, in your special circumstances?" She stopped herself when she saw the little arrowhead of a frown appear between his eyes. Craig brushed over the reference to his disability.

"You can see their point of view, I suppose. Every white man in the country wants to get out before the big black baddies take over. We would strip the country bare if there was no control."

"But, Craig, what are you going to do?"

"Stay here, I suppose. I don't have much alternative. I'll sit here and read Hiscock's *Voyaging Under Sail* and Mellor's *Cruising Safe and Simple*."

"I wish there was something I could do to help."

"There is. You can lay the table and hook a bottle of wine out of the cupboard."

Janine left more than half her steak and drank little of the wine; then she wandered across the saloon to examine his collection of tapes.

"Paganini's *Capricci*," she murmured, "now I know you are a masochist." And then her attention was attracted to the neat, square pile of the typescript on the shelf beside the tapes.

"What is this?" She turned the first few sheets and then looked up at him. Those beautiful blue eyes in the once beautiful face, now swollen and distorted with fat and speckled about the chin with angry little blemishes, made his heart plunge. "What is it?" And then, seeing his expression: "Oh, I'm sorry. It's none of my business."

"No!" he said quickly. "It's not that. It's just that I don't really know what it is—" He couldn't call it a book, and it would be pretentious to call it a novel. "It's just something I have been fiddling with."

Janine riffled the edges of the sheets. The pile was over twelve inches deep. "It doesn't look like fiddling," she chuckled, the first time he had heard her laugh since their reunion. "To me it looks like deadly earnest!"

"It's a story I have been trying to write down."

"May I read it?" she asked, and he felt panic rising in him.

"Oh, it wouldn't interest you."

"How do you know?" She lugged the huge typescript to the table. "May I read it?"

He shrugged helplessly. "I don't think you will get far, but if you would like to try—"

She sat down and read the first page.

"It's still very rough—you must make allowances," he said.

"Craig, you still don't know when to shut up, do you?" she said without looking up. She turned the page.

He took the plates and glasses through to the galley and washed them; then he made coffee and brought the pot to the saloon table. Janine did not look up. He poured her mug, and she did not look up from the page.

After a while he left her and slid through to his cabin. He stretched out on the bunk and picked up the book he was reading from the bedside table. It was Crawford's *Mariners' Celestial Navigation*, and he began to wrestle distractedly with zenith distances and azimuth angles. He woke with

Janine's hand on his cheek. She jerked her fingers away as he sat up hurriedly.

"What time is it?" he asked groggily.

"It's morning—I have to go. I didn't sleep all night. I don't know how I will get through work today."

"Will you come back?" he demanded, coming full awake.

"I have to. I have to finish reading. I would take it with me, but I'd need a camel to carry it, it's so big."

She stood over the bunk looking down at him with a strange speculation in those slanted dark blue eyes.

"It's difficult to believe that was written by somebody I thought that I knew," she mused softly. "I realize that I really knew very little about you at all." She glanced at her watch. "Oh my gosh! I have to fly!"

♦ ♦ ♦

She parked the VW under the mango trees beside the yacht a little after five o'clock that evening.

"I have brought the steaks," she called, "and the wine." She came up the ladder and ducked down into the saloon. Her voice floated up to him in the cockpit. "But you'll have to cook them. I can't spare the time, I'm afraid." By the time he got down into the saloon, she was already seated and completely engrossed in the massive typescript.

It was long past midnight when she turned the last page. When she had finished it, she sat quietly with her hands clasped in her lap, staring at the pile of paper silently.

Then when she looked up at him at last, her eyes were bright and wet with tears.

"It's magnificent," she said quietly. "It will take me a little time before I can get over it enough to talk about it rationally, and then I will want to read it again."

The following evening, she brought a fat Cornish chicken. "It's range-fed," she told him. "One more steak and you would start growing horns."

She made a *coq au vin,* and while they ate, she demanded an explanation of the characters in his typescript.

"Was Mr. Rhodes really a homosexual?"

"There doesn't seem to be any other explanation," he defended himself. "So many great men are hounded to greatness by their own imperfections."

"What about Lobengula? Was his first love really a captured white girl? Did he commit suicide? And Robyn

538

Ballantyne—tell me more about her. Did she impersonate a man to enroll in medical school? How much of that is true?''

"Does it matter?'' Craig laughed at her. "It's just a story, the way it might have been. I was just trying to portray an age, and the mood of that age.''

"Oh yes, it does matter,'' she said seriously. "It matters very much to me. You have made it matter. It is as though I am a part of it—you have made me a part of it all.''

That night when it grew late, Craig said simply, "I made up the bunk in the forward cabin; it seems silly for you to drive all that way home.''

She stayed, and the following evening she brought a valise which she unpacked into the stowage of the forward cabin, and they settled slowly into a routine. She had first use of the shower and heads in the morning while he made the breakfast. He did the cleaning and made up the bunks, while she did the shopping and any other errands for him during her lunchbreak. When she arrived back at the yacht in the evenings, she would change into a T-shirt and jeans, then help him with the work on the yacht. She was particularly good at sanding and varnishing; she had more patience and dexterity than Craig did.

At the end of the first week, Craig suggested, "It would save you a bundle if you gave up that flat of yours.''

"I'll pay you rent,'' she agreed. And when he protested: "Okay, then, I get the food and liquor—agreed?''

That night just after she had doused the gaslight in her cabin, she called through the dark saloon to his stern cabin.

"Craig, do you know, this is the first time that I feel safe since—'' She did not finish.

"I know how you feel,'' he assured her.

"Goodnight, skipper.''

Yet it was only a few nights later that he came awake to her screams. They were so anguished, so tormented and heartrending, that for seconds he could not move; then he tumbled from his bunk and sprawled on the deck in his haste to get to her. He fumbled and found the switch to the fluorescent tube in the saloon and then clawed himself down the companionway.

In the reflected light from the saloon, he saw her crouched in one corner of the cabin. Her bedclothes were hanging in untidy festoons from the bunk, her nightdress was rucked up around her naked thighs, and her fingers formed a cage across her terrified contorted face.

He reached for her. "Jan, it's all right. I'm here!" He wrapped both arms around her to try and still those dreadful cries of terror. Immediately she turned into a maddened animal, and she flew at him. Her nails slashed down his forehead, and had he not jerked away, he would have lost his eye; the bloody parallel wounds ended in his eyebrow, and thick dark blood oozed into his eye, half blinding him. Her strength was out of all proportion to her size; he could not hold her, and the harder he tried, the wilder she became. She sank her teeth into his bare forearm, leaving a crescent-shaped bite mark deep in his flesh.

He rolled away from her, and instantly she crawled back into the corner and crouched there, keening and blubbering to herself, staring at him with glittering, unseeing eyes. Craig felt his skin crawl and itch with dread and his own horror. Once again he tried to reach her, but at his first advance she bared her teeth like a rabid dog and snarled at him.

He rolled out of the cabin and dragged himself into the saloon. Frantically he searched through the tapes and found Beethoven's "Pastoral." He pressed it into the slot and turned the volume up to the maximum. The magnificent music swamped the yacht.

Slowly the sounds from her cabin dwindled into silence, and then hesitantly Janine came into the companionway of the saloon. She held her arms crossed over her chest, but the madness was gone from her eyes.

"I had a dream," she whispered, and came to sit at the table.

"I'll make some coffee," he said.

In the galley he bathed his scratches and bites with cold water and then took the coffee through to her.

"The music," she started, and then she saw his torn face. "Did I do that?"

"It doesn't matter," he said.

"I'm sorry, Craig," she whispered. "But you must not try to touch me. You see, I am a little bit mad also. You mustn't try to touch me."

◆　◆　◆

Comrade Tungata Zebiwe, Minister for Trade, Tourism and Information in the Cabinet of the newly elected government of Zimbabwe, walked briskly along one of the narrow gravel pathways that meandered through the lush gardens of State House. His four bodyguards followed him at a respectful distance. They were all former members of his old ZIPRA cadre, each of them hardened veterans whose loyalty had been tested a hundred times. Now, however, they had changed the camouflage dungarees of the bush war for dark business suits and sunglasses, the new uniform of the political elite.

The daily pilgrimage on which Tungata was intent had become a ritual of his household. As one of the senior Cabinet ministers, he was entitled to luxurious quarters in one of the annexes of State House. It was an easy and congenial walk from there, through the gardens, past State House itself, to the *indaba* tree.

State House was a sprawling edifice with white walls and gables, arched in the tradition of the great homes of the Cape of Good Hope. It had been built on the instructions of that archimperialist Cecil John Rhodes. His taste for the big and barbaric showed in the design and his sense of history in his choice of the site for State House. It was built on the spot where Lobengula's kraal had once stood before it was destroyed by Rhodes's marauders when they rode in to take possession of this land.

Beyond the great house, not two hundred paces from its wide verandas, stood a tree, a gnarled old wild plum enclosed and protected by a fence of iron palings. This tree was the object of Tungata's pilgrimage. He stopped in front of the iron palings, and his bodyguards hung back so as not to intrude on this private moment.

Tungata stood with his feet apart and his hands clasped lightly behind his back. He was dressed in a navy-blue suit with a light chalk stripe, one of a dozen that Hawkes and Gieves of Savile Row had tailored for him during his last visit to London. It fitted his wide rangy shoulders to perfection and subtly emphasized his narrow waist and the length of his legs. He wore a snowy white shirt under it; his tie was maroon with the tiny buckle and bridle logo of Gucci picked out in blue. His shoes were by the same Italian house, and he wore his expensive Western clothes with the same élan as his forefathers had worn the blue heron's feathers and royal leopard pelts.

He removed the gold-rimmed aviator-type Polaroid glasses from his face, and as part of his personal ritual, read the inscription on the plaque that was riveted to the palings.

"Beneath this tree Lobengula, the last King
of the Matabele, held his court and sat in judgement."

Then he looked up into the branches, as though in search of his ancestor's spirit. The tree was dying of old age—some of the central branches were black and dry—but from the rich red soil at its base, new shoots were bursting into vibrant life.

Tungata saw the significance of that, and he murmured to himself, "They will grow as strong as the great tree once was—and I also am a shoot of the old king's stock."

There was a light tread on the gravel path behind Tungata. He frowned as he turned, but the frown cleared as he saw who it was.

"Comrade Leila," he greeted the white woman with the pale, intense face.

"I am honored that you call me that, Comrade Minister." Leila came directly to him and held out her hand.

"You and your family have always been true friends of my people," he told her simply as he took her hand. "Beneath this tree your grandmother, Robyn Ballantyne, met often with Lobengula, my great-great-uncle. She same at his invitation to give him advice and counsel."

"Now I come at your invitation, and you must believe that I will always be yours to command."

He released her hand and turned back to the tree; his voice had a quiet, reflective quality. "You were with me when the Umlimo, the spirit medium of our people, made her final prediction. I thought it was right that you should be there when that prediction is brought to fruition."

"The stone falcons have returned to roost," Leila St. John agreed softly. "But that is not all the Umlimo's prophecy. She foresaw that the man who brought the falcons back to Zimbabwe would rule the land as once did the Mambos and Monomotapas, as once did your ancestors Lobengula and great Mzilikazi."

Tungata turned slowly to face her once more.

"That is a secret that you and I share, Comrade Leila."

"It will remain our secret, Comrade Tungata, but you and I both know that there will be need during the difficult years that lie ahead for a man as strong as Mzilikazi was strong."

Tungata did not reply. He looked up into the branches of the ancient tree, and his lips moved in a silent supplication. Then he replaced the gold-rimmed glasses over his eyes and turned back to Leila.

"The car is waiting," he said.

It was a black, bullet-proofed Mercedes 500. There were four police motorcycle outriders and a second smaller Mercedes for his bodyguards. The small convoy drove very fast, with the police sirens shrieking and wailing, and the colorful little ministerial pennant fluttering on the front of Tungata's Mercedes.

They went down the three-kilometer-long, jacaranda-lined driveway that Cecil Rhodes had designed as the approach to his State House, and then crossed the main commercial section of Bulawayo, flying through the red lights at the junctions to the geometrical grid of roads and avenues, past the town square where the wagons had laagered during the rebellion when Bazo's impis had threatened the town, down along the wide avenue that bisected the meticulously groomed lawns of the public gardens, and at last turned off sharply and drew up in front of the modern, three-story museum building.

There was a red carpet laid down the front steps of the museum and a small gathering of dignitaries, headed by the Mayor of Bulawayo, the first Matabele ever to hold that position, and the curator of the museum.

"Welcome, Comrade Minister, on this historic occasion."

They escorted him down the long corridor to the public auditorium. Every seat was already filled, and as Tungata entered, the entire gathering stood and applauded him, the whites in the gathering outdoing the Matabele as a positive demonstration of their goodwill.

Tungata was introduced to the other dignitaries on the speakers' platform. "This is Dr. Van der Walt, curator of the South African Museum."

He was a tall, balding man with a heavy South African accent. Tungata shook hands with him briefly and unsmilingly. This man represented a nation that had actively opposed the people's republican army's march to glory. Tungata turned to the next in line.

She was a young white woman, and she was immediately familiar to Tungata. He stared at her sharply, not quite able to place her. She had gone very pale under his scrutiny, and her eyes were dark and terrified as those of a hunted animal. The hand in his was limp and cold and trembled violently—still Tungata could not decide where he had seen her before.

"Dr. Carpenter is the curator of the Entomological Section." The name meant nothing to Tungata, and he turned away from her, irritated by his own inability to place her. He took his seat in the center of the platform facing the auditorium, and the South African Museum's curator rose to address the gathering.

"All the credit for the successful negotiation of the exchange between our two institutions must go to the honorable minister who today honors us with his presence." He was reading from a typed sheet, clearly anxious to have done speaking and sit down again. "It was at Minister Tungata Zebiwe's initiative that discussions first took place, and he sustained these during the difficult period when we appeared to be making little or no progress. Our great problem was in setting a relative value on two such diverse exhibits. On one hand you had one of the world's most extensive and exhaustive collections of tropical insects, representing many decades of dedicated collecting and classification, while on the other hand we had these unique artifacts from an unknown civilization." Van der Walt seemed to be warming to his subject enough to look up from his prepared script. "However, it was the honorable minister's determination to regain for his new nation a priceless part of its heritage that at last prevailed, and it is to his credit entirely that we are gathered here today."

When at last Van der Walt sat down again, there was a polite splattering of applause and then an expectant silence as Tungata Zebiwe rose to his feet. The minister had an immense presence, and without yet uttering a word, he transfixed them with his smoky, unwavering gaze.

"My people have a saying that was passed down from the wise ones of our tribe," he started in his deep, rumbling voice. "It is this: The white eagle has stooped on the stone falcons and cast them to earth. Now the eagle shall lift them up again and they will fly afar. There shall be no peace in the kingdoms of the Mambos or the Monomotapas until they return. For the white eagle will war with the black bull until the stone falcons return to roost."

Tungata paused a moment, letting his words hang between them, heavy with portent. Then he went on. "I am sure all of you here know the story of how the bird statues of Zimbabwe were seized by Rhodes's plunderers and, despite the efforts of my ancestors to prevent it, how they were carried away southward across the Limpopo River."

Tungata left the podium and strode to the curtained-off section at the back of the speakers' platform. "My friends, my comrades"—he turned to face them once more—"the stone falcons have returned to roost!" he said, and drew aside the curtains.

There was a long, breathless silence, and the audience stared avidly at the serried rank of tall soapstone carvings that were revealed. There were six of them, and they were those that Ralph Ballantyne had lifted from the ancient stone temple. The one that his father had taken on his first visit to Zimbabwe thirty years before had burned in the pyre of Groote Schuur. These six were all that remained.

The soapstone from which each of the birds was carved was of a satiny texture. Each bird crouched on top of a plinth that was ornamented by a pattern of intermeshed triangles like the teeth in a shark's jaw. The statues were not identical; some of the columns supported crocodiles and lizards that crawled up toward the bird image that surmounted it.

Some of the statues had been extensively damaged, chipped and eroded, but the one in the center of the line was almost perfect. The bird was a stylized raptor, with its long, bladelike wings crossed over its back. The head was proud and erect, the cruel beak hooked and the blind eyes haughty and unforgiving. It was a magnificent and evocative work of primitive art, and the crowded auditorium rose as one person in spontaneous applause.

Tungata Zebiwe reached out and touched the head of the central bird. His back was turned to his audience so that they could not see his lips move, and the applause drowned his whisper.

"Welcome home," he whispered. "Welcome home to Zimbabwe, bird of my destiny."

"Now you do not want to go!" Janine was shaking with fury. "After all the pains I have gone to to arrange this meeting. Now you simply do not want to go!"

"Jan, it's a waste of time."

"Thank you!" She put her face closer to his. "Thank you for that. Do you realize what it would cost me to face that monster again, but I was prepared to do it for you, and now it's a waste of time."

"Jan, please—"

"Damn you, Craig Mellow, it's you who are a waste of time, you and your endless cowardice." He gasped and drew away from her. "Cowardice," she repeated deliberately. "I say that, and I mean it. You were in too much of a blue funk to send that bloody book of yours to a publisher. I had literally to tear it away from you and send it off." She broke off, panting with anger, searching for words sharp enough to express her fury.

"You are afraid to face life, afraid to leave this cave you have built for yourself, afraid to take the chance of somebody rejecting your book, afraid to make any effort to float this thing you have built." With a wide, extravagant gesture, she indicated the yacht. "I see it now. You don't really want to get onto the ocean—you prefer to hide here, swilling gin and covering yourself with dreams. You don't want to walk; you prefer to drag yourself around on your backside—it's your excuse, your grand, cast-iron excuse to dodge life."

Again she had to stop for breath, and then she went on. "That's right, put that little-boy look on your face, make those big sad eyes—it works every time, doesn't it? Well, not this time, buster, not this time. They have offered me the job of curator at the South African Museum. I'm to see the collection safely installed in its new home, and I'm going to take it. Do you hear me, Craig Mellow? I'm going to leave you to crawl around on the floor because you're too damned scared to stand up." She flung herself out of the saloon and into the forward cabin. She began to snatch her clothes out of the stowage and throw them onto the bunk.

"Jan," he said behind her.

"What is it now?" She did not look around.

"If we are going to be there by three o'clock, then we'd better leave right away," Craig said.

"You can drive," she said, and pushed past him and went up in the cockpit, leaving him to follow at his best speed.

They drove in silence until they reached the entrance to the long, straight avenue of jacaranda trees. At the far end of it were the white gates of State House, and Janine stared straight ahead at them.

"I'm sorry, Craig. I said things that were hard to say and must have been harder to listen to. The truth is that I am as afraid as you are. I am going to face the man that destroyed me. If I can do it, then perhaps I can retrieve something of myself from the ruins. I lied when I said it was for you. It's for both of us."

The police guard came to the driver's side of the maroon Land Rover, and without a word Craig handed him the appointment card. The constable checked it against his visitors' book and then made Craig fill in his name and address and the reason for his visit.

Craig wrote: "Visit to Comrade Minister Tungata Zebiwe," and the guard took the book back from him and saluted smartly.

The wrought-iron gates swung open and Craig drove through. They turned left toward the minister's annex, with just a glimpse of the white gables and blue slate roof of the main residence between the trees.

Craig parked the Land Rover in the public car park and slid into the wheelchair. Janine walked beside him to the steps that led up onto the veranda of the annex, and there was an awkward moment while Craig negotiated them by the sheer strength of his arms. Then they followed the signs down the trestled veranda, beneath the blue wisteria and climbing purple bougainvillea to the door of the antechamber. One of the minister's bodyguards searched Janine's handbag, frisked Craig quickly but expertly, and then stood aside to let them enter the light and airy room.

There were lighter square patches on the walls from where the portraits of previous white administrators and politicians had been removed. The only wall decorations now were two flags draped on either side of the inner double doors, the flags of ZIPRA and of the new Zimbabwe nation.

Craig and Janine waited for almost half an hour, and then the doors opened and another suited bodyguard came through.

"The Comrade Minister will see you now."

Craig wheeled himself forward and into the inner room. On the facing wall were portraits of the nation's leaders, Robert Mugabe and Josiah Inkunzi. In the center of the wall-to-wall carpeting stood a huge desk in the style of Louis XIV. Tungata Zebiwe sat behind his desk, and even its size could not belittle him.

Involuntarily Craig stopped halfway to the desk.

"Sam?" he whispered. "Samson Kumalo? I did not know—I'm sorry—"

The minister stood up abruptly. Craig's shock was reflected in his own face.

"Craig," he whispered, "what happened to you?"

"The war," Craig answered. "I guess I was on the wrong side, Sam."

Tungata recovered swiftly and sat down again. "That name is best forgotten," he said quietly. "Just as what we were once to each other should also be forgotten. You made an appointment through Dr. Carpenter to see me. What was it that you wished to discuss?"

Tungata listened attentively while Craig spoke, and then he leaned back in his chair.

"From what you tell me, you have already made an application to the Exchange Control Authority for a permit to export this vessel of yours. That permit was refused?"

"That is correct, Comrade Minister," Craig nodded.

"Then what made you think I would want to or even have the authority to countermand that decision?" Tungata asked.

"I didn't really think you would," Craig admitted.

"Comrade Minister"—Janine spoke for the first time—"I asked for this appointment because I believe that there are special circumstances in this case. Mr. Mellow has been crippled for life, and his only possession is this vessel."

"Dr. Carpenter, he is fortunate. The forests and wilderness of this land are thickly sown with the unmarked graves of young men and women who gave more than Mr. Mellow for freedom. You should have a better reason than that."

"I think I have," Janine said softly. "Comrade Minister, you and I have met before."

"Your face is familiar to me," Tungata agreed. "But I do not recall—"

"It was at night, in the forest beside the wreckage of an aircraft—" She saw the flare of recognition in those brooding, smoky eyes. They seemed to bore into her very soul. Terror came at her again in suffocating, overwhelming waves; she felt the earth sway giddily under her feet, and his face filled all her vision. It took all that remained of her strength and courage to speak again.

"You won a land, but in doing so, have you lost forever your humanity?"

She saw the shift in that dark, hypnotic gaze, the almost imperceptible softening of his mouth. Then Tungata Zebiwe looked down at his own powerful hands on the white blotter before him.

"You are a persuasive advocate, Dr. Carpenter," he said quietly. He picked up the gold pen from the desk set and wrote briefly on the monogrammed pad. He tore off the sheet and stood up. He came around the desk and toward Janine.

"In war there are atrocities committed even by decent men," he said quietly. "War makes monsters of us all. I thank you for reminding me of my own humanity." He handed her the sheet of paper. "Take that to the Exchange Control Director," he told her. "You will have your permit."

"Thank you, Sam." Craig looked up at him, and Tungata stooped over him and embraced him briefly but ardently.

"Go in peace, old friend," he said in Sindebele, and then straightened up. "Get him out of here, Dr. Carpenter, before he unmans me completely," Tungata Zebiwe ordered harshly, and strode to the wide sash windows.

He stared out across the green lawns until he heard the double doors close behind him, then he sighed softly and went back to his desk.

◆ ◆ ◆

"It's strange to think that this is the same view of Africa that Robyn and Zouga Ballantyne had in 1860 when they arrived in the slaving clipper *Huron*." Craig pointed back over the stern at the great massif of Table Mountain standing perpetual guard over the southernmost tip of a continent, wreathed in the silver clouds that spilled over her weathered brow of stark rock. Around the foot of the mountain, like a necklace around the throat, were strung the white buildings with their windows shining in the early sunlight like ten thousand beacon fires.

"This is where it all began, my family's great African adventure, and this is where it all ends."

"It's an end," Janine agreed quietly. "But it's also a new beginning." She was standing in the stern, with one hand on the back stay for balance.

She wore a thin T-shirt and blue denim pants with the legs hacked off short, exposing her long brown legs. During the months of final fitting out of the yacht, in the basin of the Royal Cape Yacht Club, she had put herself on a strict diet: no wine, no gin and no white food. Her waist had fined down, and the buttocks that peeked out from under the ragged bottoms of her pants were round and tight and hard once again.

She had cut her hair as short as a boy's, and the salt sea air had made it curl tightly against her scalp. The sun had darkened her face and burned away the blemishes around the corners of her mouth and across her chin. Now she revolved slowly, taking in the wide horizon ahead of them.

"It's so big, Craig," she said. "Aren't you scared?"

"Scared as hell," he grinned up at her. "I am not certain whether our next landfall will be South America or India, but it's exciting also."

"I'll make us a mug of cocoa," she said.

"I hate this drying-out period."

"It's your own rule to have no liquor on board—you'll have to wait until South America or India, or whatever." She ducked down into the saloon, but before she reached the galley, the radio above the chart table squawked.

"Zulu Romeo Foxtrot. This is Cape Town marine radio. Come in, please."

"Jan, that's us. Take it," Craig yelled. "Someone at the yacht club saying good-bye, probably."

"Cape Town marine radio, this is Zulu Romeo Foxtrot. Let's go to Channel Ten."

"Is that the yacht *Bawu?*" The operator's voice was clear and undistorted, for they were still on line of sight to the antenna above the harbor.

"Affirmative. This is *Bawu.*"

"We have a radiogram for you. Are you ready to copy?"

"Go ahead, Cape Town."

"Message reads: 'FOR CRAIG MELLOW REGARDING YOUR TYPE-SCRIPT *Flight of the Falcon* STOP WE WISH TO PUBLISH AND OFFER ADVANCE OF £5000 AGAINST 12½% ROYALTIES ON WORLD RIGHTS STOP REPLY SOONEST CONGRATULATIONS FROM PICK CHAIRMAN WILLIAM HEINEMANN PUBLISHERS LONDON.' "

"Craig," Janine shrieked from below. "Did you hear? Did you hear that?"

He could not answer her. His hands were frozen to the wheel, and he was staring directly ahead over *Bawu*'s bow as they rose and fell gently across the distant blue horizon of the Atlantic Ocean.

◆ ◆ ◆

Two days out, the gale came out of the southeast without any warning. It laid *Bawu* over until solid green water came in over the rail and swept Janine out of the cockpit. Only her safety line saved her, and Craig struggled for ten minutes to get her back on board while the yacht paid off madly before the wind and the jib sail burst with a crash like cannon-shot.

The gale lasted five days and five nights, during which time there seemed to be no clear dividing line between mad wind and wild water. They lived in a deafening cacophony of sound as the gale played on *Bawu*'s hull like a crazed violinist, and the Atlantic graybeards marched down upon them in majestic succession. They lived with the cold in their bones, soaked to the skin, and with their hands white and wrinkled like those of a drowned man, and the soft skin torn by harsh nylon sheets and stiff, unyielding sails. Once in a while, they snatched a dry biscuit or a mouthful of cold, congealed beans, and washed it down with plain water, then crawled back on deck again. They slept in turns for a few minutes at a time on top of the bundled wet sails that had been stuffed down the companionway into the saloon.

They went into the storm as greenhorns, and when the wind dropped as suddenly as it had attacked them, they were sailors—utterly exhausted and gaunt with the terror through which they had lived, but with a new pride in themselves and the vessel that had borne them.

Craig had just sufficient strength to heave the yacht to and let her ride the smooth but still mountainous swells on her own. Then he dragged himself to his bunk, dropped his stinking wet clothing on the deck, and fell back naked on the rough blanket and slept for eighteen hours straight.

He woke to a new tumult of emotions, uncertain of what was fantasy and what was reality. Where before there had been no sensation at all, his lower body was locked in an agonizing spasm. He could feel each separate muscle, and they seemed pitted against each other to the point of tearing or bursting. From the sole of his foot to the pit of his stomach, his nerve ends felt as though they were scraped raw. He cried out as the pain threatened to swamp him, and then in the pain found suddenly the beginnings of exquisite, almost insupportable, pleasure.

He cried out again and heard his cry echoed from above him. He opened his eyes and Janine's face was inches above his, her naked body pressed against his from breast to thighs. He tried to speak, but she gagged him with her own lips and moaned into his mouth. Abruptly he realized that he was buried deeply in her heat and silken elasticity, and they were borne aloft on a wave of triumph higher and fiercer than any that the Atlantic had hurled at them during the gale.

It left them both clinging to each other, speechless and barely able to breathe.

◆ ◆ ◆

She brought him a mug of coffee once he had *Bawu* sailing again, and she perched on the edge of the cockpit with one hand on his shoulder.

"I want to show you something," he said.

He pointed at his bare leg that was thrust out in front of him on the deck cushion, and as she watched, he wriggled his toes back and forth, then from side to side.

"Oh, darling," she husked, "that's the cleverest thing I've ever seen anybody do."

"What did you call me?" he asked.

"Do you know something?" She did not reply to the question immediately. "I think that you and I are going to be all right—" Only then, she laid her cheek against his and whispered in his ear, "I called you darling, okay?"

"That's okay by me, darling," he replied, and locked in the yacht's self-steering vane, so that he had both arms free to hold her.

ABOUT THE AUTHOR

Wilbur Smith was born in Zambia and was educated in Michaelhouse and Rhodes University. He has lived all his life in Africa, and his commitment to that continent is deep.

A full-time writer since 1964, he is the author of fifteen novels. He also finds time to travel out of Africa and enjoy his other interests—such as numismatics, wild-life photography and big game fishing. He and his wife make an annual safari into the dwindling wilderness of Central Africa, and at other seasons he fishes by boat in the Indian Ocean for tuna and other game fish.

Mr. Smith lives with his wife in Constantia, South Africa.